Robert Currie

Report on the Settlement of the Shahjehanpore District

Robert Currie

Report on the Settlement of the Shahjehanpore District

Reprint of the original, first published in 1874.

1st Edition 2024 | ISBN: 978-3-36884-635-0

Verlag (Publisher): Outlook Verlag GmbH, Zeilweg 44, 60439 Frankfurt, Deutschland
Vertretungsberechtigt (Authorized to represent): E. Roepke, Zeilweg 44, 60439 Frankfurt, Deutschland
Druck (Print): Books on Demand GmbH, In de Tarpen 42, 22848 Norderstedt, Deutschland

REPORT

ON THE

SETTLEMENT OF THE SHAHJEHANPORE DISTRICT.

By ROBERT G. CURRIE, Esq., C.S.,

Settlement Officer.

ALLAHABAD:

PRINTED AT THE NORTH-WESTERN PROVINCES GOVERNMENT PRESS.

1874.

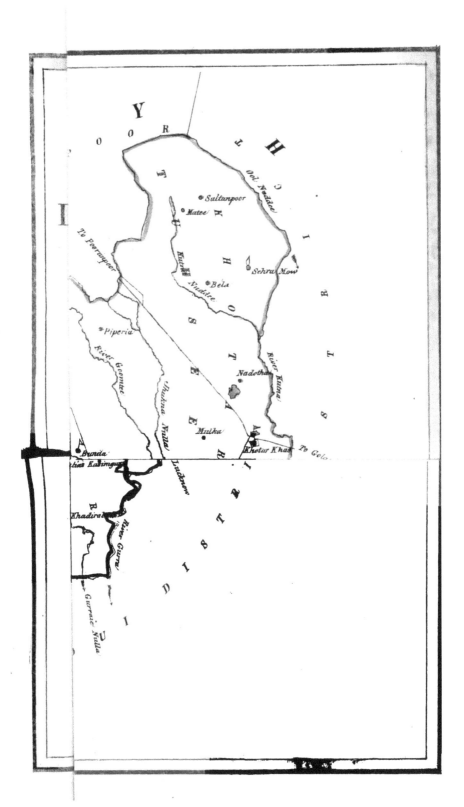

No. 123N. of 1876.

FROM

C. H. T. CROSTHWAITE, Esq.,

Offg. Secy., Board of Revenue, N.-W. P.,

To

THE OFFG. SECRETARY TO GOVERNMENT,

North-Western Provinces.

DATED NAINI TAL, THE 12TH MAY, 1876.

SIR,

SET-
OF
ENUE,
t :

, Esq.

I AM directed by the Senior Member to submit the final Settlement Report of the Sháhjahánpur district, with the following remarks.

2. The settlement of the district, including the field-survey, has been carried out from first to last by Mr. Robert Currie, with the assistance of Mr. Butt. It began in the year 1867-68, and the final report was submitted in January, 1875.

3. The total expenditure from first to last amounts to Rs. 5,86,500. The details Cost of settlemen of this charge have not been given by Mr. Currie. The cost falls at the rate of Rs. 529 per 1,000 acres, or Rs. 339 per square mile.

4. The result of the revision of assessment has been an increase to the revenue Result of present of Rs. 2,09,153, being 21·4 per cent. on the old demand. The expense of the settlement has therefore been repaid in a little less than three years. And it must be remembered that the gain is not merely financial. Hundreds of disputes of all kinds have been settled, accurate registers of rights prepared, and good village, pargana, and district maps prepared.

5. The present settlement is the tenth to which the Sháhjahánpur district has been subject since it came under the British Government. The jumma of the eighth settlement was Rs. 10,22,324. That of Mr. J. W. Muir's settlement, which has just expired, Rs. 9,83,566. The demand now assessed is Rs. 11,84,426.

6. Owing to the way in which the revenue of the earlier settlements was pushed up, Effects of earlie the district was generally in an exhausted and impoverished state when Mr. Muir ments. made his assessment, pargana Khutár alone being an exception. He was consequently obliged to reduce the jumma of every pargana except Khutár. Nevertheless his assessment was as a rule somewhat heavy at first. Punitive measures for the collection of the revenue, as well as transfers caused by its pressure, were numerous in the first ten or twelve years of the settlement. Permanent reductions were made in all cases of marked severity ; and the extension of cultivation and general improvement in the condition of the country caused all difficulty to disappear.

7. The transfers that have taken place during the period of settlement have been Transfers during very numerous, and both in his tahsíl and district reports Mr. Currie has discussed settlement. them. The number and area of transfers in the aggregate have not been shown. But the details of transfers from agricultural to non-agricultural classes are given. In 1839-40, the non-agricultural classes held 6·1 per cent. of the land, and in 1870, 17 per cent.

8. The effect which the revenue had on the transfers is approximately shown in the following table (para. 69) :—

Description of assessment.				Percentage held by non-agricultural classes.		
				In 1840.	In 1870.	Increase.
Heavy	...	...	...	8·8	30·3	21·5
Medium	...	...	...	9·6	22·0	12·4
Light	...	..	...	3·2	8·2	5·0

But before drawing any inference from these figures, we must, as Mr. Currie points out, take other circumstances into consideration. The lightly-assessed parganas are all at a distance from the city, and are owned by powerful Thákur brotherhoods, except Khutar, which was a wild, unreclaimed, and unhealthy tract. The heavily-assessed parganas lie nearer the city, and are great sugar-producers, and hence offered every incentive to the trading classes. The heavy assessment, however, gave the opportunity which enabled these classes to invest in land, if other causes supplied the motive which induced them to take advantage of it.

9. On the whole there is no reason to suppose that Mr. Muir's settlement was particularly light; and had the condition and circumstances of the country remained the same, it is probable that the increase in the assets would probably have not been more than enough to counterbalance the reduction in the standard of assessment from two-thirds to one-half.

10. But there are few districts in the North-West which have been more affected by causes tending to raise the value of land. The district covers an area of 1,733 square miles, and has a population of 949,471, being 548 to the square mile of total area, and 821 to the square mile of cultivation. Eighty-six per cent. of the people are Hindús, the bulk of whom are agriculturalists. The soil is naturally good, the climate moist, and irrigation, when necessary, is to be had. At the previous settlement, and even up to a very late date, the district was almost cut off by want of good communications from the rest of the country, and prevented from disposing of its surplus produce at a profit. Up to 1867 there was not a single metalled road to Shábjahánpur; now it is connected by metalled roads with Lucknow, Bareilly, and Fatehgarh, and the district is also intersected and thoroughly opened up by the Oudh and Rohilkhand Railway. These improvements are of so recent a date that their effect on the value of land has yet to be seen. Any rise in the revenue, which was covered by the rent-rates existing before these changes, may well be considered safe, and it must be remembered that the settlement had commenced, and in some cases the rates had been determined, before this radical alteration in the circumstances of the district had taken place. In no case have the effects of the change had time to influence the rent-rates, and through them the assessment of the district. The rise of prices and the extension of cultivation are causes that long preceded, and should have influenced the assessment.

11. The cultivated area now occupies 66·8 per cent. of the total area, and there is still 17·1 per cent. of old unbroken cultivable land. Since the last settlement the area of cultivation has increased 31 per cent. The increase of assets on that account alone must be very large.

12. Prices have risen, as Mr. Currie says, enormously. In para. 80 he gives a table showing the rise in the harvest prices of the principal crops. There is an increase in the price of wheat between the first and third decade of the settlement of 23 per cent.; between the second and third of 73 per cent., and between the second and the last five years of the third, of 95 per cent.

13. Here however, as elsewhere, we do not find that the rent-rate has risen in anything like the same proportion as the price of produce. It is curious that in the Shábjahánpur district there is hardly any batái. Rents are invariably (except in the case of exceptionally poor or uncertain lands) paid in cash, and vary with the soils. There is scarcely one village in which all the rents are paid in kind. There are

hundreds in which the rents are and have been paid in cash for the last generation or more. Even so far back as 1818 A.D., the rents of this district were usually paid n cash.

14. The rents, Mr. Currie says in para. 80 of his report, are generally low and inadequate, and are regulated more by custom than competition. They do not readily answer to any change in the prices of produce.

By comparing the present rentals of some three hundred maháls of three parganas with their rentals 20 years ago, Mr. Currie has found that there is an increase due to extended cultivation of 12½ per cent. in the rental, but the average rent-rate has increased only in one, and has actually fallen in the others. It is also found that the prevailing rates for land now are very much the same as those mentioned by Mr. Lowther as existing nearly sixty years ago (page 295 *et. seq.*, Selections from Revenue Records, North-Western Provinces, 1818-20). The areas to which the higher rates are applied have extended. But there has been no general advance in the rates corresponding to the rise in prices. The same observation has been recorded by the Settlement Officer of Etáwah.

15. There has been considerable enhancement of rents following the revision of assessment. But it has been in the form of an increase to the rents palpably below the prevailing standard of the district, and not in the shape of any increase to the old rates paid for good land.

16. The rent-rates assumed by Mr. Currie for the purposes of assessment, and sanctioned by the Board, are given by him in para. 79 of his report ; and full details of the methods by which he obtained them are to be found in the separate assessment reports for each tahsíl. It will be sufficient here to say that they are based on the rents actually paid, and have not been increased on any theoretical grounds. Mr. Currie writes that " all low and suspicious rates are eliminated, as well as all specially favourable rates for zemindar's sír, or for relations and dependants, and only genuine cultivators' rates are taken, and averages struck from large areas of all kinds of soil in all directions of each circle ; and when, for the reasons assigned, it is demonstrable that in any particular circle or pargana the existing rates are low and insufficient, as compared with similar lands in the vicinity, and a rise is not only reasonably to be expected, but certain, the assumed rates are put at such amount above the existing average rates as is estimated will correct this inadequacy and meet this certain rise. But no theoretical correctness or proper proportion between rents and prices, or value of produce, has been aimed at." It is clear that the rates thus arrived at cannot be high in the present condition of the district. In all probability rents will rise during the currency of this settlement far above them.

Rent-rates assun assessment pur]

17. Mr. Currie's system of assessment is described in section VII. of his report. It is characterized by the sound sense and sober judgment which Mr. Currie usually brings to bear on his work. The Board especially approve of his practice in causing all the assessment remarks to be written out before the jummas were declared (para. 88). Much inconvenience has been caused by Settlement Officers delaying this important work, and in some cases leaving it undone when they have been removed from the district.

System of asses adopted.

18. The value of uncultivated land has been duly taken into account in all cases, and on the other hand any circumstances, such as the number of shareholders or the caste of cultivators, rendering a lighter demand advisable, have been considered in the assessment.

19. The special arrangements made by Mr. Currie for the assessment of the *Vide* G. O. No. 1719A., Rámganga villages, instead of the usual quinquennial settlement, dated 27th October, 1871. have been the subject of separate correspondence with Government.

Assessment of Rám villages.

20. The financial results of the settlement are fully described in the eighth section of the report.

Financial results of ment.

The following statement shows the old and new revenues of each pargana : —

Pargana.	Expiring jumma, without cesses.	New jumma, without cesses.	Increase.	Percentage of increase.
	Rs. a. p	Rs. a. p.	Rs. a. p.	
Sháhjahánpur	1,07,939 6 0	1,24,219 1 0	16,277 11 0	15·1
Jumour	74,752 10 0	74,710 15 0	...	Decrease of Rs. 41-11-0
Kánt	78,963 5 0	91,740 14 0	12,776 9 0	16·2
Jalálabad	1,61,134 8 9	2,11,410 0 0	50,275 7 3	31·2
Tilhar	85,171 0 0	1,09,120 6 0	23,949 6 0	28·1
Míránpur Katra	5,971 0 0	8,510 0 0	2,539 0 0	42·5
Khera Bajhera	51,445 0 0	72,360 0 0	20,915 0 0	40·7
Jalálpur	56,125 0 0	63,005 0 0	6,880 0 0	12·2
Nigohi	61,950 0 0	77,130 0 0	15,180 0 0	24·5
Barágaon	64,345 0 0	72,950 0 0	8,605 0 0	13·4
Pawáyan	1,92,366 0 0	2,16,735 0 0	24,369 0 0	12·6
Khutár	35,110 0 0	62,535 0 0	27,425 0 0	78·1
Whole district	9,75,272 13 9	11,84,426 4 0	2,09,195 1 3 Deduct 41 11 0	} 21·4
		Net increase...	2,09,153 6 3	

21. The following statement taken from para. 105 of this report is useful for comparing the assessments of each pargana :—

Pargana.	Total population per square mile of entire area.	Agricultural population per square mile of cultivation.	Percentage of assessable area cultivated.	Percentage of 1st class soil.	Percentage of medium class soils.	Percentage of inferior soils.	Percentage of cultivated area irrigated, not merely capable of irrigation.	Percentage of superior crops.	Percentage of increase of cultivated area.	Percentage of increase of revenue without cesses.	Incidence of new revenue per acre of cultivation.
											Rs a. p.
Sháhjahánpur	981	598	79	68	28	4	51	65	17	15·1	1 14 10
Jumour	523	535	76	52	35	13	51	54	19	...	1 11 6
Kánt	504	465	83	33	42	25	36	47	18	16·2	1 4 8
Jalálabad	518	569	72	42	38	20	38	58	35	31·2	1 10 7
Tilhar	680	545	84	46	37	17	48	56	27	28·1	1 12 6
Míránpur Katra	767	592	71	47	40	13	50	54	37	42·5	1 10 9
Khera Bujhera	531	564	83	60	30	10	30	52	31	40·7	1 11 9
Jalálpur	599	570	80	60	29	11	38	55	15	12·2	1 14 4
Nigohi	504	572	73	58	30	12	35	52	23	24·5	1 11 4
Barágaon	599	584	86	56	40	4	48	66	34	13·4	2 0 0
Pawáyan	510	511	80	36	47	17	43	49	18	12·6	1 7 6
Khutár	260	370	53	35	35	30	24	32	309	78·1	0 15 7
Whole district	540	530	75	48	38	14	40	53	31	21·4	1 9 7

Assessment of Pargana Khutár.

22. The assessment of Khutár, which gives an increase of 78 per cent. on the former revenue, requires to be specially noticed. Khutár is a forest pargana in the north-east corner of the district on the boundary of Oudh. The greater part 164½ out of 203 square miles is a wild sparsely populated tract, more than half of which is uncultivated. The enormous increase of cultivation, 309 per cent., made a larger rise in the revenue unavoidable. Even after making every allowance for the circumstances of the pargana, and without discounting the increase of rental to be expected from future extension of cultivation, the rise in the revenue amounted to 78 per cent. Under these circumstances Mr. Currie recommended progressive jummas, and this course has been adopted.

23. The way in which the increase has been distributed over three periods is shown in the following statement :— *Progressive jumm*

Circle.	Current jumma.	New progressive jumma.			Difference between current and full jumma of 3rd term.			Percentage of net increase.
		Initial, 1st to 5th year,	2nd term, 6th and 7th years.	3rd term, 8th year to end of settlement.	Decrease.	Increase.	Net increase.	
	Rs.	Rs.	Rs.	Rs.	Rs.	Rs.	Rs.	Rs.
1st	16,682	23,620	24,790	25,150	399	8,867	8,468	50·8
2nd	18,428	29,530	34,420	37,385	533	19,490	18,957	102·9
Whole pargana Kháaur, ...	35,110	53,150	59,210	62,535	932	28,357	27,425	78·1

24. The necessity of a progressive jumma will be more apparent when it is stated that out of 272 maháls forming the pargana, the revenue of 16 has been left unaltered, of 20 decreased, of 236 increased. Of these last, 58 maháls in the most cultivated part of the pargana have been subjected to an increase of 72 per cent., and 178 maháls in the wilder and more backward part, to an increase of 138 per cent. It would have been cruel and impolitic to raise the demand to such an extent all at once.

25. The new jumma of the district stands at Rs. 11,84,425-4-0, being an increase of Rs. 2,09,152-6-3 on the old demand. The Board recommend the confirmation of Mr. Currie's settlement, and they concur with him in recommending that the term of settlement should be for 30 years from the 1st July, 1870, the date on which the first of the new assessments came into force. *Increase of reven*

26. In the ninth section of the report Mr. Currie explains his action regarding the records and the patwáris' circles, and in the tenth section he discusses some of the minor points connected with the settlement operations. No remarks are called for on these points, beyond the record of the Board's belief that the work has been well done. *Records and pa circles.*

27. In conclusion, I am to say that the Board consider Mr. Currie to have deserved the best thanks of Government for the way in which he has carried out the settlement of Sháhajhánpur. His ability as a Settlement Officer was well known when he began the work, and he has ably maintained his reputation. *Notice of officers,*

The final report which he submitted is also of the same character as his other work. It gives all the information that is required, in a clear and well-considered form, and the Board have pleasure in submitting it to Government.

28. The Board also desire me to bring to the notice of Government the services of the gentlemen named by Mr. Currie in para. 132 of his district report, especially those of Mr. Butt, whose industry and ability are well known to Government; and of the two Deputy Collectors, Ragbuns Sahay and Pandit Kanhya Lál, of whom the former has served from the beginning to the end of settlement, and both of whom have received great praise and recommendation from Mr. Currie.

I have the honour to be,

SIR,

Your most obedient servant,

C. H. T. CROSTHWAITE,

Offg. Secy. to the Board of Revenue,
North-Western Provinces.

CONTENTS.

INDEX TO CHAPTER I.

ERRATA OF CHAPTER I.

							for		read	
Page vii.,	*para.*	13,	*line*	30,	*for*	buted		*read*	butes.	
,,	,,	,,	,,	,,	53	,,	189,768		,,	190,023.
,,	ix.	,,	15	,,	3	,,	wood		,,	word.
,,	xi.	,,	18	,,	2	,,	114,266		,,	114,175.
,,	xix.	,,	35	,,	2	,,	cu		,,	cut.
,,	xxvii.	,,	48	,,	5	,,	superior		,,	inferior.
,,	xxxii.	,,	55	,,	33	,,	has"		,,	revenue"
,,	xl.	,,	70	,,	44	,,	except		,,	exact.
,,	xlv.	,,	76	,,	41	,,	rent		,,	rent,
,,	lvi.	,,	99	,,	43	,,	statement		,,	settlement.
,,	lviii.	,,	101	,,	form	,,	214		,,	21·4.

CHAPTER I.

GENERAL REPORT

OF THE

SETTLEMENT OF THE SHAHJEHANPORE DISTRICT.

By ROBERT G. CURRIE, Esq., C.S., *Settlement Officer.*

SECTION I.

General description of the geography, physical features, &c., of the district.

THE district of Shahjehanpore lies between 27°15′—28°30′ latitude, and 79°25′—80°25′ longitude, and forms part of the Commissionership of Rohilkhund in the North-Western Provinces, being the south-easternmost district in Rohilkhund. It is bounded on the north-east round by east to south-east by Oudh, on the south by the Futtehgurh district, and on the west by the districts of Budaon and Bareilly, and on the north-west and north by Pergunnah Poorunpore of the Phillibheet Sub-division.

Position and boundaries of the district.

The district covers an area of 1,733 square miles, and has a population, according to the census of 1865, of 935,984, and by the census of 1872 of 949,471 inhabitants, being an average by the latter of 548 individuals to the square mile.

2. It comprises four tuhseels, which are sub-divided into twelve pergunnahs, containing 2,364 *mouzahs* and 3,063 *muhals*.

The sub-division of the district into tuhseels, pergunnahs, and mouzahs.

The Jellalabad tuhseel is the only one in which there are no separate subordinate pergunnahs. Until the present revision there were no separate pergunnahs in the Shahjehanpore Tuhseel. The recurrence of villages of the same name in different directions caused endless confusion, and the existence of natural boundaries suggested the sub-division in many ways desirable, and hence, under the orders of the Board of Revenue, the tuhseel, and hitherto pergunnah of Shahjehanpore, has now been separated into three pergunnahs. The river Gurra divides pergunnah Shahjehanpore from Pergunnah Jumour, and the Gurraie *nulla* separates Pergunnah Jumour from Pergunnah Kant.

1.	2.	3.	4.	5.	6.	7.
Name of Tuhseel.	Name of Pergunnah.	Population by census of 1872.	Area in square miles.	Population per square mile.	Number of mouzahs.	Number of muhals.
SHAHJEHANPORE,	Shahjehanpore, ...	153,147	156	981	194	265
	Jumour, ...	53,340	102	525	127	183
	Kant, ...	72,596	144	504	217	301
	Whole Tuhseel,...	279,083	402	695	538	750
JELLALABAD, ...	Jellalabad,	164,356	317	518	392	584
TILHUR, ...	Tilhur, ...	86,321	127	680	211	271
	Meeranpore Kuttra, ...	9,970	13	767	12	21
	Khera Bujhera,...	46,795	88	531	137	172
	Julalpore, ...	44,924	75	599	112	187
	Nigohee, ...	56,618	113	504	152	193
	Whole Tuhseel,...	244,558	416	588	624	844
POWAYN, ...	Burragaon, ...	49,527	83	599	126	160
	Powayn, ...	159,199	312	510	427	529
	Khotar, ...	52,768	203	260	257	276
	Whole Tuhseel,...	261,494	598	437	810	965
	Whole District,...	949,471	*1,733	548	2,364	3,063

* *N.B.*—The population figures are taken from the Census Report of 1872, but the areas there given are not all correct (*e.g.*, Powayn is given at 302, and whole district as 1,723 square miles), and consequently there is a corresponding difference in the average per square mile.

A

Pergunnah Poorunpore, which up to 1865 formed a part of the Powayn tuhseel, was detached from this district and made over to Phillibheet in that year, and the independent *peshkaree* of Khotar was abolished in May 1871, and Pergunnah Khotar (after the transfer of the detached tract Pulleea to the Kheree district of Oudh in 1867) was included in the Powayn Tuhseel in lieu of Poorunpore.

3. The district extends to within three miles of the river Sardah on the north-east, and lies between it and the river Ganges on the south-west. Its greatest length is about 75 miles, and its greatest width, measured across just south of the towns of Shahjehanpore and Tilhur, is 38 miles.

General features of the district.

Where the general level is not broken by the rivers, streams, or *nullas*, the country is even and without any hills or hillocks or considerable undulations; almost a dead flat in fact, with nothing to break the m notony of the view or intercept the sight of the horizon all round except the inhabited sites of villages and numerous mango groves. It is the same unvarying *tope* and *maidan* as is to be met with all over Rohilkhund and Oudh, but not quite so bad as the Doab. It has a gradual slope of about 1¾ to 2 feet in the mile from north-west to south-east, and this is the direction of the course of all the rivers and streams and *nullas*. The general elevation above sea level is from 600 feet in the north-eastern to 500 feet in the south-western end of the district. There are slight local variations in the elevation, as the almost unvarying rule is a high sandy ridge along above the valley of a river or stream, sloping gradually back to the general level, and here and there low lying clayey dips, the commencement of ponds and drainage lines. The ordinary soil of the level country is a light loam, light both in colour and consistency when dry (light earth or soil, not sand), but turning to the dark rich colour of good mould when wetted.

There are two general divisions—the *bangar* or up lands, and the *khadir* or *terai*, the low lands in the valleys or troughs of the rivers and streams. The denominations of soil will be treated of in their proper place further on (*vide* Sec. V.) There is nothing in this district at all answering to the "*mar*" of Bareilly and Phillibheet, as no part of this district adjoins the "*Terai*" proper.

4. The Civil Station and Military Cantonment of Shahjehanpore is, however, one of the prettiest in the whole of the North-Western Provinces.

The Civil Station and Military Cantonments.

It is situated on a high piece of table-land between the rivers Gurra and Khanout, and about two miles above the confluence of these rivers. The fine mango groves and scattered trees, and graceful waving bamboos, with the church tower peeping out of the foliage, and the green valley of the Khanout, with its high ridge on the opposite side, all unite to make a very picturesque view, and the general appearance is quite park-like, even to the grass being green, and not brown and burnt. Since the mutiny the head-quarters and one wing of a European Infantry Regiment, and four companies of a Native Regiment, have been quartered here, but it has just now been done away with as a station for European troops, though certainly one of the healthiest in the whole of India. The Oudh and Rohilkhund Railway passes through the civil station and a small part of cantonments; but as it is in cutting for the greater part of the distance, it has not spoilt the appearance of the station as it would have otherwise.

5. The climate is much like that of most parts of Oudh and Rohilkhund, drier than that of lower Bengal, but moister than that of the Doab;

The climate.

and the country throughout the year, except in the months of May and June (till the rains come on), has some pretensions to looking green and fresh, and is not brown and parched like the Doab. It is quite an exception for two full months to pass at any time of the year without some rain, and usually the winter rains are pretty regular and copious about Christmas time, or during the first fortnight in January. The description given by Mr. Moens, in his report of the Bareilly settlement, is almost equally applicable here, and I take the liberty of quoting it, especially as I cannot supply the same information about the meteorological phenomena that he gives in Table I., in consequence of there being no observatory here. :—

"The meteorological phenomena of the district, and notably those attendant on the rainy season, are largely influenced by its proximity to the Himalayas and the Terai to the north. Indeed, the Oudh Terai to the eastward, lying as it does almost in the direct course of the south-east monsoon towards Bareilly (for the winds are here directed by the line of the hills into a course nearly due east) contributes not a little to determine our climate. Bareilly city itself, and all the northern pergunnahs, are fully within the limits of the heavier storms of the hills, and the rainy season consequently commences a few days earlier, and terminates a little later than in the districts more to the south, while the cold weather is of rather longer duration. The climate may therefore be termed sub-Himalayan, and presents the corresponding features of dampness, moderate heat, and partial immunity from violent hot winds, which rarely blow after sunset, and are never prolonged through the night. They usually commence to blow towards the middle or end of April, and last, with frequent intermissions of east winds, until early in June. Usually in the first fortnight of May there are storms, sometimes accompanied by rain, which temporarily lower the temperature. Early in June the west winds are displaced by southerly breezes; clouds gradually collect, and violent storms, succeeded by the regular rains, reduce the day temperature from 95° to 85° F. From this time till the middle of August is enjoyable weather. The breaks in the rains at this time are showery, cloudy, windy days, admitting of open air exercise all day long. From the middle of August to the end of September the weather is close, windless, and steamy, with occasional heavy rain, and the days and nights are oppressively hot. Gradually the temperature lessens, till, from the second week of October, a camp life in tents becomes tolerable, and from the beginning of November to the end of March the weather is unsurpassable. Clear bright days and nights, exceedingly cold from sunset to 10 A. M , render the large camp fires exceedingly enjoyable up to the first or second week in March. About Christmas time, and again at the end of January, there are two or three days of heavy rain, effectually irrigating the cold weather crops. Occasionally there are heavy mists or fogs (koer) which come on during the nights, and last sometimes as late as noon. These are considered very injurious to the spring crops, in which they produce rust (rutta). The accompanying table gives the chief meteorological phenomena for the three years from June, 1868, to June, 1871, at Bareilly station, latitude 28°21′30″ north, longitude 79°27′30″ east. Height of barometer cistern 570 feet above sea level" :—

"TABLE I.

Month.	Barometer reduced to 32°.				Thermometer in shade.		Humidity saturation, 100.				Rain-fall in month.
	4 A.M	10 A.M.	4 P.M.	10 P.M.	MAX.	MIN.	4 A.M.	10 A.M.	4 P.M.	10 A.M.	
January, ...	29·382	29·484	29·394	29·412	70·3f	44·5	85	68	53	76	·98
February, ...	·295	·368	·280	·321	78·1	5·5	83	57	43	71	·58
March, ...	·187	·298	·199	·242	86·3	59·6	77	57	40	65	1·27
April, ...	·114	·201	·090	·136	98·5	66·8	66	48	34	51	·60
May, ...	28·985	·061	28·937	28·929	105·6	77·6	63	41	35	53	·98
June, ...	·916	28·979	·865	·911	102·9	81·0	74	49	45	65	8·52
July, ...	9·18	29·015	·905	·952	95·2	78·6	83	62	59	83	9·37
August, ...	·994	·658	·960	29·025	95·2	79·0	89	63	64	83	4·91
September, ...	29·102	·182	29·079	·125	92·6	76·0	89	74	63	87	9·43
October, ...	·254	·338	·240	·264	91·3	65·8	90	62	54	79	1·55
November, ...	·391	·470	382	·403	84·1	60·9	89	61	50	78	··
December, ...	·462	·539	·448	·478	75·4	45·1	90	66	51	77	·12
Means, ...	29·168	29·249	29·148	29·183	89·6	64·8	82	59	49	72	38·31

General average barometer reading, 29·189 inches.
Mean temperature, ... 77·2° F.
Humidity, ... ·65."″

The climate of the district generally is good and healthy, the notable exception being the northernmost pergunnah, Khotar, which from its proximity to the Terai forests, and from the quantity of forest in and about it, is a very malarious part of the country, and bad fever and ague are rampant there in September and October, and again, but not so excessive perhaps, in April and May. The climate in the northern parts of Pergunnah Powayn, adjoining Khotar, is very smilar to that of Khotar, but not quite so bad. Some parts of Jellalabad about the Sote, and between the Sote and the Ganges, are unhealthy, and this unhealthiness is, I think, attributable in some measure to the water-logging of the country by damming the Sote for irrigation, but also in part to the heavy floods of the Ganges and Sote.

6. The regular rains generally set in about the 15th of June, and continue, with-

The rainfall.

out any considerable break or cessation of more than two or three days at a time, up to the middle or end of September. The average annual rainfall for the last ten years is 37 inches, the largest fall having been 54.5 inches in 1867, and the smallest 18.3 in 1868. Further details will be seen from the following table, in which the average rainfall for each month of the past ten years is given in inches and tenths of an inch. Amongst other things, it will be observed that November is the only month in which there is no rain, at least not sufficient to be registered :—

Average rainfall of the entire District for each month of the year for ten years in inches and tenths of inches.

Year.	January.	February.	March.	April.	May.	June.	July.	August.	September.	October.	November.	December.	Whole 12 months.
1863-64,	·6	...	...	·7	1·3	6·2	12·6	13·0	1·0	2·7	...	...	38·1
1864-65,	·5	·6	1·2	·2	1·2	·3	10·2	5·8	4·7	·5	·2	...	25·4
1865-66,	·8	·4	...	·4	...	1·1	13·9	8·4	6·1	...	...	·7	31·8
1866-67,	·4	2·2	...	·2	·7	1·0	12·5	7·3	2·6	...	...	...	26·9
1867-68,	1·1	1·2	·5	·6	1·9	11·9	14·9	6·8	8·8	6·5	...	·3	54·5
1868-69,	·8	·1	·7	...	...	3·7	5·6	2·4	4·8	...	...	·2	18·3
1869-70,	...	·5	1·0	...	...	2·3	6·7	5·3	11·3	7·1	...	·9	35·1
1870-71,	·9	·3	...	·5	2·9	12·3	9·4	11·6	10·8	·4	...	...	49·1
1871-72,	2·8	·7	·5	...	·6	7·3	24·7	11·8	3·5	...	...	1·7	53·6
1872-73,	·5	2	1·0	·2	1·0	8·3	11·9	9·5	4·6	...	...	·2	37·4
Average, ...	·9	·6	·5	·3	1·0	5·4	12·2	8·2	5·8	1·7	...	·4	37·0

The rainfall all over the district is very even and universal, but rather greater at the northern end (Khotar), and rather less at the southern end (Jellalabad) than in the middle parts (Shahjehanpore and Tilhur). The averages on the same ten years are Khotar 39.7, Powayn 38.9, Shahjehanpore, 38.1, Tilhur 34.5, Jelallabad 32.4. The above statistics were supplied to me by the Board's office from their registers.

7. From the foregoing it will be at once apparent that irrigation is not a *sine*

Irrigation not a sine quâ non, and easy, from the proximity of water to the surface.

quâ non in this district as it is in the Doab, and the fact of the water-level being only from 12 to 15 feet from the surface, and *kuccha* wells being made with great facility, irrigation is possible almost anywhere, and can be arranged for speedily, though no traces of wells may be visible a week or ten days before irrigation actually commences. The area actually irrigated in any one year depends, therefore, more on the season, and necessity for irrigation than on the capability of irrigation. The area entered as irrigated is that ordinarily irrigated in average years, *not* the area capable of irrigation, or a protected area, irrespective of harvest or crop. Out of a total cultivated area of all but 7½ lacs of acres, nearly five lacs are irrigable, chiefly from wells, but in some pergunnahs extensively from ponds and rivers; and there are from 87,000 to 90,000 acres of *khadir* or *terai* lands not requiring

Name of Pergunnah.	Average distance of water level from the surface of the earth in feet.
Shahjehanpore, ...	15
Jumour, ...	11
Kant, ...	14
Jellalabad, ...	13
Tilhur, ...	16
Kuttra, ...	16
Khera Bujhers, ...	17
Jelalpore, ...	16
Nigohee, ...	18
Burragaon, ...	15
Powayn, ...	12
Khotar, ...	10

irrigation. So that more than 5¾ lacs of acres, or about 77½ per cent., out of a total cultivated area of under 7¼ lacs, are either irrigable or independent of irrigation, and only (1,67,000) one lac sixty-seven thousand acres, or about 22½ per cent., are incapable of irrigation in the whole district. So long then as the present rainfall and regular winter rains continue, and the water-level remains unchanged, it seems a self-evident proposition that canals are not required in this district, and are more likely to do harm than good by raising the water-level, causing a spread of malaria, and possibly a growth of *reh*, where there is none whatever now.

8. These *kutcha* wells are very simple and primitive arrangements, and usually
Description of the various kinds of *kutcha* wells.
fall in every rains, and new ones are made in the cold season when required. They are of three kinds—the best, only constructible where the substratum about the water level is firm and not sandy, being those called *pools* or *gurras*, from which the water is raised by means of a leathern bucket, made of a single hide, and a long thick rope over a pulley ; men, and not cattle, usually being employed. These wells are similar to those commonly used throughout the Doab, but are far inferior to them, as they are only from 3 to 3½ feet in diameter, and have no cylinder of wood or bricks, but only a lining, up to just above the water-level, made of twisted stalks or twigs. They are seldom spring wells, as the real spring is not usually reached, and they never carry more than one wheel and bucket, and that much smaller than those used on masonry wells or on *kutcha* wells in the Doab, and the run is much shorter, as the water is nearer the surface. The cost of making these wells is from Rs. 3 to Rs. 5 each. The depth of water in the wells varies from five to eight feet, when the spring is tapped it reaches 12 and 15 feet, but this is very exceptional. The other two kinds of *kutcha* wells are merely small holes about two feet in diameter, made at a cost of from Re. 1 to Rs. 2, and called, the one "*chirkee*" or "*rentee*," and the other *dhenklee* or *dhooklee* ;" each is worked by only one man. In the *chirkee* the water is raised by means of a wheel on two supports immediately above the mouth of the well, with a thin rope passing over it, and an earthen pot at each end, the one ascending full as the other descends empty. The *dhenklee* is the common lever well, the earthen pot being attached by a rope to the long end of the lever, and a lump of dried clay to weight the shorter end. The lever is of wood, and works on a pivot between two earthen pillars or wooden uprights, fixed away at a short distance back from the well, so that the point of the long arm, where the string is attached, comes directly over the mouth of the well, when the water pot is lowered into the water. These are made for about Re. 1 to Re. 1-12 each. The depth of water is seldom over 4 feet, and often only 18 inches or two feet. Masonry wells are not required, and but few are to be found for purposes of irrigation, except in gardens and in the vicinity of the city of Shahjehanpore itself.

It is impossible to give any average area of irrigation per *kutcha* well as for wells in the Doab, because, in the case of the better kind of wells, the area of irrigation is practically only limited by the number of fields in the vicinity requiring irrigation. For, one watering being sufficient, and that often being a sprinkling rather than a thorough slushing, there is no restraint on area irrigated by the necessity of returning to irrigate the same fields a second and third time. Also this better kind *(pool)* is frequently constructable in any part of the area at pleasure (and not only in certain spots called *puruns*), as the inferior kinds always are, and they are therefore made wherever required, even for two or three fields only, and, though capable of irrigating a larger area than that to which water is actually given, are used for that limited area only. The *pool* well irrigates on an average about 2 *kutcha beeghas* (⅓rd acre) per diem, and the *rentee* and *dhenklee* about one *kutcha beegha*. When wheat or any large area has to be irrigated by *rentees* or *dhenklees (pool* wells not being constructible), several are usually made near together, and the water from them is united into one channel, so as to get a fair stream and good flow. For vegetables, opium, and garden products they are used singly.

B

9. The names of the rivers in the district are given in the margin, arranged in order according to their size and importance. Accounts of these will be found in the succeeding chapters; the assessment reports of the various tuhseels, each in its own place, e. g., of the Ganges, Ramgunga, Sote, and Bygool in Chapter III.; the Jellalabad report, paragraphs 19 to 24. It is sufficient to mention here that boats for traffic ply only on the first three.

The Rivers.
Ganges.
Ramgunga.
Gurra (or Deoha.)
Khanout.
Goomtee.
Bygool.
Sote.
Kutna (Western.)

All the rivers, and more especially perhaps the Gurra (which in the Bareilly district is called the Deoha), are used for floating wood down from the forests and jungles under the Himalayas, but not to any very considerable extent; not such as to constitute a regular trade in this district. The Ganges, Ramgunga, and Gurra all change their courses more or less, and cause considerable change in the position and nature of the land in their immediate vicinity; and after heavy rains the alluvion and diluvion along their banks is very considerable, the Ramgunga being the most erratic in its course and sudden in its changes of the three.

The Khanout, Goomtee, Bygool, Sote, and Western Kutna do not change their courses, or cause any alluvion or diluvion. The Khanout and Goomtee have valleys of their own, with high sandy ridges on either side, the stream wandering about through the valley, sometimes near the one, and sometimes near the other high bank, but keeping to its channel without any perceptible variation. The Bygool, Sote, and Western Kutna have no valleys or troughs of their own, but flow quietly and peaceably between high banks, and are dammed for irrigation (see reports on Tuhseel Tilhur and Jellalabad). None of these rivers rise in the district, but all, except the first three, end here. The confluence of the Khanout and Gurra takes place just below the town of Shahjehanpore; of the Bygool and Ramgunga in Pergunnah Jellalabad, and of the Kutna and Deoha (Gurra) on the confines of Pergunnahs Nigohee and Tilhur. The Sote, under the name of the Bookra Khár, enters the Ganges *khadir* in this district, but the actual confluence occurs just outside of this and within the borders of the Futtehgurh district.

10. The names of the principal streams or *nullas* are given in the margin. They have running streams near the end of their courses only, and not all of them even there throughout the year, and are all of them dammed at intervals for irrigation. Most of them are merely local drainage lines, commencing in or just on the borders of the district, and ending in some one of the rivers within it. The exceptions are the Northern Kutna, which rises from the large *pucka* Tank at Matee, in the northern part of Pergunnah Khotar, and becomes a stream just as it enters the Kheree district of Oudh. The Sukheta *nulla* which leaves this district and becomes the boundary between the Oudh districts of Kheree and

The small streams and nullas.

Stream or *nulla*.	Name of river into which it falls within the district.
Anduwee, Western ...	Bygool.
„ Southern ...	Sote.
Kutna., Northern, ...	None.
Sukheta, ...	Ditto.
Gurraie, ...	Ditto.
Kymooa, ...	Gurra.
Jhukna, ...	Goomtee.
Bhynsee, ...	Ditto.
Muhey, ...	Sote.
Tureona, ...	Bhynsee nulla.
Sukurria, ...	Khanout.
Baruh, ...	Ditto.
Reotee, ...	Bygool.
Bhagsee, ...	Gurraie nulla.
Arl, ...	Anduwee, Southern.
Burgoodia, ...	Ramgunga.

Hurdui, and the Gurrai *nulla* which enters the Hurdui district some two miles west of the Gurra, but soon joins it. There are also several old channels of the Ramgunga which are silted up at each end and in different parts, but which are flowing streams during the rains, and have deep *dibrees* in them here and there, which retain water the whole year round, and abound in large river fish.

11. There are no pieces of water in the district worthy of the name of lakes, as even the largest dry up in April or May in ordinary seasons, or else shrink to the dimensions of small ponds, and afford no irrigation to the young sugarcane in those months; the only crop which is then in

Ponds and marshes.

the ground and requiring irrigation. There are, however, numbers of large ponds and shallow marshes in different parts of the district, chiefly at the commencement of lines of drainage, or in their course before the line of drainage has assumed the form of a defined *nulla*. The largest of these cover from 150 to 280 acres (but there is one, that in Amursunda, between Powayn and Nahul, of over 300 acres), and are found in Pergunnahs Powayn, Burragaon, Shahjehanpore, Kant, and Jellalabad. There is only one of any size in Pergunnah Khotar in the two Nadothas (Dabee Dass and Hunsram), and that is a very large pond (271 acres), and never dries up completely. All these ponds, and numbers of smaller ones in which water lies after an ordinary rainy season up to November, and even the first half of December, afford very extensive irrigation to the young wheat in the months of October and November.

12. They also contain numbers of several kinds of fish which are caught with Spontaneous produce of ponds and marshes. nets of various sorts ; drag nets, casting nets, and others, in the larger ponds, but with the hands in the smaller ones when the water has been drawn off for irrigation. The large ponds and marshes abound in waterfowl of all sorts, several kinds of geese, eight or ten different kinds of ducks, and several species of teal and snipe, and afford excellent sport for some four months during the cold season. *Singhara* nuts are grown in most of the small ponds and in parts of the larger ones ; and when the ponds are favourable to the growth of the *singhara*, and men of the *dheenwur* or *kahar* caste are numerous in the neighbourhood, such ponds pay as high a rent on their area as good cultivated land.

In most of the larger ponds a species of wild rice is usually found, called *pisaie*, which is gathered and eaten as rice, and also sold as *pisaie* rice in the bazar. There is too a species of grass which also grows spontaneously in and along the edges of the shallow marshes and large ponds, the seed of which (called *sanwan* or *jharwa*) is gathered and eaten by the poor.

13. The uncultivated, but culturable, waste of the district consists chiefly of Jungle, forest, and grass lands. *dhak* and thorn bush jungle, usually with, but sometimes without grass in it, and there is but little open grazing ground or pasture land. The *dhak* tree (butea frondosa) grows to a large size if allowed, but these *dhak* jungles are usually cut down every eight or ten years, and sold for fuel or charcoal, or when not cut down incisions are made in the bark to cause the gum to exude, which is gathered and sold. Hence in the greater part of the district the *dhak* jungles do not consist of large, full-grown trees, but of mutilated and stunted trees and saplings. The largest amount of continuous *dhak* jungle is to found in the *Bunkuttee Ilaka* of the Jellalabad tuhseel. But there are large patches, and stretches of it extending through several villages in almost every pergunnah, and especially along the Oudh border. The flower of the *dhak* is used for dye, and the gum for mixing in indigo and other dyes, and for other purposes ; the wood supplies fuel and makes good charcoal, and the land on which the *dhak* grows affords grazing ground for cattle and sheep and goats, so that this *dhak* jungle and culturable waste area (as it is called) is by no means unprofitable, nor is it desirable that it should all be reclaimed and brought under the plough. The only forest or tall tree jungle is to be found in pergunnahs Powayn and Khotar. The trees are principally small *sal*, called here *koron*, but in parts *mhowa* and *asaina* trees are numerous, and the uses to which these trees can be, and are put, will be mentioned in a coming paragraph. There are several other kinds of forest trees, and creepers and shrubs scattered throughout these *koron* forests, but they call for no special notice. All further particulars and details concerning these forests will be found in paragraph 25 of Chapter V., the Powayn Tuhseel Report. The whole of this unreclaimed area, made up of forest, *dhak* jungle, open grass land, &c., which is designated old unbroken culturable waste, and is capable of reclamation, and is not barren or incapable of cultivation, amounts for the whole district to one hundred and eighty-nine thousand eight hundred acres in round numbers (189,768), or 296¼ square miles, and bears a proportion to the total area of the district of 17 per cent., and to

the malgoozaree or assessable area (*viz.*, culturable and cultivated, inclusive of groves and new fallow) of just under 20 per cent.

14. The tall thatching grass grows chiefly in shallow marshes or low lying land in which water collects and lies during the rains, land which if cultivated would produce only common rice, and the crop would be in a marked degree liable to destruction by floods. The best thatching grass is called *gándur* or *punnee*, and this is valuable, especially within eight or ten miles of the city and cantonments. It is a flat-bladed grass growing to about 3 and 3½ feet in height, with a reddish tinge in it, and, for a grass, not very hard or coarse. The price varies greatly according to the season and produce as well as the requirements, *e. g.*, the fires in the city and all the country round having been abnormally and very exceptionally numerous and severe this year (March, April, and May 1874), the demand for thatching grass will be far above average in October and November next. This *gandur* also affords the *seenk*, of which the common hand brooms are made, which are universally used by all the sweepers. This *seenk* is the reed or stalk of the *gandur* grass on which the flower and seed is produced, and only grows to broom size in the best *gandur* in moist low lying lands.

The thatching and reed grasses.

Another common grass which grows in the same places as the *gandur*, and which is used for thatching, is the *káns*. It is a taller grass, growing to a height of five and six feet, and even higher, round and coarse and brittle, and is seldom carted to any distance, but used by the poor for thatching their huts in the villages. It breaks and rots much quicker than the good *poolah*-grass, *gandur*, and is consequently of less value and cheaper. It is not the *káns* of Bundlekhund and the lower Gangetic Doab which causes so much damage to cultivation by the rapidity with which it runs over the country and refuses to be eradicated, and does not interfere with cultivation.

The third kind of grass or reed is the most valuable of all. It grows chiefly in the half-formed sandy valleys of the Ganges and other rivers, but also in any sandy damp places. It is also planted as a protection along the edges of baghs and fields, and especially where the soil is very sandy and liable to blow about and shift with the wind. The reed grows to a height of twelve and fourteen feet, ordinarily and exceptionally to eighteen and twenty feet. The stalk or reed is called *séntha*, and the grass which is a flat, broad, coarse grass *putél*, and the whole plant *sirkunduh* or *surkuruh*.

The *putél* is used for thatching. The *séntha* or reed is put to various uses; the top part, for a length of about 4½ to 5 feet, is made into screens or *sirkees*, the uses of which are numerous ; and from the strong stout part of the reed couches, chairs, and stools (*morahs*) are made. String is also made from the top part, but usually before it has flowered, ripened, and turned yellow, when it is called *moonj*.

Whereas the supply of the various kinds of thatching grass within the district is more than sufficient for the demand, and much in the northern distant portions remains uncut and gets burnt in April and May, the supply of the *sirkunduh*, or rather of the *séntha*, is not nearly sufficient, and hence what there is of it in the district is more valuable. It abounds across the Sardah in the Nepal *Terai*, where there are perfect seas of it, and quantities are brought from there in carts, and also *sirkees* are manufactured there on the spot and brought ready made into the district.

The Shahjehanpore matting (which is proof against white-ants) is made of a grass called *béb* (pronounced like the word babe) which, however, does not grow within the district but at the foot of the hills, where the roots of the hills (so to speak) spread into the plains. Quantities of this *béb* grass are brought across the Sardah with the *sirkunduh*.

15. The names of the indigenous trees of the district are given in the marginal list arranged in alphabetical order of their vernacular names. For the botanical or scientific names of most of them I am indebted to Dr. W. Jameson, Superintendent of the Government Botanical Gardens at

Indigenous trees.

Seharunpore. Where there is no regular English name in common use, the vernacular name is given, with the spelling according to the English pronunciation or vulgarization of the correct wood. I have omitted the strictly garden fruit trees, not only those which are undoubtedly foreign, such as peaches, pears, &c., but also the ordinary country-fruit

Serial Number.	Vernacular Name.	The name ordinarily used in English.	The Scientific or Botanical Name.
1	Ambh,...	Mango,	Mangifera Indica.
2	Aonla,...	Aonla,...	Emblica Officinalis.
3	Asaina,	Sein, ...	Pentaptera Glabra.
4	Amaltas,	Amaltas,	Cassia (Catharto carpus) fistula.
5	Anjain,	Anjain.	Bauhinia (Phanera) variegata.
6	Báns, ...	Bamboo,	Bambusa Arundinacea.
7	Bél,	Bail, ...	Ægle Marmelos.
8	Béree, ...	Béree, ...	Zizyphus Vulgaris.
9	Babool or Keekur,	Babool or Keekur, or thorny Acacia.	Acacia Arabica.
10	Buhéra,	Buhera,	Terminalia Belerica.
11	Bukain,	Bukain,	Melia azedarach.
12	Burgud,	The Bur, Burgod or Banyan tree.	Ficus Indica.
13	Burhul,	Jack fruit tree,	Artocarpus integufolia.
14	Dhák, ...	Dhak or Dhauk, ...	Butea Frondosa.
15	Goolur,	Goolur, Wild fig-tree,	Ficus Glomerata.
16	Goondnee,	Goondnee,	Cordia Rothii.
17	Hársinghár,	Weeping Nyctanthes,	Nyctanthes, Arbor tristis.
18	Imlee, ...	Tamarind,	Tamarindus Indica.
19	Jamun,	Wild plum,	Syzygium Jambolanum or Eugenia Jambolana.
20	Khirnee,	Khirnee,	Mimusops Kanki.
21	Khujoor,	Wild date,	Phœnix Sylvestris.
22	Koron,...	Small Sál or Saul,	Shorea (Vatica) robusta.
23	Kuchnar,	Kuchnar.	Bauhinia (Phanera) purpurea.
24	Kuthul,	Jack fruit tree,	Artocarpus lakoocha.
25	Kyth,	Keith, ...	Feronia Elephantum.
26	Lahsora,	Luhsora,	Cordia myxa, or latifolia.
27	Mahooa,	Mowa, ...	Bassia latifolia.
28	Moolsruee,	Moolsuree,	Mimusops elengi.
29	Neem, ...	Neem, ...	Azadirachta Indica.
30	Pákur,...	Citron-leaved Indian fig-tree,...	Ficus Venosa.
31	Peepul,	Peepul, Sacred fig tree,	Ficus religiosa.
32	Semul,...	Silk Cotton tree, ...	Bombax heptaphyllum.
33	Sháhtoot,	Mulberry,	Morus Indica.
34	Sheehsum or seeson,	Sissoo, Indian rose wood,	Dalbergia Sissoo.
35	Siris, ...	Siris, kind of Acacia,	Acacia Speciosa, or Mimosa Seris
36	Téndoo,	Bhueri,	Diospyros ebannm or tomentosa.
37	Tunn or Toon,	Toon, ...	Cedrela toona.

trees, such as the plantain, various kinds of oranges and limes, the loquat, guava, and pomegranate, all of which, besides several kind of grafted mangoes, are to be found, not only in the gardens of the civil and military residents, but also in the private gardens of the natives in and about all the large towns and villages. I have also omitted as not indigenous, though apparently thriving very well in many of the compounds and along some of the roads, and having become thoroughly acclimatized, the teak, *tectona grandis*, the coral-tree, *erythina stricta*, the cork tree, *millingtona hortensis*, and several others, all of them introduced, I believe, some 25 to 30 years ago, by Mr. Buller, the then Collector.

16. The principal timber trees, the wood of which is in most general use for all

The timber trees. kinds of agricultural and domestic purposes, are the mango, the bamboo, the babool or keekur, the sissoo, and the toon. The wood of the following is also used, but to a less extent, *viz.*, the asaina, the bail, the dhak, the tamarind, the wild plum, the small sál, the neem, the mowa, and the three fig trees, pakur, peepul, and goolur.

The mango wood to a great extent takes the place of deal in England, as it is a

Mango. light, cheap, easily worked wood, which cannot last long, as it is easily destroyed by white ants and the various wood insects. It is also very extensively used for firewood in the Rosa factory, and for the engines on the Oudh and Rohilkhund Railway, but it is not a good wood for fuel, nor yet for charcoal, only it is more plentiful than any other.

The bamboo is not, properly speaking, a timber tree, or a tree at all, but a giant

Bamboo. reed. Bamboos are used of all sizes, both unsplit and split, but chiefly split in thatches and screens and basket-work.

The *babool* or *keekur* is not near so plentiful in this district as across the Ganges ;
in fact there are but few *keekur* trees of any size in any part
Babool.
of the district except in pergunnah Jellalabad, between the Ramgunga and the Ganges, where they are plentiful, and grow to a large size. The wood is
hard and heavy, and very suitable for naves of wheels and agricultural purposes generally. It also makes excellent fuel, as it burns slowly, and throws out great heat, and
keekur charcoal is inferior to none. The bark is used for tanning.

Sissoo is a hard, heavy, dark coloured, well grained, handsome wood, which is put
to every kind of domestic use, *viz.*, for rafters, planks, boards,
Sissoo.
door and window-frames, and all kinds of furniture, both
European and native. Good and well seasoned sheeshum is proof against white ants
and most of the wood insects. It is of this wood, but procured from the Nepal forests,
that the gun carriages and wheels of the Indian Artillery are made.

Toon is a pretty wood for furniture, something like mahogany, of a dark colour,
but strong in substance, though light in weight. It is chiefly
Toon.
used for furniture and boxes.

The *asaina* and *koron* trees grow only in the tree forests and jungle in Powayn
and Khotar, and principally in Khotar, and not to any very
Asaina and koron.
great size, and are chiefly used for long poles (*bullees*), and for
making light country carts and cart wheels, and for door frames, as well as for charcoal.

Ebony. The ebony tree is also found in these forests, but does not
grow to any size in this district.

The best charcoal and most expensive is made of the tamarind, *koron*, and *keekur*,
but it is also extensively made of other trees, such as mango,
Charcoal.
dhak, mowa, &c.

17. The fruit trees of the list given at the commencement of the 15th paragraph, the
fruit of which is generally eaten raw or made into
Preserves or pickles, are here given in the margin,
and there are no less than 17 of them. The flowers
of the *dhak*, *weeping nyctanthes*, and *toon* are used
for dye, and the fruit of the *amaltas*, *buhéra*, and
bail for medicinal purposes, as also are the bark of
the *kachnar*, and the leaves of the *neem* tree, and the
oil extracted from its seed. The *mowa* tree is found
chiefly in the northern part of the district, and especially in the most recently reclaimed parts, and
in unreclaimed patches and the forest tracts. The
wood is hard and good, and the mowa tree is gradually disappearing, and there seem to be no young
ones coming on. Ordinarily, where the mowa tree
abounds, an intoxicating liquor is distilled from its flowers, but here the flowers are
very little used for this purpose, the country liquor being almost entirely distilled
from unrefined sugar. The pods of the *semul* produce a silky fibre (silk-cotton) which
is much used for stuffing pillows and cushions, and is very suitable for such purposes
as it is elastic and does not get so easily compressed or matted as cotton, but has not
the same warmth. The *semul* tree is to be found all over the district, but is most
plentiful north of Shahjehanpore.

Trees, the fruit and flower of which are made use of.

Number of complete list.	Common English name.
1	Mango.
2	Aonla.
7	Bail.
8	Béree.
13	Two kinds of Jack
24	fruit.
15	Wild fig.
16	Goondnee.
18	Tamarind.
19	Wild plum.
20	Khirnee.
21	Wild date.
25	Keith.
26	Luhsora.
27	Mowa.
28	Moolsuree.
33	Mulberry.

18. There are no large *oosur* plains or extensive continuous stretches of unculturable waste land in the Shahjehanpore district similar to those
Barren waste, Oosur, &c.
across the Ganges. The only part of the district where there
is anything approaching to the *oosur* plain of the Gangetic Doab is in the *Bunkuttee
Ilaqa* of Tuhseel Jellalabad, near the Ganges, and this will be found treated of in para.
27 of Chapter III, the report of that particular tuhseel. The barren and unculturable
area of the district is consequently made up almost entirely of the inhabited sites of the

city towns and villages, including the cantonments, roads, rivers, and ponds, and amounts to 114,266 acres, 178 square miles, and is less than 10¼ per cent. of the total area of the district.

19. The nodular limestone called *kunkur* (a kind of petrified clay, dug out of pits in a soft state, but hardening rapidly on exposure to the air, and found usually near marshes or ponds or in drainage lines), which is used for burning into lime for mortar, and for the metalling of the consolidated or metalled roads, was supposed to exist in only a very few parts of the district, as recently as nine or ten years ago. Now, however, it is found in most parts of the district, but chiefly in the Shahjehanpore and Tilhur Tuhseels, and Pergunnah Burragaon. Whether *kunkur* did not exist in the same quantities before, and is consequently a new growth in this part of the country, I am not prepared to say for certain; but I believe that much of it is of recent growth, and that it was searched for diligently before, and only not found because it did not exist in the same quantities that it now does. It is to this scarcity of *kunkur* that the want of metalled roads, not only in the Shahjehanpore District, but in Rohilkhund generally, is always attributed, and I believe with a great deal of truth. At all events, the increase in metalled roads has been very considerable within the last eight or nine years, and whereas the facility of obtaining funds to make these roads has been decidedly less.

20. So lately as 1867 A. D., there was no metalled road leading into or out of the cantonments, civil lines, or city of Shahjehanpore for a distance of more than a mile, and Shahjehanpore was inaccessible by any kind of wheeled conveyance from every direction. There were the metalled roads through the city, the civil lines, and cantonments, and for about a mile out on the Bareilly road in one, and on the Seetapore road in the other, direction, but nothing more, excepting the portion of Grand Trunk Road between Futtehgurh and Bareilly, which passed through Jellalabad and Tilhur of this district. Now Shahjehanpore is connected by metalled roads with Lucknow through Seetapore on one side, with Bareilly through Tilhur on another, with Futtehgurh through Jellalabad on a third, and with Powayn on the fourth side. The most recent of these is that past Kant to Jellalabad, which has only been completed this cold season (1873-74 A. D). The extent of good metalled roads, bridged and passable in all seasons of the year, including the portions of Grand Trunk Road in Pergunnahs Jellalabad, Kant, Tilhur, and Kuttra, and inclusive also of the cross roads in the city, civil lines, and cantonments, amounts to one hundred and twenty-five miles now, as against 46 miles in 1866 A. D., at the commencement of this settlement. Further particulars of the metalled and unmetalled, but made roads, as also of the common country roads, will be found for each tuhseel separately in its own special chapter (*vide* paras. 18 of Chapters II. and III., 33 and 34 of Chapter IV., and 22 of Chapter V).

21. The Oudh and Rohilkhund Railway passes across the middle of the district, entering it at the southern corner of Pergunnah Shahjehanpore, and running north till nearly opposite the city, when it bends round to the west to cross the Khanout valley at right angles, and thence runs due west past Tilhur, and with a slight inclination northwards past Meeranpore Kuttra on its way to Bareilly. Shahjehanpore is therefore now connected by rail with Lucknow on the south, and through it with Cawnpore and Benares on the East Indian Railway, and to the north-west with Bareilly and Moradabad and Chundousi in Rohilkhund, and through Bareilly with the East Indian Railway at Allygurh. This is a very different state of things to what existed in the end of 1866 A. D., when I first came to Shahjehanpore, and commenced the measurements for the new settlement, for then the railway line had not even been surveyed, and the state of the roads has already been mentioned. There are now 35 miles of the Oudh and Rohilkhund Railway passing through the Shahjehanpore District, and four railway stations, *viz.*, (1) at Kahelia, ten miles south-east of Shahjehanpore station by rail; (2) at Shahjehanpore itself; (3) at Tilhur; and (4) at Meeranpore Kuttra. The railway was only commenced just as the assessments

Marginal notes:
- Kunkur.
- Metalled roads.
- Railway.

of Tuhseel Shahjehanpore were announced in 1869, and was completed and opened right through from Lucknow to Bareilly in November 1873, as the assessments of the whole district were just completed. When the assessments of Tuhseel Tilhur were made, the railway had not been opened up to Shahjehanpore even; and the part that passes through Tilhur was made and opened after the part to the south-east of Shahjehanpore. Hence the whole district of Shahjehanpore was assessed before any improvement, consequent on the opening up of its communications with the outer world by the Oudh and Rohilkhund Railway, and the large extension of metalled roads, could have begun to develop itself.

22. The only large town in the district is the city of Shahjehanpore, which has a population of over 70,000 inhabitants. By my settlement census taken in 1867, and intended to represent the actual residents, the population is 74,003, but by the North-Western Provinces Census of 1872, taken on the night of the 18th January, it is 72,140 persons. Both enumerations omit the civil lines and cantonments. In the city are

The city of Shahjehan-pore.

Census.	Hindoos.	Maho-medans.	Others.	Total.
Settlement,...	34,800	39,177	17	74,003
N.-W. P., 1872,	34,511	37,535	87	72,140

included the inhabited sites of several *mouzahs* adjoining the outskirts of the town proper, but which are considered mohallas of the city. The omission of one of these is probably the cause of the main discrepancy between my returns of 1867 and the census of 1872. The town was founded only some 250 years ago, in the reign of the Emperor Shah Jehan, by Nawab Buhadoor Khan, Puthan, and named after the reigning Emperor. It is situated on the high ground between the rivers Gurra and Khanout, shortly before their confluence, the old fort being at the extremity of the high ground above the united valleys of the two rivers. A portion of the town is across, on the left bank of the Khanout, which is bridged by a good substantial masonry bridge, known as Hukeem Mehndi Ali's bridge. The position of the town affords great natural advantages for drainage and cleanliness, which are not thrown away. "The area occupied by the town is 1,635 square acres" (page 213, Vol. I, Census Report of 1872); but much of this is taken up by gardens and small plots of cultivation in addition to several wide roads. The gross municipal income is Rs. 52,442.

23. Tilhur is the next largest town, and the only other municipality (income about Rs. 9,000); it has a population of nearly 19,000 inhabitants, but this includes the inhabited sites of seven adjacent mouzahs, besides *kusbah* Tilhur and Hindoo Puttee, the details of which are given with other particulars in paragraph 28 of Chapter IV, the Tilhur tuhseel report. The other smaller towns, with populations of over 6,000 inhabitants, are Jellalabad, Powayn, and Meeranpore Kuttra. The only other country town or *kusbah* is Kant, which is alway honoured with the title of *Kusbah*, as it was once a place of some importance, but is now only a large village. In the census returns of 1872 it is

Tilhur and other small-er towns.

Population by Census of 1872.				
Names.	Hindoo.	Maho-medans.	Others.	Total.
Jellalabad, ...	3,687	3,440	2	7,129
Powayn, ...	4,592	1,514	3	6,109
Meeranpore Kuttra,...	4,009	2,520	...	6,529

given a population of 5,006 inhabitants, but my returns show a population of just under 4,000, and it certainly had not 5,009 *residents*, whatever the numbers there present on the night of the 18th January may have been.

24. Inclusive of these already specified, it appears from the census returns of 1872 that the number of towns and villages in this district in which the population is—

Classification of towns and villages according to number of inhabitants.

Over			50,000	inhabitants	is	1
From	5,000	to	10,000	,,	,,	6
,,	3,000	to	5,000	,,	,,	6
,,	2,000	to	3,000	,,	,,	12
,,	1,000	to	2,000	,,	,,	118
,,	500	to	1,000	,,	,,	385
,,	200	to	500	,,	,,	818
Less than			200	,,	,,	834

Further particulars of the chief and market villages will be found for each per-gunnah and tuhseel in the separate tuhseel reports.

25. The Rosa Sugar-factory is situated on the river Gurra some two miles from the city, and rather more than a mile below the junction of the Khanout and Gurra. The name of the factory is taken from that of the village in which it is situated, Rosur. It is a sugar-refinery and distillery, and not a sugar manufactory, as the juice is not pressed from the cane on the premises; but various kinds of good, clean and fine sugars are made, and rum is distilled from the coarse boiled cane-juice (*ráb* and *sheera*) which is purchased from the *ráb*-dealers and *khundsárees* in the city and various parts of the district.

The Rosa Sugar-factory.

The Rosa Factory of Carew & Co. has now the contract for supplying the British army in the Bengal Presidency with rum and sugar; and it also supplies most of the merchants and private families in this part of India, including the Punjab, the Central Provinces, and a great portion of Lower Bengal, with sugar. Mr. J. Powell, the manager, Mr. E. Macalester, the assistant manager, as well as two junior assist-ants and the engineer all reside in houses within the precincts of the factory grounds. And it is only a fair tribute to the energy, enterprise, and good taste of Messrs. Carew & Co. and Mr. Powell to say that the approach to Rosa and the grounds themselves are well planted and kept, and exceedingly pretty, and that a piece of high, barren, unsightly ground has been turned into a picturesque park with a magnificent garden.

26. The manufacture of sugar is also carried on in the city, and it is the only manufacture and trade of the city and district. But there are many kinds of what we call sugar. The refined and edible sugars, viz., *kooja* or *kund*, the white loaf sugar; *cheense*, fine powdered sugar, white (*suféd*) or brown (*lal*); and *misree*, white tablet sugar, and sugar-candy, are only made for home consumption and not for export. The sugars that are exported are— (1) the manufactured sugar, *khánd* or *shukkur*; and (2) the coarse unrefined article called *goor*. Whilst the city of Shahjehanpore is the principal mart for *khánd*, Tilhur is the principal market for *goor*, which is much made around Tilhur in preference to *ráb*. (For a description of *ráb*, *goor*, and *khánd* see Section II., para. 33 of this chapter).

Manufactures, exports, and imports.

Hitherto sugar (*khánd* and *goor*) has been almost the sole export of this district, the exchange imports being chiefly salt and cotton, but also iron and *ghee* (clarified butter). The trade has been carried on across bad roads principally by country carts, but partly also by camels, the *khánd* going chiefly across the Jumna through Delhi to Goorgaon and Hissar, and through Muttra to Bhurtpore, Jeypore, Jodhpore, &c., and the *goor* across the Ganges into the Doab and also across the Jumna in the Gwalior direction.

The railway must naturally and necessarily make a great revolution in all this, but it is needless to speculate what the results will be. Already there is a commence-ment visible, accelerated, doubtless, by the famine, or at least high prices, in Bengal; and grain of sorts has been despatched down country by rail to a much greater extent than would have been the case but for the railway.

Fine rice for the consumption of the European residents and of the well-to-do classes of natives is imported from Phillibheet and the Nepal Terai across the Sardah, as the rice grown in the district is most of it common coarse rice, eaten only by the poorer classes. Even the fine rice grown in the district is considered much inferior to the Phillibheet rice, so called from the famous mart of Phillibheet, and not from its being grown near Phillibheet itself or anywhere in that pergunnah. The exchange exports from the district are chiefly coarse *khureef* grains, bajra, &c., which are not grown in the rice-exporting parts.

27. The only other European factory of any kind in the district, besides the Rosa Sugar-factory, is the Mewna Indigo concern in the Tilhur Tuh-seel, near Khoodagunge, in Pergunnah Jellalpore. Some few years ago it was the property of Mr. Wright, late of the Customs, and latterly of

The Mewna Indigo con-cern.

D

Lieutenant-Colonel H. R. Wroughton (lately deceased), and it has been managed for the last eight or ten years by Mr. W. Gardner, whose head-quarters are at Mewna. There are four small branch factories all belonging to the head factory at Mewna, but the process of manufacture is completed at each factory, and the manufactured indigo is sent after each season to Calcutta for disposal at the public sales. The Mewna concern, moreover, is not merely an indigo factory, but one of the largest landed properties in the Tilhur Tuhseel, and indigo is not a staple or even an important crop of that tuhseel; for the area under indigo is only some 3,400 acres, and covers only about 1¼ per cent. of the cultivated area of the tuhseel, and is only one of two crops, land sown with indigo almost invariably producing a second crop in the rubbee harvest.

There is no indigo whatever grown in any other pergunnahs of the district except the five pergunnahs of Tuhseel Tilhur; but some little is grown there besides that grown for the Mewna concern, partly for seed which is sent down country and partly for kutcha indigo for local use.

SECTION II.
Agricultural Produce.

28. The chief products of the district are wheat and gram in the rubbee (or spring)
Staple products and proportion of various crops grown. harvest, and sugar-cane, rice, the millets (jowar and bajra) and several kinds of pulses in the khureef (or autumn) harvest. Special reference to the crops will be found in each of the tuhseel assessment reports and detailed crop statements giving areas and percentages of each crop in the appendices to those reports.

The following table gives the percentages only of the principal crops in each pergunnah to the total cultivated area thereof:—

Pergunnah.	KHUREEF.							RUBBEE.				
	Sugar-cane.		Rice.	Jowar.	Bajra.	Pulses, oord, moong, moth.	Cotton.	Wheat.	Gram.	Barley.	Any of these, wheat, barley or gram, mixed lands.	Double-crop lands.
	Actual.	Land prepared for next year.										
Shahjehanpore,	8·1	6·3	5·8	8·1	5·5	2·3	4·5	36·5	10·1	2·8	2·5	4·7
Jumour,	7·5	3·2	27·1	4·5	2·2	1·1	3·1	33·8	8·7	2·1	3·1	8·5
Kant,	2·7	·8	6·5	3·1	23·2	4·6	1 5	35·1	6·8	5·4	4·2	3·7
Jellalabad,	·8	·1	13·5	9·8	15·5	1·3	2·6	38·8	5 2	3·1	2·5	9·1
Tilhur,	6·8	5·5	7·6	3·7	20·7	1·1	2 5	36·2	6·8	2·1	1·1	5·1
Meeranpore Kuttra,	6·7	5·3	9·1	3·3	18·1	1·2	3·2	34·5	7·1	2·6	1·6	3·2
Khera Bujhera,	4·1	1·3	6·3	8·6	25·8	2·9	2·3	34·6	6·3	2·2	1·4	3·5
Jellalpore,	7·5	6·1	9·1	6·2	19 4	·8	4·6	29·3	6·8	1·7	1·3	8·2
Nigohee,	6·7	5·1	11·8	5·1	17·3	1·2	3·7	31·1	8·2	1·8	·7	5·2
Burragaon,	9·5	8·7	4·3	8·1	11·7	7·5	4·2	34·5	1 0·7	2·2	1·8	4·5
Powayn,	8·2	7·1	9 5	2·5	18·3	5·2	1 2	28·6	7·8	4·1	4·1	8·2
Khotar,	4·5	2·8	12·8	1·3	20·4	10·8	·6	28·5	4·8	2·5	5·5	9·5

The double-crop lands are of small extent and little importance beyond the kuchyana in the gowhanee, which is included in them.

The rest consist chiefly of rice in the khureef, followed by gram or wheat, or a mixture of wheat and barley and gram and peas; but when the rice crop has been good and has come to maturity and been reaped, the second crop is hardly ever good, and these double-crop lands do not, as a rule, pay higher rents than the good and fair average single-crop lands.

Indian-corn (mukka) is the quickest growing and earliest ripening khureef crop, and grows in any average soil, and not, like rice, only in low-lying wet lands or lands kept wet by irrigation, and hence it is the first favourite, even before rice, for double-crop lands. But no Indian-corn is grown, as a field crop, in the district, and hence there is not here, as in the Doab and in the northern pergunnahs of the Bareilly District, a double-crop area growing mukka in khureef and a good crop of wheat or barley afterwards in the rubbee.

Sugar-cane after rice is very exceptional and is seldom or never a good crop.

But little fine rice is grown in the district, the rice chiefly grown being the common or coarse rice (*sáthee dhán*).

Wheat seldom receives more than one watering, and that often a mere sprinkling, and much wheat is grown on the uplands (*bangur*) without any irrigation whatever in good seasons, when the winter rains (*mahwut*) are favourable, and it is never irrigated in the lowlands and river valleys (*khadir*).

The very small proportion of barley is remarkable. In only one pergunnah (Kant) does this crop occupy as much as 5 per cent. of the cultivated area. The enormous preponderance of wheat over barley has been remarked upon in all the separate tuhseel assessment reports.

Cotton cultivation receives very little attention, and the cotton grown in the district, besides being poor, is not sufficient for local consumption. I cannot remember having seen one single fairly good field of cotton in any year in any part of the whole district. Little or no indigo is grown in any part of the district except in the Tilhur tuhseel, in the villages in the vicinity of the Mewna indigo factories, mention of which will be found in the Tilhur tuhseel assessment report (Chapter IV., para. 52).

Very little tobacco is grown; one may pass through numbers and numbers of villages without seeing any at all. It is only cultivated by certain classes, and even then seldom, except near towns or where there is a large old *khera*.

The poppy for opium is cultivated all over the district, but chiefly in Pergunnahs Jellalabad and Kant, and the area under poppy is on the increase. It was nearly 4 per cent. in the year of measurement, and 4½ per cent. (in 1280 Fuslee) three years later.

29. This being one of the chief cane-producing districts, I have entered at some length into the subject of the cultivation of sugar-cane and the manufacture of *ráb* and *goor*. To my assistant, Mr. Butt, who has lately compiled the chapter on sugar-cane for the agricultural volume of the North-Western Provinces' *Gazetteer*, I am much indebted for many of the following details, and to that chapter I direct the reader's attention for a much fuller account than I give here, and also for the continuation of the manufacture up to sugar (*khánd*).

Sugar-cane.

30. There are two broad distinctions in the classes of sugar-cane,—the one is food-canes for eating as a sweetmeat, and the other juice-cane for producing sugar. The food-canes grown in the district are the *pounda, katáhra, kálághuna,* and *thoon*.

Varieties cultivated.

They are almost exclusively cultivated as garden crops near the city and cantonments and large country towns. They are taller and thicker than the canes grown for pressing, and are more delicate in flavour and fibre.

There are many varieties of the canes for pressing, but those chiefly grown are *dikchan, dhowr, mutnan,* and *chain,* the other varieties assimilating more or less to one or other of these kinds.

Dikchan is a tall cane about ten feet high, and averaging 2½ inches in circumference about the middle of the cane. It is chiefly grown on the uplands, and thrives in any fairly good soil, and gives a large and quick yield of juice, and may generally be distinguished by the side of any other kind by its looking a heavier and better crop.

Dhowr is much like, but not equal to, *dikchan*. It is rather hardier and requires less care. It has a somewhat thinner cane and a harder fibre, and is said to withstand floods and jackals better than *dikchan*, and is much grown in low lands (*khadir or terai*).

Mutnan is a small thin cane, usually only some five feet high, with a very hard fibre and a small yield of juice, but the juice is good and rich and gives the largest proportion of *råb*. A field of *mutnan* near a field of *dikchan* looks at first sight like a stunted ruined crop. Owing to its small stature it is never grown in *khadir* or *terai* lands.

Chain, also called *chin* or *chun*, is usually planted in *khadir* lands and in any low-lands liable to floods, as it is a very tall, thin, strong cane. It has a reddish coloured cane and a very hard fibre, and consequently gives a small yield of juice, but of good quality, as in the case of *mutnan*.

Extent of area under sugar-cane.

31. Sugar-cane is cultivated all over the district, but chiefly within a radius of 15 to 20 miles round the city of Shahjehanpore, and least of all, in the southernmost pergunnah, Jellalabad, for which, however, there is a special reason in the prejudice of the Thakoors of that pergunnah against its cultivation. The crop statements of the present settlement measurements give a total of 41,464 acres as the area actually under cane; but this is not the area of any one year for the entire district, as the measurement took several years to complete, but may be taken as a fair, though somewhat slightly low, estimate of the actual area annually under sugar-cane; and but a very small portion of this, less than 50 acres probably, is food-cane.

The areas under cane in the year of measurement and of land lying fallow under preparation for cane next year are given, with their percentages on total cultivated area for each pergunnah and tuhseel in the annexed statement :—

Name of Pergunnah.	Area in acres under cane.	Area prepared for cane next year.	*Percentages* Of land under cane.	*Percentages* Of land prepared for cane next year.
		Acres.		
Shahjehanpore, ...	5,169	4,055	8	6¼
Jumour, ...	3,258	1,400	7½	3¼
Kant, ...	1,988	562	2¾	¾
Total of Shahjehanpore Tuhseel, ...	10,415	6,017	5¾	3½
Jellalabad Pergunnah and Tuhseel, ...	964	...	¾	...
Tilhur, ...	4,214	3,386	6¾	5⅓
Meeranpore Kuttra, ...	330	279	6½	5¼
Khera Bujhera, ...	1,717	487	4	1¼
Jellalpore, ...	2,530	1,950	7½	6
Nigohee, ...	3,029	2,280	6¾	5
Total of Tilhur Tuhseel, ...	11,820	8,382	6¼	4½
Burragaon, ...	3,480	3,158	9½	8¾
Powayn, ...	11,921	10,059	8¼	7
Khotar, ...	2,844	1,789	4½	2¾
Total of Powayn Tuhseel, ...	18,245	15,006	7½	6
District Total, ...	41,464	29,405	5·6	3·9

The areas and percentages for Tuhseels Shahjehanpore and Jellalabad, of which

I had crop statements prepared for the year 1280 Fuslee, the second and third year after inspection and assessment, were larger and are given in the margin.

Pergunnah.	Area in acres.		Percentages.	
	Actual cane.	Prepared for next year.	Actual cane.	Land prepared.
Shahjehanpore, ...	6,540	5,351	10½	8½
Jumour, ...	3,653	2,735	8¼	6¼
Kant, ...	3,025	1,477	4½	2
Jellalabad, ...	1,748	116	1½	¼

32. In river valleys and low alluvial lands (*khadir*) the cultivation is much less

Cultivation.

careful than on uplands (*bangur*), the land is much less ploughed and worked, and no irrigation is needed. The hardier and tougher kinds of sugar-cane are grown, and the yield is comparatively less, and besides this, the crop is liable to partial injury or total destruction by floods, so that the *khadir*-grown sugar-cane bears about the same relation to *bangur*-grown irrigated and manured sugar-cane that *bhoor*-grown barley does to irrigated wheat, as regards their respective culture and care.

The following remarks relate entirely to the *bangur*-grown, carefully-cultivated sugar-cane produced in good or fair average soil by good and thrifty cultivators.

The land lies fallow for one whole year, a *khureef* and a *rubbee*, and during that

Ploughing.

time is ploughed from 12 times as a minimum to 45 or 50 as a maximum, from 20 to 25 ploughings being the average. One digging with the *kussee* is considered equal to five or six ploughings, but is usually only resorted to when the ground is too hard for the plough.

Manure is almost invariably given, consisting of refuse sweepings from the houses,

Manuring.

ashes, &c., and almost all the manure is given to the sugar-cane, as the custom prevailing in the Doab of having a manured zone (*gouhan* or *barah*) round the village site does not obtain in this district. It is applied shortly before planting, and is spread over and ploughed into the ground, and gives the soil a darker and richer appearance, which is observable even in the following season after the sugar-cane has been cut. The amount of manure depends entirely on the amount at the command of the cultivator, the size of his manure heap, for it is seldom or never purchased.

The planting usually takes place in February and March (*Magh* to *Cheyt*), and

Planting.

depends on the cultivators having leisure from the cutting, pressing and boiling of the last crop.

The field is ploughed; a man with a bundle of pieces of cane from 8 to 10 inches in length following the plough and dropping the pieces in lengthwise about a foot apart into the furrow;[*] after which the furrows are smoothed over and filled up with the clod-crusher (*putela*). Ordinarily the top part of the cane from about a foot below the actual arrow or head is used for seed; and only about 1½ to 2 feet of the cane, some four or five of the immature joints, which contain little or no expressible juice, are cut for this purpose from the full-grown canes. These cane-cuttings are tied up in bundles and earthed over, to keep them from drying, till required for planting six weeks or two months later.

The land lying fallow for cane is called *pundree*, and cane or any other crop sown

Pundree, porach, kharug.

after fallow is called *porach* or *poluch* or *polcha*, in contradistinction to *kharug* or *kharik*. The reason why the *pundree* area is always less than the area actually under cane is because a large amount of cane is cultivated *kharug*, following rice, *bajra*, or *kodon* in the previous *khureef*; but even then the land is fallow for at least three months. It must not be supposed that rice and sugar alternate for several years in the same field, for of course this is never the case.

---

[*] Mr. Moens, in his Bareilly Settlement Report, has, I observe, stated that the land is usually irrigated first, and that the bits of cane are thrown crosswise (*tirchha*) into the furrow; but this is certainly not the custom in Shahjehanpore, nor have I ever seen it in Bareilly.

Ratooning (*pérée rukhna*), *i. e.*, leaving the roots in the ground to sprout again and produce a second crop, is seldom resorted to except for food-canes, and not even for them as the rule.

Irrigation is seldom given before planting, only when the winter rains (*mahwut*) have been a failure, or the planting has been delayed to the
Irrigation. very end of March or beginning of April. Ordinarily two good waterings (not mere sprinklings or wettings of only two or three inches of the super-soil, as in the case of wheat) are sufficient, unless the regular rains are late, when a third is given about the middle of June. A great deal of cane is grown on the *bangur* without any irrigation (and none is ever irrigated in the *khadir*), as it is a very uncommon occurrence for April and May to pass without at least one, and generally two good falls of rain.

The ground is hoed and the surface kept loose and open until the plant is from
Hoeing. 2 to 2½ feet high, and able to take care of itself, some five or six times in all, after which little attention is paid to it, besides, in some instances, tying the canes together when they have any tendency to lie flat or straggle about much, and as a preventive against damage from jackals and pigs.

No sugar-cane is ever cut for pressing before the *Deothan* festival, which occurs
Cutting. in October or early in November, on the 11th of the bright half of the month *Kartik;* but most of the cultivators are still too busy with sowing the spring crop (*rubbee*) and harvesting the autumn crop (*khureef*), so that general and regular cane-cutting does not commence till December, and is in full swing up to the beginning or middle of February.

33. Cutting and pressing go on simultaneously, the cane being cut only as it is
Ráb and *goor.* required for the sugar-mill (*kolhu*). The pressing and boiling are usually performed by the cultivator (the exception being the *bél* system, which will be referred to presently), and what is delivered to the manufacturer (*khundsáree*) is *ráb* or cane-juice concentrated by boiling, and delivery is usually taken on the spot and the *ráb* removed at the manufacturer's expense. Cultivators working on their own capitals, and not on advances from *khundsárees*, often make *goor* instead of *ráb;* and *goor* is sold in the market, to be used as *goor* for eating or mixing as a sweetening ingredient, and *not* for making sugar (*khánd*) from. *Goor* is, in fact, a sort of unmanufactured coarse brown sugar. Tilhur is the chief *goor* market in the district, whereas most of the sugar manufactories (*khundsárs*) are in Burragaon and the city of Shahjehanpore.

The main difference between *ráb* and *goor* is that the latter is boiled rather longer over a hotter fire, and is made up into moderately dry solid balls (*bhéli*) for keeping and use as *goor;* whereas the former, *ráb*, is concentrated to only a little over crystallizing point, and retains much more moisture than *goor*, and is not intended for keeping, but for immediate conversion into manufactured sugar.

34. The price of *goor* in the open market at the height of the manufacturing
Free-sale price of *goor* season, when it is being purchased from the makers and is
and *ráb.* cheapest, is about Rs. 3-8-0 per Government maund of 82·3 ℔s. *Ráb*, as the rule, is delivered to the *khundsáree* at a price previously agreed upon, advances having been made to the producer by the manufacturer: and hence the general price for *ráb* (the *khatountee* rate of Burragaon, of which mention will be made in its proper place) is far below the free-sale or open market price, which latter is usually agreed upon at a certain amount over the *khatountee* price, and ranges from eight annas to one rupee over that rate, and now averages about Rs. 4 per *ráb* maund, or nearly Rs. 2-12-0 per Government maund, as against the Rs. 3-8-0 for *goor*.

35. The amount of juice extracted by the native *kolhu* is just 50 per cent. of
Estimate of produce. the weight of canes cu in pieces ready for the mill. The
produce of cane is always estimated by the number of *muthas*
of raw juice (*rus*) or *kulsees* of *ráb* produced per *kutcha beegah*. In estimating juice
the highest native estimate is equivalent to 100 *muthas* per acre; a good average
crop at 13 *muthas* per beegah=81¼ *muthas*, or about 2,112 gallons of juice per
acre, and 10 *muthas* as an ordinary crop per *kutcha beegah*.

Mr. Butt, taking these estimates and experiments at the Rosa Factory, has
assumed 12 *muthas* per *kutcha beegah* as a full average outturn for good land in a
cane tract, equivalent to 75 *muthas*, or 1,950 gallons of raw juice, per acre; and the
outturn of *ráb* as 21·5 per cent. of the weight of juice, and the produce in *ráb* as 37½
ráb maunds per acre, equal to rather over 55 Government maunds, or to about
4,550lbs. The produce of *goor* to *ráb* he takes as about 9 to 10 (or 19·3 per cent.
of weight of juice), and hence the average produce of *goor* is nearly 50 Government
maunds per acre.

36. Mr. Butt has taken Rs. 15 per acre as the average rent, and this is
The rent-rate. somewhat high and the average of good and above-average
sugar-cane lands and full rates. Particulars regarding sugar-
cane rates will be found under the general heading of Rent, and need not be further
alluded to here.

37. There is no appreciable difference in the cost of cultivation of what turns
Cost of cultivation and out to be a good or indifferent crop, or in the cost of manufac-
manufacture. ture of *ráb* or *goor;* but the expense of manufacture varies
directly with the amount of produce. From the expenses of cultivation have been
omitted those items which balance one another on the credit and debit side, *e. g.*,
seed and cutting, as if price is charged for seed bought, credit must be given for
seed sold; and for cutting the payment is in kind, but credit is taken for full produce,
not allowing for payment in kind. In the cost of both cultivation and manufacture
the estimate has been made as if hired labour had been employed, so that the
estimated cost is far higher than the actual expense to any cultivator; but this is
the only correct and legitimate way of making the estimate.

The expenses of cultivation proper amount to Rs. 43-7-0, and of manufacturing
ráb or *goor* to Rs. 31 per acre on an average; total Rs. 74-7-0 as under :—

Expenses of cultivation per acre.	Rs.	a.	p.	*Expenses of manufacture per acre.*	Rs.	a.	p.
Ploughing, ...	... 8	0	0	Hire of the mill or share of wear and tear, ...	1	8	0
Carriage of manure,	... 1	8	0	Ditto of boiling pan, ...	1	0	0
Planting, ...	...· 1	0	0	Labourers, ...	... 9	0	0
Irrigation, ...	... 9	7	0	Cattle, ...	... 18	0	0
Hoeing, ...	... 5	8	0	Fuel, vessels for juice and *ráb*,	1	8	0
Tieing, ...	... 0	8	0				
Carriage to the mill,	... 2	8	0				
Rent, ...	...15	0	0				
Rs.	... 43	7	0	Rs.	... 31	0	0

38. The value, expenditure, and profits per acre, (1) for *ráb*, and (2) for
Relative profits of ráb *goor*, are given as follows, for light, average, and high yields
and goor. and outturns :—

Juice in lbs.	Ráb.		Value of produce in ráb.	Expenses of cultivation and manufacture of ráb per acre.	Profits per acre.
	Government maunds.	lbs.			
			Rs.	Rs. a. p.	Rs. a. p.
14,134	36·9	3,036	100	64 1 8	35 14 4
17,668	46·1	3,795	125	69 4 4	55 11 8
21,202	55·3	4,554	150	74 7 0	75 9 0
24,736	64·5	5,313	175	79 9 8	95 6 4
28,270	73·8	6,072	200	84 12 4	115 3 8

PRODUCE PER ACRE OF

Juice in lbs.	Goor.		Value of produce in goor.	Expenses of cultivation and manufacture of goor per acre.	Profits per acre.
	Government maunds.	lbs.			
				Rs. a. p.	Rs. a. p.
14,134	33·2	2,733	116	64 1 8	51 14 4
17,668	41·5	3,416	145	69 4 4	75 11 8
21,202	49·8	4,099	174	74 7 0	99 9 0
24,736	58·1	4,782	203	79 9 8	123 6 4
28,270	66·4	5,465	232	84 12 4	147 3 8

The profits arising from the manufacture of *goor* are, therefore, shown to be much larger than those from *ráb*, and this is the general opinion. As, however, the manufacturers (*khundsárees*) take only *ráb*, and most of the cultivators are entirely dependent on advances from the *khundsárees*, they must turn out *ráb;* and do not receive the free-sale price for it, but a rate very considerably lower. Hence the great body of cultivators do not make anything approaching to the above given profits, even omitting all account of debt and interest and the other hundred and one machinations by which the *khundsárees* manage to do the cultivator, and to secure for themselves the profits that should go into his pocket.

39. The city Pathans are the principal *khundsárees* of the district, and, I think I may say without fear of contradiction, as great usurers as any of the Kulwar or Bunneah *khundsárees*, and most of them are zemindars of one or more villages in the Shahjehanpore Tuhseel. It is, of course, a great advantage to the *khundsárees* to be also a zemindar, as he has then a much greater hold on his *ráb-assamees*, besides being able to compel all cultivators residing in his villages to dispose of their *ráb* to him and to no one else, and as the rule they do not scruple to do so. This system of advances is very profitable to the *khundsáree*, and at least doubles, if it does not treble and quadruple his legitimate profits from the manufacture of *ráb* into sugar (*khánd*). The cultivator who once takes an advance seldom or never gets out of the usurer's hands, for in a very short time the accounts show that all monies due to the *assamee* for *ráb* do not more than cover advances and interest on debt, and the principal runs on to the following year undiminished if not actually increased, and the *assamee* is compelled to agree to any terms and put up with any amount of extortion on the part of the *khundsáree*.

Khundsárees and system of advances.

40. The description of the Burragaon *khatountee* I extract almost verbatim from Mr. Butt's account. The prices of all agricultural produce are annually struck in Burragaon, and according to these prices all accounts between the cultivators and the *mahajuns* are settled in the greater part of the Shahjehanpore District, and also in neighbouring parts of the Bareilly, Kheree, and Hurdui Districts. A propitious day is settled by the pundits; notices are issued, and a *punchayet* is held composed of traders, zemindars, and cultivators of the neighbourhood. Their duties are simple. The prices in the case of cereals, pulses, &c.,

Burragaon khatountee.

being on the average of the Burragaon market prices during certain terms, and these market prices are invariably accepted from the books of the leading firms.

In the case of *ráb* there is no market price, and the *khatountee* price is derived from the average price of manufactured sugar (*khánd*) for each of the three months preceding, thus :—

Suppose the average price of *khánd*, as ascertained from the entries of sales, to be as follows :—

				M.	s.	c.	
Cheyt,	...	34 per *pulla*, i. e., 3 maunds =		3	24	0	Government weight.
Bysakh,	...	32 ,,	,,				
Jeyth,	...	80 ,,	,,				

Total, ...	96, divided by 3, gives an average,	Rs.	32
	To this is added half,	... ,,	16
		Total Rs. ...	48

This figure is now taken as annas, and 48 annas, or Rs. 3 per *ráb* maund, is the *khatountee* price of *ráb* for the past season, the price according to which all transactions relating to the crop of the preceding year between the manufacturers and cultivators will be settled. The price of Rs. 3 will, however, only be allowed in the Powayn and Burragaon Pergunnahs and in Beesulpore of the Bareilly District. The *ráb* here is supposed to be the best, and for the Shahjehanpore and Tilhur Tuhseels the price is two annas per maund lower, and for Pergunnah Khotar and the adjoining Oudh districts four annas lower. Thus, with a price of Rs. 3 for Burragaon, Powayn, and Beesulpore, the price for Shahjehanpore and Tilhur will be Rs. 2-14-0, and for Khotar and Oudh Rs. 2-12-0 per *ráb* maund (121·4℔s.) The difference of two annas between Powayn and Shahjehanpore is always admitted, but the Oudh cultivators are objecting to the four-anna reduction.

The last *khatountees* for *ráb* have been as under :—

Price per ráb maund, equivalent to 1 maund 19 seers Government weight, or 121·4℔s.

Year.						Rs.	a.	p.
1868 A. D.,...	...	...	...	...	...	3	2	6
1869 ,,	...	...	...	...	...	3	4	0
1870 ,,	...	...	...	...	...	3	5	0
1871 ,,	...	...	...	...	...	3	5	9
1872 ,,	...	...	...	...	...	3	5	3
					5)16	6	6
		Average of 5 years,	...			3	4	6

41. The *bél* system prevails chiefly along the western edge of the district adjoining Bareilly and Budaon Districts, and is said to have been lately introduced from one or both of them, and since the mutiny it is extending rapidly, and will very probably largely supplant the other system of manufacture of *ráb* by the cultivator.

The bél system.

The difference of the *bél* system consists in the manufacturer (*khundsáree*) taking raw juice (*rus*) instead of concentrated juice (*ráb*) and boiling it himself. The cultivator presses the juice all the same, setting up his mill (*kolhu*) at the *bél*, which is merely a collection of mills and a boiling-house. There are usually from 12 to 20 mills at a *bél*, but sometimes as many as 30. Each *mutha* of *rus* as filled is taken over at once by the manufacturer, who receives the refuse (*kose*) for fuel. The only expenses saved to the cultivator are the cost of one labourer (the boiler) and the hire of the boiling-pan. The real advantage to him is that the *rus* is taken over indiscriminately, without any tests of whether it is good or bad, and he is relieved of the loss consequent on a small yield of *ráb* or of *ráb* of indifferent quality. The advantage to the *khundsáree* is that *ráb* is prepared in larger quantities and on a more careful process, and as there remains no motive for fraud or deception as to the quality, it is, as the rule, more uniform and superior to that purchased ready made from the cultivators.

The difference in the manufacture of *ráb* under the *bél* system consists in the boiling-pans being set up in sets of five over a furnace with a long flue, the largest pan into which the raw juice is first placed being furthest from the furnace over the far end of the flue, and the smallest, into which the heated juice is brought gradually, being immediately over the furnace. An experienced *hulwai* is employed to conduct the boiling, and *sujjee* (impure carbonate of soda) and other alkaline substances, and decoctions of bark and plants, are used to correct acidity and purify the syrup.

SECTION III.

Population—Proprietary and Cultivating Tenures.

42. The total population of the district amounts to 949,471 persons, and the details, as gathered from the census returns of 1872, are as follows :—

Population, creed, and occupation.

Males,	...	...	511,136,	percentage 54
Females,	...	...	438,333,	„ 46
Adults over 20 years of age,	...	459,667,	„ 48
Minors under ditto,	...	489,804,	„ 52
Hindoos,	...	...	822,576,	„ 86
Mahomedans,	...	...	126,599,	„ 14
Christians and others,	...	296,	„ 0

Of the 296 "Christians and others," the Christians are [*]195 Europeans, 7 Americans, 28 Eurasians ; and the rest Native Christians, mostly belonging to the Lodhipore American Mission.

Arranged according to occupation the distribution is as follows :—

Occupation.	Hindoos.	Mahomedans.	Christians and others.	Total.
Landowners, ...	23,223	3,525	...	26,748
Agriculturists, ...	567,894	39,469	1	607,364
Non-agriculturists,	231,459	83,605	295	315,359

The numbers returned as able to read and write are only 18,594, *viz.*, 18,551 males and 41 females, or less than two per cent. of the entire population, and of educated males to the male population 3·6 per cent. This is undoubtedly very incorrect, and far short of the real number. Mr. W. C. Plowden, in Section IX., paras. 121-123 of Vol. I., Census Report, admits, and in part explains, the cause of the incorrectness of the education portion of the census returns.

The total number of houses built with skilled labour are 5,589, against 138,369 built with unskilled labour, or merely mud walls and thatch.

------

[*] Amongst the 195 Europeans the troops in cantonments at that time are palpably not included, which (men, women, and children,) numbered some 600 souls, as the head-quarters and right wing of the 1st Royal Scots were then stationed at Shahjehanpore. Apparently, however, only the soldiers and their families in barracks were omitted, and all civil and military officers and their families in the civil station and cantonments were included, as they with the residents at Rosa, Mewna, and on the railway about make up that number.

These details are given in the following form at page xxxii. of Vol. II. of the North-Western Provinces' Census Report of 1872, but I have omitted as superfluous the lengthy details of different ages : —

District of Shahjehanpore.	Hindoos.		Mahomedans.		Christians and others.		Total population.	
Number of enclosures, ...	101,539		18,353		34		119,926	
Number of houses built with skilled labour.	3,493		2,055		41		5,589	
Number of houses built with unskilled labour.	158,133		25,231		5		138,369	
Total number of houses, ...	161,626		27,286		46		188,958	
Population.	Male.	Female.	Male.	Female.	Male.	Female.	Male.	Female.
Landowners, ...	13,088	10,132	1,716	1,809	...	...	14,804	11,944
Agriculturists, ...	307,769	260,125	20,526	18,943	1	...	328,296	279,068
Non-agriculturists, ...	125,305	106,154	42,504	41,101	227	68	168,036	147,323
Total, ...	446,162	376,414	64,746	61,853	228	68	511,136	438,335
Able to read and write. {12 years of age,	1,987	...	555	1	63	17	2,605	18
12 to 20 years,...	2,708	...	520	3	58	1	3,286	4
Above 20 years,	10,915	...	1,702	...	53	19	12,660	19
Total of all ages, ...	15,610	...	2,777	4	174	37	18,551	41

And at page 200 of Vol. I., the following interesting details are given for *males not less than* 15 *years of age* :—

Professional.	Domestic.	Commercial.	Agricultural	Industrial.	Indefinite and non-productive.	Total of all classes.
2,425	27,339	10,792	214,528	35,978	29,358	320,420

43. The various castes of Hindoos prevailing in the district whose members exceed two thousand in number are here given in the margin, arranged according to their numerical strength. Against every caste that has any *specialité*, peculiar trade, business or calling, I have entered the same between brackets. Nos. 1 to 8 are the agricultural classes, the Rajpoots, Brahmins, and Koormees forming the bulk of the resident proprietary community, and the members of all these eight castes being principally cultivators. The rest, from 9 to 31, chiefly ply their various trades and professions, but most of them (excepting those living in towns) also cultivate, and especially the Pasees, Dhanuks, Gadariahs, Kayeths, and Lodhas. Even the

Hindoo castes.

Serial number.	Caste, Hindoos.	Number.
1	Chumars, (skinners and leather-workers), ...	109,448
2	Kisan, ...	89,987
3	Rajpoots, ...	69,222
4	Kachees, Malee, and Murao, (gardeners), ...	65,232
5	Aheers, (cattle farmers and herdsmen), ...	62,130
6	Brahmins, (priests), ...	67,691
7	Kahar or Dheemur, (bearers, carriers, fishers, menial servants, &c)	39,374
8	Koormees, ...	28,248
9	Kolee or Koree, (weavers), ...	25,079
10	Teli, (oil-men),...	23,314
11	Gadariah, (shepherds), ...	20,593
12	Pasee, (swine-herds and village watchmen),	19,412
13	Kalal or Kalwar, (distillers, spirit-sellers, and general merchants.)	16,891
14	Dhobee, (washermen), ...	18,721
15	Barhai, (carpenters), ...	16,904
16	Bharbhunja, (grain-parchers), ...	15,507
17	Hajjam, (barbers), ...	14,897
18	Bunniah, (grain-dealers, grocers, and chandlers,) ...	14,600
19	Dhanuk, (swine-herds and village watchmen),	12,583
20	Kayeth, (writers and accountants), ...	12,323
21	Lohar, (blacksmiths), ...	11,101
22	Koomhar, (potters), ...	9,878
23	Khakrob, Bhangi, or Mehter, (sweepers and dog servants.)	6,929
24	Sonar, (gold and silver smiths), ...	5,418
25	Lodha and Beldar, (navvies or spades-men), ...	4,060
26	Goojar, (chiefly cattle-lifters), ...	3,826
27	Darzee, (tailors), ...	3,033
28	Bahelia, (bird-catchers), ...	2,994
29	Bairagee, (devotees and beggars), ...	2,177
30	Tambolee, (pān-sellers), ...	2,075
31	Goshain, (ascetics, devotees, and beggars), ...	2,068

Bairagees and Goshains take to agriculture, but they are too fond of roving and begging, and it is too good a trade for them, to become good cultivators.

44. The returns for the Mahomedans specify only four classes, *viz.*, (1) Puthan,

Mahomedans.

41,564; (2) Sheikh, 13,773; (3) Syud, 3,325; (4) Moghul, 1,167; and these constitute the genuine Mussulmans, the descendants of foreign invaders and settlers. But the "unspecified" Mahomedans bear a very large proportion indeed (over 52 per cent.) to the total Mahomedan population, and in these are included the Julahas, butchers, and the other lower classes of Mahomedans, as well as the *nou-Muslims* or converts from various castes of Hindoos, especially Rajpoots, of which there are a number in Pergunnah Jellalabad; but not one has been specified under that denomination, nor yet as a Mahomedan *fakeer*, though they are plentiful enough too.

45. Rajpoots abound in every part of the district, but they are more numerous

Rajpoot clans.

in Pergunnah Jellalabad (16,261) than in any other single pergunnah, and that is the most essentially Rajpoot pergunnah of any, as the Thakoors (Thakoor and Rajpoot are synonymous terms in this district) have

Serial No.	Name of clans.			Number.
1	Chowhan,	...	...	8,555
2	Bachal,	...	...	8,202
3	Katheriya,	...	...	6,442
4	Chandela,	...	...	6,307
5	Janghara,	...	...	6,033
6	Ponwar,	...	...	4,858
7	Rathor,	...	...	4,530
8	Kasib,	...	...	3,442
9	Gaur,	...	...	3,172
10	Gwalbansi,	...	...	2,900
11	Kuthea,	...	...	1,914
12	Sombansi,	...	...	1,717
13	Raghbansi,	...	...	1,292
14	Gautam,	...	...	1,211
15	Bais,	...	...	1,066
16	Bhadaurya,	...	...	829
17	Tomar,	...	...	728

retained their property there more than elsewhere. There are no less than fifty-four distinct clans of Rajpoots in this district, seventeen of the most important and numerous of which are given in the margin, in the order of their numerical strength. Most of the largest of these clans have tracts of country of their own, in which they originally settled, and have lived and multiplied, and in which they are the prevailing clan of Thakoors. Much the same as in the Highlands of Scotland, there are the Macrae country and Mackinnon country, and in certain parts every second or third individual is a Munro, or a Fraser, or a Macintosh, &c. And there is another similarity between the Rajpoots and the Highlanders, *viz.*, their long pedigrees and the remote antiquity of their origin.

The Thakoors are not, however, very old settlers in this district, not further back than the fourteenth century; whereas the Katherias, for a long time the most important tribe in this district, did not arrive till the sixteenth century. Until comparatively recently the Thakoors were the principal landowners, and though the dominant class, they never formed the bulk of the population in any tract of country (*vide* paras. 20-26 of Chapter IV.)

The *Bachal* country is in Pergunnah Kant, the western and south-western side of it extending into Pergunnah Jumour and just along the edge of Pergunnah Tilhur.

The *Katheria* country is Pergunnah Khotar and parts of Powayn, but they muster the strongest in Pergunnah Jellalpore of the Tilhur Tuhseel.

The *Chundelas* are all over the valleys of the Ramgunga and Bygool in the Jellalabad Pergunnah, and extend up on to the *bhoor* to the edge of the pergunnah and Bachil country, and southwards into the *bunkuttee ilaka* down to the Kutheas. There is a cluster-property of Chundelas of seventy-two mouzahs, known as the Khunder Ilaka, for details of which see paras. 14 and 34 of Chapter III., the report of Tuhseel Jellalabad.

The Jangharas.—There are two subdivisions of these, the *bhoor* and the *terai* Jangharas; those in this district being chiefly the latter, and their country the valleys of the Ramgunga and Bygool in Pergunnah Khera Bujhera, and just into Pergunnah Jellalabad.

The *Ponwars* extend from the north of the Ramgunga, in the east side of Pergunnah Jellalabad, into the east side of Pergunnahs Kant and Jumour, and generally along the boundary of this and the Hurdui District of Oudh.

The *Kasibs* are chiefly to be found in the south of Pergunnah Negohee and in the adjacent portions of Pergunnahs Shahjehanpore, Jumour, Tilhur, Powayn, and Burragaon, mostly on the borders of those pergunnahs where they touch Negohee.

The *Kuthea* country is in the western side of the *bunkuttee ilaka* of Pergunnah Jellalabad, and on either side of the Soate Nuddoe.

The *Raghbansee* and *Gautam* clans are found principally in the old Pergunnah of Bangaon in Jellalabad; the Gautams occupying the eastern side of what was formerly Pergunnah Bangaon up to the Ramgunga, and the Raghbansees the western side and extending down to the Ganges and into the *bunkuttee ilaka* up to the Kutheas.

The *Chowhans, Rathors, Gaurs* and others have no distinct tract or special country of their own, but are scattered about through the country of the other clans amongst whom they have settled, chiefly in consequence of marriage alliances. This is owing to the custom universal amongst Rajpoots of never marrying in their own clan. The whole clan is considered one family, and marriage within it is looked upon as incest. The clans are all graded or divided into (1) the highest and best; (2) the medium; and (3) the lower or inferior, and the universal rule in marriage is that the wives are taken from clans lower down in the scale, the lower clans giving their daughters with handsome dowries to superior clans. Daughters *must* be married and dowries *must* be given with the daughters, hence daughters are expensive luxuries in any Rajpoot families; in the lower clans from the heavy expenses of dowries, and in the higher from the greater difficulty of finding suitable husbands. The Chowhans and Rathors are the only clans amongst the first flight who are numerous in this district, and they are to be found pretty equally distributed through all the pergunnahs.

Landholders.

46. The following statement shows *in percentages* the proportion of separate muhals held by the principal landholding castes in each of the four tuhseels of this district :—

Caste.	Shahjehan-pore.	Jellalabad.	Tilhur.	Powayn.	Whole district.
Rajpoot, ...	23	44	44	42	36
Puthan, ...	32	13	20	9½	18
Brahmin, ...	9	3	9½	10	8½
Kayeth, ...	5	3	9½	4½	5¾
Bunniahs, Mahajuns, and Money-lenders, ...	5	1	3	5¾	4
Koormee, ...	½	...	3½	6	3

This accounts for 77 per cent. of the muhals in the district, and most of the remainder belong to these same castes, and are owned by them in various proportions, the Rajpoots having shares in more than any other of these castes. But the Bunniahs and Mahajuns have shares in many, in far more than the number of those entirely owned by them.

The Rajpoot, Brahmin, and Koormee proprietors are chiefly resident proprietors, living in some one of their villages, whilst the Puthans, Kayeths, and Mahajuns are principally residents of the city of Shahjehanpore. The proprietors of nearly six hundred muhals, or rather less than 20 per cent. of the whole district, are residents of the city, and these men own numbers of shares in different villages, so that nearly one-fourth of the entire district may be said to be owned by residents of the city, and if those mortgages which can never be redeemed be included, more than one-fourth. These, with the exception of most of the Puthans, are to all intents and purposes thoroughly non-resident proprietors. The Rajah of Powayn is the only large landed proprietor in the district, and his property is almost entirely confined to the Powayn Pergunnah, in which he is the sole proprietor of 128 muhals, and five in Khotar, and the *talookdar* of 148 muhals in Pergunnah Powayn, which are settled with the sub-proprietors. For full particulars of the Rajah of Powayn's *ilaka*, his *talookdaree* allowance, and the history of his property, as also of that of the Khotar Kutherias, see paragraph 20 of Chapter V.

For further details of resident and non-resident proprietors, their castes, &c., &c., I must refer to the following chapters (II. to V.), the separate tuhseel reports ; and I wish to direct particular attention to para. 27 of Chapter II., regarding the " incidence of Government demand on, and the balance of assets remaining with the proprietor."

Proprietary tenures.

47. The proprietary tenures have also been treated of at length in the separate tuhseel reports, and the following table gives the details for each pergunnah and the whole district :—

Pergunnah.				Total number of muhals.	Zemindaree muhals.	Putteedaree muhals.	Number of puttees in putteedaree muhals.
Shahjehanpore,	...	...	...	266	222	44	279
Jumour,	...	...	...	183	144	39	202
Kant,	...	...	...	301	155	146	777
Jellalabad,	...	...	...	504	208	296	1,796
Tilhur,	...	...	...	271	196	75	383
Kuttra,	...	...	...	21	18	3	15
Khera Bujhera,	...	...	...	172	111	61	283
Jellalpore,	...	...	...	187	108	79	265
Negohee,	...	...	...	193	160	33	111
Burragaon,	...	...	...	160	143	17	61
Powayn,	...	...	...	529	485	44	203
Khotar,	...	...	...	276	241	35	116
Whole District,		...		3,063	2,191	872	4,441

From this it will be seen that the *zemindaree* tenure preponderates very largely in all pergunnahs except Kant and Jellalabad, and on the whole district the percentage of *zemindaree* muhals is 70, against 30 of *putteedaree* muhals. In Kant and Jellalabad, however, the percentage of *putteedaree* muhals is, respectively, 48 and 58½ ; and the number of *puttees* in them is very large, being together larger than that of the rest of the ten pergunnahs of the district.

48. The chief agricultural castes, arranged in order of merit as cultivators, are :—

The chief agricultural castes and their distribution.

(1st), the Koormees ; (2nd and 3rd), the Kachees or Muraos and Kisans ; (4th) Chumars : these are all very good and amongst the first flight with no great distance between them ; then come Aheers, Brahmins, Kolis or Korees, Kahars and Pathans as medium cultivators ; and as usually inferior, Thakoors, Gadariyas, Pasees, Dhannks, and those classes who are not, strictly speaking, agriculturists.

The Koormees are most numerous in Pergunnahs Powayn, Khotar, and Tilhur. The Kachees or Muraos in Jellalabad, Powayn, Kant, Shahjehanpore, and Tilhur. The Kisans in Powayn, Jumour, and Shahjehanpore. The Chumars in Jellalabad, Powayn, Shahjehanpore, and Tilhur. The Aheers in Jellalabad, Tilhur, Powayn, and Kant. The Brahmins in Powayn, Jellalabad, Shahjehanpore, and Kant. The Kolees or Korees in Powayn and Shahjehanpore. The Pathans in Shahjehanpore, Tilhur, Jellalabad, and Powayn. The Thakoors in Jellalabad, Kant, Khera Bujhera, and Powayn. The Gadariyas in Jellalabad, Powayn, Shahjehanpore, and Kant. The Passees in Powayn, Shahjehanpore, Khotar, and Burragaon.

The following classification according to pergunnahs shows which pergunnahs are best off for the first class and medium cultivators, and which are less favoured in having fewer of the best and more of the medium and inferior castes of cultivators :—

Pergunnah.	1ST CLASS.				MEDIUM.					SUPERIOR.				Remarks giving the numbers of those castes which are the most numerous.
	Koormees.	Kachees or Muraos.	Kisans.	Chumars.	Aheers.	Brahmins.	Kolees or Korees.	Kahars.	Puthans.	Thakoors or Rajpoots.	Gadariyas.	Pasees.	Dhanuks.	
Shahjehanpore, ...	13th	4th	1st	2nd	7th	3rd	9th	8th	6th	5th	11th	10th	12th	Kisans 14,500, Chumars 13,800, Brahmins 7,500.
Jumour,...	13th	4th	1st	2nd	5th	6th	8th	7th	11th	3rd	9th	12th	10th	Kisans 16,500, Chumars 4,000, Thakoors 3,800.
Kant, ...	12th	3rd	6th	2nd	5th	4th	10th	7th	8th	1st	9th	13th	11th	Thakoors 9,839, Chumars 8,906, Kachees 7,293.
Jellalabad,	11th	3rd	5th	1st	2nd	7th	12th	6th	8th	4th	9th	13th	10th	Chumars 20,118, Aheers 19,079, Kachees 16,669, Thakoors 16,261.
Tilhur, ...	5th	4th	2nd	1st	3rd	6th	10th	9th	8th	7th	11th	13th	12th	Chumars 9,043, Kisans 8,403, Aheers 7,028.
Meeranpore Kuttra,	7th	8th	12th	4th	1st	6th	5th	2nd	3rd	10th	9th	13th	11th	Aheers 977, Kahars 853, Pathans 745.
Khera Bujhera, ...	12th	5th	9th	2nd	3rd	6th	8th	4th	10th	1st	7th	13th	11th	Thakoors 8,980, Chumars 6,299, Aheers 4,908.
Jellalpore,	3rd	6th	9th	2nd	8th	4th	7th	5th	10th	1st	11th	...	12th	Thakoors 5,523, Chumars 4,650, Koormees 3,626.
Negohee,	13th	4th	1st	2nd	6th	5th	10th	7th	9th	3rd	8th	12th	11th	Kisans 8,959, Chumars 6,294, Thakoors 4,510.
Burragaon, ...	10th	6th	5th	1st	2nd	3rd	8th	11th	7th	4th	12th	9th	13th	Chumars 7,802, Aheers 4,325, Brahmins 3,277.
Powayn,...	6th	4th	2nd	1st	7th	3rd	9th	10th	12th	8th	11th	5th	13th	Chumars 20,273, Kisans 16,702, Brahmins 15,832.
Khotar, ...	2nd	6th	5th	1st	4th	3rd	10th	11th	9th	8th	13th	7th	12th	Chumars 7,042, Koormees 5,754, Brahmins 4,932.

In this table the figures 1st, 2nd, 3rd, &c., denote that the castes under which those figures are written, and especially the cultivating members of those castes, are 1st, 2nd, or 3rd, and so on, in numerical strength in that particular pergunnah to which that line of figures is allotted. Further details under this head must be sought for in the separate tuhseel reports.

49. The following statement gives the average rural population per square mile of total area, and the actual agricultural population divided into Hindoos and Mahomedans, adults and minors, both male and female, for every pergunnah and the whole district; also the average per square mile of cultivation (1) of cultivators and their families, (2) of adult cultivators only :—

Details of agricultural population and proportion to cultivated area.

Pergunnah.	RURAL POPULATION PER SQUARE MILE OF TOTAL AREA.		HINDOO CULTIVATORS.					MAHOMEDAN CULTIVATORS.					Grand Total.	AVERAGE PER SQUARE MILE OF CULTIVATION.	
			Adults.		Minors.			Adults.		Minors.					
	By settlement returns.	By census of 1872.	Male.	Female.	Male.	Female.	Total.	Male.	Female.	Male.	Female.	Total.		Of cultivators and their families.	Of adult cultivators.
Shahjehanpore,	465	595	18,686	15,992	9,896	7,618	52,122	2,772	2,514	1,543	1,281	8,110	60,232	368	391
Jumour, ..	453	512	12,415	10,945	6,879	4,329	34,578	630	560	559	263	1,812	36,390	535	361
Kant, ..	443	495	18,809	14,694	9,175	5,909	48,587	1,027	948	649	448	3,072	51,559	465	320
Jellalabad, ..	439	506	39,797	37,670	22,499	18,860	107,846	1,841	1,584	1,068	941	5,434	113,280	369	376
Tilhur, ..	443	552	17,610	15,153	8,512	7,480	48,755	1,353	1,192	847	782	4,174	52,929	545	363
Meeranpore Kuttra, ..	397	404	1,446	1,297	714	653	4,040	243	231	118	106	698	4,738	592	392
Khera Bujhera, ..	436	503	13,495	11,013	6,844	5,412	36,764	373	314	196	143	1,028	37,792	564	376
Jellalpore, ..	403	484	10,391	8,432	5,086	4,036	27,945	564	554	324	298	1,730	29,675	570	382
Negohee, ..	391	465	12,590	10,433	6,043	6,744	37,810	1,125	1,103	558	555	3,469	41,279	572	350
Burragaon, ..	544	596	10,810	9,220	5,544	4,302	29,876	1,150	1,061	661	555	3,430	33,306	584	390
Powayn, ..	439	500	39,780	34,969	21,959	16,199	112,877	1,726	1,373	960	797	4,585	117,492	611	387
Khotar, ..	244	260	11,905	9,383	6,729	5,213	33,640	1,162	979	669	631	3,371	37,011	379	237
Whole district,	442	485	207,804	173,331	111,890	81,788	574,540	13,966	12,303	8,079	6,638	41,183	615,723	530	360

These returns are from my settlement census, and exactly the same details are not procurable from the North-Western Provinces' census returns of 1872 for complete comparison. But comparisons between them have been drawn in the separate tahseel reports and discrepancies explained. It is sufficient here to refer to the totals only, which agree very closely. The number of cultivators by the settlement returns is 615,723, and in the census of 1872 agriculturists, separate from landholders, are given as 607,364, and landholders themselves 26,748 ; but about half of the landholders, rather less, are peasant proprietors, and are as such included amongst the agriculturists in my settlement returns.

The discrepancy between the average rural population per square mile of total area in my settlement returns and the North-Western Provinces census of 1872 is mainly owing to a different interpretation in either case of " *rural*," it being almost tantamount to agricultural in the former and *rural* as opposed to non-agricutural-*urban* in the latter. Khotar is the only pergunnah in the whole district in which there is any scarcity of cultivators, or which suffers in any way from a scarcity of rural or agricultural population. In all other pergunnahs the population is not only sufficient but dense, and even including Khotar, the rural population is nearly 500 to the square mile of total area, the agricultural population is 530 to the square mile of cultivation, and the adult cultivators average 350 to the same. Khotar, as will be seen further on in the report, and by reference to Chapter V., is altogether an exception to the rest of the district, and has been treated so accordingly.

50. We now come to the cultivating tenures and distribution of the cultivated area amongst the three great divisions or classes of cultivators, viz., 1st, the proprietary cultivators (i. e., the *seer* or *khood-kasht* land); 2nd, the non-proprietary cultivators—(a) hereditary cultivators or tenants with rights of occupancy ; (b) non-hereditary cultivators or tenants-at-will. In the following statement, for the sake of simplicity, percentages only are given, and not areas :—

Distribution of the cultivated area amongst proprietary and non-proprietary cultivators, occupancy tenants, and tenants-at-will.

Pergunnah.	PERCENTAGE OF CULTIVATED AREA HELD.		
	As seer.	By tenants with rights of occupancy.	By tenants-at-will.
Shahjehanpore,	8·12	68·37	23·51
Jumour,	10·24	70·34	19·42
Kant,	25·63	63·01	15·36
Jellalabad,	20·68	55·40	23·92
Tilhur,	9·79	74·09	16·12
Kuttra,	17·65	56·43	25·92
Khera Bujhera,	20·02	65·34	12·64
Jellalpore,	16·70	64·48	16·76
Negohee,	9·84	69·34	20·82
Burragaon,	9·78	69·88	20·34
Powayn,	9·70	62·32	27·98
Khotar,	6·25	27·60	66·15
Whole District,	13·42	61·31	25·27

From this it will be seen that on the whole district about 13½ per cent. of the cultivated area is held *seer*, as cultivated by proprietors ; 25¼ per cent. only is cultivated by tenants-at-will ; and the remainder, over 61¼ per cent., is held by tenants with rights of occupancy. The largest percentages of *seer* are in Kant, Jellalabad, and Khera Bujhera, and the greater part of this is cultivated by peasant proprietors ; whilst the smallest proportions are in Khotar and Shahjehanpore, and here, too, the greater part is cultivated by the proprietors with their own stock, but some is sublet.

Except in Khotar, where land is at a discount and cultivators are at a premium, and there are large tracts dependent on cultivators residing at a distance, the smallest proportion of land held by occupancy tenants is in Jellalabad, and there even it is nearly 55½ per cent. of the total cultivated area. In Pergunnah Tilhur is the largest percentage (74) of lands held by occupancy tenants, and there the lands cultivated by tenants-at-will amount to only 16 per cent. The lowest proportion, however, of tenants-at-will is to be found in Khera Bujhera, where it is only just over 12½ per cent.; and the highest of course in Khotar, over 66 per cent.

The very large proportion of occupancy tenure is remarkable, and is, doubtless, owing to the universal prevalence of money rents all over the district with the exception of some of the worst parts of Pergunnahs Powayn and Khotar. The zemindars, too, do not appear to mind in the least their cultivators having occupancy rights, and the whole of this portion of the record has been made without almost a dispute about the tenure. Possibly this may be in some measure owing to my having caused the entry in the *khusrah* (field index) of the number of years of cultivating occupancy in every case and for every single field, and omitting all mention of the words *mouroosee* (hereditary or occupancy) and *ghair-mouroosee* (non-hereditary or non-occupancy) until the *khuteonees* (or abstract of the field indices) were made, in which separate totals were made for fields held twelve years and upwards from those held for less than twelve years ; the former becoming spontaneously *mouroosee*, and latter *ghair-mouroosee* tenures.

51. Whilst on the subject of tenures, it would be as well to dispose of the revenue-free grants and tenures. There are no complicated revenue-free tenures, but the grantees *(maafeedars)* are in every instance the proprietors of the land, the zemindars. The description of proprietary tenure *(zemindaree* or *putteedaree)* has been included in the details already given, which are for the whole district and for all muhals, both paying revenue and exempt from payment of revenue.

Revenue-free tenures and grants.

The first statement shows the total amount of revenue-free lands, under each of the three headings, according to which the registers are drawn up, for each pergunnah and the whole district, *viz., 1st.* The small grants of less than ten *beegahs* each, which are revenue-free in perpetuity conditionally upon the possession of the grantees or their heirs or assignees, and the object and intention of the grant (especially in the case of religious grants) being observed. These amount in the whole district to 4,674 acres. The only large item is in the city of Shahjehanpore (which was all revenue-free till the mutiny, and that portion only is now paying revenue which was confiscated for rebellion in 1857), and of the 2,538 acres in that pergunnah 2,048 acres are separate small grants in the city only. *2nd.* The large grants (all those not petty grants of under 10 *beegahs)* of land revenue-free in perpetuity, subject to the same conditions in the case of grants for religious purposes. Under this head also a large portion is in the city, *viz.,* 565 acres, out of a total of 1,634 in Pergunnah Shahjehanpore. The rest is scattered about in the pergunnah, but chiefly in villages in the neighbourhood of the city. In a separate form will be given the entire revenue-free *mouzahs* or *muhals* in the various pergunnahs, and the balance between the total of their areas and the amount entered under this column in this present statement represents the area of the scattered grants, being portions of *mousahs* and *muhals*, *viz.,* of
$\frac{A.~R.~P.}{7,037~1~20} - \frac{A.~R.~P.}{2,306=4,731~1~25}.$ *3rd.* The life *maafees* or grants for the lifetime only of the grantees. A separate form of these will be given further on and remarks made thereon.

N. B.—The 1st, 2nd, and 3rd refer to the following figured statement ; the numbering of the *Register* is, No. I., Maafees of more than 10 beeghas ; No. II. of less 10 beeghas ; No. III., Life grants.

The aggregate revenue-free area, inclusive of life grants, is only just over one per cent. of the total area of the district.

Table of total area in acres of revenue-free land in the Shahjehanpore District.

Pergunnah.	LAND ALIENATED IN PERPETUITY.			Revenue-free for the lifetime of grantees.
	Small grants less than 10 beegahs.	Other grants exceeding 10 beegahs in area.	Total.	
	Acres. R. P.	Acres. R. P.	Acres. R. P.	Acres. R. P.
Shahjehanpore, ...	2,538 0 25	1,633 3 25	4,172 0 10	179 1 0
Jumour, ...	243 0 25	240 0 25	483 1 10	...
Kant, ...	452 1 20	146 1 30	598 3 10	...
Jellalabad, ...	192 1 35	1,261 1 0	1,453 2 35	40 1 0
Tilhar, ...	265 0 0	777 0 10	1,042 0 10	...
Meeranpore Kuttra, ...	0 2 35	...	0 2 35	...
Khera Bujhera, ...	31 0 20	30 0 5	61 0 25	...
Jellalpore, ...	147 2 20	87 3 15	235 1 35	...
Negohee, ...	125 1 20	866 3 0	992 0 20	33 1 15
Burragaon, ...	246 1 15	242 3 30	489 1 5	117 0 0
Powayn, ...	361 3 15	362 1 15	724 0 30	...
Khotar, ...	70 2 0	1,388 2 30	1,459 0 30	...
Total, ...	4,874 2 30	7,037 1 25	11,712 0 15	369 3 15

52. The next table shows the number and names of the muhals for each pergun-

Revenue-free mouzahs and muhals. Cesses thereon under Act XVIII of 1871. Amount of alienated revenue.

nah of the district which are revenue-free in perpetuity. There is not one in any of the three pergunnahs of the Shahjehanpore Tuhseel, and there are only twelve, with a total area of 2,306 acres, in the whole district. Of these, four only are religious, not religious endowments properly speaking, but rather religious charities. Two of them are exempt from payment of cesses under Board of Revenue's Circular No. 3, dated 18th May, 1872. Upon all the others, not only of this list but throughout the district, which are not specially exempted by existing orders, cesses at 10 per cent. on the would-be revenue, *i. e.*, 5 per cent. on the estimated present "annual value," have been imposed under Act XVIII. of 1871. The total amount of these cesses for the whole district is Rs. 916-15-0. The amount of revenue alienated in the following statement of the *maafee mouzahs* and *muhals* is Rs. 3,950, but for the whole district, inclusive of all the *maafee* plots, those exempt from cesses included, it is Rs. 13,756 :—

List of muhals revenue-free in perpetuity in the District of Shahjehanpore.

Pergunnah.	Name of mouzah and muhal.	Description of maafee.	Total area in acres.	Nominal jumma assessed, i.e., revenue alienated.	Remarks.
Jellalabad, ...	Muktora, ... / Muhal maafee, ..	Charitable, for maintenance.	1,165	Rs. 1,590	10% cesses only collected, ... Rs. 150
Tilhar, ...	Shergurh, ..	Religious, ...	87	200	Ditto, ... „ 20
Ditto, ...	Oosamanpore, ... / Tiswee, ...	Charitable, for maintenance.	464	400	Ditto, ... „ 40
Negohee, ...	Chuck Lohargowan.	Ditto, ...	187	280	Ditto, ... „ 28
Ditto, ...	Ditto Sufora,	Ditto, ...	158	220	Ditto, ... „ 22
Ditto, ...	Ditto Itour, ...	Ditto, ...	159	240	Ditto, ... „ 24
Ditto, ...	Ditto Bukainya,	Ditto, ...	224	280	Ditto, ... „ 28
Powayn, ...	Sunasur, ...	Religious, ...	67	40	These being *religious* revenue-free grants, the alienated revenue of which is less than Rs. 100, are exempt from the payment of cesses under Board of Revenue's Circular No. 3, dated 18th May 1872.
Khotar, ...	Sukhchainpore,..	Ditto, ...	30	40	
Ditto, ...	Koombia, ...	Charitable, for maintenance.	220	250	Pays only 10% cesses, Rs. 25
Ditto, ...	Kesurpore, ...	Ditto, ...	323	250	Ditto, ... „ 25
Ditto, ...	Matee, ...	Religious, ...	222	250	Ditto, ... „ 25
Whole District,	12 muhals, ...		2,306	3,950	

53. The number of life-grants is now small, only five in number ; the total area
of them is only 369 acres, and the amount of revenue
temporarily alienated is Rs. 580. Revenue has been assessed on
each grant in anticipation of lapse, and to come into force from that date. Till then
cesses only at 10 per cent. on the revenue, under Act XVIII. of 1871, are collected.
It is probable that all of these grants will fall in and become subject to revenue
within the next five or six years.

Life-grants.

The following statement gives all particulars necessary for this report :—

Pergunnah.	Mouzah.	Area of life-grant in acres.	Amount of revenue assessed in anticipation of lapse of grant.
			Rs.
Shahjehanpore, ...	The city of Shahjehanpore (Dulel Bagh).	98	150
Ditto, ...	Ghoosgowan, ...	81	130
Jellalabad, ...	Bhutadewur, ...	40	50
Negohee, ...	Purajhursa, ...	33	50
Burragaon, ...	Lukhraon, ...	117	200
Whole District, ...	...	369	580

SECTION IV.

Past Settlements, Sales, Farms, and Transfers during the last Settlement.

54. The revenues of the past five settlements and of the present revision (which
is the tenth settlement since the cession) are given in the table
below for the pergunnahs as they are now constituted, but as
the jummas were assessed and without regard to subsequent alterations during the
currency of the respective settlements—

Revenues of past settlement.

Pergunnah.	Past settlements.					Present revision.
	5th.	6th.	7th.	8th.	9th. (Mr. J. W. Muir's)	
	Rs.	Rs.	Rs.	Rs.	Rs.	Rs.
Shahjehanpore Tuhseel, ...	2,68,253	2,71,965	2,76,934	2,71,880	2,67,639	2,90,671
Jellalabad, ...	1,46,309	1,45,151	1,42,909	1,39,354	1,60,610*	2,11,410
Tilhur, ...	63,877	63,062	81,486	98,432	83,258	1,09,119
Kuttra, ...	5,539	5,539	6,617	7,379	5,925	8,510
Khera Bujhera, ...	13,788	15,991	55,973	68,548	51,743	72,360
Jellalpore, ...	55,909	58,431	63,396	68,616	55,550	63,005
Negohee,... ...	38,207	38,207	58,477	74,539	63,838	77,130
Burragaon, ...	...	73,994	73,994	75,766	64,785	72,950
Powayu, ...	...	1,80,176	1,79,976	2,09,098	1,93,606	2,16,735
Khotar, ...	Not ascertainable.			†18,712	36,667	62,535
Whole District, ...	Not ascertainable correct.			10,22,894 Without Bangaon.	9,33,566 With Bangaon.	11,84,425

The interchanges from time to time of villages with the adjoining districts and
amongst pergunnahs of this district, besides the entire absorption of some pergunnahs, naturally tend to the possibility of errors of detail in the figures of the fifth, sixth,
seventh, and eighth settlements, as compared with those of the ninth settlement ; they
are given, however, for what they are worth, and are, at all events, approximately
correct. The pergunnah details of the eighth and ninth settlements do not agree with the
figures given in Mr. J. W. Muir's report of the last settlement in 1838-39 A. D., in
consequence of subsequent interchanges of villages or alteration of pergunnah boundaries, and the entire disappearance of some pergunnahs—ε. g., Morowree. And where-

---

* Including Bangaon, and Rs. 1,12,684 without it.

† This total, Rs. 18,712, is only approximately correct, it cannot be ascertained exactly.

ever the figures of this chapter differ from those in the separate tuhseel assessment reports, these are to be accepted as correct in preference to those.

55. All the settlements previous to this lately expired settlement made by Mr. J. W. Muir in 1838-39 A.D. under Regulation IX. of 1833 were short term settlements, and Mr. Muir's was the first thirty years settlement. Large enhancements had been made in most parts of the district at the seventh and eighth settlements, the two last preceding Mr. J. W. Muir's settlement, and he found the district "labouring under the pressure of a very heavy assessment." Referring to what now constitutes the Jellalabad and Tilhur tuhseeldarees he says—"The pergunnahs in question till the fourth settlement formed part of Zillah Bareilly and underwent the same processes of settlement in former times which that district did. It is well known that the Bareilly District was over-assessed, and that by Regulation VII. of 1822 settlements, by summary settlements, and by settlements under Regulation IX. of 1833, reductions, of which the aggregate may be stated at two lakhs, have at different times been granted. The seven pergunnahs of Shahjehanpore now settled had hitherto been favoured with but little relief, and it is therefore not to be wondered at that, on a total jumma of Rs. 4,66,679, I have now allowed abatements amounting in all to Rs. 79,887.

Mr. J. W. Muir's settlement; his remarks on the severity of previous settlements.

"12. The over-assessment of these pergunnahs may be traced in a great measure, more particularly in three tuhseeldaree divisions out of the four, to the great increase of revenue that was imposed under former settlements, the enhancement of jumma since 1210 Fuslee being more than the resources of the majority of estates were adequate to. The fresh revision of the assessment, particularly at the third and fourth settlements, was made the means of raising the jumma as much as possible—an object the furtherance of which was enjoined as the peculiar duty of all the pergunnah tuhseel officers, particularly of the canoongoes. To the latter rewards even were held out, and accordingly it is said that Dheeree Dhur, the canoongoe of Mehrabad, received the present of an elephant from Mr. Trant for his exertions in being instrumental in raising the jumma of that pergunnah at the fourth settlement. The consequence of these enlargements of assessment has been that the people have been kept in poverty ever since; that numbers of malgoozars have been ruined, and that, except in favourable seasons, great difficulty has" been experienced in the realization of revenue.

*   *   *   *   *   *   *

"14. The condition in which I found the people of the different pergunnahs, as I visited them one after another (independent of the considerations of temporary embarrassments arising out of the past calamitous season) proved how much they stood in need of alleviation of assessment. The great mass of the proprietors are in circumstances of extreme indigence, caused, I have reason to believe, principally by the heaviness of the jumma. The Thakoors of Mehrabad, Khera Bujhera, and Jellalpore, and the Puthans of Tilhur, are alike impoverished. The exceptions of wealthy malgoozars are very few, and those of this description met with appear to have gained their substance from other sources than the profits of their estates. It is matter of surprise how under such circumstances the jumma was realized, but this, it was found, had only been done with very great difficulty and distress to the people. Things, however, had come to a crisis, and could not have gone on much longer without a reduction of assessment."

These remarks are also to a great extent applicable to the remaining two tuhseels, Shahjehanpore and Powayn, which were also assessed by Mr. J. W. Muir, but the report of which was written by Mr. Rose in July, 1840, after Mr. J. W. Muir's death, and is not only extremely meagre but also very inaccurate. Pergunnah Khotar alone is an exception, as it invariably is in everything relating to the district generally.

56. The result of Mr. J. W. Muir's revision of settlement was a considerable reduction in every single pergunnah (except Khotar), amounting in all to nearly a lakh and a quarter of rupees (Rs. 1,22,639), or 12 per cent.; but still, with the exception of the old Pergunnah of Mehrabad (*i.e.*, Jellalabad without Bangaon, which has since been incorporated into it) parts of Pergunnahs Kant, Tilhur, and Khera Bujhera, Mr. J. W. Muir's settlement was by no means a light one. As far as one can now judge, it appears that rather more reduction was given in three of those pergunnahs just mentioned than was necessary; at all events the assessments in them were undoubtedly somewhat light as compared with the rest of the district. One striking feature of Mr. J. W. Muir's settlement is the very heavy assessments he put, or probably found and left on all Koormee villages. On the whole though, I think, that Mr. J. W. Muir's was a good settlement, that he apportioned his reductions according to the exigencies of the case as then apparent, and that he not only saved the district from impending ruin but gave a healthy impetus to industry and improvement which has borne good fruit; as is abundantly evident from this present report, and the large increase of cultivation and revenue, of which mention will be found in its proper place. Reference has been made to the past settlement of all pergunnahs in the separate assessment reports (Chapters II. to V.), to which attention is directed for any further details.

The result of Mr. J. W. Muir's settlement, a large reduction.

57. In consequence of the total destruction of all records during the rebellion of 1857-58 A.D., it has been almost impossible to obtain any detailed or authentic returns of alienations of property for the first part of the past settlement, previous to 1857, for entire pergunnahs, but such as were obtainable for the former and latter portion of the settlement have been given in the separate assessment reports. The information, however, was so meagre in many instances that it is impossible to give it in a condensed form for the whole district. I have therefore thought best to give a short resumé of such particulars as were obtained for each tuhseel separately.

The working of Mr. J. W. Muir's settlement, alienations of property.

From the following it will be seen that, with the exceptions already made in the foregoing paragraph, Mr. Muir's assessment was, as the rule, somewhat heavy at its commencement, although a considerable reduction on its predecessor, and that punitive measures for the collection of the revenue, as well as transfers, caused by its pressure, were rather numerous in the first ten or twelve years of the settlement, but became gradually less as extension of cultivation and general development and improvement took place, and after permanent reductions of revenue had been granted in all cases of marked severity. The selling price of land also rose very greatly towards the end of the settlement, to 60 per cent. and more above what it had been before the mutiny, the prices for private sales averaging in Pergunnahs Shahjehanpore, Tilhur, Negohee, and Burragaon from Rs. 12 to 22 per acre of cultivation, and from seven to twelve times the Government revenue. The average in Burragaon and Negohee alone was over Rs. 20 per acre of cultivation, and from nine and a half to twelve times the Government revenue.

58. In Tuhseel Shahjehanpore a reduction of Rs. 797 from the jumma assessed by Mr. Muir was found necessary, on the score of severity, in ten villages. Five of these villages are in Pergunnah Jumour and five in Kant. The remissions were made from time to time between 1840 and 1856 A.D., as the necessity arose in each case. Apparently there was only one sale for arrears of revenue, viz., Mouzah Arthooa of Pergunnah Kant, assessed at Rs. 500, which was subsequently reduced to Rs. 350, and kept at that sum in the present revision. There were fourteen farms for arrears of revenue, of which twelve were before the mutiny, between 1839 and 1857, and only two after it, viz., from 1858 to 1869. Over-assessment, however, was the probable or evident cause of arrears in only nine out of these fourteen farms, and in the remaining five the assessments were by no means heavy.

Tuhseel Shahjehanpore.

Nothing at all approaching to accuracy was obtainable for private transactions and alienations of property by sale and mortgage, and the returns were so palpably wrong that I was obliged to reject them altogether. They were without doubt very numerous.

59. In Tuhseel Jellalabad the information concerning punitive sales and farms

Tuhseel Jellalabad.
and private sales and mortgages is still more meagre than in Shahjehanpore, and I have nothing to add to what is contained in paragraph 38 of Chapter III., the assessment report of that tuhseel. The settlement of Mehrabad, made by Mr. J. W. Muir, was light, whereas that of Bangaon, by Mr. Robinson, was heavy. Pergunnah Bangaon was assessed in the Futtehgurh District, but transferred from it to this district before the general revision in Futtehgurh for severity of assessment took place; and it so happened that Pergunnah Bangaon, by being amalgamated with a lightly assessed pergunnah (Mehrabad), was excluded from the boon extended to the district in which it had been assessed. Pergunnah Bangaon consists of fifty-one mouzahs, in twelve of which there have been farms for arrears of revenue, and in ten of the twelve shares have also been sold and mortgaged to outsiders; there are also five other mouzahs in which there have been sales and mortgages to outsiders, three in which there have been sales, but not mortgages, and five in which there have been only mortgages. These sales and mortgages do not include any of the transactions amongst the brotherhood, which have been numerous. But in twenty-five out of the fifty-one mouzahs composing the pergunnah as transferred from Futtehgurh property has suffered, and alienations have taken place in consequence of severity of assessment. In the old Pergunnah of Mehrabad there have been a few sales and some farms for arrears of revenue, but exceptionally due merely to severity of assessment. The number of private sales and mortgages have been numerically larger, but proportionately smaller than in Bangaon, and in these private transactions also severity of assessment has not been the immediate or principal cause of transfer. In one instance only (Oomdapore) was a reduction of jumma made owing to severity of assessment, viz., from Rs. 401 to Rs. 322, and the revised jumma of the present settlement is only Rs. 360.

60. In Tuhseel Tilhur there were nine sales of muhals for arrears of revenue,

Tuhseel Tilhur.
forty-four farms, and permanent reduction of jumma in sixty-two muhals, amounting to Rs. 4,571 in all. The details of these for each pergunnah are given in the following statement, taken from para. 65 of Chapter IV.:—

Pergunnah.			Number of sales of muhals for arrears.	Number of farms of muhals for arrears.	Permanent reduction of revenue on account of severe assessment.	
					Number of muhals.	Amount of reduction.
						Rs.
Tilhur,	...	...	...	7	...	...
Kuttra,	...	...	...	...	...	...
Negohee,	...	...	18	7	42	2,402
Khera Bujhera,	...	...	...	7	13	1,593
Jellalpore,	...	...	1	23	7	576
Whole Tuhseel,		...	19	44	62	4,571

As I can add nothing to the few particulars given by Mr. G. Butt for each pergunnah in his assessment report of Tuhseel Tilhur (Chapter IV.), I merely draw attention to paragraphs 64 to 70 and 72 and 73 of that chapter, and do not reproduce them here.

61. The details about Mr. Muir's settlement of this tuhseel will be found in para-

Tuhseel Powayn.
graph 36, pages 129 to 137, of Chapter V., to which attention is directed for further particulars than the short summary here given. In Pergunnah Burragaon, though the jumma was a severe one at first, there was not one single farm or sale for arrears of revenue, but a permanent reduction of jumma in

six villages, amounting to Rs. 571, was found absolutely necessary. The proprietors who suffered most severely are the old resident village communities, viz., Thakoors, Brahmins, Aheers, and Koormees, many of whom have gone hopelessly to the wall. The total amount of Government revenue transferred during the settlement bears a proportion of 40 per cent. to the revenue of the whole pergunnah ; and the transactions themselves extend to seventy-nine muhals, or just 50 per cent. of the pergunnah.

In Pergunnah Powayn there were only two sales and four farms for arrears of revenue, but this does not, from the fact of the enormous property of the Powayn Rajah, prove any absence of severity of assessment. The transfers have been very numerous indeed, amounting to 70 per cent. in the *talookdaree* villages, and in the *khalsa* villages the changes have been nearly as great. These and other details will be found stated at length at page 135 *et seq.* of Chapter V., as already stated above.

The assessment of Pergunnah Khotar was progressive, and subsequent reductions of jumma in thirteen villages, amounting to Rs. 1,557, were found necessary. There was one sale for arrears of revenue and there were fifteen farms. No details of the private transactions are procurable, and but few of them can be in any way attributable to severity of assessment.

62. The following statements show for each pergunnah and the whole district the extent to which landed property has passed from the possession of the agricultural classes into the hands of non-agriculturists during the term of the past settlement :—

Acquisition of landed property by non-agriculturists.

Statement showing the extent to which the landed property has been transferred from the possession of the old proprietors into the hands of the non-agricultural classes in the Shahjehanpore District.

1.		2.	3.	4.	5.	6.	7.	8.	9.
Name of Pergunnah.		Total area in acres paying revenue.	Deduct area confiscated for rebellion.	Remaining.	Year.	Area occupied by agricultural classes in acres.	Per cent.	Area occupied by non-agricultural classes in acres.	Per cent.
Shahjehanpore,	...	76,263	16,878	59,385	Last Settlement, 1839-40 A. D.	58,768	98·9	617	1·1
Jumour,	...	52,063	9,215	42,848	Ditto ...	41,746	97·4	1,102	2·6
Kant,	...	78,689	4,943	73,746	Ditto ...	71,725	97·3	2,081	2·7
Tuhseel Total,	...	207,015	31,036	175,979	...	172,239	97·9	3,740	2·1
Shahjehanpore,	...	76,263	16,878	59,385	1860 A. D. ...	56,326	94·9	3,059	5·1
Jumour,	...	52,063	9,215	42,848	Ditto ...	38,130	89·0	4,718	11·0
Kant,	...	78,689	4,943	73,746	Ditto ...	71,266	96·6	2,480	3·4
Tuhseel Total,	...	207,015	31,036	175,979	...	165,722	94·1	10,257	5·9
Shahjehanpore,	...	81,471	16,878	64,593	Present Settlement, 1870-71 A. D.	57,312	88·7	7,281	11·3
Jumour,	...	56,933	9,215	47,718	Ditto ...	33,950	71·1	13,768	28·9
Kant,	...	85,757	4,943	80,814	Ditto ...	75,627	93·5	5,187	6·5
Tuhseel Total,	...	224,161	31,036	193,125	...	166,889	86·0	26,236	14·0
Jellalabad,	...	169,198	1,827	167,371	Last Settlement, 1839-40	165,619	99·0	1,752	1·0
Ditto,	...	169,198	1,827	167,371	1860 A. D.	156,124	93·2	11,247	6·8
Ditto,	...	176,523	1,827	174,696	Present Settlement, 1871-70 A. D.	161,237	92·4	13,459	7·6
Tuhseel and pergunnah the same.		...	...	...	Ditto ...	...	...	...	...

Statement showing the extent to which the landed property has been transferred from the possession of the old proprietors into the hands of the non-agricultural classes in the Shahjehanpore District—(concluded).

1.	2.	3.	4.	5.	6.	7.	8.	9.
Name of Pergunnah.	Total area in acres paying revenue.	Deduct area confiscated for rebellion.	Remaining.	Year.	Area occupied by agricultural classes in acres.	Per cent.	Area occupied by non-agricultural classes in acres.	Per cent.
Tilhur, ...	69,907	15,365	54,542	Last Settlement, 1839-40 A. D.	47,299	86·7	7,243	13·3
Meeranpore Kuttra,	6,633	...	6,635	Ditto ...	5,093	76·8	1,540	23·2
Negohee, ...	62,959	1,312	61,647	Ditto ...	53,819	87·3	7,828	12·7
Jellalpore, ...	36,507	153	36,354	Ditto ...	25,984	71·5	10,370	28·5
Khera Bujhera, ...	46,306	4,010	42,296	Ditto ...	41,113	97·2	1,183	2·8
Tuhseel Total, ...	222,312	20,840	201,472	...	173,308	86·1	28,164	13·9
Tilhur, ...	69,907	15,365	54,542	1860 A. D. ...	43,959	80·6	10,583	19·4
Meeranpore Kuttra,	6,633	...	6,636	Ditto ...	4,880	73·5	1,758	26·5
Negohee, ...	62,959	1,312	61,647	Ditto ...	38,097	61·8	23,550	38·2
Jellalpore, ...	36,507	153	36,354	Ditto ...	22,166	60·9	14,188	39·1
Khera Bujhera, ...	46,306	4,010	42,296	Ditto ...	39,023	92·3	3,273	7·7
Tuhseel Total, ...	222,312	20,840	201,472	...	148,125	73·5	53,347	26·5
Tilhur, ...	72,862	15,365	57,497	Present Settlement, 1870-71 A. D.	46,436	80·8	11,061	19·2
Meeranpore Kuttra,	7,217	...	7,217	Ditto ...	5,433	75·3	1,784	24·7
Negohee, ...	62,509	1,312	61,197	Ditto ...	36,646	59·8	24,551	40·2
Jellalpore, ...	41,598	153	41,445	Ditto ...	27,009	65·2	14,436	34·8
Khera Bujhera, ...	51,147	4,010	47,137	Ditto ...	42,987	91·2	4,150	8·8
Tuhseel Total, ...	235,333	20,840	214,493	...	158,511	73·9	55,982	26·1
Powayn, ...	168,871	1,612	167,259	Last Settlement, 1839-40 A. D.	161,810	96·7	5,449	3·3
Burragaon, ...	39,938	1,898	38,040	Ditto ...	33,079	86·9	4,961	13·1
Khotar, ...	99,386	96	99,290	Ditto ...	91,256	91·9	8,034	8·1
Tuhseel Total, ...	308,195	3,606	304,589	...	286,145	93·9	18,444	6·1
Powayn, ...	168,871	1,612	167,259	1860 A. D. ...	147,179	87·9	20,080	12·1
Burragaon, ...	39,938	1,808	38,040	Ditto ...	29,742	78·2	8,298	21·8
Khotar, ...	99,386	96	99,290	Ditto ...	87,452	88·1	11,833	11·9
Tuhseel Total, ...	308,195	3,606	304,589	...	264,373	86·8	40,216	13·2
Powayn, ...	182,793	1,612	181,181	Present Settlement, 1870-71 A. D.	144,597	79·8	36,584	20·2
Burragaon, ...	45,405	1,898	43,507	Ditto ...	34,795	79·9	8,712	20·1
Khotar, ...	120,396	96	120,300	Ditto ...	13,514	85·9	16,986	14·1
Tuhseel Total, ...	348,594	3,606	344,988	...	282,706	81·9	62,282	18·1
District Total, ...	984,611	57,309	927,302	...	769,343	82·9	157,959	17·1

DISTRICT TOTALS.

Column 4.	Column 5.	Column 6.	Column 7.	Column 8.	Column 9.
849,411	1839-40	797,311	93·9	52,100	6·1
849,411	1860	734,344	86·5	115,067	13·5
922,302	1870	769,343	83·	157,959	17·

Abstract of transfers of land to the non-agricultural classes in the Shahjehanpore District.

Pergunnah.	Percentage of area held by non-agricultural classes in 1839-40.	Percentage of area transferred to non-agricultural classes.			Percentage of area held by non-agricultural classes in 1870.
		1840-60.	1860-70.	1840-70.	
Shahjehanpore, ...	1·1	4·0	6·2	10·2	11·3
Jumour, ...	2·6	8·4	17·9	26·3	28·9
Kant, ...	2·7	0·7	3·1	3·8	6·5
Shahjehanpore Tuhseel, ...	2·1	3·8	8·3	12·1	14·2
Jellalabad Pergunnah and Tuhseel, ...	1·0	5·8	0·8	6·6	7·6
Tilhur, ...	18·3	6·1	—0·2	5·9	19·2
Kuttra, ...	23·2	3·2	—1·8	1·4	24·6
Negohee, ...	12·7	25·5	2·0	27·5	40·2
Jellalpore, ...	28·5	10·6	—4·3	6·3	34·8
Khera Bujhera, ...	2·8	4·9	1·1	6·0	8·8
Tilhur Tuhseel, ...	18·9	12·6	0·4	12·2	26·1
Powayn, ...	3·3	8·8	8·1	16·9	20·2
Burragaon, ...	13·1	8·7	—1·7	7·0	20·1
Khotar, ...	8·1	3·8	2·2	6·0	14·1
Powayn Tuhseel, ...	6·1	7·1	4·9	12·0	18·1
District Total, ...	6·1	7·4	3·5	10·0	17·0

NOTE.—The decrease during the second period in Tilhur, Kuttra, Jellalpore, and Burragaon is not a real decrease; the total area shown for 1840 and 1860 is that by the old survey, and the area by the present survey is, in each case, considerably greater, and hence, though there is a slight absolute increase in the areas held by the non-agricultural classes, the percentage on the total area is lower in 1870 than in 1860.

These statements do not profess to represent *all* transfers, but merely the former, intermediate and present proportion of the land held by strictly non-agriculturists on the one hand, and by those, on the other hand, who are not *bonâ fide* non-agriculturists. Amongst the latter, called in the first statement (Column 6) the agricultural classes, are included most of the Pathan and many Kaiyeth families, those of them at least who have been connected with the land for two and three generations or longer, many of whom have extended their properties and acquired more lands from the old original agricultural proprietors. Such men being old zemindars, and *zemindaree* their principal if not only means of livelihood, they could not be ranked amongst the *non-agricultural* classes. Hence the non-agricultural classes include only bankers, money-lenders, traders, and such like, who have more or less recently, within the last fifty or sixty years, acquired land, and whose profession is not *zemindaree*.

63. These statements, moreover, do not give any commensurate idea of the
But a small part of the transfers really shown: only the extent of profession of non-agricultural classes. extent to which lands have been transferred from the old original proprietors, except in so far as they have gone into the hands of *bonâ fide* non-agriculturists. For instance, none of those extensive transfers in Jellalabad (Bangaon especially) amongst the brotherhood appear here; and but a small portion of the enormous

transfers in Pergunnahs Burragaon and Powayn. This last is a very striking illustration of what I say, for since 1840 A.D. the resident village zemindars of Powayn have lost upwards of 60 per cent. of their property, and these statements show transfers amounting only to 17 per cent. of the area of the pergunnah during the thirty years between 1840 and 1870. And although they do show the extent of land which is in the possession of the strictly non-agricultural classes, they of course give no clue whatever to the extent to which the land remaining with the non-agricultural classes is encumbered. For though mortgagees in possession appear as proprietors, yet there are numbers and numbers of encumbered estates merely hypothecated for debt, and paying interest thereon, which are still in the possession of the old proprietors (chiefly in Jellalabad and Khotar, distant Thakoor pergunnahs), but in a fair way to part company with them.

64. On the total of the whole district, non-agricultural classes in 1839-40 held
<small>Further details of transfers to non-agriculturists, with remarks for each tuhseel.</small>
6·1 per cent. of the land, and in 1870, 17 per cent., the increase being 10·9 per cent., or almost one-eleventh of the total area of the district. The pergunnahs in which the non-agricultural classes held the largest proportion of land are (1st) Jellalpore, (2nd) Kuttra, (3rd) Tilhur, (4th) Burragaon, (5th) Negohee, all over 12 per cent.; and those in which they held the least are Jellalabad and Shahjehanpore, only one per cent. in each. Separate details for each tuhseel follow.

65. Large increases to the property of non-agriculturists naturally took place
<small>Tuhseel Shahjehanpore.</small>
in two Pergunnahs (Shahjehanpore and Jumour) of this tuhseel, in consequence of their proximity to the city, and chiefly in Jumour, as it was more highly assessed than Shahjehanpore. The acquisition by non-agriculturists in Kant has been small, as it is further from the city, has a poor light soil, and the proprietors are chiefly Thakoors of various clans, Bachels, Ponwars, &c., amongst whom a Bunniah purchaser would be loth to intrude.

66. Part of this, as already explained, viz., Mehrabad, was lightly assessed, and
<small>Tuhseel Jellalabad.</small>
part, Bangaon, was very heavily assessed. The proprietors were almost all Thakoors, and a few Pathans of the town of Jellalabad. There were no wealthy men in Jellalabad to purchase even if they dared, and no one from the city would speculate in Jellalabad from the distance and fear of the Thakoors. There are a few well-to-do Thakoors in the pergunnah who purchase when opportunity occurs. The treasurer has money lent out there and villages hypothecated, but he knows better than to take possession as a mortgagee.

67. Tuhseel Tilhur comprises five pergunnahs, about which Mr. Butt, who
<small>Tuhseel Tilhur.</small>
furnished a note on these statements, has written as follows :—

Pergunnah Jellalpore.—As to Jellalpore this (viz., the large proportion held by non-agricultural classes at the last settlement, 1839-40) is explained by the extreme severity of the previous assessments. Mr. J. W. Muir in his Settlement Report, 1838, wrote that Jellalpore was, "even at the cession, fully cultivated, and many of the villages being of old celebrated for their sugar, and the people for their industry, it came to pass that at an early period the assessment was fixed at an excessive amount, the effect of which has been that the condition of the people has hitherto been one of extreme depression. The high pressure of the Jellalpore jumma was a matter of notoriety, and I became aware of it, in the first instance, upwards of two years ago, when engaged in the settlement of the adjoining Pergunnah of Beesulpore."

The proprietors in Jellalpore had once been almost exclusively Kutheria Thakoors, but transfers here commenced early. Now the Kutherias hold few villages, but a large proportion has been purchased by Thakoors of adjoining pergunnahs, or by others included among agricultural classes. In Jellalpore, the area held by the non-agricultural classes has increased considerably, though hardly so much as might have been expected, Mr. Muir's assessment, though a reduction on the preceding one, having been very severe, and the town of Khoodagunge in the centre of the pergunnah containing many wealthy traders and money-lenders.

Pergunnah Kuttra.—In the small Pergunnah of Kuttra, the area held by the non-agricultural classes consisted of certain villages held by the English proprietor of the Meona Indigo Factory and zemindaree, and the changes since 1840 have been insignificant.

Pergunnah Tilhur.—In Tilhur no single caste ever prevailed ; and, as might be expected in a pergunnah lying round a large and important town, the non-agricultural classes had purchased to some extent before settlement. The subsequent changes require no notice, as the great change caused by the confiscation of several large estates held by Tilhur Pathans does not affect the statement.

Pergunnah Negohee.—In Negohee a descendant of Hafiz Rahmat Khan was the largest proprietor, and the sale of his villages to city bankers, a few years after settlement, chiefly causes the great increase in the area held by the non-agricultural classes.

Kassub Thakoors once held a large part of Negohee. They have gradually been disappearing, but have in great part been replaced by city Pathans or others included among the agricultural classes.

Pergunnah Khera Bujhera.—Here the change is slight. The pergunnah was very lightly assessed, is far from any town, sugar cultivation is only now commencing, and the proprietors are almost all Junghara Thakoors, a clan that hitherto has held its own well.

68. In two of the three pergunnahs of this tuhseel, Burragaon and Powayn, the assessment was heavy, and especially so in the *talookdaree* villages in Powayn. There were not very many purely agricultural proprietors in Burragaon at the last settlement, a large proportion of the so-called agricultural proprietors being an old Kayeth family resident in Burragaon itself, and Pathans of the city of Shahjehanpore. Most of the genuine agricultural proprietors have lost their property, or are deeply involved, and city Pathans are to some extent the purchasers (para. 36 of Chapter V.)

In Pergunnah Powayn the Rajah is sole proprietor of about one-third, and in this there have been no transfers. In the remainder, about 30 per cent. has passed into the hands of the strictly non-agricultural classes, and as much more has been transferred from the village zemindars to non-resident purchasers included in the agricultural classes.

Pergunnah Khotar is altogether exceptional, and at a great distance, over twenty-five miles, from the city. It was only partially reclaimed at last settlement, and is still malarious and unhealthy, and the parties with whom the settlement of a great portion was made were admitted only as farmers, and on very easy terms. Many of the Thakoor proprietors are now deeply in debt, and the treasurer has a good many villages in this pergunnah hypothecated to him. The Rajah of Pewayn has commenced acquiring property here, and may keep out the Bunniah element somewhat.

69. Doubtless, the severity of the assessment had a great deal to do with the extent of the transfers in the various pergunnahs, and eliminating exceptional cases, such as those of the large property of the Rajah in Pergunnah Powayn (a heavily assessed pergunnah), the transfer of Karamat-oollah Khan's property in Negohee

a somewhat heavily assessed pergunnah) not immediately caused by the severity of Mr. J. W. Muir's assessment; the inclusion in Pergunnah Jellalabad (a generally lightly assessed pergunnah) of the fifty-one villages of Bangaon, all very heavily assessed, the results for heavily assessed, moderately assessed, and lightly assessed pergunnahs come out approximately as given in the margin.

Description of assessment,	Percentage held by non-agri-cultural classes.		
	In 1840.	In 1870.	Increase.
Heavy, ...	8·8	30·3	21·5
Medium, ...	9·6	22·0	12·4
Light, ...	3·2	8·2	5·0

From this it would appear that severity or lightness of assessment alone governed the transfers; but this is not so, there are other causes to account for this coincidence. The lightly assessed pergunnahs are Mehrabad (the old portion of Jellalabad), Kant, Khera Bujhera, and Khotar; all of them are at a distance from the city, and very strong in powerful Thakoor brotherhoods except Khotar (which was a wild, unreclaimed, unhealthy jungle), and producing little or no sugar-cane, and containing no town or market of any importance; hence there was not only no inducement for city mahajans and Pathans, and others, to invest their money in purchasing in those pergunnahs, but everything to prevent them. Whereas of the heavily assessed pergunnahs, Jumour, Burragaon, Powayn, part of Jellalabad (viz., Bangaon) and Jellalpore, three are first class sugar-cane producing tracts, and part also of the fourth, Jumour; and Jumour lies close to the city, so that in the case of these pergunnahs there was every incentive, as well as opportunity, Bangaon alone excepted, for non-agriculturists to lay out their capital in them, and the deterrent causes were also absent.

SECTION V.

Survey ; Areas of past and present Settlement ; Soils.

70. The measurement of the district was commenced and completed under my own personal supervision and orders. The method was the plane-table; and the agency the *putwarees*, or when they were unable to measure, *ameens* accompanied by the *putwaree*. The scale of the field maps is two chains (*jureebs*) of 55 yards each in length to the inch, or 16 inches to the mile. Every field is separately mapped upon it, and barren lands, jungle, mango *baghs*, old, unbroken, waste and new fallow have each their distinctive marks, so that the map itself shows each distinct from the cultivated fields, and every field and plot has its separate number by which it can be found, and all details of name of cultivator, kind of soil, source of irrigation if irrigated, kind of crop, &c., &c., appertaining to it in the index (*hkusra*).

Measurement.

It is unnecessary here to go into minute details regarding the supervising agency, and the pains and steps taken to get good maps and correct measurements and indices. It is sufficient to mention that, with the exception of Mr. Butt, my Assistant, all the subordinates were natives, and that the final testing of the maps and indices was done entirely by Mr. Butt and myself. The results of the close agreement of our plane-table measurements with the areas of the scientific survey, and the fact of pergunnah and tuhseel maps having been made by pentograph from our field maps (*shujrahs*), sufficiently proves the accuracy and correctness of the work. The tuhseel maps which accompany this report were reduced by pentograph from our *shujrahs*, and are correct in every detail, such as except shape and size of area, position of inhabited sites, roads, large ponds, tracts of forest or jungle, and the like.

The measurement work was carried on gradually, so that the inspection and assessment might follow close upon the completion of the measurement of each pergunnah and tuhseel. I considered this preferable to entertaining large and unwieldy measurement establishments and pushing on that one part of the work, to the delay and detriment of what was to follow. The following table gives the seasons of

(1) measurement; (2) inspection; and (3) date of commencement of revised assessment of the various pergunnahs in this district :—

Name of Pergunnah.				Years of measurement.		Seasons of inspection.		Date from which new assessment came into force.
Shahjehanpore, ...	...	...	...	1867-68,	...	1867-68,	...	1st July, 1870.
Jumour,	...	...	...	Ditto,	...	1868-69,	...	Ditto.
Kant,	...	...	...	Ditto,	...	Ditto,	...	Ditto.
Jellalabad,	...	...	...	Ditto,	...	1869-70,	...	1st July, 1871.
Tilhur,	...	...	...	1868-69,	...	Ditto,	...	Ditto.
Meeranpore Kuttra,	...	...	...	Ditto,	...	Ditto,	...	Ditto.
Khera Bujhera,	...	...	...	Ditto,	...	1870-71,	...	1st July, 1872.
Jellalpore,	...	...	...	1869-70,	...	Ditto,	...	Ditto.
Negohee,	...	...	...	Ditto,	...	Ditto,	...	Ditto.
Burragaon,	...	...	...	Ditto,	...	1871-72,	...	Ditto.
Powayn, southern half,	...	...	...	Ditto,	...	Ditto,	...	1st July, 1873.
Ditto, northern half,	...	...	...	1870-71,	...	Ditto,	...	Ditto.
Khotar,	...	...	...	Ditto,	...	1872-73,	...	Ditto.

71. The areas of the past settlement according to the professional survey and
Areas of last and new settlement. the areas of the present revision of settlement according to the plane-table measurements are given in the following statements respectively. Where transfers of villages from one pergunnah to another were made before the present measurement, the areas of those villages are shown in the pergunnah to which they were transferred, so that both sets of figures are for the same local areas and limits :—

TABLE A.—*Areas of the last Settlement.*

Pergunnah.	Total area in acres.	Excluded from assessment.		Malgoozaree or assessable area.				Percentages of malgoozaree area.			
		Barren.	Lakhiraj or revenue-free.	Old unbroken waste including baghs.	New fallow.	Cultivated.	Total assessable.	Old unbroken waste.	New fallow.	Cultivated.	Total malgoozaree.
Shahjehanpore, ...											
Jumour, ...	253,215	38,729	7,885	43,019	11,332	152,249	206,601	20·8	5·5	73·6	100
Kant, ...											
Jellalabad, ...	195,275	21,625	4,452	69,155	5,343	94,700	169,198	4·08	3·1	55·1	100
Tilhur, ...	79,130	5,158	4,065	16,529	5,176	48,202	69,907	23·7	7·4	68·9	100
Meeranpore Kuttra, ..	8,156	1,383	140	2,724	190	3,719	6,633	41·0	2·9	55·1	100
Khera Buihera, ...	54,032	6,607	923	11,993	9,245	32,334	46,502	25·7	4·8	60·5	100
Jellalpore, ...	46,883	9,232	1,144	6,494	1,064	28,949	36,507	17·8	2·9	79·3	100
Negohee, ...	70,819	5,492	2,701	22,835	2,733	37,058	62,626	36·4	4·4	59·2	100
Burragaon, ...	52,343	10,611	1,794	10,021	2,732	27,185	39,938	25·1	6·8	68·1	100
Powayn, ...	200,332	27,109	4,352	29,760	15,212	123,899	168,871	17·6	9·0	73·4	100
Khotar ...	128,313	27,046	1,881	78,030	5,697	15,659	99,386	78·5	5·7	15·8	100
Whole District, ...	1,088,498	153,992	29,337	290,490	51,725	563,954	906,169	32·1	5·7	62·2	100
Percentages, ...	100	14·1	2·7	26·7	4·8	51·7	(83·2)				

TABLE B.—*Area of present Settlement.*

Pergunnah.	Total area in acres.	Excluded from assessment.		Malgoozaree or assessable area.					Percentages of malgoozaree area.				
		Barren, including cantonments.	Lakhiraj or revenue-free.	Old unbroken waste.	New fallow.	Baghs.	Cultivated.	Total assessable.	Old unknown waste.	New fallow.	Baghs.	Cultivated.	Total malgoozarees.
Shahjehanpore, ...	99,830	14,089	4,352	12,550	832	3,575	64,432	81,389	15·4	1·0	4·4	79·2	100
Jumoar, ...	64,956	7,518	511	11,698	529	1,995	43,405	56,927	20·5	0·9	3·2	75·4	100
Kant, ...	92,278	8,936	597	10,869	1,287	2,523	71,066	85,745	12·7	1·5	2·8	83·0	100
Jellalabad, ...	203,129	25,718	1,500	41,033	4,430	3,461	126,987	175,911	23·2	2·5	1·9	72·4	100
Tilhur, ...	80,809	7,066	1,031	7,307	1,505	2,763	61,147	72,722	10·0	1·9	3·8	84·3	100
Meerunpore Kuttra, ...	8,382	1,180	1	1,590	143	372	5,096	7,201	22·0	2·0	5·1	70·9	100
Khera Bujhera, ...	56,612	6,300	59	6,431	947	1,229	41,646	50,253	12·5	1·8	2·5	83·2	100
Jethalpore, ...	48,099	6,560	237	5,829	500	1,793	33,240	41,362	14·1	1·2	4·5	80·2	100
Negohee, ...	72,297	8,702	1,031	13,864	1,151	2,073	45,476	62,564	22·2	1·8	3·3	70·7	100
Burragaon, ...	59,975	6,984	605	6,043	845	2,045	36,453	45,386	13·3	2·7	4·7	80·3	100
Powayn, ...	200,171	16,379	725	34,510	3,940	7,431	147,186	183,067	13·2	2·2	4·1	80·5	100
Khotar, ...	129,702	7,813	1,459	48,289	6,271	1,790	64,080	120,430	40·1	5·2	1·5	53·2	100
Whole District, ...	1,109,240	114,175	12,108	190,023	22,380	30,350	740,204	982,957	19·3	2·3	3·1	75·3	100
Percentage, ...	100	10·3	1·1	17·1	2·0	2·7	66·8	(88·6)					

There is an increase on the total area of 20,742 acres. This is not, however, all due to difference of measurement, but a considerable portion, about 5,000 acres, is owing to the Ganges having shifted away to the south along the south-western end of the Jellalabad Tuhseel, as explained in Chapter III., paragraph 25; the percentage of increase due to difference in measurement is therefore less than 1½ (viz., 1·4) per cent. For detailed explanations of the decrease in the barren, *maafee*, and old waste areas I refer to the paragraphs concerning them in the separate tuhseel assessment reports, Chapters II. to V., as the repetition thereof here is unnecessary, and would be needlessly tedious. It must, however, be borne in mind that these areas in Chapter I. do not agree exactly with those in Chapters II. to V., as this chapter has been written last on completion of records and after correction of all figured statments, whereas the figures entered in the tuhseel assessment reports are those of the rent-rate reports, and before final scrutiny. The discrepancies are immaterial, but explanation was necessary, and where there are discrepancies the figures of this chapter are to be taken as correct.

72. The foregoing statements have percentages showing the proportion of the component parts to the area of the whole district, as well as for the details of the *malgoozaree* or assessable area ; but it may be convenient to repeat some of them here for the old and new settlement in juxtaposition. The assessable area of the district is now 88·6 per cent. of the total area, as against 83·2 at the last settlement; and similarly, the area exempted from assessment now is only 11·4 per cent., as against 16·8 per cent. at the last settlement. The *malgoozaree* or revenue-paying area is now 88·6 per cent., and of this *malgoozaree* area the percentage of actual cultivation and new fallow is now 77·6, against 67·9 at the time of the last settlement. Other details can be best seen in a tabular form :—

Distribution of the present area.

Denomination.	Percentages of total area.	
	At last settlement.	At present settlement.
Barren, including cantonments, ...	14·1	10·3
Revenue-free, ...	2·7	1·1
Old unbroken waste, ...	26·7	17·1
New fallow, ...	4·8	2·0
Uncultivated groves, ...	mostly in barren.	2·7
Cultivated land, ...	51·7	66·8

The nominal increase in the cultivated area, according to the above percentages, is 15·1 per cent. only, but the actual increase, i. e., the difference between the former and present cultivated areas, is 176,250 acres, or just over 31 per cent. Full particulars of the increase of cultivation, as well as of the extent and nature of the remaining culturable land, will be found for each pergunnah and tuhseel in the following chapters, the tuhseel assessment reports.

73. The following statement gives for each pergunnah and the whole district the irrigated and unirrigated areas of the last and new settlement, with the increase and decrease of the cultivated and irrigated areas : —

Irrigated areas of last and new settlement.

Pergunnah.	Cultivated area at last settlement in acres.			Cultivated area at present settlement in acres.			Increase in cultivated area.	Increase in irrigated area.	Decrease in irrigated area.
	Irrigated.	Unirrigated.	Total.	Irrigated.	Unirrigated.	Total.			
Shahjehanpore, ...				32,387	32,035	64,422			
Jumour, ...	78,082	74,167	152,249	22,157	21,248	43,405	26,644	2,189	...
Kant, ...				25,727	45,339	71,066			
Jellalabad, ...	39,249	55,451	94,700	48,388	78,599	126,987	32,287	9,139	...
Tilhur, ...	22,991	25,211	48,202	29,103	32,044	61,147	12,945	6,112	...
Meeranpore Kuttra,	3,257	462	3,719	2,526	2,570	5,096	1,377	...	731
Khera Bujhera, ...	8,312	24,022	32,334	12,774	28,872	41,646	9,312	4,462	...
Jellalpore, ...	25,450	3,499	28,949	12,570	20,670	33,240	4,291	...	12,880
Negohee, ...	18,242	18,816	37,058	15,937	29,539	45,476	8,418	...	2,305
Burragaon, ...	21,338	5,847	27,185	17,504	18,949	36,453	9,268	...	3,834
Powayn, ...	67,417	56,482	123,899	63,834	83,352	147,186	23,287	...	3,583
Khotar, ...	5,607	10,052	15,659	15,137	48,943	64,080	48,421	9,530	...
Whole District, ...	289,945	274,009	563,954	298,044	442,160	740,204	176,250	31,432	23,333

Net increase, ... 8,099

There are two things to be kept in mind in examining this table : *first*, that there is no canal irrigation whatever in the district, and hence there was no likelihood of any very large increase in irrigation, and certainly not of any larger proportion of irrigated to cultivated area ; *second*, that at last settlement the area supposed to be capable of irrigation, irrespective of the harvest or the crop grown, as distinguished from the area incapable of irrigation, was entered as irrigated ; whereas now that only has been entered as irrigated which was actually under irrigation at measurement, or the amount which is ordinarily under irrigation in an average year. The percentages for each pergunnah of the total cultivated area thereof irrigated at survey, the average annual irrigated area according to the entries in the *khusrahs* and other statements of the present settlement, as well as of the various sources of irrigation, are given in the following table :—

Pergunnah.	Percentage of total cultivated area irrigated at survey.	Percentage of total irrigated area irrigated from the various sources.		
		Wells.	Ponds, tanks, and nullas.	Rivers and streams.
Shahjehanpore, ...	50·5	73	19	8
Jumour, ...	51·0	46	48	6
Kant, ...	36·2	69	31	...
Jellalabad, ...	38·1	33	33	34
Tilhur, ...	47·5	82	12	6
Meeranpore Kuttra,... ...	49·6	70	15	15
Khera Bujhera, ...	30·3	48	19	33
Jellalpore, ...	37·7	72	18	10
Negohee,...	34·8	65	24	11
Burragaon, ...	47·9	77	19	4
Powayn, ...	43·4	81	16	3
Khotar, ...	23·6	80	20	...

74. The percentages of the different natural denominations of soils are given

Percentages of various soils. below for each separate pergunnah :—

Pergunnah.	Loam 1st quality (1st domut).	Loam 2nd quality (2nd domut).	Clay (*muttyar*).	Sand (*bhoor*).
Shahjehanpore, ...	67·43	23·65	6·58	2·14
Jumour, ...	53·03	11·17	35·29	·51
Kant, ...	32·82	32·05	9·81	25·32
Jellalabad, ...	42·05	25·48	21·71	10·76
Tilhur, ...	45·67	28·05	10·17	16·11
Meeranpore Kuttra, ...	46·90	32·01	10·71	10·38
Khera Bujhera, ...	59·98	15·72	15·63	8·67
Jellalpore, ...	60·32	20·14	11·23	8·31
Negohee, ...	57·78	17·40	18·36	6·48
Burragaon, ...	56·15	30·64	10·80	3·41
Powayn, ...	35·57	35·31	12·72	16·50
Khotar, ...	34·80	26·31	10·40	28·49

75. The ordinary natural soil of the district is a mixture of sand, clay and

Description of various soils. vegetable mould, and is called *domut*, the meaning of the word being two soils or mixed earth. It varies a great deal not only in different parts of the district but also often of the same pergunnah, and almost invariably with the level. Where the level is high, and there is a tendency to anything of a ridge or water-shed, there is a greater admixture of sand, all ridges and crests of undulations being sandy and usually actual sand (*bhoor*).

In depressions there is a greater stiffness and admixture of clay, the actual clay (*muttyar*) being always in hollows and depressions or low-lying land, where water collects and lies during the rains. The more even and unbroken by any drainage line or ridge the surface is, the better is the *domut*. The three soils known by the people are the *domut*, *muttyar*, and *bhoor*, but for better and more correct clssification I have introduced the second class *domut*, which is usually an intermediate soil between first class *domut* and *bhoor*. In low-lying clayey parts of the district however, as Pergunnah Jumour and the *bunkuttee ilaqa* of Pergunnah Jellalabad, it is an inferior *domut*, not a sandy soil, but a compromise between *domut* and actual clay (*muttyar*). After having measured and inspected Tuhseels Shahjehanpore and Jellalabad, and having found that a subdivision of *muttyar* would have been most useful there, I made one for use in parts still to be measured, but the very parts where it was most needed had been completed. I called it *dhunker*, a name applied to land growing rice and no other crop ; also known as *khaput*, the very hardest and poorest clay soil which is usually found in natural drainage and flood lines, and where water collects and lies for weeks on the surface of the ground during the rainy season.

As the rule, the 1st *domut* is much the best soil; the *muttyar* and the 2nd *domut* are the fair average middling soils, and much of a muchness, the *muttyar* being usually somewhat better than 2nd *domut*, especially in those pergunnahs where the worst of it has been entered as *dhunker*. The poor and bad soils are *dhunker* and *bhoor*.

There is, however, also another conventional denomination of soil, not a natural, but a made soil, the *gowhanse*, which, as its name denotes, is the land near and about the inhabited village site. It is however not universal, and is generally only to be found where there are Kachee or Murao cultivators, who grow *kucchiana* (garden crops). There are no belts or circles of artificial soil as in the Doab, the *gowhanse* of this district being a very poor substitute for the *bárak* or *gowhín* of the " Gangetic Doab." Here in Shahjehanpore the manure is always taken to whatever field or fields the cultivator sets aside for his sugar-cane, and it is quite a common thing to see the ordinary jowar and bajra crops grown in their rotation in the fields nearest the village.

The uplands are called *bangur* in contradistinction to the valleys or troughs of the rivers, which are called *khadir* or *terai*, the latter word meaning moist, damp country, and being generally applied to the damp malarious tracts between the plains proper (*Dés*) and the foot of the hills.

SECTION VI.
Rents and Rent-rates.

76. The rents throughout the entire district are almost universally in money, and *Money rents universal ; lump rents and rates.* payment by division of crops (*buttaee*) or by appraisement of standing crop (*kunkoot*) is very exceptional, and obtains only for poor and bad lands, or fields near the forest where the crop is uncertain owing to various causes, but chiefly depredations of various kinds of deer and wild pigs. There is scarcely one single village in the whole district in which rents in kind obtain throughout the whole village, and there are hundreds in which the rents have been in money, and there has been no payment in kind for a single field even for upwards of thirty years.

The rent-rates obtaining in the different pergunnahs and tuhseels have been dwelt on at length in the assessment reports of each Tuhseel (Chapters II. to V.), and omitting details there given, I confine my remarks here to the various ways in which the money rents are assessed. There are two main distinctions—the one rents, the other rates. The rents are lump rents (*chukota*) or leases : (1) so much land at such a rent the whole of a cultivator's holding at a certain total rent ; (2) lump rents on the field, such and such a field at such and such a rent ; the rent in this case often remaining the same even when the cultivator changes. The rates are of four kinds : (1) soil rates ; (2) rates on tracts (*hárs*) ; (3) all-round or summary rates, irrespective of quality or denomination of soil ; (4) crop rates. Of these, the soil rates pure and simple are the least prevalent, except that many enhancements have been decreed in soil rates. The rates on hars are the most common and the most popular, and have been retained as far as possible in enhancement of rent. The *hárs* or tracts have known local boundaries and names, such as the clay or *jhábur hár*, the *bhoor hár*, and the like, and the rate prevails throughout the entire *hár*. These *hár* rates are in point of fact, as the

M

rule, soil rates. Summary rates exist to a very large extent, but chiefly where there are no well-defined *hárs*, and the soil is very similar all over the area. Crop-rates proper obtain only in Powayn and Khotar, *i.e.*, differential rates for fine and coarse crops of either harvest.

But all over the district and in all the various kinds of rates, and to some extent even in the lump rents, sugar-cane pays a special rate : the ordinary rate being the cereal (*nijkáree*) rate, and the sugar-cane rate being from 2½ to 3 times the *nijkáree* rate.

Sugar usually occupies the ground for two years, and no rent is taken for the fallow, but the whole is collected on the crop being out. Hence the sugar-cane rate is really the rate of the land for two years, and is not therefore treble the *nijkáree* rent of two years, but of one year, and the land pays for sugar 1¼ to 1½ times only what it pays for cereals. *Kuochiana* or garden crops, including poppy, almost invariably pay a separate rate of about half as much again as the ordinary cereal rate.

77. None of the rates are on wet and dry or for irrigated and unirrigated lands,

Rent-rates on soils alone, not on irrigated and unirrigated.

though doubtless to some extent they are on the capability of irrigation, the proximity of ponds or nullahs or facility of sinking *kutcha* wells or the reverse. The almost invariable rule is that good lands are either capable of irrigation or do not require it. Where the soil is even and firm, *kutcha* wells can, as a rule, be made easily and cheaply, and they are made without the need of the zemindar's permission, and whether made or not the same rent is charged.

The assumption for good lands is that the water-level is close, the soil admits of wells being sunk, and when they are required they are made, and if not required, so much the better for the cultivator, who gets an equally good crop at a smaller expense ; but the rent-rate is the same whether he irrigates or not. High light *bhoor* or lowlying hard clay, as being inferior soils and usually incapable of irrigation, pay the lowest rates.

In working out assumed average rent-rates, therefore, the distinction of irrigated and unirrigated has been disregarded, *and the rates are on soils alone.*

78. The *beegah* on which all transactions are carried on between the zemindars

The *kutcha beegah*.

and the culti vators is the village (*gowhánee*) or *kutcha beegah*. It varies much in different parts of the district, but usually bears some nominal proportion to the *pucka* or standard *beegah* of last settlement, and runs generally from 6 to 6¼ *kutcha beegahs* to the acre. It varies, however, in different neighbouring villages and in different parts even of the same village. This subject is treated of very fully in the Tuhseel Tilhur Assessment Report (Chapter IV., para. 43), as the fluctuations are greatest in that tubseel. In Tuhseels Shahjehanpore and Powayn the proportion is generally 3¾ *kutcha beegahs* to one *pucka beegah*, and in Jellalabad usually four.

In enhancing rents it is necessary to work out rates on the *pucka beegah*, and then distribute them on the *kutcha beegah ;* and in enhancement suits I have endeavoured to fix some proportion, 3½, 3¾ or 4 *kutcha* to one *pucka beegah*, whichever was the nearest on a large area in the village concerned. It is simply impossible to force a standard *kutcha beegah* on the people so long as the Government insists on keeping up a *pucka beegah*. It was tried at last settlement and failed signally. It might have been done now if the *pucka beegah* had been dropped altogether, and the measurement made in acres, and a standard *kutcha beegah* had been fixed at onesixth of an acre. Now there is no such thing as a standard *kutcha beegah*, not even a traditional standard as in Bareilly and elsewhere.

Assumed and sanctioned average rent-rates.

79. The manner in which the rent-rates assumed as average rates for the various assessment circles, by means of which estimated rentals are obtained from soil areas, will be found detailed in each of the

separate tuhseel assessment reports. It is sufficient to state here briefly that all low and suspicious rates are eliminated, as well as all specially favourable rates for zemindars' *seer*, or for relatives and dependants, and only *genuine cultivators' rates* are taken, and averages struck from large areas of all kinds of soil in all directions of each circle ; and where, for reasons assigned, it is demonstrable that in any particular circle or pergunnah the existing rates are low and insufficient as compared with similar lands in the vicinity, and a rise is not only reasonably to be expected but certain, the assumed rates are put at such amount above the existing average rates as is estimated will correct this inadequacy and meet this certain rise. But no theoretical correctness or proper proportion between rents and prices or value of produce has been aimed at. For, even allowing that rents and rent-rates throughout the whole district are low and inadequate theoretically, it is utterly impossible for the Settlement Officer to raise them to what, in theory, and with reference to past rents and prices, as compared with existing rents and present prices and the depreciation of silver, they should now be. Any fancy work of this kind must end in the ruin of proprietors, the depreciation of the value of property, and the eventual break-down of the settlement. The actual existing rents and rates, cleared of all doubtful and palpable errors and flaws, are the real basis of the assumed rent-rates (sanctioned by the Board of Revenue) which are given for each circle and pergunnah in the annexed statement :—

Pergunnah and Circle.	Sanctioned, assumed or average rent-rates per acre on the various denominations of soil.						
	Gowhánee.	1st domut.	Muttyar.	2nd domut.	Bhoor.	Dhunker.	Standard cultivation rate.
	Rs. a. p.	Rs. a. p.	Rs. a. p.	Rs. a. p.	Rs. a. p.	Rs. a. p.	Rs. a. p.
Shahjehanpore, Domut,	8 0 0	3 12 0	2 12 0	3 0 0	2 4 0	...	3 8 0
Jumour, Muttyar,	7 8 0	3 12 0	3 8 0	3 0 0	2 4 0	...	3 4 0
Kant, Bhoor, ...	7 0 0	3 4 0	2 12 0	2 8 0	2 0 0	...	2 10 0
Jellalabad, Bhoor, ...	6 8 0	3 10 0	3 0 0	2 10 0	2 4 0	...	2 11 3
Ditto, Terai, ...	6 8 0	4 4 0	3 12 0	3 12 0	2 8 0	...	4 0 0
Ditto, Bunkuttee,	6 8 0	3 10 0	3 0 0	3 0 0	2 4 0	...	3 4 8
Tilhur, Terai, ...	7 0 0	5 0 0	4 0 0	3 8 8	2 8 0	2 8 0	4 9 6
Ditto, Bhoor, ...	6 0 0	3 4 0	2 12 0	2 8 0	1 12 0	2 0 0	2 9 4
Meeranpore Kuttra, ...	6 8 0	3 8 0	3 0 0	2 3 0	1 12 0	2 4 0	3 0 4
Khera Bujhera, Ramgunga, ...	7 0 0	4 4 0	3 12 0	3 0 0	1 12 0	2 0 0	3 14 2
Ditto, Bygool,...	6 0 0	3 4 0	2 8 0	2 8 0	1 12 0	2 0 0	2 15 2
Ditto, Bhoor, ...	6 0 0	3 0 0	2 8 0	2 4 0	1 12 0	2 0 0	2 6 2
Jellalpore, Gurra, ...	7 0 0	4 8 0	3 8 0	3 0 0	2 0 0	2 4 0	4 0 5
Ditto, Bygool,...	6 8 0	3 12 0	2 14 0	2 8 0	2 0 0	2 4 0	2 12 3
Negohee, Domut,...	6 8 0	3 8 0	3 0 0	3 0 0	2 4 0	2 4 0	3 4 7
Ditto, Kymooa,	6 0 0	3 4 0	2 12 0	2 12 0	2 0 0	2 0 0	2 13 5
Burragaon, ...	7 8 0	4 4 0	3 8 0	3 8 0	2 8 0	2 4 0	3 14 3
Powayn, Powayn,...	7 0 0	4 8 0	4 0 0	3 12 0	2 8 0	2 8 0	4 13 10
Ditto, Nahul, ...	6 8 0	4 8 0	3 12 0	3 12 0	2 4 0	2 4 0	3 15 2
Ditto, Gola, ...	6 8 0	3 12 0	3 0 0	3 0 0	2 4 0	2 4 0	3 3 8
Ditto, Tureona,...	6 0 0	3 0 0	3 0 8	2 2 0	1 8 0	1 12 0	2 7 7
Ditto, Sunwat, ...	6 0 0	2 8 0	2 4 0	1 12 0	1 4 0	1 12 0	1 11 3
Khotar, 1st Abad, ...	4 8 0	3 0 0	2 12 0	2 0 0	1 8 0	1 8 0	2 10 6
Ditto, 2nd Wairan, ...	3 12 0	2 4 0	1 12 0	1 8 0	1 2 0	1 2 0	1 9 1

80. Rents throughout the district generally, and I think in Tuhseel Shahjehanpore

Rents low and inadequate, and no rise in rents proportionate to rise in prices. especially, are low and inadequate, as they are regulated more by custom than competition, and having been in money for upwards of fifty years, they are not spontaneously affected by the variation of prices as in districts where division and appraisement of crops obtain extensively.

Prices have risen here enormously as elsewhere during the last thirty years, and there is a considerable increase in the rent, irrespective of the increase due merely to extension of cultivation ; but there is no *proportionate* increase in rent, and in money rates to the increase in prices. In fact there is very little actual increase in rates of rent—that is to say, there is no general advance in the rates themselves.

The rates quoted and found in individual cases as existing at last settlement, or at any time during the last thirty years, are almost identically the same as those now existing. Unfortunately there is nothing but the most superficial mention of rates in Mr. J. W. Muir's and Mr. Rose's reports of the last settlement, and I cannot therefore draw any detailed comparison between the *then* and the *present* rates ; nor are there vernacular records in existence showing the then rentals and rates to a sufficient extent to give any results for large areas. But I have had comparative statements prepared showing the areas and rentals at Fidda Ali's supplementary measurement, and preparation of records twenty years ago and those of the present measurement, and these, perhaps, illustrate my statement better than a comparison between the rates and rentals at time of last and present settlements would have done : —

Name of Pergunnah and Circle.	Number of muhals.	Fidda Ali's measurement twenty years ago.	Cultivated area in acres.		Rentals		Rent-rate per acre	
			Present measurement.	Of twenty years ago.	Of present time.	Of twenty years ago.	Of present time.
				Rs.	Rs.	Rs. a. p.	Rs. a. p.
Tilhur, Terai, ...	77	18,143	19,458	66,452	79,848	3 10 7	4 1 2
Ditto, Bhoor, ...	103	30,814	30,892	68,885	70,318	2 1 2	2 4 5
Negohee, Domut, ...	32	7,668	8,492	22,353	24,185	2 14 7	2 13 7
Ditto, Kymooa, ...	31	6,122	6,974	16,659	18,121	2 11 6	2 9 7
Burragaon, owned by Pathans of city, ...	30	6,580	7,204	23,252	24,017	3 6 1	3 5 4
Ditto, owned by others,	40	7,236	8,194	26,959	29,123	3 11 7	3 8 10
Total, ...	313	76,563	81,214 Increase 6 per cent.	2,18,570	2,45,607 Increase 12½ per cent.	2 13 8	3 0 4 Increase 6½ per cent.

These measurements of Fidda Ali's were made nine and ten years after the settlement, after all the excitement and disturbance in rates and rentals which accompanies and for a few years succeeds a revision of settlement had subsided, and twenty years ago from now—a sufficiently long period to allow of considerable progress being exhibited.

But what is the result? A considerable increase in rental (12½ per cent.) due to extended cultivation, but an increase in rent-rate in only one of the three pergunnahs, and an actual decrease in rent-rate in the other two. These villages have *not* been selected with the view or intention of obtaining any certain result and upholding a preconceived opinion ; but as those in which there was little or no *seer* to spoil the calculation, and in which there had been no very considerable increase in area, and where the rentals were believed to be reliable. The papers of twenty years ago are not in existence for Tuhseels Shahjehanpore and Jellalabad, as they were all destroyed in the mutiny in 1857-58 A.D.

The rates mentioned by Mr. Lowther (page 295 *et seq.*, Selections from Revenue Records, North-Western Provinces, 1818-20) as existing in 1818 are very much the same as those mentioned by me in my rent-rate report of Tuhseel Shahjehanpore in 1869, the only real difference being that I have entered into greater detail for each pergunnah and denomination of soil, whereas Mr. Lowther's returns are very condensed. But no one could now say, looking at Mr. Lowther's rates,—" Oh, yes, those rates may have possibly existed fifty or sixty years ago, but that is all changed now." On the contrary, there appears to have been very little change. There is no such thing as the 4-anna per *kutcha beegah* rate of thirty and even of fifty years ago not existing now, but having been replaced by a 5 or 6 anna rate, nor have the higher rates advanced at all proportionately with the increase in prices and the depreciation of silver.

Doubtless, when the areas are looked into to which these various rates are applied, they have increased, and so has the total cultivated area; but nothing of this sort is found, that the generality of lands which were thirty years ago paying 8 annas per *kutcha beegah* are now paying 10 annas, or that those which were paying 12 annas are now paying a rupee. There has been no general and wholesale advance, as might have been fairly expected, and hence there is no adequate relation between existing rents and the value of the present produce, as compared with the rent-rates of thirty years ago and the then value of the produce.

For instance, the average harvest price of wheat for the first decade of the past settlement was Re. 0-14-8 per maund of 82·3 lbs., but the prices were high at the commencement of the decade, owing to the famine of 1837 to 1839 A. D., and this has affected the average of the whole decade. The average of the second decade is

Harvest prices per maund of 82·3 lbs. of principal crops.						
Period.	Cane-juice or "ráb."	Jowar.	Bajra.	Wheat.	Barley.	Gram.
	Rs. a. p.	Rs. a. p.	Rs. a. p.	Rs. a. p.	Rs. a. p.	Rs. a. p.
1st decade from 1246 to 1255 Fuslee.	2 2 8	0 11 5	0 12 3	0 14 8	0 10 0	0 11 5
2nd decade from 1256 to 1265 Fuslee.	1 11 9	0 7 9	0 7 10	0 10 8	0 6 7	0 8 1
3rd decade from 1266 to 1275 Fuslee.	2 5 1	0 15 5	0 15 5	1 2 3	0 11 2	0 15 7
Last five years, or 2nd half of 3rd decade.	3 0 0	1 0 10	1 2 3	1 4 7	0 12 11	1 0 9

Re. 0-10-8 for a maund of wheat, and for the third decade it is Rs. 1-2-3, and for the last five years of the third decade Re. 1-4-7, being an increase in value between the first and third decade of 23 per cent.; between the second and third decade of 73 per cent.; and between the second decade and the last five years of third decade of 95 per cent.; and there is still a steady upwards tendency in prices, the average of the last five years since the end of the abovenamed third decade being slightly in excess of the average of the last five years of that decade. In Tuhseel Shahjehanpore the average cultivation rent-rate thirty years ago was Rs. 2-10-6, and is now Rs. 3-3-4 per acre, being an increase of Re. 0-8-10 per acre, or 20·78 per cent. In Pergunnah Negohee, the average harvest prices being the same, the average cultivation rent-rate of last settlement was Rs. 2-7-3 per acre, and now it is Rs. 2-15-11, being an increase of Re. 0-8-8 per acre, or 22·08 per cent.

81. The cause of this state of things, that the rates of rent have not increased *Explanation of the cause of rents being low, and no rise proportionate to rise in prices.* at all proportionately with the increase of prices, is, I believe, to be explained by the almost entire absence of payment in kind or appraisement, the rents being entirely in money (except only for very poor or bad lands, which the cultivators will not take at a money rent, but only on division of the actual produce). As far back as 1818, by Mr. Lowther's report it appears that very little payment in kind existed, and there is even less now—in fact none to speak of. Hence the variations of the harvest prices have not been forced on the zemindars and cultivators, and rents have not adjusted themselves spontaneously, as is the case in those districts where payment in kind or by appraisement of crop, convertible into cash at the existing harvest rates, obtains.

In such districts and villages the zemindars and cultivators fully realize the effect of the rise in prices on their rents. They see and feel each in his own way, that whereas a maund of wheat has lately been worth only about 10 to 12 annas, it suddenly becomes worth from Re. 1 to Re. 1-4-0; and the share of the zemindar in the produce ($\frac{1}{4}$ or $\frac{3}{8}$ths or $\frac{1}{3}$rd, as the case may be) is known and acknowledged, whereas here it is simply unknown and never thought of. And this no doubt is, and must continue to be, a very great obstacle to the rise of rents, either by mutual agreement or by aid of the courts, at all proportionate to the rise in prices.

82. There has been considerable enhancement of rental consequent on the revision of settlement, but owing chiefly to levelling up of palpably low and inadequate rates and correction of areas, rather than to any general rise of, or increase in, abstract rent-rates. Little or no good land, the average assumed rate whereof is 8 to 10 annas per *kutcha beegah*, now continues to pay the low rate of 4 or 4½ annas per *kutcha beegah* (about Re. 1-8-0 to Re. 1-12-0 an acre), which is the rate for inferior land, and which had gone on unchallenged for much good land from before the last settlement. Rates have levelled up to the average, but there has been no general considerable rise in the higher, and for this district full, rates on the average and good soils. It was scarcely probable, or even I might almost say possible, that under Acts XIV. of 1863 and X. of 1869 any further result could have been obtained; and the new revenue law (Act XIX. of 1873) has come too late to be of any service here for framing new rates, as the assessment of the whole district was completed six months and more before it was passed.

Enhancement of rental by levelling up of rents has already taken place.

83. Still, however, there has been a very considerable enhancement of rent, but not beyond and, as the rule, not yet quite up the amount anticipated in assessment. A commencement, however, having been made, and this district being now no longer up in a corner, on the road to *nowhere*, and without a decent road into it or out of it in any direction (as it was when the settlement operations commenced and Tuhseels Shahjehanpore and Jellalabad were assessed), but having now good metalled roads connecting it with Lucknow through Seetapore on the one side and Bareilly on the other, and the Oudh and Rohilkhund Railway crossing it and connecting it with *everywhere*, the value of produce must increase with the facility of transport, and rents ought doubtless to continue to rise. They will not, however, rise, I expect, with any giant strides, nor to any very considerable extent—not nearly to such an extent as occurred in Boolundshuhur or Meerut some seven or eight years ago. I entertain no such idea as that the assessment now concluded will ten or fifteen years hence be, as a whole, below about a fair 50 per cent. of then existing assets. I say this the more confidently as I feel convinced that the effect of the new Rent Act (XVIII. of 1873) will be to stereotype rents in a great measure *after revision* of settlement, and to check, rather than to promote, a rise in or enhancement of rates, in addition to the reason already given at the conclusion of the preceding paragraph of absence of any payments in kind. At the same time, if I am wrong in my conclusion, and rents do continue to rise largely owing to the enormous improvements in means of communication and transport, and some ten or fifteen years hence the Government revenue, which is now a full 50 per cent. of actual assets, falls to 45 or even 40 per cent. of the *then* assets, it cannot be taken as proof of the inadequacy of my assessment *now* made. I do not think it at all probable that such a state of things will come about; but if I did, I could not discount these probabilities or future contingencies so as to make an assessment which should be fair and workable now, and a correct 50 per cent. of assets any time from ten years hence to the end of the term of the settlement.

Rise in rents may continue, but nothing sudden or gigantic anticipated.

It seems absurd that one should have to defend one's-self in anticipation of an unexpected contingency; but I have the precedent of the Boolundshuhur District before me, and not having forgotten that, I deem these remarks absolutely necessary, however absurdly superfluous they may appear to the casual reader.

SECTION VII.

Assessment: explanation of the general principles adopted and refutation of the usual charges of under-assessment.

84. The charges brought against Settlement Officers and their assessments by the party who cry loudly for a heavier taxation of the land, and who talk of the inadequacy of the revised assessments of land-revenue apart from the purely theoretical rise that should have taken place

Usual charges of under-assessment.

consequent on the expenditure of so much money in roads, canals and railways, and the depreciation of silver, &c., are two-fold.

1st.—That *seer* cultivation, or the home farm of the cultivating proprietor, is admitted at the low rent (a mere nominal rate) at which it is entered in the rent-rolls ; or when otherwise rated is still under-rated, as it should be made to pay a much higher rent than the ordinary tenant-rate of the generality of the cultivators.

2nd.—That rentals are taken as they exist right or wrong, and the assessment is made thereon ; that the zemindars notoriously give in false rent-rolls, which, nevertheless, are blindly accepted and acted upon.

85. As regards the *seer*. I have invariably rated all *seer* at the general tenant-rate of the village, and only exceptionally higher when it was unmistakeably better land, and would, if held by a mere tenant, have paid a rate above the general tenant-rate. It is a great mistake to suppose that these *seer* lands are home-farms in the sense that that phrase would suggest to most people. Usually they are not situated in one spot, but scattered over the different quarters of the village, and are no better than the ordinary village lands, and if rated at the village tenant-rate or at the rate at which they sublet (when they are sublet), they are quite fully rated.

Refutation of charge of under-rating seer.

86. As regards the rent-rolls being accepted unchallenged, I must refer for details to the paragraphs headed " rentals and assets, actual and assumed" in the various assessment reports of the different tuhseels. In them will be found for each circle and pergunnah (1) the rental after due corrections for *seer ;* (2) the estimated actual assets after further correction for various omissions, *sewai* items, favoured rates of relatives and dependants ; (3) the rental resulting from the assumed average circle rent-rates; and (4) the gross assumed potential assets ; in other words, the rental on which the *jumma* was actually assessed for each separate *mouzah* and *muhal.*

Refutation of charge of blindly accepting recorded rentals, or of assessing on existing rentals uncorrected.

The percentages of (4) the gross assumed rental (the rental double of the *jumma* actually assessed) over (2), the estimated actual assets, are given in the margin for each pergunnah. It will be seen that the lowest is 6·9, and that they run mostly from 8 to 13 per cent. The point kept in view in estimating the gross potential assets for each mouzah and muhal, on which the 50 per cent. jumma is based, is the full limit to which the rental will rise immediately on the declaration of the new Government demand— that is to say, within a period of two or three years from the commencement of the new assessments ; or in other words, the equilibrium of the rental after the disturbance consequent

Pergunnah.	Percentage of assumed over actual assets.
Shahjehanpore,...	11·9
Jumour, ...	6·9
Kant, ...	9·6
Jellalabad, ...	8·8
Tilhur, ...	14·2
Meeranpore Kuttra.	26·5
Khera Bujhera,...	13·5
Jellalpore, ...	13·5
Negohee, ...	13·4
Burragaon, ...	7·4
Powayn, ...	10·3
Khotar, ...	11·8

upon a revision of the Government revenue. I think I have made it sufficiently evident that there is no such thing in my settlement as accepting blindly fictitious rentals, taking the half of them as revenue and leaving the rest and all further possible enhancements to the zemindars as their share ; thereby depriving the Government of its legitimate share of 50 per cent. of true assets.

87. The villages were all visited by the assessing officer, either Mr. Butt, my assistant, or myself, and full notes and remarks were entered daily in a pergunnah inspection note-book, in which also all area and soil details were entered.

Inspection note-books written up at the time.

Each mouzah and muhal has two pages to itself, the left hand page containing figured statements of former and present areas, all subdivision of soil areas, crops, rentals, &c., with the notes in ink, in the handwriting of the inspecting officer, on the right hand page facing the figured statements. The date on which each village was inspected has also been universally entered ; and though, at first sight, this may seem a small matter, it often proves most useful afterwards when the remarks have to be gone carefully into and studied at the time of assessment. The inspections are all made and the note-books written up *pari passu* during the cold season, or between 10th October and 15th March chiefly. The assessments are made subsequently after the inspection of the whole pergunnah is finished, and after submission of the detailed rent-rate report.

88. The procedure adopted in this district in framing the assessment, and which I have good reason to believe differs from that usually observed,

Assessment remarks written by assessing officers before declaration of jumma; their contents.

is that a separate proceeding is written in English by the assessing officer for each separate *mouzah*, and often for each *muhal* in a *mouzah*, with his own hand. It is of course largely taken from the pergunnah note-book, but is re-written, and is the result of the mature experience of the assessing officer, which often differs very materially from the first impression freely noted down at the time in the pergunnah inspection note-book. After giving a general account of the village, the quality of the soil, means of irrigation, size and number of the inhabited sites and their position, and in fact a short pen and ink sketch of the village, it proceeds to state all peculiarities worthy of notice, the existing rentals, whether sufficient or inadequate, and the reason why ; the reason for the applicability, or the reverse, of the assumed rent-rate ; the quantity and quality and actual or estimated income from the uncultivated land, and the gross rental assumed as basis of assessment, the expiring *jumma* and the new one now assessed.

What I wish to make plain is that these assessment remarks are written out fair by the assessing officer, with his own hand, *before* the *jumma* of the village is declared, and all these full and detailed reasons of assessment are *complete* before the announcement of the revised assessments. The assessing officer has, therefore, given in detail in writing (in the same way as a judicial decision is written) his reasons for coming to a certain conclusion before that conclusion is made known ; and, as far as he is concerned, the assessment is complete in every detail, and if he left the district the next day, he would leave behind him the reasons for his assessments in every single case. But this is not all ; estimates of the *jumma* of each village may be made in various ways, and worked out ever so carefully according to different rates and methods, and a man may think he is satisfied as to what the *jumma* in each case should be ; but when he comes to write down his reasons in detail, and to make them work out to one final and carefully explained result, it is impossible but that, as he goes on, he must change his imperfect, though hitherto supposed final opinion and wish to alter some few assessments at least here and there. This is avoided by the plan pursued in my settlement.

89. Each assessment proceeding in the hand-writing of the assessing officer is

Bound volumes of No. II. and III. Statements.

bound in the original vernacular *misl*, and copies of these proceedings are made under the heading of "Miscellaneous General Remarks" on the page which faces the English (translated) copies of the Nos. II. and III. Statements. Bound volumes of these statements for each pergunnah accompany this report, and for convenience I have had special books made for the purpose, omitting only the translation of the *khewat*, which is not necessary for examining into the grounds of assessment; these said books of mine are less bulky and more handy than the Board's prescribed forms. Translations have, however, been made on the Board's prescribed forms also, which have been bound in volumes, one or two to a pergunnah, and made over for record to the Collector's office. The volumes of the Nos. II. and III. Statements accompanying this report may, therefore, be kept for record in the Board's office, and not be returned to the Collector's office.

90. The assessments have not been confined to the cultivated areas only, but all

Assessment of uncultivated lands.

uncultivated land (which is not exempt from assessment as revenue-free or barren waste) has been included, always excepting the *baghs* or groves specially exempted from assessment under *existing orders, so long as the groves are kept up and the trees remain, and the land is not cleared and rendered capable of producing a crop. Ordinarily uncultivated lands are either scrub (*i. e., dhak*) jungle or grass lands, and are more or less valuable for their spontaneous produce of wood, gum, thatching grass and the like, and the actual or probable net amount has been ascertained or estimated as the case may be, and included in the gross rental of the estate. In some instances this income, especially from thatching grass, is very considerable, more so in the bunkuttee circle of Pergunnah Jellalabad than elsewhere, and in some few villages within eight and ten miles of the city and cantonments of Shahjehanpore and the town of Tilhur. Where the culturable waste remaining was good and beyond the necessary requirements for grazing the village cattle, and reclamation of waste was fairly presumable and likely to commence shortly, this has also been taken into account and discounted and a proportionate increase made (with reasons given in full in the assessment remarks) in the gross assumed rental. The *total jumma* due to anticipated extension of cultivation is small and insignificant, but in some particular and special instances it is, as regards those villages, considerable. In discounting, however, probable future increase of cultivation by reclamation of waste I have been very liberal, and have been careful not to take the same land twice over, *viz.*, first for *sewai* from grass, grazing or wood, and then again as likely to be soon reclaimed.

Board's Circular No. 22, datedd 20th October, 1869.

91. The various points which were kept specially in view in making the separate assessments on each mouzah and muhal (for the revenue is assessed, as has been already explained, on each *mouzah* and *muhal*, and the pergunnah *jummas* are only the totals of the detailed assessments) which call for particular mention are briefly, and omitting exceptional and peculiar cases, as follows :—

Special points observed in assessment requiring notice.

(*a*) *Number of proprietors.*—Allowance was made in all cases where the number of shareholders was large, and the greater part, or a very large part, of the cultivated area was held *seer*, and the actual collections from the tenants sufficed, or did not suffice to meet the Government demand. This question will be found discussed at great length and my procedure very fully explained in the Jellalabad Tuhseel assessment report, para. 34 of Chapter III.

(*b*) *Caste of cultivators.*—I accepted things as I found them and as they must remain. Certain castes and classes of cultivators are better than others, and can, and do, pay higher rents than certain other classes for land of the same quality. Where the former predominated full rates or something above the average rates could be used, whereas where the latter predominated, or prevailed to so large an extent as to neutralise the few of the better classes of cultivators, this matter received its due weight.

(*e*) *Liability of damage from floods or from wild animals.*—This, doubtless, directly affects the existing rents, but unless kept in view, villages situated in the line of the natural drainage, of the overflow of rivers or near jungle, or even abounding in *baghs* full of monkeys, are likely to get somewhat over-assessed. The villages which suffer mostly from flooding are those near the Soate and between the Soate and the Ganges in Porgunnah Jellalabad; whilst those most worried by deer, pigs and monkeys are in Pergunnah Khotar, and more or less all along the Oudh border.

(*d*) *Former surplus profits after payment of Government demand.*—This divides itself into two heads: (1) where the profits were very large, and consequently the enhancement of revenue is now very heavy, and the sudden reduction of the income of the proprietors is very serious; and (2) where the profits were small in consequence of the jumma having been heavy.

92. In the first case, where the profits on the expiring revenue were large and the increase of revenue was *very* heavy, I always gave the *mouzah* or *muhal* the benefit of any doubt in my own mind as to which of two *jummas* I should assess, and chose the lower one. I kept my assessment at an easy or bare half assets, and did not put it at quite the same

Procedure where profits were large and the increase of revenue is heavy.

o

figure as I should have assessed if the increase in revenue had been small or moderate. I used my discretion in attempting to "temper the wind to the shorn lamb" as far as I felt justified in so doing, *i.e.*, within the bounds of two or three per cent. In some instances I assessed avowedly at below 50 per cent., the chief of which are in Pergunnah Jellalabad; and this question has been treated at great length in the report on that tuhseel (*vide* Chapter III., para. 34). In the case of Pergunnah Khotar I made the assessments progressive, reaching their maximum, some at the sixth, and others at the eighth year (see Chapter V., paras. 32 and 33).

The cases in which the great increase in the rental, and the large profits over the revenue, at the end of the settlement, were in any way due to the special industry, expenditure, or other improvements of the proprietors, were very few indeed and of very small extent; and no allowance worth mentioning had to be made on this account.

93. In the second case, where the expiring *jumma* was high and the profits were comparatively small, I did not reduce the revenue right down to half assets, merely because my assumed rental or the village rental showed that the existing (*i.e.*, expiring) *jumma* was over 50 per cent. of assets; but I gave such relief as, taking all the circumstances of the case into consideration, I deemed necessary. That I did not consider myself bound by a hard-and-fast rule of assessing *all* estates, blindly and without reference to their peculiarities, at exactly half assets has been mentioned in all four separate tuhseel reports, and as this question has been the subject of special reference to the Government, North-Western Provinces, I proceed to refer to it at greater length here.

Procedure where the expiring jumma was high and the profits were comparatively low.

94. This question as regards assessments *at below* 50 per cent. was specially reported in Pergunnah Jellalabad, and will be found at length in paragraph 34 of that report, Chapter III., already several times alluded to. Sir William Muir's orders on the reference to Government in Pergunnah Powayn, concerning assessment *at over* 50 per cent. or above half assets, deal with the whole question, and I cannot do better than give the *necessary* extracts from the Government Order:—

Quotations from Sir William Muir's and Sir John Strachey's orders on references regarding assessment at above half assets.

G. O. No. 1966A., dated 13th September, 1873.

"*3rd.* His Honor is of opinion that Mr. ——— is correct in holding that the principle of assessing at half assets is not intended as a rigid and invariable rule. It is admitted, and indeed necessity under certain circumstances demand, that the Settlement Officer should go below the sum which he may arrive at by assessing at 50 per cent. on the rates prevailing in the pergunnah, in cases where from the excessive number of cultivating proprietors, or from other causes, a full assessment would press too heavily.

"*4th.* The question whether a like discretion exists where an assessment above 50 per cent. would still be a light assessment is a more doubtful one. Provided the discretion is carefully exercised, and the variation moderate, the Lieutenant-Governor does not see anything in itself inequitable or inexpedient in such a course.

"*6th.* It would be difficult to lay down any distinct rule; but the Lieutenant-Governor would not object to a discretion being left to assess such properties at a somewhat higher rate, these being a set-off to the cases in which a lower rate of assessment is admitted: provided the amount of excess above the fixed proportion is clearly stated and fully justified in the village statements."

A somewhat similar reference has been made this year from the Futtehpore District to the present Lieutenant-Governor, Sir John Strachey, and his orders quoted below fully sanction and endorse the procedure I have observed and explained as that adopted by me before I ever saw the orders now quoted:—

Extract from G. O. No. 1379A., dated the 5th June, 1874.

"2. He (the Settlement Officer) has adhered closely to his average rates and proposes an assessment which, while it would be fair enough if imposed for the first time, is not called for in the circumstances of this case. Where a village has been highly assessed, the assessment should not, in ordinary circumstances, be lowered to the half asset rate on purely arithmetical grounds. If it has borne the high assessment well, the demand should not, generally speaking, be lowered at all; if ill, the demand should be lowered, but not ordinarily to the full extent of the half asset rate."

95. The only cesses taken by landlords from their cultivators or from others

Agricultural cesses taken into consideration in assessment. residing in their villages, which have been included amongst the assessable assets, and taken into account in assessing the revenue, are what is known in this district under the name of *kharch*. It is merely a cess on rent recorded in the rentals *(nikasees)*, and virtually amalgamated with and part and parcel of the rent. In all newly arranged rents, and enhancements decreed by the Courts, the *kharch* has been consolidated with the rent, and there is no extra payment above the rate or rent decreed.

96. The foregoing is the only agricultural cess taken into consideration in assessment. No other agricultural cesses or manorial dues, such

Other agricultural cesses or manorial dues not taken into consideration in assessment, nor recorded in the wajibulurs. as income from markets, royalties *(nuzzerana)*, free labour *(begar)*, and others, a detail of the most common of which is given on the margin,* have been included in the assessable assets, or in any way taken into consideration in the assessment of the land-revenue. But very few of them, and those the least objectionable, have been recorded in the village administration

* *List of ordinary agricultural cesses.*

1. Jars of cane-juice or *rab* per sugar mill, or per field of cane, or so many canes per field.
2. So many seers of wheat per plough, or so much *bhoosa* or *kurbee.*
3. Vegetables from Kachees.
4. Free use *(begar)* of cattle, carts, or men.

List of ordinary non-agricultural cesses.

1. Market dues, and fees for buying and selling.
2. *Chantee*, or ground rent.
3. Dues from petty traders, as oil from oilmen, pots from potters, shoes from coblers, &c., &c.
4. Free labour from barbers, kehars, &c.
5. *Nuzzerana* for new houses and shops, or alterations in old ones.

papers *(wajibulurz)*, nor can they be sued for and recovered under Act XVIII. of 1873, or in any Civil or Revenue Court, except such as may be specially sanctioned by the local Government under Section 66, Act XIX. of 1873.

SECTION VIII.
Financial Results.

Tabular form showing financial results. 97. The financial results of the revision of settlement can be best seen in a tabular form, and are given in the following statement :—

Pergunnah.			Expiring jumma without cesses.			New jumma without cesses.			Increase.			Percentage of increase.
			Rs.	a.	p.	Rs.	a.	p.	Rs.	a.	p.	
Shahjehanpore,	...	...	1,07,939	6	0	1,24,219	1	0	16,279	11	0	15·1
Jumour,	...	...	74,752	10	0	74,710	15	0	...			Decrease of Rs. 41-11-0
Kant,	...	...	78,963	5	0	91,740	14	0	12,776	9	0	16·2
Jellalabad,	...	...	1,61,134	8	9	2,11,410	0	0	50,275	7	3	31·2
Tilhur,	...	...	85,171	0	0	1,09,120	6	0	23,949	6	0	28·1
Meeranpore Kuttra,	...	...	5,971	0	0	8,510	0	0	2,539	0	0	42·5
Khera Bujhera,	...	...	51,445	0	0	72,360	0	0	20,915	0	0	40·7
Jellalpore,	...	...	56,125	0	0	63,005	0	0	6,880	0	0	12·2
Nigohee,	...	...	61,950	0	0	77,130	0	0	15,180	0	0	24·5
Burragaon,	...	...	64,345	0	0	72,950	0	0	8,605	0	0	13·4
Powayn,	...	...	1,92,366	0	0	2,16,735	0	0	24,369	0	0	12·6
Khotar,	...	...	35,110	0	0	62,535	0	0	27,425	0	0	78·1
Whole District,		...	9,75,272	13	9	11,84,425	4	0	2,09,194	1	3	21·4
									Deduct 41	11	0	
						Net increase			2,09,152	6	3	

The expiring *jumma* is the revenue of the year just preceding revision, and in no one pergunnah is it the same as the *jumma* at the commencement of settlement. The explanation of the difference has been given for each pergunnah in the separate tuhseel assessment reports, and is not of sufficient importance to be repeated here. Where the figures here given differ from those in the tuhseel assessment report, these of this chapter are to be accepted as correct in preference to those. The *jumma* of Khotar is the maximum *jumma*. In this pergunnah alone is the assessment progressive, and the details are given on the margin. The increase of the *jumma* of the first term over the lately current *jumma*, i.e., the immediate rise, is at the rate of just over 51 per cent.

PROGRESSIVE JUMMAS OF PERGUNNAH KHOTAR.		
1st term of five years, from 1st to 5th year.	2nd term of two years, 6th and 7th years.	Maximum from 8th year.
Rs.	Rs.	Rs.
58,150	59,210	62,535

98. The total increase on the whole district amounts to over two lakhs and nine thousand rupees (Rs. 2,09,152), and is at the rate of 21·4 per cent. The increases in the different pergunnahs, in which there are not progressive assessments, run from 12 to 42½ per cent. In only one pergunnah, Jumour, is there a decrease, and that is really nominal, as the revenue assessed came to 17 rupees over the expiring revenue; but losses of area by diluvion, occurring after the new assessments were made, but before they came into force, necessitated a reduction of *jumma* in one or two *muhals*, which brought the total *jumma* of the pergunnah down nearly Rs. 60.

Total increase exceeds two lakhs and nine thousand rupees.

99. The foregoing statement however gives no adequate idea of the real alterations in the revenue of individual *mouzahs* and *muhals*, and what is apparently only a mild, not to say immaterial, increase of 12 or 13 per cent. on a whole pergunnah, is, when looked at by the aid of the following statement, an entire re-arrangement of the revenues of most of the *mouzahs* of which the pergunnah is made up. In fact, *teste* Jumour, the absence of any increase at all on a pergunnah by no means implies that things have remained in *statu quo ante*; for, of a total of 127 *mouzahs*, there are only sixteen in which there are no alterations of over 10 rupees, 59 in which the total decrease amounts to over 11 per cent, and 52 in which the total increase is nearly 22 per cent. These details have *not* been given in the separate tuhseel assesment reports, except for Pergunnah Khotar, (in which the net increase on the pergunnah is 78·1 per cent.), and in a somewhat different form there; so I give it in the margin for each circle in the form now used; as it is the best illustration, after Jumour, of the internal variations, whereof the pergunnah results only are usually exhibited,

The great internal alterations of jummas of mouzahs shown.

Khalsa Mahals of Pergunnah Khotar in which the assessment is

Circle.	Total.	Unaltered.	Decreased.		Increased.		Percentage of net increase.
			Muhals.	Percentage of decrease.	Muhals.	Percentage of increase.	
1st, ...	72	7	7	13	58	72	50·8
2nd, ...	200	9	13	15	178	132	102·9

and give but a faint idea of the real changes entailed by a revision of statement:—

Pergunnah.	Number of mouzahs the jumma of which has remained unaltered.	DECREASE OF JUMMA.		INCREASE OF JUMMA.		Total number of mouzahs.	Percentage of net increase of new over past jumma.
		Number of mouzahs.	Percentage of decrease.	Number of mouzahs.	Percentage of increase.		
Shahjehanpore, ...	8	47	10·1	138	37·7	193	15·1
Jumour, ...	16	59	11·2	52	31·9	127	None: but a small decrease.
Kant, ...	25	48	10·7	144	36·2	217	16·2
Jellalabad, ...	23	51	13·3	318	45·2	392	31·2
Tilhur, ...	15	14	8·4	180	37·1	209	25·1
Meerahpore Kuttra, ..	..	1	4·0	11	48·9	12	42·6
Khera Bujhera	5	9	28·1	123	57·9	137	40·7
Jellalpore, ...	24	17	11·4	71	37·2	112	13·2
Nigohee, ...	19	13	7·9	116	35·1	148	34·6
Burragaon, ...	13	29	6·7	84	39·2	126	13·4
Powayn, ...	60	61	8·9	297	22·9	437	13·6
Khotar, ...	16	20	13·6	231	110·8	267	78·1
Whole District, ..	236	363	11·1	1,755	37·7	2,354	21·4

100. In the following table are exhibited in parallel columns the revenue-rate
or incidence *per acre* of (1) the initial *jumma* of last settlement
on the then areas; (2) of the expiring *jumma* on the then areas,
i. e., the areas at the end of the settlement as shown in the new
measurements; (3) of the new *jumma* on the new areas. Land-
revenue *(jumma)* without cesses in all:—

Incidences of revenue at the commencement and end of last settlement and of new settlement compared.

Pergunnah.	Incidences on the malgoozaree or assessable area.			Incidences on the cultivated area.		
	1.	2.	3.	1.	2.	3.
	Rs. a. p.	Rs. a. p.	Rs. a. p.	Rs. a. p.	Rs. a. p.	Rs. a. p.
Shahjehanpore, ...	1 7 11	1 5 3	1 8 5	2 0 10	1 10 10	1 14 10
Jumour, ...	•1 7 2	1 5 0	1 5 0	2 0 9	1 11 6	1 11 6
Kant, ...	1 0 0	0 14 9	1 1 1	1 4 11	1 1 9	1 4 8
Jellalabad, ...	0 15 2	0 14 8	1 3 3	1 11 2	1 4 4	1 10 7
Tilhur, ...	1 3 0	1 2 8	1 8 6	1 11 7	1 6 3	1 12 6
Meerumpore Kuttra, ...	0 14 3	0 13 2	1 2 10	1 9 5	1 2 11	1 10 9
Khera Bujhera, ...	1 1 9	1 0 5	1 7 1	1 9 7	1 3 9	1 11 9
Jellalpore, ... 4.. ...	1 8 4	1 5 8	1 8 4	1 14 8	2 11 0	1 14 4
Nigohee, ...	1 0 4	0 15 10	1 3 9	1 11 7	1 5 10	1 11 3
Burragaon, ...	1 9 11	1 6 8	1 9 6	2 6 1	1 12 3	2 0 0
Powayn, ...	1 2 4	1 0 8	1 3 0	1 9 0	1 4 11	1 7 6
Khotar, ...	0 5 11	0 4 8	0 8 4	2 3 7	0 8 9	0 15 7
Whole district, ...	1 1 4	0 15 11	1 3 4	1 11 10	1 5 1	1 9 7

I have ommitted incidences on the total area, as they are utterly useless, and not
only so, but also misleading. In examining the foregoing statement, it must be kept in
view (1) that the new revised assessment is at 50 per cent. or half assets, whilst the
last one was nominally at two-thirds, or about 66 per cent. of assets; (2) that the margin of culturable waste is much smaller now than it was then, and consequently influ-
ences the assessment much less, whilst the *malgoozaree* or assessable area is now larger,
and includes much of what was formerly erroneously excluded from the assessable area
under the head of barren.

The present assumed assets for the entire district are Rs. 23,68,850; and if the
assessment had been made on these, at the proportion at which the last settlement was
made, *viz.*, 66 per cent, the revenue would have been Rs. 15,63,441 instead of
Rs. 11,84,425, and the incidence per acre of cultivation Rs. 2-1-9 against Re. 1-9-7. These
are what the figures should be if the new assessment had been made at the same proportion of assets as the old; but in reality such an assessment as this could not be made.
It would be an increase on the expiring settlement of Rs. 6,88,168, and at a rate of
rather over seventy (70) per cent.

Again, the subsequent reduction of revenue in consequence of severity of assessment had some influence (up to the extent of between three and four pie) in reducing
the incidence of the revenue at the end as compared with the beginning of the settlement; but extension of cultivation and enlargement of *malgoozaree* area were the principal causes. The increase must be looked at *not* between the incidence of the old
settlement, at time of settlement (column 1), and the new settlement (column 3), but
between the incidence at the end of the old settlement (column 2) and the beginning
of the new settlement (column 3).

101. In two of the neighbouring districts of Rohilkhund revision of settlement has

Shahjehanpore compared with neighbouring districts, Bareilly and Budaon. been in progress whilst this settlement of Shahjehanpore has been going on, and has recently been completed in both, and the settlement reports have been printed. From them I gather the details given on the margin for comparison with the results in this district. It must be kept in mind, however, that the incidence here given are those of land-revenue

District.	Percentage of increase of revenue.	Revenue rate or incidence of assessment per acre of the land-revenue (jumma).	
		On malgoozaree area.	On cultivated area.
Bareilly, ...	20·4	1 8 7	1 14 0
Budaon, ...	10·8	0 12 9	1 3 9
Shahjehanpore,	21·4	1 3 4	1 9 7

without cesses, the 50 per cent. *jumma, not* the 55 per cent. demand as shown in the tabular statements of both the Bareilly and Budaon settlement reports. The general opinion afloat about the Budaon settlement, which is also borne out by the report, is that it is an extremely light one; and when assessing pergunnahs bordering on it, the zemindars told me that my assessments were higher than those in Budaon. The Bareilly settlement again, with the exception of Tuhseel Furreedpoor, is complained of as severe, and the complaints of over-assessment have been loud and long, and though doubtless much exaggerated, yet they are not altogether without foundation. The review and revision of assessments of two pergunnahs thereof, Chaumahla and Richa, has been ordered, and is being carried out by me, but will not considerably affect the district total.

Assuming, however, that the assessment of Bareilly is somewhat high, and of Budaon somewhat low, and that an incidence of Rs. 1-12-9 and Re. 1-6-6 per cultivated acre, respectively, about represents what the incidence of each should be, if the assessments of each were equal and uniform in moderation and applicability to the status of each district, I proceed to show briefly why Re. 1-9-7 must be about fair for Shahjehanpore, and how this district escapes the charge of either undue leniency or severity of assessment.

102. First, then, let us take Bareilly. There is no pergunnah of the Bareilly District

Comparison with Bareilly. near as bad as the large pergunnah of Khotar in the Shahjehanpore District. Even the most unhealthy and worst portions of Chaumahla and Richa are not so backward in cultivation, nor do they pay such low rents as the greater portion of Pergunnah Khotar, and I know both well. It must be remembered that I am not comparing Shahjehanpore with Bareilly, plus the Pillibheet subdivision, but Bareilly proper, assessed by Mr. Moens, without that subdivision; else Poorunpoor pairs off well with Khotar. Omitting Pergunnah Khotar,

Incidence of assessment per acre of the Shahjehanpore District omitting Pergunnah Khotar.

On malgoozaree area.	On cultivated area.
Rs. a. p.	Rs. a. p.
1 4 10	1 10 7

the revenue incidences, as shown on the margin, come up somewhat nearer to those of Bareilly. But still they are, as I maintain they should be, considerably lower than Bareilly. The reasons are briefly these, that in the district of Shahjehanpore money rents have been the rule, and payments in kind the great exception, for upwards of 50 years; that now there is virtually no payment in kind. Also, as already explained in great detail in Section VI. of this report, rents throughout the district are more or less low and inadequate, and have not been materially affected by the rise in prices or change in the value of silver. In the Bareilly District, on the contrary, payment in kind abounds in all parts, and in many pergunnahs was the rule, and money rents were the exception, until the extensive commutations at the late revision of settlement. There, then, rents have been directly affected by prices and by the depreciation of the precious metals, and are consequently much higher than in the Shahjehanpore District. Then, again, there are canals in Bareilly, but not in Shahjehanpore.

But, even assuming that Bareilly and Shahjehanpore (without Khotar) are equal, still, for the reasons given, the rate of assessment of Bareilly should be not less than 8 or 10 (if not, indeed, from 10 to 12) per cent. in excess of that of Shahjehanpore. The difference between Re. 1-10-7, the rate of Shahjehanpore, exclusive of Khotar, and Re 1-12-9, the assumed moderate incidence, and Re. 1-14-0, the actual incidence of Bareilly, is 8 and 12¼ per cent. respectively.

103. I do not know much of the Budaon District personally, and cannot therefore speak as regards it with the same certainty as of Bareilly;

Comparison with Budaon.

but, from Mr. Carmichael's report, I gather that in Budaon, as in Shahjehanpore, money rents are the rule, and that there is little or no *buttaie* to speak of; that it is "a district in which the conservative element is strong, and in which therefore we should expect to find little rise (in the rent-rate) on the score of improvement or from pressure of landlords." The general impression left upon my mind by the perusal of the Budaon settlement report is that that district is not up to the standard of the Shahjehanpore District, and that rents in it are even lower and more backward than in Shahjehanpore. Hence the assessment rate per cultivated acre in the latter should be higher than that in the former, but to what extent I cannot say, even approximately.

104. No comparison can be made with the Pillibheet subdivision, as two of its pergunnahs, Jahanabad and Pillibheet, are very dissimilar

No comparison can be made with the subdivision of Pillibheet.

from the generality of the Shahjehanpore District; and the third, Poorunpoor, by far the largest of the three, similar to the exceptional pergunnah, Khotar, of this district. Moreover, revision of settlement has been ordered to a greater or less extent in all three pergunnahs, and I have been deputed to carry it out; which revision will be commenced shortly.

105. The detailed grounds of assessments of each pergunnah must of course be sought for in the separate assessment reports which follow

Tabular form for comparison of pergunnahs with one another, with explanations.

(Chapters II. to V.) ; but the following tabular statement brings together in a convenient form the principal points on which a comparison can be instituted between the various pergunnahs: from it are also ascertainable not only the causes of a higher or lower rate of assessment in each, but also the grounds of a large or small increase of revenue. In classifying the soils in this statement, I have not adhered exactly to the percentage as given in para. 74, but have put so much of the 2nd *domut* and *mutyar* as is poor soil into the "inferior soils" in addition to the *bhoor*, and the remainder into "medium class soils." The percentage of increase of cultivated area is the percentage of the difference between the cultivated areas of the last and present settlement, but most of these are subject to deductions and explanations owing chiefly to the famine and abnormally large new fallow areas of last settlement. These explanations will be found in the separate tuhseel assessment reports, e. g., para. 26 of Chapter V. shows that the actual increase due to extension of cultivation is in Powayn only 6¼ per cent. instead of 18 per cent., and in Burragaon 22¼ instead of 34 per cent:—

Pergunnah.	Total population per square mile of entire area.	Agricultural population per square mile of cultivation.	Percentage of assessable area cultivated.	Percentage of 1st class soils.	Percentage of medium class soils.	Percentage of inferior soils.	Percentage of cultivated area irrigated, not merely capable of irrigation.	Percentage of superior crops.	Percentage of increase of cultivated area.	Percentage of increase of land-revenue without cesses.	Incidence of new revenue per acre of cultivation.
											Rs. a. p.
Shahjehanpore,	981	596	79	68	28	4	51	65	17	15·1	1 14 10
Jumour,	523	538	76	53	35	12	51	54	19	...	1 11 6
Kant,	504	465	83	33	42	26	36	47	18	14·2	1 4 8
Jellalabad,	618	569	72	42	38	20	38	58	35	21·2	1 10 7
Tilhur,	680	545	84	46	37	17	48	56	27	28·1	1 12 6
Meeranpore Kuttra,	767	592	71	47	40	13	50	54	37	47·5	1 10 9
Khera Bujhera,	531	564	83	60	30	10	50	52	31	40·7	1 11 9
Jellalpore,	599	579	80	60	29	11	58	56	15	13·2	1 14 4
Nigohee,	604	572	73	68	20	12	55	52	23	24·5	1 11 4
Burragaon,	599	584	80	56	40	4	48	66	34	13·4	2 0 0
Powayn,	510	511	80	36	47	17	43	49	18	12·6	1 7 6
Khotar,	290	270	53	25	35	30	24	32	309	78·1	0 15 7
Whole district,	540	530	75	48	38	14	40	53	21	21·4	1 9 7

106. Before leaving this subject of financial results of assessment, I should
Small items of land-re-venue assessed after revi-sion of pergunnahs as re-quired. mention briefly that there are other small items of land-revenue which have not appeared in these totals, but which have been assessed from time to time as the necessity occurred after the revision of the pergunnahs in which they are situated. They are as follows :—(a) The assessment of lands taken up for the railway, and subsequently returned as not required or done with, a very small and immaterial item. (b) A religious *maafee*, in Pergunnah Jumour, resumed in consequence of the conditions not being observed, and the land sold out and out to a stranger, and assessed to revenue amounting to Rs. 35. (c) Assessment of land denuded of mango *baghs*, the trees of which had been cut and not planted again, and the land brought under cultivation subsequent to the revision of assessment of the pergunnah in which these lands had remained exempt from assessment as mango *baghs*. These
Board's Circular No. 22, dated 20th October, 1869. have been principally in Pergunnahs Shahjehanpore and Tilhur, through which the railway passes, but to some extent all over the district. Exact details cannot be given of area and revenue, as many have been assessed conditionally only : that if trees are planted within a year and kept up, the revenue shall not be enforced. And also several cases have come up recently since I had the totals made up   But approximately the area is rather under 200 acres, and the revenue assessed thereon a little over Rs. 300. (d) The last is the nominal assessment, or rather assessment at a very low rate (merely for the sake of the name of the thing) of *baghs*, the separate property of individuals, and recorded in the *khewut* as their property, both trees and land. These, under the Board's Circular just quoted, would have been exempt from revenue; but in order to prevent the acquisition of a revenue-free title, or the possibility of any mistake as to whether these lands are or are not liable to revenue, I have assessed them at usually about one-tenth of what the revenue would have been if the land was under ordinary cultivation—*e. g.*, there are some 22 acres of these in Pergunnah Kant, assessed at a revenue of Rs. 4-6-0. Of course if any of these are cut down, and the land is cultivated, they are liable to full assessment at half assets, just like any other *baghs* (under Board of Revenue's Circular No. 22, dated 20th of October, 1869).

107. The revised assessments took effect in the first pergunnahs of this district
Term proposed for set-tlement, thirty years. from 1st July 1870, and I propose that the term of the currency of the new settlement be thirty years from that date for the *whole district, viz.*, up to 30th June, 1900 A.D. There can be no question, I think, that the assessment is an adequate one, and that its term may be the full thirty years, and that a doubt can exist only as regards Khotar. I would not make an exception for Pergunnah Khotar as it is a small matter at most, the total revenue being only Rs. 62,535, and there is no prospect of any such vast improvement as took place during the past thirty years. Moreover, this pergunnah is the last assessed, and the new *jummas* of Khotar only came into force from 1st July, 1873, and then even progressive, mostly of them not reaching their maximum till 1st July, 1880, so that, the whole settlement expiring on 30th June, 1900, the term for Khotar would be twenty-seven years instead of thirty from its commencement, and only twenty years from the date of the assessment reaching its maximum.

108. The *durkhasts*, as explained in the assessment reports on the various tuhseels,
Durkhasts taken without specification of any term. have been taken without the insertion of any specific term, in conformity with instructions received from the Board in reply to a reference on this point. The wording is merely "for the term of the settlement," and also "subject to the sanction of Government," so that it rests entirely with the Government to fix the period.

SECTION IX.

Records; Putwarees' circles; Expenses of settlement.

109. The principal papers comprising the vernacular settlement *misl* are (1) the
Papers comprising the settlement vernacular *misl* record. *shujrah* or field map; (2) the *khusrah* or index thereto; (3) the *khutteonee* or detailed abstract of the former; (4) the *jumma-bundee* or rent-roll; (5) the *wajiboolurs* or administration paper; (6) the *khewat* or record of proprietary rights, and (7) the final *roobkaree* or closing proceeding There are a number of other papers, but they are chiefly tabular forms with the exception of the *durkhast* or engagement for payment of revenue, such as the Nos. II, III, and IV figured statements, the lists of groves, wells, &c., the list of revenue-free grants, and the like. These may be called the supplementary statements, and need not be further alluded to.

110. I think that a final settlement report is not the place to enter fully into a
Detailed account of contents of various settlement *misls* not necessary. lengthy disquisition on the contents, method of preparation, verification, and other details concerning these papers, or for recapitulating what has been written about them in intermediate reports during the progress of settlement. It is quite unnecessary, as monthly returns of progress of work and six-monthly and annual reports of progress have regularly been submitted, and my settlement *misls* contain all the usual papers in the prescribed forms: none have been omitted and none added. I proceed, therefore, to note only those points about the important papers of the settlement *misl* which I consider are not out of place in a final report of settlement.

111. The *shujrah* is on the prescribed scale of 16 inches to the mile, and there is
The *shujrah* and *khus-rah*. a separate *shujrah* for each *mouzah*, except when the *mouzah* is divided into two or more separate *muhals*, when there is a *shujrah* for each *muhal*, unless they are very much intermixed (*khétbut* or *khétmilk*). The *khusrah* is separate for each *muhal* under any circumstances. The *shujrahs* of this settlement have the usual prescribed distinctive marks for cultivation : unculturable land, old unbroken waste, new fallow, groves, &c., but nothing more. They have not been coloured for soil, irrigation or any thing of that sort. The measurements were all made with the plane-table by the *putwarees*, or by ameens when the *putwaree* was unable to measure. The supervision was entirely native with the exception of my assistant Mr. Butt and myself. All the *shujrahs* were tested by one of us, and the entries in the *khusrahs* at the same time, especially of soil and irrigation. The *khusrah* entries are the foundation of all the subsequent papers and statistics of cultivators' names, length of occupancy, area, denomination of soil, irrigation and its sources; and all the area columns with their details have been totalled in the *khusrahs*. This is not by any means always done in other settlements, but *all* my papers are totalled, and totals and details can be compared of the *khusrah* Nos. II. and III. and IV. Statements and *khutteonees*, and it stands to reason that this ensures greater accuracy.

112. The *khutteonee* is formed from the *khusrah* by extracting all the fields in the
The *khutteonee*. cultivating occupancy of each separate cultivator, and if there are subdivisions in the *mouzah* for each subdivision (*thokwar* and *putteewar*). Inasmuch as the smooth working and correctness of all the subsequent papers depend on the accuracy of the *khutteonee*, every endeavour has been made to ensure the greatest accuracy. For the *khutteonee* is not merely the abstract of cultivators' lands, or of lands cultivated by proprietors and tenants, but also contains complete entries of all proprietary rights, the shares and extent thereof belonging to various individuals, and as such is the basis of the *khewat* or record of rights. The plan adopted was that already explained in the last and other annual progress reports, and very similar to that adopted by Mr. Elliott in Futtehgurh, and Mr. Moens in Bareilly, *viz.*, the double slip system. The attesting Moonserims proceed to the village to be attested and attest on the spot, having duplicate slips for each separate holding, both being

corrected if neccessary at verification on the spot, and attested by his signature and that of the zemindar and *putwaree*, and one copy made over to the cultivator concerned (the other being kept for record and as the basis of the *khutteonee*). As far as possible all cases and disputes are disposed of at the time of attestation of the *khutteonee* by the Deputy Collector, or at all events are instituted then if not decided, so that they shall not stand over till the preparation of the *khewat*, and cause delay and alteration of entries at the last. The *khutteonee* is invariably prepared for the same year as the *khusrah*.

113. The *jummabundee* or rent-roll, when the *khutteonee* is properly prepared and
The *jummabundee*. the rent columns are filled up, is not necessary for the settlement *misl*, though it is very necessary as the first under the new settlement to start the *putwarees'* annual papers correctly. The *jummabundee* is sometimes for the same year as the *khusrah* and *khutteonee* (and is then especially superfluous as a part of the settlement *misl*), but not necessarily so, and oftener for a year, two or three years later, the first year of the new assessments being in force. It cannot be delayed so as to include all enhancements decreed in suits under Acts X. of 1859 and XIV. of 1863 (or latterly under Act XIX. of 1873) which are instituted after the declaration, or at all events the coming into force of the new *jummas*; but it includes all enhancements made in good time, and all mutual arrangements concerning new and increased rents, completed before or at the time of its preparation. Ordinarily the enhancement cases are not instituted until the *jummabundee* has been attested and enhancement by mutual agreement has failed.

Entirely new rent-rolls for a whole *mouzah* or *muhal* at enhanced rates have not been attempted *suo motu*, except in cases where the assessing officer considered the existing rental extremely low and inadequate as a whole, and assessed the *jumma* on a much higher assumed rental, which new *jumma* did not leave the zemindar a profit, or margin, of 35 per cent. out of his old (i. e., current) rental. But in all cases where any enhancement was necessary, every endeavour has been made to bring about a mutual arrangement between the parties, and to have the rent settled amicably out of Court.

114. The *wajiboolurz* or village administration paper is not now in these times
The *wajiboolurz*. of extensive and comprehensive legislation, circular orders and rules, as necessary or important a document as it was at the time of the last settlements. There are very few customs now which require to be recorded in the *wajiboolurz* that might not as well come into the *khewat* or *jummabundee* or final *roobkaree*, and I think that the *wajiboolurz* might with advantage be dispensed with. As, however, this view of mine was not adopted by the Board, and the *wajiboolurz* is one of the prescribed papers of the settlement *misl*, I have endeavoured to prevent its being a mere formal paper, and have looked carefully after its proper preparation and attestation by my subordinates. Nothing has been allowed into it which is in any way objectionable or inexpedient or contrary to the existing law, and subjects provided for by law have been referred to therein as so provided for. At the same time nothing necessary or needful has been omitted, and all the Board's orders respecting the entry or provision in the *wajiboolurz* of certain points have been observed. It has invariably been attested in the presence of a duly empowered officer, usually a Deputy Collector, by all the parties concerned, and their signatures attached to it ; and the fact of attestation on a certain date mentioned in the order and under the signature of the attesting officer. This refers not only to the *wajiboolurz* but to the *khutteonee*, *jummabundee*, and *khewat* also.

115. But little need be said about the *khewat*, except that it contains all details
The *khewat*. of the shares of the proprietors of the *muhal* and of all individuals who have any property therein, not omitting grantees of revenue-free land where they are the proprietors as well as grantees. With but few

exceptions all cases had been heard and decided before the attestation of the *khewat*, and if any remained, the entries were made in conformity with the decisions when given. In the *khewat*, too, is entered the apportionment or distribution of *jumma* on the various divisions and subdivisions and holdings. As far as possible this was arranged by mutual consent on the voice of the majority as to the way in which the distribution was to be effected (whether on the fractional shares, or rateably with reference to former amount, or at a summary rate on the area, or by assessment on the extent and quality of soil, irrigation &c.); or, when that was not practicable, by a district order. Number of the distributions were made by Mr. Butt in pergunnahs assessed by him, and by myself in those assessed by me, and the orders of my subordinates were all appealable to me.

116. The final *roobkaree* is the closing proceeding, recapitulating the principal points worthy of notice, and giving a short résumé or summary in a connected form, and drawn up in set paragraphs.

The final roobkaree.

117. There is one point concerning the list or statement of *baghs* which is worthy of special notice here, and it is this, that that form contains separate columns for the name of proprietor of the land and for the name of owner of the trees. The general custom in the district is that the property of the land on which *baghs* are planted vests in the zemindar even when the *bagh* itself is the property of another; the trees of the *bagh* alone so long as it exists, and not the land, being the separate property of another. Every entry has been carefully attested, and where there has been any dispute a case has been instituted and a judicial decision given. Special mention of the custom prevailing with reference to *baghs* in the *muhal* and all details concerning them have been entered in the *wajiboolurz*. Hitherto the *baghs* have been entered separately in the *putwarees'* papers without any particulars very often as to whom they belonged, and never any distinction between the property of the land as separate from the ownership of the trees. Where the *bagh* is the property of any one other than the zemindar, usually the zemindar holds a reversionary interest in the land, the owner of the *bagh* being in possession of the trees *and the land* only so long as the *bagh* remains, but without any power to plant new trees without the permission of the zemindar, whose right to the property of the land revives as soon as the trees have been cut down or the *bagh* has ceased to exist. The explanation of this is simple. Those *baghs* planted by others than the zemindars themselves must have been planted by their permission, and what was and is still given is permission to plant a *bagh* in a certain plot of land, the *bagh* to belong to the planter thereof and his heirs; but the land itself is not given. Rent is not usually taken because Government have almost all along (*viz.*, in former settlements and for the last years during the present revisions) allowed lands planted with trees, *i. e.*, *baghs*, to remain free of revenue. It is an advantage to a zemindar to have *baghs* planted about in his village, and where the permission is given to some one other than a leading cultivator to induce him to settle and bring other cultivators to settle also, a royalty or *nuzzerana* is taken, but it is quite the exception to alienate the land. Most of the cases in which others than the zemindars of the *muhal* are proprietors of the land of the *baghs*, as well as of the trees, are those in which the *baghs* have been originally planted by the zemindars themselves in their own land, and then sold to others, land and all.

Points worthy of special notice as regards baghs.

118. I had an entirely separate final scrutiny or *janch* office, through which every single settlement *misl* passed after having been prepared in the *khutteonee* and *khewat* offices, and attested and faired out before being deposited in the Collector's office. The *misls* were not given into this final scrutiny office until they were in every way complete with the exception of being bound. In this office they underwent searching tests of totals and details, and all the decided cases relating to each *misl* were given into the scrutiny office with it, and the final orders compared with the entries in the settlement *misl*, to see that the orders had been carried out and entries made accordingly. The *janch* office had my orders and instructions on all points at their fingers' ends, and a copy for reference when necessary; and every paper

Final scrutiny or test office.

was examined with special advertence to these for sins of omission and commission. No errors of any importance could thus remain, and it was frequently made manifestly evident how absolutely necessary this final scrutiny was, and how greatly it conduced to uniformity of procedure and correctness of the settlement *misl*.

119. The *misls* after having undergone the final scrutiny, and any necessary corrections having been made, were bound and deposited in the Collector's office. The bound *misl* deposited in the Collector's office is a faired original, with the principal papers signed by all the parties concerned, and the fact of attestation thereof entered in an order upon each and signed by the Deputy Collector or other attesting officer. It is *not* merely a true copy without original signatures.

Misl deposited in Collectors' office an attested and signed original.

120. Copies of the principal papers prescribed by the Board were made for the tuhseel and for the *putwarees ;* the copies are also bound, not so well as the original deposited in the Collector's office, but still fairly neatly and serviceably ; and each pergunnah of a tuhseel has its distinctive and recognizable marks in the outer binding itself, so that if several bound *misls* of one pergunnah get mixed up with those of another, they can be picked out by an illiterate menial.

Copies for tuhseel and putwarees.

121. In the four succeeding chapters will be found separate mention for each tuhseel of the arrangements made for the Putwaree Fund and the grading of the putwarees, with other necessary details. It is a subject of great regret to me to find that all this labour and trouble has been thrown away, and that the arrangement of putwarees' cirles and their pay has to be done over again under the orders and rules about to be issued under the new Revenue Act, XIX. of 1873. Under the new law the Putwaree Fund and grading system is illegal, and the arrangements made from time to time during the last four years under the law as it then existed, and in conformity with the instructions and orders of the Board of Revenue then in force, are now to be upset by retrospective effect being given to the new rules about to be issued under the new Act. Whatever alterations are necessary must be effected in the Collector's office : and all the putwarees' arrangements mentioned in para. 36 of Chapter II., para. 44 of Chapter III., para. 98 of Chapter IV., and para. 42 of Chapter V. must be considered quashed and of no effect.

Putwarees' circles; alteration of arrangements necessitated by Act XIX. of 1873.

122. The English records are (1) the No. II. and III. Statements, with miscellaneous general remarks, of which two sets have been made, as already explained in para. 89 of their chapter; they are bound up by pergunnahs (or when the pergunnah is large there are two or more volumes to the pergunnah), and the copies on the Board's prescribed form have been given into the Collector's office for record. The other copy accompanies this report, but as a manuscript only, and will not be printed.

English records Nos. II., III., and IV.

The other English record is the No. IV. general statement in the prescribed form which also accompanies this report, but will not be printed with it, as it is quite unnecessary.

123. A map of the scale of four miles equal one inch is bound into the commencement of this report, which shows the position and shape of the district, tuhseels, and pergunnahs, the principal towns and villages, rivers and streams, police-stations and post-offices. In a pocket will be found four tuhseel maps of the scale of one inch to the mile, which show the boundaries of every *mouzah*, the assessment circles, the incidence of the *jumma* per acre of cultivation, and other details, mention of which will be found in each of the separate tuhseel reports. These are photozincographed copies of maps compiled in my office by pentograph from the *shujrahs* or field maps. The fair copy for photozincography was specially made in the office of the Revenue Survey in Calcutta for that purpose.

District map and four tuhseel maps.

124. The grand total of the whole expenditure on the settlement from first to last amounts to five lakhs eighty-six thousand five hundred rupees, but it is quite impossible to apportion this to measurement, assessment, and records, or even to fix the exact amount debitable to measurement alone, so as to show what the expenses of measurement were in the gross, and what the rate was per 1,000 acres. The total additional or enhanced revenue collected since the 1st July, 1870, and inclusive of the instalments now just falling due as the settlement is concluded —*i.e.*, the total amount of enhanced revenue during the progress of the settlement, is just six lakhs of rupees, slightly over, and exceeds the expenditure by nearly fifteen thousand rupees. The revision of settlement has, therefore, more than paid its own expenses during the time that the revision and preparation of records were in progress. The whole district has been measured, the assessment revised, and a very full and careful record of rights has been prepared at an average cost of Rs. 529 per 1,000 acres, or Rs. 339 per square mile.

Expenses of the Settlement.

125. This is not a low or cheap rate as compared with other districts, but the two principal reasons are, *first*, my seniority in the service as compared to Settlement Officers who have completed settlements in other districts of the North-Western Provinces within the last three or four years, and the higher rate of pay drawn by me in consequence, and by my assistant Mr. Butt also, than that drawn by the Settlement Officers and assistants of those districts. *Second*, that all expenses of settlement have been borne by and debited to the settlement, none of the ordinary district staff having been employed in settlement without receiving pay from it, as in part of the settlements of Bijnour, Bareilly, and Budaon, where the Collector was the Settlement Officer. In Boolundshuhur, the last district settled by me, the Collector was the Settlement Officer till within the last eighteen months or so of the settlement, after which I was on a salary of Rs. 800 a month, except for the last three months, when I drew Rs. 1,200 a month. Here in Shahjehanpore, owing to lapse of years and my seniority in the service and this department, I have drawn Rs. 2,000 per mensem for more than four years, and Rs. 1,500 and Rs. 1,250 per mensem for several years respectively before that ; and my assistant Rs. 900 a month for 5½ years, and Rs. 600 before that ; whereas in no other district of those already completed has there been a Settlement Officer of the 1st grade, and but for a short time only has the Settlement Officer in them been drawing the pay of 2nd grade, Rs. 1,500 per mensem, and their assistants have been junior to and hence receiving lower salary than Mr. Butt.

Reasons for these expenses being above the average of other districts.

126. But whereas the whole of our salaries (Mr. Butt's and my own) have been debited to the settlement budget, we have both of us done a considerable amount of work, not only not strictly appertaining to Shahjehanpore settlement, but, in the case of Mr. Butt especially, quite distinct from settlement at all. Mr. Butt when first appointed to Shahjehanpore as my assistant was employed some months in laying down the boundary line between the North-Western Provinces and Oudh along the edge of this district and Pillibheet. On the occasion of the *mohurrum* riots at Pillibheet in 1871 he was specially deputed to try the riot cases at Pillibheet. He assisted from time to time in the general criminal work of the district, and supplied all the statistics and information regarding this district for the North-Western Provinces *Gazetteer*, besides writing the chapter on sugar-cane for it.

Though our salaries were charged to settlement, we did other work besides.

My own time during the last nine months has been largely taken up with the work of revision of settlemnt of the pergunnahs of the Bareilly District bordering on the Terai, inclusive of the Pillibheet subdivision.

B

Pundit Kunhya Lall, Tuhseeldar, but officiating as Deputy Collector in the settlement, has all along during the whole time of his deputation to the settlement had the arrears of rent and some other cases of his tuhseel under Act X. of 1859, and as regards them has been a subordinate of the Collector, and much of his time, at least one day in the week, was thus employed in general district work.

127.   Much of the ordinary district current work has also been taken over by
Much ordinary district work performed by the Settlement Department. and performed in the Settlement Department, especially partitions, cases for mutation of names *(dàkhil-khàrij)*, and the superintendence of the *putwarees*. All of these were taken over to the settlement from first breaking ground in a tuhseel until the completion of the records thereof, and the Collector and his subordinates were thereby relieved of a very considerable amount of difficult and irksome work. It may not be out of place to mention here that the superintendence of the *putwarees* included every thing connected with them, and the starting their papers for the first two years after measurement, in conformity with the numbers and details of the new measurements, maps, and indices. The *putwarees'* papers were then started correct in accordance with the new measurement, under the immediate supervision and direction of the Settlement Department, as soon as ever the measurements were completed and the *khutteonees* attested ; and it was not left to the *putwarees* themselves, or to the Collector's subordinates, to to make the change from the old numbers and papers of the past settlement to the new ones of the new settlement, after all records were completed and made over to the Collector's office. I believe this procedure and the extra trouble entailed on the Settlement Department is not general, though to ensure accuracy it certainly should be made so ; and is, I believe, provided for in the new rules about to issue under Act XIX. of 1873.

SECTION X.

Miscellaneous, viz., Lumberdars, Partitions, Masonry pillars, Case work, Mention of Subordinates.

128.   A re-arrangement of the *lumberdars*, the representatives of the proprietors
Lumberdars. where the shareholders are numerous, was of course necessary, and was carried out contemporaneously with the preparation and attestation of records, but before the completion of the *sBajiboolurz* and *khewat*. The principal causes of this necessity were the excessive number of *lumberdars* in some instances and the inadequate numbers in others. Sometimes there were seven or eight where two or three were in every way sufficient, and sometimes only two or three when there were numerous shareholders divided into a number of *thoks* and *puttees*, each of which should have been represented, but was not ; and thirdly, there were in some cases a sufficient number of *lumberdars* for the size of the village, its revenue, and the number of shareholders, but some subdivisions were entirely unrepresented, whilst in others the number of representatives was too large. Another cause, and by no means an infrequent or unimportant one, was that the *lumberdars* were often anything but fit representative men, being amongst the poorest, most illiterate, and least important of the shareholders, and forced into the office simply to bear the brunt of the disagreeable duties devolving on the *lumberdar*, but without any power or respect in the community, and utterly unfit for the position. And besides this, the names of men utterly out of possession and retaining no property in the *muhal* were in some few instances still borne on the list of *lumberdars*.

The remedying of these discrepancies and incongruities, and to give each separate faction and section and subdivision a representative, were the objects kept in view in the re-arrangement of *lumberdars*. The numbers of *muhals* and *lumberdars* before

and after the new measurements and re-arrangement at present settlement are given
below :—

Tehseel.	Pergunnah.				At the end of last settlement.		After revision in new settlement.	
					Muhals.	Lumber-dars.	Muhals.	Lumber-dars.
SHAHJEHANPORE,	Shahjehanpore,	...	...	...	248	379	266	472
	Jumour,	...	...	...	190	258	183	526
	Kant,	...	...	...	342	657	303	685
JELLALABAD,	Jellalabad,	...	...	...	460	1,799	504	2,192
	Tilbur,	...	...	...	268	454	271	468
	Meeranpore Kuttra,	...	...	20	20	21	25
TILHUR,	Khera Bujhera,	...	...	...	153	319	171	361
	Jellalpore,	...	...	...	162	374	187	388
	Nigohee,	...	...	...	175	252	193	289
POWAYN,...	Burragaon,	...	...	...	129	221	160	217
	Powayn,	...	...	...	440	635	529	640
	Khotar,	...	...	...	303	389	276	362
	Whole District, ...			...	2,897	5,757	3,064	6,432

The result on the whole district is an increase of 775 *lumberdars*, and the total
number of *lumberdars* is now 6,432, but these are not all separate individuals. On the
contrary, they are the number of recorded *lumberdars* in each separate *muhal*, the same
name being repeated and appearing again wherever the same individual is a *lumberdar*
in more than one *muhal*. In Powayn, for instance, the Rajah is sole proprietor of 128
muhals and has shares in some others, hence he alone accounts for upwards of 130 out
of the 640 *lumberdars* of the pergunnah.

In Pergunnah Khotar alone is there a reduction in number of the *lumberdars*, and
this is owing to the reduction in number of the *muhals* (which has been explained in
the rent-rate and assessment reports) owing to several *mouzahs* contiguous to one
another and owned by the same zemindar being measured together and made into one
mouzah and *muhal*.

129. The total increase of *muhals* from the number existing just immediately
before revision of settlement to the number after completion of
Explanation of increase in number of *muhals*.
record is 167. But this is not the sum total of complete parti-
tions effected in the Settlement Department. That, as will be seen from the following
explanation, is 193. A large number of *mouzahs* and *muhals* were amalgamated and
reduced partly by the request of the parties and partly by the spontaneous order of
the Settlement Officer. These number 138, and the total 2,897 *muhals* is first subject
to this deduction, which brings it down to 2,759. There must be added 112 *muhals*,
apart from actual partitions, as follows :—(a) 75 alluvial *muhals* in *mouzahs* where a
large portion of the area is beyond, and some portion is within, the influence of the
river and flood, and hence liable to alteration by deposit of sand or soil, as well as by
change of actual area by alluvion or diluvion : (b) the 10 cantonment *muhals* of *mouzahs*
partially in cantonments, the cantonments portion whereof have been made into
separate *muhals* : and (c) 27 *mouzahs* which had been mixed up with others and have
now been made into separate *mouzahs* and *muhals*. This makes the total number of
muhals, independent of partitions, 2,871, and the difference between this and 3,064 is
193. And this 193 is the number of complete partitions out of the 1,560 partition
cases mentioned in paragraph 131, the remainder being imperfect partitions, viz., of
puttees instead of *muhals*.

130. The triple boundary pillars at the point where the boundaries of three sepa-

Masonry boundary pillars.

rately mapped *mousahs* or *muhals* meet have all been built of solid masonry and plastered over. Also where, in consequence of disputes having arisen, or their being necessary for other reasons, permanent boundary marks were required, they have also been built of masonry, but smaller and of a different shape. The triple boundary pillars are square masonry blocks, whilst the ordinary boundary pillars are round; total height three feet, of which 1½ feet are below and 1½ feet above ground; diameter 1½ feet. The dimensions of the triple boundary pillars which I commenced making, and which are built over the whole of two tuhseels, Shahjehanpore and Jellalabad, and parts of a third tuhseel, Tilhur, are as follows:—Height above ground two feet, depth below ground one and a half feet, and three feet square. I found, however, that the cowherds made chess-boards on them, and lolled about or dangled their legs on them, amusing themselves by breaking away the corners and edges for mischief, and that the cattle made rubbing stones of them. All my attempts to keep the boys and cattle off by digging trenches and sticking brambles round these high square blocks proving fruitless, I hit upon another plan and altered the shape of the pillars, making them much lower, only nine inches above the ground, so that the boys could not dangle their legs if they sat on them, and the height was not convenient for a chess-board, nor could the cattle scrub their heads even against them. Except where there was cultivation immediately adjoining the pillar, I dug a trench round it at about two feet distance, and made a sloping side from the top of the pillar to the ditch. The dimension of these pillars are: height two feet, of which only nine inches are above ground level, length and breadth four feet square, so that the cubic contents of masonry are much the same as in the first pattern pillars. Another advantage of this improved pattern is that there is plenty of room on it for a plane-table or theodolite, and for the person using it as well.

I took great pains to secure good work as well as good materials, well-burnt bricks and good mortar, and the pillars built all over the Shahjehanpore tuhseel five and six years ago (*viz.*, those first built) are as good and as strong now as ever, and should last out the settlement, and then only a few should require replacing and repair.

In Pergunnah Khotar, wherever the old three-cornered boundary pillars were good and sound, I have not built new ones, as the expense is great there, and many ordinary boundary pillars at angles and on each side of tree and grass jungle and here and there through it at long intervals were necessary, and I wished to spare the Khotar zemindars all unnecessary expense.

All over the district where masonry pillars have been built a small ditch or trench has been dug, of from five to eight yards in length, along the boundary line, showing what the pillar defines, *i. e.*, the line on which it is built. This is useful everywhere, but especially at an angle. In the tree jungle of Khotar I had larger and deeper trenches made, and the earth heaped up as a pillar between them, even where masonry pillars were not necessary. These boundary marks should be kept up by the lines cut through the tree jungle being cleared of undergrowth every four or five years, and the trenches and mounds renewed, and all earth dug out of the trenches removed to a distance of eight or ten feet at least, or it washes in again in the rains.

131. The case-work for each tuhseel has been commented on in the assessment

Case-work.

reports of the different tuhseels, and I do not here repeat what has been said there. The following statement gives the total number of cases for the whole district, with the same details as are given in the separate assessment reports. The total number is 48,468, and this is more than the sum of the totals for the different tuhseels, as in all of them some cases were instituted after the reports were written, and especially in the headings of (1) rights and interests, and (2) miscellaneous; for those reports were written from time to time from

December, 1873, to June, 1874, as the figured statements were ready, and the records were nearly completed and being made over to the Collector's office :—

Total number of cases instituted and decided.	Rights and interests under Regulation VII of 1822.	Enhancement of rent.		Boundary disputes.	Partitions, perfect and imperfect.	Maafee investigations.	Appeals to Settlement Officer.	Miscellaneous.
		Acts X. of 1859 and XIV. of 1863.	Act XIX. of 1873.					
48,468	23,266	1,584	251	1,854	1,560	2,496	862	16,595

(columns: Details of cases instituted and decided.)

The only point requiring mention here is the number of appeals to the Judge from decisions in enhancement suits under Acts X. of 1859 and XIV. of 1873, the details of which are given below :—

Total number of cases decided.	Number of appeals instituted.	Disposal of appeals.		
		Decisions reversed.	Decisions altered or modified.	Decisions upheld.
1,584	207	19	62	126

The proportion of appeals instituted to cases decided is just over 13 per cent.; the proportion of decisions reversed to appeals instituted is 9·8 per cent.; of decisions altered or modified 29·4 per cent.; and of decisions upheld 60·8 per cent. With the exception of some four or five cases all these appeals are from the decisions of the Uncovenanted Deputy Collectors by whom these cases were chiefly decided.

132. Mr. Butt has been my Assistant throughout this settlement, and I have had many opportunities of reporting upon him, and the reports have been universally most favourable. He is not only a hard-working and most industrious officer, but also very sound in his judgment and his law, and a quick and accurate worker withal, taking a deep interest in his work and always going thoroughly into a subject and mastering it. Of his excellent abilities and intimate knowledge of his work the Government and Board of Revenue can form an opinion from his report (Chapter IV.) on his own assessments, and from parts of this first chapter in which reference has been made to him, and any further mention of them on my part is superfluous.

Mention of subordinates.
Mr. Butt.

Moonshee Rugbuns Sahai has been the Settlement Deputy Collector from the very commencement to the end of the settlement, and has received promotion from the list of supernumerary to that of permanent Deputy Collectors during that time. He is a painstaking and very hardworking officer, but not a fast workman, and rather given to long-winded decisions. He has done good honest work and given me satisfaction, and has always been favourably reported on.

Rugbuns Sahai.

Pundit Kanhya Lall, a Tuhseeldar in this district, was on deputation in this settlement with powers of a Deputy Collector for some five years. He is a man of good abilities, intelligence, and an excellent workman, not only at the desk but also in the field, and his decisions are always to the point and intelligible. He has been strongly recommended for permanent promotion, which he has well earned.

Kanhya Lall.

Moonshee Sudur-ood-deen was employed in this settlement as Deputy Collector for rather less than a year, and I was generally satisfied with his attestation work and decisions. He came when work was drawing to a close, and left in consequence of his services being no longer required, and one Deputy Collector sufficient.

Sudur-ood-deen.

Of the subordinate officials who have done the best and given me the greatest satifaction, I must mention Syud Fazal Ali, Serishtadar; Sheikh Imam Ali, Sudder Munserim; Fazl Huk, Munserim of the final scrutiny office, and Mr. G. J. Hashman, Head Clerk, all of whom, with the exception of Fazl Huk, were with me from almost the very commencement of the settlement to the end, and deserve to get permanent Government employ.

Other subordinate officials.

To one and all of these from Mr. Butt downwards I feel that I am deeply indebted for the zeal, perseverance and willingness with which they worked under me and assisted me, and enabled me to bring to a satisfactory conclusion the onerous work of this settlement, and I trust that as opportunity offers their services will not be overlooked or lost sight of.

SHAHJEHANPORE,

The 31st, October 1874.

ROBERT G. CURRIE,

Settlement Officer.

INDEX TO CHAPTER II.

ASSESSMENT REPORT OF TUHSEEL SHAHJEHANPORE.

CHAPTER II.

SHAHJEHANPORE TUHSEEL.

PREVIOUS to the cession and British rule, the portion of the Shahjehanpore
District which now forms the Shahjehanpore Tuhseel was
included in Pergunnahs Kant and Gola Raipore. It was first
formed into a pergunnah in 1803 A. D., shortly after the
cession, and then belonged to the Bareilly District. The *Tuhseeldaree* was established
in the small fort inside the city of Shahjehanpore. In 1813 A. D. the district of
Shahjehanpore was first formed, and Shahjehanpore fixed upon as the head-quarters:
from that time till 1869 the pergunnah of Shahjehanpore has remained unchanged,
and the boundaries unaltered. Some few exchanges of villages have been made with
other adjoining pergunnahs of this district, but they have been very insignificant and
immaterial, and have been no real alterations of the original boundaries of the pergunnah, which for many years past has constituted the "*Huzoor Tuhseel.*"

Present division of the Tuhseel into three pergunnahs.

2. Now at this present revision of settlement in 1869 the
Tuhseel has been divided into the three separate pergunnahs of
Shahjehanpore, Jumour, and Kant, in conformity with the
express orders of the Board. The river Gurra forms
the boundary between Pergunnah Shahjehanpore
and Pergunnah Jumour, Pergunnah Jumour itself
lying between the river Gurra and the Gurraie
Nulla, which last separates it from Pergunnah Kant.
The marginal statement gives the number of *mouzahs* and *muhals* in each pergunnah, and the area in
square miles.

Name of pergunnah.	Number of mouzahs.	Number of muhals.	Area of per-gunnah in square miles.
Shahjehanpore ...	194	266	156
Jumour ...	127	183	102
Kant ...	217	301	144
Whole Tuhseel ..	538	750	402

3. The Shahjehanpore Tuhseel is bounded on the east by the Kheree District of
Boundaries of the Tuhseel.
Oudh, the Sukheta *Nulla* forming the boundary; and from
where the Sukheta leaves the boundary by the Hurdui District
of Oudh on the south-east and south. The stream of the Gurra forms the boundary for some eight miles only, the greater part of the boundary between Hurdui and Shahjehanpore being arbitrary, and without any natural division. It is surrounded from south-west, round by west, up to north-east, by various pergunnahs of
the remaining three tuhseels of this district.

4. Each pergunnah has general features and quality of soil quite distinct from
Pergunnahs identical with soil circles. Pergun-nah Shahjehanpore the domut circle.
the other, and I had selected these pergunnahs as my soil
circles before they were made into separate pergunnahs.
Throughout the Shahjehanpore Pergunnah the surface of the
country is flat and level, except just where it is broken by the Khunout Nuddee, and
the soil is a good loam, called *domut; 1st domut* alone exceeding 65 per cent. of the
entire cultivated area, and the *bhoor,* which is the only really poor soil, being little over

Gouhanee	...	1·68
1st domut	...	65·75
2nd ditto	...	23·85
Mutyar	...	6·60
Bhoor	...	2·12

two per cent. Irrigation is, of course, needed in ordinary years,
but the soil retains moisture well and does not harden or crack,
and usually one watering is sufficient for wheat. The sub-soil
is moderately firm, and *kuchha* wells are constructable, as a rule, almost anywhere, the

water-level being from 15 to 17 feet below the surface. *Pools* or *gurras* are in very general use away from the strip of high light soil above the river banks, and *chirkees* everywhere. *Dhenklees* are but little used in this pergunnah out of the *khadir*.

5. Pergunnah Jumour, with the exception of a line varying in width from half to three-quarters of a mile along the right bank of the Gurra, in which the soil is similar to that of Pergunnah Shahjehanpore, lies low, and is composed of hard clay soil. The fault of this soil is its extreme hardness, in consequence of which it requires constant irrigation for the *rubbee* crops.

Pergunnah Jumour the mutyar circle.

Gouhanee	1·28
1st domut	51·70
2nd domut	11·17
Mutyar	35·29
Bhoor	·51

The soil percentages are given in the margin, but it must be borne in mind that much of the 1st *domut* has a very large admixture of clay in it, and is not equal to the average 1st *domut* of Pergunnah Shahjehanpore. This was my *mutyar* or clay soil circle. Although the water-level is nearer the surface (11 feet) than in either Pergunnahs Shahjehanpore or Kant, yet irrigation from *wells* is restricted, more difficult, and less certain,

1st.—Because a larger supply of water and more irrigation, and more frequent waterings are necessary for this dry, thirsty, cracking soil ; and

2nd.—Because, as a rule, the water-level is in quicksand, through which these *kuchha* wells cannot be carried, and the yield of water is poor. The principal source of irrigation is from ponds and tanks and two natural flood drains (*nullas*), called the Bhugsee and Gurraie *Nullas*, which are dammed at intervals to retain the rain-water and natural drainage into them. In a very rainy season a great part of this pergunnah is flooded several feet deep for days together, the rice and other rain harvest crops being much injured thereby, and the land does not dry soon enough to allow of its being ploughed and sown with the spring crop (*rubbee*) ; and in dry seasons there is a great want of irrigation, as the ponds and drainage lines afford a short supply of water, and the wells are bad. The *dhenklee* is more common than any other kind of well in this pergunnah, and the *pool* or *gurra* quite the exception.

6. Pergunnah Kant was my *bhoor* or sandy soil circle, and, with the exception of the valley of the Gurraie, it is all composed of light sandy soil, the denomination 2nd class *domut* being here in reality 1st class *bhoor*, and the *bhoor* downright sand. The *rentee* or *chirkee* and *dhenklee* are the kinds of wells most used in this pergunnah, as the soil is too sandy and friable to allow of *pools* being at all generally constructable. The average depth of the water

Pergunnah Kant the Bhoor circle.

Gouhanee,	1·11
1st domut,	31·71
2nd domut,	32·05
Mutyar,	9·81
Bhoor,	25·32

from the surface on the *bhoor*, omitting the valley of the Gurraie, is 14 feet, or anything from 13 to 18 feet, according to the surface level. These *kuchha* wells can be made almost anywhere, even in the worst *bhoor*, excepting that *bhoor* with a hard foundation like sandstone, off which the sand blows. This sandy soil, however, though of course not equal in productive quality to the *domut* of Pergunnah Shahjehanpore, retains moisture well, and produces very fair crops in ordinary years without the necessity of general or extensive irrigation. It also drinks up the water so fast that water can be taken a much less distance than in the *domut* and clay soil. The surface too is uneven, and hence promiscuous and general irrigation is not resorted to, except in very dry seasons.

7. The crops grown throughout the Tuhseel are very similar in kind, though not in quality or in the percentages of each kind, in every direction, and do not vary in the different pergunnahs with the quality of the soil as much as might be expected, at all events not in the spring (*rubbee*) harvest. Wheat is grown indiscriminately in good and poor soil, and even a poor crop

Produce of the soil.

of wheat is preferred to a fair or good crop of barley. Sugarcane is, of course, more grown in Pergunnah Shahjehanpore, and in the best parts of Pergunnah Jumour along the Gurra, than in the remainder of Pergunnah Jumour or in Pergunnah Kant, from the proximity of the city and the Rosa Sugar Factory, as well as from the superior natural advantages of soil and irrigation. The percentage of sugarcane to the total cultivated area is 8 per cent. in Shahjehanpore and 7½ in Jumour, but only 2¾ per cent. in Kant. Land prepared for sugarcane the following year is excepted from this, and the percentages of it for the three pergunnahs are, respectively, 6½, 3¼, and ¾.

The autumn (*khureef*) and spring (*rubbee*) harvests are just equal in Pergunnah Jumour, but in both Shahjehanpore and Kant the spring (*rubbee*) harvest is over 56 per cent. *Jowar*, *bajra*, and rice are the principal grain products of the autumn harvest; the percentage of *jowar* (8) being largest in Shahjehanpore, of rice (2·7) in Jumour, and of *bajra* (23) in Kant. The nature of the soil of each pergunnah is recognisable at once from the products of the autumn harvest, but not from those of the spring harvest. In the spring harvest wheat and gram are the principal crops, and very little barley is grown. Even in Pergunnah Kant the percentage of barley alone is only 5¾, and of wheat and barley mixed 3½, and far smaller in the other two pergunnahs. Full details of the areas and crops grown will be found in the crop statement in Appendix A., but the percentages of some of the principal staples are here given for ready reference.

Pergunnah.	PERCENTAGES OF PRINCIPAL CROPS. Rubbee or Spring Harvest.					Khureef or Autumn Harvest.					
						Sugarcane.					
	Wheat.	Gram.	Barley.	Wheat and barley mixed.	Mussoor.	Actual.	Land prepared for next year.	Jowar.	Bajra.	Rice.	Cotton.
Shahjehanpore, 1274-75 F. S.	36½	10	2¾	1½	3¼	8	6¼	8	5½	5¾	4½
Ditto, 1280 F. S.	33½	14	3¼	3½	½	10¼	8½	5¾	4¼	7¼	3½
Jumour, 1274-75 F. S.	33¾	8¾	2	1	2	7½	3¼	4¼	2	27	3
Ditto, 1280 F. S.	26¾	11½	1¾	¾	1¾	8½	6½	2	1½	29¾	3½
Kant, 1275-76 F. S.	35	6¾	5¼	3¼	2¾	2¾	¾	3	23	6½	1½
Ditto, 1280 F. S.	29¼	8¼	3¼	3½	¼	4½	2	2	25¼	8¼	1¾

The lands bearing two crops are of small extent, and, as a rule, the second crop is a poor one, unless the first crop happened to be a failure.

Pergunnah.	*Percentage of double crop lands.* Year of measurement.	1280 F. S.
Shahjehanpore, ...	4¾	6¾
Jumour, ...	8½	9
Kant, ...	3¾	5½

The reason of the double crop lands being more extensive in Pergunnah Jumour than in the other two pergunnahs is that the first crop is, almost without an exception, the common rice (*sáthee*), the principal autumn crop of the pergunnah, succeeded by gram or wheat, or wheat and barley mixed. The areas in which rice is succeeded by sugarcane are very small, being only ¼ per cent. in Shahjehanpore and Kant, and ½ per cent. in Jumour. The *kucchiana* or garden crop lands are also of small extent, being 1 per cent. in Shahjehanpore, 1½ in Jumour, and ½ in Kant. The cultivation of cotton is of the lowest order. No pains whatever are taken about it, and it appears to me that cotton is sown in almost the worst land, and not at all cared for or tended, but just allowed to take its chance. The produce is not sufficient for the necessities of the village residents even. It is extensively imported in country carts from across the Ganges. Indian corn is also very little grown, and it is conspicuous by its almost entire absence; as are also the dyes, indigo and safflower.

8. The city of Shahjehanpore is some 250 years old, having been founded in the reign of the Emperor Shah Jehan by Nawab Buhadoor Khan, Pathan, and named after the reigning Emperor. Many of the *mohullas* were called after his sons and immediate relatives, and still retain those names. There are now two principal grain and general markets, the one called Carewgunge, having been started under Carew and Co. of the Rosa Factory, and the other *Buhadoorgunge* (also called Saundersgunge), which have almost entirely monopolised the trade from the various small *bazaars* and *gunges* of 10 and 15 years ago. The population of the city, including some of the adjacent villages, which are reckoned as *mohullas* of the city, but exclusive of the civil lines and cantonments, is 74,000, of whom 8,500 are cultivators, the Hindoos nearly doubling the Mahomedans. On the total, however, the Mahomedans exceed

Cultivators.			Non-cultivators.				Grand Total
Hindoos.	Mahome-dans.	Total.	Hindoos.	Mahome-dans.	Christians.	Total.	
5,510	2,989	8,499	29,299	36,188	17	65,504	74,003

the Hindoos, being, in round numbers, 39,000 against 35,000. The Christians are all of them connected with the Lodhipore American Mission. The population of the adjacent villages included in the above is 7,713, of which the cultivators are 3,376, more than two-thirds being Hindoos; and the same proportion holds good in the non-cultivators. This specification is here made, as the inhabitants of these villages will appear again in the pergunnah population statements, irrespective of the city proper.

The only manufacture and trade of the city is sugar. Refined and edible sugars, *konja* or *kund*, *cheenee* and *misree*, are only made for home consumption, and not for export. What are exported are, (1) the first manufactured sugar *khánd* or *shukkur*, and (2) the coarse unrefined article called *goor*, a species of imperfectly manufactured coarse brown sugar, which are taken from the city to various parts of the country. The *khánd* goes across the Jumna through Delhi to Goorgaon and Hissar, and through Muttra to Bhurtpore, Jeypore, Jodhpore, &c., and the *goor* in the Gwalior direction, in country carts; the exchange imports being chiefly salt and cotton, but also iron and *ghee*. The Rosa Factory is two miles away from the city, and is famous for its sugar, and well known all over Bengal, as it supplies private families and merchants in almost every station in the North-Western Provinces, Oudh, and the Punjab with sugar, besides having the Government contract for rum and sugar for the British army. It is a sugar refinery and distillery, and not a manufactory, as it does not press the juice from the cane, but purchases the concentrated juice or *ráb*, and coarse molasses or *sheera*, from the *ráb* dealers and *khundsárees*.

9. Besides the city of Shahjehanpore, there is no town in the three pergunnahs. Jumour, from which the pergunnah has been named, is only an ordinary village, on the road between Shahjehanpore and Futtehgurh. Kant is little more than a village now, but is an old place and has been a place of some importance, and is still called *Kusbáh* Kant. Its population is nearly 4,000, chiefly Hindoo and agricultural, but the Mahomedan element is much larger than is found in the generality of large villages, and in this particular it ranks as a *Kusbáh*.

Creed.	Agricultu-ral.	Non-agri-cultural.	Total.
Hindoo	1,419	941	2,360
Mahomedan ...	1,011	576	1,587
Total, ...	2,430	1,517	3,947

10. There are only six villages in the three pergunnahs in which markets are held, the greater number of course being in Kant, as furthest from the city, and not within easy reach of Jellalabad. All of

Pergunnah.	Name of village.	Number of days in the week.	Names of the days.
Shahjehanpore,...	Sehra Mow, ...	2	Monday and Friday.
Jumour, ...	Pusgowan, alias Kasimgunge.	2	Saturday and Tuesday.
Kant, ...	Koorya, ...	2	Sunday and Wednesday.
" ...	Monuwurgunge,	3	Saturday, Tuesday and Thursday.
" ...	Kant khas, ...	2	Sunday and Thursday.
" ...	Goomtah, ...	2	Saturday and Tuesday.

these are large villages and contain many inhabitants besides the zemindars and mere cultivators, with the exception of Goomtah, which is a little bit of a village, only a few mud huts; and very little shelter obtainable on a wet day for the people who attend the market.

11. There are no statistics procurable of the population of the pergunnah at last settlement, but from the accompanying return of villages and hamlets which have been established during the last 30 years, it is probable that the increase has been considerable. At all events the fact that

Inhabited and uninhabited mouzahs and hamlets.

Pergunnah.		At last Settlement.			During currency of Settlement between 1838 and 1869.		Total at present Settlement.		
		Inhabited.	Uninhabited.	Total.	Newly inhabited.	Become deserted.	Inhabited.	Uninhabited.	Total.
Shahjehanpore,...	Mouzahs or villages, ...	161	33	194	2	...	163	31	194
	Hamlets, ...	31	4	35	10	3	38	7	45
	Total, ...	192	37	229	12	3	201	38	239
Jumour. ...	Mouzahs or villages, ...	112	15	127	1	...	113	14	127
	Hamlets, ...	14	6	20	9	1	22	7	29
	Total, ...	126	21	147	10	1	135	21	156
Kant, ...	Mouzahs or villages, ...	165	52	217	11	1	175	42	217
	Hamlets, ...	21	18	39	24	1	44	19	63
	Total, ...	186	70	256	35	2	219	61	280
Total of Tuhseel,	Mouzahs or villages, ...	438	100	538	14	1	451	87	538
	Hamlets, ...	66	28	94	43	5	104	33	137
	Villages and hamlets,...	504	128	632	57	6	555	120	675

14 *mouzahs* and 43 hamlets have been populated, and became inhabited during the last settlement, and that only one (1) mouzah and five (5) hamlets have become uninhabited, speaks very plainly of the increasing prosperity of this part of the country. Of course those villages and hamlets which were temporarily deserted during the mutiny in 1857-58 and were again occupied have been omitted from the above details. As for the uninhabited *mouzahs* and hamlets, they are most of them small, and situated amongst or near populous villages, and are most of them virtually outlying hamlets of some village, and have never been inhabited, and do not need to be. But some of them are in the thinly, or, perhaps, more properly speaking, less densely populated parts of the pergunnahs, and would benefit greatly by the location of cultivators within their areas.

2 T

12. In Pergunnahs Shahjehanpore and Jumour the average* population and areas of the *mouzahs* coincide very closely. And in all three of the pergunnahs the average rural population per square mile

Average area of mouzahs, and average population.

is high and very equal. From the rural population of Pergunnah Shahjehanpore have been omitted the inhabitants of the city proper

* Pergunnah.	Number of mouzahs.	Average area in acres.	Average area in square miles.	Average rural population.	
				Per mouzah.	Per square mile.
Shahjehanpore,	194	510	·79	374	465
Jumour, ...	127	514	·79	363	453
Kant, ...	217	425	·66	294	443
Whole Tuhseel,	538	478	·75	339	454

and of cantonments. Inclusive of the city and the native population of cantonments, the average per square mile for Pergunnah Shahjehanpore is 920 individuals. These details are given from my settlement returns. There were not three separate pergunnahs at the census of 1865. By the census of 1872 the average rural population is nearly 500 for each pergunnah and for the whole Tuhseel.

13. In the average of cultivators and their families, as also of adult cultivators,

Cultivators : their creed, caste, and proportion to cultivated area.

per square mile of cultivation (all cultivation, whether paying revenue or revenue free, being here included), Pergunnah Shahjehanpore stands first, and Pergunnah Kant last. The

†Pergunnah.	Hindoo Cultivators.					Mahomedan Cultivators.						Average per square mile of cultivation.	
	Adults.		Minors.			Adults.		Minors.					
					Total.					Total.	Total cultivators.	Of cultivators and their families.	Of adult cultivators.
	Male.	Female.	Male.	Female.		Male.	Female.	Male.	Female.				
Shahjehanpore.	18,686	15,992	9,826	7,618	52,122	2,772	2,514	1,543	1,281	8,110	60,232	598	392
Jumour,...	12,415	10,945	6,879	4,339	34,578	630	560	359	263	1,812	36,390	535	361
Kant, ...	18,809	14,694	9,175	5,909	48,587	1,027	948	649	448	3,072	51,659	465	320
Totals, ...	49,910	41,631	25,880	17,866	135,287	4,429	4,022	2,551	1,992	12,994	148,281	527	356

above statement gives the full details of the cultivating population of each pergunnah, from which it will be seen that the Mahomedan cultivators number under thirteen thousand (13,000), whilst the Hindoo cultivators exceed one hundred and thirty-five thousand (135,000). The largest proportion of Mahomedan cultivators is, as might be expected, in Pergunnah Shahjehanpore, as there are close upon three thousand in the city alone. Amongst the Mussulman cultivators, Pathans (Rohillas) are by far

† The figures according to the Census of 1872 are as follows for agriculturists :—

Pergunnah.				Hindoo.	Mahomedan.	Total Agriculturists.
Shahjehanpore,...	...	...	...	53,035	7,775	60,810
Jumour,	...	...	...	38,173	1,459	39,632
Kant,	...	...	...	46,020	3,205	49,225
Totals,		...	...	137,228	12,439	149,657

the most numerous, as they form the principal Mussulman population of the district. There is no part of any one of the three pergunnahs in which Rajpoots do not abound, and, as a rule, they are found distributed in clans, though there is always a sprinkling of other clans throughout the country of any one clan. The largest and most prevalent clans in this tuhseel are Báchil, Chouhán, Ponwar, Ráthor, Gour, and Kásib, and in this order, but members of the following clans are also numerous, viz., Bais, Budhoria, Chundéla, Goutum, Junghára, Tomar, and Sombunsee. The best cultivators who are at all plentiful are the Kisáns, Káchees, and Chumárs. They are not, as a rule, to be found in the parent villages by themselves, but often in the hamlets, and some are all distributed very universally throughout all the large and populous villages. Játs are conspicuous by their entire absence, as also Lodhas, Tuggas, and Goojurs; but Brahmins and Aheers are plentiful, and are very fair average cultivators, better than the Thakoors, but not coming up to the Koormees and Kisáns, and others mentioned amongst the best. The following seven castes compose the bulk of the cultivators in the tuhseel, and are arranged in the following table in order according to their numerical strength in each pergunnah :—

Pergunnah.	Kisáns.	Chumár.	Thakoor.	Káchee.	Brahmin.	Aheer.	Mahomedan.
Shahjehanpore, ...	1	2	5	6	4	7	3
Jumour, ...	1	3	2	4	6	5	7
Kant, ...	6	2	1	3	5	4	7
Whole tuhseel, ...	1	2	3	4	5	6	7

The Kisáns are far the most numerous, out-numbering any two of the other castes except Thakoors and Chumárs. Thakoors and Chumárs together about equal Brahmins, Káchees and Aheers together, and are about one-fourth more than the Kisáns alone. There are very few Koormees in this tuhseel.

14. Amongst the proprietary tenures, the *zemindaree* preponderates very largely in all three of the pergunnahs, the total number of *zemindaree*

Proprietary tenures.

muhals (not *mouzahs*, but separate properties in *mouzahs*,) being 521 against 229 of the *putteedaree* tenure. There are only two really *bhyachara* villages in the tuhseel, and they are in Pergunnah Kant. This, as well as the great prevalence of the *zemindaree* tenure in the *puttees* of the *putteedaree* villages, is owing to the very extensive partition and division of property. In fact, there are no *puttees* to speak of in either Shahjehanpore or Jumour in which the subordinate holding is other than *zemindaree*, and there are only 53 in

Pergunnah.	Zemindaree muhals.	Putteedaree and bhyachara muhals.	Total.
Shahjehanpore ...	222	44	266
Jumour ...	144	39	183
Kant ...	155	146	301
Total ...	521	229	750

Kant, including the two *bhyachara* villages. I attribute this very extensive subdivision of property into separate holdings to the desire of the proprietors to make their payments to Government direct, and not through a *lumberdar*. In other words, to the unnecessarily strict rules which have only quite lately, within the last two or three years, been relaxed, insisting on payment of revenue through the constituted head-men (*lumberdars*), and the steady refusal of allowing any increase to the number of *lumberdars* during

Pergunnah.	Putteedaree muhals.	Number of puttees in those muhals.
Shahjehanpore ...	44	279
Jumour ...	39	202
Kant ...	146	777
Total ...	229	1,258

the currency of the settlement. There are no entire *maafee mouzahs* or *muhals*, but the greater part of Shahjehanpore khas is *maafee*.

15. Although the *zemindaree* tenure prevails to so large an extent in this tuhseel,

Residence, creed, and caste of proprietors.

yet there is not one single large landed proprietor of any importance, not indeed one who owns ten or even seven entire *mouzahs* in this tuhseel alone, though there are several who own property here which

Caste.	Entire mouzahs.	Entire muhals, parts of mouzahs.	Shares in other mouzahs and muhals.
Pathan	89	94	17
Syud	11	1	...
Sheikh	7	5	...
Total of Mussulmans ...	107	100	17
Brahmin ...	16	5	1
Kaiyuth ...	11	7	...
Bankers and money-lenders,	26	9	8
Miscellaneous ...	1	4	...
Total of Hindoos ...	54	25	9
City Total ...	161	125	26

added to property in other pergunnahs comes up to that amount. There are also several Pathan families residing in the city whose property is extensive, but from the custom of dividing it amongst all the sons, no one individual has a property of any size or importance. Residents of the city, according to the marginal statement, are proprietors of 161 entire *mouzahs* and 125 entire *muhals*, besides owning shares in 26 other *mouzahs* and *muhals;* non-resident proprietors, *viz.*, those not residing anywhere within the tuhseel or in the city, are but few, and own in all 48 *mouzahs* and *muhals*, but most of these are residents of the district, and real absentee proprietors are almost nominal, except that many of the city *mahajuns* are as genuine absentee proprietors as if they lived two districts off. Of the proprietors resident in the pergunnah and usually

Caste.	Entire mouzahs.	Entire muhals, parts of mouzahs.	Shares in mouzahs and muhals.
Rajpoot ...	94	73	55
Brahmin ...	15	28	11
Pathan ...	10	28	3
Kaiyuth ...	14	6	4

in one of the villages owned by them, and resident proprietors in the strict sense of the term, the Thakoors or Rajpoots are far the most numerous, and after them Brahmins, Pathans, and Kaiyuths, according to the detail given in the margin.

16. The area of land held *seer* by proprietors (part only of which is cultivated

Distribution of cultivated area.

by themselves, and part sub-let to cultivators,) amounts in the whole tuhseel to 25,097 acres, or just under 14 per cent. of the total cultivated area. In Shahjehanpore much of this is *quasi* nominal *seer*, not cultivated by the proprietor himself or with his own cattle and servants, but sub-let to tenants who

Distribution of cultivated area of revenue-paying lands according to separate holdings.

Name of pergunnah.	"Seer" of proprietors actually cultivated by them or sub-let.			CULTIVATED BY TENANTS.									
				With right of occupancy.			Without occupancy rights, tenants-at-will.			Total area cultivated by tenants, irrespective of their having or not having right of occupancy.			
	Number of khatas or separate holdings.	Total cultivated area in acres.	Average of cultivated area per khata in acres.	Number of khatas or separate holdings.	Total cultivated area in acres.	Average of cultivated area per khata.	Number of khatas.	Total cultivated area.	Average per khata.	Total number of "khatas" or separate holdings of all tenants.	Total cultivated area in acres of all tenants.	Average of cultivated area per khata.
Shahjehanpore ...	480	5,233	10·91	12,469	44,216	3·54	6,423	15,008	2·33	16,650	59,224	3·55
Jumonr ...	516	4,465	8·65	9,202	30,571	3·32	4,639	8,365	1·80	12,909	38,936	3·01
Kant ..	2,012	15,399	7·65	16,606	44,533	2·70	6,619	10,858	1·64	20,925	55,691	2·66
Total ...	3,008	25,097	8·15	38,277	119,620	3·12	17,681	34,231	1·93	50,484	153,851	3·04

cannot acquire rights of occupancy. In Jumour there is much less of this, and in Kant very little, as in those pergunnahs the *seer* is, as a rule, cultivated by the small resident proprietors themselves. The average separate holding is rather over eight acres for the whole tuhseel, being highest in Shahjehanpore, where the *seer* is to a great extent *quasi* nominal, and lowest, but of much greater amount, in Kant, where it is genuine. The separate holdings (*khatas*) are for each *mouzah* and *muhal*, and, as in Shahjehanpore, there are many zemindars who have *seer* in several villages, and a few such in Jumour and Kant, therefore the actual number of *seer* holders is less, and the actual *average* per individual is larger than that shown in the marginal statement, but the area shown is correct. The actual difference, too, in the average per separate individual is not very considerable in Shahjehanpore (about 2½ acres, *viz.*, 13½ acres instead of 10·91), and hardly appreciable in Jumour and Kant. The same holds good, only to a larger extent, as regards tenants, if a separate holding be taken to represent the total cultivating occupancy of an individual or a family. The areas are strictly cor-

* Pergunnah.	Percentages of cultivated area held.		
	Seer.	By cultivators with right of occupancy.	By tenants-at-will.
Shahjehanpore, ...	8·12	68·37	23·51
Jumour, ...	10·14	70·34	19·42
Kant, ...	25·63	63·01	15·36
Whole tuhseel, ...	13·96	66·78	19·26

rect, and the proportion of lands held by each kind of tenant are correct,* and the number of *khatas* are correct *for each separate mouzah and muhal,* but the same cultivators may, and in many cases do, appear twice over and oftener in the total number of separate *khatas.* There are two reasons for this :—*First*, because a cultivator with right of occupancy frequently holds several fields as a tenant-at-will, and thus has two separate holdings in the same *mouzah.* To correct this, the area held by tenants with right of occupancy and by tenants-at-will has therefore been first shown separately ; and then *all* lands held by cultivators have been amalgamated, and in this statement the two holdings of a cultivator with right of occupancy, who also holds some lands as a tenant-at-will, have been treated as one holding. *Second*, because there are many uninhabited *mouzahs*, besides a great number of separate *muhals* and *puttees* in a *mouzah*, and the same cultivators hold lands not only in the village in which they live, but in one or more adjacent villages or *muhals*, or *puttees*, and will therefore appear as the occupants of separate holdings in each and every such village and *muhal*, and *puttee.* This is most strikingly illustrated by Pergunnah Kant, in which the population per square mile, and the agricultural population per square mile of cultivation, is smaller than in either of the other two pergunnahs, and consequently the average per separate holding should be larger, but it is smaller. And this is amply accounted for by the large number of uninhabited *mouzahs* and extensive sub-division of *mouzahs* into *muhals* and *puttees*, from the rent-rolls of which the separate holdings (*khatas*) are extracted. It is almost impossible to amalgamate these separate holdings, so that each separate holding shall represent the *total* cultivating occupancy of one individual, or one family cultivating in common. The approximate average, however, may be arrived at very closely by assuming that each separate cultivating occupancy or joint family consists of five (5) individuals, and then the result comes out 5¼ acres per separate holding in Shahjehanpore, 6 acres in Jumour, and 7 acres in Kant. This includes all cultivators, both proprietors and tenants, and all cultivated lands, whether paying revenue (*khalsa*) or free of revenue (*maafee*). For tenants only, exclusive of proprietary cultivators, it would be a little lower.

17. In order to compare the rents paid by the various castes and classes of cul-

Comparison of rates paid by the various castes and classes of cultivators.

tivators, I have had a statement prepared which will be found in the appendix (B). I have selected a number of villages from each pergunnah with the view of obtaining as fair results as possible, unbiassed and unaffected by any influence of relationship or religion. Selections, I am well aware, are open to suspicion, and in a case of this sort (*judicious*) selection could be used so as to obtain any preconceived and desired result. I have, however, selected villages, not with the view of proving by statistics a prejudged opinion, but in order to avoid all the various causes which tend to make the result of the statistics unreliable as a fair sample and pattern of the custom and existing state of things. Such, for instance, as Thakoors being the principal cultivators in a village, the proprietor whereof is a resident and one of their own kith and kin; or of Brahmin cultivators prevailing largely in a village owned by a Hindoo. Statistics of the entire tuhseel, comprising every village, would doubtless have been more satisfactory, but that was out of the question, as the labour of compiling them would have been so enormous. These statements are intended to show the difference between the rates of rent paid by cultivators of various castes, both with and without rights of occupancy, and also between the two classes, irrespective of caste, viz., cultivators with rights of occupancy and tenants-at-will. The result appears to be that in the matter of caste and creed, apart from the presence or absence of right of occupancy, there is observed the broad division between the higher and respectable castes and classes, the *sufédposh*, on the one hand, and the inferior castes or lower orders, the *lungothposh*, on the other hand. The former, or *sufédposh* division, includes Brahmins, Thakoors, Pathans, Synds, and Aheers, and the latter, or *lungothposh*, the other Mussulmans, Kisáns, and Káchees, and miscellaneous castes. The comparison must be made for each pergunnah separately, and not in the totals, as in the totals the higher or lower rent following the quality of soil of the pergunnah has an undue weight, and the totals in reality are not fair averages. In two out of the three pergunnahs the tenants-at-will pay slightly higher rates on the whole than tenants with rights of occupancy, whilst in the third (Jumour) they pay less. This, I am satisfied, is owing to the lands held by the tenants-at-will being the poorest, and decidedly inferior to those held by the occupancy tenants. Individual instances will show that, as a rule, recent cultivators, tenants-at-will, are paying considerably higher rates than old cultivators with rights of occupancy, less perhaps in Jumour than in Shahjehanpore and Kant, but undoubtedly so, nevertheless, there also.

18. In 1869, when the assessment of this tuhseel was made, there was no metalled road connecting Shahjehanpore city or cantonments with any place of importance, or even leading five miles out from Shahjehanpore in any direction. Since then a metalled road has been completed from Seetapore on the east, and to the Trunk Road at Kuttra on the north-west, thus connecting Shahjehanpore with Lucknow (through Seetapore) on the one side, and with Bareilly on the other. The *kuchha* or unmetalled road across Pergunnah Jumour and through Pergunnah Kant down to Jellalabad, where it meets the Trunk Road between Bareilly and Futtehgurh, was, and still is, in parts so excessively sandy, and was in others so low (it has now been raised), that heavily-laden carts could not travel it without difficulty at any time of the year, and in the rains it was often impassable for days together, and sometimes even for weeks. The metalled Trunk Road between Bareilly and Futtehgurh passes for some nine miles through the south-western end of Pergunnah Kant. It will then be easily understood that the district has, till quite lately, within two years, been suffering under very great disadvantages of land transport. In fact the manager of the Rosa Sugar Factory wrote as follows in answer to my enquiries on the subject in 1869 :—" In good rains the roads " here are next to impassable. Carters are averse to taking loads, and if they meet " with unfavourable weather, may be stationary for days. We therefore arrange for " boats (of about 250 maunds burden) as soon as there is any heavy fall of rain and " send to the rail at Cawnpore." These boats are sent down the Gurra, and also down the Ramgunga from Kolaghat in the Jellalabad Tuhseel. The Gurra is not navigable for anything except very small craft between November and June. The Oudh and Rohilkhund Railway traverses a large portion of Pergunnah Shahjehanpore. It was commenced just as the revised jummas were declared, and was opened between Lucknow and Shahjehanpore as the assessments of the entire district were completed, and up to Bareilly in November 1873, when this report was being written. It will doubtless cause very marked changes by the immense facility for transport which it will afford.

Means of communication.

19. The only other river in the tuhseel besides the Gurra is the Khunout, which
is a small one, and rather a stream than a river. Firewood is
The Khunout and
Gurra.
floated down this, but there is no navigation whatever upon it.
It enters Pergunnah Shahjehanpore in the north, and joins
the Gurra just below the city of Shahjehanpore, and about a mile above the Rosa
Factory; weed (*siwar*), used by the native sugar manufacturers for refining the coarse
sugar, is also floated down this stream. Neither of these rivers afford any extensive
irrigation, as they are not dammed, nor is the water turned out of them into
reservoirs or stored in any way. Water is raised from the Gurra along both
banks by the ordinary lever (*dhenklee*), and sometimes by basket lifts (*behree*), just for
the immediately adjoining lands to the distance of only a few fields. There is also
irrigation by basket lifts from the Khunout, but only for the valley lands, and these
often do not require irrigation, as they are flooded during the rains, and naturally
moist from their position. The Khunout has a well-defined valley with high banks on
either side, and the stream wanders through this valley sometimes on one side and
sometimes on the other, but it does not change its course at all. The Gurra, on the
other hand, has no defined valley or trough, nor any high ridge or broken banks, and
does change its course within certain limits very considerably, and the alluvion and
diluvion throughout its course from where it first enters until it leaves this tuhseel is
very considerable. In its course through the tuhseel it is in some parts the boundary
of villages and estates, and not in others, but from the point where it becomes the
boundary between the North-Western Provinces and Oudh, the stream is rigidly and
invariably the boundary. The Gurra has been mentioned as the boundary between
Pergunnahs Shahjehanpore and Jumour, but of course where the stream is not the
boundary of a village, that village is not partly in one and partly in the other pergunnah, but wholly in the pergunnah in which the main body of the area and principal inhabited site is situated. Where the stream is within the area of a *mouzah*, the
revenue has been assessed for the full term of the settlement, as alluvion and diluvion
counterbalance each other. In the event of extraordinary and sudden injury caused
by the river, the proprietors might claim relief under the ordinary rules in force for
the treatment of cases of alluvion and diluvion, but this is highly improbable. Where
the stream is the boundary, and loss of area on one side is gain to a village on the other
side, and *vice versâ*, separate alluvial *muhals* of lands liable to fluvial action have been
formed, the assessment whereof is liable to periodical revision without the application
of the proprietors of those estates.

20. The following figured statement gives the principal divisions of the area for
Figured statement of
area for each pergunnah
and for whole tuhseel at
present and last settle-
ment.
each pergunnah, further sub-divisions of soil of the cultivated
area appearing in the statements of the assessable area only
given in appendices C. and D :—

Name of Pergunnah.	Total area in acres.	AREA EXCLUDED FROM ASSESSMENT.			MALGOOZARRE OR ASSESSABLE AREA.							
		Barren, including roads, &c., and Cantonments.	Maafee.	Total.	Culturable.			Cultivated.				Total assessable.
					Old unbroken waste.	New fallow.	Baghs.	Irrigated.	Not irrigated.	Total.		
Shahjehanpore,	99,810	14,100	4,239	18,339	12,603	836	3,575	32,574	31,823	64,457		81,471
Jumour, ...	64,974	7,535	506	8,041	11,706	551	1,295	22,162	21,239	43,401		56,933
Kant, ...	92,244	5,912	575	6,487	10,862	1,282	2,523	25,725	45,365	71,090		85,757
Whole tuhseel,	2,57,028	27,547	5,320	32,867	35,171	2,649	7,393	80,461	98,487	1,78,948		2,24,161
Ditto last set- tlement.	2,53,070	38,729	7,885	46,614	43,019	11,333	Included partly in old	78,082 waste land	74,167 partly in	1,52,249		2,06,591 barren.

N. B.—These areas and figures were obtained and the report was written before the settlement misls
had undergone the final scrutiny previous to their being made over to the Collector's record office, and also
before the completion of the No. IV. General Statement. Hence the areas of this report differ slightly
from those of the No. IV. Statement, but the variation is slight and immaterial, and for all practical purposes the figures of this report are just as correct as those of the No. IV. Statement.

The increase in the total area by the present plane-table measurement over the survey area of last settlement is only 3,958 acres, less than 2 per cent., and is due merely to difference of measurement. The decrease in the barren area is owing to more careful definition of barren and culturable areas. It is in reality much greater than is at first sight apparent, as upwards of 3,000 acres are Military cantonments, and a great portion of this was formerly in the cultivated area, the cantonments being recent, since the mutiny of 1857. The decrease in the *maafee* area is owing to resumption of life-grants and confiscations for rebellion in 1857-58, as also to the absorption into the *khalsa* of a number of petty *maafees* whereof no traces nor of their grantees could be found at the re-investigation of all *maafees* in the present revision of settlement.

21. Of the entire *malgoozaree* or assessable area in the tuhseel, the cultivated area is 80 per cent., whilst the culturable waste is 20 per cent. From this, however, must be deducted the areas under *baghs*, 7,393 acres, and the new fallow, 2,649 acres, which reduce the percentage of actual unbroken culturable waste to below 16 per cent. There is less culturable waste proper (12¾ per cent. of the *malgoozaree* area) in Pergunnah Kant than in either of the other two pergunnahs, but most of that is good and is confined, what is not merely nominal, to about five and twenty villages, some of them along the Gurraie Nulla, several on the Oudh borders, and one in particular, Sikunderpore Kullan, in the south-west corner of the pergunnah. In Pergunnah Shahjehanpore it is 15¼ per cent. of the *malgoozaree* area, and is situated chiefly along the Oudh border and in villages adjoining the Sukheta Nulla. In Pergunnah Jumour it is 20½ per cent. of the *malgoozaree* area, but is less likely to be cultivated than in the other two pergunnahs, from its being such excessively hard low-lying clay soil, and much of it very poor. Some of it also is more or less valuable for firewood, thatching grass, and grazing, and rather out of the way and in thinly-populated parts of the pergunnah. The area under groves (*baghs*) amounts to 7,393 acres for the whole tuhseel, and is 3¼ per cent. of the assessable area. But the groves themselves are by existing orders* exempted from assessment so long as they remain, and the land is occupied by the trees. The areas and percentages for the three pergunnahs separately are as follows :—

Side note: Details of the malgoozaree or assessable area.

*Side note: * Board's Circular No. 22, dated 20th October, 1869.*

Shahjehanpore, ... 3,575 acres, 4¼ per cent. of assessable area.
Jumour, ... 1,295 ,, 2¼ ,, ,,
Kant, ... 2,523 ,, 3 ,, ,,

22. The total increase in cultivation amounts to 26,699 acres, being at the rate of 17¼ per cent. This, however, is by no means all *new* cultivation; some portion is caused by the resumption and confiscation of revenue-free lands, and a very large portion (at least 8,500 acres out of the 11,333 fallow, recently abandoned at last settlement, owing to the famine of 1838-39 A. D.) is merely the re-cultivation of lands which were formerly cultivated and only lying fallow for a year or two. But a considerable area of cultivation has been taken up for cantonments of what was cultivation at last settlement. This is almost identical with, and may be taken as a set-off against, the increase of cultivation in the revenue-paying area, from lapse and confiscation of revenue-free lands. The actual increase of *bonâ fide* new cultivation reclaimed from old unbroken waste in the past 30 years since the last settlement is therefore, in round numbers, 18,000 acres, or rather less than 12 per cent. on the former cultivated area.

Side note: Increase in cultivated area.

23. In the appendices (C. and D.) will be found detailed statements of the areas of the various soils, together with the amount of each which is irrigated, and from what source, as also the percentages of each of the different kinds of soils for each pergunnah separately, as well as for the whole tuhseel. The denominations of the various soils will be found

Side note: Details of soils and sources of irrigation.

explained at length in the general report, and it is sufficient to mention here that *gouhanee* is an artificial soil, and always adjoins the inhabited site, that it is not universal in all villages, but, as a rule, is only found where there are Káchee cultivators, who raise garden crops. The rest are natural denominations, and of them the 1st *domut* (or 1st-class loam) is the best, and the *bhoor* (sand) the worst. The percentages of the irrigated areas for the three pergunnahs are Shahjehanpore 50·53, Jumour 51·06, and Kant 36·19. The percentages of the details of the sources of irrigation to the total irrigated area are given in the margin. Well irrigation is, of course, the best of the three, and irrigation from ponds is the worst, from being the least certain, and liable to fail when most required. From these figured statements it is clear that Pergunnah Shahjehanpore is very considerably the best, and Pergunnah Kant the worst of the three pergunnahs of which the tuhseel is composed, and this is also evident throughout the report.

Name of Pergunnah.	Percentage of total cultivated area irrigated.	Percentage (of total irrigated area) of irrigation from various sources, viz.,		
		Wells.	Ponds, tanks and nullas.	Rivers and streams.
Shahjehanpore	50·53	73	19	8
Jumour	51·06	46	48	6
Kant	36·19	69	31	...
Total of tuhseel	45·52	64	30	6

24. Rents throughout the tuhseel are entirely in money, and the rents are calculated on the *kuchha* or village, *beegah*, which varies considerably in different villages and even in the same village, as there is no standard measure of a *kuchha beegah*. It runs, however, chiefly from 6 to 6¼ *kuchha beegahs* to the acre, and for all practical purposes may be taken as exactly 6 to the acre. All deduced and assumed rent-rates are, however, calculated on the standard acre, and are in no way affected by this variation in the village *beegah*. There are two grand divisions in money rents :—1st, rates ; 2nd, lump rents. The rates are of three kinds : —(1) soil rates ; (2) rates on tracts (*hars*); (3) all-round rates. There are no crop rates varying with the crop sown, but in all three of these kinds of rates it is usual to find one rate for cereals (*nijkaree,*) and a higher one, usually 2¼ times or treble of the *nijkaree* rate, for sugar-cane. The higher rate on sugar-cane is, however, not annual, but is taken only in the year the sugar-cane is produced, and nothing is paid for the year the land lies fallow under preparation for cane (*pundree*), so that, after all, the sugar rate is usually only half as much again in reality as the *nijkaree* rate. Also *kucchiana* or garden crops, vegetables, and the like, usually pay a separate rate, but often as a soil rate, under the denomination *gouhanee*. None of the rates are on wet and dry, or irrigated and unirrigated lands, but rather on the capability and possibility of irrigation, or the reverse,—on the assumption, in fact, that all good lands are either capable of irrigation or can do without it. Lump rents are only so much land at such a sum, and all-round rates are merely a summary rate per beegah, irrespective of quality or denomination. There are no belts or circles of artificial soil round the inhabited site, as is the almost unvarying rule in the Doab. Nor is irrigation a *sine quá non* here as it is there. Here, as a rule, wheat receives only one watering, and *kuchha* wells of one kind or another can be made in almost every field, except in the stiffest clay or the highest sand, and be in working order in a couple of days.

Rent and rent-rates.

25. In deducing and assuming rent-rates as basis of assessment, I have followed the existing custom of soil rates, and have not made separate rates for wet and dry. Average rent-rates are deduced from very large areas taken from all parts of each pergunnah wherever soil rates are found, or where the rent, by being applied to the area and denomination of soil according to the new measurements, is convertible into soil rates.

Deduced and assumed rent-rates.

4 т

The cultivated areas abstracted for soil rates, as well as the areas held at lump rents
by cultivators, from which
the soil rates were ob-
tained for each pergun-
nah, together with the resulting all-round cultivation rates, are given in
the margin for compari-
son with the standard
cultivation *rate* in the

Name of Pergunnah.	Area abstracted for soil rates.	Rate of rental per cultivated acre.	Area held at lump rents.	Rate of rental per cultivated acre.
	Acres.	Rs. a. p.	Acres.	Rs. a. p.
Shahjehanpore, ...	11,114	3 5 4	31,059	3 6 2
Jumour, ...	8,330	3 1 2	26,170	3 3 3
Kant, ...	7,165	2 5 10	34,470	2 6 10

next marginal statement. From these average rates are excluded all exceptionally
low and favourable rates and rents which are specially beneficial or otherwise suspicious as not genuine, and this is in itself a considerable enhancement on actual
average current rates and rents. The assumed rates taken for basis of new assessment
are put slightly *above* the rates so deduced, the point aimed at being the level to
which rates will rise within about the first three years after the declaration of the
new assessments, and by the time that the disturbance and enhancement of rents consequent on the revision of the Government revenue has subsided, and a temporary
equilibrium at least has been obtained. I have not attempted to deduce theoretically
correct rent-rates with reference to the original proportion between rents and produce,
and the subsequent rise in prices and depreciation of silver, nor yet to anticipate a still
further theoretical rise in prospect some 10 or 15 years hence, which may or may not
take place. I have accepted the position of rents being low and inadequate *theoretically*, as they undoubtedly are, but I have endeavoured to ascertain what the actual
present full rents and rates are, to what extent they are rising, and what may fairly be
assumed as the level which they will reach, or at all events may and should reach,
within the next three years or so after declaration of new assessments. More I could
not do. I could not in a day, or a year, or two years, effect what should have been the

gradual work of years. I
have therefore preferred
to be guided by things as
I found them, and to ac-
cept the position of facts
in preference to the arguments of theory. In ad-
dition to the soil rate, a
cultivation rent-rate has
been used as a check and
as a standard of compar-
ison. These rates are
given in the margin for
each pergunnah. The
No. III. Statement for
each pergunnah, *i. e.*, the
soil areas with the resulting rentals from these

ASSUMED RENT-RATES PER ACRE.			
Name of soil.	Name of Pergunnah.		
	Shahjehanpore.	Jumour.	Kant.
	Rs. a. p.	Rs. a. p.	Rs. a. p.
Gouhanee ...	3 0 0	7 8 0	7 0 0
1st domut ...	3 12 0	3 12 0	3 4 0
2nd ditto ...	3 0 0	3 0 0	2 8 0
Mutyar ...	2 12 0	2 8 0	2 12 0
Bhoor ...	2 4 0	2 4 0	2 0 0
Standard cultivation rate.	3 8 0	3 4 0	2 10 0

assumed rates, will be found in appendix C. already referred to, and the percentages of
the soils have already been given in paras. 5 to 7.

26. The current rentals or *nikasees* filed by the putwarees and attested in the
Settlement Department as existing at revision of assessment,
Rentals and assets ac-
tual and assumed. after correction for *seer* held at low or nominal rates, as also
(2) the estimated actual rentals, or rather assets after further
corrections for small omissions and under-renting to relatives and for *sewai* items,
and (3) the rental resulting from the assumed rent-rates, as well as (4) the gross

assumed assets on which the detailed *mouzahwar* and *muhalwar* assessments were made, are given below for each pergunnah :—

Name of Pergun-nah.	Rental in *nika-sees*, corrected for *seer* only.	Estimated actual assets.	Rental resulting from assumed rates.	Gross assumed potential assets	Percentage of gross assum-ed over actual assets, i.e., col. 5 over col. 3.
	Rs.	Rs.	Rs.	Rs.	
Shahjehanpore,...	2,11,798	2,31,850	2,28,492	2,48,440	11·98
Jumour, ...	1,36,675	1,39,725	1,41,721	1,49,420	6·94
Kant, ...	1,60,133	1,67,330	1,90,970	1,83,482	9·65
Total of tuhseel,	5,08,606	5,28,905	5,61,183	5,81,342	9·89

The *nikasees* being very correct and reliable, as a rule, throughout this tuhseel, the difference between the recorded and the actual assets is small. In Pergunnahs Shahjehanpore and Jumour the gross assets assumed in the detailed assessment of each *mouzah* and *muhal*, where the *mouzah* is divided into several distinct properties, is, as it ordinarily proves to be, in excess of the rental resulting from assumed average rates. The gross assumed assets include *sayer* or *sewai* income from uncultivated lands as well as anticipation of increased cultivation of those estates where an early extension of cultivation is expected. The full reasons for the assessment of each separate *mouzah* and estate are recorded in English, and constitute the remarks or reasons of assessment appended to the No. III. figured statement of each *mouzah* and *muhal*. In Pergunnah Kant, however, the gross assumed assets fall short of the rental resulting from assumed average rent-rates. The reasons for this are two-fold :—1st, the number of *mouzahs* below average in this pergunnah, or at all events, what I thought and estimated was the average of the pergunnah when I assumed the rates, is large and is not counterbalanced by the number of *mouzahs* above the average. Moreover, these, as a rule, are the *mouzahs* in which the rise in the new over the old assessment, and unwarranted by existing assets, was the greatest, and I found that I could not assess up to the estimated standard :—2nd, there are in this pergunnah several *mouzahs* containing a very large number of cultivating proprietors, both Raj-poots and Pathans, in poor circumstances, on which the full 50 per cent. assessment could not be imposed without the certainty of utter ruin to a great number of the shareholders. Although this pergunnah is out-and-out the worst of the three, yet the increase in revenue is the greatest (16 per cent). On finding that the total of my detailed *mouzahwar* assessments came out below my estimate for the whole pergunnah, I went over each assessment again in order to ascertain and satisfy myself whether the assessments were as high, and the revenue fixed was as much as could be fairly demanded, and I am fully convinced that no undue leniency was shown in any single instance, and that the assessment is as high as is, under the circumstances, fair and reasonable. Moreover, the gross assumed assets are nearly 10 per cent. in excess of the estimated actual assets existing just before revision. There is not one single wealthy or even well-to-do proprietor in the pergunnah, and almost all of the zemin-dars are entirely dependent on the land for their means of livelihood.

27. The following extracts quoted from another report just submitted to the Board of Revenue, in reply to a set of questions on settlement (Circular T. T. T. of 1871), will amply show the truth of what I have stated above, and it must be borne in mind that the greatest number of these pettiest of proprietors is in Pergunnah Kant :—" The following table prepared for Tuhseel Shahjehanpore shows the average " incidence of the present demand on petty proprietors, as well as on those who are

Incidence of the Govern-ment demand on, and the balance of assets remain-ing with the proprietor.

" not petty proprietors, but proprietors of average estates, for this tuhseel and dis-
" trict":—

Designation of proprietors.	Number of mahals.	Number of individuals.	Cultivated area in acres.	Government revenue.	Cesses at 10 per cent, and putwarees' fees.	Total demand (not including lumberdar's fees) paid into Government.	Balance of rental assets remaining.
Petty proprietors, ...	264	3,226	70,569	1,05,332	15,800	1,21,132	89,532
Others—not petty proprietors,...	475	597	1,08,379	1,85,339	27,800	2,13,139	1,57,539

Averages per individual proprietor of—

Designation.	Cultivated area in acres.	Government revenue.	Cesses.	Total demand paid to Government.	Balance of rental.	Surplus assets per mensem.
		Rs. a. p.	Rs. a. p.	Rs. a. p.	Rs. a. p.	Rs. a. p.
Petty proprietors, ...	21¾	32 10 5	4 14 4	37 8 9	27 12 0	2 5 0
Other proprietors, ...	181½	310 8 0	46 8 0	357 0 0	263 14 0	22 0 0

By this it will be seen, that in the case of petty proprietors the average per recorded proprietor of surplus rental is only Rs. 27-12-0 per annum, and Rs. 2-5-0 per mensem, out of which have to be met all incidental expenses, arrears, &c., &c. This average is, however, very greatly reduced below what is a fair average of the ordinary petty proprietors, by containing 21 coparcenary villages, in which the numbers of the shareholders are very large, no less than 1,159, and the average cultivated area per shareholder 11 acres, Government revenue *plus* cesses Rs. 16, and balance of assets Rs. 11-14-0 per annum, and 15 annas 9 pie per mensem. It is very evident that these pettiest of proprietors cannot subsist *on their property,* and it is the cause of such as these for an assessment at 40 or 45 per cent. that I have urged. After deducting these pettiest of proprietors from the detail already given of " petty proprietors," the averages of " petty proprietors" are as follows, per individual recorded shareholder (not per separate member of family) :—

Cultivated area in acres.	Total Government demand.	Balance of rental assets, per annum.	Balance of rental assets, per mensem.
	Rs. a. p.	Rs. a. p.	Rs. a. p.
33	49 9 9	36 10 0	3 0 11

In the same way, if the largest proprietors, *viz.*, those who own more than one entire village, be eliminated from the others " not petty proprietors," the average is very considerably reduced—*viz.*, to about double of that given just above. From this it will be seen that the share of the rental left to the proprietors, omitting (1) the pettiest, and (2) the well-to-do and wealthy, who are the exceptions to the rule, varies between Rs. 30 and Rs. 80 per individual recorded proprietor per annum, and out of this have to be met as already several times mentioned, all expenses and losses, which reduce the surplus profit left for food and clothing very considerably—the exact amount cannot, of course, be stated. Does it appear from this that " *too large a margin* of profits is left to the proprietor by the half-asset rate of assessment?" I say decidedly not.

28. A map of the tuhseel, on the scale of one mile to the inch, divided into per-
Map of tuhseel showing detail and cultivation rate. gunnahs, showing the boundaries of all the *mouzahs* and the cultivated and uncultivated areas, the position of the inhabited sites, the rivers, and principal *nullahs* or natural lines of drainage, as well as the principal metalled and unmetalled roads, accompanies this report. On the map is also shown the revenue-rate or incidence per cultivated acre of the Government revenue for each *mouzah*. It will be seen that the highest rates prevail round, and in the vicinity of the city of Shahjehanpore and cantonments, as rents there are higher than elsewhere, and land is at a premium. It will also be seen that the revenue-rate per cultivated acre varies in pergunnah Shahjehanpore from Rs. 1-0-7 to Rs. 3-13-9, in Jumour from Rs. 0-14-2 to Rs. 2-14-0, and in Kant from Rs. 0-14-6 to Rs. 2-14-6.

29. As already mentioned, full reasons for the amount of *jumma* assessed on
Contents of assessment remarks. every separate *mouzah* and *muhal* have been written in English and appended as remarks to the No. III. figured statement, bound books of which accompany this written report, but cannot be printed with it. It is therefore as well to explain generally what they contain and the grounds of assessment alluded to in them. A short resumé of the general features of the *mouzah* is given, taken from the pergunnah note-book written up at time of inspection, the quality of the soil in various directions, the means of irrigation, and whatever other explanation is necessary to adapt the mere figured statements to the peculiarity of the particular *mouzah* treated of. Mention is made of the former assessment and how it worked, also of the rentals of past years, of the applicability or otherwise of the assumed average rent-rates, the reasons for assuming a rental, as basis of assessment, at or above or below the rental resulting from assumed rates; also of the *sayer* or *sewaie* income from uncultivated lands, the probability and extent of increased cultivation, and the amount added to the rental assets on these accounts. Where the assumed average rates are applicable and there is no income from *sewaie* nor any room for extension of cultivation, the remarks are naturally shorter than where explanation of non-applicability of average rates and of the amount of *sewaie* income or anticipated extension of cultivation has to be given. But the remarks are brief only where there is nothing to explain. I also wish to make it clear by special mention here that in the present revision all income from uncultivated lands, as well as prospective increase from extended cultivation, has been included in the gross assessable assets, and that the mere rental of the cultivated area alone has *not* been taken as the only assessable assets. I must not omit to explain either, that in reducing *jummas* I have not stuck to the hard-and-fast rule of 50 per cent. of existing or assumed assets, merely because the declared rental, or the assumed and estimated assets, were not double of the current *jumma*. I have not lowered it exactly to what I should have done if I had been raising it by 15 to 30 per cent., but have given such fair and reasonable reduction as, taking other circumstances into consideration, the case demanded. Nor yet must it be supposed that I have left such cases as monuments of injustice and over-assessment amongst their more fortunate neighbours from a spirit of non-interference.

30. The *jummas* of the tuhseel for the last five settlements preceding the present revision are given in the margin, (the last settlement being the 9th since the cession), as also that of the present revision. The last, or Mr. J. W. Muir's 30 years' settlement was a reduction of Rs. 11,491 on the previous settlement, and was nominally at about 66 per cent. of the assets. The

Revenue of former settlements and remarks on the last one.

Jumma	of 5th	...	Rs.	2,68,253
"	of 6th	...	"	2,71,965
"	of 7th	...	"	2,56,934
"	of 8th	...	"	2,79,880
"	of 9th	...	"	2,67,389
New of present revision,	...	"	2,90,671

mention of Tuhseel Shahjehanpore in the printed report is exceedingly short, only one page of print. It was written by Mr. Rose after Mr. J. W. Muir's death, but the assessment was made by Mr. Muir, and what he wrote of the part which he reported himself, concerning the severity of the former assessment, the depressed condition of the proprietors, and the great difficulty of the realization of the *jumma*, is equally

applicable here. The following extracts are sufficient :—" The condition in which I
" found the people proved how much they stood in need of alleviation of assessment.
" The great mass of the proprietors are in circumstances of extreme indigence, caused,
" I have reason to believe, principally by the heaviness of the *jumma*. It is a
" matter of surprise how, under such circumstances, the *jumma* was realized, but this,
" it was found, had only been done with very great difficulty and distress to the
" people. Things, however, had come to a crisis, and could not have gone on much
" longer without a reduction of assessment."

  Mr. Muir's settlement was, as the rule, a moderate one, the more especially so in
consequence of its being a very considerable reduction from its immediate predecessor.
There were, however, a good many instances in which it pressed heavily, especially at
first, and further subsequent reductions, amounting to Rs. 797, had to be granted in
ten villages. There were 14 farms for arrears of revenue, chiefly during the first ten
years of the settlement, but only one sale. There were also some other scattered instances in which it proved heavy, and was the cause of property coming into the hands of
mahajuns and city Pathans, which are almost synonymous terms, for the city Pathans
are most of them sugar manufacturers (*khundsarees*), and have no qualms of con-
science, or religious scruples, against taking interest. On the whole, however, the
settlement worked well, and the reductions granted by Mr. Muir were well apportioned, and besides being a boon to the proprietors, were, I believe, a real benefit in
the long run to the Government. In Pergunnah Jumour, however, the *jummas*
pressed more heavily than elsewhere, owing, I think, to the assessments having been
based on a deduced revenue-rate for cultivation, and not on a classification of soils.

  31. When the last settlement was made the whole tuhseel was one pergunnah,
Jumma of last and pre-
sent settlement for each
pergunnah. and the subordinate pergunnahs, as already stated early in
the report, have only now been formed at the present revision.
For the sake of comparison, however, the *jummas* of the past settlement are here

Name of pergunnah.	Jumma at commencement of last settlement without cesses.	Expiring (current) jumma of last settlement without cesses.	New jumma of present revision without cesses.
	Rs.	Rs. a. p.	Rs. a. p.
Shahjehanpore,...	1,13,058	1,07,939 10 0	1,24,219 1 0
Jumour, ...	75,290	74,752 10 0	74,710, 15 0
Kant, ...	79,041	78,963 5 0	91,740, 14 0
Total of tuhseel,	2,67,389	2,61,655 9 0	2,90,670 14 0

shown for each pergunnah separately. The full explanation
of the reduction of the current
expiring *jumma* below the
jumma assessed at settlement
has been given in the rent-rate
report submitted previous to
assessment. It is sufficient to
mention here that the largest
items of decrease are Rs. 3,288
for lands taken up for public
purposes, chiefly cantonments,
and Rs. 2,923 for revenue-free lands resumed by Mr. Muir, but subsequently released
on appeal, and Rs. 797 reductions of *jumma* in the villages which were over-assessed.
The reductions for diluvion exceed enhancements for alluvion by Rs. 400. The chief
item on the increase side is Rs. 1,047 assessed on revenue-free tenures confiscated for
rebellion in 1857-58 A. D. The gross decrease was Rs. 8,326-10-0, and gross increase
Rs. 2,593-3-0, leaving a net decrease of Rs. 5,733-7-0.

  32. The increase of the new revised 50 per cent. revenue, which came into force
Increase of new, over
expiring jumma. from the 1st July, 1870 A. D., over the expiring *jumma*
amounts to Rs. 29,014-5-0, and is at the rate of just over 11
per cent. The *jumma* was originally assessed at 55 per cent. of the assets, inclusive of
cesses, according to the then existing orders, but the cesses were subsequently separated
from the revenue, and all mention of them has been omitted. To this cause,
however, is owing the existence of odd annas in the revenue, which would otherwise

have been in even rupees. In Pergunnah Shahjehanpore the increase is just over 15 per cent., and in Pergunnah Kant over 16 per cent., whilst in Pergunnah Jumour there is no increase, but a slight decrease of Rs. 41-11-0. This decrease is owing to diluvion after assessment, but just as the new *jummas* came into force. Otherwise the total *jumma* of Pergunnah Jumour was assessed at Rs. 17 over the expiring *jumma*.

Name of pergunnah.	Increase.	Decrease.	Net increase.	Percentage of increase.
	Rs. a. p.	Rs. a. p.	Rs. a. p.	
Shahjehanpore,...	16,279 7 0	...	16,279 7 0	15·08
Jumour, ...	...	41 11 0	...	...
Kant, ...	12,776 9 0	...	12,776 9 0	16·19
Total of tuhseel,	29,056 0 0	41 11 0	29,014 5 0	11·98

33. The rates or incidences per acre of the last settlement on the then areas, as well of those of the new 50 per cent. *jumma* on the present areas, are given in juxta-position in the following statement :—

Incidence per acre of last and new settlement.

Name of pergunnah.	REVENUE-RATE-PER ACRE ON					
	Total area.		Malgoozaree or assessable.		Cultivated area.	
	Last.	New.	Last.	New.	Last.	New.
	Rs. a. p.	Rs. a. p.	Rs. a. p.	Rs. a. p.	Rs. a. p.	Rs. a. p.
Shahjehanpore, ...	1 2 3	1 3 11	1 7 11	1 8 5	2 0 10	1 14 10
Jumour, ...	1 2 8	1 2 4	1 7 2	1 5 0	2 0 9	1 11 6
Kant, ...	0 13 11	0 15 2	1 0 0	1 1 1	1 4 11	1 4 8
Whole tuhseel, ...	1 0 8	1 2 1	1 4 9	1 4 9	1 12 1	1 10 0

With reference to the *revenue* rate on cultivation of the present revision being so much lower than that of the last settlement, it must be remembered that at the time of the last settlement extraordinarily large areas (11,333 acres) were lying temporarily fallow, and were not therefore included in the *cultivated* area, though virtually taken as cultivation in the assessment of revenue, whereas now at the measurements of the new settlement, the amount of recent fallow (2,649 acres) is normal. Taking rather more than 9,000 acres of the 11,333 as abnormal, and about 2,000 as normal fallow, the revenue rate per cultivated acre of last settlement becomes Re. 1-10-6. That assessment was at 66 per cent. of gross assessable assets, including far more culturable waste than remains now for the present revision, which is moreover as already stated at 50 per cent., or half assets. The incidence per cultivated acre which had been Re. 1-12-1 for the whole tuhseel, at the commencement of the last settlement, was Re. 1-7-5, at the expiration of it ; owing to the recultivation of the fallow and increase of cultivation by reclamation of waste.

34. The *kists* or instalments for payment of the Government revenue have been revised and reduced to four. Three sets were arranged by myself, with reference to what were in existence and to the wishes of the leading zemindars, whose opinions were asked, and then the zemindars were allowed to select whichever set they preferred. Only 13 *mouzahs* elected for the *khureef*, 9 annas ; 217 for half-and-half in each harvest ; and 308 for 7 annas in *khureef*, and 9 annas in *rubbee*.

Kists of instalments for payment of jumma.

Definition.	KHUREEF.			RUBBEE.		
	15th November.	15th January.	Total.	15th May.	15th June.	Total.
	annas.	annas.	annas.	annas.	annas.	annas.
In which khureef and rubbee are equal.	4	4	8	5	3	8
In which khureef is less than rubbee.	4	3	7	5	4	9
In which khureef is more than rubbee.	5	4	9	5	2	7

35. The new *jummas* and revised assessments of this tuhseel came into force from
Durkhasts or engage-ments for payment of revenue.
the 1st of July, 1870, A. D., the commencement of 1278 fuslee, and the engagements, (*durkhasts*), have been taken from that date, but without specification of any term of 20 or 25 or 30 years, merely "for the term of the settlement and until revision" and "subject to the sanction of Government." The alluvial muhals liable to periodical revision are of course an exception, and the *durkhasts* in them are taken for increase and abatement subject to the rules in force for alluvion and diluvion. In this tuhseel alone were the assessments made and the *durkhasts* taken for the 55 per cent. of assets demand, inclusive of cesses, in conformity with the then prevailing orders of the Board and Government. This 55 per cent. *jumma* has been entered in all the vernacular records and distributed as the *Government demand*, but when the orders for assessing the revenue proper at 50 per cent., and leaving the cesses to be regulated by the special Act (XVIII. of 1871) came out subsequently, I separated revenue from cesses, and every *khewut* shows the sub-division of the total 55 per cent. demand into 50 per cent. revenue and 5 per cent. cesses, as do also the lists of demand sent to the Collector's office and to the *tuhseelees*. As already explained, the revenue and *jummas* mentioned throughout this report are the 50 per cent. revenue proper, *exclusive* of cesses. The case of this *tuhseel*, and as already stated of this *tuhseel alone*, is that specially provided for in the provision clause of Section 3, Act XVIII. of 1871.

There was not one single instance of refusal to accept the settlement at the proposed *jumma.*

36. The re-arrangement of the *putwarees* circles has been affected, and entailed
Arrangement of Put-wnrees Circles and grad-ing of Putwarees.
considerable alterations, apart from the mere increase of *putwarees* and reduction of the size of over-grown circles, from the fact of many circles lying partly on each side of the River Gurra and the Gurraie *nulla* which respectively separate Jumour from Shahjehanpore on the one side, and from Kant on the other. The *putwaree* fund for the pay of the *putwarees* is made by a further cess on the zemindars, falling in Pergunnah Shahjehanpore at Rs. 4-12-0, and in Pergunnahs Jumour and Kant at 5 per cent. on the total 55 per cent. demand ; not on the mere revenue proper (*jumma mal*). The number of the *putwarees* in each grade with the salary of the grade is given in the margin. The average num-

Pergunnah.	Number of Putwarees.			
	1st grade, Rs. 13 per mensem.	2nd grade, Rs. 11 per mensem.	3rd grade, Rs. 9 per mensem.	Total.
Shahjehanpore, ...	10	20	18	48
Jumour, ...	8	14	8	30
Kant, ...	10	18	11	39
Whole tuhseel, ...	28	52	37	117

ber of *mouzahs* in each *putwaree's* circle for the entire *tuhseel* is just over 4½, and of *muhals*, separate properties in *mouzahs*, just under 6½. In Jumour there was one circle (Bunthura) which was too large for one *putwaree* but not sufficient for two, and it could not be well broken up, as the circle consisted of the entire joint property of the Bunthura Rajpoots, and so an assistant (*Gomashta*) was allowed for this circle, who is not included in the pergunnah total of 30 *putwarees*.

37. The attestation of the vernacular records of this *tuhseel* was carried on
Vernacular records and cases decided.
principally by Deputy Collector Rughbuns Sahai, but Mr. Butt attested about half of Pergunnah Kant, and I also attested re-cords, but more especially rentals, in Pergunnah Shahjehanpore chiefly, and to a small extent in the other two pergunnahs also.

The case work has also been shared by us three, the greater number of all the heavy and important cases, except partitions, falling to my own particular share, and the partitions all coming to me for sanction, by whomsoever conducted :—

Total number of cases instituted and decided.	Detail of cases instituted and decided in Tuhseel Shahjehanpore.							
	Rights and interests under Regulation VII. of 1822.	Enhancement suits under Acts X. of 1859 and XIV of 1863.	Boundary disputes.	Partitions, perfect and Imperfect.	Maafee investigations.	Appeals to Settlement Officer.	Miscellaneous.
15,783	6,181	662	230	533	1,415	137	4,525

The details of the various kinds of cases are given in the foregoing table, from which it will be readily seen that the amount of case work is very large.

There would have been many more cases for enhancement under Acts X. of 1859 and XIV. of 1863, had I not taken measures to bring about alteration of the rental and enhancement of rent by mutual agreement of the parties in all cases where my assumed rental and revised assessment showed the current rental to be low and inadequate all round, and had I not endeavoured to bring about amicable arrangements as far as possible in every instance, without a regular suit for enhancement being instituted.

The number of appeals to the Settlement Officer from his subordinates is small, but no exact percentage can be given, as so many of the cases were decided by the Settlement Officer himself. If the number of appeals to the Commissioner be added to those to the Settlement Officer, and the percentage be taken on the total of appealable cases, a fair estimate is obtainable of the appeals against the decisions of the various Officers in the Settlement Department ; the percentage is only two (2). Also of the cases appealed to the Commissioner, only six decisions have been reversed or altered, and most of these were appeals from subordinates direct to the Commissioner, before the Settlement Officer was empowered to hear appeals himself from his subordinates.

Appeals to Commissioner from decision of the Settlement Officer and his subordinates.	Number upheld.	Number reversed or altered.
30	24	6

The decisions of the Settlement Officer and of his subordinates may therefore be fairly assumed to have been good, and to have given general satisfaction to the litigants.

ROBERT G. CURRIE,

Dated December 20th, 1873.   *Settlement Officer.*

INDEX TO CHAPTER III.

ASSESSMENT REPORT OF TUHSEEL JELLALABAD.

CHAPTER III.

JELLALABAD TUHSEEL.

THE Tuhseel of Jellalabad consists of but one pergunnah, also known as, but seldom called, Mehrabad. It is situated in the southern end of the district, adjoining the Ganges and the Futtehgurh District. Pergunnah Bangaon, which formerly belonged to the Futtehgurh District, and was assessed there, and subsequently in 1842 transferred to this district, was on transfer amalgamated with and included in this pergunnah, which now contains 392 mouzahs and 504 muhals, and has a total area of 317 square miles.

Jellalabad Pergunnah and Tuhseel identical, and the southernmost in the district.

2. The boundaries of the pergunnah are almost entirely arbitrary. The Ganges was nominally the boundary between this district and Futtehgurh, and the stream is partially but only very exceptionally so now, as it has worked away to the south-west, and though the valley of the Ganges may be said to be the boundary between Pergunnah Jellalabad and the Futtehgurh District, the river itself is certainly not so : nor is there any advantage in making it so, as it is always changing its course, and may in a few years return to the edge of, or even inside, the boundary of this pergunnah. Oudh forms the boundary for some 8½ or 9 miles at the south-east end of the pergunnah, from about two miles east of the point where the metalled road from Futtehgurh enters this from that district. Pergunnahs Ooseith and Sulempore of the Budaon District form the western boundary from the Ganges to the Ramgunga, and pergunnahs of Tuhseels Tilhur and Shahjehanpore the north-western and northern boundaries.

The boundaries of the pergunnah.

3. There are three distinct tracts of soil in the pergunnah, running generally from north to south, which have been taken advantage of and made into three separate circles for assessment. The easternmost is a high sandy tract of land,—a continuation of similar land in Pergunnahs Tilhur and Kant of this district, and extending into Oudh, a mere narrow strip in the north of the pergunnah, and widening out from south of the town of Jellalabad to the Oudh border to a breadth of about five miles ; next to this, down the centre of the pergunnah, comes the Terai circle, the valleys of the Ramgunga and Bygool, which streams unite about the centre of the pergunnah, and whose valleys are one from the entrance into the pergunnah of the two rivers about five miles apart. The third tract is called *bunkuttee*, and extends from the valley of the Ramgunga to the Ganges, and is all low-lying and hard clay soil, which has never been cut away by the Ramgunga. It contains also a large extent of unreclaimed *dhák* jungle, and grass land intersected by numerous nullas, or flood drains, all leading into the Sote Nuddee, which after flowing for some distance parallel with, eventually falls into the Ganges.

The three distinct natural tracts the assessment circles.

4. The *bhoor* circle is much the smallest of the three, containing only 80 mouzahs and a total area of 31,500 acres (40 square miles). It is by far the poorest circle of the three, and very similar to the adjoining portions of Pergunnahs Tilhur and Kant ; 42¼ per cent. of the cultivated area is downright sand (*bhoor*), and nearly 33 per cent. very sandy loam, called second *domut*, but in reality only something rather better than actual sand. *Bajra* is the chief *khureef* crop, and though wheat is grown to a very great extent, the outturn of the crop is far smaller than in the other circles, as the soil is weak and light.

The bhoor circle.

5. The *Terai* circle is considerably the best in every way. The Ramgunga has at some time or another been over the whole of this area, which varies from 5 to 6½ miles in breadth for the entire length of the pergunnah, about 20 miles. The area of this circle is 82,000 acres, equivalent to 128 square miles, the *malgeozaree* or assessable area of which is 69,585 acres, nearly 109 square miles. The whole of this is alluvial deposit, and mostly of excellent quality. From its low level and the number of old beds of the Ramgunga, called *dubrees*, and the inherent humidity of the valley of the Ramgunga, the soil is naturally moist (*terai*), and does not require irrigation, and is of very uniform quality. The exceptions are where the river has left only a thin layer of super-soil over a deep deposit of sand. It produces, without irrigation and with comparatively little labor, wheat crops quite equal to the average, and in some parts equal to the best wheat crops of the *bunkuttee* circle, raised with more labor and much irrigation. Here the percentage of loam of first quality (first *domut*), including the *gowhanee*, or manured land, is 49 per cent. The second quality loam (second *domut*), which is most of it about equal to the clay (*mutyar*), being only second to the best denomination of soil, and not in itself an inferior soil, as in the other two circles, is 30 per cent.; and the really poor soil, the *bhoor*, is less than 5 per cent. of the cultivated area. This latter, with a little of the *mutyar*, represents the unformed soil and incomplete deposit in the actual flood valley or bed of the river.

6. The *bunkuttee* circle, like the *bhoor* circle on the other side of the Ramgunga valley, has never been cut away by the Ramgunga. It is the largest of the three circles, having a total area of over 89,000 acres, and nearly 140 square miles. It is of nearly, if not quite, as low a level as the *terai* circle, but there is a great admixture of hard clay in the soil, 36½ per cent. of the cultivated area being actual clay, and nearly half of the 60 per cent. of first and second quality loam having a very large admixture of clay in it. The soil of this circle is very similar to that of Pergunnah Jumour, and requires much and constant irrigation, as it otherwise hardens and chokes the growth of the stalk and roots, and cracks into large fissures: with copious irrigation and care it produces very excellent wheat, and the outturn per acre is quite equal to, and often better than, that of the *terai* circle, both for wheat and *jowar*. *Kuchha* wells cannot be made in this circle, as they can in the two others, because at or just above the water-level is a substratum of quicksand, or rather quickclay (*lelwa*), which comes up like weak mudpie or very moist mortar, and speedily hardens in the air to very heavy bluish clay, and effectually prevents the *kuchha* well being sunk through it, or water being procurable in any sufficient quantity for irrigation. Most of the irrigation in this circle is consequently from rivers or ponds, of which mention will be made further on.

7. The principal crops grown in this pergunnah are,—in the *rubbee* or spring harvest, wheat and gram; and in the *khureef* or autumn harvest, *bajra* and rice. Sugarcane is but little grown, and I believe the chief reason is the prejudice against growing it entertained by the Chundela Rajpoots of the Khunder *Ilaka*, who have a tradition that some ancestor forbad its cultivation, and assert that bad luck attends or some misfortune invariably happens to any Chundela who transgresses the order. Mr. J. W. Muir, in his report of last settlement, notices this tradition, but says he believes that the real reason is that the soil is not adapted to sugarcane. I believe that the tradition has at least as much to do with its absence as, if not more than, any peculiarity of the soil. Its almost entire absence in the Khunder *Ilaka* villages is most marked, and where it is found it is only in villages in which the cultivators are not Thakoors, but Chumars, Kisans, &c. It is only to be found very exceptionally in any Thakoor cultivated villages, whatever their clan. If there were more Koormees in the pergunnah, it would probably be found to produce more sugarcane, as they are the great sugarcane growers of the district, but are remarkable in Jellalabad by their absence. Be the cause what it may, the area under sugarcane in the year of measurement was less than one per cent., and in the second year, after the new jummas had been in force, was under two per cent. of the cultivated area. The

The Terai circle.

The bunkuttee circle.

Produce of the soil.

percentages of the principal crops for each circle and for the whole tuhseel are given

Circle.	PERCENTAGES OF PRINCIPAL CROPS.						
	Rubbee or Spring Harvest.				*Khureef or Autumn Harvest.*		
	Wheat.	Gram.	Barley.	Poppy.	*Jowar.*	*Bajra.*	Rice.
Bhoor, ...	37½	3¼	3¼	4½	2½	32¾	6¼
Terai, ...	35	8¼	2¼	4¼	12	16½	8¼
Bunkuttee, ...	42	3	3¾	1¼	11	6	22
Whole pergunnah	38½	5¼	3	3½	9½	15¼	13¼

in the margin, but full details of the crops, areas, and percentages will be found in Appendix A. These percentages are to some extent misleading and disappointing, inasmuch as they afford little or no clue to the relative capabilities of the circles, from the custom of sowing wheat even in poor land, and preferring an inferior crop of wheat to a fair crop of barley. The cotton area is only 3,100 acres, about 2½ per cent., and no more attention is paid to its cultivation here than in Shahjehanpore. The poppy cultivation is considerable, in consequence of the position of the pergunnah between Futtehgurh and Budaon, at both of which places there have been opium agencies for a long time. It is increasing now, owing possibly to a new sub-agency having been lately established in Shahjehanpore. The area under poppy in 1280 Fuslee was 4,706 acres, or 4¼ per cent. of the total cultivated area, as against 4,240 acres in the year of measurement five years previously. The most striking features of the crop statement are the small areas and percentages of barley, and of the mixed crops of barley and gram, and barley and wheat generally, and in the sandy soil of the *bhoor* circle in particular ; and the entire absence of Indian-corn, indigo, and safflower throughout the pergunnah. Some little tobacco is grown, but so little that it is not worthy of a place for itself, and is included under the heading of *kuchyana*, or garden crops, which are chiefly vegetables, and all-told amount to only 2½ per cent. The double crop lands amounted to 9 per cent. in year of measurement, but to only 6¼ per cent. last year, 1280 Fuslee, and, with the exception of *kuchyana*,

Circle.	Percentage of double crop lands.	
	Year of measurement.	1280 Fuslee.
Bhoor, ...	4½	3½
Terai, ...	8	5¼
Bunkuttee, ...	12¼	8
Whole pergunnah,	9	6½

or vegetables, are entirely wheat, barley, or gram, or two or all of them mixed after rice. As is only natural, the largest double crop area is in the *bunkuttee* circle, where the rice-land area is the largest. It is seldom, however, that a good *rubbee* crop succeeds a good rice crop. If the rice crop has been good, the *rubbee* one is usually poor, and *vice versâ*. Of the rice grown in the *bunkuttee* circle, a great deal is *kunder*, which is only ordinary rice sown in ponds and *nullas* and natural deep depressions in March and early in April, after most of the water has been drawn off for irrigation or has dried up, and cut before the rains set in, and the ponds and *nullas* are filled again.

8. The town of Jellalabad is said to have been founded in the reign of the Emperor Jellal-ood-deen, and to have been named after him. It is situated near the junction of the road from Shahjehanpore with the metalled road from Futtehgurh to Bareilly. There is a large mud fort said to have been built by Hafiz Ruhmut Khan, but very probably of older date, which is now utilised for the Government offices. The tuhseel, police station, post office, and school are all within the walls of the fort. Jellalabad is merely a country town, or *kusbeh*, of no commercial importance whatever, and without any trade or manufacture. The inhabitants are principally Mussulmans (Pathans chiefly) and Mahajuns.

The town of Jellalabad.

The zemindars are Kaiyuths, and the cultivators chiefly Brahmins. The population is over 6,000, and chiefly non-agricultural. The town has a miserable tumble-down ruined appearance, and gives the impression of being in anything but a flourishing

Agriculturists.			Non-agriculturists.			GRAND TOTAL.
Hindoos.	Mahomedans.	Total.	Hindoos.	Mahomedans.	Total.	
638	230	868	2,298	2,884	5,182	6,050

condition. There are seven *mohullas* and four *gung s*. The market days are Mondays and Thursdays. On Mondays the market is held in the zemindars' old *gunges*, which all adjoin one another, and are virtually one *gunge*, and on Thursdays in the new Government *gunge* close alongside the Grand Trunk Road.

9. There is nothing approaching to a *kusbeh* in the pergunnah besides Jellalabad, but there are a number of large and populous villages with agricultural populations almost entirely Hindoos, and chiefly Rajpoots. Details of the populations of seven of the largest villages are given in the margin. The non-agriculturists are more so in name than in reality, by far the greater number of them being day labourers employed in the fields, though not actual cultivators of fields of their own. Many, and in fact most, of the Mahomedans in these villages are *Nou-Muslims*, whose ancestors became converts to *Islam* during the reign of the Emperors, but who are in manners and appearance Hindoos,

Populations of seven of the largest villages.

Name.	Hindoos.		Mahomedans.		GRAND TOTAL.
	Agriculturists.	Non-agriculturists.	Agriculturists.	Non-agriculturists.	
Koonduria, ...	3,277	536	276	122	4,211
Khunder, ...	1,884	1,278	97	141	3,400
Mirzapore, ...	2,158	985	52	140	3,335
Zurreenpore, ...	1,762	369	25	56	2,215
Pilowa, ...	1,542	193	27	53	1,815
Keetapore Kullan,	1,271	278	62	76	1,687
Bangaon, ...	819	364	47	28	1,258

and most of them Thakoors of the same stock and with the same features as, and family likenesses to, the Hindoo fraternity amongst whom they continue to dwell.

10. *Kusbeh* Jellalabad is in the *bhoor* circle, and besides the markets held there twice a week, there are seven villages in the other parts of the pergunnah in which markets are held, a list of which, with the market days and circle in which the villages are situated, is given in the margin. Besides these there is a regular bazaar in Pirtheepore Dhai, where buying and selling goes on every day, but no special market is held. The Dhai Ghat *melas* are held on the banks of the Ganges, nearly

Name of village.	Circle.	Number of market days.	Days of the week.
Koonduria, ...	Terai, ...	2	Tuesday and Wednesday.
Futtehpore, ...	,, ...	2	Sunday and Wednesday.
Khunder, ...	,, ...	2	Ditto.
Zurreenpore, ...	,, ...	2	Ditto.
Rufflabad, ...	Bunkuttee, ...	2	Ditto.
Itmadpore Chuk, ...	,, ...	2	Ditto.
Mirzapore, ...	,, ...	2	Tuesday and Friday.

two miles away from the village itself.

11. There are no means of comparing the present population with that of the last settlement, but from the accompaying return of the number of villages and hamlets inhabited at last settlement, the number which have been established since then, and the

Inhabited and uninhabited mouzahs and hamlets.

numbers now inhabited, there can be no doubt of the great increase of population.

Pergunnah Jellalabad.	At last Settlement.			During currency of Settlement from 1838 to 1871, A. D.		Total at present Settlement.		
	Inhabited.	Uninhabited.	Total.	Newly-inhabited.	Become deserted.	Inhabited.	Uninhabited.	Total.
Village, ...	333	50	383	13	9	345	47	392
Hamlets, ...	151	12	163	84	5	230	14	244
Total,...	484	61	546	97	14	575	61	636

There are 392 *mouzahs* now, as against 383 of last settlement, owing to the separation of several villages which had distinct boundaries of their own, and were in some cases several miles apart, but were then treated as one *mouzah*. And there are now 575 inhabited villages and hamlets, against 484 at last settlement, the great increase being of course in the number of new hamlets established. Most of the villages which have become deserted during the currency of the settlement have been washed away by the Ramgunga, and some, but not all, have been re-established in some other portion of the area. With the exception of some of the poorest parts of the *bunkuttee* circle, where the waste is the most continuous and extensive, and much of it either barren or very inferior land, scarce worth cultivating, the whole pergunnah is fully inhabited, and the population is well and equally distributed.

12. The average area of *mouzahs* is smallest in the *bhoor*, and largest in the *bunkuttee* circle,—larger than in any other pergunnah or assessment circle of a pergunnah in the district. From the population of the *bhoor* circle has been deducted the non-agricultural population of the town of Jellalabad, as also from the total of the whole tuhseel, as the population shown is the rural population only.

Average areas of mouzahs and average population.

Circle.	Number of mouzahs.	Average area in acres.	Average area in square miles.	Average rural population.	
				Per mouzah.	Per square mile.
Bhoor, ...	80	393	·61	269	439
Terai, ...	178	461	·71	381	530
Bunkuttee, ...	134	667	1·04	372	356
Whole Tuhseel, ...	392	518	·80	355	439

The average population of the *bunkuttee* circle per square mile is the smallest, but in some parts the adjoining *bunkuttee* villages belong to residents of villages in the *terai* circle, as Koonduria and Purour in the north, where not only the proprietors but also most of the cultivators reside; and all down the boundary line of the *terai* and *bunkuttee* circles, residents of villages within the former cultivate to a considerable extent in the latter circle. Hence the average of 530 per square mile for the *terai* circle is somewhat above, and the average of 356 for the *bunkuttee* circle is somewhat below their respective averages, as regards the locality of the cultivation and employment of the population, but correct according to residence within the boundaries of the two circles. Also, if the very thinly-populated jungly portion of this circle be omitted, the average population in the remainder is up to the general average of the whole pergunnah. By the census of 1872 the average rural population per square mile is just over 500.

13. The proportion of Mahomedan to Hindoo cultivators is very small, the Mahomedan cultivators being chiefly confined to Jellalabad and its vicinity. Amongst the Mahomedans, as well as the Hindoos, the proportion of females—both adults and minors—to males is

Cultivators—their creed, caste, and proportion to cultivated area.

below the proper average, the Rajpoots forming a large portion of the Hindoo culti-

Hindoo Cultivators.					Mahomedan Cultivators.					Grand Total.	Average per square mile of Cultivation.	
Adults.		Minors.		Total.	Adults.		Minors.		Total.		Of cultivators and their families.	Of adult cultivators.
M.	F.	M.	F.		M.	F.	M.	F.				
39,797	31,570	22,499	13,580	107,836	1,841	1,584	1,068	941	5,434	113,270	569	376

vating community. This is no matter of surprise, as female infanticide is practised to an enormous extent in this pergunnah, and very vigorous measures are now being taken by Government for its suppression. The number of proclaimed villages in this pergunnah alone are 65, and clans 10. It is essentially a Rajpoot pergunnah, the three principal clans beginning from the south, being the Kutheas towards the Ganges, and throughout the western and south-western parts of the *Bunkuttee Ilaka*. The Chundelas all over the Ramgunga and Bygool valleys, and extending into the northern portion of the *bunkuttee* and *bhoor* circles, and the Ponwars on the north of the Ramgunga and all along the Oudh border. After these come the Rugbunsees, who occupy the western side of the old Pergunnah of Bangaon, and extend into the *Bunkuttee Ilaka*, up to the Kutheas and the Gothams in the eastern side of Bangaon. Intermixed with all of these are families of other clans, who have intermarried with them, or have settled amongst them from various causes. Consequently the Rajpoots abound throughout the pergunnah, and they have to a large extent excluded most of the ordinary cultivating classes and castes, who are better than menials. Chumars, however, they have employed largely, and there are many hamlets composed almost entirely of Chumars, and the Chumar element is very strong. The order of the principal cultivators according to their numerical strength is—(1) and (2) Chumars and Aheers almost equal, then (3) Thakoors, (4) Kachees, (5) Kisans, and with a considerable interval, (6) and (7) Brahmins and Kahars about equal. The pergunnah is not therefore very well favored in the matter of cultivators. The average of cultivators and their families per square mile of cultivation is 569, and of adult cultivators 376, being somewhat larger proportions than in Tuhseel Shahjehanpore. The 1872 census* gives a smaller number of agriculturists, but gives land-owners separate,

* Religion.	Agriculturists.	Land-owners.
Hindoo, ...	104,774	8,758
Mussulman, ...	4,658	848
Total, ...	109,432	9,606

whereas more than half of the land-owners in the pergunnah are peasant-proprietors, and as such agriculturists, which reconciles any apparent discrepancy between the census of 1872 and my settlement returns.

14. As was only probable in a pergunnah so largely composed of Rajpoot communities, the *putteedaree* and *bhyachara* tenures far exceed the *zemindaree*. In the *terai* circle, where most of the villages of the Khunder *Ilaka* and other Chundelas are situated, the *zemindaree* tenure is in a great minority. In the *bunkuttee* and *bhoor* circles the *putteedaree* and *bhyachara* muhals still out-number the *zemindaree*, but not to anything like the same extent. In the 264 *putteedaree* and *bhyachara muhals* there are no less than 1,796 separate *puttees*. Many of these *puttees* are sub-divided into a number of separate small holdings or *khathas*, and this multiplication and sub-division of holdings is on the increase with the increase of population.

Proprietary tenures.

Zemindaree Muhals,	...	208
Putteedaree ditto,	...	264
Bhyachara ditto,	...	32
		504

Subordinate sub-division of the 264 Putteedaree Muhals.	
Tenures.	Number of Puttees.
Undivided, held in common, or the property of one individual, i. e., zemindaree, ...	1,358
Divided and held in severalty, i. e., bhyachara,	438
	1,796

15. The Rajpoots are the chief proprietors in the pergunnah, and they are almost all residents in the pergunnah, and in some one of their own villages. There are only 14 entire *mouzahs*, 3 *muhals*, and parts

Residence, creed, and caste of proprietors.

	Caste.	Entire mouzahs.	Entire muhals, parts of mouzahs.	Shares in other mouzahs and muhals.
Resident proprietors living within the limits of the pergunnah.	Putban, ...	18	49	22
	Other Mussulmans, ...	3	...	3
	Total of Mussulmans, ...	21	49	25
	Thakoor, ...	160	60	96
	Brahmin, ...	8	6	8
	Kaiyuth, ...	7	6	4
	Aheer, ...	...	2	4
	Miscellaneous,	9	4	3
	Total of Hindoos, ...	205	127	140
Non-resident proprietors living outside the pergunnah.	Putban, ...	2	...	...
	Other Mussulmans, ...	3	...	1
	Total of Mussulmans, ...	5	...	1
	Thakoor, ...	4	...	3
	Brahmin, ...	2	...	1
	Kaiynth, ...	2	...	2
	Kulwar, ...	1	2	6
	Khutree, ...	...	1	2
	Total of Hindoos, ...	9	3	14

of 15 other *mouzahs* which are the property of persons not residing in the pergunnah, and more than half of these belong to residents of the district. The very great absence of the *mahajun* element is striking, but the absence is not so real as the marginal statement and foregoing remarks would suggest, as many villages are mortgaged to the treasurer and others, but the mortgagees do not take possession. When the Thakoors' property changes hands, it is purchased either by some of the well-to-do Chundelas of the Khunder *Iloka*, or by Puthans of Jellalabad.

16. The area of land held *seer* by proprietors (by far the greater part of which is cultivated by the proprietors themselves, and only a small part is sub-let to cultivators) amounts to 26,391 acres, being nearly 21 per cent. of the entire cultivated area. The same reasons as those detailed with reference to this same figured statement in Tuhseel Shahjehanpore hold good here also,—that the actual amount of *seer* and cultivation per proprietor and cultivator is somewhat larger than that shown in the statement.

Distribution of the cultivated area.

DISTRIBUTION OF CULTIVATED AREA OF REVENUE-PAYING LANDS ACCORDING TO SEPARATE HOLDINGS.

Seer of proprietors actually cultivated by them or sub-let.			Cultivated by Tenants.						Total area cultivated by tenants, irrespective of their having or not having right of occupancy.		
			With right of occupancy.			Without occupancy rights, tenants-at-will.					
Number of khathas or separate holdings.	Cultivated acres.	Average of cultivated area per khatha in acres.	Number of khathas or separate holdings.	Cultivated acres.	Average of cultivated area per khatha in acres.	Number of khathas or separate holdings.	Cultivated acres.	Average of cultivated area per khatha in acres.	Number of khathas or separate holdings.	Cultivated acres.	Average of cultivated area per khatha in acres.
5,078	26,391	5·19	33,168	70,647	2·10	18,704	30,501	1·63	51,872	101,148	2·95

The average obtained by applying the test of each separate cultivating occupancy or joint family consisting of five individuals, gives a result for the entire pergunnah, inclusive of all cultivation, both of proprietors and tenants, revenue free as well as paying revenue, of rather over 5½ acres. The number of cultivators with right of occupancy is very large, upwards of 55 per cent. of the entire cultivated area of the pergunnah being cultivated under occupancy rights. The details of the distribution of the cultivated

Circle.				PERCENTAGES OF CULTIVATED AREA HELD		
				Seer.	By cultivators with right of occupancy.	By tenants-at-will.
Bhoor,	...	...	...	15·65	63·65	20·70
Terai,	...	...	...	26·68	48·68	25·64
Bunkuttee,	...	...	...	17·35	59·15	23·50
	Total,	...		20·68	55·40	22·92

area are given in the margin for each of the three circles separately. The percentage of *seer* is the largest, and of area cultivated by tenants with right of occupancy is the smallest, in the *terai* circle, where the greater number of the Khunder *Ilaka* villages are situated, and where the Rajpoot communities have retained their hereditary property intact more generally than in the other two circles.

17. The same care has been taken here, as has been fully detailed regarding the same statement, Appendix B., in the Shahjehanpore Tuhseel chapter, to obtain reliable and genuine statistics regarding the rent paid —(1) by various castes, and (2) by tenants with right of occupancy and tenants-at-will. Villages were selected from all parts of the three circles with the same view of avoiding peculiar and abnormal conditions, and the result is very similar to that of Tuhseel Shahjehanpore. The cultivated area abstracted amounts to over 12,000 acres, 80 per cent. of which is cultivated by tenants with right of occupancy at an average rent-rate of Rs. 3-0-11 per acre, and 20 per cent. by tenants-at-will at an average rent-rate of Rs. 3-2-8 per acre. In the details of the various castes the average rate of the tenants-at-will is slightly higher than that of the tenant with right of occupancy, except in the case of—(1) Brahmins, and (2) Kisans, Kachees, &c., where there is a slight difference the other way, which is, I believe, accounted for by the fact of the area of the tenants with right of occupancy being greatly in excess of that of the tenants-at-will, and generally of somewhat better quality. As regards castes and creeds, the Puthans and Syuds pay the lowest rates; but they are principally in the *bhoor* circle, and the inferiority of the soil keeps down the rents. The Brahmins pay as high as any, and higher than most of the upper and respectable castes ; the lower castes, the *lungoth poshes*, Kachees, Kisans, Chunars, and miscellaneous castes, all pay decidedly higher rates than the respectable and upper castes, the *sufed poshes ;* the rates paid by the occupancy tenants of the *lungoth poshes* being higher than the tenant-at-will rate of the *sufed poshes.*

Comparison of rates paid by the various castes and classes of cultivators.

18. The only metalled road is the Grand Trunk Road between Bareilly and Futtehgurh, which traverses the eastern side of the pergunnah for a distance of nine miles, passing close by the town of Jellalabad. The road to Shahjehanpore from the point where it leaves the Grand Trunk Road to the edge of the pergunnah, a distance of under four miles, is, or was till quite lately (1874), one of the worst pieces of road in the whole district, being stiff clay at the Grand Trunk Road junction, and many feet below the said road, and deep flying sand from the Jellalabad eastern encamping ground to the edge of the pergunnah. There are two unmetalled roads made and kept up by the district authorities ; one leading to Dhai Ghat on the Ganges being a continuation of the road from Shahjehanpore, on which there is a great deal of traffic, as there are large Hindoo *melas* held at Dhai Ghat several times a year, and, except during the rains, the road is in fair condition and practicable for country carts and pedestrians. The other unmetalled road is called the Budaon Road, but the culverts and bridges are only made as far as the Bygool at Khunder, a distance of under five miles from Jellalabad, beyond which there is little or no through traffic on it, as a made and raised road without bridges and culverts is of less use for traffic than an ordinary country cart road. The *bhoor* and *terai*

Means of communication. Roads.

circles are therefore fairly well provided with roads, all the foregoing traversing them, the Dhai Ghat road alone going near the *bunkuttee* circle, and that only at its extreme south-eastern end. The ordinary cross-country cart roads in the *bhoor* and *terai* circles are also good, much better than those of the *Bunkuttee Ilaka*, which are bad at best, and are difficult to get along even during the cold weather. They are utterly impracticable during the rains, owing to the numerous *nullas* and water-courses and flood channels. In fact, the whole of the pergunnah across the Ramgunga is effectually cut off from the town of Jellalabad and all the Government offices throughout the rains, as there are several old channels of the Ramgunga, besides the real river, which become streams in the rains, and the floods of the Ganges and Sote unite and keep all the tributary *nullas* and flood drains which abound in the *bunkuttee* circle full for months together. So bad is the communication even for pedestrians throughout the rains, that a chuprassee or process-server attached to the tuhseel is of no use unless he is an expert swimmer.

19. This pergunnah is better off for river communication than any other in the district. It is the only one bordering on the Ganges which is of course navigable, and is much used for exporting grain and carrying thatching grass, long reed grass *(sirkunda)*, and twigs of *jhou* for wicker-work down-stream to Futtehgurh. The Ramgunga is also navigable for large boats throughout the length of its course in this pergunnah, and the traffic on it is considerable, chiefly grain of sorts down-stream, the boats often returning empty, or with light loads of iron or cloth.

River communication.

20. The Ganges flows along the south-western edge of this pergunnah, but now the actual stream of the river is the boundary only at the westernmost point, at the triple junction of the districts of Budaon, Futtehgurh, and Shahjehanpore, and for three and a half to four miles from that point between this district and Futtehgurh, and for that distance the stream is the boundary also between the villages on either side. From beyond that, the south-eastern end of Mouzah Sukhnya of this pergunnah, where it forms a triple boundary with Mouzahs Sultanpore Mujhra and Burragaon of Pergunnah Kaimgunge of the Futtehgurh District, the stream does not again touch the boundary of this district, and is not as the rule the boundary between villages. Had it been so, there would have been a still great accretion of area to villages in our district from the stream having worked gradually southwards than there has been. From the aforesaid point almost the extreme northern bank of the Ganges is the district boundary, the river itself and most of its alluvial bed, or *khadir*, being in the Futtehgurh District. The stream has, however, within the memory of living man been within the boundary of this district, and there is still a *Soate* or small *Boorh Gunga* which marks the northernmost channel of the Ganges within the present boundary of the district, and it is very probable that the stream may work over this way again within the next 30 years. The alluvial deposit in the Ganges valley is, as the rule, poor, the layer of soil being thin, and the admixture of sand very excessive. Tall reed grass *(sirkunda)*, thatching grass, and *jhou* grow abundantly in the uncultivated parts, and make up in a great measure for the deficiencies of the cultivated area of the *khadir*. Where the land is liable to considerable alteration from fluvial action, even though not actually touching the stream of the Ganges, either the whole mouzah or a separate muhal of it has been assessed for a short period of five years, liable to periodical revision under the rules in force for estates subject to alluvion and diluvion.

The rivers. The Ganges.

21. The Ramgunga enters the pergunnah at the north-western end, from having been for a short distance the boundary between the Budaon District and Pergunnah Khera Bujhera of this district. It flows in a south-easterly direction right through the middle of the pergunnah for a distance of seventeen miles, measured in a direct line, and on reaching the Futtehgurh District turns south towards the Ganges. The stream for part of the

The Ramgunga.

distance is in that, and part in this district, and fortunately is not the boundary between the districts, or even of villages anywhere, except for about a couple of miles just before it turns south. It receives the Bygool in about the middle of its course through the pergunnah, the confluence having been for the last few years about two miles south-west of Khunder, sometimes in Mundya Goojran, and sometimes in Thathur Maie: some 16 or 17 years ago the confluence was nearly three miles higher up the stream of the Bygool under Khunder. The Ramgunga has no defined valley or trough like the Ganges, but it has, nevertheless, a very broad valley of its own, between the high lands of the *bhoor* circle on the north and north-east on the one side, and the old uncut but low-lying hard clay *Bunkuttee Ilaka* on the other side. Within this valley, which contains by far the best land in, and is the most thickly populated part of, the pergunnah, the stream wanders about in the most arbitrary manner. The breadth of this valley varies from four to six miles, and is all alluvial deposit, and has all been cut away and reproduced by the Ramgunga at least once within the last 150 to 200 years, and by far the greater part of it has been removed and renewed by the stream several times within the last 70 or 80 years. Throughout the Ramgunga valley there is not one single high mound or *khera* marking the old ruined site of a village or fort, though they abound in the *bunkuttee* circle, and not one of the inhabited villages even is at all considerably raised above the level of the surrounding fields, as is invariably the case where the inhabited sites are old. The fact of a village site not being somewhat raised above the surrounding country is in itself a proof that the village is not an old one, and has not been located on that spot for any considerable number of years. The stream of the river is now, in several different places, from half to three-fourths of a mile away from where it was five years ago, when the measurements were made. It has since then cut off a large loop between Muktowra and Sohur, transferring the whole of three and parts of other villages from the right to the left bank of the stream, going into an old channel under the inhabited sites of Cuchooapore and Gubhurra, and cutting away a great part of them as well as of their areas, and the whole of the two small intervening *mouzahs*. It has cut away both village sites and nearly the whole of the area of Kundura Puharpore, and seems very inclined to betake itself to an old channel west of Atree and through the east edge of Zureenpore, some two miles away from its present channel in the areas of Noorpore, Kurhaie, Kola and Bujhera Mowa Dandee. The alluvial sandy deposit (for all the soil in this valley is a light sandy loam, and there are no traces of, or any hard substratum of, clay or kunkur, nothing but river sand) offers no resistance to the stream, and is cut away from one place and re-produced in another with astonishing rapidity. Three or four years suffice, when the deposits are soil and not sand, to reform land of a consistency and height above flood level, which gives the idea of being old land that has not been cut away for 12 or 15 years. Of course there always is, and always must be, a large area of sand and unformed alluvial deposit in the immediate valley and bed of the river on one side or other of the stream; but, as the rule, the land when formed and left by the river as done with is good, and only poor or actual sand as the exception. There is therefore no extent of locally constant uncultivated waste land in the Ramgunga valley producing *sirkunda* and thatching grass as in the *khadir* of the Ganges, and *jhou* seldom attains any age or growth as in the second, or at all events the third, year it is cut down and the land is cultivated. There is but little irrigation from the Ramgunga itself, but a good deal from its many old beds and deep hollows, called *dubrees*, which abound all over the valley.

22. The Bygool enters the pergunnah on the north, from being the boundary
The Bygool. between the Pergunnahs Khera Bujhera and Tilbur of this district, and has very little water in it for the first three or four miles of its course in this pergunnah during the cold weather, as it is dammed for irrigation a few miles higher up. It is a slow winding stream between high banks, and does not change its course materially or cause any alluvion or diluvion, and flowing in a south-westerly direction falls into the Ramgunga below Khunder, as already

mentioned. There is a little irrigation by lift, either by basket or lever well, chiefly the latter, on either side, but no attempt at damming it for irrigation in this pergunnah.

23. The Sote or Yar Wufadar is entirely a local stream which rises on the far side of the Budaon District, and enters this pergunnah from that district on the west. It runs parallel with the Ganges for a distance of nearly 18 miles, approaching it gradually, and under the name of Bookrakhar joins that river in the Futtehgurh District, and not at Dhai Ghat in this district, as stated in the description of this river in the Budaon Settlement Report. It is dammed at three places in this pergunnah for irrigation, and the entire stream is stopped and diverted into the irrigation channels, the surplus water again finding its way eventually into the bed of the river by different channels. The two principal dams are called respectively the Pilowa and Luchmunpore dams, but the Pilowa dam is some two miles up-stream from the village of Pilowa, between Kylaha and Dhukka. The third is at Budhora, at the junction of the Muhey *nulla*, and it is only second in importance to the two principal dams. There are numbers of other small dams, but they are dependent on and subservient to the two first, which are very large and important dams right across the bed of the river, completely stopping the whole stream. There are two principal *nullas* or natural flood drains, the Url and the Andowee *nuddees*, winding about the north-west part of the *Bunkuttee Ilaka* and receiving other small *nullas*, mostly natural, but partly artificial, the Url itself falling into the Andowee. The Luchmunpore dam is just below the junction of the Andowee *nuddee* with the Sote, and holds up not only all the natural drainage of the country through these *nullas*, but also all the water turned into them by the Pilowa dam seven or eight miles higher up the stream. The Budhowra dams on the Sote and Muhey *nulla* are at the tail, and hold up all the natural drainage and water led into the Ahleea and Muhey *nullas* and their tributaries which occupy the south-eastern portion of this circle. By this means the greater part of the *Bunkuttee Ilaka* is supplied with irrigation, the gentle slope of the country to the south-east allowing of a complete network of irrigating channels being kept full and running throughout the cold season ; and this system of irrigation is the mainstay and backbone of the spring harvest of this part of the pergunnah. But it doubtless is the chief cause also of the spread of *reh* and of the unhealthiness of this part of the pergunnah.

24. An elaborate inquiry has been instituted, during the preparation of settlement records, into the places at which the various principal dams (not being mere local *mends*) are made, when and by whom they are constructed, under whose management and at what expense, and by what villages the expenses are borne, and in what proportions. A formal vernacular proceeding has been drawn up showing all these details, as well as what villages are dependent on these dams for irrigation, and where only partially so, to what extent, and all necessary particulars connected therewith. The entries in the *wajiboolurz* of each village concerned has been made in accordance with the details of the said proceeding relating to that particular village. In the event of any dispute, the District Officers will only have to refer to and carry out the rules laid down in the above-named proceeding. As the demand for water is daily increasing, and the supply cannot increase (but, if anything, is rather decreasing, owing to extended cultivation retaining more of the rainfall), it is probable that disputes will arise, and the care which has now been taken to record existing facts, practices and rights, and to collate them into one general proceeding, will prove a boon to the Executive Officers of the District and to the parties themselves concerned. No water-rate or irrigation-rate or due of any kind is paid in any of the villages to the zemindar of that or any other village. The only charge on the village is its share in the expenses of making the dam on which its irrigation depends, and even where this is in money, it is *not* recovered by a water-rate separate from the rent of the land, in which, however, capability of irrigation has been included.

Marginal notes: The Sote or Yar Wufadar.

Code of rules regarding the various dams on the Sote and its tributaries.

25. The areas of the pergunnah, arranged according to the principal divisions, are given in the following form for each circle separately, according to the new plane-table measurement of the present settlement, together with the totals for the pergunnah, and also the totals according to the survey measurement of last settlement.

Figured statement of area for each circle, and for the whole pergunnah at present and last settlement.

Name of Circle.	Total area in acres.	AREA EXCLUDED FROM ASSESSMENT.			MALGOOZAREE OR ASSESSABLE AREA.						Total assessable area.
		Barren, including roads, inhabited sites, &c.	Maafee.	Total.	Culturable.			Cultivated.			
					Old unbroken waste.	New fallow.	Baghs.	Irrigated.	Unirrigated.	Total.	
Bhoor, ...	31,497	2,248	122	2,365	4,019	554	1,098	6,665	16,796	23,461	29,132
Terai, ...	82,073	11,163	1,325	12,488	11,449	819	1,448	14,243	41,635	55,878	69,585
Bunkuttee, ...	89,559	11,601	53	11,654	25,698	3,092	915	27,650	20,550	48,200	77,905
Total of Pergunnah, ...	203,129	25,007	1,500	26,507	41,166	4,456	3,461	48,558	78,981	127,539*	176,622
Total of last settlement, ...	195,275	21,625	4,452	26,077	69,155	5,343	*Included partly in old unbroken waste and partly in land exempt from assessment.*	39,249	56,451	94,700	169,198

There is an increase of 7,854 acres, equivalent to rather more than 4 per cent. This is not mere difference in measurement, but is almost entirely in the *bunkuttee* circle (*viz.*, 5,800 acres of it), and is satisfactorily accounted for by the Ganges having retreated southwards for a length of frontage of some 8 or 9 miles, thereby increasing considerably the areas of those villages forming the south-western boundary of the pergunnah. The difference attributable to measurement only is scarcely one per cent. The decrease in the *maafee* area is owing to lapse of life-grants in part, but chiefly to confiscation for rebellion during 1857-58 A. D.

26. Of the entire *malgoozaree* or assessable area of the pergunnah, the area actually under cultivation is 72¼ per cent., and the uncultivated portion is 27¾ per cent. But in order to ascertain the exact proportion of old unreclaimed culturable waste, the areas of the new fallow and *baghs* must be omitted, and then the proportion of culturable waste to actual cultivation is 33 per cent., and to *malgoozaree* area 23 per cent. for the entire pergunnah. The percentages for the three circles and for the whole pergunnah, given in the margin, show

Details of the malgoozaree or assessable area.

PROPORTIONS OF OLD UNBROKEN CULTURABLE WASTE.

Circle.	*i. e., percentage thereof*	
	On cultivation.	Of *malgoozaree* area.
Bhoor, ...	17·1	13·9
Terai, ...	20·1	16·7
Bunkuttee, ..	53·0	32·9
Whole pergunnah,	33·0	23·2

that the proportion of waste in the *bhoor* and *terai* circles is not at all excessive. In the *bhoor* circle, with the exception of some 10 or 12 villages near its southern end, the unreclaimed waste is little more than nominal; but in those specified it is considerable, and doubtless much of it will be brought under the plough during the currency of the present settlement. In the *terai* circle there is very little probability of

* There is a difference of 552 acres of cultivation in these figures in excess of the corrected totals of the No. IV. General Statement, owing chiefly to diluvion in three villages after the totals for this report had been prepared. There are other small immaterial discrepancies, as this report was completed before the No. IV. General Statement compiled from the *misls* after final scrutiny was prepared.

considerable reduction of waste and increase of cultivation, as almost all the waste is in the new land in the bed of the Ramgunga, which remains pretty constant in amount, though it varies in locality and details very considerably every four or five years. The highest proportion (53 per cent.) is in the *bunkuttee* circle, though the extension of cultivation has been greater there than in the other two circles. This culturable waste extends throughout the circle, and is principally *dhâk* jungle, with thatching grass (*poolah*) growing in it. It is most continuous up near the north-west end of the circle across the Url Nuddee, beyond the reach of irrigation to any considerable extent from the Sote dams. The income from thatching grass is large, but not so certain or constant as from cultivation, and is steadily increasing, as the grass-producing area is growing smaller. Before the present revision the income from grass alone was treble and quadruple of the Government revenue in many villages, even where there was a rental from the cultivated area of nearly double or more than double the *jumma*. Extension of cultivation will doubtless take place in this circle, but not very rapidly, and only in exceptional instances has any been anticipated in assessment, the rule having been merely to include all actual or estimated assets from the unreclaimed waste in its present state in calculating the gross rental of an estate. The area under mango groves, exempt from assessment under existing orders of the Board of Revenue, is small,

Board's Circular No. 22, dated 30th October 1869. less than 2 per cent. of the assessable area for the whole pergunnah. The *bagh* area is by far the smallest in the *bunkuttee* circle, and the groves and trees themselves are not near equal in size and growth to those in the other parts of the pergunnah and district. The details for each circle are as follows:—

Bhoor,	...	1,098	acres,	3¾	per cent. of	assessable area.		
Terai,	...	1,448	,,	2	,,	,,	,,	
Bunkuttee,	...	915	,,	1	,,	,,	,,	

27. In this *bunkuttee* circle alone is there any real *oosur* and *shorkuller* such as is

Oosur and reh infected lands of the *bunkuttee* circle. found in the *oosur* plains of the "Gangetic Doab." It is more or less scattered about throughout the *dhâk* jungle, and every here and there are found considerable continuous stretches of it, as in Pirtheepore, Kooberpore, and in Tihar, across the Url Nuddee, and in Mirzapore and several of its neighbours in the south-east end of the circle. The efflorescence shows itself a great deal all about Pilowa and in the low lands which are water-logged and super-saturated by the Sote dams. In Titree and Malon, west of the Pilowa dam, the efflorescence is as bad as any that I have ever seen along the Ganges Canal. There is nothing approaching to this in any other part of the district. Some of this *oosur* and *reh* infected land has very probably been included in the culturable waste, but, as a rule, it has been excluded and thrown into the barren area, and only where it was partial and much intermixed with the really good unreclaimed waste has it been taken in with it.

28. The total increase in cultivation is 32,839 acres, being at the rate of just 35

Increase in the cultivated area. per cent. The details for each circle are given in the margin, from which it will be seen that the increase in the *bhoor* circle is the smallest, and in the *bunkuttee* much the largest, and very considerable in the

Circle.	Percentage.
Bhoor,	... 14·7
Terai,	... 36·1
Bunkuttee,	... 45·1

terai circle. By far the greater part of this increase is genuine extension of cultivation by reclamation of waste, and only a small portion is attributable to confiscation and resumption of already cultivated revenue-free lands, and to the smaller area of new fallow now than at the last settlement. Allowing for these sets-off against the gross increase of cultivated area, the nett *bonâ fide* extension of cultivation is about 28,000 acres, and just 30 per cent. on the former cultivated area.

29. In the Appendices (C. and D.) are given for each circle detailed figured

Details of soils and sources of irrigation. statements of the areas of the various soils, with their percentages, the amount of each irrigated and unirrigated, with the source of irrigation. The soils are the same as those already mentioned in Tuhseel

10т

Shahjehanpore, and allusion has already been made to them in paragraphs descriptive

Name of circle.	Percentage of cultivated area irrigated.	Percentage of total irrigated area irrigated from various sources, viz.—		
		Wells.	Ponds and Tanks.	Rivers.
Bhoor, ...	28·40	62	37	1
Terai, ...	25·48	51	33	16
Bunkuttee, ...	57·36	14	29	57
Whole pergunnah, ...	38·07	33	33	34

of the circles. From the marginal statement it will be seen that 38 per cent. of the cultivated area is entered as irrigated. This only represents the area actually irrigated at year of measurement, or ordinarily irrigated, and is far below the area capable of irrigation. It is, in fact, below the average, which is quite 43 per cent., as the year of measurement was a favorable year, rain falling several times during the cold season, and rendering general irrigation in the *bhoor* and *terai* circles unnecessary. In neither of those circles is general irrigation needed for the rubbee in favorable seasons, and only one watering in ordinary seasons ; whereas irrigation is a *sine quâ non* in the *bunkuttee* circle even in favorable years, and usually three waterings are necessary for wheat, and sometimes more. The percentages of the various sources of irrigation are very even for the whole pergunnah, but vary exceedingly in the different circles, the irrigation in the *bhoor* circle being almost entirely from wells, and half of it from wells in the *terai* circle, but only a small proportion in the *bunkuttee* circle. In this circle the dams of the River Sote are the principal source of irrigation, and even some that is credited to ponds and tanks is in a measure due to the said dams. There are, however, several very large ponds, or more properly small lakes, which only dry up completely in May or June and afford ample irrigation throughout the cold season, and numbers of other small ones, which, however, fail unless the rains have been copious. The *bunkuttee* circle, from the hard, dry, thirsty nature of its soil, is the one that requires irrigation the most urgently, and the sources of irrigation of which are the most uncertain ; for wells, as a rule, do not answer, as already explained (in para. 6), and the extent of water in the Sote *nullas* and ponds is in the inverse ratio to the requirements,—the supply being short in a dry season, when irrigation is most urgently needed. All over the *terai* circle and in many parts of the *bhoor* circle wells (the common lever well or *dhenklee*) can be made in from one to two days at a small expense (Re. 1-8 to Rs. 3) when required ; but it must be a very exceptionally dry season that necessitates extensive use of wells in the *terai* circle. The distance of the water-level from the surface of the ground varies from 10 to 18 feet in different parts of the pergunnah and at different seasons, exclusive of the regular rains and the low *khadir* in the actual flood-beds of the Ganges and Ramgunga. It is usually between 12 and 15 feet in the *bhoor* and *bunkuttee* circles, and from 10 to 13 feet in the *terai* circle, during the irrigating season from October to March.

30. Rents throughout the pergunnah are almost universally in money ; payment

Rents and rent-rates.

in kind or by appraisement of produce being very exceptional, and entirely confined to very poor lands, or lands in which from one cause or another the crop is exceedingly precarious, and for which the cultivators refuse to pay a money rent. The beegah in use is the *kuchha* or village *beegah*, which varies slightly in some parts, but is pretty generally 3¾ to 4 *kuchha* beegahs to one Government *pucka* beegah, rather over 6 *kuchha* beegahs to the acre. All dealings between the proprietors and cultivators are transacted on this *kuchha beegha*, so much so that in ordinary conversation the rate is mentioned, and the beegah omitted as understood. The rents are paid partly by lump rents (*chukota*), partly by soil rates (*shara kismwar*), and partly by rates on *hars* or tracts (*shara harwar*). All the rates are irrespective of whether the land is or is not actually irrigated, though not altogether irrespective of the proximity of or capability of irrigation. In this pergunnah the rents and rates generally are higher than those of the Shahjehanpore

Tuhseel, and nowhere so utterly inadequate as the rates found in some parts of that tuhseel.

31. The inequality of the *kuchha* beegah in no way affects the accuracy of the deduced average rent-rates, as they are all worked out on the acre from actual correct areas, and not assumed from the prevailing rates per *kuchha beegah*. Villages of all kinds were taken in all directions of the three circles, and their areas and rents carefully abstracted, nominal rates on *seer* or favored rates for relatives or ex-proprietors being omitted, and only full rates and rents of cultivators taken. The areas thus abstracted are as follows,—in the *bhoor* circle, 11,424 acres; in the *terai* circle, 18,899 acres; and in the *bunkutt e* circle, 13,796; and the rates being, as a rule, adequate and full, and not capable of any general enhancement all round, the assumed average rent-rates, which are given in the margin, were kept very close to the deduced rates. *Gowhanee* is an artificial soil and of very small extent, and only found where there are Kachee cultivators, or where there is poppy cultivation about the village site. The rates for *gowhanee* are very similar in all three

Deduced and assumed rent-rates.

ASSUMED AVERAGE RENT-RATES PER ACRE.

Name of soil.	Name of Circle.		
	Bhoor.	Terai.	Bunkuttee.
	Rs. a. p.	Rs. a. p.	Rs. a. p.
Gowhanee, ...	6 8 0	6 8 0	6 8 0
1st Class Domut, ...	3 10 0	4 4 0	3 10 0
Mutyar, ...	3 0 0	3 12 0	3 0 0
2nd Class Domut, ...	2 10 0	3 12 0	2 0 0
Bhoor, ...	2 4 0	2 8 0	2 4 0
Standard cultivation, or all-round rate, ...	2 11 3	4 0 0	3 4 8

circles, and so no difference has been made between them. The *terai* circle rates are considerably higher throughout than those of the other circles, whilst those of the *bhoor* and *bunkuttee* are very similar for the various soils, but give very different results, in consequence of the excess of the inferior denominations of soil in the *bhoor* circle; the standard cultivation or all-round rate of the *bhoor* circle being under Rs. 2-12-0, as against Rs. 3-4-8 of the *bunkuttee* circle. In practice these rates were found much too high for the poor and inferior villages of the *terai* and *bunkuttee* circles, and other lower rates were used for them, and mentioned in the assessment remarks ; but these soil-rates are those by which the rental at assumed average rent-rates of the No. III. figured statement for each mouzah and muhal are worked out. The No. III. Statement for each separate circle, with the soil-areas, rates, and resulting rentals, will be found in the Appendix C., already referred to.

32. The rentals according to the putwarees' *nikasees* corrected for *seer* held at low or nominal rates, as also (2) the estimated actual assets after further correction for small omissions and under-renting to relatives and dependants, as well as for *sewaie* income, and (3) the rental resulting from the assumed circle rent-rates, and also (4) the gross assumed potential assets on which the *mouzahwar* and *muhalwar* assessments were eventually based, are given below for each circle separately :—

Rentals and assets, actual and assumed.

1.	2.	3.	4.	5.	6.
Name of circle.	Rental in *nikasees* corrected for *seer* only.	Estimated actual assets.	Rental resulting from assumed rates.	Gross assumed potential assets.	Percentage of gross assumed over actual assets, i.e., column 5 over column 3.
	Rs.	Rs.	Rs.	Rs.	
Bhoor, ...	60,130	62,950	63,462	65,614	4·23
Terai, ...	1,98,450	2,03,260	2,23,430	2,19,310	7·84
Bunkuttee, ...	1,36,520	1,44,800	1,61,383	1,60,226	10·65
Total of Tuhseel, ...	3,95,100	4,11,010	4,48,275	4,45,150	8·30

The *nikassee* are, if anything, more trustworthy here than in Shahjehanpore Tuhseel, as almost all the proprietors are illiterate and trust entirely to the putwarees' accounts. Consequently, there is little real concealment as regards the rent of cultivated land, but a good deal of omission regarding *sewaie* items. This, however, is almost entirely confined to the *bunkuttee* circle (as there is but little *sewaie* in the other two circles), in which the amount of *sewaie* for thatching grass, &c., not entered in the putwarees' *nikassee*, is over Rs. 4,000. Hence the difference between the supposed actual assets and the rental corrected for *seer* is considerable in the *bunkuttee* circle, but of small amount in the *bhoor* and *terai* circles. For the same reason, i. e., owing to the extensive areas of culturable waste and *sewaie* income therefrom, the percentage of gross assumed potential assets over estimated actual assets is largest in the *bunkuttee* circle. In the *bhoor* circle alone the gross assumed potential assets exceed the rental resulting from assumed average circle rates; in the other two circles they fall short of it. The explanation is that in the *bhoor* circle the presence of the town of Jellalabad raised the number of good and above average villages considerably, so that they more than counterbalanced the poor and inferior villages below the general circle average. No similar cause was present in either the *terai* or *bunkuttee* circles, and the number of villages below the general circle average proved considerably in excess of those above the average, so that in point of fact, as already mentioned, the average rates for the *terai* and *bunkuttee* circles were the averages of those circles, omitting the bad and inferior villages in them. Those below average and inferior villages in the *terai* circle are,—(1) either along the edge of the circle, partaking largely of the quality and nature of the adjoining circles, or (2) along the Ramgunga stream, with extensive areas of *kuchha khadir* in the flood-valley. In the *bunkuttee* circle they are more scattered. In neither could they have been made into a separate circle with local defined limits.

33. But the *jummas* actually assessed do not, for reasons given in the following paragraph, amount to half of the gross assumed potential assets. They are, however, for each circle in excess of the supposed actual assets at time of revision, nearly Rs. 6,000 for the whole pergunnah, and are very large increases on the old or expiring *jumma*. This will best be seen in the tabular form which follows :—

Pergunnah jummas assessable and actually assessed.

Circle.	Old, *i.e.*, current expiring jumma.	Jumma assessable at full 50 per cent. of gross assumed potential assets.	Jumma assessable at half of estimated actual assets,	New jumma actually assessed.	Percentage of new jumma actually assessed over old jumma, *i.e.*, column 5 over column 2.
	Rs. a. p.	Rs.	Rs.	Rs.	
Bhoor, ...	24,532 9 6	82,807	31,475	31,550	29·0
Terai, ...	85,786 4 3	1,09,655	1,01,630	1,02,681	19·4
Bunkuttee, ...	50,924 9 3	80,113	72,400	77,080	31·7
Total of Tuhseel,...	1,61,243 7 0	2,22,575	2,05,505	2,11,410	31·1

34. The assessment of the pergunnah has been made nominally at half-assets, or 50 per cent. of the gross rental; but partly in consequence of the very large general increase, and exceedingly heavy enhancement of revenue in special instances, and partly owing to the

Assessment—Rajpoot communities sometimes at under half-assets.

number of indigent peasant proprietors in many of the Rajpoot communities, the new assessment has in many instances not been put at 50 per cent. of potential assets. The question of extending some leniency to the Rajpoot peasant proprietors, where the enhancement of revenue was very large, and the shareholders were numerous and in bad circumstances, was the subject of a special report through the Board of Revenue to the Lieutenant-Governor; and though no definite and precise orders of the exact percentage of assets at which the revenue should be fixed were received, yet the general principle of some moderate leniency being shown was acknowledged, and the matter was left to the discretion of the Settlement Officers. The Khunder Ilaka of Chundela Rajpoots was instanced, which consists of 72 mouzahs, in 61 of which the tenure is *putteedaree* (59), or *bhyachara* (2), and the shareholders are very numerous ; the number of separate *khathas* or holdings being 894, and of the adult co-sharers and their families dependent for their livelihood, food, clothing, &c., upon the said villages, approximately 3,250. The exact number of shareholders *recorded in the khewuts of this Ilaka*, not counting the same individual twice over, is 426, and most of these are heads of families, and not single individuals. The procedure adopted was that, where the enhancement of revenue was large, sums varying commonly from 5 to 15 per cent., and exceptionally from 20 to 25 per cent., were deducted from the full actual corrected rental or *potential* rental (if actual was inadequate), and the assessment fixed at 50 per cent. of the remainder. The whole case has in every instance been fully stated in the assessment remarks appended to the No. III. figured statement, and the instance of the largest amounts of reduction are given in the margin. The details can be seen in the reasons of assessment for each muozah and mahal in the bound volumes of Nos. II. and III. Statements, to which reference is solicited. The total number of mouzahs in which this leniency has been granted are 139 and 2 mahals, and the total amount of reduction is Rs. 11,165, being just over 14 per cent. on the jummas actually assessed, which are themselves no less than 46½ per cent. enhancement on the former or expiring jummas. The marginal statements show most clearly that reduction below a full 50 per cent. assessment has only been given to any extent where the increase of the new jumma is enormous, and that, notwithstanding that requisite leniency, the increase of actually assessed over lately current revenue is nearly 47 per cent. The amount, details of which for each circle are given in the margin, seems large when looked at alone, and if added to the jumma of the pergunnah actually assessed would have made the total increase of revenue 38 per cent. instead

Name of mouzah.		Former. jumma.	New. jumma.	Amount of relaxation or reduction below a full 50 per cent. assessment.
		Rs.	Rs.	Rs.
Imliya Khoord,	...	105	200	50
Andpoor,	...	382	750	200
Banskhera Kullan,	...	200	400	80
Bunbussa,	...	35	200	60
Bhengee Khera,	...	121	500	100
Pirtheepoor Lhai,	...	3,869	4,650	500
Pilowa,	...	1,730	2,200	400
Chowkee Azumpoor,	...	458	530	122
Jeerao,	...	501	910	110
Dohee Judeed,	...	401	900	150
Oomursund,	...	275	900	100
Furreedpoor,	...	485	650	100
Kutelee,	...	670	950	150
Koondree Ilaka Khunder,	...	500	600	150
Koondura Ilaka Pyna,	...	105	280	50
Khujooree,	...	1,035	2,500	750
Khunder Khas,	...	1,400	1,600	225
Keelapoor Kullan,	...	1,517	2,000	400
Mudera,	...	425	950	150
Mulookpoor,	...	220	400	80
Munoruthpoor,	...	176	300	50
Nurainpoor,	...	138	200	50
Har Chuchora,	...	500	930	237
Kurnapoor Talooka Chowkee,	...	117	180	40
Kukrala Ditto,	...	280	400	80
Gurelee,	...	275	500	100

1.	2.	3.	4.	5.
Number of mouzahs or parts of mouzahs concerned.	Former jumma.	Full jumma at 50 per cent. of potential assets.	Jumma actually assessed.	Percentage of actual increase of new over former jumma.
141	53,440	89,535	78,373	46·65

of 31 per cent.; but I believe that no more allowance has been made than the exigencies of the case called for; and I trust that I shall be judged to have exercised a sound discretion in the amounts and instances in which I have fixed the revenue at below a full 50 per cent. of rental assets. The amount of reduction is greatest in the terai circle, not only as an actual sum, but also relatively to the lately current jumma and new revenue now assessed, as in

Circle.		Rs.
Bhoor,	...	1,157
Terai,	...	6,975
Bunkuttee,	...	3,033
Total,		11,165

that circle the Rajpoot communities with numerous shareholders prevail much more extensively than in the other two circles. It has been shown in the preceding paragraph that, notwithstanding this considerable remission, the pergunnah jumma is still Rs. 6,000 in excess of 50 per cent. of estimated actual assets existing at the time of revision. As, however, it may appear from the foregoing remarks on this question that I have been acting entirely on my own responsibility, and distributing reductions below a full 50 per cent. assessment, unfettered and unrestrained, I give extracts from the Board's orders, and my own report in reply, to show that the subject was fully entered into, and that my procedure received the approval and sanction of the Board.

Extract from Board's No. 312, dated 25th July 1870, to the Commissioner of Rohilkhund.

" 2. With reference to the measures to be adopted in regard to the Thakoor *bhyachara* communities, especially in the Khunder *Ilaka,* I am to observe that the necessity of making some reduction on the full demand in estates held by a numerous body of cultivators is fully recognized by the Board, but as no fixed rate can at present be laid down, the allowance to be granted in each case must depend upon the particular circumstances, and it will be for the Settlement Officer, when applying his rates, to determine the amount which he may think necessary.

" 3. I am to add that if Mr. Currie would furnish the Board with the results of his assessments in nine or ten *bhyachara* estates, stating in his remarks the amount of reduction he would recommend, and his reasons for so doing, orders could be passed on these reports, which would serve for his guidance in similar cases.

Extract from reply to the above by Settlement Officer of Shahjehanpore,—dated 21st November 1870.

" 2. I have delayed submitting this report until I had completed the assessment of the whole Jellalabad Tuhseel, and instead of submitting my remarks and result of assessment of only nine or ten *bhyachara* estates, I append a statement of the 58 *bhyachara* villages of the Khunder *Ilaka* of Chundela Rajpoots, and of 7 villages of a small *ilaka* of Ponwar Rajpoots, and an explanation of the grounds on which I have granted reductions.

" 3. In column 4 of that statement is shown the jumma which might be assessed on the village as regards its capabilites, with the single exception of its forming part of a *bhyachara* community. In column 5 is shown the jumma actually assessed on a reduced or modified rental lowered so as to give what I consider, under the circumstances, a sufficient amount of relief from the full assessable jumma if the village had been the property of only one individual, or only a few shareholders. In column 6 is the amount of difference between the two preceding columns, viz., the actual amount of relaxation or remission granted ; and in column 7 the actual increase retained in the new jumma over the current jumma, i. e., the old jumma just expired.

" 4. As regards the 58 villages of the Khunder *Ilaka*, it will be seen that out of a total possible enhancement of Rs. 9,602-9-9, being at the rate of 61¼ per cent., Rs. 6,232, or about 40 per cent., hav e been retained, and Rs. 3,370, or about 20¼ per cent., have been remitted. In other words, out of a total possible revised jumma of Rs. 25,200, the amount actually assessed is Rs. 21,830, or rather more than 86¼ per cent., and the amount remitted is Rs. 3,370, or rather less than 13¼ per cent.

" 5. As regards the seven villages of the Chowkee *Ilaka* of Ponwar Thakoors, out of a total possible enhancement of Rs. 585 (at 45 per cent. on the current jumma), Rs. 325 (or 25 per cent.) have been retained, and Rs. 260 (or 20 per cent.) are remitted. And out of a total possible revised jumma of Rs. 1,880, the sum of Rs. 1,620, or 86 per cent., is actually assessed, and Rs. 260, or 14 per cent., are remitted.

" 6. These figures represent the ordinary amount of remission granted in *bhya-chara* villages, in which there is a large increase in the revised jumma, *viz.*, from 13 to 15 per cent. of what the jumma would have been under ordinary circumstances ; or, in other words, a reduction of from 13 to 15 per cent. in the rental I assumed as the basis of my assessment, under the exceptional circumstances, in lieu of the full rental which would have been assumed under ordinary circumstances. But in some particular instances, as in Khujooree, where the proprietors are very numerous indeed, and the increase is over 80 and 100 per cent., a somewhat larger remission has been absolutely necessary. In Khujooree aforesaid the percentage of enhancement retained is 74 against 26 remitted, and still the actual jumma fixed is at the rate of increase of 140 per cent. upon the former jumma, *viz.*, former jumma Rs. 1,000, revised jumma, exclusive of cesses, Rs. 2,400 ; 16 per cent. of a full assessable jumma having been remitted and 84 per cent. retained.

" 7. It now remains only for me to explain the grounds upon which I have granted these remissions, and the points which have guided me in apportioning the amount remitted. First and foremost, I have not granted any remission except in those cases in which there was a considerable rise in the jumma, and the amount of remission granted has always been greatly dependent upon the extent of the increase.

" 8. *Second.*—The number and status of the sharers composing the proprietary body, and the amount of rent actually collected from the *assamees*, irrespective of the *seer* of the shareholders, have been the points next looked to.

" 9. *Third.*—When the *ilaka* is composed of a number of villages, the principal remission has been granted in those particular villages in which the resident proprietors are the most numerous, and the amount of *seer* the greatest, and consequently the amount of rent collected from *assamees* is comparatively small.

" 10. My reasons are that, *first*,—so long as there is only a slight or moderate increase, the zemindars do not raise any objection, or look for any abatement. They look upon revision of settlement as entailing some increase, and expect it as a matter of course. A small increase can be easily met, but a sudden rise of from 40 to 100 per cent. comes very hard even upon well-to-do proprietors, and is absolute ruin to those who have found it difficult to make both ends meet under a light assessment. *Secondly*, the larger the number of shareholders, the more mouths are there dependent on the surplus profits ; and it is not a mere matter of some luxury being temporarily given up, but perhaps one meal a day given up, or a daughter left unmarried for several years for want of means. So long as the cultivating shareholder's *seer* is left untouched, and the Government revenue can be paid out of the rent actually collected from *assamees*, there is no real hardship (if necessary) in assessing the jumma up to the full rental collected from the *assamees*. It is when a portion of the jumma has to be distributed over the *seer* of the shareholders, and they have to sell their produce to pay the Government *kist*, that the jumma becomes a burden; and the greater the number of shareholders, and the larger the amount of land cultivated by them, and consequently the less that is held by mere tenants, the more directly does any increase come home to each and every individual sharer."

After a further explanatory report in reply to some questions asked by the Board, their sanction was accorded in their Secretary's letter No. 155, dated 4th May 1871, to the address of the Commissioner of Rohilkhund.

35. Special arrangements have been made for all villages (with certain excep-

Special arrangements of composition of assessment for villages bordering on the Ramgunga.

tions) bordering on, or in the immediate vicinity of, the Ramgunga, by which, in lieu of a quinquennial revision of settlement, a composition has been effected, and a certain annual jumma has been assessed for the full term of the settlement, irrespective of all intermediate alluvion and diluvion. The estimate is made, and the composition based, on the average cultivated areas and rentals of the past 18 and 20 and, where procurable, 25 years, and the present and probable condition of the village. This composition principle has not been applied at all to any villages bordering on the Ganges, but to all adjoining the Ramgunga, except those which preferred the quinquennial revision arrangement, or those in which no fair and adequate composition could be made in consequence of their being at their worst, further deterioration almost impossible, and very considerable improvement possible, and even likely. The composition system could not have been introduced had the stream of the Ramgunga been the boundary between villages, but it is not (except in two instances where the stream is the boundary of the district), and the custom is *ménd-dhoora*, and not *dhar-dhoora*. The villages included in this composition scheme are many of them cluster properties along or near the river; and in these although a separate jumma is allotted to each village, yet the assessment is on the whole property, and the case of one village of a cluster property cannot be entertained separate from the property. But many also are single properties, and in these, as the rule, the stream of the Ramgunga passes through the area of the mouzah, and there are cultivated lands on both sides. The stream shifts about more or less, but does not leave the area; and the proportions of sand, water, incipient and half-formed soil, culturable waste and cultivation remain very fairly constant in extent, though altering in position and locality considerably.

The whole subject has been up before the Board of Revenue and Government, North-Western Provinces, and the composition system has, after much correspond-

* No. 1719A., dated 27th October, 1871, from Secretary to Government, North-Western Provinces, to Secretary, Board of Revenue, North-Western Provinces.

ence and explanation, been sanctioned, and a stipulation to the following effect, in conformity with the orders* of Government, has been inserted in the *wajiboolurz*, that in the event of an application for reduction of jumma being made on the plea of diluvion, and the terms of the composition being broken, the settlement of that village shall be subject to quinquennial revision from that time forward, under the rules in force for the time being for revision of alluvial estates.

All alluvial muhals on the Ganges and those on the Ramgunga to which the

† Board of Revenue's Circular No. 8., dated 2nd September 1853.

composition scheme has not been extended have been assessed, subject to quinquennial revision, under the rules in force for alluvial muhals subject in a marked degree to fluvial action.

36. With the exception of the special cases just mentioned, the assessment has

General remarks on rate of assessment.

been made for each mouzah and muhal at half-assets, or 50 per cent. of the gross actual assets, or where actual assets were insufficient of the potential rental, including all income from *sewaie* items, such as thatching-grass, wood, grazing fees, &c. In calculating the rental assets, the assumed average circle rent-rates were only used as one guide, or as a test of what the assets should be if the particular village was a fair average one for the circle, and not as the only basis of estimate. In the English assessment remarks appended to the Nos. II. and III. figured statements of each mouzah and muhal (bound books of which accompany this report) have been entered in full in English a general description of the village, its capabilities, previous and current rentals, and reasons for abiding by the result of the assumed rates, or for assessing above or below them. Reductions from severe current jummas have been freely granted where necessary, but not merely on the one ground of actual or assumed rental showing that the current revenue was above the half-asset rate ; nor have they been made, as the rule, quite down to the same amount as would have been assessed if a considerable increase on the current *jumma* was being made, instead of a decrease from it. All the various circumstances have been given full consideration, and reduction apportioned to the necessities of each particular case has been granted.

37. A map of the pergunnah, on the scale of 1 inch =1 mile, showing the boundaries and village sites of all the *mouzahs*, and the cultivated and uncultivated areas, the roads, rivers, and *nullas*, accompanies this report. In the area of each *mouzah* is written the revenue-rate or incidence per cultivated acre of the Government revenue. It will be seen that the highest rates prevail in the *terai* circle generally, and especially in the southern part of it, in what was the old pergunnah of Bangaon ; that they run chiefly from Re. 1-10-0 to Rs. 2-4-0 in the *terai* circle ; from Re. 1-8-0 to Re. 1-12-0 in the *bunkuttee* circle ; and from Re. 1-2-0 to Re. 1-7-0 in the *bhoor* circle, some few of the worst villages being as low as seventeen annas and a rupee. Where any considerable discrepancy exists in the revenue-rate of adjoining or neighbouring villages, a reference to the Nos. II. and III. Statements and assessment remarks will at once explain it.

Map of pergunnah, showing local details and incidence of revenue per cultivated acre.

38. The revenue of the last five settlements is given in the margin, but the pergunnahs as then constituted did not include the old pergunnah of Bangaon, which was only transferred to this pergunnah and district after Mr. Muir's assessment. The actual *jumma* assessed by Mr. Muir on this pergunnah was Rs. 1,12,684, a reduction of Rs. 26,770 on the previous *jumma*. The *jumma* of the pergunnah after the incorporation of the old Bangaon pergunnah from the Futtehgurh District is Rs. 1,60,610, and both *jummas* are shown for the 9th settlement for sake of comparison with the previous *jummas* and the present revision.

Revenue of former settlements, and remarks on last one.

Settlement.		Jumma.
		Rs.
5th, Jellalabad alone,	...	1,46,309
6th, „	...	1,45,151
7th, „	...	1,42,909
8th, „	...	1,39,354
9th, Mr. Muir's	...	1,12,684
9th, including Bangaon	...	1,60,610
Revised *jumma* of new settlement,	...	2,12,105

With reference to the late settlement, and its general lightness in the old pergunnah of Mehrabad, and severity in the old pergunnah of Bangaon, I make the following extracts from my rent-rate report submitted to the Board previous to assessment, and from Mr. J. W. Muir's settlement report :—

" The assessment of the old pergunnah of Mehrabad was made in 1837-38 A. D. by Mr. J. W. Muir, whilst 51 *mouzahs* composing the pergunnah of Bangaon were assessed in the Futtehgurh District by Mr. Robinson in 1839 A. D.; and whereas Mr. Muir's assessment was somewhat easy and low, Mr. Robinson's was, on the other hand, particularly heavy at first, and pressed very hard on the zemindars, the more especially as there are large proprietary Thakoor communities in almost all of the Bangaon villages.

" Pergunnah Mehrabad when assessed by Mr. J. W. Muir consisted of 331 *mouzahs*, and the *jumma* of it was reduced from Rs. 1,39,354 to Rs. 1,12,684, the revenue-rate per cultivated acre being Re. 1-8-0. Mr. J. W. Muir found the pergunnah ' labouring under the pressure of a very heavy assessment,' and gives in his report, dated

5th September 1838 A. D., his reasons for the causes and existence of over-assessment, and for the necessity of relief, as follows :—

'The over-assessment of these pergunnahs may be traced in a great measure, more particularly in three Tuhseeldaree Divisions out of the four, to the great increase of revenue that was imposed under former settlements, the enhancement of *jumma* since 1210 F.S. being more than the resources of the majority of estates were adequate to pay. The fresh revision of the assessment, particularly at the third and fourth settlements, was made the means of raising the *jumma* as much as possible, an object the furtherance of which was enjoined as the peculiar duty of all the Pergunnah and Tuhseel Officers, particularly of the Canoongoes. To the latter rewards even were held out, and accordingly it is said that Dheeree Dhur, the Canoongoe of Mehrabad, received the present of an elephant from Mr, Trant for his exertions in being instrumental in raising the *jumma* of that pergunnah at the fourth settlement. The consequence of these enlargements of assessment has been, that the people have been kept in poverty ever since ; that numbers of *malgoozars* have been ruined ; and that, except in favorable seasons, great difficulty has been experienced in the realization of the revenue.

'The condition in which I found the people of the different pergunnahs as I visited them one after another (independent of the consideration of temporary embarrassments arising out of the past calamitous season), proved how much they stood in need of alleviation of assessment. The great mass of the proprietors are in circumstances of extreme indigence, caused, I have reason to believe, principally by the heaviness of the *jumma*. The Thakoors of Mehrabad, Khera Bujhera, and Jelalpore, and the Puthans of Tilhur, are alike impoverished, The exceptions of wealthy *malgoozars* are very few, and those of this description met with appear to have gained their substance from other sources than the profits of their estates, It is matter of surprise how, under such circumstances, the *jumma* was realized ; but this, it was found, had only been done with very great difficulty and distress to the people. Things, however, had come to a crisis, and could not have gone on much longer without a reduction of assessment.'

" Mr. Robinson's assessment was, when fixed, somewhat proportionately heavier than Mr. Muir's was light. It was found necessary to grant relief to a large extent in the Futtehgurh District, and a regular revision of *jumma* was carried out, but, unfortunately for the zemindars of pergunnah Bangaon, not until after its transfer to this district, and therefore it was not included in the revision of the Futtehgurh District, and did not share in the remissions of *jumma*. There was considerable room for improvement, and the *jumma* is not now near so heavy, as can be seen from the fact that the cultivated area of those 51 Bangaon villages is now 25,148 acres, and the incidence upon it of the old (*viz.*, expiring) *jumma* is Re. 1-15-0, which is just the rate at which the new assessments of pergunnah Imrutpore, Zillah Furruckabad, made by Mr. Elliott, fall, In the early years of this settlement by Mr. Robinson there were a good many farms for balances, but there have not been any to speak of lately. There are 12 *mouzahs* out of the 51 in which there have been farms for arrears, and in ten of these shares have been sold and mortgaged ; and there are five *mouzahs* besides these in which shares have been both mortgaged and sold, and three more in which there have been sales, but not mortgages, and five in which there have been only mortgages ; so that in 25 out of the 51 *mouzahs* property has suffered from a heavy assessment. These sales and mortgages do not include any of the transactions amongst the brotherhood, which have been numerous, but apply only to dealings with outsiders. Strange to say, there have been no auction sales for balances ; they appear to have been warded off by the combined efforts of the shareholders and by the many transfers which have taken place privately amongst themselves.

" Mr. J. W. Muir undoubtedly kept his assessment purposely low, and probably had received instructions to make a light *jumma*, and to grant relief wherever it seemed there was any appearance of over-assessment. The whole tenor of his report conveys this idea.

"The collections have not been made with ease and punctuality in any part of the Tuhseel, but this is owing more to the large number of petty shareholders and to a spirit of recusancy, and a species of *eclât* which attached to late payers and defaulters, rather than to any inability to pay, or difficulty in meeting the demands of Government. There have been a few sales and a number of farms for arrears of revenue in the portion assessed by Mr. Muir, but not proportionately so many as in Bangaon; undue pressure of assessment does not appear to have been the cause, and many were purely punitive. The *jumma* of one village only (Oomdapore) was reduced from Rs. 401 to Rs. 322. The number of private sales and mortgages, though numerically much larger in this portion of the Tuhseel, is proportionately smaller than in Bangaon; but I have not succeeded in getting so sufficiently accurate and reliable returns of sales and mortgages, with details of area and price, as to enable me to give further details, or a tabular statement in this report."

39. Regarding the *Bunkuttee Ilaka*, Mr. J. W. Muir wrote :—" It is an object of vast importance that this part of the country should undergo improvement, and that the population should be increased. This end, it is to be hoped, will be gained by the benefits of a moderate assessment and a long lease." I attribute the great improvement visible in the whole pergunnah to Mr. J. W. Muir's lenient assessment. He, no doubt, relieved the proprietors and cultivators of the burden that was weighing them down, and apportioned his relief where it was most needed (as I trust I have done), and the long 30 years' lease gave them an incentive to reclaim fresh land, and to look to the plough and the soil as their sole means of livelihood, from which they could get good and ample returns. But there is another cause, the mention of which must not be omitted or forgotten, which conduced to great extension of cultivation, by stopping disputes and affrays about land amongst the Rajpoot communities generally, and in the Khunder *Ilaka* in particular. I refer to Mr. George Barnes' admirable arrangements for the Khunder *Ilaka* in 1848 to 1850, comprising the entire and careful rearrangement of the records of rights and interests of all parties, and the partitioning to every single shareholder every portion of land, both cultivated, culturable, and barren, in accordance with his share, after decision of disputed boundaries and re-measurement of all the villages concerned. Decision of boundary disputes, revision of records, and re-measurement were continued after Mr. Barnes' death by Deputy Collector Munowur-ool-zuman, who did much good honest work, and, I believe, deserved the reputation of uprightness and integrity which he earned; but things were not carried to that state of completion elsewhere after Mr. Barnes' death as in the Khunder *Ilaka* during his lifetime.

Causes of great improvement in the pergunnah, and large extension of cultivation.

40. The expiring *jumma* of the last settlement is Rs. 633 in excess of the initial *jumma*, principally owing to the confiscation and assessment of revenue-free lands after the mutiny, but for which there would have been a reduction, owing (1) to the remission for dilavion exceeding the enhancements for alluvion, (2) to a reduction of Rs. 79 in one *mouzah* for over-assessment, and (3) to small remissions for

Jummas of last and present settlement, and the rates of incidence per acre of each.

Jumma at commencement of last settlement.	Expiring (current) *jumma* of last settlement without cesses.	New *jumma* of present revision without cesses.
Rs.	Rs.	Rs.
1,60,609-0-0.	1,61,243-7-0.	2,11,410.

lands taken up for public purposes. The revenue rates, or incidences per acre, of the last settlement on the then areas, as well as those of the new *jummas* on the present areas, are given in juxtaposition in the following statement for each circle separately and for the whole pergunnah, and call for no special comments :—

Name of Circle.	Total area.		Malgoozaree or assessable area.		Cultivated area.	
	Last.	New.	Last.	New.	Last.	New.
	Rs. a. p.	Rs. a. p.	Rs. a. p.	Rs. a. p.	Rs. a. p.	Rs. a. p.
Bhoor, ...	0 12 10	1 0 1	0 14 2	1 1 4	1 3 8	1 5 7
Terai, ...	1 0 11	1 4 2	1 4 8	1 7 9	2 1 1	1 13 7
Bunkuttee,... ...	0 9 8	0 13 9	0 10 9	0 15 10	1 8 5	1 9 7
Whole pergunnah, ...	0 13 2	1 0 8	0 15 2	1 3 3	1 17 2	1 10 7

The rate per cultivated acre of the expiring *jumma* on the area at the end of the settlement (*i.e.*, the new area) is Re. 1-4-4 for the whole pergunnah.

41. The increase of the new revised assessments over the expiring *jummas*, cesses being omitted in both cases, is no less a sum than Rs. 50,166-9-0, at the rate of 31·11 per cent., as shown in the marginal statement. But this by no means represents the full increase of the new Government

Increase of new over expiring *jumma*.

Increase.	Decrease.	Net increase.	Percentage of net increase.
Rs.	Rs.	Rs.	Rs.
54,908-7-3	4,741-14-3	50,166-9-0	31·11

demand as compared with the former demand. Taking the full Government demand of new settlement, including the 10 per cent. cess and putwarees' fees, as against the revenue cesses and payment of putwarees' fees and chowkeedars' wages of the last settlement at its expiration, the increase is nearly 40 *per cent.*, and this is what must be taken into consideration in judging whether the enhancement demanded is sufficient, and as much as can be equitably and safely imposed, and not the mere excess of present bare revenue, exclusive of cesses, over the late revenue, omitting cesses and extras. I trust that in the foregoing paragraphs I have proved that, whilst showing moderation where it was necessary and expedient, I have not deprived Government of any legitimate revenue ; and also that, in raising the revenue (31) thirty-one per cent. and the total demand (40) forty per cent., I have not overstepped the limits of reasonable and fair assessment.

42. The *kists* or instalments for payment of the Government revenue have been revised, reduced to three in number, and classified as shown in the margin. The third set was found necessary to meet

Kists or instalments for payment of revenue.

the case of those villages about the western end of the Sote *nuddee*, and between

Description.	KHUREEF.			RUBBEE.			Number of *mouzahs* which selected each set of *kists.*
	15th November.	15th January.	Total.	15th May.	15th June.	Total.	
	annas.	annas.	annas.	annas.	annas.	annas.	
In which *khureef* and *rubbee* are equal.	3	5	8	5	3	8	47
In which *khureef* is less than *rubbee.*	3	4	7	6	3	9	299
In which there is little *khureef* and much *rubbee.*	1	5	6	5	5	10	46

it and the Ganges valley, in which the *khureef* harvest is very partial and insignificant, and from ⅜ths to ⅝ths of the cultivated area is usually under *rubbee*. These sets were arranged with reference to existing *kists* and the wishes of the zemindars, and then the zemindars of each *mouzah* were allowed to select one of the sets ; restriction being exercised regarding the third set, so that only those special cases for which this set was made should be allowed to elect for it. The number of *mouzahs* which selected each set are given in the last column of the said marginal statement.

43. The *durkhasts* have all been taken for this tuhseel from the commencement of 1279 Fuslee, corresponding with the 1st of July 1871,

Durkhasts or engagements for payment of revenue.

for the term of the settlement, without defining any term of 25 or 30 years, and until revision and subject to the orders of Government. The *durkhasts* show clearly in the case of villages bordering on the Ganges or Ramgunga, if the assessment is for 5 years certain, and subject to quinquennial revision, or is compounded for for the full term of the settlement. The first 5-year term expires on 30th June 1876, the end of 1283 Fuslee.

There was only one case of refusal to engage for the *jumma* assessed, and that was a regular case of recusancy. The name of the village is Surfuree. It is situated in the Ganges *khadir*, but well away from the river. The zemindar is a resident of the Futtehgurh District, and had not merely neglected the village, but wilfully thrown it out of cultivation, in order to get a low assessment. The village has been farmed for 12 years to Kirpal Singh, a Chundela Thakoor of the Khunder *Ilaka*, and 5 per cent. *malikana* is paid by the farmer into the tuhseel with the *jumma* for the proprietor.

44. The *Putwarees'* circles have been re-arranged, and the number of Putwarees increased to 88, and the *Putwarees* have been graded as

Arrangement of Putwarees' circles and grading of Putwarees.

shown in the margin. The *Putwarees'* fund for the pay of the *Putwarees* and a small balance to meet possible loss from future reduction of revenue for diluvion falls on the zemindars at 5½ per cent. on

Grade.	Number of *Putwarees.*
1st on Rs. 13 per mensem,	18
2nd on Rs. 11 per mensem,	42
3rd on Rs. 9 per mensem,	28

the revenue. The average of *mouzahs* per *Putwaree* is just under 4½, and of *muhals* 5¾, so that now there is not one *Putwaree's* circle which is too large for one man to look after properly, and consequently no excuse for arrears of work.

45. The brunt of the attestation of records and case-work of this pergunnah

Attestation of records and case-work.

has fallen on Deputy Collector Rugbuns Sahai, and very heavy work it has most undoubtedly been. This Tuhseel is by far the most troublesome and difficult in the matter of preparation and attestation of records, owing to the enormous number of *Putteedarea* and *Bhyachara mouzahs* and *muhals* and the immense number of Thakoor shareholders, and it is very creditable to Rugbuns Sahai that he has carried it through and done it thoroughly and effectually, and has lived to tell the tale. The following statement shows the number of cases under their various headings decided in this pergunnah, and by far the greater number of these of all sorts, except appeals, were decided by Moonshee Rugbuns Sahai ; the appeals and some of the heaviest cases by myself.

Total number of cases decided.	DETAIL OF CASES INSTITUTED AND DECIDED.						
	Rights and interests under Regulation VII. of 1822.	Enhancement of rent suits under Acts X. of 1859 and XIV. of 1863.	Boundary disputes.	Perfect and imperfect partitions.	Maafee investigations.	Appeals to Settlement Officer.	Miscellaneous.
12,231	6,770	298	431	417	216	53	4,046

The number of appeals to the Settlement Officer from the decisions of the Deputy Collector is very small indeed, being very considerably under one per cent. on the total, omitting miscellaneous, which are seldom appealable cases, and enhancement suits, the appeals of which lie to the Judge. The number is certainly a little kept down by some of the heaviest cases having been tried and decided by myself, and decisions in many of the serious boundary disputes and important cases of rights and interests having been submitted for my inspection and concurrence before being announced. But even then the percentage is very small, and the credit of having given satisfaction to the litigants rests most undeniably with Deputy Collector Rugbuns Sahai. The appeals beyond me to the Commissioner were quite nominal, and none of my orders were reversed.

SHAHJEHANPORE :
Datrd 19th January, 1874.

ROBERT G. CURRIE,
Settlement Officer.

TABLE OF CONTENTS OF CHAPTER IV.

SETTLEMENT REPORT OF TUHSEEL TILHUR.

CHAPTER IV.

TILHUR TUHSEEL.

1. THE Tuhseel of Tilhur is in the west of the Shahjehanpore District, and is bounded north by Beesulpore, and north-west by Furreedpore, tuhseels of the Bareilly District; south-west by Salempore *of Budaon*; while on other sides the tuhseel is bounded by pergunnahs of the Shahjehanpore District; south by Jellalabad and Kant; and east by Kant, Jumour, Shahjehanpore, and Powayn. The tuhseel averages about 30 miles in length from north-east to south-west, with an average width of 14 miles. The total area is 416 square miles, and the cultivated area 293 square miles. In the tuhseel are comprised the five pergunnahs of Tilhur, Kuttra, Negohee, Khera Bujhera, and Jelalpore.

Position of the Tuhseel Tilhur.

2. The tuhseel as now existing was constituted in 1850, when a revision of pergunnah boundaries was carried out. There had been three tuhseel divisions,—Tilhur, including the pergunnahs of Tilhur and Negohee; Jelalpore, comprising Jelalpore, Kuttra, and Murouree; and the third Khera Bujhera. The last named was the first reduced, and in 1850 Pergunnah Murouree was transferred to the Bareilly District, and Jelalpore and Kuttra were joined to the Tilhur Tuhseel. Tilhur is the only pergunnah which has remained unchanged since the settlement under Regulation IX. of 1833, but the changes in Negohee have been slight. Khera Bujhera retains all the old villages, and has received additions from the Budaon and Bareilly Districts, and from Pergunnah Kuttra. The villages of Furreedpore, Jelalpore, and Kuttra were much intermixed up to the revision of boundaries in 1850, when many transfers were made. The total area of Jelalpore remained nearly the same, but Kuttra lost half its area, and now only contains 13 square miles.

Revision of pergunnah boundaries in 1850.

3. The area included in the tuhseel was a part of the Sirkar of Budaon, and comprised in the old pergunnahs of Gola, Kant, Bareilly, and Sunaiya. Tilhur was included in Kant, Negohee in Gola, Jelalpore and Kuttra in Bareilly. The present pergunnah of Khera Bujhera was originally formed by contributions from Tilhur, Kuttra, and Furreedpore, the latter part of the old pergunnah of Bareilly, and subsequently Khera Bujhera received additions from Sulempore, and thus contains villages included in the old pergunnah of Sunaiya.

Akbar's fiscal divisions.

4. The statement below shows the number of *mouzahs* and *muhals*, the area in square miles, and the average area per *mouzah* and per *muhal*:—

Number of villages and estates.

Name of Pergunnah.	Area in square miles.	Number of Mouzahs.	Average area per Mouzah.	Number of Muhals.	Average area per Muhal.
			Acres.		Acres.
Tilhur, ...	126·5	211	584	271	299
Kuttra, ...	13·1	12	690	21	399
Negohee, ...	112·7	152	474	193	373
Khera Bujhera, ...	88·3	137	413	172	328
Jelalpore, ...	75·1	112	429	187	257
Total Tuhseel, ...	415·7	624	426	844	315

5. The police stations in the tuhseel are at Tilhur, Kuttra, Negohee, Jyntheepore in Khera Bujhera, and Khoodagunge in Jelalpore. There is thus one police station in each pergunnah, but the station boundaries do not agree with, and have been arranged without reference to, pergunnah

Civil and criminal jurisdiction.

14T

or tuhseel boundaries, nor does the civil agree with the revenue division. The Tilhur Moonsiff has jurisdiction over the pergunnahs of Tilhur, Kuttra, Khera Bujhera, and Jelalpore, but Negohee is attached to the Powayn Moonsiffee, and the Tilhur Moonsiffee also includes the distant tuhseel of Jellalabad.

6. The great bulk of the tuhseel lies between the Gurra (or Deoha) and Ramgunga
Description of the tuhseel.
rivers, pergunnah Negohee, a few Tilhur villages, and a small part of Jelalpore being on the left bank of the Gurra. From the right bank of the Gurra, Jelalpore extends only to the Bygool, but lower down Tilhur and Khera Bujhera, taken together, form a compact tract of country extending from the Gurra across the Bygool to the Ramgunga.

7. The portion of the tuhseel on the left of the Gurra is in the *doab* between the
The tract east of the river Gurra.
Gurra and Khunout. The Kutna, a tributary of the Gurra, is the boundary of Negohee on the west, with Beesulpore, Jelalpore, and Tilhur down to its junction with the Gurra, and the Khaimooa *nullah* runs down the centre of the pergunnah, and also falls into the Gurra. The tract between the Kutna and Khaimooa lies very low from Negohee khas southwards, and the prevailing soil is a hard clay of inferior quality, and in this tract a large area of *dhak* jungle still remains. There is a marked ascent from the left bank of the Khaimooa *nullah*; above this is a narrow line of light soil, and then further east a large tract of productive loam. The Jelalpore and Tilhur villages on the Negohee side of Gurra are nearly all in a narrow line between the Kutna and the Gurra; near the Kutna the soil is somewhat like that across the stream in Negohee, and the part near the Gurra is good alluvial soil.

8. Where the Gurra first enters the district in the north of Jelalpore, the high
The valley of the Gurra.
bhoor extends almost to the river, but the valley widens very soon, and for two-thirds of the course through Jelalpore, and all the course in Tilhur, there is a wide tract of low land on the right bank of the Gurra; the soil gradually improves in quality from north to south, but close to the Jumour border the soil again deteriorates, and lower down in Jumour the continuation of this tract is for the great part inferior clay; but in Jelalpore and Tilhur the soil, though firm, is not too stiff; there is fair natural drainage, water does not lie to an injurious extent, and thist tract is the best in the tuhseel, and perhaps the best in the district. The greater part of the cane grown in Jelalpore and Tilhur is grown in the valley of the Gurra, and in this tract have settled all the Koormee cultivators. The soil is alluvial, but the greater part has been untouched by the river for centuries, and is raised above the highest flood level, though there is a tradition that once, some seventy years ago, the river in flood came to the high bank by the town of Tilhur. The tract is hardly proper *terai*; good cultivation is required and pays well, and irrigation is necessary. The Bhuksee *nullah*, a mere drain, flows through the tract, for some miles in Jelalpore nearly defining the boundary, but in Tilhur it runs in the centre; and another *nullah*, the Serow or Gurrai, which rises near Kutna, from Tilhur down flows under the rise to the high *bhoor* plain.

9. South and west of the Gurra valley runs the high sandy ridge between the
The *bhoor* ridge.
valleys of the Gurra and Ramgunga. This great ridge crosses the Shahjehanpore district from north to south, extending from the Bareilly to the Hurdui district, and taking in the greater part of the Tilhur pergunnah, all Kant of the Shahjehanpore tuhseel, and parts of Khera Bujhera and Jellalabad. In the Bareilly district, and again in Jellalabad below the junction of the Ramgunga and Bygool, the Ramgunga flows close to the high land, but for about 20 miles in the Tilhur and Jellalabad tuhseels the Bygool runs under the high land, and all the country between the Bygool and the Ramgunga lies low. The Bygool first touches the district on the west of Jelalpore, where the Bygool and Gurra are but four miles apart, and in Jelalpore there is only a narrow ridge of sand above the Bygool, the descent to the valley of the Gurra coming very soon; the rivers then diverge, and the Bygool, turning towards the Ramgunga, runs in a narrow valley

through the *bhoor* ridge, and from thence down to the junction of the Bygool and Ramgunga, the Bygool assumes an appearance of undue importance, the great sandy ridge appearing to follow the course of the smaller stream.

10. The Bygool is the boundary between the Tilhur and Khera Bujhera per-

The country between the Bygool and Ram-gunga.

gunnahs, and the latter is, with the exception of a small tract of *bhoor* adjoining pergunnah Furreedpore of the Bareilly District, all low land, lying between the Ramgunga and the Bygool. In the low land are two well-defined tracts of opposing character ; in the part near the Bygool and beyond the influence of the Ramgunga, the soil is hard and stiff, and requires copious irrigation for the spring crops ; the remaining and largest portion of the pergunnah is Ramgunga *terai*, a rich alluvial soil needing no irrigation, and producing fine crops even with somewhat careless cultivation, but in parts the autumn crops are liable to injury from floods.

11. The rivers of the tuhseel are the Ramgunga, the Gurra, the Bygool, and

The rivers of the tuhseel.

the Kutna. The riparian customs on the Gurra in Jelalpore and Tilhur agree with those generally prevailing in the Shahjehanpore tuhseel. On the Ramgunga custom varies ; along the upper part of the course in Khera Bujhera the custom of *dhar dhura*, or mid-stream boundary, in the very widest acceptation prevails, and at one time this custom was followed on the entire Khera Bujhera boundary, but many years ago the river suddenly changed its course, and made for itself a new channel. A long piece of country, in places of considerable width, lies between the old and new channels, in which are entire villages that have never been touched by the river. On the new channel the custom of *dhar dhura* was never adopted, and the old custom of *mend dhura* is followed ; that is, the boundary is not affected by any change in the course of the river ; the river may turn a fertile village into a waste of sand and water, but the total area remains unchanged, and, in case of dispute, the boundary must be restored by measurement. The old channel, known as the Andhawee, is still well-defined, and is all along its course the boundary between the villages on either side. In the northern part of Jelalpore the Gurra is known as the Deoha, the name by which the river is known in Phillibheet and Bareilly, but from Khoodagunge down the river is called the Gurra. The Bygool is in Bareilly known as the Eastern Bygool, there being another stream of the same name. The Kutna is also known in Beesulpore as the Mala, from the swamp in which it rises, and might be called the Western Kutna, there being another stream of the same name in pergunnah Khotar. The Ramgunga and the Gurra are the only rivers in the tuhseel which change their course. These two rivers are hardly used for irrigation, and irrigation from the Bygool and Kutna will be subsequently described.

12. The best known *nullahs* are the Khaimooa, Bhuksee, Serow, Andhawee,

The nullahs.

Reotee, and Khara. The Khaimooa runs through pergunnah Negohee, falling into the Gurra, and supplies some irrigation in the cold weather. The Bhuksee rises in Jelalpore. The Serow, which lower down is known as the Gurrai, near Kuttra. These *nullahs* are used for irrigation in Jumour, but in Tilhur neither retains any water. The Gownaiya and the Rapettooa are larger *nullahs*, but one falls into the Bygool, the other into the Kutna, almost immediately after entering the district. The Reotee rises in Furreedpore, and falls into the Bygool in Khera Bujhera. The Khara commences at one of the deserted channels of the Ramgunga, and forming for some miles the boundary between the alluvial soil of the Ramgunga *terai* and the hard tract next the Bygool, joins the Andhawee near the Jellalabad boundary. The Andhawee is the old channel of the Ramgunga mentioned in para. 11.

13. The circles formed for assessment agree with the natural soil divisions, and

Assessment circles.

are ten in number. In pergunnah Negohee two circles were formed, the *domut* circle, including the good loam tract in the north and east of the pergunnah, and extending from the Beesulpore to the Shahjehanpore border, and the Khaimooa circle, formed of the tract of hard clay between the Khaimooa and the Kutna. In Jelalpore the circles are the Gurra circle, comprising the valley of the Gurra, and the Bygool circle, including the ridge above, and the valley of the Bygool. The Tilhur circles are the *terai* and the *bhoor*, the rich valley of the Gurra, and the sandy upland. The small pergunnah of Kuttra was not subdivided, and in Khera Bujhera three circles were formed,—a small *bhoor* circle to the north on the Furreedpore border ; the Bygool or *bunkuttee* circle, including the hard tract near the Bygool ; and the Ramgunga or *terai* circle. The *terai* circle in Tilhur and the Gurra circle in Jelalpore include, besides the actual valley of the Gurra, a line of good loam situated between the valley and the high sandy tract. The low land on the left bank of the Bygool is narrow, and generally of very poor quality, and is included in the adjoining circle, as very few villages are situated entirely in the valley, the villages on the bank of the river almost always extending up to and taking in part of the high land above the valley.

14. The total population of the tuhseel is 244,558, giving a density of
Population of the tuhseel. 588 per square mile. Full details of the population, according to the census of 1872, are given in separate statements, and the following table shows the most important facts :—

Pergunnah.	Total area in square miles.	Total population.	Total population per square mile.	Cultivated area in square miles.	Agricultural population, including land-owners and agriculturists.	Agricultural population per square mile of cultivation.
Tilhur, ...	126·5	86,321	677	95·7	56,083	586
Kuttra, ...	13·1	9,970	761	8·	5,200	650
Negohee, ...	112·7	56,618	502	71·1	44,114	620
Khera Bujhera, ...	88·3	46,725	529	66·4	38,496	580
Jelalpore, ...	75·1	44,924	598	52·2	30,249	579
Total Tuhseel,	415·7	244,558	588	293·4	174,142	594

The following table shows the population per *mouzah* in the form used in the reports for other tuhseels :—

Pergunnah.	Number of mouzahs.	Average area in acres.	Average area in square miles.	AVERAGE RURAL POPULATION.	
				Per mouzah.	Per square mile of total area.
Tilhur, ...	211	384	0·6	266	443
Kuttra, ...	12	690	1·1	433	397
Negohee, ...	152	474	0·7	290	391
Khera Bujhera, ...	137	413	0·6	280	436
Jelalpore, ...	112	429	0·6	270	403
Total Tuhseel, ...	624	426	0·7	279	419

The tuhseel as a whole is thus densely inhabited, and no pergunnah suffers from a deficiency of cultivators. The towns of Tilhur, Kuttra, and Khoodagunge cause the average total population per square mile to be highest in the pergunnahs of Tilhur, Kuttra, and Jelalpore ; but the average agricultural population per cultivated mile is very high in the purely agricultural pergunnahs of Negohee and Khera Bujhera, though they show a comparatively low average of total population. The average cultivated area per adult male agriculturist is a little over 3½ acres, and as a considerable proportion of those entered in the census returns as non-agriculturists are to a greater or less extent cultivators, the real average is somewhat lower ; but a large proportion of the adults in the census returns are not cultivators in their own right, and the average size of each holding is greater. According to the census returns the landowners are 2·4 per cent., other agriculturists 68·8, and non-agriculturists 28·8 per cent. of the total population. Details for each pergunnah are given in the Appendix. The houses built with skilled labour are only 1·6 per cent. of the total number of houses, and are almost all in the towns of Tilhur and Khoodagunge. The average number of inhabitants per enclosure and per house are 8·5 and 5·3 respectively ; and the average varies little in the several pergunnahs, the number per enclosure being a little lower in the more purely agricultural pergunnahs of Negohee and Khera Bujhera.

15. The number returned as able to read and write was only 3,124, or 1·3 per cent. of the total population of the tuhseel. All were males,
Education.
and, according to the census returns, there is not a single woman or girl in the tuhseel able to read and write. In respect of these statistics of education, the returns are evidently generally incorrect, and probably, as the rule, only those able to write in the Persian character have been returned. When taking the census of my own camp, I found that the enumerator who prepared the draft return had excluded many men well able to read and write, because they were not acquainted with the Persian character. If the same system was generally adopted, the small proportion is fully explained, very few of the rural population knowing any but the Hindee or the Nagree character.

Population according to religion.
16. The next statement shows the number and proportions of the population according to religion :—

Pergunnah.			Hindoos.	Mahomedans.	Christians and others.	Percentage of Hindoos to total population.
Tilhur, ...	...	...	70,769	15,552	13	81·9
Kuttra, ...	...	...	7,262	2,708	...	72·8
Negohee,	...	...	50,309	6,309	2	88·9
Khera Bujhera,	...	...	44,544	2,181	...	95·3
Jelalpore,	...	...	39,969	4,955	15	89·
Total Tuhseel, ...		...	212,853	30,705	30	87·5

17. The Mahomedans are generally non-agriculturists and dwellers in towns.
The Mahomedan population.
Two out of three Mahomedans are returned as non-agriculturists ; while for Hindoos the proportion is little more than 2 out of 10. Of the Mahomedans in pergunnah Tilhur, 9,100, or close on 60 per cent., are inhabitants of the town of Tilhur ; and of 2,708 in pergunnah Kuttra, 2,520 live in the town of Kuttra. Nearly half of the Jelalpore Mahomedans live either in the town of Khoodagunge, or the adjoining village of Jelalpore, the latter the old capital of the pergunnah before the rise of Khoodagunge, and a considerable proportion of the Negohee Mahomedans live in the village of Negohee. Generally in the district the towns contain a large proportion of Mahomedans, while the rural population is almost exclusively Hindoo. The towns of Kuttra and Khoodagunge, like the city of Shahjehanpore, were founded by Mahomedans. Tilhur was an old Hindoo town, but the Pathans founded several separate mohullahs ; nearly half the population is Mahomedan, and Tilhur is considered a Mahomedan town. The great bulk of the Mahomedans thus live in the towns, and the few Mahomedan villages are, almost without exception, on the old main roads connecting the towns ; in fact the old lines of communication might be traced by the scattered

Mahomedan villages. The distribution of the population thus still shows the nature of the Mahomedan settlement. They were invaders in a hostile country, for their protection founded towns, and dwelt in towns or in fortified outposts guarding the main connecting roads. The Mahomedan settlements in this tract of country are comparatively recent, and but very lately have the new immigrants commenced to settle in small parties, and spread themselves freely among the Hindoo population. Syuds and Moguls number about 1,500 and 1,000 respectively, and are almost all residents of the towns of Tilhur and Kuttra; the Pathans are between 7,000 and 8,000 in number, and are strongest in Tilhur and Kuttra. The inhabitants of the old town of Jelalpore are almost all Sheikhs, and hence nearly half the Mahomedans of the Jelalpore pergunnah are Sheikhs ; and the Sheikhs of Jelalpore are almost the only men entitled to call themselves so, many of the others being Jullahas or Dhoonas, and some descendants of converted Hindoos, though in Shahjehanpore, owing to the late advent of the Mahomedans, there has never been any large addition to the ranks of Islam by conversion. Jullahas and Dhoonas number over 6,000 and nearly 4,000, respectively, and, as might be expected, a very large proportion of each are residents of Tilhur. These are the only classes important from their numbers. Mewatees are only found in one village in the Khera Bujhera pergunnah. Cheepees, Hujjams, Durzees, Kassubs, and Meemars are found in small numbers in the towns, and Fakeers are scattered over the tuhseel.

18.   Brahmins number nearly 13,000, and Kayeths 3,000, both castes being

The Hindoo population Brahmins and Kayeths. evenly distributed through the several pergunnahs. The Brahmins are generally Kanoujias, the Kayeths nearly all Suksenas.

19.   The Bunniahs number 3,000, the Kulwars about 5,000. They are the

Bunniahs and Kulwars. chief traders and money-lenders, and are nearly all non-agriculturists. They are found in every large village, but in greater numbers in the towns.

20.   The most important caste, politically, is that of the Thakoors or Rajpoots.

The Thakoors. They number 22,950, distributed as per margin. By the census of 1865 the number was 19,480. In other pergunnahs there are only slight variations, but in Khera Bujhera the number has risen from 6,207 to 8,960. This great difference is of course due to errors in one or both of the enumerations, but the later record is most probably nearer the truth. In pergunnah Tilhur Thakoors never prevailed, and the Thakoors are found almost exclusively near the border of the pergunnah, the prevailing clans of the neighbouring pergunnahs extending across the boundary. There are thus Bachils on the Kant, Chundels on the Jellalabad, Jungharas on the Khera Bujhera, Katherias on the Jelalpore, and Kassubs on the

* Pergunnah.	Number.	Percentage on total population.
Tilhur, / ...	3,771	4·4
Kuttra, ...	188	1·4
Negohee, ...	4,510	8·
Khera Bujhera,...	8,960	19·2
Jelalpore, ...	5,523	12·3
Tuhseel, ...	22,950	9·4

Negohee border, but very few Thakoors in the centre of the pergunnah. In Kuttra there are Thakoors in only one village,—a village which geographically should belong to Khera Bujhera. In Negohee Kassubs, in Khera Bujhera Jungharas, and in Jelalpore Katherias, are the prevailing clans.

21.The Kassubs are found thinly scattered over the *doab* between the Gurra

The Kassubs. and the Khunout, including the pergunnah of Negohee and parts of Powayn and Shahjehanpore. They once possessed all this tract of country, and were probably the first Thakoor settlers in the present district of Shahjehanpore. The Katherias later on were at least nominal rulers of this Kassub country, but I believe that the possession of the Kassubs was little interfered with until the Gours took possession of Powayn, and the Mahomedans of Negohee. The Kassubs have not prospered, and a large proportion of the villages found in their possession at cession have since been alienated. In this tuhseel they now only hold some 20 villages in Negohee, and some shares in Tilhur villages. The clan numbers just 1,000 in Negohee, and 540 in the adjoining part of Tilhur. Kassubs rank low in the Thakoor scale, though claiming to be an off-shoot from the Kuchwahas : their tradition is that this branch of the Kuchwahas settled in Caahmere, and that part then emigrated again, and settled in their present tract of country. They claim to be of the same clan as the Maharajah of Jummoo, and state that the relationship was recently recognized by the Maharajah.

22. The Bachil country is chiefly in the Shahjehanpore tuhseel, and they are
The Bachils. found in very small numbers in the Tilhur tuhseel, except on the border of the Kant pergunnah. The Bachils commonly state that they settled in their present tract of country in the time of Jyechund of Kunouj. This would put the date of their arrival in the twelfth century, and though the clan probably arrived at a later date, there is no doubt of their having been long settled here, probably before any Thakoor clan, except the Kassubs.

23. The Jungharas are found in large numbers in Khera Bujhera and in the
The Junghara clan. neighbouring pergunnahs of Bareilly and Budaon ; there are two well known sub-divisions, the *bhoor* and the *terai* Jungharas. The *bhoor* Jungharas are chiefly found in the Bareilly district, the great majority in the Shahjehanpore and Budaon districts being *terai* Jungharas. The Jungharas claim descent from the Tomur Kings of Delhi, the predecessors of Pirthee Raj. Their account is that on the succession of Pirthee Raj to the Delhi throne, many of the Tomurs left Delhi in disgust at the accession of the Chowhan. Five brothers led five separate parties, and the youngest of the five crossed the Ganges, and first settled in Sumbhul. He had two sons, one of whom moved to the present Boolundshuhur district. The other, Huns Raj, had three sons, and they moved east from Sumbhul. One settled on the high land east of the Ramgunga, and from him are descended the *bhoor* Jungharas ; of the other two, who were by a second marriage, one was the ancestor of the *terai* Jungharas, now found in Bareilly and Shahjehanpore, and the other of the Budaon Jungharas. Some of the *bhoor* Jungharas state that the ancestors of the *terai* Jungharas were sons of a woman of the clan, and that hence their descendants rank lower. This account is not admitted by the *terai* Jungharas, but the difference in rank is not denied. The names of the two branches are from the countries in which they settled. The *bhoor* Jungharas settling on the high upland above the valley of the Ramgunga, the others in the valley of the river. The earlier names in the list may be altogether or in part incorrect, but from the time the tribe settled in their present country pedigrees in detail exist, and these are probably fairly correct. It appears that on the average about 14 generations have passed, and their settlement here may then be put as in the 15th century, or nearly 300 years later than the alleged emigration from Delhi ; and as the founders of the present branches are given as grandsons of the son Anang Pal, it is clear that if the tribe is a branch of the Tomurs, and left Delhi either on the accession, or, as might be more probable, on the defeat of Pirthee Raj, many names have been omitted. The Jungharas have so far prospered better than any other Thakoor clan in the district, and the villages lost by the clan have been compensated for by these conferred in reward for service rendered in the mutiny to Captain (now Colonel) Gowan and others in Khera Bujhera. The Jungharas in Khera Bujhera now number 3,150.

24. There are few Katherias in the tuhseel, except in Jelalpore, where they number
The Katherias. 2,781. The Katherias settled in the present Shahjehanpore district in the 16th century. They moved east under two brothers, the younger of whom settled in Gola, and is represented by the Rao of Nahul in Powayn. The Katherias of Shahjehanpore and eastern Bareilly all belong to the Nahul branch, and claim descent from Rao Hurree Singh, the younger of the two brothers. Rao Hurree Singh settled at Gola on the Khunout : he or his successors acquired the old pergunnah of Gola, and the *zemindaree* of the pergunnah was conferred on Rao Bikram Singh in 1645 A. D. by a *firman* of the Emperor Shah Jehan,

which is now in the possession of Rao Jeet Singh of Nahul. Rao Bikram Singh moved from Gola to Nahul, and the Raos of Nahul remained rulers of the pergunnah for 70 or 80 years, when they came into collision with the Pathans, who obtained Negohee, and then the Katherias were ousted from Powayn by their allies and connections, the Gours. A full account of the Katherias should more properly be given in the Powayn report. The Katherias of Jelalpore are a branch of the Nahul family, but there is a sub-division similar to that between the *terai* and *bhoor* Jungharas, and these *Jelalpore* Katherias are looked down on by, and rank lower than, the rest of the clan. All the Jelalpore, and many of the Beesulpore, Katherias belong to this inferior branch. The Jelalpore Katherias were once proprietors of large part of the pergunnah, but now only retain a few villages. They are generally in very poor circumstances, and are the most turbulent and troublesome clan in the district, except perhaps the Jellalabad Chundels.

25. The prevailing clans settled in considerable numbers in definite tracts in the tuhseel are thus the Jungharas, Katherias, Bachils, and Kassubs, Other Thakoor clans. but with all are mixed other Thakoors of various clans, who have settled singly or in small numbers, chiefly on account of marriage connections with the local clans. Chowbans and Rathores are most numerous, especially among the Katherias, who give their daughters only to the very highest clans, and some 20 other clans are represented in the tuhseel.

26. The Thakoor settlements are all of comparatively recent date, none probably Distribution of the before the 14th century, and the Katherias, long the most Thakoors. important tribe in the present district, only arrived in the 16th century. Till comparatively recently the Thakoors were almost exclusively the landowning class. They came and subdued the tracts of which they remained rulers, till dispossession by a stronger clan, or by the Mahomedans. They were the dominant class, but never formed the bulk of the population in any tract. The distribution of the Thakoor population shows that, though coming as conquerors, their rule was freely accepted by the people. The Mahomedans never ventured to settle in small parties, but among the Thakoors successive branches continually left the family residence, and settled in their allotment of country. This system continued so long as the Thakoors retained power, and we thus find each clan scattered in small numbers over its own tract of country. When the Thakoors' power was destroyed, and especially after the cession, when their property was reduced, and acquisition of new villages became impossible, the existing distribution of the clans became stereotyped; but there has not yet been time for them to multiply into large communities, except in the case of one or two exceptional and exceedingly prolific families, and consequently there are no *Bhyachara* villages in the tuhseel. Generally, indeed, in the district the proprietary tenures are of too recent date to have yet developed into the complicated holdings found in districts where sub-division has gone on for a much longer time.

27. The most important cultivating castes are the Koormees, Kisans, Aheers, The cultivating classes. Muraos, and Chumars, and the following statement shows their numbers and distribution :—

Pergunnah.	KOORMEES.		KISANS.		AHEERS.		MURAOS OR KACHEES.		CHUMARS.	
	Population.	Percentage on total agricultural population.	Population.	Percentage on total agricultural population.	Population.	Percentage on total agricultural population.	Population.	Percentage on total agricultural population.	Population.	Percentage on total agricultural population.
Tilhur, ...	5,891	9·6	8,493	14·8	7,028	12·5	6,170	11·	9,043	16·1
Kuttra, ...	429	5·2	62	1·2	977	18·8	384	7·4	750	14·4
Negohee, ...	613	1·4	8,959	20·3	2,924	6·6	3,999	9·1	6,294	14·2
Khera Bujhara,	57	0·1	626	1·1	4,908	12·7	3,678	9·5	5,299	16·3
Jelalpore, ...	3,566	11·7	1,487	4·9	1,916	6·3	2,356	7·7	4,650	15·3
Tuhseel, ...	10,056	5·8	19,587	11·1	17,753	10·2	16,587	9·5	27,036	15·5

Koormees, Kisans, Aheers, and Muraos are purely agriculturists, and, with the exception of a few Koormee and Aheer land-owners, are mere cultivators. The Chumars also may practically be counted as purely cultivators. These castes, with the Brahmins, Thakoors, and Kahars, make up all the agricultural castes found in considerable numbers. The Brahmins are generally, but not universally, cultivators, and are devoid of any caste scruples on the subject. Almost every Thakoor is a cultivator, either of his own *seer*, or as a tenant. The Kahars number 12,852, and though they alone work as boatmen and palkee or banghee bearers, a large proportion are chiefly agricultural, and follow other work at odd times. As might be expected, they are strongest near the Ramgunga in Khera Bujhera. Koormees are hardly found in Khera Bujhera or Negohee, but are strong in Tilhur and Jelalpore. Koormees are gregarious, and are almost always found in tracts of good soil, and they are only found in the best parts of Tilhur and Jelalpore, in the rich tract on the right bank of the river Gurra. They are the best and the most prosperous cultivators in the district. They are generally *Gungaparee* Koormees, and say that the settlement here was of comparatively recent date. Kisans are numerous in Tilhur and Negohee. They too are good cultivators, but far from equal to the Koormees. Aheers are very strong in a great part of Khera Bujhera and in the southern part of Tilhur, and are always mentioned as the first settlers in this tract of country; they are fair average cultivators; they commonly have good cattle, but are generally found in tracts either of light soil or of alluvial deposit, where very careful or laborious cultivation is less required. The Muraos have the garden cultivation exclusively in their own hands, and on a larger scale also are excellent and careful cultivators. The Chumars and Muraos are more evenly distributed than most other castes. Grading these castes as cultivators, I should put them in the following order,—Koormee, Murao, Kisan, Chumar, Aheer, Thakoor, Kahar, Brahmin. The position of the castes in material prosperity does not follow their grading as cultivators. The Koormees, though usually paying high rents, are the most prosperous, but they are in comparably the best cultivators, and, what is more important, commonly manage to keep out of the bunniah's books. After them will rank Thakoors, Brahmins, and Aheers. All these castes have some little position to maintain, and are accustomed to a standard of living to which they are expected to conform ; and all will make a stand when the exactions of landlord or money-lender would lower this position and standard. The other castes are of much lower rank, and according to native feeling should think themselves well off if supplied with the barest necessaries of existence. A landlord would generally prefer Kisan and Chumar tenants, as they can be most easily managed, and will submit quietly to exactions it might be dangerous to try with Thakoors or Aheers. These are the only important castes, Guderias, with a population under 6,000, coming next in number. The various castes of village servants are found of course all over the tuhseel; the Telees number over 5,000, the others range from 2,000 to 4,000. Many castes common elsewhere are almost entirely absent. Jats and Lodhas number only a few hundred each. Passees are only found on the border of Powayn, in which pergunnah they are one of the prevailing castes. In only one village in the tuhseel are there many Goojurs, and the village is not far from the triple junction point of the districts of Budaon, Bareilly, and Shahjehanpore, a suspicious position for a caste with their general character. The tuhseel is thus, on the whole, fortunate in its cultivating classes, and also in their distribution; and, so far as their numbers go, we have rather to fear evils resulting from over than from under population. Population is increasing fast, and even now there is certainly no lack of cultivators.

Dhobees—washermen.
Barhais—Carpenters.
Lohars—Blacksmiths.
Telees—Oilmen.
Koomhars—Potters.
Bhurjees—Corn parchers.
Nais—Barbers.
Dhanooks { Here the village watchmen.
Mehtars—Sweepers.

28. *Towns of the Tuhseel.*—Tilhur, the chief town in the tuhseel, and the second town in the district, is situated on the Bareilly road, 12 miles from Shahjehanpore, and the Oudh and Rohilkhund Railway

Tilhur,

passes the town. The total population is 18,910. The town is situated in several *mouzahs*, and in the returns of the census of 1865 these *mouzahs* were treated as separate towns or villages, and the total population was not shown. Details of the population by the census of 1872 are given in the following statement:—

Mouzah.	HINDOOS.			MAHOMEDANS.			CHRISTIANS AND OTHERS.			TOTAL POPULATION.		
	Male.	Female.	Total.	Male.	Female.	Total.	Male.	Female.	Total.	Male.	Female.	Total.
Kusbeh Tilhur, ...	1,363	1,367	2,730	1,285	1,297	2,582	3	2	5	2,651	2,666	5,317
Hindoo Puttee, ...	1,735	1,674	3,409	1,317	1,293	2,610	...	...	...	3,052	2,967	6,019
Moazzimpore, ...	1,010	831	1,841	663	615	1,278	...	...	...	1,673	1,446	3,119
Oomrpore, ...	418	382	800	885	1,009	1,894	...	...	...	1,303	1,391	2,694
Nuzrpore, ...	132	110	242	110	114	224	...	...	...	242	224	466
Behareepore, ...	223	172	395	15	13	28	...	...	...	238	185	423
Bunwareepore, ...	144	126	270	65	72	137	...	...	...	209	198	407
Sheregurh, ...	44	40	84	151	152	303	2	1	3	197	193	390
Munsoorpore, ...	39	...	39	35	1	36	...	...	...	74	1	75
Total, ...	5,108	4,702	9,810	4,526	4,566	9,092	5	3	8	9,639	9,271	18,910

There are fourteen *mohullahs* in Kusbeh Tilhur, seven in Hindoo Puttee, and five in Moazzimpore, the other *mouzahs* not being sub-divided into *mohullahs*. Tilhur is said to have been founded by Rajah Tilok Chund, a Bachil Thakoor, in the time of Akbar, but the Mahomedan settlers first made Tilhur a place of importance. Tilhur and Hindoo Puttee form the oldest part of the town, but almost all trade and business is carried on in and about Moazzimpore, and the chief Pathan families resided in Oomrpore. The three principal markets—Datagunge, Nizamgunge, and Birreeagunge,—are all in Moazzimpore. The Datagunge bazar is the most important in Tilhur, and most of the leading traders and money-lenders live in Datagunge. This *mohullah* owes its origin to a Mahomedan official. It was surrounded by a high brick wall, a great part of which is still in good preservation, and the gunge consists of a street with substantial masonry houses and shops, and a high gateway at each end. Mahomed Oomr Khan, a Yusufzai Pathan, founded Oomrpore; his son Mungul Khan, Nazim under Hafiz Rahmut Khan, was killed in the engagement with Shuja-ood-Doula and the English troops. Mungul Khan built a large fort and residence outside Oomrpore, close to the present Bareilly road, the buildings and enclosing walls of which cover a large area; it remained in the possession of Mungul Khan's descendants up to the mutiny, when, with their other property, it was confiscated for rebellion; and all the Government offices, which before the mutiny had been in an old fort in *mohulla* Khuttreean of Kusbeh Tilhur, at the other end of the town, were established in Mungul Khan's fort, where they still remain. The fort is in Mouzah Munsoorpore, of which it forms the only *abadee*. Moazzimpore is on and south of the Bareilly road; Tilhur and Hindoo Puttee are further east, separated from Moazzimpore by a large tank. Sheregurh is south of Tilhur and Oomrpore; Nuzrpore, Behareepore, and Bunwareepore are all north of Moazzimpore and the Bareilly road. The railway passes north of the town, and the station is more than a mile from the business part of the town, but a good metalled road to the station is now being made. Tilhur is not noted for any special manufacture or trade, except for the work of its *kamangars* in *palkees* and varnished boxes. The town was once famed for the bows and arrows made by the *kamangars*, and received the name of *kaman-ka-shahr*, a name still commonly used. The most important trade, as in each town of the district, is in sugar; and Tilhur is principal market for *goor*, which comes in large quantities from the country round, and is purchased by traders for export. Comparatively little *goor* is made in other parts of the district. Tilhur has recently been made a municipality, but the great length and straggling character of the town, the number of petty roads branching out on each side, and the large groves round the town, must render collection of the *octroi* duties difficult and expensive.

29. Kuttra, with a population of 6,529, is six miles from Tilhur, at the junction of the road from Shahjehanpore to Bareilly with the Rohil-khund Trunk Road; the road from Phillibheet *via* Beesulpore and Khoodagunge also joins the Trunk Road at Kuttra. Kuttra is not a place of much trade or importance, but it has improved of late, and the population has risen rapidly ; and, as there is now a railway station at Kuttra, the town may perhaps do more justice to its marked advantages of position.

Kuttra.

30. Khoodagunge is in Pergunnah Jelalpore, on the right bank of the Gurra, distant 12 miles from Tilhur, and 7 from Kuttra. It is a new town, having been founded little more than 100 years ago, but it has a population of 6,194 ; there are many wealthy traders, and considerable business is done in sugar. The population of Khoodagunge was under-stated in the census returns of 1865, part of the town included in mouzah Luchmeepore having been entered separately.

Khoodagunge.

31. There are five villages with population above 2,000,—Sumdhana (2,052) in Tilhur, Khimeria (4,012) and Gurhia Rungee (2,966) in Khera Bujhera, Mujhla (2,224) and Jelalpore (2,395) in Jelalpore. The village of Negohee has a population of 1,848, Khera Bujhera of 1,922. Markets are held in the towns and villages given in the following statement :—

Chief villages.

Pergunnah.			Name of village.			Number of days in the week.	Days on which market is held.
Tilhur,	...	...	Milkeepore,	...	...	2	Tuesday and Saturday.
Ditto,	...	...	Bowree,	...	...	2	Sunday and Thursday.
Kuttra,	...	...	Kuttra,	...	...	2	Sunday and Thursday.
Negohee,	...	...	Negohee,	...	...	2	Tuesday and Saturday.
Ditto,	...	...	Raghopore Sekunderpore,	...		2	Wednesday and Saturday.
Ditto,	...	...	Dhukia Tiwaree,		...	2	Sunday and Thursday.
Ditto,	...	...	Sunda,		...	2	Monday and Friday.
Ditto,	...	...	Arelee Ismailpore,		...	2	Wednesday and Saturday.
Ditto,	...	...	Zindpoora,		...	2	Tuesday and Saturday.
Khera Bujhera,	...		Khera Ruth,	...	...	2	Monday and Thursday.
Ditto,	...	...	Dubhowra,		...	2	Tuesday and Saturday.
Ditto,	...	...	Gurheea Rungee,		...	2	Monday and Friday.
Jelalpore,	...	...	Khoodagunge,	...		2	Wednesday and Saturday.
Ditto	...	...	Mujhla,	...	...	2	Tuesday and Friday.

The market days in the town of Tilhur are Monday, Wednesday, and Friday.

32. *Communications.*—The Oudh and Rohilkhund Railway crosses the tuhseel from the Jumour Pergunnah of Shahjehanpore to the Bareilly District, a distance of 14 miles, passing through the Tilhur and Kuttra pergunnahs. The railway stations in the tuhseel are at the towns of Tilhur and Kuttra, and there is also a station at Futtehgunge, the first village in the Bareilly District. The railway has only been open a few months, and it is too soon to form an opinion as to the effect of the railway on the trade of the district ; but the rail, if freely used, should take sugar and *goor*, the main exports, to Allygurh, and bring salt ; and from Hatrass and Chundowsee cotton; sugar is now sent by cart over bad roads to the markets across the Jumna, and the railway ought to be used both for export and import carriage. Piece-goods and iron will of course be imported by rail, but it is doubt-ful when and to what extent the railway may be used for the transport of the more bulky goods—sugar, salt, and cotton.

The Railway.

33. There are two metalled roads in the tuhseel,—one, the road from Shahjehanpore to Bareilly, through Tilhur to Kuttra, where it joins the Rohilkhund Trunk Road; the railway follows closely the line of this road. The Rohilkhund Trunk Road from Futtehgurh to Bareilly enters Pergunnah Tilhur from the Kant Pergunnah, and running due north for nine miles to Kuttra, unites with the metalled road from Shahjehanpore; from Kuttra the road turns to the north-west, and four miles further crosses the Bygool by a bridge built some fifty years ago by Hakeem Mehndee Ali, the Oudh Wazeer, and enters the Bareilly District. Both these roads have been metalled within the last few years; eight or nine years ago there was not a metalled road in the district outside the city and station of Shahjehanpore. A third road, that from Khoodagunge to Kuttra, is to be metalled for part of the distance.

Metalled roads.

34. The principal unmetalled roads are the following:—The Budaon road, partly raised, but unbridged, which runs from Tilhur across the Tilhur and Khera Bujhera pergunnahs to the Ramgunga and the Budaon border; this road received but little repair, and is in great part superseded by a new road from Hakeem Mehndee's bridge on the Bygool, which runs along the north-west border of Khera Bujhera. The Powayn and Khoodagunge road, raised and partly bridged, crosses the Kutna under Mujhla, and the Gurra under Khoodagunge, by ferry. From Khoodagunge there is a road south to Kuttra, which is to be metalled in part; one north to Beesulpore and Phillibheet, crossing the Gurra at Bhoondee; and another east to Furreedpore,—the two last unmade roads. The road from Phillibheet to Shahjehanpore, which is raised and bridged, runs through the eastern part of Negohee nearly from north to south, passing by the village of Negohee. There are other roads, such as the roads from Tilhur to Khoodagunge, from Tilhur to Negohee, and from Tilhur to Mudnapore on the Trunk Road, which are little more than village tracks, but along which considerable traffic passes. Village cart tracks abound, and the only part of the tuhseel in which any difficulty ever arises is part of Khera Bujhera, where in the rains many small nullahs are filled by the Ramgunga and render communication sometimes difficult; but at that season water carriage is always available, and Khera Bujhera, little cane being grown, exports considerable quantities of grain down the Ramgunga.

Unmetalled roads.

35. *The landholders.*—The *zemindaree* tenure prevails in each pergunnah, as will be seen from the following statement, and there is not a single *bhyachara* village in the tuhseel. On the average there are four *puttees* in each *putteedaree muhal*:—

Tenures.

Pergunnah.	Total number of muhals.	Zemindaree muhals.	Putteedaree muhals.	Number of puttees in the putteedaree muhals.
Tilhur, ...	271	196	75	333
Kuttra, ...	21	18	3	15
Negohee, ...	193	160	33	111
Khera Bujhera, ...	172	111	61	283
Jelalpore, ...	187	108	79	265
Total, ...	844	593	251	1,007

36. The statement in Appendix (G.) gives the number of entire villages, and of separate estates, parts of villages held entirely by each caste, and the estates in which the caste holds the larger part of the shares,

Caste and residence.

and the statement shows also the estates held by residents of the tuhseel and by non-residents. The following abstract supplies a large part of the information :—

Pergunnah.	Division by Race.													Division by Residence.	
	Brahmin.	Thakoor.	Kayeth.	Bunniah.	Koormee.	Other castes or proprietors of mixed castes.	Total Hindoos.	Pathan.	Sheikh.	Other Mahomedan.	Total Mahomedan.	English.	Grand Total.	Proprietors residing in the tuhseels.	Proprietors residents of other tuhseels.
	Number of muhals held by each class.													Number of muhals.	
Tilhur,	33	86	20	7	6	15	167	80	5	7	92	12	271	229	42
Kuttra,	...	2	...	9	...	...	11	5	...	2	7	3	21	20	1
Negohee,	17	58	14	12	8	18	127	59	6	...	65	1	193	86	107
Khera Bujhera,	9	144	9	1	...	6	169	2	...	...	2	1	172	155	17
Jelalpore,	10	79	38	5	6	2	150	23	3	2	28	9	187	149	38
Tuhseel, { Number, ...	79	369	81	25	29	41	634	169	14	11	194	26	844	639	206
{ Percentage,...	9½	44	9½	3	3½	5	74½	20	1½	1	22½	3	100	76	24

Thakoors hold 44 per cent., Pathans 20, Brahmins and Kayeths each 9½ per cent., and all others in the aggregate only 17 per cent. of the estates in the tuhseel. Bunniahs are as yet recorded proprietors of only three per cent. of the muhals, but are mortgagees of many ; and in very many others the proprietors are so hopelessly in the hands of the money-lenders, that the final transfer is merely a question of time, the bunniah at present finding it more profitable to take as much as he can from his debtor, and allow him to have the trouble of collection and management of the village. Most of the Kayeth villages are held by representatives of the old Canoongoe families. The Koormees, as the rule, have purchased from their savings as cultivators. The estates held by castes not given in the statement are shown in the margin ; 76 per cent. of the estates are held by proprietors living in the tuhseel, and in this class are included the English villages, as the manager with full authority from the proprietor lives in the tuhseel. In Negohee alone are many estates held by non-resident proprietors. Further details for each pergunnah are given in the following paragraphs.

Kulwar, ... 3
Aheer, ... 8
Sonar, ... 2
Khuttree, ... 7
Kahar, ... 1
Teloe, ... 1
Syad, ... 3
Mogul, ... 7
Nakkal, ... 1

37.   At the last settlement Mahomedans, nearly all Tilhur Pathans, held close on half the villages of the pergunnah, but now hold less than one-third ; the change has been caused by confiscation for rebellion, and the majority of the confiscated villages were at settlement the property of two men,—one the representative of Mungul Khan, mentioned in para. 28, the other a grandson of Hafiz Rahmut Khan ; the latter, Mahomed Tukkee Khan, was allowed to retain one village for his support, and he is still alive and lives in his village of Burheepore. The confiscated villages were chiefly conferred on Thakoors and Brahmins of Khera Bujhera, and Thakoors now hold almost one-third of the villages, and Brahmins nearly one-eighth. Of the Thakoor villages more than half are held by Jungharas of Khera Bujhera, or of villages near the Khera Bujhera border, one-fourth by Bachils near the Kant border, and the rest by Katherias of Sootha, a village near the Jelalpore border, and by Chundelas of the Jellalabad Pergunnah. Tilhur is not a Thakoor pergunnah, but the adjoining Thakoor tracts overlap the boundary. Most of the Thakoor, Brahmin, and Kayeth villages are held by single proprietors, or by a small number of sharers. In several of the Pathan villages there are many sharers, but the Pathan zemindars almost all live in the town, and very seldom cultivate themselves.

Pergunnah Tilhur.

17 T

38. Of the 12 mouzahs in Kuttra, Mahomedans, Pathans, or Moguls have four
Pergunnah Kuttra. entire mouzahs and separate muhals in three mouzahs, the other
muhals in which belong to Colonel Wroughton. Koormees
have three (nine muhals), Thakoors one, and the twelfth is held by a number of sharers,
chiefly Thakoors.

39. In Negohee, at the time of last settlement, nearly half the pergunnah belonged
Pergunnah Negohee. to Nawab Karamat Ullah Khan, a grandson of Hafiz Rahmut Khan; but of the 65 villages held by him in 1838, only
two remained in 1845. Fifteen were sold for arrears of revenue, thirty-five were sold
under decree of Court, and thirteen by private sale. The two remaining villages and
four revenue-free chucks were in possession of mortgagees at the mutiny, and the rights
of the mortgagors, the heirs of Karamut Ullah Khan, were confiscated for rebellion.
As only three other villages in the pergunnah were sold for arrears of revenue, high
assessment can hardly have been the cause of the loss of this estate, though possibly
the settlement accelerated the final ending. Kassub Thakoors of Dhukia Rugha held
twenty-two villages, Kassubs of Azimabad nine, and Chowhans of Dhukia Tewaree five
villages. The Chowhans still retain four out of the five, but the usual fortune of the
clan has attended the Kassubs, and the Dhukia Kassubs now retain only eight villages,
the Azimabad Kassubs only shares in four villages. A considerable part of Nawab
Karamat Ullah's property passed into the hands of a Hindoo banking firm in the city.
The partners in the firm have since separated, and the villages have been divided. One
of the partners was a Brahmin, the other a Bunniah. Pathan sugar manufacturers of
the city have acquired many villages, and fully half of the present proprietors are
monied men of the city. The resident proprietors are chiefly Thakoors, who hold 31
entire villages and 27 muhals, all but six held by resident proprietors. Koormees hold
eight muhals, and all the Koormee proprietors might be considered resident, though in
fact some live outside the borders of the pergunnah.

40. In Khera Bujhera the proprietors are generally Junghara Thakoors; this
Pergunnah Khera Buj-
hera. clan holding nearly ¾ths of the pergunnah, and five muhals
are held by other Thakoors who have acquired through mar-
riages with the Jungharas. Brahmins and Kayeths, who hold nine muhals each, are
the only other castes holding any considerable number of villages. Mahomedans have
only two villages, both recently acquired, and fifty years ago I believe every village in
the pergunnah was held by Jungharas. Twenty muhals in the north of the pergunnah
are held by bhoor Jungharas, and terai Jungharas hold the rest. The leading families are those of Khera Ruth (bhoor Jungharas), Gurheea, Khimeria, Gobindpore,
and Soorjoopore. There are no really large proprietary communities; generally each
body of sharers holds at least two or three villages, and in many instances a few sharers
hold nine or ten villages.

41. In Jelalpore the proprietors are now of many castes. Mr. J. W. Muir in
Pergunnah Jelalpore. 1839 wrote:—" The *malgoozars* throughout the whole pergunnah
are nearly all Katheria Thakoors;" but even then this account
was not quite accurate, as at the last settlement many villages were held by Brahmins,
Kayeths, and Junghara Thakoors, though the majority were held by Katherias. Since
Mr. Muir wrote there have been great changes. Now Thakoors only possess a little
over 40 per cent. of the *muhals*, and more than half of those are held by residents of
the pergunnahs of Khera Bujhera, Furreedpore, Beesulpore, and Tilhur, most of whom
have purchased from resident proprietors. Kayeths hold nearly one-fourth of the
muhals, and ten are held by one family, residents of Khoodagunge. Many villages have
been purchased by city Pathans, and one of these is now the largest proprietor in the
pergunnah, his villages all purchased during the term of settlement. The remaining
proprietors are Brahmins, Koormees, Kulwars, Bunniahs, Kuttra Moguls, and the
English proprietor of the Meona indigo factory; some of the Brahmins are of old
standing, the others have nearly all purchased during the term of settlement. Not a

single proprietor or family holds more than ten villages, very few more than two or three. There are two comparatively large Katheria communities, those of Newada and Mujhla, each with two or three villages.

42. The following statements show the areas held in each pergunnah as *seer*
Area held as seer and by each class of tenants. by cultivators with rights of occupancy, and by tenants-at-will, with the percentage to the total cultivated area.

On the tuhseel total, fourteen per cent. of the area is *seer*, either cultivated by the proprietors or sub-let, sixty-nine per cent. is held by tenants with rights of occupancy, and seventeen per cent. by tenants-at-will; the *seer* percentage is highest in Khera Bujhera, and nearly all is there cultivated by the proprietors.

The average area held by each tenant according to this statement is a little under three acres, but, as has been explained in the Shahjehanpore Tuhseel Report, the actual area is greater, many tenants cultivating in more than one *muhal* or *puttee*, and thus one name may recur several times.

The average area per adult male agriculturist came out a little over 1½ acre (para. 14). The census shows all over 12 years of age as adults, and taking one holding to each family of five, the average size of the holding is over five acres.

DISTRIBUTION OF CULTIVATED AREA OF REVENUE-PAYING LANDS ACCORDING TO SEPARATE HOLDINGS.

| Name of Pergunnah. | Seer of proprietors actually cultivated by proprietors, or sub-let. | | | Cultivated by Tenants. | | | | | | Total area cultivated by tenants, irrespective of their having or not having rights of occupancy. | | |
| | | | | With right of occupancy. | | | Without rights of occupancy, tenants-at-will. | | | | | |
	Number of khathas or separate holdings.	Total cultivated area in acres.	Average cultivated area per khati in acres.	Number of khathas or separate holdings.	Total cultivated area in acres.	Average cultivated area per khatha.	Number of khathas.	Total cultivated area.	Average per khatha.	Total number of khathas or separate holdings of all tenants.	Total cultivated area in acres of all tenants.	Average cultivated area per khatha.
Tilhur, ...	927	6,025	6·5	13,407	45,560	3·4	4,406	9,909	2·2	17,813	55,469	3·1
Kuttra, ...	109	913	8·4	811	2,917	3·6	594	1,340	2·3	1,405	4,257	3·0
Negohee, ...	351	4,435	12·6	8,241	31,223	3·8	4,192	9,371	2·2	12,433	40,594	3·3
Khera Bujhera,...	747	9,155	12·3	8,498	27,175	3·2	3,135	5,260	1·7	11,633	32,435	2·8
Jelalpore, ...	880	5,570	6·3	8,575	22,091	2·6	3,980	5,566	1·4	12,555	27,657	2·2
Total, ...	3,016	26,098	8·7	39,532	128,966	3·3	16,307	31,446	1·9	55,839	160,412	2·9

| Pergunnah. | | | | | PERCENTAGE OF CULTIVATED AREA HELD | | |
					As seer.	By cultivators with rights of occupancy.	By tenants-at-will.
Tilhur, ...	{ Actual area, ...	...	...	...	6,025	45,560	9,909
	{ Percentage, ...	...	...	...	9·79	74·09	16·12
Kuttra, ...	{ Actual area, ...	...	...	...	913	2,917	1,340
	{ Percentage, ...	...	...	...	17·65	56·43	25·92
Negohee, ...	{ Actual area, ...	...	...	...	4,435	31,223	9,371
	{ Percentage, ...	...	...	...	9·84	69·34	20·82
Khera Bujhera	{ Actual area, ...	...	...	...	9,155	27,175	5,260
	{ Percentage, ...	...	...	...	20·02	65·34	12·64
Jelalpore, ...	{ Actual area, ...	...	...	...	5,570	22,091	5,566
	{ Percentage, ...	...	...	...	16·70	64·48	16·76
Tuhseel, ...	{ Actual area, ...	...	...	...	26,098	1,28,966	31,446
	{ Percentage, ...	...	...	...	13·99	65·15	16·86

The areas in these statements do not agree exactly with those given elsewhere in the report, as the figures have been compiled from the completed misls. The difference is very small, and the preparation of the tuhseel report could not be delayed until the final results from all completed papers should be ready. The areas elsewhere given agree with those contained in the rent-rate reports; but, as I have stated, the difference is almost immaterial, and chiefly due to some alterations consequent on diluvion subsequent to survey.

43. Any account of the manner in which rents are paid in this tuhseel is almost
Rent customs. unnecessary, as the customs agree exactly with those described in the report for the Shahjehanpore Tuhseel. As in that tuhseel rents are, with the exception of a few fields here and there, exclusively money rents, partly lump rents, and partly rates per *beegah*; the rates, all-round rates for the entire holding, rates on *hars* or tracts, or rates varying from field to field. All-round rates are practically almost the same as lump rents, and both are less liable to enhancement than *har* rates, which again are more likely to remain unchanged than rates varying from field to field.

The last in parts of the tuhseel vary most capriciously, and of two adjoining fields of similar quality, one will often be found to pay 5 or 6 annas, the other 10 or 12 annas per *beegah*. In places too enhancement has commonly been effected, not by raising the rate per *beegah*, but by reducing the size of the village *beegah*, and thus villages are found where one rate per *beegah* is paid all over the village; but in the poorer *hars* only does the old *beegah* remain, and in the superior part the *beegah* will be from 15 or 16 to 19 *biswas* by the old measurement, according to the enhancement effected. Enhancement is also effected by an increase in the rate of *kharch*, and in the *terai* part of Tilhur a statement that the rent of 'a field is eight annas per *beegah* conveys but little information; it may be without *kharch* on a *beegah* one-sixth of the acre, or it may be with 5 annas in the rupee *kharch* on a *beegah* little more than one-eighth of an acre, the rate in one case being 3, in the other over 5 rupees per acre.

At the last survey there were four distinct *pucka beegahs* used, and in each pergunnah an attempt was made to introduce a new *kuchha beegah*, bearing a definite proportion to the survey *beegah* of the pergunnah; this attempt met with only partial success, the people commonly reverted to the old, or *gowhanee, beegah*, and the new, or *captanee, beegah* was only partially adopted. Starting with these variations, the size of the *beegah* has been often reduced by the zemindars, and many real changes in area have taken place without correction of the record. In two or three villages of the tuhseel there is a special rate for cotton, but, with this exception, the only crop rates are for sugarcane and for *kuchyana* or garden crops; and, as in Shahjehanpore, there are no wet and dry rates, and no circles of artificial soil round the village site. In one property in Khera Bujhera the recorded rate was looked on as a standard for average seasons, the landlord being entitled to demand some addition in favorable, and bound to grant some remission in unfavorable, seasons,—but this custom is now almost extinct; it was worked to the advantage of the landlord, and only remained in full force so long as the landlord's power and influence remained undiminished. On the death of the proprietor the estate was divided, his heirs have little influence, and the tenants have resisted, and now never pay more than the standard rate, and look for no deduction from it.

44. In this tuhseel also the *putwarees*' papers have been found on the whole to show
Real rental seldom concealed. fairly the actual rentals; the papers are not free from errors and mistakes, and in some few cases have been found quite unworthy of trust, but generally the rent entries are correct, and systematic concealment of the true rental is very rare. Enhancement has commonly been postponed pending settlement; sometimes land has been purposely allowed to remain waste, or the cultivation of the superior crops to some extent discouraged; but the landlords are themselves too much dependent on the papers for collection of their rents to be able to afford

false *nikasees* with rents paid exclusively in money. The cultivators are generally in debt to the *bunniahs*, but, as respects the landlord, are independent, and are, as the rule, ready enough to assert their rights against him.

In Tilhur, the first pergunnah I inspected in this tuhseel, on constantly finding the greatest variations in rates paid for similar soil in adjoining villages, I could not at first believe that the rents were correctly recorded, but more extended inquiry convinced me that the entries represented actual facts, and that the low rates recorded proved under-renting, and not fictitious entries. In 1870 I wrote as follows:—

" I have now had considerable opportunities of forming an opinion as to the trustworthiness of the recorded rents, as I have myself attested a very large number of *khutsounees* and *jummabundees* in the Kant Pergunnah, adjoining Tilhur; have attested many *khutsounees* in Tilhur, and have inspected both pergunnahs, and decided very many enhancement cases, and disputes of every description relating to entries in the *khutsounee*. I find that the tenants are, as a rule, ready to dispute the slightest attempt at alteration of their rents, and I believe that the rents actually paid are almost always entered." (Para. 14 of Tilhur Rent-rate Report.) Trial of enhancement cases after assessment fully bore out this view. Practically, it makes little difference whether an inadequate rental is attributed to low rents or to false entries. I quote again from the Tilhur Rent-rate Report,—" Rs. 1,83,705 is then the actual *nikasee* with the all-round tenant-rate applied to *seer*, but without any allowance for land held rent-free or under-rented, and my assumed rental is Rs. 2,08,554, or 13·5 per cent. in excess of the actual *nikasee*. There is a close agreement between these figures and those given by Mr. C. A. Elliott in paragraph 54 of his Chibramow Rent-rate Report; the Chibramow declared rental at the actual rent-rate was Rs. 1,84,364, and Mr. Elliott's assumed rental was Rs. 2,07,326; the Tilhur actual rental is Rs. 1,83,705, and my assumed rental Rs. 2,08,554.

" The estimated rentals of the pergunnahs agree very closely, and bear nearly the same proportion to the declared rental. This close agreement in the proportion between the declared and assumed rentals, to which the accidental agreement in the total sums attracted my attention, brought to my notice that I might have arrived at almost the same result by adopting Mr. Elliott's plan of calculating roughly, that an addition of two annas in the rupee is required to bring the declared up to the true average rental, as Rs. 1,83,705 × 1¼ = 2,06,668, or only 0·9 per cent. less than my assumed rental. Mr. Elliott, as I understand, considers that the greater part of this addition is due to cases of under-renting, but that part is due to fraudulent under-statement of rents actually paid: here I have made no allowance for under-statement of rent, or fabricated *nikasees*; my rates are based on rents actually paid and declared, and I attribute the difference between my rates and the actual all-round rate solely to land under-rented, not to land the rent of which is incorrectly entered, but the final result is much the same whether low entries of rent be attributed to actual low rents or to fictitious entries. I may hold that a village, the recorded rents of which are decidedly below the average rents paid for similar land, is under-rented, while another officer might decide that the entries were incorrect, but in either case the result would be identical, and the village would be assessed at the full average rate of its class." (Para. 19.)

45. The statement on the following page gives the total area and the principal sub-divisions for each pergunnah by the present survey, compared with the areas recorded at the last settlement ;—

Comparative statement of area at present and last settlement.

Pergunnah.	Total area in acres.	AREA EXCLUDED FROM ASSESSMENT.			MALGOOZAREE OR ASSESSABLE AREA.								Total.
					Culturable land not cultivated.				Cultivated land.			
		Barren.	Revenue free.	Total.	Old waste.	New fallow.	Groves.	Total.	Irrigated.	Not irrigated.	Total.	
Tilhur, ... { Last settlement, ...	79,130	5,158	4,065	9,223	16,529	5,176	...	21,705	22,991	25,211	48,202	69,907
{ Present settlement,	80,988	7,139	987	8,126	7,363	1,501	2,763	11,627	29,199	32,106	61,235	78,562
Kutra, ... { Last settlement, ...	8,156	1,383	140	1,523	2,724	190	...	2,914	3,257	462	3,719	6,633
{ Present settlement,	8,380	1,162	1	1,163	1,595	143	372	2,110	2,535	2,572	5,107	7,217
Negobee, ... { Last settlement, ...	70,819	5,492	2,701	8,193	22,835	2,733	...	25,568	18,242	18,816	37,058	63,696
{ Present settlement,	72,095	8,574	1,012	9,586	13,753	1,153	2,073	16,979	15,844	29,686	45,530	62,509
Khera Bujhera, ... { Last settlement, ...	54,032	6,507	923	7,530	11,923	2,245	...	14,168	8,312	24,022	32,334	46,502
{ Present settlement,	56,533	5,338	48	5,396	6,480	966	1,229	8,675	12,879	29,593	42,472	51,147
Jelalpore, ... { Last settlement, ...	46,888	9,232	1,144	10,376	6,494	1,064	...	7,558	25,450	3,499	28,949	36,507
{ Present settlement,	48,054	6,232	224	6,456	5,846	547	1,793	8,186	12,604	20,808	33,412	41,598
Total Tuhseel, ... { Last settlement, ...	2,59,090	27,872	8,973	36,845	60,595	11,408	...	71,913	78,259	72,010	150,262	222,175
{ Present settlement,	2,66,050	28,445	2,272	30,717	35,073	4,310	8,230	47,577	72,991	114,765	187,756	235,333
{ Increase, ...	7,030	573	...	...	...	...	...	...	...	42,755	37,494	13,158
{ Decrease, ...	...	...	6,701	6,128	25,468	7,098	...	24,336	5,261	...	...	...
Percentage of increase or decrease, ...	2.7	2.1	74.8	16.6	42.1	62.2	...	33.8	6.7	59.4	24.9	5.9

N.B.—Groves are not separately shown in the statements of the last settlement, but were included partly in the barren area, and partly in the old waste.

The increase in total area is at the rate of 2·7 per cent. The new survey shows an increase generally, but this is a slightly higher rate of increase than in any other tuhseel. The increase is greatest in Khera Bujhera, and there is only in the Ramgunga circle, and is due to alluvion. In other pergunnahs the difference is not very great. There is a large decrease in the revenue-free area, which now only aggregates 2,272 acres, or 0·8 per cent. of the area of the tuhseel. The barren area comes to almost the same total by each survey, and the variations in detail do not require explanation.

46. The following table shows conveniently the present distribution of the *malgoo-zaree* area :—

Detail of the assessable area.

Sub-divisions of assessable area.	PERCENTAGE OF TOTAL MALGOOZAREE OR ASSESSABLE AREA.					
	Tilhur.	Kuttra.	Negohee.	Khera Bu-jhera.	Jelalpore.	Total tuh-seel.
Cultivated, ...	84	71	73	83	80¼	79½
Old waste, ...	10	22	22	12½	14	15
New fallow, ...	2	2	2	2	1¼	2
Groves, ...	4	5	3	2½	4½	3½
Total { parts of 100, ..	100	100	100	100	100	100
{ in acres, ...	72,862	7,217	62,509	51,147	41,598	235,333

The results for the tuhseel agree closely with the figures for the Shahjehanpore tuhseel, the percentages of which are given marginally for comparison. A comparatively large area of unbroken waste remains in Kuttra, but the total assessable area of the pergunnah is little over 7,000 acres, and in Negohee alone does any considerable area of old waste remain; the waste in Negohee amounts to 13,753 acres, of which a great part is low-lying *dhák* and thorn jungle in the poorest part of the pergunnah; the soil generally hard inferior clay; practically very little valuable waste remains, and, except in Negohee and Kuttra, the waste is either poor uneven land on and immediately above the rise from the valley of the Bygool, or new alluvial soil, hardly yet fit for the plough, in the valleys of the Ramgunga and Gurra. There is a little *dhák* jungle near the Bygool in Khera Bujhera, and a little waste in the *bhoor* part of Tilhur.

Marginal note:
Cultivated, 80
Old waste, 15½
Fallow, ... 1¼
Groves, ... 3½
Total, { 100
{ acres 234,161

47. The increase in cultivation amounts to 37,494 acres, at the rate of just 25 per cent. The rate of increase in each pergunnah is given below :—

Increase in cultivated area.

Kuttra, ... 37 per cent.
Khera Bujhera, ... 31 „
Tilhur, ... 27 „
Negohee, ... 23 „
Jelalpore, ... 15 „

The increase has been greatest in Kuttra. In Khera Bujhera the increase was chiefly in the Bygool circle, where cultivation has increased 50 per cent. In Tilhur the increase was greatest in the *bhoor* circle. Jelalpore was in the most advanced state at the last settlement, and there was little room for extension of cultivation. Negohee has not kept pace with the rest of the tuhseel, but the waste was the poorest, and population less dense than in any other pergunnah. The increase of 25 per cent. in the cultivated area is not all due to extension of cultivation. The increase in the total area accounts for some, and the decrease in the revenue-free area for a considerable part of the increase, and some of the additional cultivation is land which had temporarily fallen out of cultivation in consequence of the unfavorable seasons immediately preceding the last settlement. I give the areas.*

	*Last settlement.	Present settlement.
Revenue-free,	8,973	2,272
Fallow, ...	11,408	4,310
Cultivation,	150,262	187,756
Total, ...	170,643	194,338

The lapsed and resumed revenue-free holdings were almost exclusively cultivated land. The increase is here 23,695 acres, or at the rate of 14 per cent., and this probably fairly enough shows the rate of increase caused by real extension of cultivation.

48. The soil denominations used throughout the district will be explained in the several reports, and the detailed soil statements are given in the appendices. The following statement gives the proportion of each soil in each assessment circle and pergunnah :—

Details of soils.

Soil.	Tilhur. Terai circle.	Tilhur. Bhoor circle.	Tilhur. Pergunnah.	Pergunnah Kuttra.	Khera Bujhera. Ramgunga circle.	Khera Bujhera. Bygool circle.	Khera Bujhera. Bhoor circle.	Khera Bujhera. Pergunnah.	Negohee. Domut circle.	Negohee. Khymua circle.	Negohee. Pergunnah.	Jelalpore. Gurra circle.	Jelalpore. Bygool circle.	Jelalpore. Pergunnah.	Total Tuhseel.
Gowhanee, ...	3	1½	2	3½	2¼	1½	1½	2	1½	1	1	¾	½	¾	1½
1st Domut, ...	64	30	43¾	43	65	62	24½	58	62½	42½	56¼	67½	29½	59½	53
Mutyar, ...	15	5	9½	7½	12	22	7½	14½	11	16¾	13½	9	4½	8½	11
2nd Domut, ...	14½	37½	28	32	14½	8½	35½	15¾	17	18½	17½	16	38½	20½	21½
Bhoor, ...	1½	26	16	10½	5½	3½	31½	9	5½	9	6½	3¾	25	8½	11
Dhunker, ...	2	½	1	3½	½	2	½	¾	2¾	12½	5½	3	2	2¾	2½
Total, ...	100	100	100	100	100	100	100	100	100	100	100	100	100	100	100

A glance at this statement shows that the *Terai* circle in Tilhur, the Ramgunga circle in Khera Bujhera, the Gurra circle in Jelalpore, and the *Domut* circle in Negohee are the four best in the tuhseel. The Khera Bujhera Bygool circle appears to follow very closely, but with respect to this circle the soil percentages are somewhat deceptive, much of the 1st *domut* being hard soil that might almost as well have been entered as *mutyar*. The high 2nd *domut* and *bhoor* percentages show the light sandy character of the soil in the *bhoor* circle of Tilhur and Khera Bujhera, and in the Bygool circle of Jelalpore. The *dhunker* percentage in the Khymua circle of Negohee shows the proportion of the poorest clay soil.

49. The detailed statements for each pergunnah are appended to the report. The following statement gives the proportion of the total cultivated area occupied in each circle and pergunnah by the more important crops :—

Agricultural produce.

Crop.	PERCENTAGE OF TOTAL CULTIVATED AREA OCCUPIED. Tilhur. Terai circle.	Tilhur. Bhoor circle.	Tilhur. Pergunnah.	Pergunnah Kuttra.	Negohee. 1st or domut circle.	Negohee. 2nd or Khymua circle.	Negohee. Pergunnah.	Khera Bujhera. Ramgunga circle.	Khera Bujhera. Bygool circle.	Khera Bujhera. Bhoor circle.	Khera Bujhera. Pergunnah.	Jelalpore. Gurra circle.	Jelalpore. Bygool circle.	Jelalpore. Pergunnah.	Total Tuhseel.
Sugarcane, ...	10	4¾	6¾	6½	7½	5	6¾	2¾	5¼	4¾	4	8½	5½	7½	6¼
Land prepared for cane, ...	8½	3½	5½	5¼	6	3¼	5	0¼	2¼	2	1½	6½	3½	6	4½
Cotton, ...	4	1	2¾	3¼	3¾	4	3¾	2½	3½	0¾	2½	5	3½	5	3½
Garden crops, ...	1½	0¾	1	1½	1	1½	1	1½	1½	1	1½	1	½	1	1
Jowar, ...	6	2½	3¾	3½	5	4¾	5	11	8½	1	8½	6½	2½	6	5½
Bajra, ...	7¾	30	20¾	18	16½	19½	17½	29½	17½	31½	25¾	16½	32¾	19½	21
Rice, ...	12½	4	7½	9	8½	17½	11½	4	10	5	6½	9½	7½	9	8½
Wheat, ...	36	37	36½	34½	31½	29½	31	33½	34½	37½	34½	29½	29	29½	33½
Gram, ...	6¾	6	6½	7	8½	17½	11½	4	10	5	6½	7	5¾	6¾	6¾
Barley, ...	2	2	2	2½	2	1½	1¾	1¾	3½	2½	2½	1¾	1½	1¾	2
Urhur, ...	3½	5	4½	5½	5½	3½	5	1½	1¾	5½	2	3½	4½	3½	3¾
Total autumn crops, ...	51½	48	49½	48¾	49½	56¾	51½	54½	52½	48	52¾	55½	57¾	56	51¾
Total spring crops, ...	48¾	52	50¾	51½	50¾	43½	48½	45½	47¾	52	47½	44½	42½	44	48½
Producing two crops, ...	7	3¾	5½	3¾	5¾	3¾	5½	4½	4½	2½	3¾	9¾	3½	8¾	5½

Wheat occupies one-third, bajra one-fifth, cane, including the actual crop and land fallow for the crop of the next year, one-ninth, and rice one-twelfth of the cultivated area. The proportion of land under each spring crop varies little, while the variations in the *khureef* percentages show the different qualities of the sub-division, the cane and *jowar* percentage being high in the best soil, the *bajra* percentage highest in the worst. The Ramgunga *terai* is an exception, and land there is under *bajra* that with more careful cultivation should be under more valuable crops.

50. The principal autumn crops are sugarcane, *jowar*, *bajra*, rice, cotton, and the various pulses, *mote, oorud*, &c., grown with the tall millets.

Autumn crops.

With the exception of wheat, sugarcane is the most important crop of the district; the valley of the Gurra grows much cane, the area in the Tilhur *terai* circle being 10, and in the Jelalpore Gurra circle 8¼ per cent. of the total cultivated area. A good deal is also grown in the Negohee *domut* circle. Little is found on the sandy uplands, and in Khera Bujhera till lately cane was seldom, if ever, grown, but the cultivation is spreading rapidly through the pergunnah, though as yet the cane area is not great. *Jowar* shows a higher percentage in the superior circles, as it requires a good and rather stiff soil. *Bajra* is always grown to some extent in each circle, while in the Ramgunga *terai* and the light sandy tracts it is the main autumn crop; but in this tuhseel there are no tracts in which *bajra* is grown year after year as the sole crop; almost every field in the very lightest soil grows a spring crop in alternate years, the general custom in the *bhoor* tracts being that the whole *har* will be under *bajra* in one year, and under wheat the next. In these tracts the wheat and *bajra* areas are always in large blocks, and not in scattered fields. The *bajra* percentage ranges from 7¾ in the Tilhur *terai* to 30 in the Tilhur *bhoor* circle. Cotton occupies a somewhat larger proportion of the area than in the other tuhseels of the district, but it is a crop to which little attention is paid; the cotton is of inferior quality, and the produce meets but a small part of the local wants, most of the cotton used being imported. Rice is extensively cultivated in all the low-lying tracts, whether of good or bad soil; much is grown in Negohee in soil hardly capable of producing any other crop, and in the Tilhur *terai* rice is grown in soil that produces excellent wheat and sugarcane. The inferior descriptions of rice only are commonly grown, and rice is often followed by a second crop, a great part of the area producing two crops, being land in which gram or other spring crop has followed rice. Maize is hardly grown in the tuhseel.

51. Wheat and gram are the main spring crops, barley is but little cultivated; and even in the lightest soil wheat is almost always sown in preference to barley; wheat as well as barley can, as the rule, be grown without irrigation, and though a heavier crop of barley should be obtained, the lighter crop of the superior grain may pay best, and we may assume that our cultivators are the best judges on this point.

Spring crops.

52. This is the only tuhseel in the district in which indigo is grown. There is one very small concern under native management where a little *kuchha* indigo is made, but the cultivation is almost confined to the indigo grown on advances from the Meona factory. The chief factory is at Meona, near Khoodagunge, in Jelalpore, and there are branch factories at Khiria in the same pergunnah, at Kuttra, at Jugut in Khera Bujhera, and at Bunthree in Tilhur. The Meona concern is not solely an indigo factory, but also one of the largest landed properties in the tuhseel. Many of the villages are near the Bygool, some in Tilhur, and some in Khera Bujhera, three are in Kuttra, one in Negohee, and a good many in Jelalpore. Of the indigo cultivation, about one-third is grown in villages belonging to the factory; the average area under indigo is about 3,400 acres; but a much smaller area is shown by the crop statements. The crop is sown after the close, and cut before the commencement, of the field season, during which, except when a field is kept for seed, no visible trace of the crop remains; and hence, as indigo is never the sole crop of the season, an accurate record of indigo cultivation is probably never obtained.

Indigo.

The process of manufacture is completed at each factory, and the manufactured indigo is each season sent to Calcutta for disposal at the public sales. The concern is an old one, having been first started early in the century by a French adventurer named Debois. It has changed hands many times, and Lieutenant-Colonel H. R. Wroughton has lately become the recorded proprietor. Indigo can hardly be considered one of the important crops of the tahseel; it is grown in but little over one per cent. of the cultivated area, and then is one only of two crops taken during the year.

53. Irrigation is chiefly from wells, and the wells in use in the district will be fully described in the district report. In the Ramgunga valley irrigation is unnecessary, except for garden crops.

Irrigation.

54. In the valley of the Gurra, in Tilhur, and Jelalpore, and in the good tract in the east of Negohee, *pul* wells are generally used; in these tracts, where the superior *pul* wells can be made, the soil is harder, with more clay mixture than in the upland tracts, and requires irrigation, and in these tracts irrigation is the rule in ordinary seasons. These *pul* wells are worked with the rope and leathern bucket and the sloping run, but the labor employed is almost invariably that of men. The bucket is rather smaller than where cattle are employed, but the buckets follow at much shorter intervals, and the men can keep up the work for a much longer time in the day. It is universally believed that irrigation would cost much more if cattle were substituted for men, and for work at the well bullocks of a class superior to the ordinary run of our plough cattle would be required.

Irrigation in the superior tracts of Tilhur, Negohee, and Jelalpore.

55. In the sandy upland tract the area irrigated varies greatly from year to year. The wells used in light soil are the *churkhee*, the wheel with two pots, and the *dhenklee* or lever wells, and these can generally be constructed. Here and there are very small pieces where the soil is almost pure sand, in which wells can hardly be dug; but these are exceptional. In the most exceptionally dry season of 1868-69, almost all this tract was irrigated, though only by most unremitting labor; the crop was average or nearly average, and, owing to high prices caused by scarcity elsewhere, the year was a most paying one for our agriculturists. In that season it was quite exceptional to see an unirrigated wheat field. The next year, 1869-70, it was quite as exceptional to see one irrigated. The rains were good, and followed by suitable falls in the cold weather, and hardly a well was dug in any tract of light soil in the district. In the two following years also there was very little irrigation. In these tracts irrigation is rather the exception than the rule, though almost all can be irrigated, and only in very dry seasons, such as 1868-69, is irrigation general. The wells are dug where wanted, are ready for use in about three days, and the cost averages little more than one rupee.

Irrigation in the upland tracts.

56. There remain the low tracts of hard clay, one in the west of Negohee near the Kutna, the other in the east of Khera Bujhera near the Bygool. Wells do not, as the rule, answer satisfactorily in either tract. Water is close enough to the surface, but is commonly found in quicksand, and, where wells can be made, the supply is small, while this hard dry soil requires a thorough flooding. Fortunately the adjoining rivers supply the water required.

Irrigation in the low clay tracts of Negohee and Khera Bujhera.

57. The river Kutna is dammed each year at Barah on the Negohee and Tilhur border, and a large head of water is obtained; the river can be crossed only by boats for many miles above the dam. Distributing channels take the water to villages three and four miles from the river, and there are few villages in the hard tract of Negohee to which the Kutna does not afford some irrigation, and it gives full irrigation to the small line of hard soil on the right or west bank. The Khaimooa *nullah* is dammed in several places by the zemindars of the villages on the banks, and furnishes some little irrigation.

Irrigation from the Kutna in Negohee.

58. The Bygool is dammed each year at Shunkerpore, and irrigates a large
Irrigation from the By- part of the Bygool circle in Khera Bujhera, and also a good
gool in Khera Bujhera. many villages in Tilhar. These dams on the Kutna and the
Bygool are constructed by Colonel Wroughton, the proprietor of the Meona indigo
factory and *zemindars*. In each case Colonel Wroughton is zemindar of one of the
villages touching the river at the point where the dam is made. There is a branch
factory at Khiria, not far from the Kutna dam, and two at Buathrée and Jugut, near
the Bygool dam. The dams are made primarily for the sake of the indigo cultivation,
but are constructed as soon after the rains as the state of the rivers allow, and are
always made in time to give irrigation to the spring crops. One year only did I hear
the cultivators complain of the Bygool dam not being made in good time, but that
year the Bygool carried a most unusual volume of water; the river carried away the
first dam, and a second had to be constructed in another place. The dams are earth-
work embankments, and are cut each year when the rains set in. The Kutna dam was
first constructed by the Meona factory, but the Bygool dam is of older date, and the
right to construct the dam was acquired with the villages about Buathree purchased
from former Thakoor proprietors. The Thakoors of Gobindpore, some six miles up the
river in a direct line, have the right to construct a dam every third year. Their dam
was made in 1869-70, but the river furnished also a fair supply for the lower or Shunkerpore dam. In 1872-73, on account of disputes among the Thakoors, the Gobindpore dam was not made. The greater part of the hard tract urgently needing river
irrigation is near the Shunkerpore dam. The distribution of the supply might be
improved; some water is comparatively wasted by being taken to villages where other
irrigation is possible, while a few villages that could be irrigated and urgently need
water receive none; but, on the whole, present arrangements work well and quietly.
The general irrigation rate is 2 annas a *beegah*, or about 12 annas an acre, for all
crops except *koonder* rice, which pays double. The rate is moderate, and is, I believe,
collected without difficulty.

59. The tuhseel has thus good irrigation facilities. In the broad valley of the
Irrigation from each Gurra and the loam tract of Negohee the very best *kuchha* wells
source. can generally be constructed. The Ramgunga valley never
requires irrigation, and though the cultivators allow the upland sandy tracts to remain
unirrigated in ordinary seasons, they do so, as I have proved, from choice, not necessity;
wells can be made, but irrigation is not necessary, and in average seasons fair wheat
crops are produced without irrigation. To the low hard clay tracts the Bygool and
Kutna give water, and land quite incapable of being irrigated is practically almost
non-existent. The following statement gives the percentage of irrigation from each
source. The areas in detail are given in Appendix :—

Pergunnah.			Percentage of total cultiva- ted area irri- gated at sur- vey.	Percentage of total irrigated area irrigated from the various sources.		
				Wells.	Tanks and nullahs.	Rivers and streams.
Tilhur, ...	...	...	47·5	82	12	6
Kuttra, ...	...	...	49·6	70	15	15
Negohee,	...	...	34·8	65	24	11
Khera Bujhera,	...	...	30·3	48	19	33
Jelalpore,	...	...	37·7	71	18	10
Total Tuhseel,	...		38·8	70	17	13

60. The area actually irrigated, not the irrigable area, is here given. Except a
The irrigated, not the little of the worst *bhoor* and some poor clay, almost every field
irrigable, area recorded. is irrigable. The percentage of irrigation is the percentage to

the total cultivated area, and this statement does not show the proportion of irrigation to the area under crops ordinarily irrigated in dry seasons. In the Tilhur pergunnah at survey the actual was 88 per cent. of the possible irrigation, as given in the marginal table, taken from the rent-rate report.

Circle.	Percentage of actual irrigation to total cultivation.	Percentage of actual to possible irrigation, i. e., of actual irrigated area to total area under all crops irrigated in dry seasons.
Terai, ...	56·5	95
Bhoor, ...	41·5	82
Pergunnah Tilhur, ...	47·5	88

61. The areas recorded as irrigated at the last settlement are clearly incorrect, as in Kuttra and Jelalpore, where the areas returned as irrigated were 3,257 and 25,450 acres, the total areas cultivated being 3,719 and 28,949 acres; in these pergunnahs probably the area capable of being irrigated was given, but throughout the tuhseel the old record of irrigation has been found generally incorrect.

Former record of irrigation incorrect.

62. There is no canal in the tuhseel. The Shahjehanpore branch of the Sardah Canal was to have passed through the very best part of Negohee, where certainly it was not wanted. I believe there are proposals for bringing a canal down the *Doab* between the Ramgunga and the Gurra; it appears to me that a canal is not needed, and is never likely to pay, but if the canal and canal irrigation were to be strictly restricted to the high sandy ridge, it would undoubtedly traverse the part of the district best suited for the introduction of canal irrigation, and even if a failure, should be a comparatively harmless failure.

Canals.

63. The following statement gives the land revenue for each of the past five settlements and that now assessed :—

Revenue of former settlements.

Land Revenue assessed at each Settlement.

Pergunnah.	5th settlement.	6th settlement.	7th settlement.	8th settlement.	9th settlement.	Present revision.
	Rs.	Rs.	Rs.	Rs.	Rs.	Rs.
Tilhur, ...	63,877	63,062	81,486	98,432	83,258	1,09,119
Kuttra, ...	5,539	5,589	6,617	7,379	5,925	8,510
Negohee, ...	38,207	38,207	58,477	74,539	63,833	77,130
Khera Bujhera, ...	13,788	15,991	55,973	68,548	51,743	72,360
Jelalpore, ...	55,909	58,431	63,396	68,616	55,550	63,095
Tuhseel, ...	1,77,320	1,81,280	2,65,949	3,17,514	2,60,309	3,30,124

This statement shows that very large enhancements were effected at the 7th and 8th settlements, and these enhancements were undoubtedly more than the country could then prosper under. Mr. J. W. Muir, who made the 9th settlement, that under Regulation IX. of 1833, pronounced all these pergunnahs to have been laboring under the pressure of a very heavy assessment, the enhancement of revenue subsequent to 1210 Fuslee having been more than the resources of the majority of the estates were adequate to. Mr. Muir goes on to state that, as the consequence of these enhancements, the people have been kept in poverty, numbers of *malgoozarees* had been ruined, and, except in favorable seasons, great difficulty had been experienced in the collection of the revenue (paras. 11 and 12 of Mr. J. W. Muir's report of 5th September 1838). The revenue assessed at the 8th settlement was higher than that of the 6th settlement by Rs. 1,36,284, or 75 per cent.

64. Mr. Muir, it will be seen, granted large reductions in each pergunnah amounting in the aggregate for the tuhseel to Rs. 57,205, or 18 per cent. on the revenue of the 8th settlement. Mr. Muir's assessments, and the necessity for the reductions granted, were examined and discussed in the pergunnah rent-rate reports. In Tilhur, Kuttra, and Khera Bujhera I considered that Mr. Muir had granted unnecessarily large reductions, but in Jelalpore I looked on the reduction granted as insufficient, and I attributed this to Mr. Muir having over-estimated the quality of his 1st class circle in Jelalapore. He assumed for this circle an average revenue-rate of Rs. 2-8 per acre, and for the 1st class villages of Tilhur a revenue rate of Rs. 2-4, while I think the Tilhur circle much superior, and believe that Mr. Muir would have been nearer the mark had he assumed a rate of Rs. 2-8 for the Tilhur, and one of Rs. 2-4 for the Jelalpore villages. In his detailed assessment Mr. Muir assessed above his assumed rate in the Tilhur, and below it in the Jelalpore circle, the actual revenue-rate being Rs. 2-6-9 for the Jelalpore, and Rs. 2-6-5 for the Tilhur circle; but, even so, I believe that the Tilhur villages were too leniently, and the Jelalpore too heavily assessed. Mr. Muir's assumed rates cannot be compared with those of the present settlement, as the old circles are not the same as the circles now formed. In Negohee the settlement pressed heavily at first, and Mr. Currie considered the pergunnah an exception to Mr. Muir's general tendency to leniency. In three pergunnahs the assessment was certainly light and in two somewhat severe, but on the whole the settlement may be said to have worked well, and there have been few sales or farms for arrears, except in Negohee and Jelalpore.

Mr. J. W. Muir's settlement under Regulation IX. of 1833.

65. The following statement shows the number of farms and sales for arrears of revenue, and permanent reductions on account of severity of assessment :—

Sales and farms for arrears of revenue, and permanent reductions on account of over-assessment.

Pergunnah.	Number of sales of muhals for arrears.	Number of farms of muhals for arrears.	Permanent reduction of revenue on account of severe assessment.	
			Number of muhals.	Amount of reduction.
				Rs.
Tilhur, ...	...	7	...	...
Kuttra, ...	...	...	...	...
Negohee, ...	18	7	42	2,402
Khera Bujhera, ...	...	7	13	1,593
Jelalpore, ...	1	23	7	576
Tuhseel, ...	19	44	62	4,571

66. There were no sales, farms, or reduction of revenue in Kuttra. In Tilhur, the largest of the pergunnahs, there were only seven farms, three within a few years of settlement and four immediately after the mutiny; two estates were farmed twice, and consequently the number of estates in which farms took place is only five.

Pergunnahs Kuttra and Tilhur.

67. In the part of the present pergunnah of Khera Bujhera assessed by Mr. Muir, there were only two farms, one of an entire *mouzah* and one of a small share of 1¼ *biswahs*. The other farms and all the cases of reduction of revenue were in villages settled in Bareilly or Budaon, and subsequently transferred to Khera Bujhera, and were chiefly in the villages, thirteen in number, settled as part of Furreedpore by Mr. Conolly. Reductions were granted in seven of these thirteen villages; of the remaining six, one was settled with a farmer, and the proprietors subsequently sold out, three were farmed for arrears, and in only two, both the property of non-resident proprietors holding other villages, can Mr. Conolly's settlement be said to have worked. Two of the villages transferred from

Pergunnah Khera Bujhera.

Budaon were farmed for arrears of revenue, and the revenue assessed in a lump on a cluster of six villages forming one property was reduced as too severe.

68. In Jelalpore one Katheria village was sold in 1845 A.D. ; fourteen entire villages and shares in nine others were farmed for arrears, twenty-one of these farms were within a few years of settlement, and the remaining two immediately after the mutiny ; nearly all were Katheria villages, and in all but two or three there have been, since the farms, transfer under decree of Court. The reductions of revenue were all in villages on the boundary between the superior and inferior tracts of the pergunnah, which were assessed as of uniform good quality, though each contained a considerable proportion of inferior soil ; many mistakes of this kind occurred, and could not be avoided, the settlement not having been founded on a close inspection of the villages.

Pergunnah Jelalpore.

69. The eighteen sales for arrears in Negohee all took place between 1838 and 1842 A.D., and of the eighteen villages, fifteen belonged to Nawab Keramat Oollah Khan, (para. 39) ; of the seven farms, six were before 1846, three of entire villages, and three of shares in villages, and the only farm of later date was of a small *muhal* and of a small *mouzah.* The reductions were granted in 1847 A.D., and of the forty-two villages, twenty-four had been in the Nawab's property, and thirteen belonged to the Kassub Thakoors of Dhukia and Azimabad. The reductions came too late to save these properties, but since then, as stated above, there has been no sale, and only one farm for arrears of revenue.

Pergunnah Negohee.

70. Mr. Currie was unable to obtain any accurate information concerning the circumstances of these sales and farms in Negohee, and it is doubtful how far they can be attributed to severity of assessment, and how far to neglect and mismanagement on the part of the proprietors ; but the fact remains that almost all the sales and farms have taken place in the portions of the tuhseel, the pergunnahs of Jelalpore and Negohee, and the villages transferred to Khera Bujhera from Bareilly and Budaon, which for other reasons have been considered the most heavily assessed. Another point deserving notice is, that almost all these sales and farms occurred within a very few years of settlement, and as Mr. Muir's settlement was a reduction on the preceding one, it may be that the arrears accrued before settlement, or were caused by the scarcity of 1837 and following years, and that, in the part assessed by Mr. Muir, the sales and farms should be attributed to the severity of the preceding settlement, rather than to Mr. Muir's revision.

Causes of sales and farms.

71. The initial revenue of the last settlement was Rs. 2,60,309, and at the present revision the amount of the expiring revenue was Rs. 2,60,662, the net increase during the term of settlement being Rs. 353. The net increase or decrease in each pergunnah, and details of the increase and decrease for the tuhseel, are here given. Details of the increase and decrease for each pergunnah were given in the rent-rate reports, but here details for the total tuhseel will be sufficient :—

Alterations in the revenue during the term of settlement.

Pergunnah.				Initial jumma.	Net increase.	Net decrease.	Expiring jumma at present revision.
				Rs.	Rs.	Rs.	Rs.
Tilhur,	...	...	...	83,253	1,918	...	85,171
Kuttra,	...	...	...	5,925	46	...	5,971
Negohee,	...	...	...	63,833	...	1,883	61,950
Khera Bujhera,	...	...	...	51,743	...	298	51,320
Jelalpore,	...	...	...	55,550	575	...	56,125
	Tuhseel,		...	2,60,309	2,534	2,181	2,60,537

Detail of gross increase.	Rs.	a.	Detail of gross decrease.		Rs.
Assessed on resumed revenue-free holdings, ...	2,511	8	Remissions for diluvion, ...		902
Assessed on alluvial additions, ...	3,548	8	Ditto for land taken up for public purposes, ...		354
Increase in revenue of a Jelalpore village, ...	120	0	Ditto on account of severe assessment, ...		4,571
Total, ...	6,180	0	Total,	...	5,827

72. In this district, in consequence of the destruction of records in 1857, it has
Transfers of landed property. been found most difficult to procure any accurate information relating to the prices obtained for property sold. In each pergunnah report statements of transfers were given, but all were not in the same form, and in several pergunnahs the information obtained from the tuhseel office was clearly often incorrect, and consequently I have not given these statements in the present report. In Tilhur I expended considerable labor in attempting to eliminate all fictitious sales, but I did not show the details for each decade of the settlement.

In Negohee Mr. Currie found the returns of prices during the two first decades either entirely wanting or unworthy of credit. In Khera Bujhera and Jelalpore I sub-divided the term of settlement into two periods, taking the mutiny as the division, but was able to ascertain the price of only a small proportion of the transfers. Under these circumstances I have omitted these statements. The areas shown were deceptive, as many properties recurred several times, some villages having changed hands three or four times since settlement, and the general account of the land-owners contained in this report should give a much more accurate view of the changes that have occurred.

From the statistics procured it would appear that since the mutiny the average price per acre has been about 60 per cent. above the average price during the term from settlement to 1857, but the data are imperfect, and I believe that the increase in selling value has been very much more than 60 per cent.

73. I give in Appendix H. extracts from a statement lately submitted, showing
Acquisition of land by non-agricultural classes. the extent to which land has passed from the possession of the agricultural into the hands of the non-agricultural classes during the term of settlement, and I give here an abstract showing the percentages held by the non-agricultural classes:—

Pergunnah.	Percentage of area held by non-agricultural classes in 1839-40.	Percentage of area transferred to non-agricultural classes 1840 to 1870.	Percentage of area held by non-agricultural classes in 1870.
Tilhur, ...	13·3	5·9	19·2
Kuttra, ...	23·2	1·4	24·6
Negohee, ...	12·7	27·5	40·2
Khera Bujhera, ...	2·8	6·0	8·8
Jelalpore, ...	28·5	6·3	34·8
Tuhseel, ...	13·9	12·2	26·1

But a small proportion of the transfers of landed property are here included, as only transfers to the non-agricultural classes are shown, and many city Pathans and money-lending Brahmins were included as belonging to the agricultural classes. To quote from a note written by me when the statement was submitted:—" In other parts of the district also small village zemindars have been to a great extent replaced by new purchasers, many of whom are included among the agricultural classes. In many cases the successors are men bonâ fide belonging to the agricultural community, but in many instances the purchasers are agricultural only in name, and have made their money solely by money-lending or sugar manufacture: many Brahmins and Koormees are as sharp money-lenders as any Bunniah or Kulwar. The city Pathans too have little claim to count among the agricultural classes; many have made money in Government service, and the rest of the wealthy men among them by sugar manufacture, while in their dealings with the cultivators they are as hard and unmerciful as any Bunniah."

74. The pergunnah of Negohee was inspected and assessed by Mr. Currie, and **The present settlement.** the other four pergunnahs, Tilhur, Kuttra, Khera Bujhera, and Jelalpore, by me. An account of the method of inspection, manner of working out rates, and principles of assessment, is given in the general report, and separate remarks for this tuhseel are not called for. In this report the special results for the tuhseel are given and explained, but all general subjects come more fittingly into the general district report.

75. The assumed rent-rates sanctioned by the Board of Revenue for each circle **Assumed average rent-rates.** and pergunnah are given in the following statement. The soil percentages have been already given in paragraph 46, and the soil areas, with the rates and resulting rentals, are given in full detail in Appendix C. :—

	ASSUMED RENT-RATES PER ACRE.									
Soil.	Pergunnah Tilhur.		Pergunnah Kuttra.	Pergunnah Negohee.			Pergunnah Khera Bujhera.		Pergunnah Jelalpore.	
	Terai circle.	Bhoor circle.		Domut circle.	Khaimooa circle.	Ramgunga circle.	Bygool circle.	Bhoor circle.	Gurra circle.	Bygool circle.
	R. a. p.	R. a. p.	R. a. p.	R. a. p.	R. a. p.	R. a. p.	R. a. p.	R. a. p.	R. a. p.	R. a. p.
Gowhanee, ...	7 0 0	6 0 0	6 8 0	6 8 0	6 0 0	7 0 0	6 0 0	6 0 0	7 0 0	6 8 0
1st Domut, ...	5 0 0	3 4 0	3 8 0	3 8 0	3 4 0	4 4 0	3 4 0	3 0 0	4 8 0	3 12 0
Mutyar, ...	4 0 0	2 12 0	3 0 0	3 0 0	2 12 0	3 12 0	2 8 0	2 8 0	3 8 0	2 14 0
2nd Domut, ...	3 8 0	2 8 0	2 8 0	2 8 0	2 12 0	3 0 0	2 8 0	2 4 0	3 0 0	2 8 0
Bhoor, ...	3 8 0	1 12 0	1 12 0	2 4 0	2 0 0	1 12 0	1 12 0	1 12 0	2 0 0	2 0 0
Dhunker, ...	2 8 0	2 0 0	2 4 0	2 4 0	2 0 0	2 0 0	2 0 0	2 0 0	2 4 0	2 4 0
All-round incidence on cultivation, ...	4 9 6	2 9 4	3 0 4	3 4 7	2 13 5	3 14 0	2 15 2	2 6 2	4 0 5	2 12 3

There are thus ten circles, each with six rates, but many of these rates are repeated in the various pergunnahs for the same or some other soil, and the separate rates used in the assessment of the tuhseel number seventeen, and range from Re. 1-12-0 to Rs. 7. It will be seen that, with one exception, the rates are all multiples of four annas ; the rates are approximate average rates, and have been fixed in figures that can readily be tested and applied as new areas and fresh villages are met in the daily work of inspection.

76. The all-round incidence on the total cultivated area of the rental resulting **All round incidence agrees with crop and soil grading.** from the assumed rates furnishes a fair test of the relative quality of the various circles, and the following statement shows that the grading thus arrived at agrees closely with that given by the soil and crop percentages :—

Pergunnah.	Circle.	All-round incidence on cultivation of rental given by assumed rates.	Percentage of superior soils, Gowhanee, 1st Domut, and Mutyar.	Percentage of superior crops, sugarcane, jowar, garden crops, cotton, and wheat.
		R. a. p.		
Tilhur, ...	Terai, ...	4 9 6	82	66
Jelalpore, ...	Gurra, ...	4 0 5	77½	56½
Khera Bujhera, ...	Ramgunga, ...	3 14 0	79½	51
Negohee, ...	1st or Domut, ...	3 4 7	74½	54½
Kuttra, ...	...	3 0 4	54	54½
Khera Bujhera, ...	Bygool, ...	2 15 2	85½	54½
Negohee, ...	2nd or Khaimooa, ...	2 13 5	60½	47½
Jelalpore, ...	Bygool, ...	2 12 3	34½	44½
Tilhur, ...	Bhoor, ...	2 9 4	36½	49½
Khera Bujhera, ...	Bhoor, ...	2 6 2	33	46½

The Ramgunga circle crop percentage shows badly, as in the Ramgunga *terai* a rather careless style of cultivation prevails, and sugarcane is little grown. The soil .percentages, on the other hand, represent the two circles where hard clay soil is common, the Khera Bujhera Bygool, and the Negohee Khaimooa circle, as better than they really are, each circle containing much hard 1*st domut*, approaching *mutyar* in character, and much *mutyar* generally of very inferior quality.

77. There is very great difference in the quality of the circles, the all-round incidence ranging from Rs. 4-9-6 to Rs. 2-6-2 ; but in statements made out for each pergunnah without circle sub-divisions, there will appear much less difference, each pergunnah with a good circle having also a circle of inferior quality. The rentals resulting from the assumed rent-rates give the all-round rates on the cultivated area for each pergunnah shown in the margin. As a pergunnah, Jelalpore ranks first in quality, the greater part of the pergunnah being in the good circle. Tilbur ranks second, Khera Bujhera third, Negohee fourth, and Kuttra last.

Great variations in quality of circles, but pergunnahs of more uniform quality.

Pergunnah.					All-round incidence on cultivation.
					Rs. a. p.
Tilbur,	...	...	...	...	3 6 6
Kuttra,	...	...	...	...	3 0 4
Negohee,	...	...	...	...	3 2 6
Khera Bujhera,	...	...	...	...	3 5 6
Jelalpore,	...	...	...	...	3 12 2
			Tahseel,	...	3 6 2

78. The next statement gives for each pergunnah—(1) the rental at revision of settlement as obtained from the putwarees' papers, corrected only for *seer* at low rates ; (2) the estimated actual rental after corrections for *seer*, rent-free holdings, lands under-rented to relatives or connections of the proprietors, &c.; (3) the rental resulting from the assumed average rent-rates ; and (4) the gross assumed assets on which the detailed village assessments were finally made.

Rentals, actual and assumed.

Pergunnah.	Recorded rental corrected for seer.	Estimated actual rental.	Rental resulting from assumed rates.	Gross assumed assets.	Percentage of gross assumed assets over estimated actual rental.	Percentage of gross assumed assets over rental resulting from assumed rates.
	Rs.	Rs.	Rs.	Rs.		
Tilbur, ...	1,83,705	1,91,170	2,08,544	2,18,238	14·2	4·6
Kuttra, ...	12,131	13,450	15,488	17,020	26·5	9·9
Negohee, ...	1,28,305	1,36,000	1,43,613	1,54,260	13·4	7·4
Khera Bujhera, ...	1,20,482	1,27,550	1,41,888	1,44,720	13·5	2·
Jelalpore, ...	1,00,064	1,11,000	1,25,766	1,26,010	13·5	0·2
Tahseel, ...	5,44,667	5,79,170	6,35,299	6,60,248	14·0	3·93

The rental for the tahseel of Rs. 6,35,299, given by the assumed average rent-rates, is 9·9 per cent. in excess of the estimated actual rental of Rs. 5,79,170 ; the excess is a little over an anna and a half in the rupee, and this therefore is about the average enhancement of rents calculated on. The assets finally assumed for the detailed assessment include any *sewaee* items or allowance for increase of cultivation, and the total sum assumed is 14 per cent. above the estimated actual rental ; the percentage is almost constant in the other pergunnahs, but in the little pergunnah of Kuttra, where rents were abnormally low, and the *sewaee* income of more importance than in the other pergunnahs, the difference is greater. The assets finally assumed are 3·9 per cent. in excess of the rental resulting from the average rates, and this difference is chiefly due to the additions made for *sewaee* income, or for prospective increase in cultivation, and is greatest in Kuttra and Negohee, where most waste remains.

21 T

79. The difference was calculated on and explained in the rent-rate reports, in
each of which a final estimate of the revenue to be assessed
was given. The aggregate of these final estimates amounts to
Rs. 3,26,430, supposing assets of Rs. 6,52,860, and the total of
the detailed village assessments comes to Rs. 3,30,124, suppos-
ing assets of Rs. 6,60,248, the sum shown in the preceding statement. The revenue of
Rs. 3,30,124 assessed in detail is only 1·1 in excess of the sum of Rs. 3,26,430 estimated
before the assessments in detail were made. The actuals were slightly in excess of
the final estimate in each pergunnah, except in Negohee, in which the figures agree.

Assessments actually made in detail agree almost exactly with estimates reported before assessment.

80. The net increase of revenue obtained by the present revision of assessment
is Rs. 69,462, at the rate of 26·65 per cent. Particulars are
given in the following statement :—

Increase of new over expiring revenue.

Pergunnah.	Expiring jumma at present revision.	Total enhance-ment.	Total reduction.	Net increase.	New revised revenue.	Percentage of increase.
	Rs.	Rs. a.	Rs. a.	Rs.	Rs.	
Tilhur, ...	85,171	24,804 8	856 8	23,948	1,09,119	28·1
Kuttra, ...	5,971	2,569 0	30 0	2,589	8,510	42·5
Negohee, ...	61,950	15,823 0	643 0	15,180	77,150	24·5
Khera Bujhera, ...	51,320	23,618 0	2,703 0	20,915	72,360	40·7
Jelalpore, ...	56,125	10,086 0	3,206 0	6,880	63,005	12·2
Tuhseel, ...	2,60,537	76,900 8	7,438 8	69,462	3,30,124	26·65

81. The next statement shows at a glance some of the most important facts for
each pergunnah, and is here inserted before the explanation of the increase in each
pergunnah :—

1.	2.	3.	4.	5.	6.	7.	8.	9.
Pergunnah.	Population per square mile.	Agricultural popula-tion per square mile of cultivation.	Percentage of assess-able area cultivated.	Percentage of increase in cultivated area.	Percentage of superior soils.	Percentage of superior crops.	Percentage of increase of land revenue.	Incidence of new reve-nue on cultivation.
								Rs. a. p
Tilhur, ...	680	586	84	27	55	55½	28·1	1 12 6
Kuttra, ...	767	650	71	37	54	54	45·9	1 10 8
Negohee, ...	501	620	73	23	71	52½	24·5	1 11 1
Khera Bujhera, ...	531	580	83	31	74½	52	40·6	1 11 3
Jelalpore, ...	599	579	80	15	69	55	12·2	1 14 2
Tuhseel, ...	588	594	79½	25	65½	54	26·72	1 12 1

82. The increase in land revenue is greatest in Kuttra, but the incidence of the
revenue lighter than in any other pergunnah. The increase
in the cultivated area is 37 per cent.; and in this pergunnah,
for reasons stated at length in the rent-rate report, my assumed rates were considerably above the actual rates. As I stated in the rent-rate report (para. 17),—
"It should be remembered that Kuttra, though a separate pergunnah, contains only
12 villages, and that hence the case is that of a cluster of villages paying exceptionally low rents. I apply to these exceptional instances rates founded on the rates
actually paid in the neighbourhood." There has been a steady and rapid increase
in the rental of the pergunnah, an increase due chiefly to increase of cultivation ; there
is still a large margin of culturable waste, and ample room for enhancement of rents.
To quote again from the rent-rate report,—"There is no apparent reason why the
nikasees should not continue to increase, at least at the same rate, during the whole

Increase in Kuttra.

term of settlement; and if so, any *jumma* now assessed on the pergunnah must, at the end of the term, be even lighter than Mr. Muir's *jumma* now is, and very probably the revenue will have to be raised 50 or 60 per cent." The circumstances of the pergunnah appeared to me to fully justify the heavy increase in the revenue, and my proposed rates were sanctioned by the Board of Revenue.

83. Khera Bujhera comes next, with an increase in land revenue at the rate of 41·7 per cent. There has been, in this pergunnah also, a large increase in the cultivated area, at the rate of 31 per cent., and an examination of the rents recorded in the *bundphantas* of Mr. Muir's settlement proved that Mr. Muir's assumed rates were considerably below the actual rates prevailing in his time. The old assessment was a very light one, and in part to this, and in part to the great increase in cultivated area, is due the increase of revenue. In this pergunnah rents had risen very little, but I did not therefore pitch my assumed rates much above the actual rates. " But seldom do I expect to assume for assessment rentals very greatly above the actual rentals; rents are less likely to rise in Khera Bujhera, the proprietors are of one caste, and are resident landlords, population is less dense, there is no town in the pergunnah, and it lies apart from all main lines of communication; there are comparatively few tenants of the good cultivating castes, and, partly owing to the liability to inundation, a rougher style of cultivation prevails. We should expect rents to be more dependent on custom, and less on competition, than in Tilhur, and I believe that rents have risen less than in Tilhur, and are less likely to rise in the future; further, when the enhancement of revenue is, in any case, extremely heavy, the rates assumed should be moderate." (Rent-rate Report, paragraph 27). Khera Bujhera I look on as one of the most lightly assessed pergunnahs in the district, and the revised revenue as rather less than 50 per cent. of a full rental; but I consider an increase of 40½ per cent. quite as much as could be safely taken from the pergunnah, a pergunnah held almost exclusively by Thakoor proprietors. Kuttra and Khera Bujhera, the two pergunnahs in which the percentage of increase is the highest, are also the pergunnahs in which, looking to present capabilities and possible improvement, the revised assessment is the lightest.

84. Tilhur is on the whole inferior in natural capabilities to Khera Bajhera, as, though its *terai* circle is the best circle in the tuhseel, the greater part of the pergunnah is included in the *bhoor* circle; but in Tilhur rents have risen more than in Khera Bujhera. The pergunnah contains a large and important town, the proprietors are of various castes and classes, the pergunnah is traversed by several main roads, and a very large proportion of the cultivators are of the best cultivating castes. There was less room for extension of cultivation at the last settlement, and the waste remaining was brought under cultivation much sooner than in Khera Bujhera; the assessment of the last settlement, though far from severe, was not nearly so light as in Khera Bujhera, and the revised assessment gives an increase on the expiring revenue of 28·1 per cent. The incidence of the new revenue is Re. 1-12-6 per acre, or 1¼ anna higher than in Khera Bujhera.

85. In Negohee Mr. Muir's assessment was not a light one, but considerable reductions were subsequently granted, cultivation has advanced 23 per cent., and though the pergunnah is a purely agricultural one, containing no town, and off the main lines of communication, rents have risen more than in Khera Bajhera, the new purchasers having raised rents more than the Thakoors of Khera Bujhera. In Negohee also a large area of culturable waste still remains, which though generally most inferior soil, is of value for the wood, grass, and grazing; and hence in this pergunnah some of the increase of revenue is due to allowances for *sayer* income, or anticipation of immediate increase of cultivation, while in the rest of the tuhseel, excepting Kuttra, little waste remains, and the *sayer* income is insignificant. The percentage of increase in revenue is 24·5.

86. In Jelalpore, though the incidence of the revised assessment is higher, and
I believe the pergunnah to be now more heavily assessed than

Increase in Jelalpore. any other in the tuhseel, the increase is small, and the new
assessments were most favorably received by the proprietors. The zemindars, as the
rule, look chiefly to the amount of increase in the revenue, and this being here of small
amount, the assessment was received as, and is generally considered, a light one. The
pergunnah was on the whole very heavily assessed at the last settlement, though the
assessment was an unequal one; and as it was fully cultivated, the increase in cultivated
area is only at the rate of 15 per cent., and but a part of this is actual extension of
cultivation; much was due to land revenue-free at settlement, but since resumed and
assessed, and part is accounted for by the exceptionally large area fallow at the last
settlement. The increase due to actual reclamation of culturable waste is only about
8 per cent. on the old cultivated area. In this pergunnah my assumed rates were
pitched considerably above the actual rates, but the revised assessment is only 12·3
per cent. above the expiring *jumma* of the last settlement, and is Rs. 5,611, or 8 per
cent., less than the revenue of the 8th settlement,—this being the only pergunnah of
the tuhseel in which the new revenue is less than that of any previous settlement.

87. I do not think it necessary in this report to discuss many questions that
have been plainly stated, and fully explained in the five rent-

Many questions fully treated in former reports now not again discussed at length. rate reports. These reports contained full reasons for each
conclusion arrived at, and showed to what extent, and on what
grounds, rates were assumed above the actual rates, and discussed at length many
points here only briefly mentioned. The detailed assessments agree so closely with the
estimates in the rent-rate report, that the final results now shown may be said to be
the same as the results estimated in the rent-rate reports, the revenue actually assessed
being only 1·1 above the estimate, 'and accordingly there is no important departure
from sanctioned rates to be explained, and I here only note the more salient points,
and commonly give conclusions arrived at without explanation, where the proof was
given at length in the earlier reports.

88. The incidence per acre of the initial revenue of the last settlement on the
then areas, and of the revenue now assessed on the present

Incidence per acre of revenue of former and of present settlement. areas, are shown in the following statement:—

| | REVENUE-RATE PER ACRE ON | | | | | | | |
| Pergunnah. | Total Area. | | Assessable (malgoozaree) area. | | Cultivated area. | | Aggregate of cultivated area and new fallow. | |
	Last settlement.	Present settlement.	Last settlement.	Present settlement.	Last settlement.	Present settlement.	Last settlement.	Present settlement.
	Rs. a. p.	Rs. a. p.	Rs. a. p.	Rs. a. p.	Rs. a. p.	Rs. a. p.	Rs. a. p.	Rs. a. p.
Tilhur, ...	1 0 10	1 5 6	1 3 0	1 7 11	1 11 7	1 12 6	1 8 11	1 11 10
Kuttra, ...	0 11 7	1 0 3	0 14 3	1 2 10	1 9 5	1 10 8	1 8 3	1 9 11
Negohee, ...	0 14 5	1 1 1	1 0 4	1 3 9	1 11 7	1 11 1	1 9 8	1 10 5
Khera Bujhera,...	0 15 4	1 4 7	1 1 9	1 6 7	1 9 7	1 11 3	1 7 11	1 10 8
Jelalpore, ...	1 2 11	1 4 11	1 8 4	1 8 2	1 14 8	1 14 2	1 13 7	1 13 8
Tuhseel, ...	1 0 1	1 3 10	1 2 9	1 6 5	1 11 9	1 12 1	1 9 9	1 11 6

The revenue-rate on the total assessable and cultivated areas of each settlement
are here shown, and I have added a column giving the rate on the aggregate of cultivation and fallow. The area fallow at the last settlement was exceptional, and hence

the old revenue-rate on cultivation is deceptive, and makes the assessment appear higher than it really was.

89. For comparisons with the rates of other pergunnahs the revenue-rate per cultivated acre should be used, but the rates on the aggregate cultivated and fallow area show more fairly the difference between the rates of the last and present settlement. Comparing these latter rates, it will be seen that the rate of the present settlement is higher in each pergunnah, and that for the entire tuhseel the increase is 1 anna 9 pie per acre.

Rates to be used in comparisons.

90. The increase in the revenue-rate on cultivation alone is over 4 pie per acre; and this increase, small as it appears, proves that the assets now assumed at assessment are more than 66 per cent. above those assumed at the last settlement, the present settlement at half-assets being made on an area 25 per cent. greater than that formerly settled at two-thirds assets. Had the assessment been made on the present assumed assets, at the old proportion of two-thirds of the assets, the revenue of the tuhseel should have been Rs. 4,40,419,—an increase on the expiring revenue of Rs. 1,79,757, at the rate of 69 per cent ; and the revenue-rate on cultivation should be Rs. 2-5-6 per acre on the aggregate of cultivation, and fallow Rs. 2-4-8 per acre. These are what the figures should be if the proportion of assets taken had remained unchanged, but practically it would have been utterly impossible to put on any enhancement approaching that here shown.

Increase in assets supposed by new assessment, and revenue resulting, had the Government share of the assets not been lowered.

91. I may remark here that in every statement in this report the revenue given is the land revenue proper, the 50 per cent. demand without cesses of any kind, and all percentages and rates are made out on this 50 per cent. assessment. I note this particularly, as comparison may be made with the revenue-rates of the adjoining pergunnahs of the Bareilly and Budaon districts; and in the Bareilly and Budaon Settlement Reports the percentages of increase and the revenue-rates are those of the 55 per cent. demand, the total of land revenue and cesses at 10 per cent. on the land revenue. The revised land revenue gives a revenue-rate of Re. -1-12-1 per cultivated acre, but the incidence of the 55 per cent. demand is Re. 1-15-0 per cultivated acre.

All figures, rates, and incidences those of the land revenue proper. The half-assets demand.

92. Hitherto the revenue has been paid in four or five instalments, and the proportion paid at each instalment has in some pergunnahs varied most capriciously. The instalments are now four in each pergunnah, and fall due on the 15th November, 15th January, 15th May, and 15th June. The proportion payable at each instalment is not uniform for the entire tuhseel, but the classification has been much simplified. In Kuttra and Khera Bujhera there is one class only in each pergunnah, in Tilhur and Jelalpore two, and in Negohee three classes, as shown in the following statement :—

Revenue instalments.

Pergunnah				Number of muhals in each class.	Autumn instalments (khureef kists).			Spring instalments (rubbee kists).		
					15th November.	15th January.	Total.	15th May.	15th June.	Total.
					As.	As.	As.	As.	As.	As.
Tilhur,	...	...	...	97	3	3	6	5	5	10
Ditto,	...	...	...	174	3	4	7	4	5	9
Kuttra,	...	...	...	21	3	4	7	4	5	9
Negohee,	...	...	...	49	3	4	7	4	5	9
Ditto,	...	...	...	140	4	4	8	4	4	8
Ditto,	...	...	...	4	4	6	10	3	3	6
Khera Bujhera,	...	...	...	172	3	3	6	5	5	10
Jelalpore,	...	...	...	43	3	3	6	5	5	10
Ditto,	...	...	...	144	3	4	7	4	5	9

The two classes in Tilhur and Jelalpore correspond. Khera Bujhera agrees with the first Tilhur arrangement, Kuttra and one Negohee class with the second Tilhur class, and thus there are now only four separate sets of *kists* in the tuhseel.

93. In Tilhur, Kuttra, Khera Bujhera, and Jelalpore the instalments were settled

Instalments fixed by assessing officer in four pergunnahs.

by the assessing officer, and the villages classified in the pergunnahs where distinct classes were found necessary. The landowners were then invited to bring forward any objections they might have to the arrangements made, but very few petitions were presented, and the arrangements made have been generally approved. The instalments were fixed, and the villages classified, with regard to the value of the produce in each harvest, the wishes of the proprietors, and the arrangements heretofore existing. In Khera Bujhera I should have formed a second class, but that the payment of 10 annas of the revenue in the spring instalments was found to prevail in all parts of the pergunnah, and the proprietors almost all were in favor of this arrangement.

In Tilhur and Jelalpore the superior villages in the valley of the Gurra are included in the first class, paying 10 annas in the spring instalments.

94. The only petitions of objection received were from two or three zemindars of

Objections brought forward.

the Tilhur *terai* circle, who asked that the November instalment might be largely increased, on the ground that they then received a great part of the sugarcane rents. It is true that rent for cane is very commonly paid months before the crop is ripe, but it is so paid from the advances made to the cultivator by the sugar manufacturer; often, indeed, the manufacturer pays the rent direct to the landlord. The fact that rents are thus paid is commonly adduced by land-owners and native officials as a strong argument in favor of a large November instalment; but it does not appear to me that a custom which compels a tenant to borrow money to pay his rent months before he receives any return from his crop, should be in any way countenanced in the arrangement of the revenue instalments. No special February cane *kist* has been fixed, and February is in my opinion too early. Pressing the cane commonly lasts well into March. To justify a February instalment of revenue, the cultivator should be able to dispose of his produce early in January, but not one-half the cane will then be pressed; and allowing one month between the disposal of the produce of the tenant, and the collection of the revenue from the landlord, April would be early enough for the special cane *kist*, and this comes so close to the May and June instalments, that any separate cane *kist* is unnecessary.

95. In Pergunnah Negohee, as in the Shahjehanpore Tuhseel, three separate sets

Instalments in Negohee.

of instalments were drawn out by Mr. Currie, and the zemindars were allowed to select the arrangement they preferred, and but few selected the arrangement by which the largest share of the revenue is payable in the autumn instalments.

96. The revised assessment of Pergunnahs Tilhur and Kuttra came into force on

Engagements for payment of revenue.

the 1st July 1871; those of Negohee, Khera Bujhera, and Jelalpore on the 1st July 1872. As in Shahjehanpore, the engagements have been taken, not for a specified term of 20 or 30 years, but for the term of settlement and until revision. In the case of alluvial *muhals* on the Ramgunga and Gurra, engagements have been taken for short terms, subject to quinquennial revision under the rules for alluvion and diluvion in force. In Tilhur and Khera Bujhera the primary term before the first regular examination has been fixed at five years, and the alluvial estates in these pergunnahs will come under examination in 1876 and 1877 respectively; had the same term been fixed for Jelalpore, the examination of villages on the Ramgunga in Khera Bujhera, and on the Gurra in Jelalpore would have come on in the same year, and might cause an inconvenient pressure of work; to avoid this, six years has been fixed as the first term for the Jelalpore alluvial estates, which accordingly will come under examination in 1878. After the first term the examination will, under the present rules, be quinquennial, and the estates of Tilhur, Khera Bujhera, and

Jelalpore will thus, at the expiry of each term, come under examination in three consecutive years.

97. In Negohee " there are four *maafee mouzahs*, which were till quite lately only

Revenue-free villages.

portions of *mouzahs*, and are still distinguished by the appellation *chuck* prefixed to the name of the parent *mouzah*, from which they have been separated, as they are in reality now separate *mouzahs*. " (Mr. Currie's Negohee report (para. 2). These four revenue-free *chucks* were the property of Nawab Keramat Ullah Khan, and were in possession of mortgagees at the mutiny, when the rights of the mortgagors, the heirs of Keramat Ullah, were confiscated and sold, and the mortgagees purchased. They still remained revenue-free. In Pergunnah, Tilhur there are two revenue-free villages—Oosmanpore Tiswee and Sheregurh,—the former granted by Shuja-ood-Doula to a hakeem who attended him during illness, and the village is still held by the hakeem's descendants.

Sheregurh was originally a *maafee chuck* in *mouzah* Kusbeh Tilhur, and has been long held as a religious *maafee* by a family of Syuds, who were among the very earliest Mahomedan settlers in Tilhur. These are the only revenue-free villages in the tuhseel, and the aggregate revenue-free area is only 2,272 acres (para. 45). There is also one permanently-settled village in Pergunnah Tilhur,—Habeebpore, *alias* Bhandkhiria, which was granted by the Nawab Wazir to some Tilhur *nakkdls* in perpetuity, subject to a *nuzzurana jumma* of Rs. 59. The grant was after cession confirmed by Government, and the descendants of the grantees are still in possession.

The following statement gives the areas of these villages, and shows the amount of revenue alienated. In each village the *maafeedars* are also zemindars. The small revenue-free patches amount in the aggregate to 993 acres:—

Pergunnah.	Name of village.	Description.	Total area in acres.	Revenue now paid.	Revenue assessable, if village were not revenue-free.
				Rs.	Rs.
Tilhur, ...	Habeebpore,	Held on payment of a *nuzzurana jumma*, ...	188	59	350
Ditto, ...	Sheregurh,	Religious *maafee*, ...	87	...	200
Ditto, ...	Oosmanpore Tiswee,....	Charitable *maafee*, ...	464	...	400
Negohee,...	Chuck Itowa,	Ditto,	159	...	240
Ditto, ..	Chuck Bakainia,	Ditto,	224	...	280
Ditto, ...	Chuck Safora,	Ditto,	158	...	220
Ditto, ...	Chuck Lohurgawan,...	Ditto,	187	...	280
	Total,	...	1,467	59	1,970
					59
					1,911

98. The alteration in the system of payment of putwarees, by which they are

Arrangement of putwarees' circles, and grading of putwarees.

paid fixed salaries from the fund, has made it possible to arrange the circles so as to distribute the work fairly. Hitherto each putwaree has been paid by fees, generally at the rate of half-anna for each rupee of rental ; and consequently in low-rented and backward tracts the circles were much too large for the putwarree to do his work thoroughly. In the more fertile tracts, where rents are high, the alterations now made in the circles have been unimportant, but in the poorer tracts, especially where there has been a large increase in the cultivated area, it has been necessary to form many additional circles.

The following statement shows the grades and number of putwarees of each grade :—

Pergunnah.	Number of Putwarees.			
	1st grade, Rs. 13 per mensem.	2nd grade, Rs. 11 per mensem.	3rd grade, Rs. 9 per mensem.	Total.
Tilhur, ...	15	24	9	48
Kuttra, ...	...	2	2	4
Negohee, ...	10	14	8	32
Khera Bujhera, ...	9	13	7	29
Jelalpore, ...	7	12	6	25
Tuhseel, ...	41	65	32	138

The putwarees' cess has been fixed at the rate of 5¼ per cent. on the revenue (*jumma mal*) in three pergunnahs, and at 6 per cent. in Tilhur and Kuttra. The fund suffices for all expenditure, and leaves a small surplus to cover cost of stationery and miscellaneous expenditure. On the average, each putwaree has 4·5 mouzahs containing 6·1 muhals, with an aggregate area of 1,928 acres in his charge, and receives a salary averaging Rs. 133-9-0 per annum.

SHAHJEHANPORE, }
31st January 1874. }

GEORGE BUTT,
Assistant Settlement Officer.

POSTSCRIPT.

The foregoing report of Tuhseel Tilhur was written by Mr. Butt at my request, as *Foregoing report written by Mr. Butt, as greater part of this tuhseel was assessed by him as my assistant.* the assessment of the entire tuhseel, with the exception of Pergunnah Negohee, was made by him, and he was in direct charge of the measurements and vernacular records of the tuhseel almost from first to last. The rent-rate reports were written by Mr. Butt of each pergunnah assessed by him, and submitted by me to the Board of Revenue for sanction of the proposed rates ; and the detailed assessments made by Mr. Butt on receipt of sanction of the proposed rates were looked into by me before announcement of the *jummas*. Again, after announcement of the *jummas*, a term of one month was allowed for objections to be presented by the zemindars against Mr. Butt's assessments ; and all objections lodged were taken up my me as appeals, and the assessment was carefully gone over, and, if necessary, reduction was granted. The objections presented were numerous, but the instances in which any alteration was made were few, and the sums reduced were, as the rule, small ; for I did not hesitate to remit such small sums as 10 and 15 rupees where necessary, and, of course, I did not come across any instances in which severity of assessment called for a large reduction.

Deputy Collector Rugbuns Sahai had charge of the measurements of Pergunnahs *Vernacular records and case-work.* Tilhur and Khera Bujhera at first for a short time ; but Mr. Butt, with Pundit Kunhiya Lall (Tuhseeldar of Tilhur), as his Sudder Moonserim, soon took them over, and remained in charge of the measurement till completion of the entire tuhseel.

The brunt of the case-work fell on Mr. Butt and Pundit Kunhiya Lall (who was invested with powers of a Deputy Collector under Regulations VII. of 1822 and IX. of 1833, and Act XIV. of 1863, as soon as the measurements were completed). The attestation of the vernacular records fell chiefly to the share of Pundit Kunhiya Lall, and the whole tuhseel was in fact attested by him, with the exception of the greater part of Pergunnah Negohee and some few villages in Pergunnahs Tilhur and Khera Bujhera, which were made over to Moonshee Sudur-ood-deen on Pundit Kunhiya Lall's becoming ill and being obliged to take leave.

Besides most of the heavy and important cases being decided by Mr. Butt, he also heard and decided some of the appeals whilst officiating for me from the end of April to the end of December 1872:—

Total number of cases instituted and decided.	DETAILS OF CASES INSTITUTED AND DECIDED IN TUHSEEL TILHUR.						
	Rights and interests.	Enhancement.	Boundary disputes.	Partitions.	Maafee investigations.	Appeals to Settlement Officer.	Miscellaneous.
11,842	5,664	570	627	359	455	322	3,845

The details of the various cases are given in the table above, amounting in all to nearly 12,000. The number of enhancement suits is large, but still very many enhancements were adjusted mutually without a regular suit, and the 570 mentioned above are all separate suits, and they were all heard and decided under Acts X. of 1859 and XIV. of 1863, as this part of the work was completed before the passing of the new Rent Act, XVIII. of 1873.

The number of boundary disputes is very large, almost equal to the number in the two tuhseels of Shahjehanpore and Jellalabad together, but this is partly owing to cases having been made of insignificant and trivial disputes, such as in Shahjehanpore were summarily decided by me vivâ voce on the spot, and not allowed to come to a disputed case.

The number of appeals to the Settlement Officer is much swollen by objections to Mr. Butt's assessments having been taken up by me as appeals, as already mentioned. These number 190, so that the appeals from the judicial decisions of the Settlement subordinate officers is reduced to 132, or rather less than 2 per cent. of appealable cases, and, as already explained in the annual reports, the proportion of decisions reversed is very small. Separate details for the enhancement suits appealable to the Judge cannot be given for each tuhseel, but particulars of these cases will be found in the general report.

The number of appeals to the Commissioner is very small: only ten and five of these were appeals against the assessments, but all were thrown out, and no order of the Settlement Officer in this whole tuhseel has been reversed on appeal by the Commissioner of the Division, and I believe that not one single appeal was carried on to the Board of Revenue.

SHAHJEHANPORE,}
   23rd April 1874. }

ROBERT G. CURRIE,
Settlement Officer.

INDEX TO CHAPTER V.

ASSESSMENT REPORT OF TUHSEEL POWAYN.

CHAPTER V.

TUHSEEL POWAYN.

Tuhseel Powayn is now made up of the three Pergunnahs Powayn, Burragaon, and Khotar. Khotar was an independent Peshkaree
until May, 1871, when the Peshkaree was abolished and Khotar
was incorporated into this tuhseel in lieu of
Poorunpore, which was transferred from this
District to Phillibheet in 1865. It comprises
810 mouzahs and 965 muhals, and has a total area
of 598 square miles.

Pergunnahs comprising Tuhseel Powayn.

Pergunnah.	Mouzah.	Muhals.	Area in Sq. Miles.
Burragaon,	126	160	83
Powayn,	427	529	312
Khotar,	257	276	203
Whole tuhseel,	810	965	598

2. It is the northernmost tuhseel in the district, extending up to the commencement of the Ool nuddee and forest grants in Oudh and
Phillibheet, and to within three and a half and four miles of
the river Sardah. It is bounded on the north-east and east by the Kheree District of
Oudh, on the north and north-west by Pergunnah Poorunpore of Phillibheet, on the
west by Pergunnah Beesulpore of Bareilly, and on the south-west and south by Pergunnahs Negohee and Shahjehanpore of this district.

The boundaries of the tuhseel.

3. Of the three pergunnahs contained in this tuhseel, the southernmost, Burragaon, and the northernmost, Khotar, were assessed by me,
and the largest one, Powayn, by my assistant, Mr. Butt. I
take them in order from south to north, which is also the order
of time in which they were inspected and assessed.

*Pergunnah Powayn as-
sessed by Mr. Butt, the
other two by myself.*

4. The Sukheta *nulla* commences in the northern end of Pergunnah Burragaon,
in a series of only partially connected ponds and hollows.
About the centre of the pergunnah it assumes the form of a
shallow natural drain, and only becomes a well-defined nulla
on reaching the edge of the pergunnah, whence it becomes the natural boundary between
Pergunnah Shahjehanpore and Oudh. The soil in the north-eastern and eastern part
of the pergunnah near the Sukheta, and to the east of it, is mostly a firm clayey loam,
with stiff clay in the depressions, whilst the north-western, western, and southern
parts of the pergunnah, which lie along on the high ground between the Sukheta and
the Khunout nuddee are composed of a light sandy loam; but there is no wide belt of
bad sandy soil along above the high bank of the Khunout. The tract of fourteen villages on the south of the Khunout is similar to that in the *domut* circle of Negohee and
in Pergunnah Shahjehanpore, of which it forms a continuation. The water level
throughout the pergunnah is generally from fourteen to fifteen feet below the surface,
except in the tract south of the Khunout, where it is from twenty to twenty-three
feet. These are the averages for the *pool* or *gurra* wells from which water
is raised by the leathern bucket, which are constructible over the greater portion
of the pergunnah. The averages for the *dhenklees* and *rentees* is less, as they
are usually made in the low-lying lands, where water is close, or in the light sandy
tracts, where the soil is too friable for the *pool* wells. In these tracts, of course,
the water level for them is the same as for other wells, but the average is spoilt by the
greater number of them being in low lands, where water is within seven and eight feet
of the surface, and in this *pool* or *gurra* wells are never made. The *khadir* of the

*Description of the na-
tural features of Pergun-
nah Burragaon.*

Khunout is in bad odour just now, owing to the heavy floods of the last few years (1869 to 1872), which have destroyed the sugarcane, and waterlogged all the low lands and prevented their producing good rubbee crops. Mr. Rose, who wrote the report of the last settlement of this pergunnah, says :—" The Khunout, famous for the sugarcane produced along its banks, runs through the pergunnah." This excessive flooding is said to be quite a new feature, but there is no mistake about the truth of it. The rates show that the land was considered good, and the higher parts of it are still good, but the cultivators are relinquishing the real *terai* and *khadir* parts, as they have suffered severe losses for the last four years consecutively.

5. I make the following extract from my rent-rate report of the reasons for not making two or more assessment circles in Pergunnah Burragaon :—

No necessity for classification of Pergunnah Burragaon into soil circles. " Mr. J. W. Muir at last settlement divided the pergunnah into three classes for assessment, but the description of the classification is very vague ; the only explanation given by Mr. Rose being ' the first two classes are chiefly in the east and north, the best and south villages forming the third class.' Beyond this I have no means of ascertaining what villages were contained in each classification. The last assessment [having been made on all-round revenue rates on cultivation, without any separate soil rates, probably such classification was necessary. Now by using soil rates I find that a separate classification into circles is unnecessary here, the differential rates on soils giving quite sufficient variation in the resulting all-round cultivation rates between good and indifferent villages. Moreover the bad villages (what few there are) are scattered here and there throughout the pergunnah, and could not be formed into a circle with geographical limits." The proportions of the various soils are, 1st domut (including gowhanee) 55 per cent. ; mutyar or clay 10 per cent. ; 2nd domut, which is, as a rule, not a bad soil, but only 2nd and inferior to 1st domut, and about equal to mutyar, 30½ per cent. Dhunker and bhoor, the poor soils, under 4½ per cent.

6. The following description of Pergunnah Powayn is taken from Mr. Butt's rent-rate report written previous to assessment :—

Description of the natural features of Pergunnah Powayn. "(1.) The Pergunnah of Powayn formed part of the old Pergunnah of Gola, a division which included the present tuhseel of Powayn, the Pergunnah of Negohee, and part of Poorunpore. Gola included ten *tuppehs* and 1,544 villages, the names of the *tuppehs* being Negohee Khas, Kodurna, Pilkunna, Jewan, Islamabad, Charkee Deoree, Hawelee, Matee, Mujhwa, and Aurungabad. Jewan, Islamabad, Charkee Deoree, Aurungabad, and part of Hawelee form the present Pergunnah of Powayn. The boundary of the pergunnah was not fixed with regard to the old sub-divisions, but was marked so as to include the country held by the Gour Rajahs of Powayn, and contains all the villages found in their possession at the cession. The main portion of the pergunnah is a compact tract of country extending from Pergunnah Burragaon and the Oudh border on the south, to the pergunnah of Poorunpore of Phillibheet on the north, separated from Khotar on the east by the river Goomtee, and from Beesulpore on the west by the river Khunout.

"(2.) In the central part of the pergunnah the soil improves in quality from north to south, and the southern part, near the Pergunnah of Burragaon, is a well cultivated and densely populated tract ; the soil usually a firm and fertile loam, with occasional small patches of low and hard clay near the larger tanks or *jhaburs*.

The southern portion.

"(3.) The soil near the river Goomtee deteriorates from north to south; at the northern extremity of the pergunnah the Goomtee is a small stream, and the rise from the valley is slight; but twelve miles lower down it receives on the right, or Khotar bank, a considerable tributary, the Jhukna, and eight miles lower the Bhynsee falls into the Goomtee. Below the junction of the Goomtee and Jhukna the valley is much wider, the rise from the low land great, and above the rise for some distance back is the very poorest sandy soil.

The Goomtee ridge.

"(4.) Near the Khunout, on the contrary, the sandy ridge is more marked along the first part of the river's course. The Khunout changes less in character than the Goomtee. It receives no important tributary, and the volume of water is nearly as great, and the rise as marked, when the river first touches, as when it leaves the pergunnah. Along the upper part of the Khunout the soil above the valley is in fact a ridge between the Khunout and the Bhynsee, and hence of a light sandy nature, while lower down, almost as soon as the rise from the valley is stopped, the soil improves and becomes of the normal character.

The Khunout ridge.

"(5.) In the northern part of the pergunnah near Poorunpore the soil is generally of a somewhat sandy character, but there are numerous dips or depressions, and in these the soil is a good *mutyar*. These depressions wind about, and a few, those nearest the Khunout, unite and form the Bhynsee *nullah*, and the others unite and form the Tureona *nulla*. The Bhynsee is the first to assume the form of a regular *nulla*, and for some distance runs nearly parallel with the Khunout, then running to the south-west to the junction of the Tareona, from which point it first turns south, and then runs nearly in a semicircle till it falls into the Goomtee near the Oudh border. There is a marked rise from the right bank of the Bhynsee, and a line of light poor soil is found along the ridge. Where the Bhynsee is close to the Khunout this ridge unites with the Khunout ridge, but lower down is a narrow line extending but a short distance back from the rise. There is very little rise from the left bank of the Bhynsee before the Tureona joins it, and this tract, drained by the Bhynsee and Tureona, has no land raised very much above the level of the depressions. These depressions, the drainage lines, are wide shallow dips, from a quarter to half a mile wide generally, and form in the aggregate a considerable portion of the area of this part of the pergunnah. The soil is *mutyar*, but *mutyar* of a character that resembles alluvial deposits. It never cakes or hardens, requires no irrigation, and almost invariably produces two crops in the year. Heavy floods occasionally injure the autumn crop of rice, but the spring crops, except in very exceptional places, are good even after the heaviest rains.

The northern portion.

"(6.) The valley of the Khunout is narrow, and the land is raised above the level of the river. The soil is fertile and, as a rule, produces sugarcane and good spring crops; but the excessive floods for the last few years have rendered the produce inferior, and much land has been left too wet for cultivation."

The valley of the Khunout.

"(7.) The valley of the Goomtee is generally rice land, and the floods have here been most destructive, hardly a maund of rice having been produced during the last three years. For two years the rice sown was swept away, and this year (1280 F.S.) hardly any attempt has been made at cultivation, and only in unusually raised parts can any crop, except rice, be grown. This failure of the crops in the low lands is due to the excessive floods we have had each of the last three years (1872), and not to any wilful deterioration. All admit that the valley of the Goomtee, as a rule, produces excellent rice.

The valley of the Goomtee.

"(8.) The pergunnah also includes a tract of country lying between the river Khunout and Negohee, almost detached from the rest of the pergunnah and separated from it and from Burragaon by the Khunout. The Khunout bounds this piece north-east and south, and three tributaries of the Khunout flow through it, joining the Khunout on the Burragaon border. One of these, the Sakerrea *nulla*, is the most important tributary received by the Khunout, and flows in a well-defined valley with sandy ridges on each side. There is very little poor soil, but the Khunout and the nullas leave no space for any tract of good soil, and it is of only second class quality, and on the Negohee border are tracts of hard clay where little *dhak jungle* remains."

Detached tract west of the Khunout.

7. The division of the pergunnah into five assessment circles is thus explained by Mr. Butt in the same rent-rate report written before assessment, and dated 23rd February, 1873 :—

The circle arrangement, Pergunnah Powayn.

" (9.) For assessment I have found it necessary to form five circles. The detached tract between the Khunout and Negohee forms the Gola

The Gola circle.

circle, so called from the old town and present village of Gola,
situated on the river Khunout.

" (10.) The Powayn circle includes the villages lying round Powayn *khas*, and
extends from Pergunnah Burragaon to the commencement of

The Powayn circle.

the light poor soil above the Bhynsee and Goomtee. It takes
in the greater part of the Koormeeát, a small tract north of Powayn, where the cultivators are almost exclusively Koormees, and the circle is a good one. No river or *nulla*
touches the circles, and the variations in quality are chiefly due to slight local alterations in level.

" (11.) The Nahul circle extends along the Khunout, lying between that river and
the Powayn circle, and reaching from Burragaon on the south

The Nahul circle.

to the commencement of the line of poor soil crossing the pergunnah along the course of the Bhynsee on the north. The circle thus has one long
narrow line of low land along the Khunout, and another narrow line of poor soil on the
rise from the valley ; for the rest the soil is fair loam, but somewhat inferior to the
average of the Powayn circle, and three small nullas, tributaries of the Khunout,
break the level ; and in the southern part of the circle there are two considerable tracts
of clay soil where much *dhak jungle* yet remains. This circle receives its name from
the large village of Nahul.

" (12.) The Sunwat circle takes in the poorest *bhoor* soil in the pergunnah. The
doab between the Bhynsee and Goomtee is locally known as the

The Sunwat circle.

Sunwat, and adopting the name, I have extended the bounds.
The circle includes the Sunwat proper, the line of poor soil between the Powayn circle
and the rivers Bhynsee and Goomtee, and five bhoor villages across the Goomtee,
between Khotar and Oudh. These form a compact tract in the east of the pergunnah,
and from this the circle extends north-west, just taking in the poor line along the
upper part of the Bhynsee, till this narrow ridge unites with the ridge above the Khunout, and from this point the circle follows the Khunout to the Poorunpore border,
including a few very poor villages, and a large piece of stunted forest on the Khunout.
This circle is an extremely poor one. Excepting the uncertain valley of the Goomtee,
the soil is of the very lightest description, population very thin, and a large part of the
circle most unhealthy.

" (13.) The Tureona circle includes the remainder of the pergunnah, and is a
compact tract in the north-east extending from the Goomtee

The Tureona circle.

to the Sunwat circle, and including the low-lying country
drained by the Tureona and Bhynsee depressions. Along this circle the rise from the
valley of the Goomtee is comparatively slight, the *bhoor* above it is of less pronounced character than lower down, and extends but a short way back. The rest of the
circle may be almost described as a series of undulations ; the dips being the depressions
in para. 5, and the slightly raised parts all of a sandy character."

The percentages of soils in the various circles can be most conveniently given and

Circle.	Gowhanee.	1st Domut.	Mutyar.	2nd Domut.	Dhunker.	Bhoor.
Gola, ...	·6	40·6	10·5	35·8	·4	12·1
Powayn, ...	·9	65·2	10·3	19·6	1·1	2·9
Nahul, ...	·4	47·0	15·9	25·9	1·4	9·4
Sunwat, ...	·4	10·9	7·7	43·4	·7	36·9
Tureona, ...	·6	31·7	14·4	40·6	1·1	11·6
Totals of pergunnah,	·6	35·0	11·7	35·2	1·0	16·5

read in
a tabu-
lar form,
and a
glance
at the
margin-
al state-
ment
will at

once show that the Powayn is the best, and the Sunwat by far the worst circle.

This will also be still further proved by the percentages of various crops given in para. 10.

8. The description of the natural features of Pergunnah Khotar is given in the form of extracts from my own rent-rate report, written previous to assessment in May, 1873 :—

Description of the natural features of Pergunnah Khotar and extent of forest.

" (9.) The length of the pergunnah is from north to south, or rather from nor-nor-west to sou-sou-east, and is just twenty-five miles ; the average breadth being ten miles, till near the sou-sou-east end, where it narrows into a point. The Ool nuddee, here a mere open glade and broad shallow drainage line through the forest, forms its north-eastern boundary, separating it from the grants and *terai* forests of the Kheree district. The Ool on the north-east, and the river Goomtee on the south-west, are its natural boundaries, but on the west and east along its sides it has no continuous natural boundaries. The pergunnah is divided into two almost equal parts by a broad belt of forest of from one and a half to two miles in width, which extends across from the Kutna on the east, just where it becomes the pergunnah boundary, to the Jhukna nulla on the west, where, after forming the boundary for a short distance, it enters the pergunnah,—this belt only just not effecting a junction with the forest which surrounds the entire north of this boundary. This forest is widest and densest along the northern end, and the Ool, where it averages two to two and a half miles in width for a distance of twelve miles. It is narrowest on the west, where it is only from a quarter to half a mile in width in this district, and rather less across the border in Phillibheet ; and where it has been pierced through by reclamation, and disconnected by cultivation for the distance of about half a mile. The forest also extends southwards along the Kutna from where it goes out of the pergunnah into the boundary till where it leaves the pergunnah altogether and enters the Kheree district, a distance of nearly 10 miles, usually from half to three-quarters of a mile in breadth. Wherever there is forest along the boundary of this pergunnah and Oudh, there is much more across the boundary, and the Oudh forest grants extend down as far as, and march with the forest on our boundary. The total forest area, as already mentioned, is nearly 29,000 acres,—about 45 square miles.

" (10.) This forest consists chiefly of small *sal*, here called *koron*, which does not *Forest.* grow to sufficient size to be of any use as large timber, or for logs. There are several other kinds of forest trees, but none of them timber trees, except the *mhowa* and *asaina*, which are not plentiful, except in a few of the villages. Apparently there have been some fine trees besides *peepul* and *burgat*, which still remain throughout this forest, but they have been cut, and no care is taken of the forest, and the trees have no fair chance ; the custom of cutting *bullees* (which may be cut at Rs. 2 per 100) preventing the growth and development of the young trees, each *bullee* being in fact a young tree. There is, however, abundance of wood well fitted for agricultural implements, country carts, wheels, door frames, and the like, as also for firewood and charcoal. These forests harbour herds of deer, principally *neelgai* and *cheetul*, and also pigs, which swarm out during the night to feed, and render constant night-watching absolutely necessary, in order to save the crops anywhere within half a mile of the forest. In some parts the monkeys are very numerous, and do an immense amount of damage.

" (11.) The Jhukna nulla enters the pergunnah from Perguunah Poorunpore on *The bhoor and sandy tracts near Jhukna and Goomtee.* the west, and flows southwards towards the Goomtee, into which it falls about the middle of the south-western end of the pergunnah, from the junction of the Jhukna and Goomtee to the Oudh border on the south-east ; the ridge above the valley of the Goomtee, averaging one and a quarter to one and a half mile in width, consists of uneven sandy soil, mostly the worst description of flying *bhoor* with sand hills. This light sandy soil continues up-stream on the left bank of the Jhukna nulla for an average width of one mile as far as the forest ; but though the soil is principally *bhoor*, it is fairly level, and does not run up into sand hills. The tract between the Jhukna nuddee and the Goomtee is all light sandy soil, not like ordinary *bhoor* in appearance, having more of an earthy and less of a sandy appearance, but gritty, and not a bit better than ordinary *bhoor* in productive qualities, and some quite as bad as the worst *bhoor*. This is called the Mujhra Illaka, and this and the ridge above the Jhukna *nulla* and river Goomtee are the portions already alluded to as unirrigated, and as a rule incapable of irrigation.

"(12.) The rest of the cultivated area of the pergunnah consists of two blocks, the

Other parts of the per-
gunnah good loam and
clay.

one east of the Jhukna and north of the Goomtee ridges, and south of the strip of forest which crosses the pergunnah from side to side; the other, the Chandpore *Illaka*, north of that belt and completely surrounded by forest. The soil in both of these is very similar, being usually a moderately light but good loam, with good clay in the depressions. Of these two blocks, however, the soil of the southern is rather better than that of the northern, but chiefly owing to its superior advantages of denser population and better cultivators, and the proximity of the greater portion of the northern block to the surrounding forest.

"(13.) *Kuchha* wells are, as a rule, constructible all over both these blocks, or, in

Kuchha wells, *dhenklees*,
and *pool* wells.

other words, throughout the pergunnah, with the exception of the *bhoor* ridges above the Goomtee and Jhukna, including the greater part of the Mujhra *Illaka*. The *dhenklee* or *dhooklee*, the ordinary lever well, is chiefly used, but in Chandpore and several of its neighbours in the northern block, and in some eight or ten villages in the middle of the southern block, *pool* wells (the ordinary large leathern bucket raised by four or six men) are constructible without cylinders, and are in general use. There are very few masonry wells for irrigation, but some of the *kuchha pool* wells have a wooden cylinder up to above water-level."

9. The description of my assessment circles is also taken from the same report :—

"(26.) For purposes of assessment, I have divided the pergunnah into two circles.

The two assessment
circles of Pergunnah
Khotar.

The 1st or best circle, which I have called the inhabited (*ábád*) circle, comprises the best villages about Khotar, and is in fact that piece described in foregoing paragraphs as the southern block, and Chandpore and some of its neighbours in the northern block, those now fully inhabited and cultivated, and well away from the forest and malarious tracts. The second circle is everything else: all the bad parts of the pergunnah, the thinly inhabited and unhealthy portions along the forest, the Mujhra *Illaka*, and the ridges above the Jhukna and Goomtee, which I have designated *jungle wairan*.

"The following statement shows the contrast between the two circles most forcibly as regards population, cultivation, and unreclaimed waste :—

Circle.	Number of mouzahs.		Total area in square miles.	Population by settlement returns.	Average population per square mile.	Assessable area in acres.			
	Inhabited.	Uninhabited.				Cultivated.	New fallow.	Baghs.	Culturable waste.
1st, *Abád*, ...	62	7	39½	28,510	750	18,549	590	1,245	1,170
2nd, *Jungle wairan*, ...	97	91	164½	20,777	126	45,528	5,649	545	47,120
Total, ...	159	98	203	49,287	244	64,077	6,239	1,790	48,290

" The average population of 750 to the square mile may give an erroneous impression, unless it is borne in mind that the villages contained in this first circle supply cultivators for the adjoining portions of the second circle, and that many of the villages in the first circle are unnaturally large, in consequence of the unhealthiness of the second circle; but still the fact remains that many of the villages in the second circle are dependent for cultivators on the residents of villages at a distance of from two to five miles off.

"Again, of the ninety-seven inhabited villages in the second circle, eleven are very small and insignificant, and some fifteen more are little else than small hamlets, the walls of the houses not even being built of earth, but only screens of dry grass and small branches. There are therefore only some seventy real reliably inhabited villages worthy of the name, instead of ninety-seven in the second circle.

"The superiority of the first over the second circle, both as regards irrigation and quality of soil, is shown by the next statement, in which are given the details of the cultivated area, divided first into irrigated and unirrigated, and second into soils irrespective of irrigation, but in the order of merit of the soils themselves. *Gowhanee* is an artificial soil, and there is but little of it in either circle. The good natural soils are, first class *domut* and *mutyar*; the inferior and poor soils are second class *domut*, *bhoor*, *dhunker*.

Circle.	DETAILS OF THE CULTIVATED AREA (IN ACRES), WITH PERCENTAGES.															
	Irrigated.		Unirrigated.		Gowhanee.		1st Domut.		Mutyar.		2nd Domut.		Bhoor.		Dhunker.	
	Acres.	Percentage.	Acres.	Percentage.	Acres.	Percentage.	Acres.	Percentage.	Acres.	Percentage.	Acres.	Percentage.	Acres.	Percentage.	Acres.	Percentage.
1st, *Abad*, ...	8,442	46	10,167	54	60	...	10,953	59	2,114	11½	4,355	23½	1,858	6	9	...
2nd, *Jungle wairan*,	6,706	14	36,820	86	127	...	11,140	24½	4,026	9	12,531	27½	17,229	38	484	1

"The cultivation in the second circle is of course much inferior to that in the first, and consequently the finer crops are grown to a less extent. It is unnecessary to recapitulate the reasons, as they are patent. The fact and extent will be seen at a glance from the statement in the following paragraph, which shows the percentages of the principal crops grown in each circle. But even this comparison of the crops does not in itself give a sufficiently strong idea of the very decided inferiority of the style of cultivation adopted in the second as compared with the first circle, chiefly because here also, as generally throughout the district, a poor crop of wheat seems to be preferred to a moderate or good crop of barley. Land being plentiful, and cultivators comparatively scarce, they take up more than they can cultivate carefully and properly. The land is not thoroughly ploughed, and receives nothing in the shape of manure, as the cultivators' homes are far off, but is given rest instead, after two or three years of continuous cropping, and hence there is always a large fallow area recovering its fertility."

10. Pergunnah Burragaon is famed for its sugarcane, which is grown very generally all over the pergunnah, and the percentage of sugarcane is larger than that of Shahjehanpore. It is probable, too, that the sugarcane area will increase, as, besides Burragaon being a great sugar manufacturing place itself, almost all of the Puthan proprietors are *khundsarees* or sugar manufacturers. The area of lands bearing two crops in the year is 1,623 acres, or 4¼ per cent. of the total cultivated area, and is principally a *rubbee* crop after rice. The wheat crops of the pergunnah are very good, and are better in lands that are of the inferior denominations and look poor, than in what are similar lands in appearance and denomination in any other pergunnahs of the district.

Produce of the soil.

The detailed crop statement, with the areas and percentages of each kind of crop, is given in the Appendix (A.), but a statement showing percentages only of the principal crops grown is given here to facilitate comparison in the various circles. Re-

Harvest	Crop	Pergunnah Burragaon.	PERGUNNAH POWAYN.						PERGUNNAH KHOTAR.		
			Golai.	Powayn.	Nabui.	Sunwat.	Tureona.	Whole Pergunnah.	1st Circle.	2nd Circle.	Whole Pergunnah.
AUTUMN (KHUREEF.)	Sugarcane, actual, ...	9½	7½	11	10¼	4¼	8¼	8¼	9	2⅞	4¼
	Land prepared for next year's cane, ...	8¾	7¼	10¼	9¼	3¼	6¼	7	6	1½	2¼
	Jowar, ...	8	5¼	6¼	3¼	...	3¼	6	⅛	1½	1½
	Bajra, ...	11½	20¼	8	10	32¼	15	18¼	7½	25½	20¼
	Cotton, ...	4¼	3¼	2¼	2¼	¼	¼	1¼	¼	¾	¼
	Rice, ...	4¾	3	7¼	8¾	6¼	15	9½	16¼	11	12¾
	Oord, i. e., Mash, ...	¾	¾	¼	¼	5	8¼	4	5¾	8¼	7¼
	Kodon, ...	¼	1	2¼	2¼	1	3¼	2	5	5¼	5¼
SPRING (RUBBEE.)	Wheat, ...	34¼	36	33¼	33¼	18	30¼	28¼	36¼	25¼	28¼
	Barley, ...	2¼	1¼	1¼	2¼	9¼	2	1½	2¼	2¼	
	Gram, ...	10¼	10¼	10¼	11¼	4¼	5¼	7¼	5¼	3¼	4¼
	Wheat and Barley mixed, ...	¾	¼	1	1¼	8¼	2	3¼	1¼	6¼	
	Double crop lands, ...	4¼	2¼	8¼	8	5	13¼	8¼	17¼	6	9¼

garding the crop statement of Pergunnah Powayn, Mr. Butt remarks,— "Cane and wheat are the great staples, and even in the poor tracts a remarkably large area is devoted to cane. Cotton is little cultivated, is commonly sown in inferior land, and receives little care or attention; maize is not grown, and very little *jowar* is found in the north of the pergunnah, where the high lands are too sandy, and the low lands too wet for this crop. The sugarcane, *jowar*, and *bajra* percentages in the autumn harvest furnish a good test of relative fertility, and the area under barley and *goojai* in the Sunwat circle deserves notice, as in all other tuhseels the percentage under wheat has been found very nearly the same in all tracts, and did not vary with the quality of the soil. The Tureona depressions account for the large area under rice in that circle, and also for the large (*dofuslee*) double crop area, most of which is rice or *kodon*, followed by mixed crops of gram, *masoor*, *ulsee*, peas, and *bijra*."

The large double crop area in Pergunnah Khotar is owing to the large amount of rice grown there, with a rubbee crop, chiefly gram or linseed (*ulsee*), to follow.

11. The climate of Pergunnah Burragaon and of the greater part of Pergunnah

Climate.

Powayn is good—much the same as that of the district generally; but it is not so good in the Sunwat and Tureona circles. And in the northernmost part of the Tureona circle, about Gooluria, it is of a Terai character and unhealthy, similar to the climate of Pergunnah Khotar.

The climate of Pergunnah Khotar is of course very much affected by the forest within the pergunnah, being, as it is, a continuation of the Terai forests, and it partakes very largely of the unhealthiness and insalubrity of the regular Terai climate. The most unhealthy parts are those along the edge of the forest up to about a mile from it, and in the Mujhra *Illaka*, between the Goomtee and the Jhukna. Fevers are very prevalent here, and there are two regular fever seasons, the one in April and May, and the other just as the rains are over, in September and October. During these seasons three-fourths of the population are fever-stricken, and the cultivators gather their spring and autumn harvest alternately burning with fever and shivering with ague. There is little wonder then that these parts are thinly inhabited. The people assert that the Jhukna nulla is so deadly that no one can live within a mile of it; and that although several attempts have been made to locate villages within that distance, the residents have most of them died, and the villages become deserted; and to all appearances this is quite true. The water in some of these unhealthy parts is said to be very injurious,—I mean the well water; and this is very probably the case, as in the rains the water level is so high near the forest that a vessel can be filled from the well with the hand without the necessity of a rope. In the oldest reclaimed and thoroughly cleared parts of the pergunnah there is not so much fever, but acclimatization is necessary even there.

12.   Powayn is hardly worthy of the name of a *kusbah* or country town, and would not be one but for the *moonsiffee* and tuhseel and police offices being here, and in the absence of any other country town anywhere within the limits of the tuhseel.   The population, as shown in the margin, is

The town of Powayn.

Agriculturists.			Non-agriculturists.			
Hindoo.	Mahomedan.	Total.	Hindoo.	Mahomedan.	Total.	Grand Total.
1,050	230	1,280	3,435	1,220	4,655	5,935

nearly 6,000, and the proportion of the Mahomedan to the Hindoo population is smaller here than in any of the towns in the district.   One great reason of Powayn not having grown into a larger and more flourishing country town is, I believe, because it is the residence of the Rajah of Powayn, who has all along exercised very considerable *zemindaree* functions in it, and has treated it as a mere village, and the land occupied by houses as his especial private property, and not as a *kusbah*, and has been in the habit of taking very heavy and, I consider, illegal dues from any resident who builds a house, or enlarges or alters it, or sells it. All this has doubtless tended to keep the place from spreading and growing, as no one can do anything in the way of making bricks, building a new house, or altering an old one, without the Rajah's permission, or sell or buy a house or premises without paying the Rajah one-fourth of the price.   I have refused to enter any detailed mention of this in the settlement records, as none of these dues and demands have been taken into account in assessment, and because I consider that they should not be acknowledged, and have the authority of entry in the settlement records accorded to them.

There are no good rows of conveniently situated and well-built shops, nor is there anything worthy of the name of a *bazaar*, but markets are held here twice a week, just like those in ordinary villages.

13.   Neither Burragaon nor Khotar have any pretensions to being more than large villages; Khotar Khas is made up of the inhabited sites of Khotar, Kurruckpore, and Narainpore, which all adjoin one another. Khotar, now that the *Peshkaree* has been removed from there, is a place of no importance, and no trade of any kind is carried on there.   Burragaon, though in size nothing more than a large village, is, however, of considerable note and importance from the fact that the prices for all agricultural produce, and especially the *rab* rates, which are struck there hold good, not only for the immediate neighbourhood, but also for a great part of this district, and the adjoining pergunnahs of Bareilly on the one side, and of Kheree and Hurdui on the other.   A description of the Burragaon *khutountee* will be found under the head of sugarcane in the general report.   The Mahomedan population in both Burragaon and Khotar is very small, and the non-agricultural population, with the exception of a few leading

Population of Burragaon and Khotar and of seven of the largest villages in the tuhseel.

Name.	Hindoos.		Mahomedans.		Grand Total.
	Agriculturists.	Non-agriculturists.	Agriculturists.	Non-agriculturists.	
Khotar Khas (including Kurruckpore and Narainpore,....	1,518	1,587	155	226	3,486
Burragaon, ...	797	998	145	389	2,329
Nahul, ...	1,721	1,557	56	245	3,579
Jewan, ...	1,246	1,004	56	144	2,450
Punduria, ...	2,268	439	17	39	2,763
Dulelpore, ...	2,164	455	32	...	2,651
Tanda, ...					
Moondia, ...	1,034	775	21	62	1,892
Koomiran, ...					
Banda, ...	1,125	245	230	86	1,686
Gooluria, ...	1,219	325	76	56	1,676

bunniahs and mahajuns, is made up chiefly of petty dealers and day-labourers.   The names and populations of the other large villages of over 1,600 inhabitants are given in the margin.   All of these are in Pergunnah Powayn, and although there are many fine large flourishing and populous villages in both Burragaon and Khotar, yet they run mostly from

1,000 to 1,500, and not one of them comes up to 1,600 inhabitants. If, however, the marginal statement was enlarged to include them, a still larger number would have to be added from Powayn.

14. Inclusive of Powayn Khas, there are 38 villages in the Powayn Pergunnah where markets are held, and twice a week at all of them. In the Gola circle there are only two, and in the Sunwat circle there is only one; but the former circle is small, and near market villages in the Nahul circle, and in Pergunnahs Burragaon and Negohee; and the latter (Sunwat), though not a small circle, has no single village in it which is as much as five miles distant from one or more of the market villages of the Tureona, Nahul, or Powayn circles. Burragaon pergunnah is well provided with markets, and is also situated between Shahjehanpore and Powayn. The inhabited parts of Khotar are also well off for markets, close and handy: for several of the villages in the first circle,

Market villages and market days.

Pergunnah.	Circle.	Name of village.	Number of market days.	Days of the week.
POWAYN.	Powayn.	Bungawan, ...	2	Sunday and Thursday.
		Bilsundee Khoord,	2	Monday and Thursday.
		Powayn Khas, ...	2	Sunday and Wednesday.
		Jewan, ...	2	Tuesday and Friday.
		Moondia Koormeesn,	2	Saturday and Wednesday.
	Tureona.	Indulpore, ...	2	Saturday and Tuesday.
		Biraheempore, ...	2	Sunday and Wednesday.
		Bunda, ...	2	Monday and Thursday.
		Pundaria Dulelpore,	2	Tuesday and Saturday.
		Deokullee, ...	2	Wednesday and Saturday.
		Guluria, ...	2	Sunday and Thursday.
		Mohee-ood-deenpoor,	2	Monday and Friday.
	Sunwat,	Dhurmspoor, ...	2	Ditto ditto.
	Gola,	Bilundpoor, ...	2	Ditto ditto.
		Chena Rora,	2	Thursday and Sunday.
	Nahul,	Bhugwuntpoor, ...	2	Wednesday and Sunday.
		Ruroos, ...	2	Ditto ditto.
		Nahul, ...	2	Tuesday and Friday.
		Nuguria Boozoorg,	2	Saturday and Thursday.
		Total, 19 Villages,	38	
BURRAGAON.	Burragaon.	Budreepoor Hudeera,	2	Saturday and Wednesday.
		Burragaon, ...	2	Monday and Thursday.
		Bhunderee, ...	2	Saturday and Wednesday.
		Kuttya, ...	2	Saturday and Friday.
		Ghoor Khera, ...	2	Ditto and Tuesday.
		Muhao Doorga,...	2	Monday and Friday.
		Total, 6 Villages,	12	
KHOTAR.	1st or abdd.	Bela, ...	2	Sunday and Wednesday.
		Pipuria Bhugwunt,	2	Thursday and Monday.
		Rontapoor, ...	2	Saturday and Tuesday.
		Morarpoor, ...	2	Ditto ditto.
		Nurainpoor Bikrumpoor,	2	Wednesday and Sunday.
		Humeerpoor, ...	2	Monday and Thursday.
	2nd	Sultanpoor, ...	2	Wednesday and Friday.
		Moradpoor, ...	2	Tuesday and Saturday.
		Total, 8 Villages,	16	
		Total of Tuhseel 33 Villages,	66	

as Bela for instance, are within easy reach of the inhabited villages of the second circle.

15. There are no census returns of the population of this tuhseel at last settle-
Inhabited and uninhabited mouzahs and hamlets. ment, so that comparison of actual numbers is impossible, but from the accompanying statement. :—

Pergunnah.	Description.	At last settlement.			During currency of settlement from 1838 to 1871 A.D.		Total at present settlement.		
		Inhabited.	Uninhabited.	Total.	Newly inhabited.	Become deserted.	Inhabited.	Uninhabited.	Total.
Powayn, {	Mouzahs, ...	362	95	427	11	1	372	55	427
	Hamlets, ...	9	44	53	11	...	20	47	67
	Total, ...	371	109	480	22	1	392	102	494
Burragaon, {	Mouzahs, ...	108	18	126	9	...	117	9	126
	Hamlets, ...	6	6	12	10	...	16	1	17
	Total, ...	114	24	138	19	...	133	10	143
Khotar, {	Mouzahs, ...	92	165	257	70	3	159	98	257
	Hamlets, ...	6	18	24	9	3	12	17	29
	Total, ...	98	183	281	79	6	171	115	286
Whole tuhseel, {	Mouzahs, ...	562	248	810	90	4	648	162	810
	Hamlets, ...	21	68	89	30	3	48	65	113
	Total, ...	583	316	899	120	7	696	227	923

showing the inhabited and uninhabited mouzahs and hamlets at the last and present settlement, a very considerable increase in population is evident, and a spreading out thereof into a larger number of separate villages and hamlets. In Pergunnahs Burragaon and Powayn the increase in the number of newly inhabited villages is not large, as those pergunnahs were generally thickly populated, and almost fully cultivated at last settlement, with certain exceptions. The great increase is in Khotar, where I estimate that the population is now more than treble what it was at Mr. J. W. Muir's settlement. There were 265 mouzahs then, but the number has been reduced by eight at the present settlement, by measuring in one the several contiguous uninhabited areas belonging to the same proprietor. As this, however, would have caused confusion, and have been an apparent error in the table, I have there shown the total 257 for last settlement the same as now. Similarly in Pergunnah Powayn there were 440 mouzahs, but 13 chiefly small and uninhabited areas were doubled up and measured with others at the request of the proprietors, principally the Rajah, and the present total 427 has been shown as the former and present number in the tabular statement. Of the 70 villages newly inhabited in Pergunnah Khotar during the currency of the settlement, some 12 or 15 are very small and insignificant, but the rest are *bonâ fide* villages which have remained inhabited for 25 years and more, and have been steadily increasing. Again, of the villages inhabited at last settlement, most of them have increased in size more or less, and in 42 of them the improvement and increase of population has been very considerable. Many have doubled and trebled the number of their then residents, and some which then had populations of only 50 and 60 inhabitants, have now grown into flourishing villages with from 500 to 1,000 inhabitants.

In the entire tuhseel there are now 696 inhabited villages and hamlets against 583 at the time of the last settlement in 1838-39.

16. The average mouzah area for the entire tuhseel, though somewhat raised by
Average areas of mouzahs and average population. Pergunnah Khotar, is considerably smaller than that of both Tuhseels Shahjehanpore and Jellalabad, but much about the same as that of Pergunnahs Negohee, Khera Bujhera, and Jelalpore.

Khotar contains some very large mouzah areas, but also many very small ones, which more than counterbalance the large ones in the average :—

Pergunnah.					Number of mouzahs.	Average area in acres.	Average area in square miles.	Average rural population.	
								Per mouzah.	Per square mile.
Powayn,	...	...	...	...	...	427	466	·73	357	489
Burragaon,	...	...	...	...	...	126	421	·65	358	544
Khotar,	...	...	...	...	...	257	505	·78	192	244
Whole Tuhseel,	...	...	...	...	810	472	·73	293	397

The average rural population per mouzah and square mile for Pergunnahs Powayn and Burragaon is well up to the average of other pergunnahs of the district, and Pergunnah Burragaon indeed is considerably above the average, the rural population per square mile in it being denser than in any of the three pergunnahs of the Shahjehanpore Tuhseel, and also of Pergunnah Jellalabad, but surpassed by several of the pergunnahs of the Tilhur Tuhseel.

Khotar, as is abundantly evident from various parts of this report, is only partially reclaimed and inhabited, there being no less than 98 uninhabited mouzahs and some 45 square miles of forest, besides other culturable waste, and hence the average population per square mile in it is far lower than that of any other pergunnah, in the district. The above details are all given from my settlement returns, and for comparison with them, the averages per mouzah and square mile for each pergunnah, according to the general census of 1872, are now given in the margin. The total population in each pergunnah is somewhat larger by the census of 1872 than by my settlement returns prepared in 1870-71.

Pergunnah.	Average rural population by census of 1872.	
	Per mouzah.	Per square mile.
Powayn,...	365	500
Burragaon,	393	596
Khotar, ...	205	260

17. In the following form are shown for each pergunnah and each circle the average per square mile of cultivation, (1) of cultivators and their families, and (2) of adult cultivators only.

Cultivators—their creed, caste, and proportion to cultivated area.

Pergunnah	Circle	Hindoo Cultivators					Mahomedan Cultivators					Total cultivators.	Average per square mile of cultivation.	
		Adults.		Minors.			Adults.		Minors.				Of cultivators and their families.	Of adult cultivators.
		Male.	Female.	Male.	Female.	Total.	Male.	Female.	Male.	Female.	Total.			
Powayn,	Nahul, ...	7,438	6,600	4,330	3,083	21,451	264	228	176	149	817	22,268	571	373
	Gola, ...	4,360	3,624	2,317	1,713	12,014	166	158	75	56	455	12,469	498	332
	Sunwat, ...	6,442	5,714	3,893	2,653	18,702	472	338	383	176	1,369	19,971	338	219
	Tureona, ...	12,758	11,164	6,917	5,352	36,191	422	370	265	172	1,219	37,410	519	343
	Powayn, ...	8,752	7,567	4,502	3,398	24,219	408	279	171	244	1,102	25,331	723	466
	Whole pergunnah,	39,750	34,669	21,959	16,199	112,577	1,725	1,373	960	797	4,852	117,439	511	337
Burragaon,	...	10,810	9,220	5,544	4,302	29,876	1,150	1,061	661	558	3,430	33,306	584	390
Khotar,	1st Circle, *abad* ...	6,464	5,647	3,606	2,821	18,538	398	345	238	190	1,171	19,709	680	444
	2nd Circle, *jungle wairun*,	5,341	4,236	3,133	2,392	15,102	764	534	461	441	2,200	17,302	243	153
	Whole pergunnah,	11,805	9,883	6,739	5,213	33,640	1,162	879	699	631	3,371	37,011	870	537
	Whole tuhseelee, ...	62,365	53,772	34,242	25,714	176,093	4,044	3,313	2,320	1,986	11,663	187,756	485	319

The totals as given in Vol. II., Census, North-Western Provinces, 1872, are quoted in the margin. The numbers agree very closely indeed with my returns in Pergunnahs Burragaon and Khotar. In Pergunnah Powayn, however, there is a difference of over 7,000 between the census return of 1872 and my settlement census of 1870-71 ; and I believe the mistake is in the 1872 census—that many of those enter-

Pergunnah.	Hindoo.	Mahomedan.	Total Agriculturists.
Powayn,	104,620	4,427	109,047
Burragaon,	29,993	3,276	33,269
Khotar,	34,295	3,530	37,825

ed as non-agriculturists are in reality agriculturists, and have been included as such in the settlement returns ; e. g., my returns show over 2,000 Kulwar and Bukkal cultivators and nearly 2,300 carpenters. There are no details yet published of 1872 census, only totals ; but it is probable that most of these men have in the census appeared as non-agriculturists, from being of non-agricultural castes. The foregoing statement shows most clearly the inferiority of the Sunwat circle, in the matter of resident cultivators, to the other circles of Pergunnah Powayn, as also of the 2nd (*jungle wairan*) circle of Khotar to the 1st (*abdi*) circle. This matter of the cultivators congregating in the 1st circle, and going long distances to cultivate in the 2nd, has been already dwelt upon in paragraph 9.

The best cultivators in these pergunnahs are—(1) Koormees, (2) Muraos or Kachees, (3) Kisans and Chumars ; all amongst the first flight in the order given, and there are but few really bad cultivators, the carpenters perhaps being the worst, as they almost all of them ply their own trade in addition to cultivation, and hence grow little or no cane, and pay less attention to the cultivation of their fields than those who ply no other trade. They are most numerous in Khotar, and specially in the villages in the northern half of the pergunnah near the forest. The following table, showing the percentage of the various cultivators in each pergunnah, arranged in approximate order of merit as cultivators, will show that all three pergunnahs are well favoured in the matter of cultivators : —

Pergunnah.	*Caste of cultivators and percentage of each caste.*											
	Koormee.	Murao or Kachee.	Kisan.	Chumar.	Brahmin.	Puthans, i. e., Rohillas.	Other Mahomedans.	Aheers.	Kulwars and Bukkais.	Rajpoots or Thakoors.	Miscollaneous, chiefly Khateeks, Aruks, and Pasees.	Carpenters.
Powayn, ...	10·8	9·9	14·9	15·2	13·8	1·3	8·1	9·6	2·8	6·0	4·1	3·0
Burragaon, ...	3·9	8·5	7·2	22·7	9·9	4·5	8·4	13·9	3·7	8·7	6·2	1·8
Khotar, ...	15·0	7·8	7·5	12·2	13·3	1·3	10·3	9·5	2·0	6.7	6·7	7·1

The Aheers vary the most. In Burragaon they are cultivators certainly quite up to the average, excepting only the first four castes, as they cannot keep herds there, and must devote themselves entirely to cultivation ; whereas in Khotar, where there much grazing land, they are amongst the worst cultivators.

The Thakoors, from being to a great extent intermixed with some of the best classes of cultivators, are under those circumstances fairly good cultivators ; but where they are in numbers, and not intermixed, they are lazy and bad cultivators. Pergunnahs

Powayn and Khotar being part of the old Kutheria country, one would have expected to find the Kutheria clan of Rajpoots mustering very strong; but such is not the case, for the Rajpoots do not muster very strong, and there are numbers of various clans besides Kutherias, but all scattered about here and there, and not in clusters. Again, the Gours having wrested the Pergunnah Powayn from the Kutherias, one might have naturally supposed there would have been many Gours, but the members of this clan do not number 500, including women and children.

The Rajah of Powayn is a Gour, and a good big one, but his clan is chiefly conspicuous by its absence. In Burragaon amongst the miscellaneous are included Lodhas or Beldars, and to a considerable extent, and they too are good cultivators. The foregoing table of the percentages of the various classes of cultivators hardly bears out Mr. Rose's remarks on the cultivators of the pergunnah, when, in writing the report of Mr. J. W. Muir's settlement, he said:—"The cultivators are mostly Koormees, Kisans, and Lodhas, all noted for their industry and skill." Probably it was just as incorrect then as it is now.

18. The *zemindaree* tenure obtains very generally, and the number of *putteeda-ree muhals* is very small, and there is not one real *bhyachara* village in any one of the three pergunnahs. The reason of this great preponderance of the *zemindaree* tenure is, that in Burragaon the chief proprietors

Proprietary tenures.

Pergunnah.	Zemindaree muhals.	Putteedaree and Bhycharra muhals.	Total.
Powayn, ...	485	44	529
Burragaon,	143	17	160
Khotar, ...	241	35	276
Total,	869	96	965

are Puthans residing in the city and a Kayuth family in Burragaon, an old *Canoongoe* family. In Powayn the Rajah alone is the zemindar of 128 *muhals*, and of those which were taken from him at last settlement and settled with *mokuddums* and *malikana* given to the Rajah, not one was settled with a body of resident *quasi*-peasant proprietors, but chiefly with one or two individuals; and most of those have been sold out and their place has been taken by city Puthans, Mahajuns, Bunniahs, Kulwars, &c. In Khotar again there are no proprietors, except the Rajah of Khotar's sons, of older date than Mr. J. W. Muir's settlement. The whole pergunnah was portioned out by Mr. J. W. Muir to various members (individuals chiefly, families exceptionally) of the Kutheria brotherhood, all clansmen and Scotch cousins of the Rajah of Khotar when not nearer relatives, with the exception of the *khana khalee* villages, which were given by him in farm to any one who would take them, excepting only the Rajah himself and his sons. Special mention of this will be found in the next paragraph but one. The number of *puttees*

Pergunnah.	Putteedaree muhals.	Number of puttees in those muhals.
Powayn, ...	44	203
Burragaon,	17	61
Khotar, ...	35	116
Total,	96	380

also in the *putteedaree muhals* is not large, averaging only four to each *muhal*, and in most instances the subordinate tenure of the *puttee* is *zemindaree* and owned by only one individual or family. In Burragaon there is no revenue-free village, and there is only one in Pergunnah Powayn, and that one (Sunasar) pays no cesses,[*] as the jumma would be less than Rs. 100. The number of the talookdaree *mouzahs* in Powayn is 105, and of *muhals*, including the *mouzahs*, 148, in which the Rajah of Powayn receives *malikana* from the sub-proprietors with whom the settlement is made.

*Board's Circular No. 3, dated 18th May, 1872. This *malikana* is collected with the revenue, and paid to the Rajah from the *tuhseelee* treasury. It is now 10 per cent. on the revenue (*vide* para. 20). In Pergunnah Khotar there are four revenue-free *mouzahs*, three of which pay cesses on an assumed or nominal *jumma*, but the 4th, Sookchainpoor, is exempt under Circular 3 quoted above.

All these *maafee* and *talookdaree mouzahs* and muhals have been included in the preceding tabular statements of this paragraph according to their respective tenures.

19. The following table shows the number of entire *mouzahs* and *muhals* held by members of the various castes in each pergunnah of the tuhseel resident within the tuhseel itself:—

Residence, creed, and caste of proprietors.

Caste and creed.	Powayn.			Burragaon.			Khotar.			Whole Tuhseel.		
	Entire Mouzahs.	Entire Muhals, parts of Mouzahs.	Shares in other Mouzahs or Muhals.	Entire Mouzahs.	Entire Muhals.	Shares in other Mouzahs or Muhals.	Entire Mouzahs.	Entire Muhals.	Shares in other Mouzahs or Muhals.	Entire Mouzahs.	Entire Muhals.	Shares in other Mouzahs or Muhals.
Thakoor,	187	25	21	7	0	2	146	14	21	340	39	44
Brahmin,	33	17	23	4	2	2	16	0	1	52	19	26
Koormee,	30	16	14	1	0	1	12	0	3	43	18	20
Kaiyuth,	4	1	5	22	2	1	1	0	1	27	3	7
Kulwar,	11	2	7	1	1	2	3	0	2	15	3	11
Bukkal,	8	1	4	1	0	1	2	0	1	11	1	6
Aheer,	7	4	5	2	0	0	0	0	0	9	4	5
Kisan,	4	1	0	0	0	0	0	0	0	4	1	0
Miscellaneous Hindoos,	3	1	2	0	0	0	2	0	0	5	1	2
Puthan,	0	6	2	1	3	2	0	1	2	1	4	6
Other Mussulmans,	2	0	1	2	0	1	7	1	0	11	1	2
Total,	288	69	86	41	8	12	189	16	31	518	93	129

There are 129 *mouzahs* and *muhals* in which various castes have shares, and in the above statement the same *mouzah* or *muhal* is not repeated, but is credited to that caste which predominates in it, or owns the greatest part of it; *e. g.*, the Thakoors are the chief proprietors in the 44 villages against their name, but other castes have also small shares, and in like manner Thakoors have shares in many of the remaining 85 *mouzahs* and *muhals*. These remarks apply equally to the table of non-resident proprietors.

The next table gives the non-resident proprietors, those living in the city of Shahjehanpore, or elsewhere beyond the limits of the tuhseel, but by far the greater number, Thakoors excepted, in the city itself. Pergunnah Burragaon is no distance from the city, and the city Puthans are not strictly non-resident or absentee landlords as regards that pergunnah.

Caste and creed.	Powayn.			Burragaon.			Khotar.			Whole Tuhseel.		
	Entire Mouzahs.	Entire Muhals.	Shares in other Mouzahs or Muhals.	Entire Mouzahs.	Entire Muhals.	Shares in other Mouzahs or Muhals.	Entire Mouzahs.	Entire Muhals.	Shares in other Mouzahs or Muhals.	Entire Mouzahs.	Entire Muhals.	Shares in other Mouzahs or Muhals.
Thakoor,	9	1	0	4	2	0	12	0	1	25	3	1
Brahmin,	11	5	1	2	1	5	6	1	3	19	7	9
Kaiyuth,	5	0	1	3	2	0	5	0	1	13	2	2
Kulwar,	5	0	0	5	1	0	0	1	0	10	2	0
Bukkal,	9	2	1	0	0	6	1	0	0	10	2	1
Khutbree,	1	0	0	2	2	0	0	0	1	3	2	1
Other Hindoos,	2	2	0	0	0	0	1	0	0	3	3	0
Puthans,	17	6	6	45	14	5	6	0	0	68	20	11
Other Mussulmans,	0	0	0	6	0	0	0	0	0	6	0	0
European,	0	0	1	0	0	0	0	0	0	1	0	1
Total,	59	17	10	67	22	10	32	2	6	158	41	26

From the foregoing statements it will be seen that out of the 965 *muhals* in the entire tuhseel, all but (158+41) 199 and portions of 26 others are owned by proprietors resident within the tuhseel. Of the *muhals* belonging to non-resident proprietors, nearly half are owned by city Puthans, and most of them are in Pergunnah Burragaon, and as regards these, as shown above, the city Puthans are not really absentee proprietors. The Rajah of Powayn alone is sole proprietor of 128 entire *muhals* and *mouzahs* in Pergunnah Powayn, besides 5 in Pergunnah Khotar, but he has not one single village in Pergunnah Burragaon. Of the other Thakoor proprietors, by far the greater number are Kutherias, but other clans, chiefly Chowhan, Kasib, and Junghara, are represented, many of whom, however, especially in Khotar, have inherited property by marriage into the Kutheria clan. The principal non-resident Thakoor proprietors are the Chundélas of Goongchai and the Kutheras of Jutpoorah in Pergunnah Poorunpore.

20. It is necessary here to interrupt the continuity of the report upon things

Former history of Powayn and Khotar, with special reference to arrangements made at the last settlement by Mr. J. W. Muir.

as they now exist, and to bring in an account of the previous history of Pergunnahs Powayn and Khotar, as it bears upon the present distribution of property in them, and also in order to explain various phrases and references in different parts of this report, which would be otherwise incomprehensible. The extracts on this subject regarding Pergunnah Powayn are taken from Mr. Butt's rent-rate report :—

" 16. The purely fiscal history of the pergunnah can hardly be rendered intelli-

Acquisition of Gola by the Kutherias.

gible without a brief sketch of the recent history and the origin of the Gour *Talooka*, and for present purposes the history of the pergunnah may commence with the Kutheria Thakoors, from whom the province derived its old name of Kather. The names of the first Kutheria settlers were Rajah Khurruk Sing, the elder brother who settled in the western part of the province, and Rao Hurree Sing, the younger brother from whom all the Kutherias of this district and also of the eastern part of Bareilly claim descent. Rao Hurree Sing appears to have established himself in Gola on the river Khunout in the latter half of the 16th century; his successors obtained possession of all the old pergunnah of Gola, and a *firmán* of the Emperor Shahjehan, dated 1055 H., conferred on Rao Bikram Sing the *zemindaree* of the whole pergunnah. Rao Bikram Sing moved from Gola to Nahul, where the head of the family has since resided, and the royal *firmán* is in the possession of his descendant, Rao Jeet Sing of Nahul.

" 17. The Kutherias continued to hold the pergunnah of Gola for 70 or 80 years

The Kutherias succeeded by the Gours.

from the date of the *firmán.* They then came into collision with the Puthans, who were pushing on from the recently founded city of Shahjehanpore. The Kutherias had been weakened, several cadet families having separated and received portions of the pergunnah, and there was now no powerful government in the country. The contest with the Puthans was an unequal one. The modern pergunnahs of Burragaon and Negohee, the latter included in Gola as tuppeh Negohee, came into possession of the Puthans, and in one of the engagements Rao Gopal Sing fell in fight, leaving a widow and two infant sons. The Ranee was of a Gour family, and she fled with her children to her own relations and prayed for their assistance. Bhoput Sing and Himmut Sing, Gour Thakoors of Chundra Mahole in Oudh, were leaders of a force which re-established the Kutherias in Nahul, and some of the Ranee's relations remained and managed on behalf of the infant Kutherias. Further disputes with the Puthans arose, and the Gours were again called on for aid, and were again successful, but Oodhee Singh, son of Bhoput Sinh, and leader of the second expedition, settled in the Kutheria territory and founded the town of Powayn.

" The Kutherias having no acknowledged leader, were soon almost completely supplanted by the Gours of Powayn, who are also said to have succeeded in gaining the favor of Hafiz Rahmut Khan, and from about the middle of the last century the Gour Rajahs held possession of the country included in the present pergunnah of Powayn. The first offshoot from the Nahul family had crossed the Goomtee and settled in Khotar, and the Gours never obtained any territory across the Goomtee.

" 18. Oodhee Singh was succeeded by Juswunt Singh, Bhugwunt Singh, and Rug-

Rajah Ruggoonath Singh recognized at cession.

goonath Singh, and at cession Rajah Ruggoonath Singh was in possession of the present pergunnah of Powyan, with perhaps the exception of a few villages still held by the Kutheria Thakoors of Nahul and Jewan. Immediately after cession, Rajah Ruggoonath Singh was, in a *perwanah* dated 18th August, 1802, recognized as zemindar by Mr. Wellesley, the Deputy Governor, and his right was recognized at the 1st and 2nd settlements.

"19.   At the 3rd settlement the assessment was an extremely severe one, the Rajah refused to engage, and, on account of his refusal, settlement was made with farmers, and the Rajah was excluded from the management of the whole pergunnah from 1218 to 1225 Fuslee, but received a *nankar* allowance.   On the expiry of this term the Rajah's right of re-entry was declared positive and indefeasible, and he was admitted to engage for such villages as he agreed to take at the jummas then paid by the farmers.   The Rajah selected 284 villages, for which he was re-admitted to engagements from 1225 F., but he still declined to engage for 253 villages, which therefore remained in the hands of the farmers,—usually the village *mokuddums*.   The villages for which the Rajah then declined to engage—as the rule the least productive and most severely assessed villages—have ever since remained in the hands of the farmers or their successors, and in these villages the present Rajah has no rights either as zemindar or talookdar.   There does not appear to have been any formal or regular investigation of the proprietary right in these villages, and it would appear that the Rajah's continued refusal to accept the *jummas* fixed in 1217 F. S. was accepted as a tacit relinquishment of any proprietary rights.   The Board in 1835 incidentally mention that the Rajah had occasionally made efforts to regain possession; but the nature of the efforts is not stated, and Mr. J. W. Muir, writing in 1839, stated that the Ranee's right of property in these villages was not acknowledged.

Settlement with farmers, and subsequent re-admission of the Rajah to engage for selected villages.

" Rajah Ruggoonath Singh remained in possession of the villages for which he accepted engagements up to his death in 1825, when he was succeeded by his widow.

"20.   The settlement operations under Regulation VII. of 1822 were concluded by Mr. H. Swetenham, the Collector, and he (report of 31st May, 1831) considered the Ranee to have a good title to all the villages.   A claim by the Rao of Nahul, based on the royal *firmán*, was dismissed as barred by limitation.   Some claims were put forward by the village *mokuddums*, but Mr. Swetenham, though considering many the lineal descendants of the original village *zemindars* dispossessed by the Kutherias, held that, about 85 years having elapsed since the acquisition of the villages by the Gour Rajahs, an honest and just title had been established, no matter how fraudulent or unjust the original acquisition might have been.   This report, with subsequent reports by Mr. Swetenham and the Commissioner, was four years later submitted by the Board of Revenue with their report No. 491 of the 13th October, 1835, and the Board considered that ' the local authorities, by whom the question of proprietary title had to be investigated, were persons who had not apparently applied their minds previously to the contemplation of the relative position in which individuals possessing an interest in land can stand to each other under the present system of revenue administration, and the point therefore to which their most particular attention should have been directed on this occasion was not treated in a way calculated to give satisfaction.'

Mr. Swetenham's settlement under Regulation VII.

" The Board held that the precise character of these *mokuddummee* tenures had never yet been fully investigated, and that the position of the Powayn *mokuddums* was not clear from the enquiries made, but that, on the general revision of the settlement, the question could be enquired into and finally disposed of.

" The villages then remained as they had been left in 1817,—those settled with *mokuldums*, on account of the Rajah's refusal, remaining with them, and those selected by the Rajah in the *malgoozaree* possession of the Ranee.

"21.   The settlement under Regulation IX. of 1833 was made by Mr. J. W. Muir, and he, in letters of the 11th December, 1838, and 24th January, 1839, reported on the state of the pergunnah and applied for instructions.   Mr. Muir's views are clearly stated in the following paragraphs extracted from his report No. 147 of the 11th December, 1838 :—

Mr. Muir's settlement under Regulation IX. with village zemindars.

'The Regulation VII. settlement was founded on a wrong system altogether. It was made with the talookdars, whereas it ought to have been concluded, had the principles of settlement now recognized been adopted, with the *mokuddums* or village proprietors.

'3. The Powayn tenures are most simple. The Ranee, although recorded as zemindar of the 250 mouzahs included in her talooka, can only be considered in the light of talookdar or superior, while in every village there exist village proprietors or *mokuddums*. These *mokuddums*, according to the analogy of all similar cases that I have met with, are fully entitled to engage directly with Government, while a sufficient provision in the shape of *malikana* is made for the talookdar.

'4. Besides the Ranee's talooka, there are 180 other mouzahs of Pergunnah Powayn settled with the *mokuddums* and village zemindars, and in which the Ranee's right of property is not acknowledged. Now these 180 mouzahs, with the exception of some in the possession of certain Kutheria zemindars, were originally similarly circumstanced with the villages now forming the Ranee's talooka. The Rajah was formerly talookdar of the whole pergunnah, exclusive of the Kutheria villages, and the selection of the mouzahs now forming his widow's talooka was owing entirely to accident. At the 4th settlement the whole pergunnah was settled with the *mokuddums* and villages proprietors, which arrangement continued in effect till 1224 Fuslee. At the 5th settlement, however, Rajah Ruggoonath Singh was allowed to engage for the villages comprised in the talooka which he picked out in consequence of their superior capabilities, and not in consequence of any difference in the *tenures*. Hence the Rajah became *malgoozar* of all the finest sugar and Koormee villages in the pergunnah, while the poor unproductive *mouzahs* were allowed to remain, and are still, in the hands of these *mokuddums*.

'5. It follows that the difference in the circumstances of the villages now engaged for by the *mokuddums*, and those composing the Ranee's talooka, is not owing to any intrinsic distinction in the *mokuddummee* tenures of the two sets of *mouzahs*, which originally were precisely of the same nature. It appears to me therefore that it would be manifest injustice to allow the *mokuddums* of the Ranee's talooka to continue deprived of their rights for a further period of 20 years, while their more fortunate brethren in the same pergunnah, but out of the pale of the Ranee's talooka, are blessed with a *mokuddummee* settlement. It does not follow that because a mistake was made with regard to the tenures under the settlement by Regulation VII. of 1822, that that mistake should be perpetuated, which would be equivalent to the total extinction of the *mokuddummee* rights. I am therefore of opinion that when the Regulation VII. leases expire, the future settlement of the talooka should be made with the *mokuddums*.'

" Mr. Muir's proposals were approved of and detailed enquiries were entered on.

22. " Mr. Muir did not live to superintend the enquiry which was concluded by Mr. MacCutchan, Deputy Collector, under the control of Mr. Rose, Mr. Muir's successor.

Result of the investigation of subordinate proprietary rights.

" The result was that out of the 247 villages till then held by the Ranee, in 126 no subordinate rights were established, while in 121 the rights of inferior proprietors were held to be established, village settlements were made with them, and a *talookdaree* allowance fixed. This allowance, or *malikana* as it has been always termed, has been collected with the revenue and paid from the treasury to the *talookdar*.

" The total jumma of these villages amounted to Rs. 59,049, the *talookdaree* allowance to Rs. 15,475, or a little over 26 per cent. on the revenue, the allowance having been generally fixed at 26 per cent. on the revenue, or the nearest sum in even figures.

" 23. The villages for which Rajah Ruggoonath Singh in 1817 refused to engage were by Mr. Muir settled with the farmer *mokuddums* as zemindars with full power of alienation; in a few of these

The khalsa villages.

28 P

no proprietors were discovered, and they (18 in all) were settled with farmers'; but subsequently, in accordance with Government Notification No. 4158 of 28th November, 1851, proprietary rights were conferred on these farmers.

"All these villages, with the Kutehria villages, are commonly known as *khalsa* villages, as also are a few villages held by Gour Thakoors, connections of the Rajah's,—the term thus including all estates in which the Rajah is neither zemindar nor talookdar.

"24. On the ground of the mismanagement and exactions of the Ranee's *karindahs* the talooka was, on Mr. Muir's recommendation, placed under the management of the Court of Wards. Fifteen villages were left practically in the management of the Ranee, and 111, the remainder of the villages in which the Ranee was decided to be sole proprietor, were leased to farmers for a term of 10 years, or till the death of the Ranee. The Ranee was a few years later released from the control of the Court of Wards, and soon after she instituted a number of suits against the *mokuddums* of the *malikana* villages. She obtained decrees in 19 suits, but on appeal in nine cases the lower Court's decision was reversed and the rights of the *mokuddums* upheld.

Claims in the Civil Court.

"The questions of principle were decided in these cases, and it appears there was some understanding that the result of these appealed cases should be held as ruling cases to govern the claims the Ranee was about to institute in respect of other villages. The Lieutenant-Governor's minute, printed in the Thomason Despatches, was written before the decision of these cases in appeal, and the result of the appeals rendered the course suggested by Mr. Thomason unnecessary,—and Mr. Buller did not complete the enquiries.

"25. The Ranee of Powayn died at the close of 1850, and eventually, Government having disputed his title, Rajah Juggunnath Singh, the present Rajah, was recognized as her successor, and as the adopted son of Rajah Ruggoonath Singh. Rajah Juggunnath Singh was of the same family, being descended from Bagh Rao, brother of Oodhee Singh, and son of Bhoput Singh, both mentioned above.

Rajah Juggunnath Singh succeeds.

"26. On Rajah Juggunnath Singh's succession, a reference was made as to whether the *malikana* or *talookdaree* allowance should be continued at the full amount fixed at settlement, and there appears to have been much correspondence on the subject, but it is not known on what grounds the final orders in the case were passed. The allowance was continued at the full amount, and the arrears held in deposit pending final orders were paid to the Rajah, but the vernacular records existing do not show the reasons for the decision, and the correspondence cannot be traced in the Office of the Board of Revenue.

Reference as to talookdar's allowance.

"27. Copies of a few of the letters have been recently filed before the Settlement Officer by the Rajah, and it appears that Mr. Barnes, the Collector (No. 369, dated 30th December, 1851, to Commissioner), pointed out that the Powayn *talooka* had been settled on the same principles as *talooka* Moorsan in Allygurh, and that, according to Government orders in that case, a *talookdar's* allowance was only remuneration for management, and without management the right could not hold good; and that though, in the case of Moorsan, Government had continued the money payments recommended, this was only for life, and the subject would be open to revision on the *talookdar's* demise.

Mr. Barnes's report.

"The Rajah had remonstrated against any reduction of the allowance, as an infringement of the settlement concluded with the Ranee, and this objection had been considered valid by the Commissioner (No. 59 of March, 1851, to Board), but Mr. Barnes now stated that there was nothing in the vernacular records opposed to a revision of the allowance.'

A full report, accompanied by the foregoing extracts, was submitted by me to the Board of Revenue, and by the Board to the Government, and the *talookdaree* or *malikana* allowance of the Rajah of Powayn has, by the order quoted in the margin, been reduced to 10 per cent. on the revenue of each *talookdaree mouzah* and *muhal*. This is a great pecuniary loss to the Rajah, as his *malikana* at the end of the settlement was Rs. 13,081, but will now be only Rs. 5,591, as the total revenue of the 148 *talookdaree muhals* has increased but little, and is Rs. 55,910.

No. 1684A ,dated Nynee Tal, 8th August, 1873, fron Secretary to Government, North-Western Provinces, to Secretary to Board of Revenue, North-Western Provinces.

The history of Pergunnah Khotar is sufficiently detailed in a report submitted by me to the Government, North-Western Provinces, explaining the case of the sons of the late Rajah of Khotar (Rajah only by assumption at first, and subsequently by courtesy; there is no Rajah now), and representing that their case is a hard one, and that they are entitled to the generosity and favourable consideration of Government; and I make the necessary extracts from the said report :—

"2. From the time of the cession up to the revision of settlement by Mr. J. W. Muir in 1838-39 A.D., Rajah Khoshal Sing had been in possession of the entire Pergunnah of Khotar, and the settlements had been concluded with him, *viz.*, four different settlements extending over a period of 35 years. The 2nd settlement mentioned by Mr. Muir in his report of 1st July, 1838, para. 4, as having been made with Gopal Sing, Neyt Sing, and Keeruth Sing, was for five years, but they held it only one year, fell into arrears, and it was transferred to Rajah Khoshal Sing on payment of arrears. In fact Rajah Khoshal Sing and his ancestors had held uninterrupted possession of Pergunnah Khotar for upwards of one hundred years, the first settlers there being the younger branch of the Nahul family in Powayn, to whom the trans-Goomtee tract was given as their portion. They being across the Goomtee, and in a part of the country only thinly inhabited and consisting chiefly of *jungle* and malarious forest, remained to a great extent undisturbed, or at all events escaped the attacks of the Puthans and Gour Rajpoots, who overran Powayn and extinguished the rule of the elder branch. As in the case of many other families, the younger offshoots and relatives of the Khotar family never asserted any title to a share in the property, and the Rajah for the time being remained sole lord, providing for his relatives and clansmen. This state of things continued down to close upon the time of Mr. J. W. Muir's settlement, for quite 30 years from the commencement of the British rule, beside the seventy years or so before it.

"3. Mr. J. W. Muir, the Settlement Officer of Shahjehanpore, in his report to the Board of Revenue, through the Commissioner, regarding the tenures and condition of Pergunnah Khotar, stated that Rajah Khoshal Sing of Khotar, with whom the settlements of the whole pergunnah had been made in a lump, was only a *farmer*, and that the settlements which had been made with him were only farming settlements; that he was the head of a clan of Kutheria Rajpoots in whom vested whatever proprietary' rights there were, but that 'in the light of a proprietor the *Rajah* was only a petty sharer, and a single individual amongst many brethren ;' that the only investigations into proprietary rights that had ever been made were by Mr. Trant at the 3rd, and Mr. Christian at the 4th settlement ; that the results arrived at by both were the same, *viz.*, that the zemindaree rights in a certain number of villages vested in a clan of Kutheria Rajpoots, and that there were a large number of *mouzahs*, either chiefly or entirely forest and unreclaimed waste, without any acknowledged proprietors.

From J. W. Muir, Esq., Settlement Officer, to 8. Davidson, Esq., Offg. Commissioner, Rohilkhund, No. 73, dated 1st July, 1838.

"4. 'That Mr. Christian settled the whole pergunnah with Khoshal Singh in farm, evidently on the understanding that this arrangement was entered into with the consent of his brethren.' The Rajah, Khoshal Sing, was entered in Mr. Trant's records as part proprietor in 32 *mouzahs*, the names of Busunt Sing and Bhoop Sing

being specified as co-sharers, and in Mr. Christian's records (settlement book and
roobkaree) as joint proprietor with others, without any specification of the names or
number of individuals or their shares, in 31 mouzahs. Mr. Christian's record being that
of the past settlement, and more recent and reliable than Mr. Trant's, and the number
of *mouzahs* in a wild unreclaimed forest tract, like Pergunnah Khotar then was, being
at best uncertain before there was any regular *mouzahwar* survey, or such things as
village maps had been thought of, was accepted as correct, and the number of *mouzahs*
without acknowledged proprietors, those allotted to different branches and families of
the Kutheria brotherhood, was then set down at 241. This included the detached portion called Pullia, which is not now part of Pergunnah Khotar, but was separated from
it in 1868 and transferred to the Kheree District of Oudh.

" 5. Mr. J. W. Muir thus arguing, in the said report, that Rajah Khoshal Sing
had no proprietary rights, beyond his shares, in those 31 *mouzahs*, and had no right
whatever to a renewal of his farming lease either in the villages belonging to the brotherhood, or in the villages without acknowledged proprietors, recommended to the Board
that 'the past system of *farming out the pergunnah* in a lump should be abolished and a
mouzahwar settlement be introduced.' The reasons he gave for the exclusion of the Rajah
were for gross mismanagement in reduction and throwing down of cultivation, and
oppression of his own clan and brotherhood, for being suspected of harbouring thieves .
and *dacoits* and interfering with police arrangements, and also for the acknowledgment of the just rights of the Kutheria brotherhood, and the benefits likely to accrue
to Government by extension of cultivation and enhanced revenue, consequent on a
mouzahwar settlement.

" 6. Regarding the *mouzahs* without any acknowledged zemindars, Mr. Muir left
it to the Board to say whether first investigations should be made in them, or whether the
existing records should be accepted as correct, and they should be treated as the property
of Government. Some few of them were inhabited and partially cultivated, but most of
them were forest tracts uninhabited and uncultivated.

" 7. The Board in their reply approved of and sanctioned Mr. Muir's proposals,
and ordered a *mouzahwar* settlement of the cultivated *mouzahs*
with the resident proprietors, and no further investigation in the
case of the waste *mouzahs*, which, they remarked, had already
been proved to belong to Government, holding that Rajah
Khoshal Sing was only a farmer of the entire pergunnah, and
that all the leases had been farming leases.

From H. M. Elliott, Esq.,
Secretary, Sudder Board
of Revenue, to the Offi-
ciating Commissioner of
the 3rd or Rohilkhund
Division, No. 210, dated
14th August, 1838.

" 8. In conformity with the above orders, Mr. J. W. Muir, in December, 1839
A. D., appointed a *punchayet* to apportion to the Kutheria brotherhood their respective
villages and shares of and in those villages which were borne on Mr. Christian's records
as belonging to the Kutheria Thakoors. No fresh investigations were made about these
or about the *khana khalee* villages, which latter were, as well as the former, taken from
Rajah Khoshal Sing and the *khana khalee* villages settled by Mr. Muir in farm (*mus-
tajuree*) with different individuals, *any one who would come forward except the Rajah*, at
progressive jummas.

1. Khundsar.
2. Deorua.
3. Jamooneea.
4. Mullookpoor.
5. Deoree.
6. Khotar khas.
7. Resseon khoord.

" 9. The Kutheria property recorded villages were settled
in *zemindaree* with the families and individuals to whom they
were allotted by the *punchayet*. The *punchayet* awarded the five
entire villages and portions of two others marginally noted to
the Rajah in lieu of his part shares in 31 mouzahs.

" 10. In March, 1841, the Board submitted their report to Government, North-
Western Provinces, the paragraphs of which bearing on
this subject are 19 to 26. After explaining the mistaken
policy which had hitherto been continued of farming the entire pergunnah in
a lump to Rajah Khoshal Sing, and the necessity, expediency, and justice

No. 83, dated 5th March,
1841.

of the change, as well as of the recognition and admission to settlement of the Kutheria brotherhood, the Board recommend in the 23rd paragraph that Government will confirm the arrangements made with the individuals who undertook the engagements of the various mouzahs without any acknowledged proprietors, the

From J. Thomson, Esq., Secretary to Government, North-Western Provinces, to H. M. Elliott, Esq., Secretary, Board of Revenue, North-Western Provinces, No. 559, dated 26th April, 1841.

property of Government, 'as proprietary grantees entitled to renew their engagements as proprietors on the completion of their present contract.' This proposal the Government sanctioned in the following words, para. 3 :—' The suggestions contained in paras. 17 and 23 of your letter under acknowledgment are severally approved and confirmed.'

"11. The English correspondence obtained from the Board ends here, but in a vernacular *roobukarec* of Mr. Buller, the Collector of Shahjehanpore, dated 5th March, 1846 A. D. (of which I obtained an authenticated copy), reference is made to English correspondence on the Khotar *khana khalee* villages, ending with Commissioner's letter No. 35, dated 26th February, 1846, and instructions are issued for the substitution of the word *mokuddum* in place of *mustajir* in the *khewuts* of the *khana khalee* villages, and the entry of the shareholders' names in the proper column, which had hitherto remained blank *(khana khalee)*, and for acknowledgment of the power of alienation and disposal of the property by sale, mortgage, &c. This was carried out in the khewuts of 1253 F. S., and completes the alienation of these *khana khalee* villages from the Rajah of Khotar and the conferment of the proprietary title on the newly created farmers, thence called *mokuddum* proprietors.

"12. In January, 1846, Rajah Khoshal Singh instituted a suit in the Civil Court of the Sudder Suddoor at Bareilly for some of the villages and mesne profits, and got a decree, which, however, was never executed : apparently it was reversed on on appeal to the Sudder Nizamut. Another case for the entire pergunnah was also instituted and lost, but no details can be given, as copies are not procurable. Nothing further is ascertainable than that the Rajah went into the Civil Courts and tried to recover the pergunnah, but failed.

"13. On the occasion of the Lieutenant-Governor's visit to Shahjehanpore in 1844, the Rajah presented a petition to Mr. Conolly, the Commissioner of Rohilkhund, stating how he had been deprived of the entire pergunnah and reduced to great straits, which was referred to Mr. Buller, the Collector, for report. In

From F. P. Buller, Esq., Collector of Shahjehanpore, to H. Pidcock, Esq., Officiating Commissioner of Rohilkhund Division, No. 82, dated 7th April, 1845.

his report Mr. Buller set forth that now, from being the Rajah of Khotar, and holding the entire pergunnah, and enjoying a large income, he had been deprived of everything except his *maafee* villages, and that they had been resumed and assessed (for by Board's orders of 14th August, 1838, he was not

allowed to engage for the villages awarded to him as his own property) and reduced to a 'state of extreme destitution.' Mr. Buller also says :—' I have been informed, and believe the story, that during his attendance on Mr. Conolly, he was dependent on the Ranee of Powayn, who was also a follower of the camp, for his daily food, and that his sudden return home, of which Mr. Conolly complains in his order on the Rajah's petition, was owing to his want of means to cover the expenses of marching.' In the 5th paragraph of his letter Mr. Buller continues :—' Meanwhile the pergunnah has been gradually increasing in prosperity. It is on this account, and the great profits enjoyed by the Government by the new settlement, that a restoration of a portion of his former income is solicited on behalf of Rajah Khoshal Singh. As his father and grandfather before him also, under the Native Governments, held nearly the sole management of the pergunnah, the fall of the family, which at this moment consists of about 100 persons immediately dependent on Khoshal Singh, and the severity of their punishment, is of course most severely felt. Under the circumstances, therefore, perhaps the allowance of Rs. 500 per mensem for his life may be considered not too liberal.'

"14. This recommendation for a pension of Rs. 500 per mensem for the life-time of Rajah Khoshal Singh was eventually sanctioned by the Governor-General in Council, 'subject to the confirmation of the Honourable the Court of Directors,' and intimation thereof was sent to the North-Western Provinces' Government by letter No. 537, from G. A. Bushby, Esq., Secretary to Government of India, dated 9th August, 1845. The said allowance was drawn by the Rajah during his life, and ceased on his death in November, 1855 A.D.

"15. The heirs of Rajah Khoshal Singh have at the present revision of settlement brought a claim before me to recover all the villages settled in *zemindaree* with the various members of the Kutheria brotherhood, as well as all the *khana khalee* villages settled at first in farm with outsiders, on whom the proprietary rights were subsequently conferred in 1841, as already mentioned. This claim, however, has been dismissed by me, as effectually barred by limitation, as well as by the fact of the Rajah's having taken his case into the Civil Courts and failed to get a decree.

"16. The heirs of the Rajah are therefore completely debarred from obtaining any redress at law. But from what has gone before, and from other points which I am about to mention, I think it must be acknowledged that the Rajah received extremely harsh treatment, and that his sons still residing in Khotar are entitled to some consideration and generosity at the hands of Government." No reply has yet been received from Government to this application (May 20th, 1874), but if received before the whole report has been printed and bound, the substance of the reply will be inserted at the end of the appendices of this chapter.

21. The following statement gives the distribution of the cultivated area amongst—

Distribution of the cultivated area amongst the various classes of cultivators. (1) the proprietary cultivators, i. e., *seer*; (2) the cultivators with rights of occupancy; and (3) tenants-at-will. The striking feature here is the increased size of the holding in each instance over the holdings in the three other tuhseels :—

Distribution of cultivated area of revenue-paying lands according to separate holdings.

Names of Pergunnahs.	Seer of proprietors actually cultivated by them, or sub-let.			Cultivated by Tenants.								
				With rights of occupancy.			Without occupancy rights, i. e., tenants-at-will.			Total area cultivated by tenants, irrespective of their having or not having rights of occupancy.		
	Number of *khathas* or separate holdings.	Cultivated area in acres.	Average of cultivated area per *khatha* in acres.	Number of *khathas* or separate holdings.	Cultivated area in acres.	Average of cultivated area per *khatha* in acres.	Number of *khathas* or separate holdings.	Cultivated area in acres.	Average of cultivated area per *khatha* in acres.	Number of *khathas* or separate holdings.	Cultivated area in acres.	Average of cultivated area per *khatha* in acres.
Burragaon, ...	294	3,567	12·09	7,477	25,488	3·40	3,020	7,403	2·45	10,497	32,891	3·13
Powayn, ...	1,333	14,284	10·71	22,941	91,809	4·00	18,277	41,224	2·25	41,218	133,033	3·22
Khotar, ...	260	4,004	15·40	5,170	17,686	3·42	11,936	42,387	3·55	17,106	60,073	3·51
Whole Tuhseel,	1,887	21,855	11·58	35,588	134,983	3·79	33,233	91,014	2·74	68,821	225,997	3·28

The average amount of cultivation per each separate holding, deduced in the same way as it has been done in the three foregoing tuhseels (by assuming that each holding consists of a family of five individuals), comes also to well above the average of those tuhseels, viz., to 6¼ acres for the whole tuhseel, and the same for Pergunnah Powayn, 5¼ acres for Pergunnah Burragaon, and 8¾ acres for Khotar.

Burragaon, as the best populated pergunnah, with the largest amount of old culti-

Pergunnah.	Percentage of cultivated area held		
	Seer.	By cultivators with right of occupancy.	By tenants-at-will.
Burragaon, ...	9·78	69·88	20·34
Powayn, ...	9·70	62·32	27·98
Khotar, ...	6·25	27·60	66·15
Whole Tuhseel, ...	8·82	54·46	36·72

vation and the smallest number of uninhabited villages, has the largest proportion of right-of-occupancy cultivation, and Khotar, as the very reverse, has a small proportion thereof, and by far the larger portion of its cultivation is by tenants-at-will. Powayn comes between the two, as it should do, with a proportion cultivated by tenants-at-will rather larger than the average of the pergunnahs of other tuhseels. The percentage of *seer* throughout this tuhseel is of course small, and far below the general district average, as there are few *putteedarees* or *bhyachara* villages here, and the Rajah of Powayn alone is the proprietor of so large a portion of that pergunnah. But what *seer* there is in all three of the pergunnahs is, as the rule, genuine *seer* cultivated by the proprietors, and only exceptionally sub-let.

22. The metalled road connecting Powayn with Shahjehanpore passes through Burragaon itself, and down nearly through the centre of the pergunnah. There are no metalled roads in any other part of the pergunnah of Powayn, and the town itself is down near the southern end of the pergunnah, under three miles from Burragaon and 17½ miles from Shahjehanpore; there is moreover a serious break in this metalled road at the Khunout, where there is no bridge except a bridge of boats, and a mile of excessively bad, sandy, raviny road. There once was a masonry bridge, but it was carried away some 20 years ago by a very heavy flood, and there may be another some day; but it has been in contemplation and supposed to be on the point of commencement for the last seven years, and lately bricks have been collected for it, but no commencement has been made. There are several large unmetalled roads in Pergunnah Powayn, all starting from the point where the metalled road ends, i. e., from Powayn itself. They are—(1) that leading to Nigohee and Kundagunge, on which the bridges and culverts have not yet been built, and so it is never used; (2) the road through Nahul to Beesulpore in the Bareilly District, which has some bridges and culverts, and is passable except in the rains, when parts of it where culverts should have been put in are flooded or injured by water; (3) the road running north through Bunda and Goolurea to Poorunpore and Madho Tanda in Pergunnah Poorunpore, which is a fairly good and passable road except in the rains, but several small bridges are required, and especially one at the Bhynsee nulla; (4) the road leading to Khotar. This is the most important of all the unmetalled roads, being the direct road from several of the *ghâts* on the Sardah into Shahjehanpore and on to Futtehgurh. There is a large traffic on it of carts bringing wood from the grants on the Oudh borders as well as in Khotar pergunnah, and from Nepal across the Sardah. This has small bridges and culverts, but the Goomtee is unbridged, and there is nearly a mile of bad sandy road there like that at the Sindhowlee *ghât* on the Khunout. Here too there was once a masonry bridge, which also went some twenty years ago in the same flood which swept away the Khunout bridge, but the difference here is that no attempt at rebuilding it has ever been made, nor, as far as I know, contemplated. It certainly would be a great advantage to Pergunnah Khotar if this bridge was rebuilt. Pergunnah Khotar rejoices in another road, or what may some day be a road, leading from the river Kutna, two miles east of Khotar itself (and being a continuation of a road from the Kheree District), in a north-westerly direction to Poorunpore. There are, however, no bridges or culverts on it between Khotar and the Jhukna, and where it passes through the forest it is little else than a cut and cleared line through the jungle.

Means of communication —Roads.

There are fair country cart-roads (leeks) all over all three pergunnahs, which are good and passable for country carts except during the rains.

23. The rivers are the Khunout and the Goomtee, and neither of them is of any size, nor do they afford any water carriage, or act as means of communication. Mention of the Khunout *khadir* has already been made in the earlier part of this report (chapter II). The Goomtee is a small and sluggish stream, and takes its rise near Madho Tanda of Pergunnah Poorunpore, and where it first enters this pergunnah is only a *nulla*. From where it becomes the boundary between Pergunnahs Powayn and Khotar it is very tortuous, whence its name, and it has a defined valley of its own, but does not change its course at all. The banks of the valley are high and uneven, and the valley itself swampy, and hence there is no irrigation on the uplands from the river. During the cold season the valley appears to be nothing but a snipe jheel, but in ordinary years rice is grown in it in the rains, and the land is much sought after as growing good rice; but for the three or four years before this last dry year (1873 A. D.), the floods have been so very heavy that no rice has been produced. The Kutna nuddee rises in the northern end of Pergunnah Khotar, its visible and ostensible source being the large brick-lined tank of the *maafee* village Matee, which is upwards of a mile in length. At first it is a mere drain, and only aspires to the standing of a *nulla* on going out on to the edge of the pergunnah and forming the boundary, and is scarcely worthy of the name of a *nuddee* where it leaves the pergunnah and enters the Kheree District, some 13 miles of stream, but about 10 miles direct, lower down. It does not afford any irrigation to speak of, and whatever there is, is more properly pond than river irrigation. The Burhowa nulla, which joins the Jhukna soon after it enters Pergunnah Khotar, and the Jhukna nulla itself both have small streams in them, and well defined valleys with high banks like the Goomtee, and the rice cultivation in them has suffered a similar fate.

Rivers and Streams.

24. The principal divisions of the area of each pergunnah are given in the accompanying statement, and further details and sub-divisions of the cultivated area will be found in Appendices C. and D., which relate to the assessable (*malgoozaree*) area only :—

Figured statement of area for each pergunnah and for whole tuhseel at present and last settlement.

Pergunnah.	Total area in acres.	AREA EXCLUDED FROM ASSESSMENT.			MALGOOZAREE OR ASSESSABLE AREA.						
		Barren, including roads, village sites, &c.	Maafee	Total.	Culturable.			Cultivated.			Total assessable.
					Old unbroken waste.	New fallow.	Baghs.	Irrigated.	Not irrigated.	Total.	
Powaya, { new,	199,961	16,505	683	17,168	94,095	3,950	7,431	63,987	83,330	147,317	182,792
{ last,	200,382	27,109	4,352	31,461	29,769	15,912	*	67,417	56,482	123,899	168,871
Burragaon, { new,	52,995	6,988	602	7,590	6,052	850	2,045	17,458	19,0 0	36,458	45,405
{ last,	52,343	10,611	1,794	12,405	10,031	2,732	*	21,318	5,847	27,185	39,938
Khotar, { new,	129,664	7,809	1,459	9,268	48,290	6,239	1,790	15,150	48,927	64,077	120,396
{ last,	128,313	27,046	1,881	28,927	78,039	5,597	*	5,607	10,052	15,659	99,386
Whole Tuhseel, { new,	382,620	31,302	2,724	34,026	78,437	11,039	11,266	96,595	151,257	247,852	348,594
{ last,	380,988	64,766	8,027	72,793	117,811	23,641	*	94,362	72,381	166,743	308,195

There is an increase of only 1,632 acres in the total area by the present plane-table measurement over the professional survey area of last settlement, being a difference of less than a half (43) per cent. This is the only tuhseel in which the boundaries are not in any way liable to change, and alteration by fluvial action—and here, as should consequently have been the case, the new total areas of each separate pergunnah, as well as of the whole tuhseel, agree very closely with the old ones. The large decrease in the barren area is owing to more careful classification at the present settlement, and it is greatest in Khotar, where one-fourth, or 25 per cent., of

* At last settlement the baghs were included in the old waste, and not shown separately.

the uncultivated area in every *mouzah* was, by then existing orders, thrown into the barren area, quite irrespective of the fact of its being barren or not. The decrease in the *maafee* area is owing to lapse and resumption of life-grants, the entire disappearance of many petty grantees, and the absorption of their grants into the revenue-paying area, and lastly to confiscation for rebellion in 1857-58.

25. Of the entire *malgoozaree* or assessable area, the area actually under cultivation is more than 80 per cent. in Pergunnahs Powayn and Burragaon, but only 53 in Pergunnah Khotar, and even that, as mentioned elsewhere in this report, is rather above the average annual cultivated area, the year of measurement having been an exceptionally favourable year. In order, however, to show clearly what land remains to be reclaimed, and what the margin for extension of cultivation really is, the areas of new fallow and *baghs* must be omitted, as a constant and necessary quantity on which no considerable indent can be made.

Details of the malgoozaree or assessable area.

Percentage of malgoozaree area.

Pergunnah.	Cultivation.	Culturable and cultivated.
Powayn, ...	80·5	19·5
Burragaon, ...	80·3	19·7
Khotar, ...	53·2	46·8

We have then, as shown in the margin, 16 acres of reclaimable waste only remaining for every 100 of actual cultivation in both Powayn and Burragaon, but the very large margin of 75 in Pergunnah Khotar. In the Powayn, Tureona, and Gola circles there is but little real reclaimable waste, but a considerable amount in parts of the Sunwat and Nabul circles; but none of it is likely to be speedily reclaimed, though doubtless none but the worst and poorest for cultivation, or, what is equally remunerative almost, for grass and wood in its uncultivated state, will probably remain at the next revision of settlement. In Pergunnah Khotar the unreclaimed waste is principally small *sál* forest or tree jungle (of which an account has been already given in the earlier paragraphs of this report), and situated in the 2nd circle. There is no forest, and but little really good and reclaimable waste in the 1st circle.

Proportions of old unbroken culturable waste.

Pergunnah.	i.e., PERCENTAGE THEREOF To cultivation.	Of malgoozaree area.
Powayn, ...	16·3	13·2
Burragaon, ...	16·6	13·3
Khotar, ...	75·3	40·1

Old unbroken waste, but
open land, ... 19,500
Forest and tree jungle, ... 28,790
————
48,290

The area under mango groves exempt from assessment, so long as the trees remain and the groves are kept up, is very considerable—in both Powayn and Burragaon above the general average, but small in Khotar for obvious reasons:—

Board's Circular No. 22, dated 20th October, 1869.

Powayn, ... 7,431 acres, 4 per cent. of assessable area.
Burragaon, ... 2,045 ,, 4¾ ,, ,,
Khotar, ... 1,790 ,, 1½ ,, ,,

The *baghs* in all three pergunnahs are very fine, but I think that some of the oldest *baghs* in Khotar can show the most magnificent trees of any. It is to be hoped that the *baghs* planted during the last 30 years, and those which will be planted hereafter, will follow the good example of those which have gone before them.

A good many fine mango groves were, I regret to say, cut down in Burragaon pergunnah just before and after measurement, and the land on which all those cut then, or up to the present time, stood has been assessed to revenue.

26. The increase in the cultivated area of present settlement as compared with that of the last settlement at its commencement, and the percentage of increase, is as follows:—

Increase in the cultivated area.

				Acres.	Per cent.
Powayn,	...	...	...	23,416	18·8
Burragaon,	...	...	...	9,273	34·1
Khotar,	...	...	...	48,418	309·1

About Pergunnah Powayn Mr. Butt gives the following clear and detailed explanation in his rent-rate report, from which it will be seen that the actual increase of *bonâ fide* new cultivation instead of being over 18 per cent. is less than 7 per cent.:—

"The statement shows an increase in cultivation of nearly 19 per cent. To ascertain the real increase due to actual extension of cultivation, I add the fallow to the cultivation of each settlement, and also add 3,000 acres to the former area,—this addition being on account of the *maufee* area; the decrease in which is 3,720 acres, and this area was almost exclusively cultivation. The figures then are—

			Last settlement.	Present area.
			Acres.	Acres.
Recorded cultivation,	...	...	123,899	147,317
Fallow,	...	...	15,212	3,950
Cultivated *maafee* now resumed and included in cultivated area,	...	...	3,000	...
Total,	...	...	142,111	151,267

"The actual increase due to extension of cultivation therefore appears to be little over 9,000 acres, at the rate of less than 6½ per cent.

"It then appears that a great part of the increase in cultivation is due to the small proportion found fallow at the present survey. The fallow at the former survey was almost all land that had fallen out of cultivation immediately before settlement, in consequence of the calamitous seasons so frequently mentioned by Mr. J. W. Muir.

"The present survey followed a season of scarcity and high prices; but in this district crops in each harvest were nearly average, and in consequence of the continuance of the high prices and favourable rains next year, every cultivator took up as much land as he could procure, and much poor soil, not worth cultivating in ordinary seasons, was ploughed and cultivated. The present survey thus took cultivation at the very maximum. Since survey, prices have fallen, especially harvest prices; the rains have been excessive; there has been unusual sickness in the northern part of the pergunnah; and in 1871 enormous loss of cattle. Cultivation has receded, and is now in the poorer portions of the pergunnah much below the area found at survey and shown in the statements. These remarks apply chiefly to the Sunwat and Tureona circles, especially to the Sunwat, in much of which land is commonly allowed to be fallow for some years in almost a regular rotation."

The same causes as those explained in the foregoing quotation from Mr. Butt's rent-rate report of Pergunnah Powayn tended to make the recent fallow of last settlement in Pergunnah Burragaon abnormally large, and of this new measurement somewhat below a full average, but not to so great an extent in either case here as in Powayn. From the 9,273 acres of increased cultivation must be deducted some 1,900 for excess over average of new fallow at last settlement, and about 1,100 acres of what was then *maafee* and under cultivation, which reduces the genuine increase of cultivation by reclamation of waste to 6,200 acres in round numbers, and the percentage to rather over 22½.

The increase in Pergunnah Khotar on the contrary is most of it *bonâ fide*, as the gain to the cultivated area from formerly cultivated *maafee* is very insignificant, and the large excess of new fallow at last settlement over the average pretty well counterpoises the lesser amount of new fallow than an ordinary average at the present measurement. Assuming the corrected cultivated area of last settlement to be 19,500 acres (instead of 15,659), and of the present settlement to be 60,000 acres (instead of 64,077), the *bonâ fide* increase in cultivation by reclamation of waste is 41,000 acres, or just over 210 per cent. Of these 41,000 acres, about 22,000 acres were forest and tree jungle, and the remainder was either light scrub and thorn jungle or open grass land. Seventy thousand acres represent the total reclaimed area of the Pergunnah (Khotar), but the whole amount is never under cultivation in any one year, and ordinarily the fallow area (owing partly to paucity of cultivators and partly to poverty of soil) is nearly double of that here shown, certainly not under 10,000 acres. The year of measurement was an exceptionally good year, as explained by Mr. Butt in a preceding quotation about Powayn, and the cultivated areas obtained for quite three-fourths of this pergunnah were maximum cultivated areas—far above the ordinary average.

	Acres.
Cultivation,	... 64,077
New fallow,	... 6,239
Total,	... 70,316

27. Notwithstanding the large increase in the cultivated areas of Pergunnahs Powayn and Burragaon, it will be seen from the table in para-

Irrigated areas and sources of irrigation.

graph 24 that there is a very considerable decrease in the irrigated areas of both pergunnahs. This is, however, merely nominal, and owing to difference of procedure adopted then and now. Now *that* only is entered as irrigated which was actually irrigated in the year of measurement, or the amount which is ordinarily irrigated every year, *i. e., irrigated* and not *irrigable;* whereas at last settlement the *irrigable* area, and not the *irrigated*, was entered. This is patent from the amount entered at last settlement—54 per cent. of the total cultivated area in Powayn, and 78 per cent. in Burragaon. The percentages of the area entered as irrigated to the whole cultivated area, as well as the subordinate details of the sources of irrigation, are given in the table in the margin. The

Pergunnah.	Percentage of cultivated area irrigated	Percentage of total irrigated area irrigated from various sources.		
		Wells.	Ponds and tanks.	Rivers.
Powayn, ...	43·4	81·1	16·4	2·5
Burragaon, ...	47·9	76·8	18·9	4·3
Khotar, ...	29·6	80·4	19·4	·2
Whole Tuhseel, ...	38·9	80·2	17·3	2·5

general inferiority of the Sunwat circle, and the small extent of irrigation in it, bring down the pergunnah average to below that of Burragaon; but omitting the Sunwat circle, the percentage of irrigation in the two pergunnahs would be almost identical, a slight excess in favour of Pergunnah Powayn. Similarly the percentage of the whole pergunnah of Khotar is very much reduced by the careless cultivation of a great part of the 2nd circle, that especially cultivated by *pahees* from a long distance. The proportion in the 1st or best circle is not far behind that of the other two pergunnahs, and the 2nd is in every way an exception and a law unto itself.

Circles of Pergunnah Powayn.	Percentage of cultivated area irrigated.
Powayn, ...	53·5
Nahul, ...	48·7
Gola, ...	44·0
Tureona, ...	46·5
Sunwat, ...	29·9

Circles of Pergunnah Khotar.	Percentage of cultivated area irrigated.
1st, *Ábád*, ...	45·4
2nd, *Jungle wairan*, ...	14·7

In all the body of Pergunnah Burragaon, as well as in the Powayn, Nahul, and Gola circles of Pergunnah Powayn, and in parts of the 1st circle of Pergunnah Khotar, the well in ordinary use is the *kuchha pool* or *gurra* well, worked by men instead of cattle; whereas on the light and sandy ridge of Burragaon above the Khunout, and universally throughout the Sunwat and Tureona circles of Pergunnah Powayn, and in the 2nd circle of Pergunnah Khotar, and some parts of the 1st circle, the *dhenklee*, or common lever well, *kuchha* of course, is used. These latter cost from Re. 1 to Rs. 2, and the former from Rs. 3 to Rs. 5 each.

The water-level is near the surface of the ground, and *dhenklees* can be made almost anywhere and everywhere, but irrigation is not a *sine quâ non*, and the extent of it depends upon and varies greatly with the season. It is least required in the Tureona circle of Pergunnah Powayn and the northern part of Pergunnah Khotar than elsewhere, as the former approximates to a *terai* character of soil and climate, and the latter adjoins the Sardah *terai*, and the dewfall from the proximity of the forest is very large. In Burragaon I have given the average depth of water-level below the surface of the earth at 15 feet: this is for the body of the pergunnah. In the tract across on the south

Pergunnah	Circle.	Distance of water-level from surface of the earth in feet.
KHO-TAR POWAYN	Burragaon, ...	15
	Gola, ...	16½
	Powayn, ...	14
	Nahul, ...	12
	Sunwat, ...	9¼
	Tureona, ...	7¼
	1st Circle, ...	9½
	2nd Circle, ...	10½

of the Khunout, at the junction of Pergunnahs Shahjehanpore and Nigohee, it is from 20 to 23 feet, and the wells are all *pool* wells.

28. In the appendices (C. and D.) will be found full details of soil areas divided into irrigated and unirrigated, and the percentage of each kind of soil for each circle and pergunnah, arranged in order of merit, the 1st *domut* being the best natural soil; the *mutyar* and 2nd *domut*, usually about equal, the middling kind; and *dhunker* or mere rice land, and *bhoor*, the worst. The percentages alone are here given to facilitate comparison of one pergunnah with another, and the circles with each other, though mention of them has already appeared in different forms earlier in this report :—

Details of soils.

Percentage of cultivated area occupied by each denomination of soil.

Name of soil.	Pergunnah Burragaon.	Pergunnah Powayn.						Pergunnah Khotar.		
		Powaya Circle.	Nahul Circle.	Gola Circle.	Tureona Circle.	Sunwat Circle.	Whole Per-gunnah.	1st Circle.	2nd Circle.	Whole Per-gunnah.
Gowhanee,	.7	.9	.4	.6	.6	.4	.6	.3	.3	.3
1st Domut,	54.4	65.2	47.0	40.6	31.7	10.9	35.0	59.0	24.5	34.5
Mutyar,	10.1	10.3	15.9	10.5	14.4	7.7	11.7	11.4	8.8	9.5
2nd Domut,	30.6	19.6	25.9	35.8	40.6	43.4	35.2	23.5	27.5	26.3
Dhunker,	.8	1.1	1.4	.4	1.1	.7	1.0	...	1.1	.2
Bhoor,	3.4	2.9	9.4	12.1	11.6	36.9	16.5	5.8	37.8	28.5
Total,	100.	100.	100.	100.	100.	100.	100.	100.	100.	100.

29. In Pergunnah Burragaon the rents are entirely in money, not differential rates on crops (as is so common in the adjoining pergunnah of Powayn), excepting always sugarcane, which almost invariably pays a special rate; nor yet are they, strictly speaking, rates on soils, but chiefly on *hars* or tracts, and on the presence or absence of means of irrigation (not on irrigation itself) or the capacity of land to produce crops without the necessity of irrigation. Also *chukota* or lump rents, and summary or all-round rates, irrespective of denomination or quality of soil, are very prevalent.

Rents and rent-rates.

Concerning Pergunnah Powayn, Mr. Butt writes as follows in his rent-rate report:—"In the Sunwat circle and the poorest part of the Tureona circle, payment of rent by division or estimate of the produce prevails extensively. The share taken as rent ranges from one-sixth to one-third of the produce, but one-fourth is the usual rate.

" Lump rents for the entire holding are quite exceptional in this pergunnah, and the total area so held is little over 1,700 acres,* or 11 per cent. of the cultivated area. In the superior part of the pergunnah a large part of this area is held by favoured tenants, while in the poor tracts the land so let is generally of over average quality, as no tenant will pay a lump rent for land the cultivation of which is uncertain, and thus these rents are of an abnormal character.

*Circle.	Area in acres.	Incidence per acre.
		Rs. a. p.
Powayn, ...	5,472	3 3 0
Nahul, ...	2,567	2 12 6
Gola, ...	2,725	2 11 6
Tureona, ...	2,012	2 11 6
Sunwat, ...	4,383	2 0 0

" Rents are generally paid by rates per *beegah :* a special rate for sugarcane is almost universal, as is the case generally in the district, but differential rates for other crops prevail to a considerable extent, and this custom is confined to the Powayn Tuhseel.

"The lower rates are only in favour of the poorest *khureef* crops; rice, *jowar,* and cotton pay the normal or *rubbee* rate; *bajra* sometimes does; and the crops always, where differential rates prevail, paying lower rates are *mash* or *oorud, moth* and *kodon.* A reference to the crop statement will show that the area under these crops is of small extent, except in the Sunwat and Tureona circles. In the Gola circle the custom is exceptional, and in the Powayn and Nahul circles commonly the lower *khureef* rates are customary only in the poor parts of a village—*hars* which pay 5 or 6 annas for *rubbee* will be 3 or 4 annas for coarse *khureef* crops, while *rubbee* rates of 8 or 10 annas will be constant for all crops except sugarcane. The abatement is often only one or two annas, very commonly one anna for *bajra* or *kodon,* and two annas for *moth* and *oorud.* These differential rates do not then, as the rule, very materially lower the total *nikasee,* and may be almost disregarded, except in parts of the Sunwat and Tureona circles. In many good villages near Powayn in which these coarse crops are hardly ever grown, differential rates are still known, but can be looked on as little more than a tradition running on from the days when cultivation was more rough, and coarse crops were extensively grown. In this respect I believe there has been a vast improvement, and that cane and wheat now occupy much land which thirty years ago produced commonly *bajra* and *oorud.*"

Money rents prevail almost universally throughout Pergunnah Khotar, and there is very little division or appraisement of crops, and where it is found it is forced on the zemindars by the cultivators, and for fields only surrounded by or close alongside of jungle, where the damage from monkeys, deer, and pigs is out of the way and excessively severe, rates are the rule, and lump rents the exception. The rates are on *hars* or tracts principally, and so they are soil rates in reality, though not in name, except in the villages bordering on the forest, where proximity to the forest, and consequent damage, or distance therefrom, irrespective of the quality of the soil, regulates the variation in the rate. A special rate for sugarcane is usual, but not universal, and in some few villages in the 1st circle there are crop rates similar to those existing in Powayn.

30. In this tuhseel, as in the rest of the district, the assessment rent-rates are on
Deduced and assumed rent-rates. soils only, and not on wet and dry, or irrigated and unirrigated areas or soils. In Burragaon, for reasons detailed in the rent-rate report (which are briefly these, that in many villages the real existing rates and
Burragaon. rents were inadequate, having remained unchanged since the last settlement, and in others, especially in the villages belonging to the city Puthans, the recorded rentals and rates were not reliable, but purposely concealed), I had to frame my soil rates more from selected villages than in any other pergunnah. The areas, however, of each kind of soil were large, and the villages of all kinds, and from every part of the pergunnah. The deduced rates were per acre—*gowhanee,* Rs. 7-3-10; 1st *domut,* Rs. 3-13-3; 2nd *domut,* Rs. 3-5-8; *mutyar,* Rs. 3-4-4; *bhoor,* Rs. 2-8-0; and *dhunker,* Rs. 2-4-0. The assumed rates are considerably in excess of

these for all except the *bhoor* and *dhunker*, and will be found mentioned with those of the various circles of Powayn and Khotar towards the end of this paragraph.

In order to show fully the procedure adopted by Mr. Butt in obtaining his assumed rent-rates for the various circles of Pergunnah Powayn, I give somewhat lengthily extracts from his rent-rate report:—

Powayn.

"There is fair ground for assuming rates somewhat above actual rates, that is, for anticipating some general enhancement.

"50. To take the Tureona circle. In village after village I have found that the rates now prevailing were fixed when the villages were first made over to farmers more than sixty years ago. I do not profess to be able to work out what percentage of rise in the rent-rate should have taken place, and theoretical conclusions are of little use in practical assessment, but there are other and more tangible grounds. This circle adjoins the 4th or Goongchai circle of the Poorunpore Pergunnah. The Goongchai circle is in fact a continuation of the Tureona circle, and is of character inferior to the greater part of the Tureona circle,—inferior in soil, crops,* health, and position, and yet rents are higher. In Goongchai circle the chief proprietors are influential Thakoors of Goongchai who have gradually raised rents. Rents there are exclusively crop rates, and there is no enhanced rate for cane. The rates are as follows :—

* The following crop abstract shows the difference, although the Tureona is for the entire circle including a poor tract, that over the Goomtee near the Sanwat Circle :—

Crops.	Tureona percentage.	Goongchai percentage.
Cane, including pundree,	15¼	11
Rubbee crops, ...	41¼	39
Rice, jowar, cotton and garden crops, ...	15¼	18
Total, ...	71¼	68
Bajra, oorud, kodon, moth,	28¼	32

	Rs. a. p.
Sugar, rice, and spring crops, ...	3 2 0 per acre.
Ordinary khureef, ...	2 5 6 „
Oorud and moth, ...	1 2 9 „

These rates applied to the Tureona crop areas give a rental as follows :—

	Rs. a. p.		Rs.
1st class crops at	3 2 0	...	1,03,444
2nd ditto „	2 5 6	...	20,420
3rd ditto „	1 2 9	...	4,959
		Total, Rs.	1,28,823

"In the Tureona circle crop rates are not so universal, but generally prevail in the part adjoining the Goongchai circle, though commonly the classification is somewhat different from that found in the Goongchai circle. The Goongchai rate of 8 annas per *beegah* for rice and spring crops runs up to the edge of the Tureona circle, and in the circle is found in villages held for some time by the Goongchai Thakoors, and also in a few other villages, while in adjoining and similar villages rates of 6 and often 5 or 4 annas will prevail. Then in villages where the old rates of 4 to 6 annas prevail, land relinquished will be often at 8 or 10, or even 12 annas. Where crop rates prevail the most common rate for *rubbee* crops and rice is almost equal to Rs. 2-8 per acre, and the *nikasee* at prevailing crop rates, taking the Goongchai classification of the crops, comes to Rs. 1,02,200,—a result agreeing closely with the actual rental, but far below the rental at Goongchai rates. The Goongchai rates are those given by the Settlement Officer as the actual rates, and were used for assessment. They agree exactly with

	Rs.
1st class crops at 2-8 ...	82,755
2nd ditto „ 1-10 ...	14,156
3rd ditto „ 1-4 ...	5,289
Total, ...	1,02,200

my own enquiries, and the recent assessment of the Goongchai circle is considered a fair one by the people. I have ridden through most of the Goongchai circle, and it is admitted to be inferior naturally to most of the Tureona circle, so that I have here good grounds for assuming rates considerably above the actual rates.

"This great difference in rent-rates between two portions of the same tract of country separated by an arbitrary boundary at once attracted my attention, and I satisfied myself of the facts while in the neighbourhood ; and on seeing Mr. LaTouche's report some months subsequently, I found that the facts there recorded agreed with what I had ascertained on the spot.

" It is only where rent-rates are still in a somewhat primitive state, and all-round rates commonly prevail throughout whole tracts, that a difference between the rents of neighbouring tracts of country is so palpable.

" In the southern part of the pergunnah many rates are found in each village, and the pergunnah is separated from adjoining pergunnahs by natural boundaries, and is not similar either to Khotar across the Goomtee, or to Beesulpore across the Khunout.

" To the south the pergunnah adjoins Burragaon, but in these tracts a close acquaintance with village rates is necessary in order to institute a comparison, and the results for the pergunnah of Burragaon are not applicable, since, though parts resemble the adjoining part of. Powayn, the pergunnah as a whole is inferior to the Powayn circle.

" I have hence, in the southern part of the pergunnah, obtained my data solely within the pergunnah by comparing the rates of similar villages, and enquiries into the dates of fixation, the manner and amount of enhancement effected. The result is that the variations in detail in the more advanced part of the pergunnah point to con- clusions almost identical with those obtained by a different process in the Tureona circle.

" In these enquiries I have not used the rates paid in Koormee villages, not only for the reason that Koormees can bear up under rents that no other cultivators could pay, but also, and chiefly, because at all the past settlements these villages have been most cruelly assessed, and the high rent-rates paid by Koormees are in great part due to the extremely severe assessment of all villages in which Koormee cultivators prevail.

" In the poor Sunwat circle I have kept my rates as low as possible. The con- dition of the circle does not justify me in calculating on any enhancement of rents, and material improvement must take place before any considerable enhancement of revenue can be effected. In a backward tract like this circle, no close adherence to assumed rates is to be expected; but the rates being low, I expect the detailed assess- ment to be well above the jumma at assumed rates.

" In the Tureona circle my assumed rates are not quite equal to the Goongchai rates. The enhancement there has been gradually effected during the last fifty years, and in a tract of country of almost *terai* character, and with large tracts of waste near, I cannot at once assume so great an enhancement, but in the detailed assessment I shall bear in mind that my average rates are lower than what rates *ought* to be, and work up to the fair standard whenever the circumstances of the village allow of my doing so."

In Pergunnah Khotar I put my assumed rent-rates at the average actual cur- rent rates as deduced from existing rents, without any addition
Khotar.
for future increase or rise. I omitted the best Koormee villages paying what, in this pergunnah, were exceptionally high rates, which would have merely spoilt any average, and treated those villages separately. The reasons I gave in my rent-rate report are as follows :—

" Throughout the pergunnah, even in the thoroughly cultivated and well inhabited parts of the 1st circle, rates are much lower, omitting the best Koormee villages, than in any other part of the district, except the adjoining poor parts of Pergunnah Powayn, —lower than they are anywhere else for similar advantages of soil and irrigation.

" But they are very much lower still in the 2nd circle. There is no prospect of any appreciable rise in rates in the generality of the 2nd circle villages, as land is at a discount and cultivators are at a premium ; nor is there any reasonable probability of any immediate considerable and general rise in the 1st circle villages, whilst there is so much good land within four and five miles to be had at such extremely low rates. I do not mean to say that there will not be enhancements in particular instances ; of course there will be; but what I do intend to say is that there cannot, and will not, be in this pergunnah any general revolution of rents and rise of rent-rates."

The assumed average soil rates per acre, *viz.*, the sanctioned rent-rates used for assessment in the different pergunnahs and circles of this tuhseel, are given in the following table :—

Denomination of Soil.	Pergun-nah Bur-ragaon.	Pergunnah Powayn.					Pergunnah Khotar.	
		Powayn circle.	Nahul circle.	Gola circle.	Tureona circle.	Sunwat circle.	1st circle, Abad.	2nd circle, Jungle Wairdn.
	R. a. p.	R. a. p.	R. a. p.	R. a. p.	R. a. p.	R. a. p.	R. a. p.	R. a. p.
Gowhanee, ...	7 8 0	7 0 0	6 8 0	6 8 0	6 0 0	6 0 0	4 8 0	3 12 0
1st class Domut, ...	4 4 0	4 8 0	4 8 0	3 12 0	3 0 0	3 8 0	3 0 0	2 4 0
Mutyar, ...	3 8 0	4 0 0	3 12 0	3 0 0	3 0 0	2 4 0	2 12 0	1 12 0
2nd class Domut, ...	3 8 0	3 12 0	3 12 0	3 0 0	2 2 0	1 12 0	2 0 0	1 8 0
Dhunker, ...	2 4 0	2 8 0	2 4 0	2 4 0	1 12 0	1 12 0	1 8 0	1 2 0
Bhoor, ...	2 8 0	2 8 0	2 4 0	2 4 0	1 8 0	1 4 0	1 8 0	1 2 0
All-round incidence, ...	3 14 3	4 13 10	3 15 2	3 3 8	2 7 7	1 11 3	2 10 6	1 9 1

The above rates are those by which the rental at assumed average rent-rates of the No. III figured statement for each *mouzah* and *muhal* are worked out. The No. III statement for each separate circle, with the soil areas, rates, and resulting rentals, will be found in Appendix C., already more than once referred to.

31. In the next table are given for each pergunnah and circle the following

Rentals and assets, ac-tual and assumed.

particulars :—(1) the rentals according to the putwarees' *nikasees* corrected for *seer* held at low or nominal rates ; (2) the estimated actual assets after further correction for small omissions, or wilful omissions, as well as under-renting to relatives and dependants ; (3) the rental resulting from the assumed average circle rent-rates ; and (4) the gross assumed potential assets on which the *mouzahwar* and *muhalwar* assessments were eventually based.

Name of pergunnah and circle.	Rental in *ni-kasees* corrected for *seer* only.	Estimated actual assets.	Rental result-ing from as-sumed rates.	Gross as-sumed poten-tial assets.	Percentage of gross assumed over actual assets, *i.e.*, col. 5 over col. 3.
	Rs.	Rs.	Rs.	Rs.	Rs.
Burragaon, ...	1,29,060	1,35,800	1,41,926	1,45,900	7 43
Powayn, { Powayn, ...	80,600	87,000	95,902	96,590	11·1
Nahul, ...	78,100	85,000	97,122	93,960	10·5
Gola, ...	44,500	49,000	51,388	54,550	11·3
Tureona, ...	1,00,400	1,06,000	1,14,344	1,16,320	9·7
Sunwat, ...	58,580	66,000	64,831	72,050	9·1
Whole Pergunnah, ...	3,62,180	3,93,000	4,23,587	4,33,470	10·3
Khotar, { 1st circle, *Abad*, ...	44,850	47,350	49,253	50,300	6·28
2nd circle, *Jungle Watran*,	56,680	60,400*	71,300	70,170	16·20
Whole Pergunnah, ...	1,01,530	1,07,750	1,20,553	1,20,470	11·84
Whole Tuhseel, ...	5,92,770	6,36,550	6,86,068	6,99,840	9·34

* These estimated actual and gross potential assets of the 2nd circle of Pergunnah Khotar do not include the *Sewaie* items from the large forest areas, but are on the cultivated and *malgoozaree* areas, omitting the forest villages and large jungle areas, the *jummas* on which, as mentioned further on in the report, amount to Rs. 2,300.

The *nikasees* in this tuhseel are on the whole fairly reliable and correct, but perhaps less universally so here, especially in Burragaon and Powayn, than in the district generally. In Burragaon the *nikasees* of most of the villages of the Puthan proprietors residing in the city are open to suspicion, and some are certainly incorrect, not to say wilfully falsified, with the view of misleading the enquirer into the actual rental of the village. In parts of Powayn rents in kind prevail, and in these villages the *nikasees* are untrustworthy, where not utterly wrong, and they cannot be so implicitly relied upon in all of the Rajah's villages as in those of illiterate zemindars, who depend entirely on the putwaree's *nikasees*, and keep no separate accounts of their own. In Khotar there is perhaps less inaccuracy than in either of the other two pergunnahs; in fact accuracy is the rule, and concealment or inaccuracy is the exception there.

In Pergunnah Burragaon the gross assumed potential assets (*i.e.*, double the amount of the *jumma* actually assessed) are nearly 7½ per cent. over the estimated actual assets, owing partly to (1) some miscellaneous *sewai* items, and (2) to some slight anticipated extension of cultivation in a few villages, but chiefly (3) to the rates and rentals being absurdly low and inadequate in some villages, notably those of Mirza Abootoorab Khan of Lucknow, quite apart from those in which there was any wilful concealment.

In the five circles of the Powayn Pergunnah the excess of gross assumed over actual assets runs from 9 to 11 per cent., being just over 10 per cent. on the entire pergunnah. The former are, as they should be, somewhat in excess of the rental at average circle rates in all the circles except the Nahul circle. In the quotations from Mr. Butt's rent-rate report have already been given in detail his reasons for assuming his rates and the probable results, which having turned out as anticipated, call for no further remarks.

The reason for the actual assessments having been made in the Nahul circle at a lower figure than that resulting from the average circle rates is, that there are great variations in quality in that circle, owing to the river Khunout and the *nullas* running into it, and some poor low-lying pieces near the *dhak* jungle. The poor and inferior villages assessed at below circle rates more than counterbalanced the good and average ones assessed at or slightly above the circle rates.

This first circle of Pergunnah Khotar calls for no special remarks here beyond this, that but little enhancement of rent, and still less reclamation of waste, has been anticipated. In enhancement nothing beyond the levelling up of exceptionally low rates in some of the fully cultivated and well populated villages to the ordinary rates existing in other neighbouring villages in every way similarly circumstanced. There is nothing precarious about the cultivation of this first circle, nor anything special or peculiar in it, as compared with other pergunnahs of this district.

32. In the 2nd circle, on the contrary (the one I have named *Jungle Wairan*), there is the greatest dissimilarity to anything to be found in any other part of the district, in consequence of the insalubrity of the climate, the paucity of resident cultivators, and the large area entirely dependent on cultivators residing at distances varying from 3 to 8 miles. The explanation of the procedure I adopted naturally divides itself into two parts—1st, the villages in which there is a large cultivated area and only a moderate or small proportion of culturable waste; 2nd, the forest villages, in which the cultivation is insignificant and the forest and culturable waste amount to three-fourths and upwards of the assessable area. And I proceed to quote from my rent-rate report:—

Explanation of the various special grounds of assessment of the 2nd circle of Pergunnah Khotar.

" 1st.—In the villages with a large cultivated area I ascertain and satisfy myself of, and enter in my assessment remarks, the average annual cultivated area as distinct from the cultivated area at measurement, which, as already mentioned, was an exceptionally large amount, and take that average cultivated area as the basis of assessment, I make no addition for culturable waste in anticipation of possible, but distant extension of cultivation, but include in the assessable assets all *sewai* items for grass, grazing dues, &c. If these are not ascertainable correctly, I add revenue at the rate of one rupee for every 10 to 12 acres of really good culturable waste, after deducting and allowing free 10 acres of waste for every 100 of actual cultivation.

"2nd.—The forest villages with little or no cultivation. Here I, of course, take whatever certain cultivation there is, and assess upon it ; and where I know that there will be speedy reclamation of waste and extension of cultivation by ordinary spread of cultivation without any special expenditure on the part of the zemindar, this is also kept in view. As regards the forest, I take as assessable assets whatever the actual ascertainable assets are, if I consider them sufficient, or else estimate the revenue as about to be explained. Many, in fact most, of these forest *mouzahs* are let or farmed out, and I find that although the zemindars and lessees have no idea of the actual forest area, and the leases are for the entire forest in the lump, and not at any rate of so many *beegahs* to the rupee, yet that on comparing the leases with the forest areas, they run at from 15 to 10 acres to the rupee, according as it is considered an inferior or good forest. These forests have been much neglected and have been thought nothing of, as there were miles and miles of better forest with finer trees close by, from which trees could be cut and timber felled without any one asking for payment. Now, however, since the *Terai* forests across the Sardah have been given to Nepal, and the Oudh forests have been allotted to grantees, and wood cannot be got for the mere cutting and carrying away, the zemindars are just beginning to pay attention to their own forests, and it is beginning to dawn upon them that these *koron* jungles of theirs may after all be worth something. Again, the grazing fees across the Sardah in Nepal have this year been doubled, and this will raise the value of any grazing land on the confines of this district. Also, within the last two months, the Oudh and Rohilkhund Railway has been opened between Lucknow and Shahjehanpore, and the demand for firewood is very large and constantly increasing, as the engines burn wood, and not coal. I consider, therefore, that I am fully justified in assuming that these forests and forest lands and waste lands are becoming more valuable every year, and that I am not putting on too heavy an assessment, nor yet making a present of these forest lands at a merely nominal *jumma* in computing the revenue rate at about 1½, *one*, and ¾ of an anna per acre for good, medium, and indifferent waste lands respectively ; in other words, putting on one rupee of revenue for every 10 or 12 acres of good, for 15 to 16 acres of medium, and for 18 to 20 acres of inferior, forest and grazing ground. I do not even propose putting on the whole of this now, but gradually by the eighth year, as will be explained presently."

"31. I do not anticipate any great reclamation of waste and retrogression of forest and increase of cultivation and population, such as has taken

place in the last 35 years. I believe that there will be some and a considerable amount, and my object in proposing a light assessment now is to promote it; but in assessing I do not include in my estimate any prospective considerable increase in cultivation, anything that I have not ample and sufficient grounds for being convinced will take place immediately. My reasons for thinking that there will not be any such great increase in population and cultivation in the next 20 or 25 years as there has been in the last is, that then Oudh had not been annexed to the British Government, and cultivators flocked in from there. Now there is a strong competition all round for cultivators. The Kheree District in Oudh has been assessed, as has also Pergunnah Poorunpore in Phillibheet, and cultivators are at a premium in the *Bhoor Illaka* of Kheree and all over the adjoining parts of Poorunpore. Some of the immigrants from Oudh of 20 and 25 years ago have lately returned there, and any considerable enhancement of rent here, or any pressure on the *asamees*, would send them off in numbers. The grantees, too, all along the border offer very advantageous terms to cultivators, who will squat in the new villages on their grants."

The gross assumed potential assets (Rs. 70,170) are over 16 per cent. in excess of the estimated actual assets (Rs. 60,400), but more than 1,000 less than the rental assumed at average rent-rates ; and this apparently unaccountable anomaly requires explanation, more especially as I have said that the rates assumed were actual current rates, and that no addition for probable rise of rates has been made. It is simply this, the rental resulting from assumed rates (Rs. 71,300) is worked out on the cultivated area of measurement, which, as already explained, was a maximum, and not an average area ; had it been worked out on the average area (on which the detailed *mouzahwar* assessments have been based) it would have been some Rs. 5,000 to 5,500 less, and then the gross assumed potential assets would have been as they should be, (considering that they include some *sewai* items and anticipated extension of cultivation), some Rs. 5,000 or more in excess of the rental resulting from the assumed rates. But the rental resulting from assumed rent-rates would still be some Rs. 5,000 or 6,000 more than the estimated actual assets. How is this ? Because although no enhancement of existing *rates* above rates generally found was anticipated, yet a levelling up of exceptionally low rates (in all except the most unhealthy and thinly populated parts, which are cultivated from a distance, and in which there will be no increase in rates for years) is certain. *Rentals* will increase without any general rise in *rates*, merely by existing rates which obtain in neighbouring villages spreading into fairly good and similarly circumstanced villages in which they had not yet been introduced, simply because the *jumma* was a mere flea-bite, a tenth or a twentieth of the rental only, and the old rates at which the land had been first reclaimed were running on till revision of settlement. For instance, one village is still paying rent-rates of 3 and 3½ annas per *kuchha beegah*, though there is no culturable waste remaining nor any forest within a mile, whilst its neighbour is paying 4 and 5 annas for exactly similar land growing the same crops, both of them inhabited and cultivated by the same classes and castes of cultivators. The 4 and 5 anna rate may rise a little in the latter (no rise, however, has been anticipated), but the 3 and 3½ anna rate in the former is sure to level up to the 4 and 5 annas of its neighbour. In all such cases, as well as in all where the rise in revenue is large, the assessments are progressive, and the initial *jumma* for the first period of five years is at half of the declared current rental (the *nikasee*), and the maximum *jumma* is not reached till in some cases the 6th, and in others the 8th year. So that there are five years at the least for this levelling up to accomplish itself, before it is trenched upon by the Government demand.

33. In Pergunnah Khotar alone is the assessment progressive, and the reasons for my recommending it were briefly the enormous increase in revenue and the depressed condition of the pergunnah, owing to recent cattle-plague. The reasons as given in full in my rent-rate report follow as quotations, and I may here add that that report was forwarded by the Board of Revenue to the Government, North-Western Provinces, and provisional sanction to the progressive assessments, as proposed by me, was granted by the Lieutenant-Governor :—

Assessment of Pergunnah Khotar progressive.

" 32. I trust I have made it plain that a lenient assessment is not only the best policy, but is absolutely necessary. But however low the assessment is pitched, it is an enormous increase on the present revenue, and of course chiefly so in the 2nd circle. This alone would be a sufficient reason for making the assessment progressive, and not imposing the whole burden at once. But besides this there is another very strong and urgent reason, and that is, that just now the pergunnah generally is in a low and depressed condition in consequence of the severe cattle disease of two years ago. Both zemindars and cultivators are suffering from the effects of the cattle disease and the loss of numbers of plough oxen, and to impose now, at once, what would be anything like a fair and reasonable *jumma* for Government to demand would be simple ruination, and would throw back

Reasons for a progressive assessment.

the pergunnah 12 or 15 years. The cultivated area has considerably decreased in the last two years, and is now below its average, whereas in the year of measurement it was at its maximum. This decrease of cultivation is *not* wilful or intentional on the part of the zemindars (though in one or two exceptional instances some advantage of the general depressed state of things has been taken to make some villages look their worst), but *bonâfide* beyond their control, and owing to the loss of plough cattle, and the cultivators being in straitened circumstances. To merely defer the settlement for a year would not in any way meet the case, for the pergunnah will require several years to recover the effects of the late cattle disease, the more particularly as neither of these last two years has been a good one, the *khureefs* having been destroyed or much injured by floods and excessive rain, and the *rubbees*, which promised well, turning into disappointment and delusion. Nor yet would a meagre progressive assessment reaching its limit in the 4th or 5th year be a sufficient deferment of the great burden of enhancement. What I propose, and wish to have sanctioned, is that the terms of the progressive jummas may be, the initial *jumma* for the first five years, the 2nd term *jumma* for two years, and the 3rd term *jumma* the full assessment from the 8th year up to the end of the settlement.

" I do not propose a progressive assessment because I am anticipating any very great extension of cultivation or enhancement of rent, or because I am in the smallest degree over-estimating existing assets, for I trust I have explained that I am not doing anything of the sort. But I do consider it absolutely necessary, in order to take off the sting of the very great enhancement, and to allow the zemindars time to retrench their expenditure according to their reduced means, and to remove the necessity of their being almost forced to try for enhanced rents, where the mere mention of the subject would drive away hundreds of cultivators, for the joint benefit in fact of the Government, the zemindar, and the ryot. I merely propose to defer and work gradually up to *jummas* which under ordinary circumstances would be imposed at once, but which, if imposed at once here, would be a cut-throat policy in Government, and utter ruin to three-fourths of the proprietors."

34. A map of the tuhseel, on the scale of one mile to the inch, divided into pergunnahs, and showing the different assessment circles and other details mentioned in the Shahjehanpore and Jellalabad tuhseel reports, accompanies this report. The one thing to be borne in mind when looking at the revenue rate per cultivated acre marked in each village, as well as when running the eye over the No. IV. general statement, is, that when there is but little cultivation, and the bulk of the assessment is on the forest or unreclaimed area, the rate or incidence of revenue per cultivated acre is abnormal, and the one to be consulted is the rate on the *malgoozaree* area. I have therefore, in the second circle of Khotar, given the *malgoozaree* rate or incidence per acre of revenue on the assessable area, as well as the incidence per cultivated acre.

Map of the tuhseel.

35. The assessment remarks of this tuhseel are perhaps more full and elaborate than those of any other pergunnah in the district, as there was more to write about in them and more requiring explanation, especially in Pergunnah Khotar. These assessment remarks are appended to the English Nos. II. and III. figured statements, which accompany this report in the form of bound volumes. If the map mentioned in the previous paragraph be opened, and the reasons required for the assessment of any village which seems by the revenue rate therein mentioned to be considerably higher or lower than its neighbours, they will be found full and clear in the said assessment remarks.

Bound volumes of Nos. II. and III. statements and assessment remarks.

The question of assessment at exactly half assets, or keeping to a hard-and-fast rule of precisely 50 per cent., was brought up by the Board commenting adversely on a passage in Mr. Butt's rent-rate report of Powayn, and the whole question was referred to the Government of the North-Western Provinces for orders. The result was that the procedure observed, not only in this pergunnah, but in the assessment of the whole district was authoritatively laid down by the Lieutenant-Governor to be correct. For full details of this subject I must refer to the general report of the whole district. It is sufficient to mention here, that where the old proprietors have given place to the trading and money-lending classes, or where the current *jumma* was heavy and a reduction necessary, the assessments have not been kept down to exactly 50 per cent. of existing or potential assets, but have been put at a figure which, all other circumstances being taken into consideration, was (for reasons given in full in the assessment remarks) considered to be applicable to the particular case. There were only a few scattered instances, chiefly in Powayn, of the necessity of assessment at below half assets.

36. The *jummas* of the last four settlements are given in the margin for per-
Revenue of former settlements, and remarks on the last one.
gunnahs Burragaon and Powayn. They cannot be ascertained even approximately for Khotar, as it was assessed or farmed in a lump, and included Pullees, which no longer forms part of this pergunnah. The *jumma* assessed on pergunnah Burragaon by Mr. J. W. Muir was Rs. 68,985, and on pergunnah Powayn Rs. 1,91,367, but some villages were subse-

Settlement.		Burragaon. Rs.	Powayn. Rs.
5th,	...	73,994	1,80,176
6th,	...	73,994	1,79,976
7th,	...	78,248	2,09,098
8th, Mr. J. W. Muir's,		64,735	1,93,606

quently transferred from Burragaon to Powayn, Negohee and Shahjehanpore, which reduced the amount of Burragaon *jumma* and raised that of Powayn. The *jummas* marginally noted are those assessed by Mr. Muir on the villages which still constitute these pergunnahs.

When Mr. J. W. Muir assessed Burragaon 35 years ago, he found the existing
Burragaon.
jumma a very heavy one, and granted a decrease on the old *khalsa* lands of over Rs. 10,000. He wrote in para. 13 of his printed report :—

" 13. The collections were made with regularity previous to the late unfavourable
Former assessment.
seasons, but since the drought of 1245F. there has been considerable distress, and the existing rate on cultivation, Rs. 2-10-8, being out of all proportion high compared with the other pergunnahs of the district, it was determined to allow a large reduction."

In my rent-rate report I explained that, notwithstanding that amount of reduction, the *jumma* was still a very heavy one at the commencement of the settlement, and even at the end of it was still heavy where there had not remained a very considerable margin for improvement at the commencement. I cannot do better than give extracts about this from my rent-rate report :—

" 13. Notwithstanding the large decrease and extensive relief allowed by
Mr. Muir's assessment a heavy one notwithstanding the reductions granted.
Mr. Muir, the assessment was still a heavy one; and the fact of there not having been one single sale or even farm for arrears of revenue does not, in this instance, prove that the assessment was not a heavy one, or that it was realized with ease and punctuality. A subsequent reduction of *jumma* in six villages, amounting to Rs. 571, was found absolutely necessary in this pergunnah, besides decreases in several of the villages transferred to other pergunnahs. Also the assessments of many of the villages must have broken down had not the proprietors of them been owners of other villages elsewhere. The Kayeth *ilaka* of 22 villages must have been sold up or farmed (and was heavily mortgaged for some years), had not Bhowanee Sahai reduced his expenses to the very lowest possible limits, by which means he managed with difficulty to tide over the period, until increase of cultivation and a gradual increase in rental enabled him to lay by money and pay off the heavy debt with which the property had become burdened just before and during the first few years of the settlement. Had these villages belonged to resident proprietors, or by fours and fives to several individuals, they must have changed hands, and probably most of them would have been sold or farmed for arrears. It must also be remembered, and acknowledged as a powerful reason for there not being any sales and farms at all,

that however heavy this assessment was, it was lighter than the preceding one ; and doubtless Mr. Muir arranged his reductions so as to meet the most urgent cases and in order to prevent sales and farms, and that the subsequent reductions were granted with the same view. The proprietors who have suffered most severely are the old resident village communities, *viz.*, Thakoors, Brahmins, Aheers, and Koormees; and these have, as was only to be expected, gone sadly to the wall,—most of them past all hope of recovery through any remission that can now be granted to them.

"14. For the first and second decades no traces whatever of the prices paid are obtainable, and therefore I have given the following figured statement for them separate from that for the third decade :—

Transfers of property during past settlement shown in decades.

1st Decade.

Kind of transfer.	Entire mouzahs or muhals.	Of mouzahs or muhals.	Parts or shares				Cultivated area in acres.	Government revenue.
			Shares.					
			Biswa.	Bis-wansee.	Kuch-wansee.	Tis-wansee.		
								Rs. a. p.
Private sale, ...	13	19	90	16	0	0	3,570	7,413 10 1
Private mortgage, ...	2	3	10	16	13	5	541	1,282 2 7
Auction sale by decree of Civil Courts.	3	12	38	12	6	9½	1,221	3,163 7 0
Total, ...	18	34	140	4	19	14½	5,332	11,859 3 8

2nd Decade.

								Rs. a. p.
Private sale, ...	10	38	152	16	1	13	3,699	7,580 2 5
Private mortgage, ...	5	4	36	2	10	...	855	2,189 8 0
Auction sale by decree of Civil Courts.	...	47	101	7	3	3½	1,801	3,740 7 5
Total, ...	15	89	290	5	14	16½	6,355	13,510 1 10

By the end of the second decade 43 per cent. of the cultivated area, and nearly 40 per cent. of the Government *jumma* had been transferred from the original proprietors. The transfers are usually the greatest during the first decade, but here they increase in each decade ; the *jumma* value of the property transferred being greater in the third than in either of the preceding decades, and the amount of cultivated area only slightly less than that of the second decade.

3rd Decade.

Kind of transfer.	Entire mouzahs or muhals.	Of mouzahs or muhals.	Parts or shares				Cultivated area in acres.	Government revenue.	Price.	Average price per acre.	Years' purchase on Government jumma.
			Biswa.	Biswansee.	Kuchwansee.	Tiswansee.					
								Rs. a. p.	Rs.	Rs. a. p.	
Private sale, ...	7	20	69	7	17	2½	1,392	3,124 10 11	30,780	21 12 0	9½
" mortgage,	23	12	43	11	12	3	4,024	10,288 14 10	56,528	14 0 9	5½
Auction sale by decree of Civil Courts, ...	...	16	70	3	12	13½	732	1,933 13 9	not ascertainable.		
Total.	30	48	183	3	1	18½	6,148	15,347 7 6	...	...	...
Grand Total of 30 years, ...	63	171	613	13	16	9½	17,835	40,716 13 0	...	...	...

"The total amount of Government revenue transferred during the settlement bears a proportion of 40 per cent. to the whole pergunnah *jumma*. These transfers, however, are not quite so wholesale or sweeping as would appear from the foregoing statements, as rather more than one-half of the *mouzahs* and *muhals* in the pergunnah escaped all kinds of transfers, and the transactions detailed above were confined to 79 *mouzahs* and *muhals*,—the same property being transferred in some instances several times over. I am not inclined to place much reliance on the correctness of the returns of price paid. Under the circumstances it is wonderfully high, if true; the average per cultivated acre agreeing very closely with that of pergunnah Negohee, where the expiring assessment was light, whereas here it is heavy—certainly not light. The Kayeths' *ilaka*, mentioned in paragraph 13 as having been heavily mortgaged, is not included in these statements, as it was merely in debt or hypothecated, and not transferred."

Mr. Butt has, in his rent-rate report of pergunnah Powayn, explained with great detail the past assessments of this pergunnah, and has shown that Mr. J. W. Muir's was a heavy assessment, and that in many instances it continued so to the last; though of course the general improvement and extension of cultivation during the currency of the settlement, nearly 35 years, gave room for enhancement at the end where room for improvement remained at the commencement of the settlement. The following extracts are taken from that report:—

Powayn.

"29. I have been able to obtain but very meagre statistics of the revenue assessed at the earlier settlements.

"On the cession the entire pergunnah was settled with Rajah Ruggoonath Singh at a lump sum of Rs. 92,000.

"Detailed village assessments do not appear to have been made out, and at first the Nahul and Jewan Katheria villages were also settled with the Rajah, but were very soon restored to the Katherias.

"The same total *jumma* remained to the end of the second settlement, or for a term of six years. Village assessments were made at the third settlement in 1808, and the pergunnah *jumma* was raised from Rs. 92,000 to Rs. 1,37,503, an enhancement of nearly 50 per cent.

"The Rajah refused to engage for the enhanced *jumma*, and the whole pergunnah was settled with former *mokuddums* for a term expiring in 1817. The Rajah then engaged for more than half the villages at the *jummas* paid by the farmers, but still refused to engage for the rest. Many of the farmers had relinquished, large balances had accrued, and I find that in 1817 the Collector was authorized to offer these villages to the highest bidder if he could get no one to engage at the *jumma* of the expiring settlement. Subsequently the settlement of the villages in the possession of the Ranee was revised, under Regulation VII., by Mr. Swetenham. This revision was ordered apart from any general revision of the settlement of the district, and primarily with the object that the tenures might be investigated; but Mr. Swetenham's enquiries did not meet with the approval of the Board (para 20). Mr. Swetenham proposed an enhancement of Rs. 22,774 on the *ilaka*, but this was deemed high by the Board, and the enhancement reduced to Rs. 15,811 on a former *jumma* of Rs. 97,216.

"Mr. Swetenham had assumed gross rentals, deducted 7½ per cent. to cover cost of collection, and then allowed one-sixth of the net rental as zemindars' profits. The Board modified this proposal by increasing the zemindars' profits to 20 per cent., or one-fifth of the net rental remaining after deduction of 7½ per cent. to cover cost of collection. The assessment was then, as sanctioned, 80 per cent. of the net rental. The assessments of the villages in the hands of the *mokuddums* were also revised and enhanced, but no reports on the subject now exist. The totals for the pergunnah, as found in the No. IV. statement of the last settlement, are—

Jumma of 1st settlement.	Jumma of 2nd settlement.	Jumma of 3rd settlement.	Jumma of 1245F.
Rs. 92,000	Rs. 92,000	Rs. 1,37,503	Rs. 2,09,098

"The *jumma* of the pergunnah had thus within thirty years (1808-1838) been raised from Rs. 92,000 to Rs. 2,09,098. The first settlements may have been light, but there is no doubt that the later enhancements were most excessive.

"30. The assessment under Regulation IX. was completed by Mr. J. W. Muir, but the report was written by his successor, Mr. Rose. Mr. Muir did not frame soil or crop rates, but assessed by the aid of all-round revenue-rates on cultivation, and his assessment was nominally at two-thirds assets, or 66 per cent.

"The following table, extracted from the printed report, shows the classes, rates, and *jummas* :—

Class.	Deduced revenue-rate on cultivation.	Cultivated area in acres.	Jumma demandable at revenue-rates.	Jumma actually fixed.	Rate on cultivation by new jumma.
	R. a. p.		Rs.	Rs.	R. a. p.
First, ...	3 0 0	12,539	37,617	37,482	2 15 10
Second, ...	2 4 0	23,316	52,461	50,283	2 2 6
Third, ...	1 12 0	33,717	59,005	60,695	1 12 9
Fourth, ...	1 0 0	53,181	53,189	42,907	0 12 11
	Total, ...	122,753	2,02,264	1,91,367	1 9 0

					Incidence on	
					Cultivation.	Malgoozaree.
				Rs.	Rs. a. p.	Rs. a. p.
Former *jumma*, ...				2,09,098	1 11 4	1 4 6
New *jumma* (including resumed *maafee*), ...				1,91,367	1 9 0	1 2 3
	Decrease, ...			17,731	...	...

"The revenue assessed on resumed *maafee* was Rs. 1,450, so that the actual reduction amounted to Rs. 19,181, at the rate of over 9 per cent. In the three better classes the detailed assessment agreed closely with the result at average rates, but fell far under in the poorest and largest circle,—the cause assigned being the extreme poorness of the soil.

"The reduction granted by Mr. Muir was almost confined to the villages comprised in the Powayn *talooka*, from which it would appear that these villages had been most severely assessed owing to the revision under Regulation VII.

" The following figures are taken from No. IV. statement :—

		Third settlement jumma.	Jumma of 1245 Fuslee.	Mr. Muir's settlement under Regulation IX.	Incidence of Regulation IX. jumma on		
					Total area.	Malgoozaree.	Cultivation.
			Rs.		Rs. a. p.	Rs. a. p.	Rs. a. p.
Khalsa villages,	...	64,058	86,693	84,688·	0 13 4	0 15 7	1 6 2
The Ranee's *ilaka*,	...	73,445	1,22,405	106,689	1 1 5	1 5 1	1 11 7
Total,	...	137,503	2,09,098	191,377	0 15 4	1 2 2	1 8 11

"The *jumma* of the Ranee's *talooka*, settled by Mr. Muir, agreed almost exactly with the sum estimated, five years before, as a fair demand by Mr. Robinson, then Collector of Shahjehanpore, who, in consequence of a difference of opinion between the Board and Commissioner with respect to the pressure of Mr. Swetenham's Regulation VII. settlement, had undertaken a searching enquiry into the capability of the *talooka*. The Board, in applying for sanction to Mr. Muir's settlement, note the coincidence as striking and satisfactory, Mr. Muir never having had an opportunity of seeing the former correspondence, and having arrived at his conclusions by a totally different process.

" 31. Mr. Muir's assessment was no light one, although a considerable decrease on the preceding assessment. The former assessments had been extremely severe, and there can be little doubt that Mr. Swetenham's assessment of the Ranee's *ilaka* must have broken down had there been then small landholders. It worked simply because the property was held by one wealthy proprietor. The fact that Mr. Muir granted a reduction is, then, no proof that his assessment was a light one; and the fact noted with satisfaction by the Board, the agreement of Mr. Muir's estimate with that made five years before by the Collector, Mr. Robinson, seems to me to prove that Mr. Muir's *jumma* was more than two-thirds of the assets, since I find that Mr. Robinson's estimated *jumma* was calculated at 75 per cent. of the gross assets, and seasons of distress and scarcity having intervened, the assets can have but little increased between Mr. Robinson's enquiry and Mr. Muir's settlement.

" It is generally reported through the pergunnah that in the assessment of the Ranee's *ilaka*, the sums formerly paid by the lessees under the Ranee were fixed as the sums to be paid by the village *zemindars*, and then divided into Government revenue and *talookdar's* allowance. It might be held the village *mokuddums* should be able to pay to Government as *zemindars* what they have paid to the Ranee as lessees, but the part of the payment credited as revenue would undoubtedly be more than 66 per cent. of the assets. I have found in many instances that the total demand from the new village *zemindars* did agree very closely with the old leases from the Ranee, and I am convinced that there is much ground for the opinion current in the pergunnah. The Ranee's *zemindaree* villages were all settled with farmers, and the proprietors' profits in these villages were fixed at the same percentage on the revenue as the *talookdar's* allowance in the *talookdaree* villages. Mr. Muir fixed the *jumma* and the additional sum to be collected with it; and the subsequent enquiry decided whether this additional sum was to be considered proprietary profits or *talookdar's* allowance.

Where Messrs. M'Cutchan and Rose found no village *zemindars*, the *mokuddums* placed in possession were merely farmers, and the additional sum became the Ranee's profits under Court of Wards' management. Where subordinate rights were admitted the *mokuddums* became *zemindars*, and the additional sum the *talookdar's* allowance. The Ranee, so long as the estate remained under the Court of Wards, received exactly the same percentage of profits from the *talookdaree* as from the *zemindaree* villages. ·

" My own belief is that the Ranee's *ilaka* was all round assessed at full 70 per cent. of the assets. In the *khalsa* villages Mr. Muir granted less reduction, but the preceding assessment had not been so severe, and Mr. Muir's *jumma* was on the total probably not more than two-thirds of the assets.

" 33. The cases of farm or sale for arrears of revenue have been very few,—only three entire villages, and shares in three others; and in only two cases can severe assessment be assigned as the cause. These two villages were sold for arrears of revenue, and in each considerable reduction in the revenue had to be granted.

" One, assessed at a *jumma* of Rs. 878, was farmed for five years from 1253 *Fuslee;* and very soon after the expiration of the term of farm, balances again remained, and the village was brought to sale. The *jumma* was then reduced to Rs. 650, and the village was purchased by a Pathan of the city for Rs. 550.

" The other, a small village adjoining my Powayn, but included in my Sunwat circle, was very heavily assessed at Rs. 200. It was sold for arrears in 1258 *Fuslee,* and after the sale was twice transferred by private sale within six years, when it was a second time brought to sale for arrears of revenue. This time no purchaser was found; the village was bought in by Government, the *jumma* reduced from Rs. 200 to Rs. 76, and the village re-settled with the old proprietors : they, a year or two ago, sold the village for Rs. 530, and the purchaser asserts that he was taken in and paid double the value of the property.

" The four cases of farm for arrears of revenue require no detailed notice. In three of the four only, shares or separate small *muhals* were farmed; and in the one case where the whole village was farmed, the farm was taken by one of the proprietary body.

" The instances of reduction of *jumma* or transfer for arrears do not prove any general over-assessment; but generally in this district estates have been farmed or sold only when the proprietors were unable to dispose of the property by private sale.

" 34. The transfer statement shows the permanent transfers during the term of settlement divided into four terms, two before and two subsequent to the mutiny. This statement, compiled from the tuhseel records, is only of value as showing the increase in the value of landed property. It does not show the proportion of the area transferred, as many estates have been sold several times during the term of settlement, and thus the same property may appear two, three, or even four and five times in the statement. I give details separately for the *talookdaree* and the *khalsa* villages. The latter might be expected to show a higher average price, but as a large proportion of the *talookdaree* villages are in the superior tract of the pergunnah to the south, and most of the others are in the north of the pergunnah, the average price per acre is higher in the case of the *talookdaree* villages. The average price is still low, but has risen steadily, and is more than double the average price during the ten years following settlement; but the uncertainty caused by the Ranee's claims in the Civil Courts, and the various investigations ordered, must have at first made the *talookdaree* villages of little selling value. The majority of the transfers, where the price has not been ascertained, took place before the mutiny, and this explains the apparent increase in the latter term :—

Transfer Statement.

		TRANSFERS IN TALOOKDARES VILLAGES.												
		Transfers by private sale.						Transfers under decree of Court.						
Term.	Number of mohals in which transfers took place.	Total shares in talwa.	Area in acres.	Jumma.	Total Price.	Price per acre.	Years' purchase of jumma.	Number of mohals.	Shares in talwa.	Area in acres.	Jumma.	Total Price.	Price per acre.	Years' purchase of jumma.
				Rs.	Rs.	Rs. a. p.					Rs.	Rs.	Rs. a. p.	
Settlement to 1849, ...	17	144	2,613	2,727	12,389	4 11 10	4·55	8	48	934	1,278	1,922	1 15 2	1·43
1850 to 1856,	19	115	2,340	2,621	19,008	8 0 8	6·97	13	108	2,487	2,861	10,757	4 5 2	3·77
1857 to 1864,	35	200	5,136	6,083	36,966	7 3 2	6·1	16	98	1,678	2,288	9,743	5 13 11	4·26
1965 to 1971,	38	230	5,237	5,896	56,303	11 ·2 1	9·88	10	70	1,180	1,811	11,117	9 6 9	6·14
Total, ...	109	689	15,726	17,329	1,25,669	8 4 1	7·83	47	324	6,279	8,229	33,439	5 9 1	4·1
Transfers where price cannot be ascertained,	122	1,010	20,944	25,938	...	...	...	131	1,149	24,735	28,432	...	...	...
GRAND TOTAL,	231	1,709	36,170	43,367	...	...	...	178	1,473	31,014	36,660	...	...	...

		TRANSFERS IN "KHALSA" VILLAGES.												
Settlement to 1849, ...	16	140	2,634	2,722	9,095	3 7 3	3·43	5	24	690	517	2,050	2 15 6	3·97
1850 to 1856,	23	161	3,697	3,414	16,781	4 8 3	4·91	16	106	1,720	1,995	12,063	7 0 2	5·1
1857 to 1864,	56	586	13,762	11,531	75,464	5 14 9	6·84	19	168	9,639	6,718	37,363	3 13 11	5·54
1965 to 1871,	53	656	16,840	14,808	93,383	5 8 8	6·19	5	18	611	593	5,570	9 1 10	9·41
Total, ..	149	1,543	36,933	32,475	1,94,723	5 6 8	5·96	45	316	12,647	9,823	56,945	4 8 0	5·79
Transfers where price cannot be ascertained,	168	1,919	41,630	33,643	...	...	...	110	961	24,618	24,122	...	...	...
GRAND TOTAL,	317	3,462	77,563	65,918	...	...	...	155	1,277	37,265	33,945	...	...	...

" 35. The transfer statement shows that a large part of the area must have been transferred, and I now show the extent of these transfers. The information now given is taken from my own notes of the villages of the pergunnah. About one-third are held in *zemindaree* by the Rajah of Powayn ; and the Rajah, retaining all villages settled with the Ranee, has gained ten or twelve others by decree or purchase.

" One-fourth of the *mouzahs* are *talookdaree* or *malikana* villages, the remainder (about $\frac{7}{11}$ths of the pergunnah) are the *khalsa* villages.

" I first take the *talookdaree* villages in which the village *mokuddums* were admitted to engagements at the last settlement. In these the transfers have been most numerous, and 70 per cent. of these villages have passed finally from the village *zemindars;* while of those still remaining, many are mortgaged, and in others the proprietors are deeply in debt. Two clusters of villages, held respectively by Katheria and Bais Thakoors, comprise one-fourth of the villages remaining, and in each case the proprietors are heavily in debt and poor. At settlement these village proprietors were of the following castes :—

Caste.		Proportion of villages held.	Caste.		Proportion of villages held.
1. Koormee,	...	over one-fourth,	7. Kisan,	...	
2. Thakoor,	...	nearly one-fourth,	8. Guddee,	...	Collectively about one-tenth.
3. Brahmin,	...	one-fifth,	9. Goshain,	...	
4. Aheer,	...		10. Kulwar,	...	
5. Pathan,	...	nearly equal ; and collectively about one-fifth,			
6. Jat,	...				

" The Pathans, Jats, Guddees and Goshains have all disappeared; the Kisans and Aheers only retain some shares. The one Kulwar village remains, and the proprietors, money-lenders of very bad repute, have purchased many villages and shares, now holding in whole or part some 20 villages, chiefly in the immediate neighbourhood of the original village, their sole property at settlement.

"The new proprietors are almost exclusively of the money-lending classes,—Bunniahs, Kulwars, city Brahmins, or Pathan *Khundedrees.* Koormees of Khiria, in the Burragaon pergunnah, have purchased several in the Gola circle, but they too are money-lenders, and often purchased at sales under their own decrees.

" In the *khalsa* villages the changes have been nearly as great. Nearly forty villages were held by Kutheria Thakoors of Nahul and Jewan, by Jungharas of Gooleria, and by Gours of the Rajah's family. Most of these villages still remain; but, with the exception of Gooleria, the proprietors are very deeply in debt. The remaining *khalsa* villages had been in 1817 generally given in farm to the village *mokuddums*, but many farmers broke down, and a few years later the farms were given to any one willing to take them and able to furnish security. Very many of the original village *mokuddums* had disappeared before Mr. Muir's settlement, and had been replaced by successful farmers of other villages, or by men of substance in the neighbourhood.

" Even so, notwithstanding that natural selection had thus been working for more than twenty years before Mr. Muir's settlement, more than 60 per cent. of these villages have left the hands of the proprietors recorded at settlement, and but few now remain with the representatives of the original farmer *mokuddums.*

" In the southern part of the pergunnah the new proprietors are of the same class as in the *talookdaree* villages, but most of these villages are in the northern part of the pergunnah, where money-lenders or traders of the city, Burragaon, and Powayn, do not appear to care for purchasing. Bunniahs of the Beesulpore pergunnah have purchased several villages, but many have come into the hands of Thakoor landowners of the adjoining pergunnahs, and of Brahmins, Thakoors, or Koormees of the pergunnah.

" The radical change in the proprietors of the *talookdaree* villages might have been anticipated, as the Government revenue with the *talookdar's* allowance came to 83½ per cent. of the assumed assets, leaving only 16½ per cent. as profits for the village *zemindars*; but the change has been nearly as great in the non-*talookdaree* villages, although village settlements had been introduced more than 20 years earlier, and the cause must, in part at least, be sought elsewhere, and cannot altogether be attributed to undue severity of the assessment. The result of the village settlement is very different from what must have been expected and intended, and in this respect the settlement must be looked on as a failure; but I am inclined to assign as the chief cause the unfitness of the *mokuddums* for the duties they were allowed to undertake, —some were mere cultivators, others were village headmen who had often held leases under the Rajah, but they were not therefore qualified to succeed under our system.

" One result of the sweeping changes in the proprietary body is that now, as the rule, the proprietors are wealthy men, and seldom need there be hesitation in raising the revenue from regard to the condition of the *zemindar*."

There had been no separate *mousahwar* assessments before this last settlement of Mr. Muir's, but the whole pergunnah had been settled (in farm)

Khotar.

with Rajah Khooshal Singh of Khotar. The history of its being taken from him and given to others will be found in a former part of this report (para. 20).

The following extracts from my rent-rate report give all the necessary details about Mr. J. W. Muir's settlement,—its working and extreme lightness in all but a few instances :—

"22. Mr. Muir made the settlement a *russudee* or progressive one for all but 33 *mouzahs*, the progressive *jummas* extending to a maximum period of 15 years, but many of them not increasing after the eighth year, by which time the full *jumma* was reached. The initial *jumma* of first year was Rs. 21,859, of the fifteenth year Rs. 36,667, and the current and expiring *jumma* is Rs. 35,110. Mr. Muir's initial *jummas* in the 33 *mouzahs* were none light, and mostly heavy, and especially so in the Koormee villages, which was his rule throughout the district. In the *russudee* villages it was of course impossible but that some of his expectations should be disappointed, and the anticipated improvement not attained ; but as the rule the *russudee* assessments have proved light and been a success, and have broken down only as the exception. Remissions, *i.e.* reductions of *jumma*, have been granted to the amount of Rs. 1,557 in 13 of the *russudee* villages, some as far back as the twelfth year of the settlement ; and some since, and partly in consequence of the mutiny. There was one sale, and there have been 15 farms for arrears of revenue ; all except four being amongst the *russudee* villages. Of the 15 villages farmed, however, only three are amongst those to which reduction was granted. The settlement was made by Mr. Muir for a term of twenty years only, but the period was prolonged by ten years to thirty years by the order of Government, and it has overrun the thirty years by five years, as the term of the whole district expired on 3rd June, 1868 A.D., and this pergunnah has remained till the last for revision. Some few of the *jummas* are still high, and rather above half assets, chiefly in those villages where the assessments were not progressive ; but as a rule, in all except those 33 villages and some 15 others, say 50 in all, the *jummas* have been exceedingly low for the last 15 to 20 years, and the rentals have been from three to five times the Government revenue. Looking back at the difficulties under which Mr. Muir laboured, and the almost utter darkness in which he must have been groping, I think that he succeeded in a most wonderful way in making a settlement most advantageous to Government, as well as to those who entered into engagements with Government, and that his conjectures and anticipations of advancement and improvement have been more than realized. It is no fault of his that for the last 15 years the Government revenue of more than half the pergunnah has been less than one-third of the rental, for, as already stated, he made his calculations and arrangements for twenty years, and the extension to thirty years was made after his death."

(marginal note) *Mr. Muir's assessment. Subsequent reductions and farms for arrears.*

37. The expiring *jumma* of the last settlement is in each pergunnah somewhat less than the *jumma* originally assessed. In Burragaon the amount is Rs. 430, which is thus made up,—a reduction of 571 rupees in six villages over-assessed, and an increase of 141 rupees assessed on lapsed and resumed *maofees*. In Powayn the amount is Rs. 1,240, the details of which are a decrease of Rs. 2,001, being reductions of assessment subsequently made in 23 *mouzahs*, and an increase of Rs. 761, of which Rs. 729 were

(marginal note) *Jummas of last and present settlement for each pergunnah.*

Name of pergunnah.	Jumma at commencement of last settlement without cesses.	Expiring (current) jumma of last settlement without cesses.	New jumma of present revision without cesses.
	Rs.	Rs.	Rs.
Burragaon, ...	64,735	64,305	72,950
Powayn, ...	1,93,606	1,92,364	2,16,735
Khotar, ...	36,667	35,110	62,535
Whole tuhseel, ...	2,95,008	2,91,781	3,52,220

increases of *jumma* in 1849 A.D. in 10 *mouzahs*, and 32 summary assessments on resumed and lapsed *maofees*.

The *jumma* was progressive at last settlement in Khotar, and is so also now, and the maximum *jumma* has in both cases been entered ; the separate tract, Pulleea, which no longer forms part of this pergunnah, has been altogether omitted. The expiring *jumma* is Rs. 1,557 less than the maximum originally assessed by Mr. J. W. Muir on the villages now forming the pergunnah, and is the amount of *jumma* reduced in 13 villages which were over-assessed, as already explained in a previous paragraph.

88. These new *jummas* came into force in pergunnah Burragaon from the 1st of July, 1872 A.D., and in pergunnahs Powayn and Khotar from the 1st July, 1873 A.D. In all three the *jumma* is the revenue proper or *jumma mal* without cesses. In the margin are given the amount of increase and percentage for each pergunnah, amounting to Rs. 60,439 for the whole tuhseel, at the rate of 20·72 per cent. In pergunnah Khotar, however, the whole of this increase does not come into force at once, but gradually, and this can best be seen in the following form :—

Increase of new over expiring jumma.

Pergunnah.	Increase.	Percentage.
	Rs.	
Burragaon, ...	8,645	13·44
Powayn, ...	24,369	19·68
Khotar, ...	27,425	75·11
Whole tuhseel, ...	60,439	20·72

Circle.	Current jumma.	New progressive jumma.			Difference between current and full jumma of 3rd term.			Percentage of net increase.
		Initial, 1st to 5th year.	2nd term, 6th and 7th years.	3rd term, 8th year to end of settlement.	Decrease.	Increase.	Net increase.	
1st, ...	16,682	23,620	24,790	25,150	899	8,867	8,468	50·8
2nd, ...	18,428	29,530	34,420	37,385	533	19,490	18,957	102·9
Whole pergunnah Khotar.	35,110	53,150	59,210	62,535	932	28,357	27,425	78.1

The increase is enormous, but so far as a 50 cent. of assets assessment is a light one, I believe this to be light. Where the *jumma* is progressive (and it is progressive wherever the increase is large) I have put the *jumma* of the first term at only one-half of the average declared current *nikasee*, without corrections for *seer* or low and favourable rates; and in some exceptional cases, where the increase is five and six-fold or more, at even less than half the *nikasee*. The real pressure, however, of the increase is not even adequately represented by the above table, but may be realized from a perusal of the following statement :—

Circle.	NUMBER OF KHALSA MUHALS, AND EXPIRING JUMMA THEREOF, IN WHICH THE ASSESSMENT IS					
	Unaltered.		Decreased.		Increased.	
	Muhals.	Jumma.	Muhals.	Jumma.	Muhals.	Jumma.
First, ...	7	1,314	7	3,041	58	12,327
Second, ...	9	881	13	3,461	178	14,086
Totals, ...	16	2,195	20	6,502	236	26,413

The total amount of decrease on the seven *muhals* in the 1st circle is Rs. 899, and on the thirteen in the 2nd circle Rs. 533, being 13 and 15 per cent. respectively. The actual increase on the 58 *muhals* in the 1st circle is Rs. 8,867, or 72 per cent., and on the 178 *muhals* in the 2nd circle it is Rs. 19,490, or 138 per cent. Surely this will convince the most hard-hearted that a gradual increase by means of a progressive assessment was urgently needed.

39.   The rates or incidences of the last settlement on the then area at the commencement of settlement are compared with those of the new
settlement (cesses omitted in both cases) on the present areas
in the following table :—

Incidence per acre of the last and new settlement.

Name of Pergunnah.	Total area.		Malgoozaree or assessable area.		Cultivated area.	
	Last.	New.	Last.	New.	Last.	new.
	Rs. a. p.	Rs. a. p.	Rs. a. p.	Rs. a. p.	Rs. a. p.	Rs. a. p.
Burragaon, ...	1 3 9	1 6 0	1 9 11	1 9 8	2 6 1	2 0 0
Powayn, ...	0 15 6	1 1 4	1 2 4	1 3 0	1 9 0	1 7 6
Khotar, ...	0 4 7	0 7 8	0 5 11	0 8 4	2 3 7	0 15 7
Whole tuhseel, ...	0 12 5	0 14 9	0 15 4	1 2 0	1 11 7	1 6 9

The reason of the revenue-rate per cultivated area of the new settlement being
less than that of the last settlement in pergunnahs Burragaon and Powayn is owing
chiefly to the extraordinarily large recently abandoned (i.e., new fallow) area at last
settlement, and the amount thereof at the present measurement being below average ;
and, secondly, to the fact of the old settlement having been at certainly quite 70 per
cent. of the assets, whereas the new one is professedly at about half assets, and is in
these two pergunnahs about 52 or 53 per cent. of present assets.

In pergunnah Khotar the rate is given of the maximum *jumma*, which was assessed
chiefly on anticipated extension of cultivation, which anticipation has been moreover fully realized, for the incidence per cultivated acre, which was Rs. 2-3-7 at the
commencement of the settlement, was only 8 annas and 9 pie at the end of it.   The
foregoing statement, however, gives only the result of the entire pergunnah of Khotar.
The following are the details for the two circles :—

Circle.	INCIDENCE PER ACRE OF THE NEW JUMMA	
	On malgoozaree area.	On cultivated area.
	Rs. a. p.	Rs. a. p.
First, ...	1 2 8	1 5 8
Second, ...	0 6 1	0 13 2

The marginal statement shows the incidence of the expiring *jumma* on the area

Pergunnah.	Rate per acre	
	On malgooza-ree area.	On cultivated area.
	Rs. a. p.	Rs. a. p.
Burragaon, ...	1 6 8	1 11 11
Powayn, ...	1 0 10	1 4 3
Khotar, ...	0 4 8	0 8 9
Whole tuhseel, ...	0 13 1	1 2 10

at the expiration of the settlement for each pergunnah.   Burragaon's, which was Rs. 2-0-1 at
the commencement, was
Re. 1-11-11 at the end, and has
been now raised to Rs. 2, whilst
that of Powayn, which was
Re. 1-9 at the commencement,
was Re. 1-4-3 at the end, and has been increased to Re. 1-7-6.   Khotar has been
mentioned above.

40.   Throughout the three pergunnahs of this tuhseel the *kists* were fixed, in conformity with the wishes of the majority of the zemindars, at
half for the *khureef* and half for the *rubbee.*

Kists or instalments for payment of revenue.

The second *khureef* instalment is later in this tuhseel than in any other, as it is

Khureef.			Rubbee.		
15th November.	15th February.	Total.	15th May.	15th June.	Total.
Annas. 4	Annas. 4	Annas. 8	Annas. 4	Annas. 4	Annas. 8

the northernmost, and the ripening and gathering of the millets and pulses of the *khureef* harvest, and commencement of sugarcane pressing is later than in other parts of the district. There was no need for making any of the other *kists* later here than in other pergunnahs.

41. The *durkhasts* of pergunnah Burragaon were taken from the 1st of July,

Durkhasts or engagements for payment of revenue.

1872 A.D., the commencement of 1280 Fuslee, and for pergunnahs Powayn and Khotar from the 1st July, 1873 A.D., the commencement of 1281 Fuslee, and for revenue *(jumma mal)* only, without cesses. The cesses are entirely separate, and are regulated by Act XVIII. of 1871. As in other pergunnahs, so also here, no period for the settlement has been entered in the *durkhasts*, which are merely "for the term of the settlement, and until revision" and also "subject to the sanction of Government."

In pergunnah Burragaon there was one refusal to engage at the proposed *jumma*, *viz.*, in *mouzah* Simra; and the village has been farmed for twelve years to the zemindars of the Burragaon Kayeth family, who own most of the neighbouring villages.

In pergunnah Powayn there was no case of refusal to engage, and only one in Khotar.*

42. In the re-arrangement of *putwarees'* circles very slight alterations were

Arrangement of putwarees' circles and grading of putteedarees.

found necessary in pergunnahs Powayn and Burragaon, but considerable reduction of very large and unmanageable circles in pergunnah Khotar. In Khotar six new circles were made, and even now the circles in that pergunnah are full large, but the tenures are simple. The *putwaree* cess falls on the zemindars at 5¼ per cent. in pergunnah Burragaon, and at 6 per cent. in pergunnahs Powayn and Khotar on the revenue *(jumma mal)*.

The number of *putwarees* in each grade, with the salary of the grading, is given in the margin; but in pergunnah Khotar I made the salary of the lowest grade Rs. 10 per mensem, as the circles are large and the

Perguanah.	Number of putteedarees.			
	1st grade, Rs. 13 per mensem.	2nd grade, Rs. 11 per mensem.	3rd grade, Rs. 9 per mensem.	Totals.
Burragaon, ...	6	14	10	30
Powayn, ...	21	39	33	93
Khotar, ...	10	16	6	32
Whole tuhseel, ...	37	69	49	155

climate is bad; and for these reasons the Khotar *putwarees* have been treated liberally in the grading also.

The marginal table shows the averages per *putwaree* in each pergunnah. Many of the

Pergunnah.	Averages per putteedaree.		
	Number of mouzahs.	Number of muhals.	Cultivated area in acres.
Burragaon, ...	4¼	5¼	1,215
Powayn, ...	4⅓	5⅓	1,584
Khotar, ...	8	8½	2,002

mouzahs in pergunnah Khotar are uninhabited, and the average of inhabited *mouzahs* per *putwaree* is just under five. There is one circle in the pergunnah in which all the mouzahs are uninhabited.

* The one case is that of *Mouza* Kujra, and is a peculiar one; the refusal to engage being chiefly owing to an erroneous order of the Deputy Magistrate taking security from the zemindar to keep the peace towards cowherds who tended their masters' cattle in the neighbouring jungles and drove them into the standing crops of this village, causing very extensive damage. The case is separately reported.

43. Every officer in the Settlement Department of this district has had more or less to do with the case-work and attestation of records of this tuhseel as it was the last; and not one of the three pergunnahs even has been the *specialité* of any one of them. The heavy cases have all been disposed of by me, amongst which are numbered the two claims of the Rajah of Powayn for 109 and 179 *mousahs* respectively, and of the sons of the late (so called) Rajah of Khotar to the whole of that pergunnah.

Attestation of vernacular records and case-work.

In the following statement the enhancement suits under Act XIX. of 1873 are shown separately, and these were one and all of them decided by Mr. Butt between the end of December and end of March. The other enhancement cases under Acts X. of 1859 and XIV. of 1863 were also chiefly decided by him, but partly by the Uncovenanted Deputy Collectors :—

Total number of cases decided.	DETAILS OF CASES INSTITUTED AND DECIDED.							
	Rights and interests under Regulation VII. of 1822.	Enhancement of rent suits under		Boundary disputes.	Perfect and imperfect partitions.	*Moofus* investigations.	Appeals to Settlement Officer.	Miscellaneous.
		Acts X. of 1859 and XIV. of 1863.	Act XIX. of 1873.					
9,965	4,331	54	251	566	151	410	327	3,875

Of the 327 appeals to the Settlement Officer from the decisions of his subordinates, 33 are appeals in the 251 enhancement suits under the new Land Revenue Act, and 244 are objections against Mr. Butt's assessments in pergunnah Powayn, so that there are only fifty appeals against decisions under all the other heads, which is less than one per cent. in appealable cases, omitting miscellaneous cases.

The appeals against the enhancements under Act XIX. of 1873, " the North-Western Provinces Land Revenue Act," are rather numerous — 33 out of 251,—being at the rate of over 13 per cent. ; and most of them are extremely frivolous, simply objecting to any enhancement of rent at all on the part of the cultivators, and of not granting separate *kharch* or cesses over and above the rent on the part of the zemindars, for they look upon their consolidation with the rent as a myth. In twenty-six cases Mr. Butt's orders have been upheld and the appeal dismissed *in toto*, and in seven only his decision has been reversed or modified.

In the 244 objections against Mr. Butt's assessments in Powayn, taken up by me and disposed of as appeals, reductions of various amounts, from ten to fifty rupees chiefly, were granted in sixty muhals, aggregating a sum total of Rs. 1,420. The appeals were rejected and the assessments upheld in 184.

Up to the time of the assessment of pergunnahs Powayn and Khotar, the number of appeals, or even petitions not being regular appeals, to the Commissioner against the assessments in the other three entire tuhseels, and pergunnah Burragaon of this tuhseel, numbered only 17 ; whereas now, in pergunnahs Powayn and Khotar alone, the number of appeals to the Commissioner against the assessments is no less than 171. This can only be accounted for by the late commotion in Bareilly and Phillibheet, and general outcry against those assessments, and the news that in consequence thereof an enquiry into the assessments of parts at least of those districts has been ordered by Government. For here the assessments have been made on the same principles and by the same officers as in the other three-fourths of the district, from which, as stated above, there were only eight appeals and nine petitions of objection on first hearing the new *jumma*, which, however, were not followed up with copies of orders and grounds of appeal. All those eight appeals in other parts of the district were dismissed, but none of these later appeals have yet been decided on their merits. Some forty-two have been rejected as not having been instituted within the term of limitation, counting the 60 days from the date of the publication of the translation of the Land Revenue Act in the *Government Gazette.* Not one single appeal, I believe, was given in within six months of the announcement of the *jummas* (except of course the appeals to me from Mr. Butt's assessments), as at that time the Bareilly and Phillibheet zemindars had not formed their committee for objecting against and bringing into public notice " the over-assessment of the Bareilly District."

Amongst the appeals to the Commissioner against judicial decisions, which are very few in number, the only ones worthy of special notice are those of the Rajah of Powayn in his two claims abovementioned, both of which were dismissed, and I am not aware whether he has carried them on to the Board or not. The result of the appeals in this tuhseel has, so far, been as good as in other tuhseels, not one single order having been reversed by the Commissioner on appeal.

ROBERT G. CURRIE,

Settlement Officer.

SHAHJEHANPORE :

June 25th, 1874.

APPENDICES.

(a) Crop statement for each circle and pergunnah, and for entire tuhseel,

(c) Statement showing details of the cultivated area, the sanctioned average rent-rates, and the deduced rentals for each assessment circle.

(d) Statement of soils, with percentages and detail of irrigated area for each pergunnah, each circle, and the entire tuhseel.

(e) Statement showing the population of each pergunnah, and of tuhseel, by the census of 1872.

(f) Statement showing the number of houses and enclosures.

(g) Statement showing number of estates held by each caste in each pergunnah, distinguishing those held by resident and by non-resident proprietors.

(h) Statement showing the extent to which landed property has been transferred from the agricultural to the non-agricultural classes.

INDEX

APPENDICES TO THE FOUR TUHSEEL REPORTS OF THE SHAHJEHANPORE DISTRICT.

APPENDICES.

APPEN

Assessment Report of

Crop

Pergunnah.	Season.	Number.	Description.	Grand Total.	Khureef. Sugar-cane. Present year.	Khureef. Sugar-cane. Land prepared for next year.	Cotton.	Kuchians.	Jowar.	Bajra.	Oord.	Moat.	Rice.	Kodon.	Shama.
Shahjehanpore.	Year of measurement, 1274-75 F. S., ...	1	Area in acres, ...	64,457	5,109	4,055	2,862	780	5,208	3,563	1,143	252	3,740	592	5
		2	Percentage, ...	100	8	6¼	4½	1¼	8	5½	1¾	½	5¾	1	...
	1280 F. S., ...	3	Area in acres, ...	64,457	6,540	5,351	2,168	517	3,710	2,925	616	100	4,644	378	...
		4	Percentage, ...	100	10¼	8½	3½	¾	5¾	4½	1	...	7¼	½	...
Jumour.	Year of measurement, 1274-75 F. S., ...	5	Area in acres, ...	43,401	3,258	1,400	1,277	755	1,847	864	216	177	11,764	2	...
		6	Percentage, ...	100	7½	3¼	3	1¾	4¼	2	½	½	27	...	...
	1280 F. S., ...	7	Area in acres, ...	43,401	3,653	2,735	1,424	280	838	524	242	33	12,965	...	...
		8	Percentage, ...	100	8½	6½	3¼	½	2	1¼	½	½	29¾	...	...
Kant.	Year of measurement, 1275-76 F. S., ...	9	Area in acres, ...	71,090	1,988	562	994	863	2,185	16,403	1,749	1,442	4,674	18	2
		10	Percentage, ...	100	2¾	¾	1½	1¼	3	23	2½	2	6½	...	...
	1280 F. S., ...	11	Area in acres, ...	71,090	3,025	1,477	1,268	406	1,332	17,940	667	796	5,868	...	...
		12	Percentage, ...	100	4¼	2	1¾	½	2	25¼	1	1	8¼	...	...
Whole Tuhseel,	Year of measurement, 1274-75-76 F. S., ...	13	Area in acres, ...	1,78,948	10,415	6,017	5,133	2,398	9,240	20,830	3,108	1,871	20,178	612	7
		14	Percentage, ...	100	5¾	3½	3	1¼	5¼	11¾	1¾	1¼	11¼	...	...
	1280 F. S., ...	15	Area in acres, ...	1,78,948	13,218	9,556	4,860	1,203	5,880	21,389	1,525	929	23,477	378	...
		16	Percentage, ...	100	7½	5½	2½	¾	3½	12	1	½	13	½	...

Land bearing two

Pergunnah.	Season.	Number.	Pergunnah.	Kuchians.	Rice, afterwards Sugar-cane.	Rice, afterwards Linseed.	Rice afterwards Wheat.	Rice, afterwards Wheat and Barley mixed.	Rice, afterwards Gram.	Rice, afterwards Barley.	Rice, afterwards Joar.	Oord, afterwards Gram.	Oord, afterwards Gram and Barley mixed.	Jowar, afterwards Gram.	Rice, afterwards Bajra.	Flax, afterwards Gram.	Indian-Corn, afterwards Kuchians.
Shahjehanpore.	Year of measurement 1274-75 F. S., ...	1	Area in acres, ...	664	124	121	236	131	1,210	80	57	3	9	11	4	22	44
		2	Percentage, ...	1	¼	¼	¼	¼	1¾	¼	...	...	...	...	...	...	...
	1280 F. S., ...	3	Area in acres, ...	517	140	150	280	138	2,938	150	30	...	...	10	...	4	20
		4	Percentage, ...	1	¼	¼	½	¼	4½	¼		...	...	...	...	...	...
Jumour.	Year of measurement,	5	Area in acres, ...	691	183	150	544	228	1,769	84	...	8	...	9	2	...	...
		6	Percentage, ...	1½	½	½	1¼	½	4	¼	...	...	...	...	...	...	...
	1280 F. S., ...	7	Area in acres, ...	280	98	210	380	282	2,360	185	...	...	...	5	...	...	...
		8	Percentage, ...	¾	¼	½	¾	¾	5½	½	...	...	...	...	...	...	...
Kant.	Year of measurement,	9	Area in acres, ...	394	87	41	322	175	1,879	335	...	-	...	...	...	...	...
		10	Percentage, ...	¾	¼	...	½	¼	1¾	¼	...	...	...	...	...	...	...
	1280 F. S., ...	11	Area in acres, ...	406	141	72	531	250	2,141	387	...	...	...	...	...	...	...
		12	Percentage, ...	¾	¼	...	¾	¼	3	½	...	...	...	...	...	...	...
Whole Tuhseel.	Year of measurement,	13	Area in acres, ...	1,699	394	312	1,102	534	4,258	499	57	11	9	20	6	26	44
		14	Percentage, ...	1	¼	¼	½	½	2½	¼	...	...	...	...	...	...	...
	1280 F. S., ...	15	Area in acres, ...	1,203	379	432	1,191	670	7,439	722	30	...	...	15	...	...	20
		16	Percentage, ...	¾	¼	¼	¾	½	3¾	½	...	...	...	...	...	...	...

Dated Shahjehanpore, the 20th December, 1873.

DIX A.

TUHSEEL SHAHJEHANPORE.

Statement.

Indigo.	Indian-Corn.	Mundoos.	Flax and Hemp.	Turmeric.	Lahee.	Til.	Churree.	Total of Khureef.	RUBBEE. Wheat.	Gram.	Wheat and Barley mixed.	Barley.	Gram and Barley mixed.	Linseed.	Safflower.	Mussoor.	Poppy, *viz.*, Opium.	Urhur.	Peas.	Melon and Cucumber.	Total of Rubbee.	Number.
1	144	10	308	1	20	2	4	27,859	23,894	6,476	1,108	1,717	381	298	1	2,092	134	409	8	80	36,598	1
...	¼	...	½	...	...	...	...	43¼	36½	10	1¾	2¾	¾	½	...	3¼	¼	¾	...	¼	56¾	2
...	115	8	537	...	25	...	30	27,264	21,556	9,082	2,048	1,964	1,359	220	...	278	90	445	...	75	37,117	3
...	¼	...	¼	...	...	...	...	42½	33½	14	3¼	3½	2¼	½	...	½	...	¾	...	...	57½	4
...	1	2	59	1	1	1	1	21,626	14,749	3,824	388	832	843	131	3	862	109	26	8	...	21,775	5
...	...	...	½	...	...	...	...	50	33¾	8¾	1	2	2	¼	...	2	¼	...	...	...	50	6
...	10	...	35	...	...	3	10	22,752	11,585	4,953	303	748	2,363	76	...	254	361	...	...	10	20,658	7
...	...	...	½	...	...	...	...	52¼	26¾	11¼	¾	1¾	5¼	¼	...	½	¾	...	...	...	47½	8
8	50	8	13	20	74	12	18	31,083	24,879	4,793	2,300	3,667	709	98	58	1,973	833	557	123	22	40,007	9
...	¾	...	...	...	¼	...	...	43¼	35	6¾	3¼	5¼	1	¼	...	2¾	1½	¾	¼	...	56¾	10
...	15	...	902	...	85	...	24	33,798	24,116	5,896	2,470	2,715	761	...	...	163	1,247	...	...	...	37,363	11
...	...	...	1½	...	¼	...	...	47½	34¼	8	3½	3¾	1	...	...	¼	1¾	...	...	...	52½	12
9	195	20	308	22	95	15	23	80,568	68,522	15,098	3,796	6,126	1,933	527	57	4,927	1,076	992	139	102	98,389	13
...	...	...	...	...	...	...	...	45	35½	8½	2¼	3½	1¼	½	...	2½	½	½	...	...	55	14
...	140	8	1,074	...	110	3	64	83,814	57,257	19,931	4,821	5,427	4,488	296	...	695	1,608	445	...	25	95,143	15
...	...	...	½	...	...	...	...	46¾	32	11	2¾	3¼	2¾	...	..	¼	1	½	...	...	53¼	16

crops in the year.

Indian-Corn, afterwards Wheat.	Fodder, afterwards Barley.	Fodder, afterwards Kucchiana.	Flax, afterwards Wheat.	Indian Corn, afterwards Sugar cane.	Flax, afterwards Linseed.	Flax, afterwards Lahee.	Joar, afterwards Mussoor.	Joar, afterwards Wheat.	Flax, afterwards Sugar-cane.	Fodder, afterwards Sugar-cane.	Gram, afterwards Cucumber.	Rice, afterwards Oord.	Mundoos, afterwards Barley.	Linseed afterwards Barley.	Sugar-cane, afterwards Barley.	Rice, afterwards Flax.	Oord, afterwards Sugar-cane.	Oord, afterwards Linseed.	Oord, afterwards Joar.	Joar, afterwards Peas.	Rice, afterwards Mundoos.	Rise, afterwards Wheat and Gram.	Bajra, afterwards Gram.	Rice, afterwards Mussoor.	Total.	Number.
13	1	11	1	2	3	8	3	6	15	4	141	1	8	105	38	75	3	8	14	...	1	...	...	...	3,177	1
...	...	...	...	...	...	...	...	...	...	...	½	...	...	¼	...	¼	...	...	...	...	...	...	...	...	4½	2
25	...	...	...	...	...	...	...	...	...	...	...	...	...	...	...	...	...	...	...	...	...	...	...	...	4,398	3
...	...	...	...	...	...	...	...	...	...	...	...	...	...	...	...	...	...	...	...	...	...	...	...	...	6¾	4
...	...	...	...	...	...	...	...	...	...	...	...	...	...	...	...	...	...	...	...	4	...	3	30	10	3,719	5
...	...	...	...	...	...	...	...	...	...	...	...	...	...	...	...	...	...	...	...	...	...	...	...	...	8½	6
...	...	...	...	...	...	...	...	...	...	...	...	...	...	...	...	...	...	...	...	...	...	...	...	...	3,800	7
...	...	...	...	...	...	...	...	...	...	...	...	...	...	...	...	...	...	...	...	...	...	...	...	...	9	8
...	...	...	...	...	...	...	...	...	..	...	...	...	...	...	...	...	...	...	...	...	...	39	12	...	2,684	9
...	...	...	...	...	...	...	...	...	...	...	...	...	...	...	...	...	...	...	...	...	...	...	...	...	3½	10
...	...	...	...	...	...	...	...	...	...	...	...	...	...	...	...	...	...	...	...	...	...	50	25	12	4,015	11
...	...	...	...	...	...	...	...	...	...	...	...	...	...	...	...	...	...	...	...	...	...	...	...	...	5½	12
[illegible]	1	11	1	2	3	8	3	6	15	4	141	1	8	106	38	75	3	8	14	4	1	42	42	10	9,580	13
...	...	...	...	...	...	...	...	..	...	...	...	...	...	...	...	...	...	...	...		...	...	...	...	5¼	14
[illegible]	...	...	...	...	...	...	...	...	...	...	...	...	...	...	...	...	...	...	...	...	...	50	25	12	12,213	15
...	...	...	...	...	...	...	...	...	...	...	...	...	...	...	...	...	...	...	...	...	...	...	...	...	6¾	16

APPEN

Assessment Report

Crop

Khureef.

Circle.	Season.	Number.	Description.	Grand Total.	Sugar-cane. Present year.	Sugar-cane. Land prepared for next year.	Cotton.	Kucchiana.	Jowar.	Bajra.	Oord.	Most.	Rice.	Kodon.
Terai.	Year of measurement, 1276-77 F. S.,	1	Area in acres,	55,607	437	...	1,699	1,399	6,621	9,174	876	...	4,765	...
		2	Percentage, ...	100	¾	...	3	2½	12	16½	1½	...	8½	...
	1280 F S., ...	3	Area in acres,	55,607	916	...	1,694	800	4,707	7,366	914	...	470	...
		4	Percentage, ...	100	1½	...	3	1½	8½	13½	1½	...	7½	...
Bunkut-tee.	Year of measurement,	5	Area in acres,	48,147	299	...	1,080	1,356	5,111	2,861	395	...	10,851	...
		6	Percentage, ...	100	½	...	2	3½	11	6	¾	...	22	...
	1250 F. S., ...	7	Area in acres,	48,269	441	...	1,184	879	5,418	3,023	6,064	...	10,291	267
		8	Percentage, ...	100	1	...	2½	2	11½	6½	1½	...	21	½
Bhoor.	Year of measurement,	9	Area in acres,	23,431	248	...	322	474	540	7,661	221	...	1,586	...
		10	Percentage, ...	100	1	...	1½	2	2½	32½	1	...	6¾	...
	1280 F. S., ...	11	Area in acres,	23,531	391	116	321	197	525	7,925	149	89	1,504	...
		12	Percentage, ...	100	1¾	½	1½	¾	2½	34½	¾	½	6½	...
Whole Tuhseel.	Year of measurement, 1276-77 F. S.,	13	Area in acres,	127,185	984	...	3,101	3,229	12,272	19,696	1,492	...	17,202	...
		14	Percentage, ...	100	¾	...	2½	2½	9½	15½	1½	...	13½	...
	1280 F. S., ...	15	Area in acres,	127,707	1,748	116	3,199	1,876	10,650	18,314	1,727	89	15,865	267
		16	Percentage, ...	100	1¾	½	2½	1½	8½	14½	1½	½	12½	½

Land bearing two

Circle.	Season.	Number.	Description.	Kucchiana.	Rice, afterwards Sugarcane.	Rice, afterwards Linseed.
Terai.	Year of measurement, 1276-77 F. S., ...	1	Area in acres,	1,399	...	...
		2	Percentage, ...	2½	...	...
	1280 F. S., ...	3	Area in acres,	800	...	...
		4	Percentage, ...	1½	...	...
Bunkut-tee.	Year of measurement,	5	Area in acres,	1,356	...	...
		6	Percentage, ...	3½	...	...
	1280 F. S., ...	7	Area in acres,	879	...	...
		8	Percentage, ...	2	...	...
Bhoor.	Year of measurement,	9	Area in acres,	474	...	...
		10	Percentage, ...	2	...	...
	1280 F. S., ...	11	Area in acres,	197	...	...
		12	Percentage, ...	1	...	...
Whole Tuhseel.	Year of measurement, 1276 F. S., ...	13	Area in acres,	3,229	...	...
		14	Percentage, ...	2½	...	...
	1280 F. S., ...	15	Area in acres,	1,876	...	...
		16	Percentage, ...	1½	...	...

Dated Shahjehanpore, the 19th January, 1874.

DIX A.

OF TUHSEEL JELLALABAD.

Statement.

Sweet potatoes.	Lobees.	Churree or Fodder.	Miscellaneous.	Total of Khureef.	Rubbee. Wheat.	Gram.	Wheat and Barley mixed.	Barley.	Gram and Barley mixed.	Linseed.	Safflower.	Mussoor.	Poppy, *viz.*, Opium.	Urhur.	Peas.	Miscellaneous.	Total of Rubbee.	Number.
...	...	...	500	25,471	19,392	4,745	254	1,284	1,484	...	...	334	2,463	...	...	177	30,136	1
...	...	...	¾	45¾	35	8¾	½	2½	2¾	...	...	½	4½	...	...	...	54½	2
...	...	206	682	21,355	27,280	6,430	514	1,355	5,291	...	...	269	2,796	...	295	322	34,552	3
...	...	½	1½	38¼	31	11¼	1	2½	9¼	...	...	½	5¼	...	½	½	61¾	4
764	...	...	284	23,001	20,671	1,237	325	1,534	425	...	...	...	699	...	...	255	25,146	5
2	...	...	½	48	42	8	¾	3¾	1	...	...	...	1¼	...	...	¼	52	6
689	...	...	581	23,170	18,311	1,478	520	2,302	1,018	...	...	...	1,019	...	...	451	25,099	7
1½	...	...	½	48	37½	3½	1	5½	2¼	...	...	...	2¼	...	...	¾	52	8
...	...	...	148	11,200	8,735	722	435	800	374	...	...	...	1,078	...	...	87	12,231	9
...	...	...	½	47¾	37½	3¼	2	3½	1½	...	...	...	4½	...	...	¼	52¼	10
...	129	...	67	11,413	8,199	940	745	741	512	...	...	...	891	...	...	90	12,118	11
...	½	...	...	49¾	32½	4½	3½	3½	2½	...	...	...	4½	...	...	¼	50½	12
764	...	...	932	59,672	48,798	6,704	1,014	3,621	2,283	...	...	334	4,240	...	...	519	67,513	13
½	...	...	¼	47	38½	5¼	¾	3	1¾	...	...	½	3¼	...	...	¼	53	14
689	129	206	1,830	55,938	43,790	8,848	1,789	4,398	6,821	...	...	259	4,706	...	295	863	71,769	15
½	½	½	1¼	44	32	7½	1½	3¾	5¾	...	...	¼	4¼	...	½	½	56	16

Crops in the Year.

Rice, afterwards Wheat.	Rice, afterwards Wheat and Barley mixed.	Rice, afterwards Gram.	Rice, afterwards Barley.	Rice, afterwards Wheat and Gram.	Miscellaneous.	Total.	Number.
503	...	221	...	2,043	241	4,407	1
1	...	½	...	3¾	¼	8	2
...	...	1,761	...	...	1,333	6,894	3
...	...	3¾	...	...	¼	5¾	4
3,585	...	...	392	1,428	286	6,047	5
5	...	...	¾	3¼	½	12¾	6
1,197	...	876	278	442	353	4,025	7
2½	...	2	½	¾	¼	8	8
95	87	...	...	374	112	1,142	9
½	½	...	...	1½	¼	4¾	10
65	...	324	...	...	240	826	11
½	...	1¾	...	...	¼	3½	12
,183	87	221	392	3,845	639	11,596	13
3½	½	¼	¾	3	½	9	14
,262	...	2,961	278	442	926	8,745	15
¾	...	2½	½	½	½	6¼	16

APPEN

ASSESSMENT REPORT OF

Crop Statements for each Assessment Circle, each

Pergunnah.	Circle.			Total cultivated area.	Sugar-cane. Actual crop of the year.	Sugar-cane. Land fallow for crop of succeeding year (pundree).	Garden crops.	Cotton.	Jowar.	Bajra.	Rice.	Mash or Oorud.
						CROPS OF THE AUTUMN						
TILHUR, ...	Terai, ...	1	Acres, ...	25,015	2,511	2,109	367	992	1,493	1,931	3,078	118
		2	Percentage, ...	100	10	8½	1½	4	6	7¾	12¼	½
	Bhoor, ...	3	Acres, ...	36,220	1,703	1,277	279	336	807	10,829	1,460	181
		4	Percentage, ...	100	4¾	3½	¾	1	2¼	30	4	½
	Total, Pergunnah, ...	5	Acres, ...	61,235	4,214	3,386	646	1,328	2,300	12,760	4,538	299
		6	Percentage, ...	100	6¾	5½	1	2¼	3¾	20¾	7½	½
KUTTRA, ...	Kuttra, ...	7	Acres, ...	5,107	330	279	77	168	158	921	458	31
		8	Percentage, ...	100	6½	5½	1½	3¼	3¼	18	9	¾
NIGOHEE, ...	1st or Doomut,	9	Acres, ...	32,153	2,367	1,837	298	1,217	1,638	5,266	2,793	146
		10	Percentage, ...	100	7½	6	1	3¾	5	16¼	8½	½
	2nd or Khaimooa, ...	11	Acres, ...	13,377	662	443	161	550	619	2,599	2,328	54
		12	Percentage, ...	100	5	3¼	1¼	4	4¾	19½	17½	½
	Total, Pergunnah, ...	13	Acres, ...	45,530	3,029	2,230	459	1,767	2,257	7,865	5,121	200
		14	Percentage, ...	100	6¾	5	1	3¾	5	17¼	11½	½
KHERA BUJHERA, ...	Ramgunga or Terai, ...	15	Acres, ...	22,085	629	67	329	505	2,398	6,553	883	462
		16	Percentage, ...	100	2¾	¼	1½	2¼	11	29½	4	2
	Bygool or Bunkuttee,	17	Acres, ...	14,086	784	299	171	445	1,185	2,427	1,415	148
		18	Percentage, ...	100	5½	2¼	1¼	3¼	8½	17¼	10	1
	Bhoor, ...	19	Acres, ...	6,301	304	121	59	50	65	1,946	331	20
		20	Percentage, ...	100	4¾	2	1	¾	1	3½	5	½
	Total, Pergunnah, ...	21	Acres, ...	42,472	1,717	487	559	1,000	3,648	10,946	2,629	630
		22	Percentage, ...	100	4	1¼	1¼	2¼	8½	25¾	6¼	1½
JELLALPORE, ...	Gurra, ...	23	Acres, ...	26,443	2,148	1,706	265	1,432	1,723	4,270	2,534	144
		24	Percentage, ...	100	8½	6½	1	5	6½	16¼	9½	½
	Byghool, ...	25	Acres, ...	6,969	382	244	81	222	194	2,288	519	28
		26	Percentage, ...	100	5½	3½	½	3¼	2¾	32¾	7½	½
	Total, Pergunnah, ...	27	Acres, ...	33,412	2,530	1,950	296	1,654	1,917	6,558	3,053	172
		28	Percentage, ...	100	7½	6	1	5	6	19½	9	
WHOLE	TUHSEEL, ...	29	Acres, ...	187,756	11,820	8,382	2,037	5,912	10,280	39,030	15,799	1,332
		30	Percentage, ...	100	6½	4½	1	3¼	5½	21	8½	

DIX A.

TUHSEEL TILHUR.

Pergunnah, and the entire Tuhseel (para. 49 of Report).

(KHUREEF) HARVEST.

Moat.	Kodon.	Indigo.	Samakh.	Mundooa.	Flat and Hemp.	Lahee.	Til.	Kakoon.	Koondher rice.	Maize.	Lobia.	Moong.	Guar Moong.	Turmeric.	Total Khureef.	
43	13	65	1	...	38	1	12	1	...	5	...	2	1	...	12,781	1
¼	...	½	...	...	¼	...	...	...	...	...	...	...	...	...	51¼	2
215	7	222	1	3	4	2	17	2	83	...	...	...	...	...	17,428	3
½	...	½	...	...	...	...	...	...	¼	...	...	...	...	...	48	4
258	20	287	2	3	42	3	29	3	83	5	...	2	1	...	30,209	5
½	...	½	...	...	...	...	...	...	¼	...	...	...	...	...	49¼	6
17	8	44	...	1	...	...	4	...	...	...	...	2	...	...	2,493	7
¼	½	¾	...	...	...	...	...	...	...	...	...	...	...	...	48¾	8
35	129	13	4	4	60	2	2	...	...	...	1	...	...	...	15,813	9
¼	½	...	...	...	¼	...	...	...	...	...	...	...	...	...	49¼	10
100	59	9	...	6	6	2	5	...	...	...	...	...	...	...	7,605	11
¾	½	...	...	...	...	...	...	...	...	...	...	...	...	...	56¾	12
135	188	22	4	10	66	4	7	...	...	...	1	...	...	...	23,418	13
½	½	...	...	...	...	...	...	...	...	...	...	...	...	...	51½	14
91	...	6	...	31	5	1	56	1	33	...	...	3	1	...	12,034	15
½	...	...	...	¼	...	...	¼	...	¼	...	...	...	...	...	54½	16
92	8	249	...	31	...	2	3	3	89	...	...	10	1	2	7,364	17
¾	...	1¾	...	¼	...	...	...	...	¾	...	...	...	...	...	52¼	18
76	...	28	...	4	...	...	2	...	...	...	...	5	8	...	3,019	19
1¼	...	½	...	...	...	...	...	...	...	...	...	...	...	...	48	20
259	8	283	...	66	5	8	61	4	122	...	...	18	10	2	22,437	21
½	...	¾	...	½	...	...	¼	...	¼	...	...	...	...	...	52¾	22
96	144	185	9	9	31	...	31	2	3	7	...	9	29	...	14,693	23
...	½	¾	...	...	¼	...	¼	...	...	...	...	...	½	...	55½	24
16	21	52	5	...	12	...	9	1	...	...	...	1	1	...	4,026	25
¼	¼	¾	...	...	¼	...	...	...	...	...	...	...	...	...	57¾	26
42	165	237	14	2	43	...	40	3	3	7	...	3	30	...	18,719	27
...	½	¾	...	...	¼	...	...	...	...	...	...	...	...	...	56	28
711	389	873	20	82	156	10	141	10	208	12	1	28	41	2	97,276	29
½	¼	½	...	...	...	...	...	...	...	...	...	...	...	...	51¾	30

APPEN

ASSESSMENT REPORT OF

Crop Statements for each Assessment Circle, each

Pergunnah.	Circle.			Crops of the					
				Wheat.	Gram.	Barley.	Goojai or wheat and barley mixed.	Bijra or gram and barley mixed.	Linseed.
TILHUR, ...	Terai, ...	1	Acres, ...	8,768	1,648	485	51	149	28
		2	Percentage, ...	36	6¾	2	½	½	...
	Bhoor, ...	3	Acres, ...	13,379	2,174	763	272	131	20
		4	Percentage, ...	37	6	2	¾	½	...
	Total Pergunnah, ...	5	Acres, ...	22,147	3,822	1,248	323	280	48
		6	Percentage, ...	36¼	6½	2	½	½	...
KUTTRA, ...	Kuttra, ...	7	Acres, ...	1,718	354	133	42	39	7
		8	Percentage, ...	34½	7	2½	¾	¾	...
NIGOHEE, ...	1st or Doomut, ...	9	Acres, ...	10,132	2,842	610	139	62	541
		10	Percentage, ...	31½	8½	2	½	¼	1¾
	2nd or Khaimooa, ...	11	Acres, ...	3,960	795	170	25	28	227
		12	Percentage, ...	29½	6	1½	¼	¼	1¾
	Total Pergunnah, ...	13	Acres, ...	14,092	3,637	780	87	167	768
		14	Percentage, ...	31	8	1¾	¼	¼	1¾
KHERA BUJHERA,	Ramgunga or Terai, ...	15	Acres, ...	7,331	1,328	378	10	367	...
		16	Percentage, ...	33¼	6	1¾	...	1¾	...
	Bygool or Bunkuttee,	17	Acres, ...	4,809	910	453	50	78	7
		18	Percentage, ...	34½	6½	3¼	½	½	...
	Bhoor, ...	19	Acres, ...	2,344	381	139	12	1	3
		20	Percentage, ...	37½	6	2¼	¼	...	...
	Total Pergunnah, ...	21	Acres, ...	14,484	2,619	970	72	446	10
		22	Percentage, ...	34½	6¼	2¼	¼	1	...
JELALPORE, ...	Gurra, ...	23	Acres, ...	7,727	1,845	452	142	234	197
		24	Percentage, ...	29½	7	1¾	½	1	¾
	Byghool, ...	25	Acres, ...	2,018	395	110	48	17	33
		26	Percentage, ...	29	5¾	1½	¾	¼	½
	Total Pergunnah, ...	27	Acres, ...	9,745	2,240	562	190	251	230
		28	Percentage, ...	29½	6¾	1¾	½	¾	¾
WHOLE	TUHSEEL, ...	29	Acres, ...	62,186	12,672	3,693	714	1,183	1,063
		30	Percentage, ...	33¼	6¾	2	½	¾	½

Dated Shahjehanpore, the 31st January, 1874.

DIX A.

TUHSEEL TILHUR.

Pergunnah, and the entire Tuhseel (para. 49 of Report)—(concluded.)

SPRING (RUBBEE) HARVEST.

Masoor.	Urhur.	Peas.	Poppy.	Oats.	Surson.	Kussumba (safflower.)	Aksa.	Chaina.	Melons.	Total rubbee.	Area producing two crops (do-fuslee).	
168	818	52	40	15	10	...	1	...	I	12,234	1,753	1
½	3½	½	½	...	...	...	...	...	...	49¾	7	2
25	1,777	16	222	7	1	1	3	1	...	18,792	1,347	3
...	5	...	¾	...	...	...	...	...	...	52	3¼	4
193	2,595	68	262	22	11	1	4	1	1	31,026	3,100	5
½	4¼	...	½	...	...	...	...	...	...	50¾	5	6
6	275	21	7	3	1	...	3	...	5	2,614	205	7
...	5½	½	...	...	...	...	...	...	...	51½	3½	8
56	1,764	8	116	9	29	18	...	...	14	16,340	2,102	9
½	5½	...	½	...	...	...	...	...	...	50¾	5¼	10
16	458	1	83	...	7	2	...	...	...	5,772	590	11
...	3½	...	¾	...	...	...	...	...	...	43¼	3¾	12
72	2,222	9	199	9	36	20	...	...	14	22,112	2,692	13
...	5	...	½	...	...	...	...	...	...	48½	5½	14
151	265	42	62	25	2	14	26	9	21	10,031	923	15
¾	1¼	¼	¼	...	...	...	¼	...	...	45½	3¾	16
81	362	24	14	23	1	1	...	1	8	6,722	585	17
½	1¾	¼	...	¼	...	...	...	...	...	47¾	3¼	18
24	339	12	3	2	4	...	...	18	...	3,282	151	19
½	5¼	¼	...	...	...	...	...	¼	...	52	2	20
256	866	78	79	50	7	15	26	28	29	20,035	1,659	21
½	2	¼	¼	¼	...	...	¼	...	...	47½	3½	22
112	903	7	42	16	5	...	14	...	54	11,750	2,659	23
½	3¼	...	¼	...	...	...	...	...	¼	44½	9½	24
16	299	1	6	...	...	...	...	...	...	2,943	249	25
¼	4¼	...	...	...	...	...	...	...	...	42¼	3¼	26
128	1,202	8	48	16	5	...	14	...	54	14,693	2,908	27
½	3½	...	...	...	...	...	...	...	½	44	8½	28
655	7,160	184	595	100	60	36	47	28	103	90,480	10,564	29
½	3¾	...	¼	...	...	...	...	...	...	48¼	5½	30

APPEN

ASSESSMENT REPORT OF

Crop Statement of land produc

Pergunnah.	Circle.	Number.		Kuchhiana.	Rice, afterwards wheat.	Rice, afterwards barley.	Rice, afterwards pundree.	Rice, afterwards gram.	Rice, afterwards linseed.	Rice, afterwards mussoor.	Rice, afterwards various crops, chiefly wheat, barley, gram, and peas, 2 or 3 mixed.	Bajra, afterwards various crops, chiefly indigo, linseed, pundree, gram, or melons.
TILHUR, ...	Terai, ...	1	Acres, ...	367	89	25	61	777	13	135	81	29
		2	Percentage,...	1½	½	¼	¼	3¼	...	½	¼	...
	Bhoor, ...	3	Acres, ...	279	50	66	11	217	9	14	30	414
		4	Percentage,...	¾	¼	¼	...	¾	...	...	...	¾
	Total Pergunnah,	5	Acres, ...	646	139	91	72	994	22	149	111	443
		6	Percentage,...	1	¼	¼	...	2	...	¼	¼	¾
KUTTRA, ...	Kuttra, ...	7	Acres, ...	77	9	5	...	76	4	...	5	28
		8	Percentage,...	1½	¼	...	...	1½	...	...	...	...
NIGOHEE, ...	1st or Domut, ...	9	Acres, ...	298	151	300	27	303	417	20	84	138
		10	Percentage,...	1	½	1	...	1	1¼	...	...	½
	2nd or Khaimoos,	11	Acres, ...	161	12	10	10	105	219	1	25	13
		12	Percentage,...	1¼	...	...	...	¾	1¾	...	...	...
	Total Pergunnah,	13	Acres, ...	459	163	310	37	408	636	21	109	151
		14	Percentage,...	1	½	¾	...	1	1½	...	...	½
KHERA BUJHERA, ...	Ramgunga or Terai,	15	Acres, ...	329	15	26	...	168	2	...	18	230
		16	Percentage,...	1½	...	¼	...	¾	...	...	...	1
	Bygool or Bunkuttee.	17	Acres, ...	171	20	8	16	54	8	1	16	137
		18	Percentage,...	1¼	¼	...	¼	½	...	...	...	1
	Bhoor, ...	19	Acres, ...	59	6	2	18	34	...	...	4	12
		20	Percentage,...	1	...	...	¼	½	...	...	...	...
	Total Pergunnah,	21	Acres, ...	559	41	36	29	256	10	1	38	379
		22	Percentage,...	1¼	¼	¼	...	¾	...	...	...	¾
JELALPORE, ...	Gurra, ...	23	Acres, ...	265	56	44	32	567	249	27	67	694
		24	Percentage,...	1	¼	¼	¼	2	1	¼	¼	2¼
	Bygool, ...	25	Acres, ...	31	15	4	1	62	42	3	7	56
		26	Percentage,...	½	¼	...	...	1	¾	...	...	¾
	Total Pergunnah,	27	Acres, ...	296	71	48	33	629	291	30	74	660
		28	Percentage,...	1	¼	¼	...	2	1	...	¼	2
TOTAL	TUHSEEL, ...	29	Acres, ...	2,037	423	490	171	2,363	963	201	337	1,661
		30	Percentage,...	1½	¼	¼	...	1½	½	¼	...	¾

DIX A.

TUHSEEL TILHUR.

ing two crops in the year.

Jowar, afterwards gram.	Jowar, afterwards pundree.	Jowar, afterwards various crops, chiefly indigo, mussoor, wheat, or gram.	Jowar, afterwards linseed.	Indigo, afterwards wheat.	Indigo, afterwards various crops, chiefly gram or barley.	Cotton, afterwards pundree.	Cotton, afterwards other crops, chiefly linseed, gram, or indigo.	Maize, afterwards wheat, barley, or pundree.	Oorud, afterwards gram, pundree, or indigo.	Sugar-cane, afterwards indigo.	Wheat, afterwards koonder or indigo.	Miscellaneous.	Total.	Number.
31	37	27	...	12	7	3	13	3	31	...	...	12	1,753	1
¼	¼	...	...	...	...	...	...	...	...	...	...	...	7	2
5	8	16	...	133	38	2	6	...	5	...	21	18	1,347	3
...	...	...	...	½	...	...	...	...	...	...	...	...	3¼	4
36	45	43	...	150	45	5	19	3	36	...	21	30	3,100	5
...	...	...	...	¼	...	...	...	...	...	...	...	...	5	6
1	...	...	...	...	...	...	...	...	...	...	...	...	205	7
...	...	...	...	...	...	...	...	...	...	...	...	...	3¼	8
89	10	54	26	5	1	1	13	...	45	...	...	120	2,102	9
...	...	...	...	...	...	...	...	...	...	...	...	...	5¼	10
...	...	12	1	...	...	5	...	...	6	...	...	10	590	11
...	...	...	...	...	...	...	...	...	...	...	...	...	3¾	12
89	10	66	27	5	1	6	13	...	51	...	...	130	2,692	13
...	...	...	...	...	...	...	...	...	...	...	...	...	5¼	14
70	10	22	...	...	...	3	4	...	3	...	...	23	923	15
¼	...	...	...	...	...	...	...	...	...	...	...	...	3¾	16
6	3	33	...	11	38	11	43	...	1	...	...	8	585	17
...	...	...	...	...	...	...	...	...	...	...	...	...	3¼	18
12	1	1	...	4	1	1	1	...	...	...	...	...	151	19
½	...	...	...	...	...	...	...	...	...	...	...	...	2	20
88	14	56	...	15	39	15	43	...	4	...	...	31	1,659	21
½	...	...	...	...	...	...	...	...	...	...	...	...	3½	22
148	76	168	79	5	27	27	92	5	2	59	2	58	2,659	23
½	¼	½	¼	...	...	⅛	...	...	...	¼	...	...	9½	24
...	2	10	1	2	4	...	6	...	...	1	...	2	249	25
...	...	...	...	...	...	...	...	...	...	...	...	...	3¼	26
148	78	178	80	7	31	27	98	5	2	60	2	60	2,908	27
½	¼	¼	¼	...	...	...	¼	...	...	¼	...	...	8¼	28
362	147	343	107	177	116	53	178	8	93	60	23	251	10,564	29
½	...	¼	...	...	...	...	...	...	...	...	...	...	5½	30

APPEN

ASSESSMENT REPORT OF

Crop

Name of Circle.	Description.	Number.	Grand Total.	Sugar-cane. Present year.	Sugar-cane. Land prepared for next year.	Khureef. Cotton.	Kucchiana.	Jowar.	Bajra.	Moat.	Rice.
TIROWNA, ...	Area in Acres, ...	1	46,217	4,025	2,936	79	274	158	7,035	553	6,871
	Percentage, ...	2	100	8¾	6½	¼	¾	¼	15	1½	15
SUNWAT, ...	Area in Acres, ...	3	38,030	1,635	1,253	247	219	391	12,391	756	2,476
	Percentage, ...	4	100	4½	3¼	¾	½	1	32½	2	6½
POWAYN, ...	Area in acres, ...	5	22,582	2,529	2,346	609	205	1,471	1,794	159	1,751
	Percentage, ...	6	100	11	10½	2¾	1	6½	8	¾	7¾
GOLA, ...	Area in acres, ...	7	15,898	1,210	1,145	534	135	857	3,217	55	461
	Percentage, ...	8	100	7¾	7½	3½	¾	5¾	20½	¼	3
NAHIL, ...	Area in acres, ...	9	24,590	2,522	2,379	508	176	834	2,486	176	2,167
	Percentage, ...	10	100	10¼	9¾	2½	½	3½	10	¾	8¾
TOTAL PERGUNNAH, POWAYN,	Area in acres, ...	11	147,317	11,921	10,059	1,977	1,009	3,711	26,923	1,699	13,726
	Percentage, ...	12	100	8½	7	1½	¾	2½	18¼	1	9¼
BURRAGAON, ...	Area in acres, ...	13	36,458	3,480	3,158	1,507	296	2,921	4,249	...	1,574
	Percentage, ...	14	100	9½	8¾	4½	¾	8	11¾	...	4¼
KHOTAR, 1ST CIRCLE,	Area in acres, ...	15	18,549	1,648	1,140	121	124	124	1,403	339	3,094
	Percentage, ...	16	100	9	6	¾	¾	¾	7½	1¾	16¾
KHOTAR, 2ND CIRCLE, ...	Area in acres, ...	17	45,528	1,196	649	200	167	793	11,661	1,362	5,017
	Percentage, ...	18	100	2¾	1½	½	¼	1¾	25¼	3	11
WHOLE TUHSEEL, ...	Area in acres, ...	19	247,852	18,245	15,006	3,805	1,596	7,549	44,236	3,400	23,411
	Percentage, ...	20	100	7½	6	1½	¾	3	17¾	1½	9½

Land bearing two

Name of Circle.	Description.	Number.	Kucchiana.	Rice, afterwards sugar-cane.	Rice, afterwards linseed.
TIROWNA, ...	Area in acres, ...	1	274	229	239
	Percentage, ...	2	¾	½	¾
SUNWAT, ...	Area in acres, ...	3	219	120	116
	Percentage, ...	4	½	¼	¼
POWAYN, ...	Area in acres, ...	5	205	22	41
	Percentage, ...	6	1	...	¼
GOLA, ...	Area in acres, ...	7	135	4	33
	Percentage, ...	8	¾	...	¼
NAHIL, ...	Area in acres, ...	9	176	23	87
	Percentage, ...	10	¾	...	½
TOTAL, PERGUNNAH POWAYN, ...	Area in acres, ...	11	1,009	398	516
	Percentage, ...	12	¾	...	½
BURRAGAON, ...	Area in acres, ...	13	296	...	58
	Percentage, ...	14	¾	...	¼
KHOTAR, 1ST CIRCLE, ...	Area in acres, ...	15	124	316	221
	Percentage, ...	16	¾	1¾	1¼
KHOTAR, 2ND CIRCLE, ...	Area in acres, ...	17	167	30	439
	Percentage, ...	18	¼	...	1
WHOLE TUHSEEL, ...	Area in acres, ...	19	1,596	744	1,243
	Percentage, ...	20	¾	¼	½

Dated Shahjehanpore, the 29th May, 1874.

DIX A.

TUHSEEL POWAYN.

Statement.

				Rubbee.						
Kodon.	Oord.	Miscellaneous.	Total of Khureef.	Wheat.	Gram.	Wheat and Barley mixed.	Barley.	Urhur.	Miscellaneous.	Total of Rubbee.
1,440 3¼	3,678 8¼	172 ¼	27,221 59	13,994 30¼	2,590 5½	975 2	991 2	84 ¼	362 ¾	18,996 41
398 1	1,938 5	439 1	22,143 58	6,558 18	1,888 4¾	3,305 8½	3,625 9¾	73 ...	438 1	15,887 42
517 2¼	75 ¼	102 ½	11,558 51	7,493 33¼	2,374 10½	210 1	290 1¼	404 1¾	253 1¼	11,024 49
140 1	126 ¾	26 ...	7,906 50	5,715 36	1,600 10	41 ¼	202 1½	218 1¼	216 1¼	7,992 50
552 2¼	178 ¾	46 ¼	12,019 49	8,151 33½	2,811 11¼	453 1¾	669 2¾	153 ¾	334 1¼	12,571 51
3,047 2	5,990 4	785 ½	80,847 65	41,911 28½	11,263 7¾	4,984 3¼	5,777 4	932 ½	1,603 1	66,470 45
207 ½	231 ¾	135 ¼	17,758 48¾	12,582 34½	3,900 10¾	384 ¾	824 2¼	304 1	786 2	18,700 51¼
938 5	1,077 5¾	43 ...	10,051 54	6,792 36¾	986 5¼	234 1¼	293 1¾	62 ¼	131 ¾	8,498 46
2,433 5¼	3,778 8¼	512 1¼	27,768 61	11,438 25¼	1,730 3¾	2,940 6½	1,262 2¾	92 ¼	298 ½	17,780 39
6,625 2¾	11,076 4½	1,475 ½	136,424 55	72,723 29½	17,879 7¼	8,442 3½	8,156 3¼	1,410 ½	2,818 1	111,428 48

Crops in the year.

Rice, afterwards wheat.	Rice, afterwards wheat and barley mixed.	Rice, afterwards gram.	Miscellaneous.	Total.
222 ¼	167 ¼	2,195 4¾	2,837 6	6,163 13¼
30 ...	22 ...	832 2¼	466 1¼	1,805 4½
21 ...	87 ½	923 4	598 2½	1,897 8¼
4 ...	7 ...	73 ½	199 1½	455 2¾
27 ...	21 ...	1,048 4½	576 2½	1,958 8
304 ...	304 ...	5,071 3¾	4,676 3¼	12,278 8¼
... ...	56 ¼	491 1¼	729 2	1,623 4½
53 ¼	68 ¼	1,635 8¾	875 4¼	3,292 17½
53 ...	174 ¼	1,113 2½	852 2¾	2,828 6
410 ¼	602 ¼	8,310 3¼	7,125 2¾	2,004 8

APPENDIX B.

ASSESSMENT REPORT OF TUHSEEL SHAHJEHANPORE.—(para. 17).

Statement showing the rent-rate per acre on the area cultivated by cultivators of different castes with and without right of occupancy.

Pergunnah.	BRAHMANS — With rights of occupancy. Area in acres.	Incidence per acre. Rs. a. p.	BRAHMANS — Tenants-at-will. Area in acres.	Incidence per acre. Rs. a. p.	THAKOORS — With rights of occupancy. Area in acres.	Incidence per acre. Rs. a. p.	THAKOORS — Tenants-at-will. Area in acres.	Incidence per acre. Rs. a. p.	PATHANS AND SYUDS — With rights of occupancy. Area in acres.	Incidence per acre. Rs. a. p.	PATHANS AND SYUDS — Tenants-at-will. Area in acres.	Incidence per acre. Rs. a. p.	AHEERS — With rights of occupancy. Area in acres.	Incidence per acre. Rs. a. p.	AHEERS — Tenants-at-will. Area in acres.	Incidence per acre. Rs. a. p.
Shahjehanpore, 40 villages.	390	3 0 0	122	2 15 8	446	2 5 10	107	2 13 7	707	3 0 5	239	2 13 7	570	2 10 7	186	2 10 6
Jumour, 30 villages,	165	2 12 3	28	2 9 6	1,164	3 0 6	187	3 3 3	104	2 15 1	92	2 4 8	87	3 3 1	50	5 0 10
Kant, 50 villages,	947	2 1 6	178	2 3 10	1,622	2 4 8	391	2 5 0	47	1 10 6	19	2 3 11	1,457	1 15 4	185	2 5 10
Total, ...	1,453	2 5 11	328	2 8 9	3,232	2 9 10	685	2 9 11	858	2 15 1	350	2 10 6	2,114	2 3 3	421	2 11 8

Pergunnah.	OTHER MUSULMANS — With rights of occupancy. Area in acres.	Incidence per acre. Rs. a. p.	OTHER MUSULMANS — Tenants-at-will. Area in acres.	Incidence per acre. Rs. a. p.	KHARS AND KACHHES — With rights of occupancy. Area in acres.	Incidence per acre. Rs. a. p.	KHARS AND KACHHES — Tenants-at-will. Area in acres.	Incidence per acre. Rs. a. p.	MISCELLANEOUS — With rights of occupancy. Area in acres.	Incidence per acre. Rs. a. p.	MISCELLANEOUS — Tenants-at-will. Area in acres.	Incidence per acre. Rs. a. p.	GRAND TOTAL OF ALL CASTES OF CULTIVATORS — With rights of occupancy. Area in acres.	Incidence per acre. Rs. a. p.	GRAND TOTAL — Tenants-at-will. Area in acres.	Incidence per acre. Rs. a. p.
Shahjehanpore, 40 villages.	90	2 9 3	84	2 13 6	1,336	3 7 3	831	3 3 4	723	2 13 7	459	3 1 2	4,192	2 15 11	3,028	3 0 3
Jumour, 30 villages,	37	3 3 10	15	2 3 7	3,518	3 3 9	564	2 14 9	637	3 3 4	199	2 11 10	4,812	3 3 7	1,185	2 14 7
Kant, 50 villages,	39	2 12 6	31	2 7 7	1,769	2 7 10	677	2 6 1	1,370	2 5 5	383	2 5 9	7,341	3 4 4	1,864	2 6 5
Total, ...	156	2 11 6	130	2 10 10	6,723	3 1 1	2,072	2 13 6	2,730	2 10 7	1,041	2 11 9	16,345	2 11 7	5,097	2 11 10

Dated Shahjehanpore, the 30th December, 1873.

APPENDIX B.

ASSESSMENT REPORT OF TUHSEEL JELLALABAD.—(para. 17).

Statement showing the rent-rate per acre on the area cultivated by Cultivators of different castes with and without right of occupancy.

1	2	3				4				5				6			
		BRAHMINS.				THAKOORS.				PATHANS AND SYUDS.				AHEERS.			
		With rights of occupancy.		Tenants-at-will.		With rights of occupancy.		Tenants-at-will.		With rights of occupancy.		Tenants-at-will.		With rights of occupancy.		Tenants-at-will.	
Pergunnah.	No. of villages abstracted.	Area in acres.	Incidence per acre.	Area in acres.	Incidence per acre.	Area in acres.	Incidence per acre.	Area in acres.	Incidence per acre.	Area in acres.	Incidence per acre.	Area in acres.	Incidence per acre.	Area in acres.	Incidence per acre.	Area in acres.	Incidence per acre.
			Rs.a.p.		Rs.a.p.		Rs.a.p.		Rs.a.p.		Rs.a.p.		Rs.a.p.		Rs.a.p.		Rs.a.p
Jellalabad, ...	40	893	3 0 3	116	2 14 8	1,035	2 11 1	212	3 3 10	259	2 5 2	67	2 5 9	2,111	2 13 5	533	2 13 9

1	2	7				8				9				10			
		OTHER MOOSULMANS.				KISANS, KACHEES AND CHUMARS.				MISCELLANEOUS.				GRAND TOTAL OF ALL CASTES OF CULTIVATORS.			
		With rights of occupancy.		Tenants-at-will.		With rights of occupancy.		Tenants-at-will.		With rights of occupancy.		Tenants-at-will.		With rights of occupancy.		Tenants-at-will.	
Pergunnah.	No. of villages abstracted.	Area in acres.	Incidence per acre.	Area in acres.	Incidence per acre.	Area in acres.	Incidence per acre.	Area in acres.	Incidence per acre.	Area in acres.	Incidence per acre.	Area in acres.	Incidence per acre.	Area in acres.	Incidence per acre.	Area in acres.	Incidence per acre.
			Rs.a.p		Rs.a.p		Rs.a.p.		Rs.a.p.		Rs.a.p.		Rs.a.p.		Rs.a.p.		Rs.a.p
Jellalabad, ...	40	107	2 14 1	65	3 3 4	2,818	3 5 6	692	3 4 2	2,541	3 0 10	688	3 6 6	9,744	3 0 11	2,374	3 2 8

The 19th January, 1874.

APPENDIX C.

ASSESSMENT REPORT OF TUHSEEL SHAHJEHANPORE.

Tabular statement of soils, sanctioned average rent-rates, and deduced rentals.

Pergunnah.	GOWHANEE.					1ST DOMUT.					2ND DOMUT.				
	Irrigated.	Not Irrigated.	Total.	Rate.	Value assumed at average rent-rates.	Irrigated.	Not Irrigated.	Total.	Rate.	Value assumed at average rent-rates.	Irrigated.	Not Irrigated.	Total.	Rate.	Value assumed at average rent-rates.
				Rs.a.p.	Rs. a. p.				Rs.a.p.	Rs. a. p.				Rs.a.p.	Rs. a. p.
Shahjehanpore,	891	193	1,084	8 0 0	8,672 0 0	25,009	17,375	42,384	3 12 0	1,58,940 0 0	5,111	10,268	15,379	3 0 0	46,137 0 0
Jumour, ...	506	51	557	7 8 0	4,177 8 0	15,141	7,311	22,452	3 12 0	84,195 0 0	2,372	2,478	4,850	3 0 0	14,550 0 0
Kant, ...	729	75	803	7 0 0	5,621 0 0	11,631	10,888	22,519	3 4 0	73,186 12 0	7,878	14,907	22,785	2 8 0	56,962 8 0
Total,	2,126	318	2,444	...	18,470 8 0	51,781	35,574	87,355	...	3,16,321 12 0	15,361	27,653	43,014	...	1,17,649 8 0
Percentages of soils to total area.	...	...	1·19	...	...	··	...	48·82	...	...	...	...	24·04	...	...

Pergunnah.	MUTTAR.					BHOOR.					TOTAL AREA.			
	Irrigated.	Not Irrigated.	Total.	Rate.	Value assumed at average rent-rates.	Irrigated.	Not Irrigated.	Total.	Rate.	Value assumed at average rent-rate.	Irrigated.	Not Irrigated.	Total.	Value assumed at average rent-rates.
				Rs.a.p.	Rs. a. p.				Rs. a p	Rs. a. p.				Rs. a p
Shahjehanpore,	1,436	2,806	4,242	2 12 0	11,665 8 0	127	1,241	1,368	2 4 0	3,078 0 0	32,574	31,883	64,457	2,26,492 8 0
Jumour, ...	4,132	11,185	15,317	2 8 0	38,292 8 0	11	214	225	2 4 0	506 4 0	22,162	21,239	43,401	1,41,721 4 0
Kant, ...	1,873	5,106	6,979	2 12 0	19,192 4 0	3,614	14,390	18,004	2 0 0	36,008 0 0	25,735	45,365	71,090	1,90,970 8 0
Total, ...	7,441	19,097	26,538	...	69,150 4 0	3,752	15,845	19,567	...	39,592 4 0	80,461	98,487	178,948	5,61,184 4 0
Percentages of soils to total area. ...	...	...	14·83	...	...	...	...	10·95	...	{ Percentage of irrigated and unirrigated.	45·52	54·48	...	...

The 30th December, 1873.

Name of Circle.	Gowhanee.					1st Domut.					2nd Domut		
	Irrigated.	Not Irrigated.	Total.	Rate.	Value assumed at average rent-rates.	Irrigated.	Not irrigated.	Total.	Rate.	Value assumed at average rent-rates.	Irrigated.	Not Irrigated.	Total.
				Rs. a. p.	Rs. a. p.				Rs. a. p.	Rs. a. p.			
Terai, ...	1,008	249	1,257	6 8 0	8,170 8 0	9,247	18,226	27,473	4 4 0	1,16,760 4 0	2,413	14,352	16,765
Bunkuttee, ...	552	35	587	6 8 0	3,815 8 0	13,373	7,405	20,778	3 12 0	77,917 8 0	3,146	4,880	8,026
Bhoor, ...	346	74	420	6 8 0	2,730 0 0	1,433	1,686	3,119	3 10 0	11,306 6 0	2,568	5,129	7,697
Total, ...	1,906	358	2,264	...	14,716 0 0	24,053	27,317	51,370	...	2,50,984 2 0	8,127	24,361	32,488

Dated Shahjehanpore, the 19th January, 1874.

Pergunnah.	Circle.	Gowhanee.					1st Domut.					Mutyar.				
		Irrigated.	Not Irrigated.	Total.	Sanctioned average circle rent-rate.	Value at average circle rate.	Irrigated.	Not Irrigated.	Total.	Sanctioned average circle rent-rate.	Value at average circle rate.	Irrigated.	Not Irrigated.	Total.	Sanctioned average circle rent-rate.	Value at average circle rate.
Tilhur, {	Terai, ...	603	128	731	7 0	5,117 0	11,065	4,887	15,952	5 0	79,760 0	989	2,774	3,763	4 6	15,052
	Bhoor, ...	328	124	452	6 0	2,712 0	6,446	4,385	10,831	3 4	35,201 0	542	1,287	1,829	2 1	5,030
	Total pergunnah, ...	931	252	1,183	...	7,829 0	17,511	9,272	26,783	...	1,14,961 0	1,531	4,061	5,592	...	20,082
Kuttra, ... {	Kuttra, ...	149	30	179	6 8	1,065 8	1,384	829	2,213	3 8	7,745 8	104	276	380	3 0	1,140
Negohee, {	1st or Domut, ...	264	66	330	6 8	2,145 0	9,246	10,906	20,152	3 8	70,582 0	591	2,929	3,520	3 0	10,560
	2nd or Khaimooa,...	126	17	143	6 0	858 0	2,847	2,832	5,679	3 4	18,457 0	623	1,629	2,252	3 12	6,193
	Total pergunnah, ...	390	83	473	...	3,003 0	12,093	13,738	25,831	..	88,989 0	1,214	4,558	5,772	...	16,753
Khera Buj- { hera, {	Ramgunga or Terai,	315	261	576	7 0	4,032 0	2,861	11,448	14,329	4 4	60,892 0	321	2,321	2,642	2 12	9,908
	Bygool or Bunkut- tee.	152	42	194	6 0	1,164 0	5,157	3,585	8,742	3 4	27,226 0	1,191	1,916	3,107	2 8	8,557
	Bhoor, ...	59	23	82	6 0	492 0	790	769	1,559	3 0	4,677 0	85	367	452	2 8	1,130
	Total pergunnah, ...	526	326	852	...	5,688 0	8,828	15,802	24,630	...	92,795 0	1,597	4,604	6,201	...	19,595
Jelalpore, {	Gurra, ...	150	34	184	7 0	1,288 0	8,823	9,064	17,887	4 8	1,492 0	403	1,947	2,330	3 8	8,22.
	Bygool, ...	23	2	25	6 8	163 0	1,175	882	2,057	3 12	7,714 0	32	278	310	2 14	89.
	Total pergunnah, ...	173	36	209	...	1,451 0	9,998	9,946	19,944	...	9,206 0	435	2,225	2,660	...	9,11.
	Total Tuhseel, ...	2,169	727	2,896	...	19,034 8	49,814	49,587	99,401	...	3,13,696 8	4,881	15,724	20,605	...	65,68.

DIX C.

OF TUHSEEL JELLALABAD.

sanctioned average rent-rates, and deduced rentals.

		Mutyar.						Bhoor.					Total area.			
Rate.	Value assumed at average rent-rates.	Irrigated.	Not Irrigated.	Total.	Rate.	Value assumed at average rent-rates.	Irrigated.	Not Irrigated.	Total.	Rate.	Value assumed at average rent-rates.	Irrigated.	Not Irrigated.	Total.	Value assumed at average rent-rates.
Rs. a. p.	Rs. a. p.				Rs. a. p.	Rs. a. p.					Rs..a.p	Rs. a. p.				Rs. a. p.
3 12 0	62,868 12 0	1,370	6,368	7,738	3 12 0	29,017 8 0	205	2,440	2,645 2 8 0		6,612 8 0	14,243	41,635	55,878	2,23,429 8 0
3 0 0	24,078 0 0	10,470	7,199	17,669	3 0 0	53,007 0 0	109	1,031	1,140 2 4 0		2,565 0 0	27,650	20,550	48,200	1,61,383 0 0
2 10 9	20,204 10 0	583	1,704	2,287	3 0 0	6,861 0 0	1,735	8,203	9,938 2 4 0		22,360 8 0	6,865	19,796	23,461	63,462 8 0
...	1,07,151 6 0	12,423	15,271	27,694	...	88,885 8 0	2,049	11,674	13,723	...	31,538 0 0	48,558	78,981	127,539	4,48,275 0 0

DIX C.

TUHSEEL TILHUR,

rent-rates, and the deduced rentals for each assessment circle of Tuhseel Tilhur.

	2nd Domut.					Bhoor.					Dhunker.				Total.			
Irrigated.	Not Irrigated.	Total.	Sanctioned average circle rent-rate.	Value at average circle rate.	Irrigated.	Not Irrigated.	Total.	Sanctioned average circle rent-rate.	Value at average circle rate.	Irrigated.	Not Irrigated.	Total.	Sanctioned average circle rent-rate.	Value at average circle rate.	Irrigated.	Not Irrigated.	Total.	Total value; rental at circle rates.
1,367	2,262	8,629 3 8		12,701	78	326	404 2 8		1,010	...	536	536 2 8		1,340 0	14,109	10,913	25,015	1,14,980 0
5,755	7,796	13,551 2 8		32,877	1,956	7,484	9,440 1 12		26,520	...	117	117 2 0		234 0	15,027	21,193	36,220	1,03,574 0
7,122	10,058	17,180	...	46,578	2,034	7,810	9,844	...	27,530	...	653	653	...	1,574 0	29,129	32,106	61,235	2,18,554 0
743	889	1,632 2 8		4,080	155	375	530 1 12		927 8	...	178	178 2 4		389 4	2,535	2 572	5,107	15,345 0
1,148	4,302	5,450 3 0		16,350	297	1,542	1,749 2 4		3,935	...	952	952 2 4		2,142 0	11,456	20,697	32,153	1,05,664 8
617	1,857	2,474 2 12		6,903	175	1,018	1,193 2 0		2,886		1,636	1,636 2 0		3,272 0	4,388	8,989	13,377	37,969 0
1,765	6,159	7,984	...	23,153	382	2,560	2,942	...	6,321	...	2,588	2,588	...	5,414 0	15,844	29,686	45,530	1,43,633 0
205	3,006	3,211 3 0		9,683	37	1,195	1,232 1 12		919	...	95	95 2 0		190 0	3,759	18,326	22,085	85,574 0
462	775	1,237 2 8		3,392	125	408	538 1 12		913	...	273	273 2 0		546 0	7,087	6,999	14,086	41,818 0
704	1,523	2,227 2 4		5,021	395	1,575	1,970 1 12		3,448	...	11	11 2 0		22 0	2,033	4,268	6,301	14,790 0
1,371	5,304	6,675	...	18,046	557	3,178	3,735	...	5,300	...	379	379	...	758 0	12,879	29,593	42,472	1,42,182 0
846	3,380	4,226 3 9		12,678	74	942	1,016 2 0		2 032	...	780	780 2 4		1,755 0	10,296	16,147	26,443	27,470 0
838	1,839	2,677 2 8		6,692	240	1,517	1,757 2 0		3,514	...	143	143 2 4		322 0	2,308	4,661	6,969	19,296 8
1,684	5,219	6,903	...	19,370	314	2,459	2,773	...	5,546	...	923	923	...	2,077 0	12,604	20,808	33,412	46,766 0
12,685	27,629	40,314	...	1,11,227	3,442	16,382	19,824	...	45,624 8	...	4,716	4,716	...	10,212 4	72,991	1,14,765	187,756	3,66,480 12

41

APPENDIX C.

ASSESSMENT REPORT OF TUHSEEL POWAYN,

Tabular Statement of soils, sanctioned average rent-rates, and deduced rentals.

Name of Circle.	GOWHANEE.					1ST DOMUT.				
	Irrigated.	Not irrigated.	Total.	Rate.	Value assumed at average rent-rates.	Irrigated.	Not irrigated.	Total.	Rate.	Value assumed at average rent-rates.
				R. a. p	Rs. a. p			Rs.	Rs. a. p.	Rs. a p
Powayn, ...	188	26	214	7 0 0	1,498 0 0	9,106	5,621	14,727	4 8 0	66,271 8 0
Tureona, ...	267	20	287	6 0 0	1,722 0 0	9,794	4,888	14,682	3 0 0	44,046 0 0
Sunwat, ...	148	29	177	6 0 0	1,062 0 0	2,312	1,820	4,132	2 8 0	10,330 0 0
Gola, ...	79	17	96	6 8 0	624 0 0	3,859	2,602	6,461	3 12 0	24,328 12 0
Nhil, ...	86	10	96	6 8 0	624 0 0	7,382	4,168	11,550	4 8 0	51,975 0 0
Total Pergunnah Powayn, ...	766	102	870	...	5,530 0 0	32,453	19,099	51,552	...	1,96,851 4 0
Burragaon, ...	208	46	254	7 8 0	1,905 0 0	11,657	8,195	19,852	4 4 0	84,871 0 0
Khotar 1st Circle, ...	58	2	60	4 8 0	270 0 0	6,357	4,596	10,953	3 0 0	32,859 0 0
Khotar 2nd Circle, ...	109	18	127	3 12 0	476 4 0	3,806	7,334	11,140	2 4 0	25,065 0 0
Total Pergunnah Khotar, ...	167	20	187	...	746 4 0	10,163	11,930	22,093	...	57,924 0 0
Whole Tuhseel, ...	1,143	168	1,311	...	8,181 4 0	54,273	39,224	93,497	...	3,39,146 4 0

Name of Circle.	MUTTAR.					2ND DOMUT.					BHOOR.				
	Irrigated.	Not irrigated.	Total.	Rate.	Value assumed at average rent-rates.	Irrigated.	Not irrigated.	Total.	Rate.	Value assumed at average rent-rates.	Irrigated.	Not irrigated.	Total.	Rate.	Value assumed at average rent-rates.
				R. a. p	Rs. a. p				R. a. p	Rs. a. p				R. a. p	Rs. a. p
Powayn, ...	1,009	1,306	2,315	4 0 0	9,260 0 0	1,675	2,771	4,446	3 12 0	16,672 8 0	119	517	636	2 8 0	1,590 0 0
Tureona, ...	1,338	5,213	6,551	3 0 0	19,653 0 0	9,123	9,671	18,794	2 2 0	39,987 4 0	995	4,384	5,379	1 8 0	8,068 8 0
Sunwat, ...	746	2,153	2,899	2 4 0	6,522 12 0	6,156	10,356	16,512	1 12 0	28,896 0 0	2,033	12,012	14,045	1 4 0	17,556 4 0
Gola, ...	678	997	1,675	3 0 0	5,025 0 0	2,007	3,675	5,682	3 0 0	17,046 0 0	373	1,546	1,919	2 4 0	4,317 12 0
Nhil, ...	1,447	2,441	3,888	3 12 0	14,580 0 0	2,725	3,653	6,378	3 12 0	23,917 8 0	342	1,985	2,327	2 4 0	5,235 12 0
Total Pergunnah Powayn, ...	5,218	12,110	17,328	...	55,040 12 0	21,686	3,126	51,812	...	126,469 4 0	3,862	20,444	24,306	...	36,768 4 0
Burragaon, ...	1,343	2,342	3,685	3 8 0	12,897 8 0	4,148	7,009	11,157	3 8 0	39,049 8 0	102	1,126	1,203	2 8 0	3,075 0 0
Khotar 1st Circle, ...	470	1,644	2,114	2 12 0	5,813 8 0	1,427	2,928	4,355	2 0 0	8,710 0 0	130	928	1,058	1 8 0	1,587 0 0
Khotar 2nd Circle, ...	306	3,720	4,026	1 12 0	7,045 8 0	1,878	10,653	12,531	1 8 0	18,796 8 0	609	16,611	17,220	1 2 0	19,372 8 0
Total Pergunnah Khotar, ...	776	5,364	6,140	...	12,859 0 0	3,305	13,581	16,886	...	27,506 8 0	739	17,539	18,278	...	20,959 8 0
Whole Tuhseel, ...	7,337	19,816	27,153	...	80,797 4 0	29,139	50,716	79,855	...	1,93,925 4 0	4,703	39,111	43,814	...	60,802 12 0

Name of Circle.	DROONKER.					TOTAL AREA.			
	Irrigated.	Not irrigated.	Total.	Rate.	Value assumed at average rent-rates.	Irrigated.	Not irrigated.	Total.	Value assumed at average rent-rates.
				Rs. a. p.	Rs. a. p.				Rs a. p.
Powayn, ...	...	244	244	2 8 0	610 0 0	12,097	10,485	22,582	95,902 8 0
Tureona, ...	...	524	524	1 12 0	917 0 0	21,517	24,700	46,217	1,14,343 12 0
Sunwat, ...	...	265	265	1 12 0	463 12 0	11,395	26,635	38,080	64,830 12 0
Gola, ...	...	65	65	2 4 0	146 4 0	6,996	8,902	15,898	53,387 12 0
Nhil, ...	...	351	351	2 4 0	779 12 0	11,982	12,608	24,590	97,122 0 0
Total Pergunnah Powayn,	...	1,449	1,449	...	2,926 12 0	63,987	83,330	1,47,317	4,83,586 4 0
Burragaon, ...	...	280	280	2 4 0	630 0 0	17,458	19,000	36,458	2,41,926 0 0
Khotar 1st Circle, ...	...	9	9	1 8 0	13 8 0	8,442	10,107	18,549	49,255 8 0
Khotar 2nd Circle, ...	...	484	484	1 2 0	544 8 0	6,708	38,820	45,528	71,500 4 0
Total Pergunnah Khotar,	...	493	493	...	558 0 0	15,105	48,927	64,077	1,20,555 4 0
Whole Tuhseel, ...	...	2,222	2,222	...	4,114 12 0	96,595	151,257	247,852	6,86,067 8 0

Dated Shahjehanpore, the 29th May, 1874.

APPENDIX D.

ASSESSMENT REPORT OF TUHSEEL SHAHJEHANPORE.

Tabular Statement of soils, with percentages thereof, and details of irrigated areas.

Name of Pergunnah.	Culturable not cultivated, in acres.		Name of soil.	Cultivated area in acres.						Percentage of soils to cultivated area.
				Irrigated from				Not irrigated.	Grand Total.	
				Wells.	Ponds.	Rivers.	Total.			
Shahjehanpore.	Baghs,	3,575	Gowhanee, ...	891	...	...	891	193	1,084	1·68
			1st Domut, ...	18,525	4,593	1,891	25,009	17,375	42,384	65·77
	Old waste,	12,903	2nd Domut, ...	3,958	687	466	5,111	10,238	15,379	23·85
	New fallow,	836	Mutyar, ...	353	775	310	1,436	2,806	4,242	6·58
			Bhoor, ...	47	59	21	127	1,241	1,368	2·12
Total,...	... ...	17,014		23,774	6,112	2,688	32,574	31,883	64,457	100
			Percentage of	irrigated	and un	irrigated	50·53	49·47	...	...
Jumour.	Baghs,	1,295	Gowhanee, ...	400	106	...	506	51	557	1·28
			1st Domut, ...	7,753	6,242	1,146	15,141	7,311	22,452	51·75
	Old waste,	11,706	2nd Domut, ...	907	1,243	222	2,372	2,478	4,850	11·17
	New fallow,	531	Mutyar, ...	1,099	3,002	31	4,132	11,185	15,317	35·29
			Bhoor, ...	3	7	1	11	914	225	·51
Total,...	... ...	13,532		10,162	10,600	1,400	22,162	21,239	43,401	100
			Percentage of	irrigated	and un	irrigated	51·05	48·94	...	...
East.	Baghs,	2,523	Gowhanee, ...	689	40	...	729	74	803	1·11
			1st Domut, ...	8,282	3,349	...	11,631	10,868	22,519	31·71
	Old waste,	10,862	2nd Domut, ...	5,782	2,096	...	7,878	14,907	22,785	32·05
	New fallow,	1,282	Mutyar, ...	630	1,243	...	1,873	5,106	6,979	9·81
			Bhoor, ...	2,588	1,026	...	3,614	14,390	18,004	25·32
Total,...	... ...	14,667		17,971	7,754	...	25,725	45,365	71,090	100
			Percentage of	irrigated	and un	irrigated	36·19	63·81	...	...

Dated Shahjehanpore, the 20th December, 1873.

APPENDIX D.

ASSESSMENT REPORT OF TUHSEEL JELLALABAD.

Tabular Statement of Soils with percentages thereof, and details of irrigated areas.

Name of circle.	Culturable not cultivated, in acres.			Name of soil.	Cultivated area in acres.						Percentage of soil to cultivated area.
					Irrigated from				Not irrigated.	Grand Total.	
					Wells.	Ponds.	Rivers.	Total.			
Terai.				Gowhanee, ...	826	114	68	1,008	249	1,257	2·24
	Baghs, ...	1,448		1st Domut, ...	4,626	2,726	1,895	9,247	18,226	27,473	49·10
	Old waste, ...	11,449		2nd Domut, ...	1,234	940	239	2,413	14,352	16,765	30·00
	New fallow, ...	810		Mutyar, ...	451	728	191	1,370	6,363	7,738	13·80
				Bhoor, ...	93	104	8	205	2,440	2,645	4·86
Total, ...	...	...	13,707	...	7,230	4,612	2,401	14,243	41,635	55,878	100
				Percentage of irrigated and unirrigated, ...				25·48	74·52	100	...
Bunkuitee.				Gowhanee, ...	333	78	141	552	35	587	1·22
	Baghs, ...	915		1st Domut, ...	2,221	3,924	7,228	13,373	7,405	20,778	43·11
	Old waste, ...	25,589		2nd Domut, ...	428	1,232	1,486	3,146	4,880	8,026	16·65
	New fallow,	3,092		Mutyar, ...	1,084	3,518	5,868	10,470	7,199	17,669	36·66
				Bhoor, ...	36	24	49	109	1,031	1,140	2·36
Total, ...	......	...	29,596		4,102	8,776	14,772	27,650	20,550	48,200	100
				Percentage of irrigated and unirrigated, ...				57·37	42·634	100	...
Bhoor.				Gowhanee, ...	322	24	...	345	74	420	1·79
	Baghs, ...	1,098		1st Domut, ...	718	678	37	1,433	1,686	3,119	13·29
	Old waste, ...	4,129		2nd Domut, ...	1,757	796	15	2,568	5,129	7,697	32·81
	New fallow, ...	554		Mutyar, ...	139	444	...	583	1,704	2,287	9·75
				Bhoor. ...	1,237	498	...	1,735	8,203	9,938	42·36
Total, ...	...	...	5,681	...	4,173	2,440	52	6,665	16,796	23,461	100
				Percentage of irrigated and unirrigated, ...				28·41	71·59	100	...
Totals of Jellalabad Tuhseel.				Gowhanee, ...	1,481	216	209	1,906	358	2,264	1·77
	Baghs, ...	3,461		1st Domut, ...	7,565	7,328	9,160	24,053	27,317	51,370	40·23
	Old waste, ...	4,167		2nd Domut, ...	3,419	2,968	1,740	8,127	24,361	32,488	25·48
	New fallow, ...	4,456		Mutyar, ...	1,674	4,690	6,059	12,423	15,271	27,694	21·71
				Bhoor, ...	1,366	626	57	2,049	11,674	13,723	10·76
Total, ...	...	...	48,984	...	15,505	15,828	17,225	48,518	78,981	1,27,539	100
				Percentage of irrigated and unirrigated, ...				38·07	61·93	100	...

ROBERT G. CURRIE,

Settlement Officer.

Dated Shajehanpore, 13th January, 1874.

APPENDIX D.

ASSESSMENT REPORT OF TUHSEEL TILHUR, SHAHJEHANPORE DISTRICT,

Tabular Statement of Soils with percentages and details of irrigated areas for each pergunnah and for the whole tuhseel.

Culturable, but not cultivated, area in acres.		Name of Soil.			CULTIVATED AREA IN ACRES.						Percentage of soil to total cultivated area.
					Irrigated area.				Not irrigated.	Grand Total.	
					Irrigated from wells	Irrigated from tanks.	Irrigated from rivers.	Total irrigated.			
Pergunnah Tilhur.											
		Gowhanee,	...	...	826	87	18	931	252	1,183	2
		1st Domut,	...	...	14,450	1,797	1,264	17,511	9,272	26,783	43½
Groves,	2,763	Mutyar,	...	...	828	436	267	1,531	4,061	5,592	9¼
Old waste,	7,363	2nd Domut,	...	...	5,715	1,079	328	7,122	10,058	17,180	28
New fallow,	1,501	Bhoor,	...	...	1,857	170	7	2,034	7,810	9,844	16
		Dhunker,	...	...	...	...	...	...	653	653	1
Total,	11,627	Total,	...		23,676	3,569	1,884	29,129	32,106	61,235	100
Pergunnah Kuttra.											
		Gowhanee,	...	...	131	16	2	149	30	179	3½
		1st Domut,	...	...	948	213	223	1,384	829	2,213	43
Groves,	372	Mutyar,	...	...	30	59	15	104	276	380	7¼
Old waste,	1,595	2nd Domut,	...	...	512	83	148	743	889	1,632	32
New fallow,	143	Bhoor,	...	...	139	6	10	155	375	530	10½
		Dhunker,	...	...	...	...	...	...	173	173	3½
Total,	2,110	Total,	...		1,760	377	398	2,535	2,572	5,107	100
Pergunnah Nigohee.											
		Gowhanee,	...	...	359	20	11	390	83	473	1
		1st Domut,	...	...	8,201	2,650	1,242	12,093	13,738	25,831	56½
Groves,	2,073	Mutyar,	...	...	352	658	204	1,214	4,558	5,772	13½
Old waste,	13,753	2nd Domut,	...	...	1,120	447	198	1,765	6,159	7,924	17¼
New fallow,	1,153	Bhoor,	...	...	242	118	22	382	2,560	2,942	6¼
		Dhunker,	...	...	...	...	...	...	2,588	2,588	5½
Total,	16,979	Total,	...		10,274	3,893	1,677	15,844	29,656	45,530	100

APPENDIX D.

ASSESSMENT REPORT OF TUHSEEL TILHUR, SHAHJEHANPORE DISTRICT.

Tabular Statement of Soils with percentages and details of irrigated areas for each pergunnah and for the whole Tuhseel.—(concluded).

Culturable, but not cultivated, area in acres.		Name of Soil.			CULTIVATED AREA IN ACRES						
						Irrigated area.					
					Irrigated from wells.	Irrigated from tanks.	Irrigated from rivers.	Total irrigated.	Not irrigated.	Grand Total.	Percentage of soils to total cultivated area.

Pergunnah Khera Bujhera.

Culturable		Name of Soil			Wells	Tanks	Rivers	Total irrig.	Not irrig.	Grand Total	%
		Gowhanee,	...	...	444	46	36	526	326	852	2
		1st Domut,	...	...	3,986	1,561	3,281	8,828	15,802	24,630	58
Groves,	1,229	Mutyar,	...	...	389	713	495	1,597	4,604	6,201	14¼
Old waste,	6,480	2nd Domut,	...	...	884	143	344	1,371	5,304	6,675	15½
New fallow,	966	Bhoor,	...	...	501	13	43	557	3,178	3,735	9
		Dhunker,	...	...	...	...	...	...	379	379	½
Total,	8,675	Total,	...		6,204	2,476	4,199	12,879	19,593	42,472	100

Pergunnah Jelalpore.

		Gowhanee,	...	...	167	5	1	173	36	209	½
		1st Domut,	...	...	7,387	1,642	969	9,998	9,946	19,944	59½
Groves,	1,793	Mutyar,	...	...	147	254	34	435	2,225	2,660	8½
Old waste,	5,846	2nd Domut,	...	...	1,112	329	213	1,654	5,219	6,903	20¼
New fallow,	547	Bhoor,	...	...	214	76	24	314	2,459	2,773	8½
		Dhunker,	...	...	...	...	...	...	923	923	2¾
Total,	8,186	Total,	...		9,027	2,306	1,271	12,604	20,808	33,412	100

Total Tuhseel.

		Gowhanee,	...	...	1,927	174	68	2,169	729	2,896	1½
		1st Domut,	...	...	34,972	7,863	6,979	49,814	49,587	99,401	53
Groves,	8,230	Mutyar,	...	...	1,746	2,120	1,015	4,881	15,724	20,605	11
Old waste,	35,037	2nd Domut,	...	...	9,343	2,081	1,261	12,685	27,629	40,314	21¼
New fallow,	4,310	Bhoor,	...	...	2,953	383	106	3,442	17,382	19,824	11
		Dhunker,	...	...	...	...	...	...	4,716	4,716	2½
Total,	47,577	Total,	...		50,941	12,621	9,429	72,991	111,765	187,756	100

N. B.—Statements for each circle in Pergunnahs Tilhur, Nigohec, Khera Bujhera, and Jelalpore follow. Pergunnah Kuttra was not subdivided into circles.

GEORGE BUTT.

APPENDIX D.

Assessment Report of Tuhseel Tilhur, Shahjehanpore District.

Tabular Statement of Soils with percentages and details of irrigation for each assessment circle in the Tuhseel.

Culturable, but not cultivated, area in acres.		Name of Soil.	Cultivated area in acres. Irrigated Area. Irrigated from wells.	Irrigated from tanks.	Irrigated from rivers.	Total irrigated.	Not irrigated.	Grand Total.	Percentage of soil to total cultivated area.
		Terai Circle, Pergunnah Tilhur.							
		Gowhanee, ...	522	66	15	603	128	731	3
		1st Domut, ...	9,396	844	825	11,065	3,881	15,952	63¾
Groves,	1,525	Mutyar, ...	707	143	139	989	2,774	3,763	15¼
Old waste,	2,738	2nd Domut, ...	1,081	166	120	1,367	2,262	3,629	14½
New fallow,	290	Bhoor, ...	77	1	...	78	326	404	1½
		Dhunker, ...	...	...	...	...	536	536	2
Total,	4,548	Total, ...	11,783	1,220	1,099	14,102	10,913	25,015	100
		Bhoor Circle, Pergunnah Tilhur.							
		Gowhanee, ...	304	21	3	328	124	452	1¼
		1st Domut, ...	5,054	953	439	6,446	4,385	10,831	30
Groves,	1,238	Mutyar, ...	121	293	128	542	1,287	1,829	5
Old waste,	4,603	2nd Domut, ...	4,634	913	208	5,755	7,796	13,551	37½
New fallow,	1,211	Bhoor, ...	1,780	169	7	1,956	7,484	9,440	26
		Dhunker, ...	...	...	...	...	117	117	¼
Total,	7,079	Total, ...	11,893	2,349	785	15,027	21,193	36,220	100
		1st or Domut Circle, Pergunnah Nigohee.							
		Gowhanee, ...	247	10	7	264	66	330	1¼
		1st Domut, ...	6,606	1,817	823	9,246	10 906	20,152	62½
Groves,	1,609	Mutyar, ...	248	261	82	591	2 929	3,520	11
Old waste,	6,254	2nd Domut, ...	753	238	157	1,148	4,302	5,450	17
New fallow,	568	Bhoor, ...	114	75	18	207	1,542	1,749	5¼
		Dhunker, ...	...	...	...	...	952	952	2¾
Total,	8,431	Total, ...	7,968	2,401	1,087	11,456	20,697	32,153	100
		2nd or Khaimooah Circle, Pergunnah Nigohee.							
		Gowhanee, ...	112	10	4	126	17	143	1
		1st Domut, ...	1,595	833	419	2,847	2,832	5,679	42½
Groves,	464	Mutyar, ...	104	397	122	623	1,629	2,252	16¾
Old waste,	7,499	2nd Domut, ...	367	209	41	617	1,857	2,474	18½
New fallow,	585	Bhoor, ...	128	43	4	175	1,018	1,193	9
		Dhunker, ...	...	...	...	...	1,636	1,636	12¼
Total,	8,548	Total, ...	2,306	1,192	590	4,388	8,989	13,377	100
		Ramgunga, or Terai Circle, Pergunnah Khera Bujhera.							
		Gowhanee, ...	284	24	7	315	261	576	2½
		1st Domut, ...	1,738	785	358	2,881	11,448	14,329	65
Groves,	2,645	Mutyar, ...	162	142	17	321	2,321	2,642	12
Old waste,	281	2nd Domut, ...	68	40	97	205	3,006	3,211	14½
New fallow,	420	Bhoor, ...	8	...	29	37	1,195	1,232	½
		Dhunker, ...	...	...	...	...	95	95	5½
Total,	3,346	Total, ...	2,260	991	508	3,759	18,326	22,085	100

APPENDIX D.

ASSESSMENT REPORT OF TUHSEEL TILHUR, SHAHJEHANPORE DISTRICT.

Tabular Statement of Soils with percentages and details of irrigation for each assessment circle in the Tuhseel.-- concluded.)

Culturable, but not cultivated, area in acres.		Name of Soil.			CULTIVATED AREA IN ACRES.					Not irrigated.	Grand Total.	Percentage of soil to total cultivated area.
						Irrigated Area.						
					Irrigated from wells.	Irrigated from tanks.	Irrigated from rivers.	Total irrigated.			

Bygool, or Bunkuttee Circle, Pergunnah Khera Bujhera.

Culturable, but not cultivated		Name of Soil			Wells	Tanks	Rivers	Total irrigated	Not irrigated	Grand Total	Pct
		Gowhanee,	...	...	104	19	29	152	42	194	1¼
		1st Domut,	...	...	707	705	2,911	5,157	3,585	8,742	62
Groves,	3,080	Mutyar,	...	...	44	530	478	1,191	1,916	3,107	22
Old waste,	395	2nd Domut,	...	...	636	49	233	462	775	1,237	8¼
New fallow,	593	Bhoor,	...	...	382	...	14	125	408	533	3½
		Dhunker,	...	...	...	...	...	...	273	273	2
Total,	4,018	Total,	...	...	1,825	1,303	3,665	7,087	6,999	14,086	100

Bhoor Circle, Pergunnah Khera Bujhera,

Culturable, but not cultivated		Name of Soil			Wells	Tanks	Rivers	Total irrigated	Not irrigated	Grand Total	Pct
		Gowhanee,	...	...	56	3	...	59	23	82	1¼
		1st Domut,	...	...	707	71	12	790	769	1,559	24½
Groves,	805	Mutyar,	...	...	44	41	...	85	367	452	7¼
Old waste,	290	2nd Domut,	...	...	636	54	14	704	1,523	2,227	35½
New fallow,	216	Bhoor,	...	...	382	13	...	395	1,575	1,970	¼
		Dhunker,	...	...	...	...	...	...	11	11	31½
Total,	1,311	Total,	...	...	1,825	182	26	2,033	4,268	6,301	100

Gurra Circle, Pergunnah Jelalpore,

Culturable, but not cultivated		Name of Soil			Wells	Tanks	Rivers	Total irrigated	Not irrigated	Grand Total	Pct
		Gowhanee,	...	...	145	4	1	150	34	184	¾
		1st Domut,	...	...	6,473	1,470	880	8,823	9,064	17,887	67½
Groves,	3,323	Mutyar,	...	...	138	244	21	403	1,947	2,350	9
Old waste,	344	2nd Domut,	...	...	590	130	126	846	3,380	4,226	16
New fallow,	1,538	Bhoor,	...	...	53	20	1	74	942	780	3
		Dhunker,	...	...	...	...	...	...	942	1,016	3½
Total,	5,205	Total,	...	...	7,399	1,868	1,029	10,296	16,147	26,443	100

Bygool Circle, Pergunnah Jelalpore.

Culturable, but not cultivated		Name of Soil			Wells	Tanks	Rivers	Total irrigated	Not irrigated	Grand Total	Pct
		Gowhanee,	...	...	22	1	...	23	2	25	¼
		1st Domut,	...	...	914	172	89	1,175	882	2,057	29½
Groves,	2,523	Mutyar,	...	...	9	10	13	32	278	310	4½
Old waste,	203	2nd Domut,	...	...	522	199	117	838	1,839	2,677	38½
New fallow,	255	Bhoor,	...	...	161	56	23	240	1,517	1,757	2
		Dhunker,	...	...	...	...	...	...	143	143	25
Total,	2,981	Total,	...	...	1,628	438	242	2,308	4,661	6,969	100

Dated Shahjehanpore, the 31st January, 1874.

GEORGE BUTT,
Assistt. Settlt. Officer.

APPENDIX D.

ASSESSMENT REPORT OF TUHSEEL POWAYN.

Tabular Statement of Soils, with percentages thereof and details of irrigated areas.

Name of circle.	Culturable, not cultivated, area in acres.		Name of soil.	Irrigated.				Not irrigated.	Grand Total.	Percentage of soil to cultivated area.
				Wells.	Ponds.	Rivers.	Total.			
Powayn.			Gowhanee, ...	187	1	...	188	26	214	·9
	Baghs, ...	2,126	1st Domut, ...	7,485	1,621	...	9,106	5,621	14,727	65·2
	Old waste, ...	2,176	Mutyar, ...	604	405	...	1,009	1,306	2,315	10·3
	New fallow, ...	266	2nd Domut ...	1,347	328	...	1,675	2,771	4,446	19·6
			Bhoor, ...	68	51	...	119	517	636	2·9
			Dhunker, ...	...	...	...	...	244	244	1·1
	Total, ...	4,568		9,691	2,406	...	12,097	10,485	22,582	100
Tureona.			Gowhanee, ...	259	8	...	267	20	287	·6
	Baghs, ...	1,843	1st Domut, ...	8,545	1,113	136	9,794	4,888	14,682	31·7
	Old waste, ...	2,223	Mutyar, ...	1,065	237	36	1,338	5,213	6,551	14·4
	New fallow, ...	430	2nd Domut, ...	8,234	741	148	9,123	9,671	18,794	40·6
			Bhoor, ...	914	61	20	995	4,384	5,379	11·6
			Dhunker, ...	...	...	...	...	524	524	1·1
	Total, ...	4,496		19,017	2,160	340	21,517	24,700	46,217	100
Sunwat.			Gowhanee, ...	148	...	...	148	29	177	·4
	Baghs, ...	1,100	1st Domut, ...	1,942	299	71	2,312	1,820	4,132	10·9
	Old waste, ...	10,681	Mutyar, ...	439	151	156	746	2,154	2,899	7·7
	New fallow, ...	2,509	2nd Domut, ...	5,094	948	114	6,156	10,356	16,512	43·4
			Bhoor, ...	1,714	300	19	2,033	12,012	14,045	36·9
			Dhunker, ...	...	...	...	...	265	265	·7
	Total, ...	14,290		9,387	1,698	360	11,295	96,635	98,030	100
Goila.			Gowhanee, ...	79	...	...	79	17	96	·6
	Baghs, ...	948	1st Domut, ...	3,386	416	57	3,859	2,602	6,461	40·6
	Old waste, ...	2,990	Mutyar, ...	198	137	343	676	997	1,675	10·5
	New fallow, ...	237	2nd Domut, ...	1,466	436	105	2,007	3,675	5,682	35·8
			Bhoor, ...	246	94	33	373	1,546	1,919	12·1
			Dhunker, ...	...	...	...	...	65	65	·4
	Total, ...	4,175		5,375	1,083	538	6,996	8,902	15,898	100

APPENDIX D.

ASSESSMENT REPORT OF TUHSEEL POWAYN.

Tabular Statement of Soils, with percentages thereof and details of irrigated areas,--(continued.)

Name of circle	Culturable, not cultivated, area in acres.		Name of soil.	CULTIVATED AREA IN ACRES.						Percentage of soil to cultivated area.
				Irrigated.				Not irrigated	Grand Total	
				Wells.	Ponds.	Rivers.	Total.			
Nahil.			Gowhanee, ...	83	3	...	86	10	96	·4
	Baghs, ...	1,414	1st Domut, ...	5,442	1,857	83	7,382	4,168	11,550	47·
	Old waste, ...	6,025	Mutyar, ...	806	460	181	1,447	2,411	3,883	15·9
	New fallow, ...	508	2nd Domut, ...	1,897	782	96	2,725	3,653	6,378	25·9
			Bhoor, ...	240	69	33	342	1,985	2,327	9·4
			Dhunker, ...	...	...	...	...	351	351	1·4
	Total, ...	7,947		8,468	3,121	393	11,982	12,608	24,590	100
Total Pergunnah .wayn.			Gowhanee, ...	756	12	...	768	102	870	·6
	Baghs, ...	7,431	1st Domut, ...	26,800	5,306	347	32,453	19,099	51,552	35·
	Old waste, ...	24,095	Mutyar, ...	3,112	1,390	716	5,218	12,110	17,328	11·7
	New fallow, ...	3,950	2nd Domut, ...	18,038	3,185	463	21,686	30,126	51,812	35·2
			Bhoor, ...	3,182	575	105	3,862	20,444	24,306	16·5
			Dhunker, ...	...	...	...	...	1,449	1,449	1·
	Total, ...	35,476		51,888	10,468	1,631	63,987	83,330	1,47,317	100
Burageon.			Gowhanee, ...	198	10	...	208	46	254	·7
	Baghs, ...	2,045	1st Domut, ...	9,525	1,997	135	11,657	8,195	19,852	54·4
	Old waste, ...	6,152	Mutyar, ...	539	517	287	1,343	2,342	3,685	10·1
	New fallow, ...	852	2nd Mutyar, ...	3,095	771	282	4,148	7,009	11,157	30·6
			Bhoor, ...	54	9	39	102	1,128	1,230	3·4
			Dhunker, ...	...	...	...	...	280	280	·8
	Total, ...	8,947		13,411	3,304	743	17,458	19,000	36,458	100
Khotar 1st circle.			Gowhanee, ...	58	...	...	58	2	60	·3
	Baghs, ...	1,245	1st Domut, ...	4,934	1,423	...	6,357	4,596	10,953	59·
	Old waste, ...	1,170	Mutyar, ...	319	151	...	470	1,644	2,114	11·4
	New fallow, ...	590	2nd Domut, ...	1,171	256	...	1,427	2,928	4,355	23·5
			Bhoor, ...	129	1	...	130	928	1,058	5·8
			Dhunker, ...	...	...	...	...	9	9	...
	Total, ...	3,005		6,611	1,831	...	8,442	10,107	18,549	100

APPENDIX D.

ASSESSMENT REPORT OF TUHSEEL POWAYN.

Tabular Statement of Soils. with percentages thereof and details of irrigated areas.—(concluded.)

Name of circle.	Culturable, not cultivated, area in acres.		Name of soil.	Irrigated. Wells.	Ponds.	Rivers.	Total.	Not Irrigated.	Grand Total.	Percentage of soils to cultivated area.
Khotar, 2nd circle.			Cowhanee, ...	108	1	...	109	18	127	·3
	Baghs, ...	545	1st Domut, ...	3,160	629	17	3,806	7,334	11,140	24·5
	Old waste, ...	47,120	Mutyar, ...	193	99	14	306	3,720	4,026	8·8
	New fallow, ...	5,649	2nd Domut, ...	1,597	280	1	1,878	10,653	12,531	27·5
			Bhoor, ...	517	91	1	609	16,611	17,220	37·8
			Dhunker, ...	...	...	..	...	484	484	1·1
Total, ...	...	58,314		5,575	1,100	33	6,708	38,820	45,528	100
Total Pergunnah Khotar.			Gowhanee. ...	166	1	...	167	20	187	·3
	Baghs, ...	1,790	1st Domut, ...	8,094	2,052	17	10,163	11,930	22,093	34·5
	Old waste, ...	48,290	Mutyar, ...	512	250	14	776	5,364	6,140	9·6
	New fallow, ...	6,239	2nd Domut, ...	2,768	536	1	3,305	15,581	19,886	26·3
			Bhoor, ...	646	92	1	739	17,539	18,278	28·5
			Dhunker, ...	...	...	.	...	493	493	·8
Total, ...	...	56,319		12,186	2,931	33	15,150	48,922	64,077	100
Total Tuhseel Powayn.			Gowhanee, ...	1,120	23	...	1,143	168	1,311	·5
	Baghs, ...	11,266	1st Domut, ...	44,419	9,355	499	54,273	39,224	93,497	37·7
	Old waste, ...	78,437	Mutyar, ..	4,168	2,157	1,017	7,687	19,816	27,153	10·9
	New fallow, ...	11,039	2nd Domut, ...	23,901	4,492	746	29,139	50,716	79,855	32·2
			Bhoor, ...	2,882	676	145	4,703	39,111	43,814	17·7
			Dhunker, ...	...	...	...	...	2,222	2,222	1·
Total, ...	...	1,00,742		77,485	16,703	2,407	96,595	1,51,257	2,47,852	100

SHAHJEHANPORE SETTLEMENT OFFICE :
The 29th May, 1874.

ROBERT G. CURRIE,
Settlement Officer.

ASSESSMENT REPORT OF TUHSEEL

Statement showing the population of each Pergunnah

Pergunnah.	Landowners.						Agriculturists.					
	Hindoos.		Mahomedans and others.		Total.		Hindoos.		Mahomedans and others.		Total.	
	Male.	Female.	Male.	Female.	Male.	Female.	Male.	Female.	Male.	Female.	Male.	Female.
Tilhur, ...	836	572	199	199	1,035	771	27,152	22,989	2,146	1,990	29,298	24,979
Kuttra, ...	88	57	32	44	120	101	2,283	1,971	363	362	2,646	2,333
Negohee, ...	365	295	66	41	431	336	21,697	18,186	1,789	1,981	23,480	19,867
Khera Bujhera, ...	924	731	4	5	928	736	19,739	16,025	590	478	20,329	16,503
Jelalpore, ...	778	652	61	70	839	722	14,862	12,080	921	825	15,783	12,905
Total Tuhseel, ...	2,991	2,307	362	259	3,353	2,666	85,733	71,251	5.803	5,336	91,536	76,587

Statement showing number and percentage of population able to read and write,—(para. 15).

Pergunnah.						Educated, i.e., able to read and write.			Percentage of total population able to read and write.
						Hindoos.	Mahomedans and others.	Total.	
Tilhur, ...						1,001	229	1,230	1·4
Kuttra, ...						105	9	114	1·1
Negohee,...						514	31	545	0·96
Khera Bujhera, ...						463	16	479	1·0
Jelalpore, ...						712	44	756	1·7
Total Tuhseel, ...						2,795	329	3,124	1·3

Note.—The educated are all males ; not one single female in the Tuhseel was recorded as able to read and write.

Dated Shahjehanpore, the 31st January, 1874.

D I X E.

TILHUR, SHAHJEHANPORE DISTRICT.

and of the Tuhseel, according to the census of 1872,—(para. 14 of Report).

NON-AGRICULTURISTS.						TOTAL POPULATION.						Grand Total.
Hindoos.		Mahomedans and others.		Total.		Hindoos.		Mahomedans and others.		Total.		
Male.	Female.	Male.	Female.	Male.	Female.	Male.	Female.	Male.	Female.	Male.	Female.	
10,428	8,792	5,574	5,344	16,102	14,136	38,416	32,353	8,019	7,533	46,435	39,886	86,321
1,677	1,186	1,069	888	2,746	2,024	4,048	3,214	1,464	1,244	5,512	4,458	9,970
5,321	4,445	1,589	1,149	6,910	5,594	27,383	22,926	3,438	2,871	30,821	25,797	56,618
3,898	3,827	614	490	4,512	3,717	24,561	19,983	1,208	973	25,769	20,956	46,725
6,258	5,339	1,713	1,365	7,971	6,704	21,898	18,071	2,695	2,260	24,593	20,331	44,924
27,582	22,989	10,659	9,186	38,241	32,175	116,306	96,547	16,824	14,881	133,130	111,428	244,558

Statement showing total number, and proportion to total population of each class, landowners, agriculturists, and non-agriculturists,—(para. 14.)

Pergunnah.	Non-agriculturists.		Agriculturists.		Landowners.		Total Population.
	Number.	Percentage of total.	Number.	Percentage of total.	Number.	Percentage of total.	
Tilhur, ...	1,806	2·1	54,277	62·9	30,238	35·7	86,321
Kuttra, ...	221	2·2	4,979	49·9	4,770	47·9	9,970
Negohee, ...	767	1·3	43,347	84·2	12,504	14·5	56,618
Khera Bujhera, ...	1,664	3·5	36,832	78·8	8,229	19·6	46,725
Jelalpore, ...	1,561	3·5	28,688	63·9	14,675	32·6	44,924
Total Tuhseel, ...	6,019	2·4	168,123	68·8	70,416	28 8	2,44,558

APPENDIX F.

ASSESSMENT REPORT OF TUHSEEL TILHUR, SHAHJHANPORE DISTRICT.

Statement showing the number of enclosures and houses in each Pergunnah,—(para. 14).

Pergunnah.	Number of Enclosures.				Number of Houses.			Average No. of Inhabitants.	
	Hindoos.	Mahomedans.	Christians and others.	Total.	Houses built with skilled labour.	Houses built with unskilled labour.	Total No. of Houses.	Per enclosure.	Per house.
Tilhur, ...	7,977	1,991	...	9,968	535	15,697	16,232	8·7	5·3
Kutira, ...	750	282	...	1,032	17	1,787	1,804	9·6	5·5
Negobee, ...	5,963	774	...	6,737	4	10,526	10,530	8·4	5·4
Khera Bujhera, ...	5,401	304	5	5,710	17	8,811	8,828	8·2	5·3
Jelalpore, ...	4,530	626	1	5,157	186	8,200	8,386	8·7	5·3
Total Tuhseel, ...	24,621	3,977	6	28,604	749	45,091	45,770	8·5	5·3

Dated Shahjehanpore, the 31st January, 1874.

APPENDIX G.

ASSESSMENT REPORT OF TUHSEEL TILHUR, SHAHJEHANPORE DISTRICT.

Statement showing the number of estates held by each caste, distinguishing those held by resident and by non-resident proprietors.

HINDOO PROPRIETORS.

Pergunnah		Brahmin — Entire mouzahs	Brahmin — Entire mubahs, parts of mouzahs	Brahmin — Aggregate of shares	Brahmin — Total	Thakoor — Entire mouzahs	Thakoor — Entire mubahs	Thakoor — Aggregate of shares	Thakoor — Total	Kayth — Entire mouzahs	Kayth — Entire mubahs	Kayth — Aggregate of shares	Kayth — Total	Bunniah — Entire mouzahs	Bunniah — Entire mubahs	Bunniah — Aggregate of shares	Bunniah — Total	Asheer — Entire mouzahs	Asheer — Entire mubahs	Asheer — Aggregate of shares	Asheer — Total	Koormee — Entire mouzahs	Koormee — Entire mubahs	Koormee — Aggregate of shares	Koormee — Total	Aheer — Entire mouzahs	Aheer — Entire mubahs	Aheer — Aggregate of shares	Aheer — Total	Miscellaneous Hindoo — Entire mouzahs	Miscellaneous Hindoo — Entire mubahs	Miscellaneous Hindoo — Aggregate of shares	Miscellaneous Hindoo — Total	Total Hindoos — Entire mouzahs	Total Hindoos — Entire mubahs	Total Hindoos — Aggregate of shares	Total Hindoos — Total
TILHUR	Residents of the Tuhseel	8	14	3	25	39	19	13	71	10	13	1	14	1	…	5	6	…	…	…	…	4	2	…	6	2	…	…	2	8	4	…	12	72	42	22	136
	Residents of other Tuhseels	7	1	…	8	5	2	8	15	6	…	…	6	…	1	…	1	…	…	…	…	…	…	…	…	…	…	…	…	…	1	…	1	18	5	8	31
	Total	15	15	3	33	44	21	21	86	16	13	1	20	1	1	5	7	…	…	…	…	4	2	…	6	2	…	…	2	8	5	…	13	90	47	30	167
KUTRA	Residents of the Tuhseel	…	…	…	…	1	…	1	2	…	…	…	…	…	…	…	…	…	…	…	…	1	…	…	1	…	…	…	…	…	…	…	…	2	8	1	11
	Residents of other Tuhseels	…	…	…	…	…	…	…	…	…	…	…	…	…	…	…	…	…	…	…	…	…	…	…	…	…	…	…	…	…	…	…	…	…	…	…	…
	Total	…	…	…	…	1	…	1	2	…	…	…	…	…	…	…	…	…	…	…	…	1	…	…	1	…	…	…	…	…	…	…	…	2	8	1	11
NEGOHEE	Residents of the Tuhseel	11	4	2	6	29	20	3	52	1	1	1	…	…	…	…	…	1	1	…	1	…	3	…	3	3	2	1	6	…	…	1	…	36	27	6	69
	Residents of other Tuhseels	…	…	…	11	2	3	1	6	12	…	1	13	12	…	…	12	1	…	…	1	5	…	…	5	…	…	…	…	5	4	1	10	48	7	3	58
	Total	11	4	2	17	31	23	4	58	13	1	1	20	12	…	…	12	1	1	…	2	5	3	…	8	3	2	1	6	5	4	1	10	84	34	9	127
KHERA BUJHERA	Residents of the Tuhseel	2	4	4	6	89	44	5	138	1	1	…	…	1	…	…	1	1	1	…	…	…	…	…	…	…	…	…	…	4	1	…	5	97	50	7	154
	Residents of other Tuhseels	…	…	…	…	2	4	…	6	5	2	…	…	…	…	…	…	…	…	…	…	…	…	…	…	…	…	…	…	1	…	…	1	8	7	…	15
	Total	2	4	4	9	91	48	5	144	6	3	…	…	1	…	…	1	1	1	…	1	…	…	…	…	…	…	…	…	5	1	…	6	105	57	7	169
JELALPORE	Residents of the Tuhseel	3	12	3	18	19	36	17	72	20	2	24	3	…	…	1	4	1	1	4	6	3	3	…	6	…	…	1	…	…	…	…	84	72	22	128
	Residents of other Tuhseels	1	1	…	2	2	5	…	7	4	1	6	…	…	…	1	1	…	…	1	1	…	…	…	…	…	…	…	…	…	…	1	1	10	11	1	22
	Total	4	13	3	20	21	41	17	79	24	3	30	3	…	…	1	5	1	1	4	6	3	3	…	6	…	…	1	…	…	…	1	44	83	23	160
TOTAL TUHSEEL	Residents of the Tuhseel	13	34	10	57	177	119	39	335	46	24	3	44	5	1	5	11	1	1	4	2	16	8	…	24	2	2	1	3	12	5	…	17	241	199	58	498
	Residents of other Tuhseels	19	3	…	22	14	2	9	34	6	4	1	37	12	2	…	14	1	…	…	1	…	…	…	5	…	…	…	…	7	5	1	13	84	30	12	196
	Total	32	37	10	79	188	133	48	369	46	30	5	81	17	3	5	25	2	1	…	3	16	…	…	29	2	2	1	8	19	10	1	30	335	229	70	694

APPENDIX G.

ASSESSMENT REPORT OF TUHSEEL TILHUR, SHAHJEHANPORE DISTRICT.

Statement showing the number of estates held by each caste, distinguishing those held by resident and by non-resident proprietors.—(concluded.)

MAHOMEDAN PROPRIETORS.

Pergunnah.		Syad.				Pathan.				Mogul.				Shaikh.				Miscellaneous Mahomedans.				Total Mahomedans.				English.				Grand Total.			
		Entire mouzahs.	Entire mahals, parts	Aggregate of shares.	Total.	Entire mouzahs.	Entire mahals, parts of mouzahs.	Aggregate of shares.	Total.	Entire mouzahs.	Entire mahals, parts of mouzahs.	Aggregate of shares.	Total.	Entire mouzahs.	Entire mahals, parts of mouzahs.	Aggregate of shares.	Total.	Entire mouzahs.	Entire mahals, parts of mouzahs.	Aggregate of shares.	Total.	Entire mouzahs.	Entire mahals, parts of mouzahs.	Aggregate of shares.	Total.	Entire mouzahs.	Entire mahals, parts of mouzahs.	Aggregate of shares.	Total.	Entire mouzahs.	Entire mahals, parts of mouzahs.	Aggregate of shares.	Total.

Dated Shahjehanpore, the 31st January, 1874.

APPENDIX II.

ASSESSMENT REPORT OF TUHSEEL TILHUR, SHAHJEHANPORE DISTRICT.

Statement showing the extent to which landed property has been transferred from the agricultural to the non-agricultural classes—(para. 73 of Report).

1. Name of Pergunnah.	2. Total area in acres paying revenue.	3. Deduct area confiscated for rebellion.	4. Remaining.	5. Year.	6. Area held by agricultural classes in acres.	7. Per cent.	8. Area held by non-agricultural classes in acres.	9. Per cent.	10. Remarks.
Tilhur, ...	69,207	15,365	54,542	Last Settlement 1839-40, A. D.,	47,299	86·7	7,243	13·3	The areas given are the mulgoozaree or assessable, not the total areas. In the agricultural classes are included, in addition to classes purely agricultural, others, such as Pathan, Brahmin, and Kayeth families long connected with the land. In the non-agricultural classes are included money-lenders, bankers, and others of similar class who have no old connection with the land.
Kutira, ...	6,533	...	6,533	„	5,093	76·8	1,540	23·2	
Negobee, ...	69,259	1,312	61,947	„	53,819	87·3	1,828	12·7	
Khera Bujhera, ...	46,306	4,010	42,296	„	41,113	97·2	1,183	2·8	
Jelalpore, ...	36,507	153	36,354	„	25,984	71·5	10,370	28·5	
Tuhseel Total, ...	222,312	20,840	201,472	„	173,308	86·1	22,164	13·9	
Tilhur, ...	72,862	15,365	57,497	Present Settlement 1870-71, A. D.,	46,436	80·8	11,061	19·2	
Kutira, ...	7,217	...	7,217	„	5,433	75·3	1,784	24·7	
Negobee, ...	65,509	1,312	61,197	„	36,646	59·8	24,551	40·2	
Khera Bujhera, ...	51,147	4,010	47,137	„	42,987	91·2	4,150	8·8	
Jelalpore, ...	41,598	153	41,445	„	27,009	65·2	14,436	34·8	
Tuhseel Total, ...	235,333	20,840	214,493	„	158,511	73·9	55,982	26·1	

GEORGE BUTT,
Assistant Settlement Officer.

SHAHJEHANPORE, }
31st January, 1874. }

45

ORDERS OF GOVERNMENT.

No. 154 OF 1881.

RESOLUTION.

REVENUE DEPARTMENT.

Dated Allahabad, the 26th January, 1881.

READ—

Letter from the Secretary, Board of Revenue, No. 123N., dated 12th May, 1876, submitting the
final Settlement Report of the Sháhjahánpur district,

OBSERVATIONS.—The district of Sháhjahánpur is the most eastern of those constituting the sub-Himálayan division of Rohilkhand. It is a plain of 1,733 square miles in extent, about 500 feet above the level of the sea. By the census of 1872 the population was 949,471, giving an average of 548 people to the square mile. The average rainfall is 37·2 inches, of which 33·3 fell during the five months from June to October. The climate is moist, and irrigation for crops in ordinary years is not a necessity ; but 77½ per cent. of the cultivated area is either irrigable, or from its low-lying position never requires irrigation. Kucha wells are the chief source of irrigation ; they strike the water-level at 12 to 15 feet from the surface, but the experience of 1877 has shown that this source of water-supply is not an unfailing one.

The total area of the district is 1,109,240 acres, of which 740,204 are cultivated, being in excess of the area shown as cultivated at beginning of the last settlement by 176,250 acres. The culturable area as yet un-reclaimed amounts to 296½ square miles, equal to 17 per cent. of the total area. It lies chiefly in pargana Khutar, and consists of tracts used as grazing lands or covered with scrub forest or small sál trees.

Previous to 1867 the chief means of communication were the three rivers—the Ganges, Rámganga and Garra—and country roads. Since that year the district has been crossed by the Oudh and Rohilkhand Railway, and the headquarters connected by metalled roads with Luck-now, Fatehgarh, and Bareilly, and tahsíl Pawayan.

The chief towns, Sháhjahánpur, with a population of 70,000, and Tilhar, of 19,000, are the centres of the important sugar trade of the district. Nearly 6 per cent. of the cultivated area is under sugarcane, the juice of which is locally manufactured into coarse and refined sugar, and forms the main article of export.

Wheat is the predominant crop, averaging from 28 to 38 per cent. of the cultivation, and is extensively grown, even on the uplands, with-out irrigation. The other crops are mostly in the kharíf rice and bajra, (the other millet, juar, being much less grown), and in the rabi gram, juar, and bajra.

The soil is generally of a loamy character, consisting of a mixture of sand, clay and vegetable mould, known locally as *dúmat*. In the depressions this changes to clay (matiár), and on the crests of the undula-tions to sand (bhúr). An artificial soil, called gauháni, is found with the

1

market garden cultivation near some village sites, but it never forms a regular belt, as is the case in the Doáb, the reason being that generally the cultivator's stock of manure is used for his cane-fields, wherever these may happen to be, and not kept for the lands near the village site.

2. The proprietors of villages hold them generally on a zamindari tenure. The chief of them are Rájputs, who own 38 per cent. of the land, Patháns own 18 per cent., and the Hindu trading classes only 4 per cent. In parganas Khera-Bajhera, Jalálabad and Kant the sír land or home cultivation of the proprietors amounts respectively to 16, 20, and 25 per cent. of the cultivated areas, these parganas being largely in possession of peasant proprietors. Of the total cultivated area 13 per cent. is held as sír.

Except in the forest circle of Khutar, the cultivators are sufficiently numerous, and more than half belong to the most industrious classes. They hold 61 per cent. of the land with occupancy rights. Mr. Currie remarks that the landholders do not object to the acquisition of these rights by their tenants. This is fortunate and rather singular, as in the adjoining districts, Pilibhít and Bareilly, it is understood the reverse is the case.

3. Rents are paid in cash, except in a few places where, the crops being very uncertain, the landholder takes a share of the produce. They vary in their rates according to the quality of the soil, but are not affected by the actual fact of irrigation, for, as a general rule, good lands are either capable of irrigation or do not need it. The rent for sugarcane, however, is always a special rate, equal to nearly three times the ordinary rate, on account of the *two* years the crop occupies the ground.

The rents are regulated by custom rather than competition, so much so that the higher rates remain much as they were in 1818. The general average has, however, been raised about 6½ per cent. by the enhancement of the *lower* rents.

Yet during the 30 years preceding 1870 there was a great increase in prices. Owing to the famine of 1837-39 the prices of the first decade of that period give an abnormal average: but taking the second decade, we find the average price of wheat to have been Re. 0-10-8 per maund of 82·3℔. In the last decade it was Re. 1-2-3, an increase of 73 per cent. Evidently, therefore, as the general standard of rent has remained unchanged, there is no adequate relation between the existing rent and the present value of the produce, as compared with the relation existing 30 years ago.

Mr. Currie considers the landholders have not raised their rents mainly because, from the absence of payments in kind, the variation of the harvest prices has not been forced on their attention. But this alone is not a sufficient explanation. It is quite as likely that, as a rule, the old proprietors, living in close communication with their tenants, do not inter-fere with the customary rates, unless there has been an enhancement of the Government demand. Owing also to the extent of culturable land not yet brought under the plough, there was probably not that briskness of competition for land which furnishes an incentive and an opportunity for enhancement.

4. The settlement under Regulation IX of 1833 was the ninth in this district since the cession : it extended from 1840 to 1870. The previous settlements had all been for short terms. Mr. J. Muir, the Settlement Officer, was of opinion that the revenue had been assessed with undue severity, and made a reduction of Rs. 1,22,639, equal to 12 per cent. of the total amount. Notwithstanding this, Mr. Currie considers generally the ninth settlement was not borne easily at first. Punitive measures for its collection and private transfers were numerous, but became less when the area under cultivation extended, and permanent reductions had been made in all cases of marked severity.

What proportion was borne by the demand as originally assessed to the assets is not given. In section 80, however, Mr. Currie has shown that there has been an enhancement of the average rent-rate by about 6½ per cent. Now, taking the present estimated actual assets and the *cultivated* areas as given in the several tahsíl reports, we have a general rent-rate of Rs. 2-14-6 per acre. This should be then about 6½ per cent. in excess of the rent-rate at the commencement of last settlement. The average rent-rate then must have been Rs. 2-8-7 per acre of cultivation. According to section 100, the incidence of the revenue at its commencement was Re. 1-11-10, which therefore was 68 6 per cent. of the assets. But, as noted in various places in the tahsíl assessment reports, the cultivation was, owing to special causes, very much reduced at the time the old measurements were made, and therefore the incidence per cultivated acre of the revenue is higher than it should be. Allowing for this, the old demand must have been at its imposition nearly up to 66 per cent. of the assets. At the close of the period, owing to reductions, increase of cultivation and rent-rates, it had sunk to an incidence of Re. 1-3-4 per cultivated acre, which was only 44·6 per cent. of the assets.

5. Mr. Currie shows that during the currency of the last settlement there occurred extensive transfers of property from the agricultural to the commercial classes. At the beginning of the period the landed estates owned by the latter amounted to only 6 per cent. of the district estates ; at its close the percentage had increased to 17 per cent. In pargana Jamaur the increase was from 2·6 to 28·9 per cent.

Eliminating all special cases, Mr. Currie finds that in those parganas where the Government demand of the last settlement was light, only 5 per cent. of the estates were during its currency transferred to the commercial classes ; in those where the assessment was heavy, the percentage transferred amounts to 21 per cent. ; while in those where the assessment was of a medium character, the transfers amounted to 12 per cent. Mr. Currie, however, points out that there were special attractions to capital in the heavily assessed parganas, which were absent in those lightly assessed, where, moreover, special causes existed deterring city capitalists from investments in land. Hence in the first the transfers were accelerated by the eagerness of the purchasers and checked by their absence in the other.

The inference Mr. Currie draws is, therefore, that the transfers were in part only caused by the severity of the assessment. The main causes were doubtless those which have been at work generally in these provinces during the last 40 years. The various rights in the land had been carefully defined, the principles upon which the Government share was to be assessed had been fixed, and a settlement to run for a whole generation had been sanctioned. For the first time landed property offered a secure investment to the commercial classes, whose capital, moreover, had greatly increased. Thus the means of purchasing and the inducements to it increased simultaneously. Doubtless this was the main reason for the great increase in the price of land, which was 60 per cent. higher during the period after the mutiny than before. The prices in parganas Sháhjahánpur, Tilhar, Nigohi and Baragaon were from 7 to 12 times the Government revenue.

6. The rents actually paid formed the basis for the rent-rates sanctioned by the Board of Revenue for the assessment of the district. All favorable rents paid by connections of the landholders and all low and suspicious rents were eliminated. The rents paid by *bona fide* tenants remained. Of these, large areas consisting of the various soils were taken from all directions in each assessment circle, and the rates per acre deduced. Where, however, the rates were found to be low in comparison with those paid for similar land with similar advantages in the neighbourhood, and the circumstances indicated a rise of rents to be certain, then the rates were enhanced so much as appeared required to correct their inadequacy and to meet the anticipated rise. The aim of the assessing officer was to ascertain what the actual present full rents and rates are, to what extent they are rising, and what may fairly be assumed as the level which they will reach, or at all events may and should reach, within the next three years or so after the assessment. Since, as noted above, the actual rates do not vary, as the land is irrigated or not, no wet rates were assumed.

In assessing an estate the Settlement Officer applied these assumed rates to show what the assets should be if the estate was a fair average one. He sought to estimate the amount to which its rental would rise when the disturbance consequent on the revision should cease. The estate was inspected, and every point of importance noted in the pargana book opposite the statistical abstracts relating to the estate. When every village in the pargana had been inspected, the actual assessment of each was undertaken. The reasons which influenced the Settlement Officer in fixing the revenue were written out for each estate at length in the manner of a judicial decision, and thus the whole process by which the assessment was arrived at was put on record before the new demand was announced.

Where the Settlement Officer found more culturable waste than was required for the village grazing, and considered its reclamation was likely to commence shortly, he made a proportionate increase in the gross assumed rental, on which he calculated the revenue; otherwise he simply included the actual income from such lands in the gross rental. Reductions were made where estates were liable to injury from floods or wild animals. The fact, also, that certain castes of cultivators do actually pay lower rents than others was accepted and allowed due influence.

In G. O. No. 1960A., dated 13th September, 1873, this Government laid down that the Settlement Officer might exercise his discretion in assessing below 50 per cent. of the assets, where, on account of the large number of cultivating proprietors, or from other causes, a demand at that rate would be oppressive. Where, on the other hand, an assessment above that rate would be light, the Settlement Officer was allowed the same discretion in moderately exceeding the rate. Again, in G. O. No. 1379A., dated 5th June, 1874, it was distinctly ruled—"Where a village has been highly assessed, the assessment should not in ordinary cases be lowered to half assets on purely arithmetical grounds. If it has borne the high assessment well, the demand should not, generally speaking, be lowered at all ; if ill, the demand should be lowered, but not ordinarily to the full extent of half assets."

The detailed application of a reduced assessment to certain villages will be noticed below, in connection with the assessment of the Jalálabad Rájput villages. Generally, where the Settlement Officer found in such estates that the old demand bore a very low ratio to the assets, he fixed the demand 2 or 3 per cent. below the full half, and where there was any doubt which of two sums should be fixed, he selected the lower. Where he found, on the other hand, that the old demand was more than 50 per cent. of the assets, he gave such relief as he deemed necessary, never, however, making a reduction on merely arithmetical grounds. Mr. Currie remarks that the cases where allowance had to be made for special profits arising from the industry or expenditure of the proprietors were very rare and trifling.

With one exception, the cesses taken by landholders from their tenants were not included in the assets on which the demand was calculated. The exception was that known locally as *kharch*, or village expenses, which is virtually a portion of the rent.

7. The result of the revision carried out on these principles has been an enhancement of the revenue from Rs. 9,75,273 to Rs. 11,84,425, an increase of Rs. 2,09,152, equal to 21·4 per cent. of the old assessment. The incidence of the former demand at its expiration was Re. 0-15-1 on the assessable acre and Re. 1-5-1 on the cultivated acre. This has been now raised to Re. 1-3-4 and Re. 1-9-7 respectively. The practical result, therefore, is enhancement of the demand by Re. 0-6-3 on each acre of cultivation. Taking the parganas individually, the rate of the demand on cultivation, excluding the backward tract of Khutar, where it is necessarily low, varies from Re. 1-4-8 in Kant to Rs. 2 in Baragaon, and the gradation of rates corresponds closely with what might have been inferred from the relative rank in regard to the elements detailed

2

in para. 105, on which the assessment is based. These rates are compared in para. 100 with the incidence on the present area of the demand of the last settlement. In one pargana, Jamaur, the incidence is unchanged. . In the others there is an increase per cultivated acre, varying from 2 annas 11 pies in Kant to 8 annas in Khera-Bajhera.

8. In order to show the proportion borne by the new demand to the assets, Mr. Currie has, in each of the assessment reports of the four tahsils, calculated the actual assets on the basis of the village rent-rolls. These are, he considers, as a rule, trustworthy records. Taking these returns, he corrects them for small omissions, places the full village tenant rate on the sír and land under-rented to relatives of the proprietor, and adds the siwai items. The rental thus calculated he calls the "actual assets" of the proprietors. For the whole district it amounts to Rs. 21,54,635. Of this sum, the demand fixed is 54·9 per cent. The Settlement Officers have then taken as revenue nearly 5 per cent. more than the half. This excess is accounted for by the principles of the assessment already explained.

The assumed rates by which the assessment of each village was guided were the full ones paid by *bond-fide* tenants. These were of course applied to the assessment of under-rented villages. Moreover, where in a circle these full tenants' rates were low, compared to those paid in the neighbourhood, they were, as already explained, enhanced. Some enhancement was also made for prospective extension of cultivation. Thus the grounds on which the Settlement Officers fixed the demand above half the actual assets were simply that the proprietors could obviously, without any injustice to their tenants, raise their rentals to the full amount assumed as the potential assets. The following statement shows for each pargana—

(1) The recorded rental corrected for sír only ;

(2) The estimated actual assets ;

(3) The rental at assumed rates ; and

(4) The gross assumed potential assets, of which half was assessed as the demand.

			Corrected rental.	Estimated actual assets.	Rental from assumed rates.	Potential assets.	Demand.
			Rs.	Rs.	Rs.	Rs.	Rs.
Sháhjahánpur	...	...	2,11,798	2,21,850	2,28,492	2,48,446	1,34,219
Jamaur	...	...	1,36,675	1,39,725	1,41,721	1,49,420	74,701
Kant	...	...	1,60,133	1,67,380	1,90,970	1,83,482	91,741
			...	5,28,905	5,61,183	5,81,342	...
Jalálabad	...	...	3,95,100	4,11,010	4,46,275	4,45,150	2,11,410
Tilhar	...	...	1,83,705	1,91,170	2,08,544	2,18,238	1,09,120
Kátra	...	...	12,131	13,450	15,486	17,020	8,510
Nigohi	...	...	1,28,805	1,36,000	1,43,613	1,54,260	77,180
Khera-Bajhera	...	...	1,20,482	1,27,550	1,41,888	1,44,790	72,360
Jalálpur	...	...	1,00,064	1,11,000	1,25,766	1,26,010	63,005
			...	5,79,170	6,35,299	6,60,248	...
Baragaon	...	...	1,29,060	1,35,800	1,41,928	1,45,900	72,950
Pawayan	...	...	3,62,130	3,93,000	4,23,587	4,33,470	2,16,735
Khutar	...	...	1,01,530	1,07,750	1,20,553	1,20,470	62,535
			...	6,36,550	6,86,068	6,99,840	...

The few cases in which the potential assets are less than the rental from assumed rates are explained in the tahsíl reports. They are generally those of tracts in which there were large bhaiachára communities, with innumerable petty holdings. Mr. Currie has explained in para. 113 his procedure in regard to enhancement of rents and the preparation of new rent-rolls, and it was unquestionably judicious. The preparation of an entirely new rent-roll *suo motu* for every village would have enormously delayed the completion of the settlement.

How far actually enhancement of rents was effected during the course of the settlement or before the submission of the report there is nothing to show.

The increase on the old demand is readily explained by the considerations noted above. That was only 44·6 per cent. of the assets : 5·4 per cent. more had to be taken to bring it up to the half assets, and the excess beyond was justified by the low rents and extensive culturable waste.

9. The cost of the revision amounts to Rs. 5,86,500, being an average of Rs. 339 per square mile. The seniority of the Settlement Officers employed was the main cause of the high cost. Measured by the increase of revenue, the outlay was financially a complete success, resulting in an income equal to above 35 per cent. of the capital expended.

10. Before concluding, it is necessary to notice certain peculiarities in the assessment of the four tahsíls, of which the district consists.

A separate report on each of these is given, in which the specialities of each assessment circle are detailed at great length and the general principles of assessment are re-stated. It is unnecessary to follow these. The table at section 105 gives the principal points on which a comparison between the parganas can be instituted. An examination of this shows, as remarked above, that the incidence of the revenue varies in accordance with the advantages the pargana possesses in population, extent of cultivation, class of soil, &c. The only exception to this is the small pargana of Katra, consisting of 12 villages much under-rented.

There has been a considerable increase of revenue in every pargana except Jamaur. In this the old revenue of Rs. 74,753 has been practically maintained, no increase being possible owing to the severity of the old assessment. In assessing, however, the Settlement Officer has taken the potential assets as nearly 7 per cent. higher than the actual assets, and yet no increase has been possible.

11. Beyond the case of pargana Jamaur just noted, there is nothing calling for special remark in the assessment of tahsíl Sháhjahánpur. Some remarks are, however, perhaps required on the elaborate calculations in section 27 *et seq.*, regarding the balance of assets remaining to the proprietors after the deduction of the revenue. Taking 21 coparcenary villages, the Settlement Officer calculates that the surplus rent gives an income of Re. 0-15-9 a month to each proprietor, and remarks—" These proprietors cannot subsist on their property, and it is the claim of these for an assessment at 40 to 45 per cent. that I have urged."

There is a double fallacy in this. First, it is a mistake to treat of these people as though they were *landlords* living solely on rents: they are peasant proprietors getting some additional income by renting a portion of their property, but their chief income is derived from the profits of their cultivation. In para. 16 of this chapter, Mr. Currie has shown that the average size of a *tenant's* holding is six acres, while the average *sir* land cultivated by the proprietor is eight acres. Obviously then, if a tenant can live on six acres and pay his rent, the peasant proprietor can live on eight acres, paying to Government only half the amount which a tenant would pay, and receiving nearly Re. 1 a month clear profit from the rents of his tenants.

Secondly, it is assumed that the landholders have a right to be supported exclusively from the rents. What they have a right to is the portion which, by prescription or the direct or indirect sanction of the ruling power, they have been allowed to enjoy. If this has been large, they will certainly be supported by rents, but if small, then the rents will be only a supplement to some occupation by which they earn their living. From a mere statement of the average amount enjoyed by a proprietor, no inference can be drawn regarding the *fairness* of the assessment. The assessment depends on the rental value of the land, not on the size of individual holdings. If the holdings are so small that when assessed at the same rate as other land they are insufficient for the support of the proprietors, this consequence does not furnish any ground for impeaching the fairness of the settlement.

A similar criticism is applicable to the calculation, whereby, omitting the most petty and the most wealthy proprietors, Mr. Currie finds the average income of a shareholder to be from Rs. 30 to Rs. 80 a year, and considers this not too large a margin. Obviously, whether it is so or not must depend on the amount of the assets which the Government has allowed the landholder to appropriate, and the continued enjoyment of which he has been allowed to expect. If his share is so small that the produce is insufficient to support him and his family, any assessment would be too heavy, but it does not follow that the right of the State should be foregone in his favor.

12. The first peculiarity in the assessment of the Jalálabad tahsíl occurred in the Bankati circle. This consists mostly of a hard clay soil, requiring much water. Owing to a peculiarity in the subsoil, kucha wells cannot be worked, and the irrigation is chiefly from rivers and ponds, but especially from the river Sot. Of the assessable area, 53 per cent. is uncultivated, being covered with scrub (dhák) jungle and grasses used for thatching, and having interspersed in it considerable stretches of real usar, the *reh* efflorescence being specially noticeable where there is superabundant irrigation from the dams on the Sot. Mr. Currie did not consider this would come rapidly under cultivation, and accordingly, in assessing the revenue, has only calculated on a possible extension in exceptional cases. As a general rule he simply included in the assets the actual or estimated profits from these lands.

The actual assets of the circle, calculated as above, amount to Rs. 1,44,800, of which sum the demand is 55·3 per cent. The excess of

5·3 per cent. is explained on the general principles above detailed, and the fact of the large culturable area just noticed.

13.   The chief proprietors in this tahsíl are Rájputs, holding their estates on a *pattidari* or bhaiáchára tenure.   These estates are sub-divided into a number of small holdings, which are increasing in multiplicity with the population.   The sír holdings amount to 21 per cent. of the cultivation, the average extent of a sír being about six acres.

In assessing many of these communities, Mr. Currie, with the concurrence of the Commissioner and the Board of Revenue, fixed the Government demand considerably below half the potential assets.

The case may be shortly stated thus :   The numerous co-sharers in these properties subsist more or less on the share of the rents they have hitherto been allowed to enjoy; they have, moreover, multiplied to the extent that their present income is just sufficient to afford them the necessities of their standard of living.   If now their income has been largely made up of rent, and the old assessment has been low, then the demand cannot
* To the Commissioner of Rohilkhand, dated 18th June, 1870. be enhanced without trenching on the income required to supply the family with necessaries; or, as Mr. Currie wrote in his original report* regarding these communities, "If the new assessment is made at the full rate, they will be improved off the face of the earth."

Mr. Currie found 141 villages in which he thought it necessary to fix the revenue in a reduced proportion to avoid this result.   His method of procedure was to first calculate on each the gross potential assets, and to compare the 50 per cent. demand on this with the existing demand. Where the enhancement would have been large, he deducted from the potential assets from 5 to 15 per cent., and in exceptional cases from 20 to 25 per cent., and fixed the demand at one-half the remainder.   This procedure resulted in a jama 14 per cent. less than the full demand, the total loss of revenue amounting to Rs. 11,165.   Yet the new demand was an enhancement of 46·5 per cent. on its predecessor.

The general principle by which this procedure was directed was undoubtedly correct, and in accordance with the G. O. of 1873 quoted above.   And as in every case the demand actually imposed is considerably in excess of the old demand, and if calculated at a full half of the potential assets would have implied a very large diminution of the share hitherto enjoyed by the proprietors, there is no reason to interfere with the Settlement Officer's proceedings.   But unquestionably Mr. Currie was wrong in the theoretical arguments by which he justifies them, and especially in what he says as to his mode of treating sír lands. He considers there is no real hardship in assessing the demand up to the full rental from tenants leaving the sír untouched.   But when proprietors have to sell their *sír* produce to pay the revenue, " the jama becomes a burden to them in proportion to the amount of the land cultivated."

But let a proprietor hold 12 acres with a renting power of Rs. 3 an acre, which represents (say) one-third of the produce, and assume the old revenue to be Rs. 8. Now, deducting the revenue, if the proprietor cultivates his holding, his income will be Rs. 100 ; if he rents it, it will be Rs. 28. In the first case, the enhancement of his revenue to the full Rs. 18 will reduce his income 10 per cent. only, *viz.*, to Rs. 90 ; in the second case, it will reduce it nearly 36 per cent., *viz.*, to Rs. 18. Whence it appears that where a proprietor is mainly dependent for his support on the *cultivating* profits of his holding, the low revenue of the former settlement may be enhanced without much affecting his income ; if, however, he has been chiefly dependent on the rental which the low assessment left at his disposal, the revenue cannot be enhanced without trenching on his income very seriously. Indeed, it is obvious that the smaller the proportion in which his income is constituted by rents, the less he will feel the increase of the demand calculated on the rent. Mr. Currie therefore is quite wrong in saying there is no real hardship in assessing the demand up to the rental from tenants leaving the sír untouched ; there will be no hardship if the income from the rents has been small in proportion to the cultivating profits from the sír ; if, however, the reverse has been the case, there may be excessive hardship.

With regard to the remark that there is a special hardship in making the proprietor sell his produce to pay the revenue, there is no speciality in this ; every tenant has to do it in a far greater proportion.

To what extent the assessment of particular estates was affected by these erroneous principle does not appear from the detailed statements submitted to the Board : these do not give the grounds for the reduction in the particular cases. Taking a general review of the result of these reductions, however, it is obvious that if these proprietors must have been ruined by an assessment at the full rate, they cannot have been saved by the present reductions.

In the original report on the subject above quoted, Mr. Currie directed special attention to the Khander ilaka of the Chandela Rájputs, stating it to be a fairly representative case of the Rájput communities in question. It consisted of 72 estates, on which 3,250 people of the proprietary families were dependent. In this proportion the number of people dependent on the (141) estates now in question must have been about double the number, 6,500 souls. The reduction made, therefore, was such as to increase the income of each by nearly Re. 1-12-0 a year, an amount not likely to save them from ruin, if that was imminent from an enhancement of the demand to a full rate.

As observed, in reviewing the Etáwah settlement report, while un- questionably the principle of the Government order that proprietary cultivating communities should be assessed leniently is right, especially if an assessment at full rates would involve a great enhancement of the previous demand, there is a limit to the indulgence with which they should be treated. Pushed to an excess, it would imply that no assessment should be imposed when the community had multiplied to such an extent and property become so sub-divided that individual holdings no longer yield a sufficient income for bare subsistence. Apparently, if sub-division go on until holdings are too small to furnish full employment for the proprietor and his family, any leniency encouraging it, and, tending to increase the burden on the land, is a mistaken policy.

Mr. Currie is mistaken in assuming that the assessment of these villages was the subject of a report by the Board to Government.

The Board directed the Settlement Officer to use his discretion in applying the sanctioned rates to these villages, and to report the result of his assessment in some of the estates. This he did, and the Board sanctioned the assessments without reference to Government, and His Honor does not doubt that the discretionary power they have of assessing at less than the full demand was, on the whole, and with reference to all the circumstances, rightly exercised. The assessment made is not a full one, but is a fair enhancement on that which it superseded.

14. Tahsíl Tilhar was assessed by Mr. George Butt, who wrote Chapter IV. of the Report. There is, however, little or nothing calling for remark in its assessment. It is a fair specimen of the district and was assessed on the principles detailed in the general review, appeals being allowed from Mr. Butt to Mr. Currie. Mr. Butt's assessments will be better noticed in connection with pargana Pawáyan. The result in tahsíl Tilhar has been an enhancement of the old jama of Rs. 2,60,537 by 26·6 per cent. up to Rs. 3,30,124. The incidence on the cultivated acre of the old jama was Re. 1-6-3, that of the present is Re. 1-12-1.

This chapter, written by Mr. Butt, is particularly full in all details regarding his procedure and its results.

15. Of the three parganas forming tahsíl Pawáyan, one, that of Pawáyan itself, was assessed by Mr. G. Butt, Assistant Settlement Officer. The rest of the tahsíl was assessed by Mr. Currie himself.

There are several points treated of in this chapter which require special notice.

The first is the assessment of pargana Khutar.

This pargana covers an area of 203 square miles, including 45 square miles of forests.* Only 53 per cent. of the assessable area is cultivated, though the area under the plough during the currency of last settlement increased 210 per cent.

* These are private property and demarcated into mauzas.

For assessment purposes the pargana was divided into two circles, the inhabited (ábád) portion, with an average population of 750 people to the square mile, and the forest (wairan) portion, an unhealthy tract with a population of only 126 to the square mile.

The assumed rates were deduced simply from those actually current in the pargana, no attempt being made to raise the standard to that of the rest of the district. There resulted an all-round rate of Rs. 2-10-6 in the inhabited circle and of Re. 1-9-1 in the forest circle. These may be compared with Mr. Butt's rates in the adjoining and similar portion of the Pawáyan pargana. In the Tariona circle the rate was Rs. 2-7-7, and in the very unhealthy Sunwat circle Re. 1-11-3. In the other circles of this tahsíl the assumed rate varied from Rs. 3-3-8 to Rs. 4-13-10.

The assessment of the inhabited circle of Khutar was carried out on the same method as that of the rest of the district.

The forest circle villages were divided into two classes:—(1) Those with a large cultivated area and a small proportion of culturable waste. The *average* cultivated area of these was taken as the basis of assessment, with an addition on account of the grazing dues, &c. No addition for possible extension of cultivation was made. (2) The villages in which the forest and culturable waste cover two-thirds of the assessable area. The actual cultivation in these was assessed, and wherever Mr. Currie considered a speedy extension of cultivation would occur without any special expenditure by the proprietor, he made an addition to the potential assets on this account. Where the actual income from the forest and waste land was ascertainable and sufficient, he simply assessed the revenue upon it. Where, however, this was not the case, he was guided by the incidence of leases, and assessed Re. 1 on every 10 to 12 acres of good forest, 15 to 16 of medium, and 18 to 20 of inferior.

In this manner the gross potential assets worked out to Rs. 70,170. Of this sum, about Rs. 60,000 was actual rental, Rs. 5,000 the forest income, and additions for anticipated extension of cultivation. The remainder is due to the application of full circle rates to villages where very low rents prevailed for no special reason, except perhaps that the old demand was but $\frac{1}{10}$th to $\frac{1}{20}$th of the assets.

The former revenue was increased by 78·11 per cent., from Rs. 35,110 to Rs. 62,535. The incidence of the revenue on the *assessable* area rose from Re. 0-4-8 to Re. 0-8-4 per acre.

16. Mr. Currie in his rent-rate report recommended that in those estates where excessive enhancement occurred, the full revised demand should be introduced gradually, on the ground that a sudden curtailment of the landholders' incomes must have a ruinous result to them, and at that time more especially, as the agriculture of the pargana was, owing to the cattle plague, in a depressed condition. He was also of opinion that it would compel the landholders to attempt to raise their rents, which would drive away the cultivators and thus actually injure the pargana. The report in question was forwarded to the Government by the Board for orders. In G. O. No. 1820A., dated 25th August, 1873, to the address of the Secretary to the Board, Government approved of Mr. Currie's suggestion and sanctioned the progressive assessment "provisionally." The period of the progressive revenue has now expired, and the full amount was taken from July, 1880.

17. In section 20 of chapter V. Mr. Currie enters at considerable length into the history of the Rájas of Khutar. In March, 1874, he submitted a report on the subject to Government, which led to correspondence which continued down to May, 1876. It is not necessary to recapitulate the case here. It is sufficient to note that Mr. Currie was supported by the Commissioner and Board of Revenue in recommending that a pension of Rs. 250 a month should be granted to the family, and a loan of Rs. 22,000 advanced on easy terms by Government to clear their estates of debts. This Government obtained sanction to the loan from

the Government of India, on the condition that it was to be repaid within nine years from the profits of the estates, the sír land being left to the family for their maintenance. In the opinion of Government there was no sufficient reason brought forward for granting the pension. But Mr. Currie, on being informed of this, declared the profits of the estates would not suffice to liquidate the loan in less than 21 years ; that the *sir*, moreover, was insufficient for the support of the family ; and consequently, without the grant of the pension, the loan on the terms proposed would be useless. On this, Government, in No. 855, dated 31st May, 1876, to the Secretary to the Board, directed that the question of the loan must be allowed to drop, and the proprietors left to arrange as best they could for their own interest.

18.—The assessment of pargana Pawáyan was effected by Mr. G. Butt.

He found the rents prevailing in the Tariona circle of this pargana abnormally low. It is a continuation of the Gungchai circle in pargana Puranpur, zila Pilibhít, from which it is separated by a merely arbitrary boundary. The rents in Gungchai are, however, considerably higher than in Tariona, though in all points affecting its renting power it is inferior. Mr. Butt therefore based his rents on those prevailing in Gungchai, and found them correspond closely to those which the Settlement Officer of Puranpur (Mr. LaTouche) had adopted. In applying them, however, to Tariona, Mr. Butt reduced them, as he considered it would have been imprudent to enhance the rents suddenly up to the standard of the Gungchai rates. The resulting enhancement evidently was not excessive. The corrected rentals for the circle were Rs. 1,06,000; and Mr. Butt calculated his demand on potential assets amounting to Rs. 1,16,320, only 9·7 per cent. higher than the actuals. The old demand for this circle is not given.

19. The remainder of the tahsíl was assessed on the principles already detailed. In pargana Pawáyan generally the rent-rolls, especially in the villages belonging to the Rája of Pawáyan, were not considered to be so trustworthy as those of the rest of the district. Moreover, in the poor Sunwat circle rents in kind prevail, giving every facility for understating the assets. Hence from the corrected rentals of the jamabandis no certain inference can be drawn regarding the proportion borne to the assets by the revised demand. The total of the corrected rental is Rs. 3,93,000, while the potential assets have been taken as Rs. 4,33,470, which is 10·3 per cent. higher. Even on these inaccurate papers the demand is not higher in Pawáyan than the average of the district : the demand is only 55 per cent. of the corrected rental.

The Rája of Pawáyan has repeatedly complained that the pargana has been over-assessed, and applied for reduction of the demand. His petition was made the subject of full enquiry, and was finally rejected by Government Resolution No. 3618, dated 13th December, 1878. In a minute on this petition, Mr. G. Butt, then Secretary to the Board, wrote :—
"There are few parganas the assessment of which has been more examined. It was the last pargana assessed by me ; and by that time the agitation against the Bareilly settlement was going on, and to this cause

is greatly, in my opinion, due the comparatively large number of appeals.
............Mr. Currie invited objections to my assessments, and spent
some time in the pargana examining the assessments and disposing of
objections. There were 89 appeals by the Rája to the Commissioner or
to the Board, resulting in a total reduction in revenue of Rs. 400.........
Mr. Simson, as Commissioner, went through the pargana and examined
the work with Mr. Currie when disposing of appeals, and Mr. B. Colvin,
............his successor, did the same the following cold weather."

20. The engagements from the landholders were taken to hold good
for such period as Government should sanction. The revised assessment first took effect from 1st July, 1870, in tahsíl Sháhjahánpur, and in
the other parganas from the same dates—in 1871, 1872, and 1873, the last
being that of Khutar. Mr. Currie is of opinion the period of settlement
for the whole district should be fixed at the 30th June, 1900. The
maximum demand in Khutar was reached in July, 1880; and as this
pargana is the least advanced and most lightly assessed, Mr. Currie
thought the shorter period in its case would be advisable.

21. The general results of the report may be thus briefly sum-
med up :—

The district ranks high in the chief elements of productiveness,
moisture, a healthy climate, good soil, and an industrious and dense
population. The landholders belong chiefly to the agricultural classes,
and the cultivators to the most hardworking castes. Measured by these
circumstances and the present prices of produce, the standard rents are
undoubtedly low, and the tendency to a rise, now apparent, will be increased by the improvements in the means of communication recently
made. It is impossible, however, to calculate to what extent or within
what period this rise will occur. In fixing the standard rates for assessment, therefore, the Settlement Officer did not take this into consideration. He deduced his rates simply from those he found in existence, but
raised abnormally low rates to his standard. Working on this safe basis,
he has been able to increase the revenue by 21·4 per cent., from Re. 1-3-4
on the cultivated acre to Re. 1-9-7.

22. The detailed assessment reports show the laborious care and
general discrimination with which the innumerable circumstances affecting the rents have been treated, and the prudence with which the claims
of the landholders and tenants have been considered without a sacrifice
of the rights of Government. The work, as a whole, is a striking display
of patient treatment of details and sound judgment in the application of
principles, and it reflects much credit on Mr. Currie and Mr. Butt, the
early death of both of whom the Government must sincerely deplore
and regret.

23. It is abundantly clear there need be no hesitation in sanctioning
the settlement of this district for the full term of 30 years. It will, however, be convenient to adopt Mr. Currie's suggestion, and to fix the year
1900 as the termination of the period for the whole district.

C. ROBERTSON,
Secy. to Govt., N.-W. P. and Oudh,

ORDER.—Ordered that a copy of this Resolution be forwarded to the Secretary to the Board of Revenue, North-Western Provinces, for the information of the Board.

Ordered also that a copy (with copy of report) be forwarded to the Secretary to the Government of India, Home, Revenue and Agricultural Department, with the recommendation that the settlement of the Sháhjahánpur district be confirmed as proposed.

C. ROBETSON,
Secy. to Govt., N.-W. Provinces and Oudh.

Extract paras. 1 and 2 of a letter from the Officiating Under-Secretary to the Government of India, Home, Revenue and Agricultural Department (Revenue), to the Secretary to the Government, North-Western Provinces and Oudh, No. 254, dated Simla, the 2nd May, 1881.

I AM directed to acknowledge the receipt of the report on the settlement of the Sháhjahánpur district, and of the resolution of His Honor the Lieutenant-Governor thereon, No. 154, dated the 26th January last.

2. In reply I am to say that the Governor-General in Council confirms the orders of His Honor the Lieutenant-Governor sanctioning this settlement and fixing its duration. The period of settlement will accordingly be thirty years in the part of the district where the revised assessments took effect from the 1st July, 1870, and in other cases also will extend to the 30th June, 1900.

———

No. 776 OF 1881.

REVENUE DEPARTMENT, N.-W. P. AND OUDH.

Dated Naini Tal, the 16th May, 1881.

COPY of the above forwarded to the Secretary to the Board of Revenue, North-Western Provinces, for information.

R. SMEATON,

Offg. Secy. to Govt., N.-W. P. and Oudh.